DAWN
OF
GODS
&
FURY

ALSO

A
DAWN
OF
GODS
&
FURY

K.A. TUCKER

ISBN 978-1-990105-42-5 (paperback)

ISBN 978-1-990105-40-1 (ebook)

Edited by Jennifer Sommersby

Cover design by Hang Le

Published by K.A. Tucker Books Ltd.

Manufactured in the United States of America

To the many characters who brought this story to life in a way I couldn't imagine when I typed those first words.

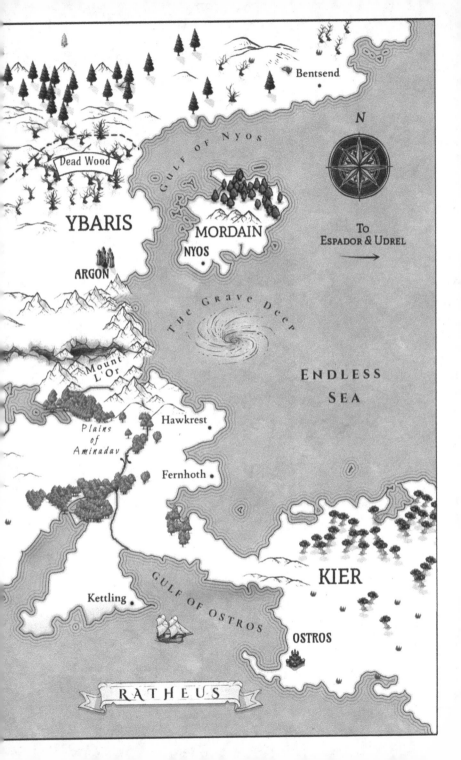

1

ANNIKA

"Is there *nothing* palatable on this fates-forsaken ship?" I inspect a bruised apple under the oil lamp's glow before tossing it back into the bushel of spoiling produce.

The *Tempest*'s cook—a brawny man with a tufted gray beard—pauses in his task of fileting the day's catch to eye me. That's all any of these sailors do—offer stares but no words for their princess.

"Well?" I snap. "Does no one's tongue work around here, save for your *delightful* captain's?" Who I would pitch overboard if I didn't think his crew would toss me in after him.

"Eat your day's rations when they're given, or someone else gladly will," he finally answers, his voice gruff.

"You mean that slop of soggy oats and salted pork? Is that what you deem adequate for a member of Islor's royal family?" Corrin would beat this mortal with a wooden spoon if she were here, and I would enjoy watching.

"Pardon me for bein' so boorish. Is there somethin' *else* I can get ya?" he asks with mock sincerity, holding up his hand. The radiant two-crescent moon emblem is a taunting beacon in the gloom of the scullery kitchen.

"I would have to be on my deathbed to take your vein even *without* that mark," I sneer. The man can't have seen soap in weeks. Few of the sailors on this ship have. I can barely stand the smell below deck.

"Ya may be there soon enough." And by the grin, he doesn't look at all disappointed.

I've never been spoken to by a mortal in such a disgraceful manner. "What is your name, sailor?"

"Why?"

"So I may provide it to my brother *the king* when I next see him. I'm sure he will love hearing how you relished in the idea of my suffering."

He snorts. "Name's Sye, an' we all saw what we were runnin' from back there. Not much of a king without a throne to sit on. Besides, he's likely dead, or soon will be."

I flinch at his callousness. My twin may have left me in Cirilea to deal with a rebellion, and we may barely tolerate each other, but ... all I have left are my brothers. That, and a city ablaze and shadowed by a beast like none I've seen before. "Perhaps I am the only royal family member left, then, which would make me queen."

"Well then, *queen*, you can grab yerself a biscuit and quit pestering me. I got work to do." He brandishes his cleaver toward a shelf where the basket of hardened bread sits and then lops off the head of a fish.

The block of kitchen knives to my left taunts me. I could probably put one of those through this filthy mortal's jugular before he had a chance to yell. Little good killing the cook will do me, though. I'll still be stuck on this ship and with hungry sailors, no less.

"Don't get no silly ideas," Sye warns, his eyes also on the knife block. "There's a lot of us and only one of you."

"I'm not a savage." I make a point of snatching *two* biscuits—twice the day's ration—plus a bruised apple.

Sye scowls. "Be off, then!"

A jug of mead sits nearby. On impulse, I snake my arm around it and, hugging the awkward cask against my chest, I saunter up the stairs with my head held high, trying not to stumble under the weight.

Hudem's silver moonlight shimmers off the seawater, highlighting the absence of land.

"Must we sail so far from shore?" I complain to anyone listening.

"If we don't wish to punch a hole in the hull and sink to our deaths," Captain Aron answers from the helm.

"I assumed we were already as good as dead once the sirens find us."

"If the winds don't pick up, we won't get that far."

The air is stale and warm, the ship's sails sagging. There's barely a ripple over the water.

He peers at me, then at my loot. "I see you found the kitchen."

"And your foul cook."

He smirks. "Sye's a stickler for rations. You must have really annoyed him to get away with all that."

I flop onto the floor and yank out the cork. "I figured, by the time I reach the bottom, all my problems will vanish."

"Couldn't find what you're really hankering for down there, *Your Highness*?" comes that grating voice.

I count to five before I gift Tyree my attention, to find crystal blue eyes locked on me. The Ybarisan prince doesn't have to spell out his meaning. At least a quarter of the sailors on this ship brandish glowing marks, and I wouldn't trust the unmarked ones. But I haven't fed in *days*. If I'd had any inkling of the looming rebellion, I wouldn't have wasted time making nice with Dagnar. I would have simply sunk my teeth into his vein.

"You look dreadful." Worse than before, his olive complexion now a sickly pallor.

"Can't imagine why," he drawls, twirling the dagger I stabbed him with before his fist clamps onto the bronze handle forged from Aminadav's horn. "Not just a merth blade, is it?"

"I guess my father foresaw my need for a special weapon." I was sixteen when he gifted me the blade and warned me to never use it unless under dire circumstances, for even a minor scratch could prove fatal.

Tyree shifts and winces. The belt, confiscated from my dress, is soaked in his blood, the wound still leaking more than a day later. "What exactly is it doing to me?"

I shrug. "I've never stabbed anyone before. Glad you were the first, though."

He gives the blade another twirl. "Perhaps I should repay the favor."

That Tyree *hasn't* stabbed me yet is shocking. "I'm still more valuable to you alive."

He flashes me that cocky, infuriating smile and reaches out a hand toward me, the smooth onyx cuff around his wrist a pretty shackle. Atticus secured the matching set on the enemy Ybarisan to cripple his access to his elven affinity—to what, I haven't deduced yet. It made no difference in the end. He still managed to escape, kill several guards, and kidnap me. "Show a dying male some compassion and bring me a drink."

I yank the cork out of the cask, top up my metal cup, and guzzle it down, splashing mead down my ruined dress.

He grins. "Hey, Captain, isn't my future wife a sight to behold? Can you imagine what she'll be like on our wedding night?"

"That is *never* happening!" I hiss, whipping the empty cup at Tyree's head.

He snatches it from the air with those quick reflexes I keep underestimating, even as he slowly bleeds out.

And now I don't have a mug.

"I'll have that drink now." He waves it in the air. "It's the least you could do, seeing as I saved you from that mob."

"I would have been fine. I know every place to hide in that castle."

His eyes lack their usual wickedness as he heaves a sigh and offers a more conciliatory, "Please, Annika. I'm tired and thirsty and I'd love something to dull this pain."

A twinge of guilt stirs inside me. He could have hurt me in retaliation a hundred times over, but he hasn't.

"Look, I'll even tuck the dagger in here." He winces as he turns, sliding the blade into the wooden crate he's perched on, out of easy reach.

With reluctance, I drag myself to my feet and lug the jug over.

An overwhelming waft of that sweet neroli oil makes me inhale sharply. My incisors burn, begging to release. It reminds me what a bad idea it is to be this close when I haven't fed in so long. But I also know his blood is as toxic as the marked mortals on this ship and would deliver me to an agonizing grave just as swiftly.

Tyree keeps quiet as I fill the cup and watch him drink, that sharp jut in his columnar throat bobbing with each swallow. It really is too bad he is so hateful. Even I can admit he has physical appeal, his thick, dark locks collecting at his nape in a sexy wave, his square jaw a contrast to lush lips.

What would his Ybarisan blood taste like?

I've heard it's euphoric.

Orgasmic.

"So, how does it work?" Tyree's attention is on the glowing Hudem moon above, nearly at its peak. "If you fucked me right now, we'd be guaranteed an offspring, right? Annika, help save my bloodline for me." He holds out his arms, presenting his waiting hips for me. "I can see you want it."

That's not how it works—we aren't in the nymphaeum, and he isn't an Islorian immortal—but I don't answer, instead snatching the mug from his hand and upending it over his crotch. Hollers from every sailor on the deck, including the captain, sound as I stroll away.

"Relax, I didn't waste it all." Besides, that was well worth it. Maybe the stench of mead will drown out his more appealing scent that now trails me back. I pour myself another cup full and watch Hudem's moon as it swells until the silver is nearly blinding. In all my years, I've never seen it so brilliant and so low before, but I've also never been at sea for it.

"Is that typical for it to be so bright on the water?" Tyree asks, noticing it as well.

"Aye, I don't spend much time ponderin' that moon. It's never brought me any good," Captain Aron mutters, but he studies it with a perplexed look.

Either way, it is a beautiful view.

I take a deep breath, inhaling the warm sea air as the silver globe begins to dim, passing the height of Hudem—another that will surely make its way into Islor's history books, with my family's slow demise.

But ...

I frown.

Something has changed.

I whip around.

Tyree is still there, still breathing.

Still watching me like a predator waiting patiently for an opportunity with its prey. I move toward him, toward the scent of his tempting Ybarisan blood.

"Is something the matter, Annika?" He eyes me warily.

"No. I just ..." I inhale again. I can still catch the scent of his blood, of all the mortals' blood around me.

But the unmistakable craving that plagued me only moments ago is suddenly gone.

In the far distance, an unearthly screech fills the night.

2

SOFIE

"Watch yourself, my love." Elijah's grip on my hand tightens as I step over a corpse.

"I am watching." But even with my keen eyesight and the rays of light from the silver moon above, it is a challenge to avoid limbs as we move toward the castle. A grand path of destruction has been carved through the royal garden, the ashy remains of trees still smoldering. Statues that were likely once grand have crumbled. "What manner of creature caused such carnage?" Surely, it was no mortal being. The manicured lawn wears gouges from a beast's claws.

"A powerful one who will bow to me before long."

I steal a glance up at my husband, still in disbelief that after almost three centuries, I am walking alongside him again, in flesh and blood, his hand within mine.

He feels different. Those endless years in the Nulling have hardened him. I suppose it is to be expected that he would not be the same.

"What sparked this battle, I wonder." I have seen the aftermath of war before—cities toppled, bodies left to claim or rot.

"Weak kings." Elijah's jaw is firm, resolute.

I open my mouth to ask him what he means—and how he knows —when a cluster of blood-streaked elven soldiers rushes through the castle doors.

"Ah, good, you've found us." Elijah's voice is cordial—dare I say, cheerful.

"Declare yourselves!" a burly soldier demands, moving ahead of the others, gripping the pommel of his sword as if prepared to attack.

But Elijah remains composed, unruffled. "I am your king."

The male chuckles, stirring amusement from the others. "Our king is in the east, fighting Islor's traitors."

"That king is no longer the ruler of anything but his own failures. I rule here now."

The soldier's eyes flare with new understanding. "You have proclaimed treason against the crown. The penalty for that is death." He raises his sword point toward Elijah's chest.

I call forth threads of my affinity—I did not come this far only to lose my love to a blade—but before I can throw up a shield, Elijah raises his free hand and the soldier erupts in flames. The others leap away as his shrieks echo.

My pulse races, throbbing in my ears.

Elijah did not have an affinity to Malachi.

"Who am I?" His voice booms into the night.

The question is for the soldiers, but I squeeze my eyes shut against the answer that screams inside my head. *No, no, no ... it cannot be.*

A beat passes and then, one by one, the soldiers kneel, murmurs of "Your Highness" slipping from their lips.

I grit my teeth as I turn to regard my husband, my true love, the soul I have clung to for nearly three hundred years, the fog lifting as reality sinks in.

This was Malachi's plan all along.

I do not dare utter the accusation, and yet I don't need to. His lips peel back with a knowing smile. "Come, my queen, and we will rule everything together."

3

ROMERIA

Dawn paints the sky in sweeping shades of pink lemonade and wisteria, ignorant of the blood that soaks the earth and the countless bodies that litter it.

"Is it over?" Adrenaline and fear have kept me standing all these hours, through a night that felt endless at times. Now my legs wobble and my arms hang limp. I've never been so tired in all my life, not even when I was living on the street and sleeping with one eye open, guarding against threats.

"For the moment." Zander sidles up to me, his own breathing labored, his armor drenched in inky blood. He never left my side as each creature crawled out of the rift, carving through any that managed to escape the blades and arrows in the gory battle in front of us.

I graze a fingertip along the new silver line on his throat—a near-fatal strike by a wolflike beast who used the cover of a charging nethertaur to get too close. I healed him instantly with my key caster magic while battle raged around us.

Zander's jaw tenses as he collects my hand and kisses my knuckles. A silent thank-you for saving his life, perhaps.

On the other side of him, Abarrane plunges her sword into a cloaked heap that I'm certain is already dead.

I shudder, recognizing the body as that of a hag—a horrid monster that walked upright as if human, but with the black eyes and gray skin of something undead. When I saw the first one appear last night, its layers of jagged teeth revealed with an ungodly shriek, I screamed and incinerated it with a bolt of fire. Five more emerged behind it, their stench burning my eyes. Zander piggybacked off my flame to dispatch them.

I'd rather face a grif than another of those.

"Most of these beasts prefer the cover of night. We'll have the day to recuperate." Jarek saunters over to a nethertaur's corpse to wipe his blade across it, shedding clinging innards. Where Zander flanked my left, my faithful Legion commander slaughtered without mercy at my right. Now he looks like a movie poster for a wartime battle, his normally blond braids stained black.

"Are you telling me we'll have to do this *again* tonight?" I shake my head, a touch of hysteria in my otherwise weak voice. Is there enough time to rest?

"Perhaps not. These beasts do not appreciate the stink of their own kind's death, so they may be deterred. Eventually, they'll find somewhere else to climb up." He winces when he stands upright, pressing his palm against his side, a poor attempt to patch the gash where a beast tore through his warrior leathers and into his ribs.

"Jarek." I reach for my affinities without thought so I can heal him, but there isn't a single thread to grasp. The well has run dry after hours of launching flames and icicle arrows and stone bullets and everything else I could think of. At some point in the night, wielding my affinities became second nature, as innate as breathing. Now, without access to them, I feel naked.

"That thing moved faster than I expected." He juts his chin at a small creature that reminds me of a hyena—only with blue skin and scales lining its spine. "Thankfully, its claws were unimpressive."

"Impressive enough to cut you open," I counter. "We can get you to a healer on the Ybarisan side—"

"I'm *fine*, Romeria. It's just a scratch. Do not mother me." Soot-colored eyes pierce me as he uses my first name rather than my title. He's the only one who dares speak to me that way, especially in front of others. Jarek and I have always had an unorthodox relationship, but I appreciate it.

"There are many others, far worse off." Zander waves his sword outward, drawing my attention to the gory scene.

With daylight breaking, I can finally grasp the carnage at the rift. Countless beasts lie in still heaps, while blood-covered soldiers—Islorian and Ybarisan alike—wander among them, giving an aimless kick here and a blade poke there as if to ensure the carcasses won't revive.

There are also fallen soldiers in the mix.

My heart clenches as I scramble to search faces, but it's impossible to discern people in helmets and blood. "Where is Elisaf? And Radomir? And ... and—"

"Elisaf is over there." Zander points to a single figure surveying the slaughter in an exhausted daze, much like us.

My old nighttime guard meets our gaze then and begins moving for us.

A wave of relief overwhelms me. "What about the others?"

"They will find us soon enough."

"What if they don't? What if ..." I can't bring myself to finish that sentence. We started the battle with them surrounding us, but where are they now? I can't handle losing another person. The fissure in my heart from Gesine's death is still too raw.

"Then they fought bravely, and we will continue the fight in their honor," Zander says calmly, as if he can sense my rising panic.

"Your Highness!" Gaellar calls out then, limping forward, a gangly squire at her side.

"Glad to see you, Commander." Zander dips his head. "The rift army fought bravely."

"They did. But if not for your presence, I fear the outcome would have been vastly different." She regards me and where I saw only apprehension before—for a Ybarisan princess turned queen, for a key caster—now I see something entirely different. Something like awe.

What must I have looked like, with my silver eyes glowing while I conjured weapons out of thin air? At least I changed out of that winged dress and crown before Hudem, replacing them with far more practical leathers that Abarrane procured.

"Your Highness." She bows.

"Do you know how many we've lost?" Zander asks.

"Not nearly as many as stand. But that is not why I've found you. Riders approach from the south."

Zander turns in the direction, but the view is blocked by a sea of tents and bodies. "Which banner do they fly?"

"Kettling's."

A muscle in his jaw ticks. "That must be the army Atticus has sent."

"They've crested the hill. Their cavalry is moving quickly."

"To help or to hinder us?"

"They have not sent a messenger ahead of them for any sort of parley. Perhaps they saw the battle and are coming to aid." But the expression on Gaellar's face belies her worry.

"And when they see that we are not fighting Ybaris?" Zander surveys the battlefield.

"They will return their focus to Atticus's false claim to the throne," Abarrane retorts with certainty, reaching for her sword's pommel.

Gaellar pulls her wounded body upright. "The rift army is with you, Your Highness."

Zander sighs heavily. "I appreciate that."

Their meaning becomes clear. "Are you all insane?" I exclaim. "We can't fight them!"

Zander smirks at my outburst, but there's no amusement in that look. "No, we cannot join another battle on the heels of one," he agrees. "But we may have little choice if we cannot hold them off long enough for them to see reason."

"Bellcross is not far behind." Though it was hard to gauge yesterday, flying high above in Caindra's clutches. "Did you see the purple banner?"

Gaellar looks to the squire beside her, who shakes his head fervently.

"Still, they might think twice about attacking with another army at their back."

"Lord Rengard is marching here to fight against the Ybarisan army, not Islor," Zander says. "I do not know that he will be eager to involve his men. And we cannot fight against our own people. We need *all* of them."

"What are your orders then, Your Highness?" Gaellar waits expectantly for an answer Zander doesn't have.

Weary silence hangs over our small group as we struggle to see the solution. We were in a similar position only days ago, facing a vast army of Ybarisans and a ruthless queen on the other side of the bridge—enemies we could not afford to fight when a far bigger enemy waited in the wings.

We had one considerable advantage then. Well ... technically, two, if I include myself.

"Fine. We meet them at the front line and explain it to them," I say.

Zander snorts. "You make it sound so simple."

"It is. And they'll listen."

"And why is that?"

"Because we have *her*." I point to the beast that sits perched on the wall, the sunrise a contrast against her webbed wing and indigo scales.

As if Caindra can hear me, she tips her head back and releases a deafening roar in answer.

Zander's lip curls with a grim smile. "Let us make our way to meet them, then."

Gaellar spins on her heels and leads us through the fray.

As Zander predicted, legionaries meet us along the way, coated in blood and gore, but granting me a wave of relief that they all seem accounted for.

Jarek and Drakon clasp each other's wrists, their wordless greeting laden with meaning. "That must be stemmed." Jarek points to the gash that stretches across the redhead's forehead, just below his hairline, painting his face in rivulets of crimson. It's a head wound that would likely kill any mortal. The legionary will no doubt wear the silver scar with honor once it's healed, but for now, it's a ghastly sight.

"It's nothing—"

"Stop for a moment," Jarek commands, ignoring Drakon's protests as he tears a strip of canvas off a nearby tent and fastens it around his forehead.

Drakon winces as Jarek secures it before gesturing to fall in line behind us.

"What?" Jarek snaps when he sees me smiling up at him.

"Nothing. I just remember being accused of *mothering* recently."

"He is still weak from his time with the saplings and too stupid to accept that Nulling beasts can kill him," Jarek mumbles, grimacing as he peers down at his oozing side.

"Speaking of being stupid ..." I let my soft chide fade as we trail Zander, who cuts through the soldiers at a punishing pace, Elisaf at his flank. Those able to step out of the way do so, murmurs of "Highness" slipping from their lips. They wear expressions varying from pain to exhaustion to delirium, but all are marked with that same confused, surreal glaze. It must come with their sudden lack of desire for blood. Some of them have lived hundreds of years, driven by the base need.

"Did you notice the ground?" Zander points at the chartreuse blades of grass where trampled weeds and hard soil used to exist, glancing over his shoulder at me.

"Has to be the nymphs."

"I imagine so."

My thoughts drift to Ulysede. Hudem's moon has passed, and these mysterious creatures have arrived. What does that mean for us, other than freedom from the blood curse that has plagued these people for two thousand years? We know virtually nothing about them, though Gesine said seer visions labeled them anarchic, happy to collect their pound of flesh in turn for favors.

Has Islor traded one curse for another?

"We will have answers soon enough," Zander says, as if reading my mind.

"What sort of Nulling beast does *that*?" Elisaf draws our attention to a body lying in the fresh grass.

I frown as I get a better look at the skull tucked into the helmet. "Whoever it is, it looks like they died years ago." Bony fingers still grip the pommel of a sword. The soldier is nothing more than a skeleton dressed in metal, the flesh and muscle picked clean.

"There are more like this. I saw at least a dozen that way." Elisaf points behind him.

"Aye, we saw them too," Drakon calls out from behind, pressing his hand against his leaking forehead, the canvas soaked. "But we did not see what felled them."

Zander's scowl is deep as he studies the few creatures lying around us for a long moment. "There is nothing we can do for these soldiers now, save for giving them a proper burial. We must focus on the living." He moves on.

But my feet are stalled as I take in the suffering around us. "The living" includes many who are barely doing so if the agonizing moans hint at the truth. I cringe at a soldier in Ulysede's golden armor doubled over, his hands on his stomach to keep his guts from spilling out. Horik once arrived in the same manner after a fight with a hag, and it took Gesine all night to save him. Nearby, a pale-faced soldier uses a nethertaur corpse for support, his left arm hanging at his side, attached by nothing more than tendons.

"Romeria," Zander calls out, realizing I'm not following him. "We must continue."

I shake my head in a silent refusal to go on, to walk past as the others can. Some of these soldiers won't survive their brutal wounds, despite their elven ability to heal. "We need to divide all the soldiers into groups, those with the worst injuries in one area, so they can be treated first."

With a sigh, Zander retraces his steps, his expression softening. "You cannot heal *any* of them. Not until you rest," he says gently. "And even then, you will not be able to help all of them."

"I know. But there are healers across the bridge."

"You assume they aren't busy repairing limbs and flesh on their side."

"There are no sides anymore. We're all in this together." He's right, though. We have no idea how Ybaris managed with the barrage of beasts. The sky was alight with constant blasts of fire and rocky explosions from Mordain's Shadows. Anything that got through them would have met Ybarisan blades, led by Kienen.

Is my new Ybarisan commander alive? God, I hope so. He's the only person I trust in Ybaris, other than Agatha, the old caster and Gesine's coconspirator who stowed away in a wagon to find me.

Could the Master Scribe have survived last night?

Zander purses his lips but nods. Waving over a soldier, he relays the order to gather and separate the injured by severity.

"Bring the most critical to the officers' tents," Gaellar adds.

Zander turns to Elisaf. "Bring back healers on orders of Ybaris's queen. As many as they can spare."

Elisaf inhales sharply—no one is keen on crossing the rift after seeing what crawled and flew out of it—but he nods. "Consider it done." He marches back the way we came.

Zander collects my hand. "Is that better?"

"No," I grumble, watching as able-bodied men hoist those unable to walk. "I feel so helpless."

He offers a soft smile. "I know you ache for others in a way my kind doesn't seem capable. And it is commendable. But we have done what we can by delegating that work. Now we have a pressing issue that we cannot delegate to anyone else."

"The Kettling army."

"The Kettling army. Atticus's army." He jerks his chin at Abarrane. "Get us horses."

In minutes, we're in saddles, our small company making ground quickly, soldiers parting for us as we charge past the camp's outer borders.

Gaellar wasn't exaggerating. The cavalry is a thundering cloud rolling across the vast terrain, the green flag waving high in the air.

"They are not slowing down," Jarek notes, his gelding shifting on its front legs, likely sensing its rider's apprehension.

"We'll make them slow down." I slide out of my saddle, my legs nearly buckling from exhaustion. "Hold on to him, will you?" I toss my reins to Jarek.

Zander frowns. "Where do you think you're going?"

"I'd rather not get thrown off a horse today." I put some distance between myself and the others before I seek out the terrifying creature on the wall, like a monstrous, fire-breathing gargoyle. She hasn't moved, but I can feel her violet eyes on me, even from this distance.

I swallow my apprehension, praying this works. "Caindra! I need you!"

With a shrill screech that ricochets through the skies, the dragon launches herself into the air, her mammoth wings pumping with enough force to swirl dust below.

A mixture of awe and trepidation swells inside me as I watch her massive body sail toward us, the sun glinting off her scales, highlighting the indigo and rose gold.

Our horses dance and tug on their reins as they sense the predator's approach. It would be nothing for her to pluck them in her claws. I've seen her do it before.

Zander slides from his saddle and joins me on the ground. "How did you know she would come?"

"I didn't. It was a hunch." I sense a connection between her and me. Maybe it's that I know her secret—her alterative life as a brothel owner, hiding in plain sight among commoners and kings alike—or maybe it's that she has declared herself an ally.

My attention is on her, but Zander's deep brown eyes never leave my face, his hand smoothing over my hip. "Will you ever cease to amaze me?"

I reach up to draw a fingertip along the angular line of his jaw. Even with his golden-brown hair and face streaked in beast blood, he is the most attractive male I've ever met. "I hope not. We have *a lot* of years ahead of us. Could get stale."

He cups my jaw and places a soft kiss against my lips. "I welcome those years, stale or otherwise."

"I don't think it's the best time for *this*," I whisper against his lips.

"Perhaps not, but I certainly needed it."

"So did I." I close my eyes and revel in his closeness, wishing I could melt into his arms and remain there … forever.

The ground shudders beneath Caindra as she lands in the clearing.

With a heavy sigh, Zander peels away, brushing something off my shoulder.

"What was that?"

"A piece of something's tooth." He misses my grimace of horror as he turns toward the army. "Your plan worked."

Bellows carry over the rush of hooves, more green flags waving high in the air. Soon, the lines slow to a canter, then to a trot, until a wall of soldiers on horses a dozen-deep forms fifty feet away.

"Of course it worked. Who would be stupid enough to pick a fight with our fiercest ally?" I edge closer to where Caindra stoops. It's the first time I've been near her since before Hudem's moon. "Thank you," I whisper, reaching out to slide my hand over her snout. "You saved us." Had those wyverns that emerged from the rift attacked, this morning would look very different.

We might not be standing here.

If she understands me, she gives no hints. Does Caindra even remember the form she once occupied as the Goat's Knoll barkeep and master of secrets, now that the nymphs are here and she's relegated to remain as a dragon? I guess I'll never know. There's no way to ask her.

I catch my reflection in her violet eyes—of Princess Romeria's face that I've had to accept as my own in this world. My grimace returns in an instant as I take in my wild, windswept mane, standing on end and held in position by crusted blood. Smears of black coat my cheeks and forehead. "Why didn't anyone tell me I look like *this*?" I only ever touched these beasts with my affinities.

"Like you survived a battle?" Zander's voice is laced with humor. "I did not realize you would be so vain."

"I look like I dove into a vat of ink!"

"And I can't wait to help you wash it off," he counters, his voice low and contrary to our current predicament.

Jarek strolls up alongside Abarrane, their horses abandoned with Gaellar, their swords drawn. "You've looked better." He inhales. "Smelled better too."

A puff of hot air from Caindra's snout breezes over me.

"Oh, that's funny, huh?" I scoff.

I get a second huff in return. At least she no longer seems two seconds from slicing Jarek's body in half with her claws.

"What is the plan now?" Jarek's narrowed eyes size up the soldiers.

Zander shares his intense gaze. "We wait to see who they send for parley—"

"There!" Abarrane aims her sword end toward the purple flag hoisted high in the distance.

Beside me, Zander's shoulders sink with relief as Bellcross's envoy cuts through the wall of horses. "This changes everything. Come. We will meet them halfway."

"Make sure she behaves." Jarek points an accusatory finger at Caindra, who snarls in response.

I catch his eye roll as he's turning away. "Of course she'll behave. Lord Rengard is our *ally* and we need this army." I toss Caindra a knowing stare and then rejoin the others.

A company of twenty horses and riders move toward us with a noticeable gap between, forming two groups.

I pick out Lord Rengard first, his armor gleaming in the morning sunlight, the telltale purple plume marking him. Even the ominous situation doesn't diminish the smile on his lips as he climbs out of his saddle. The soldiers wearing Bellcross's crest on their shields scramble off to follow their lord while the ones wearing eastern green remain on their horses, their expressions guarded.

"It has been some time since I've seen you covered in beast blood, Your Highness." Lord Rengard clasps hands with Zander the same way he did when they met the morning he delivered supplies for our long journey north to Stonekeep. It's as if a vast army of thousands of men isn't standing nearby, awaiting orders.

"You answered my call, dear friend."

"We rode as hard as we could. I am sorry it was not hard enough."

"Do not fear, you will have your opportunity to defend Islor before long."

Lord Rengard studies Zander's face, a mixture of wonder and confusion there. "The last we spoke, you were chasing prophecy into Venhorn. It seems you found it."

Zander smirks. "So it would seem."

"It also seems you left some important details out of your letter." He regards Caindra.

"It was far too much to include, but all will be explained in due time."

Lord Rengard's interest swings to me. It's a moment before he dips his head in greeting. "Princess Romeria."

"*Queen* Romeria," Zander corrects. "Of Ybaris and Ulysede."

His eyebrows arch. "In due time, indeed."

With that greeting finished, Zander turns his attention to the other half. "The eastern army, sent here by my brother." He has adopted an imposing voice. "Who leads you now, for I know it is not General Adley."

Abarrane chuckles. It was her blade that severed Lord Adley's son's head from his body, after all.

"I am Amos. I lead these men," a male announces. He has no

feather plume or stately armor, nothing to suggest his high rank. He looks too young to command an army, though I know looks can be deceiving in his kind. Still, he puffs out his chest.

"Your Highness," Abarrane hisses, chiding the officer much like Boaz once did to me. "You are in the presence of Islor's true king."

Zander pats the air to rein in her temper. "And who are you to Lord Adley for him to name you general of Kettling's army?"

Amos pauses on his answer, as if deciding how much truth he has to offer. "I am no one to Lord Adley. I've never spoken to him. He did not name me ... Your Highness," he falters, glancing at Abarrane. "The king did."

"The king. As in my brother," Zander says evenly. "Explain."

"His Highness left the city walls to give us our orders to march here at once. I was not in command at the time. I was not even second-in-command. But he relieved my superiors and told me I was in charge."

"Superiors. Plural."

"Yes. Four of them, Your Highness." Amos swallows. "He pulled them into a tent one by one, and I guess he did not like what they had to say."

Zander twists his lips in thought. "So Adley is giving my brother as much issue as he gave me. Not surprising," he murmurs, more to himself. "And what were his exact orders?"

"His Highness sent us here, to the rift, to battle against the enemy Ybarisan invaders." Amos's eyes land on me, his expression hard.

A deep rumble vibrates my core as Caindra snarls, her lips curling upward to reveal her fangs.

The young general's face pales, earning Abarrane's and Jarek's snickers.

Zander ignores them, moving closer, seemingly unfazed that Amos sits on his horse and he is without his. "And did he give you any other orders, Amos? Anything regarding me or Her Highness?" He watches him closely.

Amos keeps his focus on Zander, as if afraid to look at me again for even a fleeting second. "He said we are to aid the rift army in the name of Islor, and that he would arrive soon to deal with our traitors."

Zander inhales deeply. "Then you will be happy to know you can follow your orders without issue, General. How far behind is the infantry?"

"A half-day's march, at most."

"Rift Commander!" Zander reaches behind him and Gaellar trots forward, reins for our horses in hand.

We remount, and I follow Zander as he moves toward the wall of cavalry, my heart thumping in my throat. I wish I could erect an air shield in case of stray arrows. Surely, no one would attempt something as foolish as to shoot either of us.

Even battle weary and covered in blood, Zander sits regal atop his horse. "Soldiers of Islor! My name is Zander. Some of you know me as king, while others will refuse to address me as such. In these coming dark days, it does not matter which side you choose as long as you listen to me now, for time is not our ally." His deep voice carries, riveting all eyes to him as he lets his stallion pace several steps to the right, then to the left. "Cirilea is in the throes of rebellion, and we do not know its fate. King Atticus left for the east to fight against Kier soldiers, welcomed into our lands by eastern lords who plotted to carve up Islor for themselves. They are the true traitors to Islor, and they will be judged for their treason."

Amos's eyes widen, the news a genuine shock to him.

"But Islor has far bigger woes than simple traitors. The rift is open."

Gasps sound.

A curse slips from Lord Rengard's lips.

Zander searches the faces before him, studies the range of terror, fear, and anger painted on them. "As I am sure you have all noticed by now, we have entered a new age, one with hope for all. The blood curse that has plagued us for two thousand years has ended. The poison that taints Islor's mortals is no longer our concern. That is thanks to *Queen* Romeria of Ybaris!"

I struggle against the urge to shrink as countless eyes grip me.

"Queen Neilina is dead. Under Queen Romeria's reign, the Ybarisans are no longer a threat to Islor. There will be no battle against them. We are now united against a common enemy, and with Ybaris and Mordain at Islor's side, we *will* prevail!" His voice projects confidence that I let seep into my bones, hoping it will ferment.

But, aside from the odd whinny or hoof scrape, the army remains silent. No cheers, no claps, nothing to hint where the people of Islor's heads are at, which king they believe in.

Do they believe him?

Will they follow him?

Zander nods, more to himself. "The rift welcomes your swords as we battle for the future of Islor. Our realm will need every one of you in the coming days." Abruptly, he turns.

I canter alongside him, back to where Lord Rengard and General Amos wait.

"Have them move into camp as soon as possible," Zander orders, his tone giving away nothing of his mood.

"When do you anticipate another attack?" Lord Rengard asks.

Zander peers up into the clear blue sky. "As soon as the sun goes down."

ELISAF GREETS us as we arrive back at camp, Caindra's shadow passing over on her way to her stone perch.

"You have returned already."

"I did not need to cross the bridge. The Ybarisans were on their way here. Her Highness's new commander and Mordain's Shadow leader."

I sigh with relief. Two of my only allies survived the night. Not that I should expect less with the skilled fighters, but a part of me worried that the other Ybarisans might be more of a threat to Kienen than the Nulling beasts, given his allegiance to me.

"They brought a dozen healers with them, at Kienen's request. Some of their strongest."

"Proving his worth yet again." Zander nods with satisfaction. "Where are they now?"

"The healers are at work in the tents. The others wait near the gates, but—"

"Best speak to them at once." Zander kicks his heels to his horse.

"They found Lord Telor," Elisaf says in a rush, stalling him. "He is wounded. A healer is with him, but she did not appear confident when she saw him." His tawny face furrows. "How he still breathes is beyond me."

Zander's gaze flitters to me, and I see the question in his eyes. Lord Telor is perhaps his most powerful ally in Islor's political arena, even more so than Lord Rengard. But what is more, he is an old friend.

I shake my head. Not even a spark of my key caster affinities shows itself yet.

Elisaf hesitates. "If you have anything important to say, I would say it now. He is there." He nods toward the large canopy nearby.

"Go to him," I urge. "We'll find Kienen and Solange."

"Fine." Zander hops off his horse and rushes toward the tent, but not before aiming an accusatory finger my way. "Do not cross to the Ybarisan side without me." To Jarek, he echoes, "Do not allow her to cross into Ybaris without me." With that, he ducks into the tent.

"'Do not *allow* her.' Funny," Jarek says dryly. "Does he not know you?"

I attempt to laugh but can't even muster the energy, the night's chaos and the aftermath weighing more heavily on me with each passing moment. The sun beats down, but it won't be long before it is gone and a new wave of terror arrives. "You should go and find a healer. You look pale."

"Later. Others need them far more. But you need rest, Romeria," Jarek says softly.

It's so rare to hear him use a tone that isn't abrasive, gruff. "I know, but we don't have time for that. Kienen and Solange didn't cross to sightsee." They must need to speak with me. "I need to get back to Ulysede to understand what has happened now that the nymphs are officially here. And we need to know how bad the situation is in Cirilea. And what about Atticus in the east?" Bexley made it sound as though he would not survive the coming battle.

"Jarek is right," Elisaf agrees, a rare occurrence between the two of them. "Take a few hours. Let's find you a tent and—"

Caindra's deafening roar cuts off his words. It's a warning, much like the one she issued last night as the Nulling beasts approached.

Heads whip toward the rift, and we all watch as a red wyvern sails out, its wings pumping hard. Soldiers shout alarms and rush for weapons.

But it doesn't seem to have any interest in us as it climbs higher into the sky.

A glint of gold in its claws catches my notice. "What is that ... It's carrying something."

Jarek's eyes narrow. "Or some*one*."

The sun's rays catch shimmering fabric fluttering in the wind, a body cradled.

My stomach drops with dread.

No. It can't be.

4

ANNIKA

"I vow to reward you with a ruby pendant thrice the size of that ring upon delivering me to Northmost."

"I don't believe you," Captain Aron drawls, his hands slung lazily over the *Tempest*'s wheel. The sunrise brought with it a dull breeze, just enough to billow the sails. His crew cheered.

My mouth gapes. "You are questioning the integrity of a royal family member's vow?"

He sighs. "And where is this pendant now? In your boot?"

"No. In the vault, where all our most valuable jewels are held." I add in a scoff, "Who keeps jewelry in their boot?"

"Your companion has promised me a pendant to get you to Westport, and it's in his boot."

"He is *not* my companion. He is my *captor*," I hiss. "And you are aiding in his crime against the royal family. That is punishable by death. *Plus* that pendant in his boot isn't worth nearly as much as the one I offer. I should know. They're both mine!" Tyree stripped me of my jewels as soon as we reached the docks. My ring, he used to barter our way onto the ship and then, when the captain balked at this notion of sailing to Skatrana's port, he begrudgingly sweetened the deal with *my* necklace. As if he were parting with *his* dearest belongings.

"Still, I think I'll stick to the guaranteed prize, not the one many leagues from here, in a city under attack."

My rage swells. Does this fool have any idea the treasures hidden in our coffers? "If you were smart, you would insist on taking the other ring he pilfered from me too." A white pearl set in a gold band crafted in the shape of the sea's coral. A gift from Zander.

"He has more jewels to present?" Captain Aron eyes the Ybarisan, leaning back against a wooden crate, his complexion ashen.

Despite his poor condition, Tyree grins. "Not in my boot. That one, I secured in a safer place." He pats his crotch, and I grimace.

"That can't be comfortable," Captain Aron notes, swinging his attention back to the horizon. "Or secure."

"Oh, trust me, it's secure. I'm keeping it extra safe for the princess." The mongrel winks at me.

"From what I've heard, it would fit just as well on your cock as it does on my pinky finger." I turn my back to them as the captain bursts into laughter, and watch my lands in the far distance. Waves break over rock just under the surface. I see what the captain meant last night. Whatever waits there would surely tear apart our hull.

"What's the big rush to get off the boat, anyway?" Tyree calls out.

"He's right. Given what we saw in Cirilea, we're safer at sea," Captain Aron adds.

"Surely, we are not." The sirens are not a tall tale meant to keep people from these waters. He, of all people, should know that.

The captain studies my ruined dress. "If it is blood you require, I would be willing to barter mine for a price. I did not take any poison."

I turn away, not to hide my disgust at the proposition, though it is vile—he is a filthy, hairy brute with pocked skin and yellowed teeth—but to hide my panic. Given the circumstances, I should be happy I am no longer desperate. But I don't like not having answers.

Why do I no longer crave blood? Hudem's moon flares and the need is suddenly *gone*? Just like that? Is it only me who is afflicted in this way? And what has happened to make this possible? All these questions I need answers to, and I will not get them in Westport. *If* we even make it there.

But from Northmost, I could travel to Bellcross and to Lord Rengard. Theon will know what is happening. He might also have a way to contact Zander. They have been friends since childhood. He would choose Zander over Atticus, that much is certain.

"Your not-companion will have a better chance of surviving his injuries through Westport, into Ybaris, where there are healers," Captain Aron says, as if that might sway my mood.

"She is the one who stabbed me in the first place!" Tyree's bellow of laughter carries. "I assure you, Annika will wait until I am too weak to stand and then put me in a wagon and slit my throat."

"And then I will take my dagger back from your corpse," I muse.

"See? At least she is honest." Tyree smiles. "From Westport, she will run to Shadowhelm and beg for safe haven from the king and queen—"

"I do not beg," I snap.

He goes on, ignoring me. "Given Annika was once betrothed to their human son, they may grant it."

"I *still* am betrothed to him." Technically, anyway. Mother made the arrangements, and no one has officially called it off. "And how did you know about that?" Very few did.

"After all that Ybaris accomplished, you are still surprised by what I know?" Tyree sighs heavily. "I've never understood it, though. Why would a human king and queen wish a plague upon their people?"

"Because they understand the value of an alliance, unlike *other* royal families who are too stupid and hateful to see through their ignorance."

"I think she's talking about me," Tyree mock whispers.

The captain shakes his head, but he's grinning, entertained by our bickering.

"And I would not have infected him."

"But you would have fed off him." The amusement has slipped from his face.

I shrug. "If he permitted it."

"I'm sure you could be very persuasive." There's a cold glint in his eyes. "It's neither here nor there now."

Wait. "Why do you say that?" What does Tyree know about what is happening to me? Is this something else the Ybarisans have caused?

"Because you are now betrothed to me."

Right. That foolishness. "I am not! I never agreed to it."

"Minor detail."

"Your mother never agreed to it either, and Atticus never intended to honor it. He certainly won't now that you've abducted me. He'll have your head for this. He'll have *all* your heads!" I waggle a finger at the sailors nearby. Some sneer, but most duck to avoid my attention, especially the ones whose emblems glow. Why is their blood still poison to me when I do not crave it?

Tyree tucks his hands behind his head as if relaxed. The sun glints off the multitude of silver scars across his sinewy forearms, where the legionaries subdued his elven affinity with a merth blade over the past weeks. "See what I have to look forward to, Captain?"

I smile through my simmering rage. "It is a good thing you will be dead soon, then."

He shrugs. "Maybe not. There are sometimes healers in Westport."

"Likely not powerful enough for that." I nod toward his thigh. The wound still oozes blood. The dagger Father gifted me has proven as lethal as he warned.

"I have heard rumor of a powerful caster traveling with the exiled king and Ybarisan princess," Captain Aron says, veering the conversation back to Islor. "In the Venhorn Mountains, which is only a few days' travel from Northmost."

"Yes, I know of Caster Gesine," Tyree says, his humor from a moment ago evaporating. "Even if I could find her, I imagine she'd kill me faster than my future wife will."

"I like her already," I quip, earning Tyree's eye roll. How Zander joined forces with such a caster is another answer I'd like, but my eldest brother has been carrying many secrets.

"That might be a more graceful death than the one the sea promises us if we cannot avoid this folly." Captain Aron sets his sights on the northern horizon.

5
ROMERIA

The stench of death curls my nostrils as we ride through camp toward the bridge. Few soldiers are idle, working as teams to heave carcasses toward the rift. Those too big to move are surrounded by kindling, awaiting flames at nightfall. According to Radomir, once a sapling who survived in these mountains among the Nulling beasts, the combination of burning beast flesh and fire is a compelling deterrent.

"There!" I spot Kienen and Solange near our gates, where Elisaf said they would be. They look as battle-worn as the rest of us—streaked in blood, their bodies weighed down with exhaustion. With them are a handful of Ybarisan soldiers and Agatha, the tiny old Master of Scribes, hidden within a cloak.

Jarek, Elisaf, and I slide out of our saddles and stride to greet our allies, the smile on my face unbidden and wide, despite my troubled thoughts.

"Your Highness." Solange offers a militant bow. Her face and lengthy chestnut-brown braids are relatively clean, thanks to the black mask and helm of her uniform, now tucked under her arm. "I did not expect to see glee from you." Her expression remains stony. No one would ever accuse the Shadow leader and Mordain's Second in the hierarchy of the Casters' Guild of being warm and fuzzy.

"I'm relieved to see you all in one piece." And invigorated, knowing I trusted right. "Thank you for bringing the healers. Elisaf was on his way to ask for them."

Kienen dips his head. His youthful face has been wiped clean, but all around his hairline is proof that he battled hard. "We assumed your night was as eventful as ours, and that you could use the aid."

"Good assumption." I could kiss him right now. "How bad is it over there?" I jut my chin toward Ybaris.

"Most civilians made it a safe distance away before the flood of beasts emerged. There were unavoidable deaths, but not nearly as many as we anticipated." Kienen peers up at Caindra, a silent acknowledgment of the vital part she played in the battle, sending the wyverns away. "Everyone is fatigued."

"The casters are resting to recoup their affinities, as I plan to shortly." Solange peers at the carnage around us. "It would be wise for you and your soldiers to find a tent and gather your strength."

"My people are quite happy to feel the sun on their faces, in case this is the last chance to do so," a deep voice announces from behind us.

I'm momentarily stupefied by Radomir's new—or rather old—face as he joins us, even though I'd already seen it within the safety of Ulysede. Once a hideous creature of the night, the nymphs' return has given the saplings a second chance at life, returning them to their former elven versions.

Still, I struggle to accept that this is the same person who strapped Annika to a boulder and tossed her over the bridge my first night here. They are two different people in every way. "But they are sleeping in shifts. Your Highness." He bows to me and nods at Kienen, who matches it immediately. The two of them were our sworn enemies upon first meeting. Zander was prepared to kill them both and struggled with trusting them. They seem to have bonded over that similarity.

"And how many of *your people* have fucked off to the mountains already?" Jarek, ever the cynical one, asks.

Radomir pauses as if weighing his answer. "One that I know of," he admits. "And I promise Your Highness that when this battle is over, I will personally hunt him down and deliver his punishment with my blade."

"Don't waste energy worrying about a few deserters. We have reinforcements on their way in." I tell them about the two armies that just arrived. But that is not at the forefront of my mind. "Did you see the red wyvern that came out?"

"It was rather hard to miss," Kienen says.

"Right. But did you see what was in its grasp? Tell me it's not what I think it is."

"We noticed." Solange's shrewd gaze darts to Agatha, who worries her thin lips. "And we cannot tell you that unless you wish to invite lies, Your Highness."

Beside me, Jarek curses.

"So, you're saying it's possible that Neilina survived the fall into the rift." Forget for a moment the token blade I drove through her throat.

"The queen did not survive the fall." Solange nods toward her elder—a clear sign that this is her explanation to deliver.

"There are only two ways to remove a gold collar from the elementals' necks. Either by Queen Neilina's touch or by her death." From within her satchel, Agatha produces a shimmering ring. "They all opened last evening."

"You are telling us that the elementals are no longer collared." Panic fills Jarek's voice. "They can all summon the fates at any time."

"As opposed to Ybaris's queen forcing them to?" Solange retorts crisply.

"They are no longer collared," Agatha confirms. "But I do not believe you should be worried about elementals rushing to meddle with the fates."

I don't care about uncollared elementals now. "Why would that wyvern carry Neilina's body out of the rift?"

"A good question, indeed. We seem to understand little about what is and isn't possible when the fates are scheming. That is becoming clearer with each new day." Agatha's wrinkled forehead lifts with a knowing stare. "I often wondered about that garish token encircling Queen Neilina's neck, what purpose it might serve her. Or, more likely, what purpose it might serve the donor."

Aoife. "The fates never give without taking." And Aoife gave Neilina Princess Romeria—a deadly weapon to use against Islor.

Her nod is subtle. "We may have just witnessed the true cost of that summons so long ago. Queen Neilina undoubtedly fell into the rift, and surely, *she* did not survive. As for who came out, though ... another version of Neilina, as we have a different version of Romeria? Perhaps. But I fear it is something far worse."

My curse echoes Jarek's from a moment ago as I grasp what the caster is suggesting. "Aoife has been here before." And we know that Malachi wishes to come back. It's the entire reason Sofie sent me to Islor in the first place. "Are you telling me we may have not one fate to worry about, but two?"

Agatha's pinched expression confirms I'm not wrong in my suspicions. "I wish I could say otherwise."

My stomach swirls with sudden nausea. "How are we supposed to fight against not just Malachi but Aoife?"

"We've done it once and obviously succeeded, though how remains a mystery."

A mystery that may be answered within that vast library the nymphs have been protecting all these years. Gesine was adamant it held vital information for me, for our future. "How fast can we get those scribes to Ulysede?"

"We sent letters yesterday as soon as we parted ways and received a response from the Prime at sunrise." Agatha and Solange share another look, and this time the elderly caster dips her head, deferring to her superior.

"The Prime has declared that she will not comply with the request for scribes."

"What does *that* mean? Romeria is the queen of Ybaris. Did you make it clear that this is a command, not a request?" Jarek stares down the Shadow.

Solange takes a step forward, challenging him. "Her Highness's needs could not have been clearer had I inked it in her own blood."

"And yet she ignores us."

"Lorel is certainly not ignoring Queen Romeria." By Agatha's tone, more bad news is to come. "The Prime has obviously learned of the lengths the scribes have undertaken to aid prophecy and had announced that all scribes must face judgment for treason against their guild. She has also learned that I am here and has demanded that the Shadows escort *me* back to Mordain so I may be suitably punished for my crimes."

"And yet she was willing to turn a blind eye to Neilina forcing Ianca to summon a fate in the first place," Solange mutters. "She even had the audacity to suggest that was an impossibility in front of the council."

"The queen who ensured Lorel's role as Prime?" Agatha snorts. "What else would you expect of someone who puts politics before integrity? But that queen is dead and, I assure you, Lorel will still not admit culpability."

"And a new Ybarisan queen changes *everything*."

"Which is why Lorel has chosen this path."

The two casters lob words back and forth as if we're not standing here.

"Why would the Prime want to make me an enemy?" I interrupt.

"Because she assumes you already are one. She has professed you a false queen and Mordain free of Ybaris's rule." Agatha's face turns grim. "After she interrogates the scribes in hopes of uncovering every last shred of knowledge about what has taken place in Ybaris and Islor, she will execute them."

My stomach drops. "How many?"

"I fear all of them." Pain fills the old caster's wrinkled face.

"But she can't!" We need the scribes.

"Without Neilina, Lorel knows her position as Prime is threatened and she will do whatever she feels necessary to maintain it," Solange says with more than a hint of bitterness. "Using the opportunity of a new ruler to assert full independence from Ybaris is her best move."

"And how do *you* feel about that?" Kienen cuts in, quiet up until now, his steady gaze on Solange.

She glares at him. "What point are you trying to make with an audience here, Ybarisan soldier? You know *exactly* how I feel," she snaps back, and I can't help but sense they know each other beyond their current roles. "It is no secret I have long since wished for my realm to be out from beneath Ybaris. We are discarded as children and then expected to return as servants once our affinities are of use. Now here we are, summoned to the rift to fight in a war between two royal families over land and power, expected to do their bidding. We have played puppets to Queen Neilina's whims for far too long."

"Queen Neilina is dead," I remind her.

"Yes, by *your* hand. Whether Lorel knows of your path here by Malachi's will is yet to be determined, but once she does, she will use that to turn the entire guild against you. She can be very persuasive in her methods."

"Do you support your Prime?" Jarek's voice is filled with challenge, the unspoken question hanging in the air. *Will Solange betray us?*

Solange meets it with squared shoulders. "I do not support Lorel," she says slowly, clearly, daring anyone to oppose her words. "She must be stopped before she causes irreparable damage to my people and to all our realms. I am no fool, and I am here, witnessing the dangers to all firsthand, not hiding in Nyos's protected towers. Whether I wish to be here or not, here is where Mordain *must* be." She casts a hand. "But how long before Lorel recalls us all to Mordain?"

Panic strikes me. "She wouldn't do that, would she?" We can't afford to lose any elementals to this Prime's schemes.

"She will if she thinks it will give her an advantage," Solange says without missing a beat.

I shake my head, my fury building. "If she is not going to send the scribes here, then we have to go get them. *Now*, before she has a noose around all their necks." Or whatever method of murder Mordain relishes in.

"If you wish to never leave Mordain." Solange's warning sounds like a threat, and Jarek grips his sword's pommel in response, a move not missed by the caster.

She rolls her eyes at him. "I am merely stating facts."

"Mordain has shields for protection," Agatha elaborates. "Its connection to the elements is exceptionally strong."

"It's a pulse." That's what Wendeline called it.

"Yes. And that pulse has allowed the guild to build powerful wards to guard it from its enemies. Even your beast will not be allowed to get close to Nyos's walls. Certainly not your legionaries, for no Islorian immortal has been able to cross the threshold since the day Prince Rhionn stole away with Caster Farren."

"Are you saying I can't break down those wards?" Not that I would know how. But Gesine never mentioned this. Maybe it's because she basically warned me against ever setting foot on Mordain soil.

The tiniest smirk touches Solange's lips. "You are powerful, but you are not *all*-powerful, Your Highness. And you are certainly not indestructible."

"I'm well aware of that." I have scars across my shoulder to prove it.

"Even if *I* escort you through, Lorel will bind your affinities the moment you pass the guild's gates." Solange shakes her head. "Did Gesine teach you nothing?"

"Caster Gesine had a lot to teach in a very short time," Agatha snipes, defending her ardent pupil. She turns to me, adjusting her tone to one of lecturer. "As Prime, Lorel wears the Ring of Minerva, the first known guild leader of the caster era. It is akin to a ruler's crown, and it strengthens her connection to her affinity. As a regular caster, her abilities with Aoife's element were adequate. Now, they are easily triple that in strength. That is why she rarely ever leaves Nyos and why she certainly won't now. But it also allows her to tap into the power of Mordain, manipulating the wards to suit her needs with a few whispered words. It is how Mordain controlled key casters in the past."

"Like Farren."

"Precisely. The wards can work on those who create *and* those who manipulate. Both casters and elven. Queen Neilina herself never set foot in Nyos. Some say it was because she deemed herself above attending to anyone, but I suspect she knew the risk, if Lorel decided to bind her. Regardless, Lorel will not allow you access to your affinities while you are anywhere near her."

"But we need the scribes to figure out how to get rid of Malachi when he gets here," I say weakly.

"Then I suggest you come up with a better plan than showing up at Nyos's gates and demanding she release them, because I assure you, Lorel will be waiting for you," Solange cautions.

I look to Agatha, hoping she might have an idea. She was the true puppet master behind ensuring this prophecy came to pass.

All she has for me, though, is a sympathetic smile laced with worry. "Perhaps rest for all will allow us fresh ideas."

"How much time do we have before this Prime knows we are not giving her the Master Scribe?" Elisaf asks. An excellent question.

"She will expect an immediate response from me and a departure with due haste."

"And how long does it take to get to Mordain by horseback?"

"For others, three days. For a group of Shadows? The trip can be completed in a day and a half at most, riding hard with rest only for the horses. We could make excuses for an additional day, due to lame animals and issues with the cargo."

We need to buy time. "So, you lie and tell her you're sending Agatha back, and then we have until tomorrow night before the Prime starts looking for her." Which means the Master Scribe can't be seen on the Ybarisan side again. That's fine—I need to get her to Ulysede, where she will be safe.

"I know the perfect messenger for this task," Agatha cuts in. "Look for Baedriya. She rode here with me and seems to have a good head on her shoulders—"

A cascade of stone chunks tumbles from the rift wall then, interrupting our dire conversation. Caindra, shifting from one clawed foot to another and back again.

"She is troubled," Radomir notes, watching closely. "There is something in the rift. Something coming."

He's right. Her attention is riveted to the canyon in the earth.

My stomach roils. Is this the moment Malachi makes his grand appearance? Bexley did say he wouldn't crawl out of the Nulling like a fiend, but maybe he'll fly out on the back of a wyvern?

"On your horse *now*, Romeria," Jarek commands, goading me toward my saddle with a firm hand on my back. Others follow suit, Solange hauling Agatha up with a holler from the elderly caster.

We're backing our horses away when two mammoth forms shoot out from the rift and up into the sky, issuing earsplitting roars.

"Fates," Elisaf whispers as we watch their wings spread wide. "They are of her kind."

Caindra launches herself upward toward them, answering their calls with one of her own.

I gape as the beasts soar high above and shouts of panic erupt in the camp. They're identical to Caindra, save for the color of their scales—one a burnt orange, the other a vibrant chartreuse.

More dragons.

"She's not attacking them!" Jarek yells over the commotion as we struggle to steady our bucking horses.

In fact, their sky dance of spiraling dives and spins appears friendly, their wings grazing each other's with each pass.

It dawns on me. "She's been waiting for them." Caindra's astute guard from her perch today wasn't just to ward off enemies. She was anticipating her kind's arrival, either with expectation or hope.

In a triangular formation, with Caindra in the lead, the three dragons sail toward us.

"Stand down!" Radomir's voice booms as he hollers at soldiers armed with arrows and swords to back away.

The ground trembles as they land, Caindra flanked by the others.

"Fates." Kienen's sword dangles in his grip, useless. "The orange one is even larger than her. I didn't think that possible."

Larger and fiercer looking, its jade-green eyes cold as they size us up. A deep gouge through its scales hints at a battle fought long ago. What could do *that* to a dragon?

The chartreuse one on Caindra's right side is much smaller, its yellow eyes narrowed as it drags its claws through dirt.

"Romeria," Jarek warns through gritted teeth as I slide off my horse and move forward.

"Everyone, stay back."

"As if." With a curse, Jarek joins me on foot. "You are determined to see me eaten by one of these things."

"Put your sword away," I warn him, keeping my gaze ahead. "It might agitate them."

After a moment, he complies, wincing with the simple movement.

Caindra tips her head back with a roar before swinging it to the side to rub snouts with the orange one.

"I think it's okay," I whisper, advancing toward her.

"And if you are wrong?"

"Then neither of us will know any better because we'll both be dead."

I feel his glare at my cheek, but I keep my eyes on Caindra and her companions, my heart pounding as we get closer, until we're standing within their shadows.

The chartreuse dragon's snout twitches as it scents us, and it emits a growl.

Jarek is in front of me in a split second, his hand gripping his pommel.

"A lot of good that'll do." I move around his back but stay there. Maybe that is a warning not to come any closer. "Caindra?"

Her lips unfurl to show fangs. She swings her mammoth head toward the smaller dragon and issues a warning snarl in response.

Long beats pass and then the orange and green dragons sink forward and dip their heads toward the ground.

Jarek shakes his head and whispers more to himself, "That is as good a bow as you'll get from such a beast."

Behind us, horse hooves pound with approaching riders. "Romeria!" Zander shouts, charging toward me, Abarrane on his heels.

The orange beast's head swings in that direction and a low rumble vibrates inside my chest with its growl.

I rush forward, my hands in the air. "He's with me! He's *with me*!" Can it understand me as Caindra does?

Zander leaps off his horse and runs toward me, freezing when I hold up my palm to stall him.

Another few beats pass, and the orange dragon dismisses him, returning its attention to Caindra.

Slowly, Zander approaches my side.

"How is Lord Telor?" I ask.

"I ... he ..." Zander stumbles over his words, caught off guard by the question. "Still breathing. The caster claims there are traces of a powerful caster's affinities within him. Yours, I assume, from when you healed him. She believes that is what has kept him alive this long." His wide-eyed gaze drifts over the beasts in front of us. "I heard the commotion and rushed here. There are three of them now."

"I know. Isn't it amazing?"

Zander glares with accusation at Jarek. "And your Legion commander allowed you this close to them without a shred of your affinities intact?"

"There he goes again with that word *allowed*," Jarek mutters.

I ignore their bickering. "I think they know each other." Maybe *more* than know.

"That is a welcome thing. I would not want that orange one as her enemy."

We watch as Caindra and the others take turns bumping each other with their snouts, like long-lost friends, reunited.

"You know what this means, right?" I can't help my broad smile. "We have three dragons on our side now."

"We have *three* dragons," Zander echoes. He checks the sun in the sky. "And the timing for their arrival could not be better. We have much to do."

"I need to go to Mordain." I give him a rushed version of what we just learned from Solange and Agatha, who hang back with the others.

"I agree. *We* need to go to Mordain," Zander counters. "But there is little you can do until you have regained use of your affinities—"

"But she's going to—"

"And even less we can do for those scribes without a solid plan," Zander cuts me off, his voice taking on a lecturing tone. He steps forward, settling his hands on my shoulders as if he's about to deliver unwelcome news. "Right now, you *must* go with Caindra to Ulysede, Romeria, to rest and learn what you can of these nymphs. They could prove more helpful to us yet."

"Or they could cause her great harm," Jarek counters, his expression dark.

"Prophecy has made her their queen," Zander answers crisply. He doesn't like being challenged by anyone, but especially not the male who spends more time with me than even he does. "They built and hid an entire city for her protection."

"And left it in the ward of a devious serpent who plays mind games. I do not like this plan." Jarek emphasizes that with a headshake.

"And I do not care what you like. She will be safer there than anywhere else. Especially with you to protect her, *legionary*."

Jarek's jaw clenches, but he doesn't respond.

"If you two are done deciding where *I* should go … What about you? It doesn't sound like you're coming with me." I can't help the forlorn tone in my voice.

"I will be there soon, I promise." Zander collects my hands in his. "But first I must learn what has happened to Atticus. And I must reclaim my city."

My mouth gapes. "You're going to Cirilea *now*?" The memory of how I left it—in flames and chaos, with Gesine's lifeless body slung over Zorya's shoulder—flares in my mind.

"I must. I cannot waste a moment."

"But Malachi is coming." And very likely aiming for that same throne.

"All the more reason to secure it before he has the chance. I will present myself as the king returned and make it known the strength of my allies should anyone choose to challenge me. Abarrane will come with me. Once that is done, I will find you in Ulysede."

That's as much an order from Zander to stay put as I have ever received. "But what about the rift? Those fucking *things* are going to crawl up out of the Nulling again tonight and—"

"That is not our role."

"But I'm a key caster." That is exactly my role.

"Last night, you needed to be a key caster, and you did so remarkably. But today, you are a queen, and kings and queens do not sit idly waiting for mindless beasts to emerge from the ground each night when so many political pieces are in play. We have important work that no one else can do," he says evenly. "Between Gaellar, Kienen, and the Shadows, the rift is in capable hands. I will leave Elisaf to guard over Lord Telor, one of our most valuable allies. Send Caindra to patrol tonight while you rest, if she is willing. And I will return to you as soon as I am able." Zander's intention dawns on me as he eyes the orange dragon with grim determination.

Beside me, Jarek curses.

Abarrane's face fills with horror. "Fates, no. Absolutely *not*."

6

ZANDER

My boots land on the grass with a soft thud. I brace my hands on my knees and grant myself a moment to settle after the terrifying flight that began moments after Romeria invited help from Caindra's companion. The request, spoken out loud as a question —*Would it be possible?*—hung like sodden undergarments for a few beats and then, without warning, the orange dragon charged forward, scooping up Abarrane and me in its claws before I had time to react.

I'm not sure I breathed the entire time in the air.

I appreciate Jarek's stark warning when I suggested the swifter form of transportation. There were moments when I was sure I would slip through its grip and plummet to the ground, and other moments where I felt it might drop me intentionally. How Romeria handles such travel with grace is beyond me.

"Do they make saddles large enough for these creatures?" This dragon must have a name, as Caindra does. I wish I had one to use.

Abarrane answers by leaning over and heaving the meager contents of her stomach, her complexion a sickly green.

If this were under different circumstances, I would mock her for her fragility. But I can't find the humor in anything as I take in the carnage over the rolling green hills normally known for their fertile soil. Now, they're drenched in the blood of countless bodies, lying scattered in various states of dress, most wearing Cirilea's flame crest on their armor. An odor lingers in the air, the beginnings of rot. These bodies have been here for days.

Tents are slashed and caved in, suggesting a surprise overnight attack while soldiers slept. Aside from a horse grazing by the tree line, a curious green bird that flutters around us, and copious flies laying eggs, there are no signs of life.

Kier's silver and red banner flutters in the light breeze next to the green and gold of Kettling. There is no mistake who has claimed victory over this massacre.

My molars grind as I regard my faithful Islorian soldiers, dead thanks to the games of those in power and those who angle for it. I should have killed Adley years ago. Someone else would have risen to his place, though. Maybe someone worse.

Still, I should have killed him.

Abarrane wipes the spittle from her jaw. "When I pledged my sword, it was to die in battle, not plummeting to my death from a beast's grip."

"Be thankful we had the option. It would have taken days to reach here by horseback. Though I cannot say this sight brings me comfort." Especially not after the battleground we just left.

I survey the surrounding forests. Plenty of places for enemies to lie in wait within the trees. "Surely, there are scouts watching us this very moment." Waiting for Cirilea to send in reinforcements so they can slaughter them too. Where exactly Kier's army is, I would like to know. "I imagine they'll reconsider an ambush, given our orange friend."

"Our *orange friend* is as likely to kill us as our enemies." Abarrane eyes the dragon warily.

"They do not know that." Perhaps I should ask it to char the trees with its fiery breath—if it shares that skill with Caindra.

But we didn't come here for another battle. We came to learn what has become of my brother, Islor's current king. "I will corral that gelding over there and then make my way among the dead to—"

The ground trembles as the dragon launches itself into the air.

The horse barely has time to whinny before it's snatched from its grazing spot. Its bones crunch as the dragon devours it, Abarrane and I looking on. The entire spectacle—how quickly a beast this size can pounce on its prey of choice—has me reaching for flame in case I must defend myself. But there isn't a hint of one anywhere near us to fuel my affinity. I have nothing but my blade—futile against this beast if it decides it's still hungry.

The dragon returns to its initial spot, casting a wide shadow over the hill.

"You were saying?" Abarrane asks dryly.

I sigh. "We will search the dead on foot."

"YOUR HIGHNESS!" Abarrane calls out, hovering at a cluster of bodies. We scoured the entire camp and, not finding Atticus among the debris, moved on to a smaller battleground to the west.

My stomach clenches as I navigate toward her. Despite how deeply my brother betrayed me, despite the reality that his demise will make my reclaiming my throne a smoother process, the thought of him dead—by my hand or another's—does not bring me the satisfaction I once thought it might.

I brace myself as she flips over a male riddled with wounds, including one earned by an ax cleaved into his armor.

A wave of relief swarms me as I note the beard. "That is not Atticus."

"No, it is Kazimir, which is the next best thing. He is a growth on your brother's arse. Where he is, Atticus is always near, especially in battle."

I scan the bodies for the familiar blond curls and polished armor. "And yet he is not here." I add after a moment, "Which means Kier has likely taken him captive." An Islorian king in chains is a powerful bartering chip. Though, a usurper whose realm is in the midst of rebellion? Maybe not as valuable as Kier's ruler hopes.

Kazimir's eyelids flutter.

"He lives." Abarrane stoops to check his pulse. "Barely."

"Barely is good enough for the healers if we can get him there in time."

"He will not survive the trip."

"He has survived this long. Let us pray he can hang on. Kazimir may be the only one who can convince Atticus to ally with us, for Islor's sake." He is certainly the best one to shine a light on where my brother's head has been these last days, and how hard he will battle me for the throne once I reclaim it. "The Kiers will not kill Atticus as long as they think he is valuable."

Abarrane snorts. "Knowing your brother and his silver tongue, King Cheral will believe he is blessed by Malachi himself."

"So be it. This is where our search for Atticus must end, then. May the fates grant him strength in whichever dungeon they place him."

"And this Kierish army?"

I scan the sun's placement in the sky. We're moving into midafternoon. "As much as I would like to find them and have the dragon blaze a path through their ranks, I have a throne to reclaim."

7

ATTICUS

B riny sea air. That's the first thing I note when I regain consciousness.

The second is the way my body sways with the soft lull of waves, and the jarring pain in my right shoulder. What was it that ... *oh, right.* An ax found its way between the joint in my armor, cutting through my chain mail and nearly cleaving me in half. That's what toppled me. Why my head throbs, I can't recall.

A gruff male says something in Kierish and another laughs.

In all the years I've walked this earth, why had I not bothered to learn that language? It would be useful now.

Agony splices my skull as a palm strikes my cheek.

"We know you are awake," says the man, his accent thick, his words stilted. He smells of stale ale and horseradish.

I wait until the pain subsides and then crack an eyelid. We're in the wooden hull of a ship. On our way to Ostros, no doubt, so this mortal swine can deliver me to his king for a prize. A quick scan around reveals I am alone with these two.

"You are looking for your army?" The soldier grins, flashing crooked teeth. "They are dead. Every last one of them. I made sure of it."

With a snarl, I flex against the restraints binding my wrists behind my back, the desire to tear this man's head from his shoulders invigorating. But all I achieve is more pain and a searing burn against my skin.

"Special chains that even your kind cannot break," he says with a chuckle. "I am surprised you survived, usurper king."

"Should have left me there. I doubt I'll be much use to King Cher-al," I croak, my throat raw. Zander will reclaim his throne the moment he discovers it's empty and leave me to rot in a Kierish dungeon.

Perhaps I deserve it.

I lick my dry lips.

"Thirsty?" The soldier lifts his arm in front of my face, just out of reach. He hisses as he jabs a thumb into a gash above his elbow. A fresh stream of crimson trickles from the spot.

It stirs nothing.

Not a clench in my stomach, not a burn at my gums. In fact, the scent of this human's blood is as sour and unappealing as the rest of him.

A deep bellow of laughter sails from my lips, filling the ship's hull.

She did it. Romeria was telling the truth.

With a scowl, the soldier swings the blunt handle of his ax toward my temple.

Everything goes black.

8

ROMERIA

I stare in amazement as we descend toward Ulysede's golden gates. The craggy, inhospitable wasteland of yesterday is now bursting with lush trees and a cobblestone road fit for a royal entranceway. When Caindra first veered in this direction, I had no idea where she was taking us.

Caindra lands in a clearing, setting Jarek and me down on the stone.

"She didn't toss you this time." It's become a favorite thing for her to do—cast my Legion commander to the ground like trash, sending him tumbling.

"For once." Jarek winces as he pulls himself upright, pressing his arm against his side. He's paler than he was when we left. It could be the flight—he hasn't adapted as well to the air as I seem to have—but I'm worried. If it were just a scratch, his elven body would have healed by now.

"I should have made the casters take a look at you." I don't know if I'm more annoyed with him for dismissing me or with myself for relenting to his stubbornness.

"I'll be fine." He peers up at the sky. "I'd be more worried about the old witch. I heard her screaming."

I hold my breath as the smaller chartreuse dragon swoops toward us. Thankfully, it sets Agatha down with the tenderness of a beast who somehow knows the fragile cargo it carries.

Agatha wobbles on her feet, and Jarek dives to catch the elderly caster a moment before her legs give out.

"Goodness, much thanks." She tests the fasteners on her leather satchel before smoothing windswept strands of wiry gray hair that escaped her bun during flight. Whatever is in that bag must be important to her. She hasn't been apart from it since we met. "I will be happy to *never* do that again."

I offer an apologetic smile. "Safer and much faster than traveling through the mountains."

"Be that as it may, I made peace with my sins while in flight and convinced myself that I would not reach this place." Her eyes widen at the view behind me. "But I am so glad I have."

Clanking metal and throaty grunts draw our attention to Ulysede's grand gate—the first of two to enter the secret nymph city hidden for thousands of years.

My breath catches at the line of living, breathing gargoyles that now mark the tunnel's walls within. They're identical to the statue versions, in size and ferocity, with rippled gray skin, elongated snouts, and webbed wings tucked behind their shoulders. Deadly spears sit within their grips, their claws nearly as long as the blades. When I first saw the stone versions, I wondered if they might be daaknars—Malachi's favorite underworld demons and the beast that attacked me that first night. Now that I see the live version, I'll admit they aren't as terrible, but still fearsome nonetheless.

They aren't the only creatures to occupy the tunnel. Scantily clad faeries with pointed ears regard us with curiosity, their wings fluttering behind them. They're child size, the tops of their heads barely reaching the gargoyles' waists, but they show no hint of nervousness around the soldiers.

Jarek is suddenly beside me again. "For the record, I do not trust these beings, and I am against walking into this place without your full affinities returned."

"Yes, you've made your position clear."

"And yet you do not listen."

I don't have the energy for this fight. "I'm the Queen of All, aren't I?"

"Unless you've served your purpose by opening the nymphaeum." He eyes them as a warrior sizing up his adversaries. They in turn watch him with equal wariness. Or maybe it's the two giant dragons behind me that they're cautious of. "We know nothing of these nymphs, other than they have the power to hide an entire realm, and they can undo the fates' work. That is troublesome enough for me."

But are they the agents of chaos people have come to believe them to be? "Gesine said everything to do with the fates was mostly guesswork." Fed by vague foretelling and a few old books. Ingrained beliefs that have survived millennia, only to be proven false within weeks. According to Lucretia, they were never banished by the fates. It was the nymphs themselves who chose to leave this world, taking away their power and, with it, the ability for the fates to walk this realm in flesh and blood. And the key to releasing them from their self-imposed exile had nothing to do with the nymphaeum door in Cirilea, but the one at Stonekeep.

"Yes, and it seems we have been wrong about much," Agatha says, as if reading my mind. "We are all in a state of great learning now, myself included." She smooths her hands over her skirts. "But your commander is right to be concerned."

"We must be more than *concerned*." Jarek spares her a sideways glance, as if suspicious of her agreement.

"I guess there's only one way to find out, because we can't stand here all day." I step forward.

The gargoyle on the end snarls something in another language, and as one, the line of guards drops to a knee. Meanwhile, the faery-nymphs bow deeply.

"That's a good sign," I murmur. "And I didn't even need my crown."

"The one you lost?" Jarek throws back.

"I did *not* lose it. It vanished." Along with the wings and dress, from the tent where I left it with a servant, on my way to battle last night. He shook as he described the moment it disappeared from his guard, afraid I would punish him.

I check Caindra's position, who seems preoccupied with a tiny green bird that flutters near her snout.

"You trust her far too much for my liking," Jarek whispers, as if afraid the dragon will hear him disparage her.

"I don't think she would have brought me here if I had to worry about my safety. And besides, if it were up to you and Zander, we would never trust *anyone*, and then where would we be?" Without Kienen and Radomir, who have proven invaluable ten times over. I give him a knowing smirk.

Two lean, leather-clad figures emerge from the shadows of the tunnel then.

A rare, genuine smile stretches across Jarek's face as he takes in his fellow legionaries. "I never thought I would be happy to see your ugly faces."

"Nor I yours, Commander," Zorya retorts, her one good eye crinkling with her grin.

That their swords sit holstered in their scabbards as they pass the nymphs tells me a lot. The tension slides from my shoulders.

"It seems we've missed a worthwhile battle." She passes through the gate. "You look ill. And injured."

"It's just a scratch," Jarek snaps.

Zorya gives me a once-over from head to toe, before dipping her head in greeting.

One of the faery-nymphs—the female in a gauzy green dress that leaves little to the imagination—reaches with clawed fingers for Loth's arm as he passes. The quiet legionary shoos her away like a horse switches his tail against a fly, earning her titters.

The same gargoyle who snarled at the guard earlier shouts at her now and, with a jolt, she and her companion dash out.

And vanish.

My mouth hangs as familiar childish giggles touch my ears and, a moment later, an invisible fingertip skates across my cheek. I follow the sound of their laughter down the stone path, but they never reappear.

"Yes, they can live among us without us having a single clue." Zorya confirms my unspoken question, her tone dripping with displeasure at that notion.

Jarek glares at Agatha. "Did your seers tell you about *that*?"

"I do not recall such a thing." But by Agatha's wondrous smile, it doesn't disturb her as much as it does us.

Zorya's eye narrows. "You've brought another *witch* here?"

I stifle the urge to groan. I thought we had moved past the legionaries' loathing for casters. "This is Agatha. She is Mordain's Master Scribe, and she knows more about prophecy than anyone else."

"If it appeases you any, warrior, my own guild wants to execute me for my part in all this," Agatha says.

Zorya sniffs—the only sign that the caster's words might mollify her displeasure.

I add gently, "Gesine trusted her."

That earns a flinch. But when Zorya regards the old woman again, her expression has softened a touch. "I recall your name."

Gesine spoke of her often.

Agatha nods, her own grief painted on her face. "She was like a daughter to me."

Behind us, the gargoyles remain on one knee. "Anything we should know before we go in there?"

Zorya peers over her shoulder, sizing up the nymphs. "They are expecting you, and they grow impatient."

"Then let's get to it." With my head held high, I stroll into my city covered in beast blood.

"FATES," Agatha whispers, her clouded eyes alight with awe as we pass the second portcullis and step into Ulysede, Loth and Zorya at our flank. The gargoyles march behind us, their footfalls pounding against the stone.

My own reaction to the view isn't much different, and I've been here before. But everything has changed now. What was once an empty city of elaborate stone buildings and summer flowers is now teeming with life. In every direction I look, there are groups of nymphs, perusing wares at wooden carts, devouring pretzels on iron benches, admiring the spray of water fountains. They've all paused to stand and gape, equally curious about the newcomers. More gargoyles and faeries, as well as little goblin-like figures with pot bellies and lengthy arms—they're all so different from one another, save for the fact that they all have wings.

"They're like the statues," I note. Do they know who I am?

"They *were* the statues," Zorya says. "The stone crumbled at the height of Hudem's moon, and these creatures emerged. I have never heard a sound so shrill and terrifying in all my life, and that is saying something."

"But are they *all* nymphs? Like, different breeds of them?"

Jarek jerks his chin toward Agatha. "What do you know of this?"

"Only ramblings in scripture." The caster watches with interest as a little goblin child splashes in the nearby fountain. "A seer named Norae told of a world of nymphs as different from each other as water and sand. Different in temperament and in power."

"Gesine did not speak of this," Zorya counters. She and the elemental caster had grown close in their time in Ulysede, and it's clear the warrior held her knowledge in high regard.

"I have spent nearly eight decades living among the oldest forgotten scriptures, of which there are many. Gesine knew much, but

I know far more." Agatha smiles sadly, as if saying her old pupil's name reminds her of what she has lost. "Norae's visions were singular and largely disregarded, by myself included, I must admit. As I stand here now, it seems we should have paid closer attention."

Gesine did allude to there being more than one depiction of the nymphs—some friendly, while others were ... not, but there's no point splitting hairs over what she told to whom.

A blond faery-nymph dressed in pink silk, much like the one at the gate when we arrived, skips past, pawing at Zorya's belt.

The warrior snarls, swatting her hand. "*Those* do not know boundaries."

"Norae drew such a creature." Agatha frowns. "But I cannot recall the name she gave them."

"What about the others?" I point toward the gargoyles. "Did she draw them too?"

"They are also familiar, but it has been too long. I apologize, Your Highness. If I could gain access to Mordain's records—"

"No, it's okay. I'm sure Lucretia has the answers we need." If the sylx is willing to share them. Besides, the library inside must have books on these creatures. I turn to the legionaries. "What have they told you so far?"

"Told us?" Zorya snorts. "They do not speak to us. They giggle and grunt and stare. *Those* have yet to make a sound." She points to a short, hairless goblin-nymph with webbed feet to match its wings. "The only reason we know they wait for you is because that blasted crypt serpent's voice fills my head with words. She will not relent." Zorya's face pinches with pain. "And she plays cruel games."

"Tell me about it," Jarek grumbles, his gaze landing everywhere but on me. "She is probably watching us right now."

From the direction of the castle, the crowd stirs as a row of tall forms clad in black leather cut through, moving soundlessly toward us. The faeries and goblins scamper out of their path. Even the gargoyles who tower over them step back in deference.

"And what are they?" I ask.

"Another breed of nymphs. They guard the throne and scare the children," Loth says.

I can see why. The closer they get, the more I can make of their features—sharp cheekbones, papery white skin, hairless skulls that have bones protruding from the top like tiny horns. Their bodies are tall and lean and sculpted for battle, and they move with purpose, bows strapped to their backs.

48

"The Cindrae," Agatha whispers in a gasp, her eyes wide with disbelief, as if surprised she could recall the name. "Those, I remember. Norae said they were a vicious breed."

I reach for threads of my affinities, only to remember that there is nothing to grasp.

They form a line and regard us through black irises that match the wings on their backs. Not a hint of friendliness gleams within.

Jarek steps forward, half shielding me, his hand on a dagger.

One of them bows. "Your Highness." Its voice is an ethereal rasp that is neither male nor female.

"So they *can* speak," Zorya says. "That would have been helpful *hours* ago."

The Cindrae ignores her. "I am Oredai, your ambassador. We will escort you from this point forward."

"She doesn't need an escort. She has me." Jarek falters a step as he shifts position.

Two of the faery-nymphs dart in from the other side, their nimble hands groping his wound.

He shoves them back with a grimace and yanks a dagger from its scabbard, aiming the point at the closest one's throat. "Try it again, I dare you."

They skitter back with hisses.

"Why does he refuse aid?" Oredai cocks his head as if confused. "Allow the wisps' healing hands now."

"*Those* are not healing hands," Jarek snaps, pointing at these so-called wisps' clawed fingers. "And I am Her Highness's commander. *You* do not give me orders."

So it's going to be a pissing match.

Oredai studies him through those cold, dark eyes for a long beat before settling back on me.

Can the great elven warrior not handle a little discomfort for his own benefit?

I frown at the velvety soft male voice that suddenly fills my head.

Oredai's lips part in a knowing smile that reveals a mouthful of canines—sharp and pointed, they look capable of tearing flesh.

"He can," I answer tentatively, unnerved by the sudden mental intrusion.

Jarek's head swings between the two of us. He scowls. "'He can' what?"

Order your commander to take the wisps' healing.

I grit my jaw at his demanding tone. "Last I checked, *I* was the queen. Has something changed?"

Smug humor flickers across Oredai's face. "As you wish."

"I saw one of them heal a cut on a mortal child's leg earlier," Loth admits, eyeing the two wisps who cower near Jarek's side. "They do seem capable."

Mention of a child reminds me of the hundreds of mortals I brought from Cirilea into Ulysede only days ago. So distracted by the nymphs, they had temporarily slipped my mind. "Where is everyone?"

"In the castle," Zorya confirms. "They are safe."

"I need to see them." I was distraught after Gesine's death and then Caindra came and I left. I never had a chance to speak to Corrin or Gracen. To thank them for their help that day—and their trust.

"The queen must attend the elders," Oredai announces, gesturing in the direction of the castle, his meaning clear.

"*Now?*" I look pointedly down at my blood-crusted clothes.

"*After* you've rested, and His Highness returns." Jarek stares at me. He means after my affinities are back so I can defend myself.

"The queen *must* attend the elders," Oredai pushes, repeating himself.

"The *queen* just fought a battle against the beasts that now plague us with your return. She must rest. The elders can wait," Jarek says evenly, stepping forward, earning sharp hisses from the group of Cindrae.

Oredai displays his pointed teeth as he stares down my commander.

I didn't notice Loth and Zorya drawing their blades, but now they stand at the ready.

"Jarek ...," I warn. We know nothing of this nymph breed—what their powers are, their skill level. Surely now is not the time for him to pick a fight, injured and with only two legionaries at his side.

"Please don't fight me on this, Romeria." A hint of pleading laces his weary voice.

"I would heed your commander's caution, Your Highness," Agatha whispers. "You do not take orders from anyone, including them."

I have plenty of questions for these elders, but the more time I spend with this Cindrae, the more reluctant I become to meet their leaders.

The queen must attend the elders.

I open my mouth to argue.

Once she has rested.

Oredai holds his gritted smile as he silently acquiesces to our demand.

"Thanks for the compromise," I mutter.

"We shall escort you to the castle." As one, the wall of Cindrae turn on their heels and move silently through the crowd toward the horses.

I share a glance with my small company and then we follow.

AN ODD SENSE of peace flows through me as we cross the bridge, the river's crystal blue water beneath rippling under the midday sun. Ahead is the castle of white walls and blue spires that is technically mine but does not feel like it.

It reminds me that I now have another castle to rule from in Argon —one that I, Romy Watts from New York City, have never stepped inside.

"Thank the fates nothing flew out of *these*," Loth murmurs, and we all nod with agreement as we pass under the archway formed by the two nymph statues that stand several stories tall.

By the time we step through the castle doors, my legs wobble with exhaustion. And yet a wide smile stretches across my face, listening to the peals of laughter inside. The great hall is much the same, with a water fountain in its center and a grand staircase at the far end. Notably empty are the pedestals where nymph sculptures used to sit.

Now mortal children streak through the vast space while pot-bellied goblins chase after them in what appears to be a game of tag, their awkward gait comical.

"See? They are fine," Jarek announces, impatience in his voice. "You can go upstairs and—"

"Fates, Your Highness!" Dagny is the first to spot me.

I hold up my hands in surrender as she rushes toward me, bowing and bobbing like a clucking hen with each step, as only Dagny can do.

"You look like you've been to Azo'dem and back!" she blusters.

"I'm fine! Really." But she's not far off because last night was as close to hell as I can imagine.

"Can you believe what's happened here?" She waves a hand around the space. "One minute it's us and a lot of statues, and then the next thing we know, there's all these creatures runnin' around! Or flyin', I suppose, 'cause some of them fly when they want to. It was terrifying at first, but they're not so bad at all." She glares at the wall of Cindrae behind us. "Most of them, anyway. Even the big—"

"The queen must rest now." Jarek cuts off her rambling at the kneecaps—the seamstress is known to babble.

I spare him a glare, but it morphs into a frown. His complexion has turned ashen. "Jarek, you look—"

"I'm fine," he growls.

"Go upstairs and rest."

"Gladly." His hand grips my elbow, his meaning clear. He won't leave me alone with these nymphs for one second.

"We'll get ya sorted right away, then, Your Highness." Dagny wipes her hands on her apron. "Corrin! Corr—"

"I'm right behind you, ya daft fool." The stern-faced lady's maid glares at her with annoyance before turning her focus to me. "Your Highness." Her chest heaves with a sigh. "I hope you don't expect me to salvage that outfit."

"At least I changed out of my dress."

Her stony face breaks with a smile. "It is good to have you back. Will the king be along shortly?"

I don't have to ask which king she means. She's always been loyal to Zander. "Yes. I hope so." I can't blame him for leaving me and rushing out to reclaim his throne the second he had a chance. After all, he lost it because of me. But what will he find while he's out there? A dead brother? A realm that has turned against him, no matter who his allies may be?

She claps her hands. "I've sent someone to draw your bath, and I'm sure you're famished. Your meal will be ready by the time you've scrubbed yourself clean."

Same old Corrin. "Settling in just fine, I see." She ran the entire household in Cirilea's castle, and it's becoming clear she's stepped into the role here.

"It is certainly a change." Her suspicious gaze flitters to Oredai before dismissing him with a displeased sniff.

I introduce Agatha. "She is the Master Scribe from Mordain. She will be spending a lot of time in the library. Please help her settle in so she can rest."

"Speaking of rest ..." Jarek grits his teeth.

"Okay! I'm going!" He's not usually *this* pushy.

Commotion stirs as Pan and Eden dash out from a hallway in

hysterics, Gracen's daughter Lilou in Eden's arms. Right behind them is Mika, his curly mop of brown hair damp with sweat.

Pan's feet falter. "Romy! You're back!"

I grin. He's the only one who calls me that.

"I do not have the energy for this." Jarek sways on his feet.

Eden quickly searches out the legionary she sometimes shares a bed with. Her eyes light up with excitement when she finds him next to me.

But her face twists with shock in the next moment as he slumps to the marble floor.

I drop to my knees, my panic exploding as I seize his jaw. "He's unconscious." Or worse. His skin is gray and cold. I plead with my affinities to rise, but they will not come.

He is not long for this world.

"What?" I erupt, glaring up at the Cindrae leader. "What do you mean?"

He reeks of vrog toxin. It is leaching the life from his body. It may already be too late to heal now.

"Why didn't you tell me this?" My anger echoes through the grand space, suddenly quiet as bystanders wait.

Oredai smirks in response.

I recommended you order him to accept healing.

"You …" I grit my teeth. Now is not the time. "Get him upstairs with your best healers. And it better not be too late, for your sake." I leave the unspoken threat dangling in the air.

His amusement vanishes in an instant. He snaps his fingers. The closest gargoyle scoops up Jarek's limp body and runs up the main stairs with surprising speed; a dozen wisps take flight behind him.

I chase after them, my heart pounding in my ears, Loth and Zorya on my heels.

By the time we reach his chambers, Jarek is already stripped of his warrior leathers and lying in bed, draped in a white sheet speckled in blood. A long, thin line drags across his rib cage, where the claw of this vrog opened his skin. It might have been little more than a scratch at the start, but now it's angry and red and swollen, with a black, tar-like liquid oozing out.

The wisps hover around his body, their giggles contrary to the grim task ahead.

Tears prick my eyes. "You stubborn idiot!" He should have gone to the casters when he had the chance.

Oredai slides in silently behind me. "They must remove the poison."

"And how do they do that?"

"There is only one way."

My mouth drops as one of them shoves its clawed fingers into the wound.

Jarek's eyes open with his bloodcurdling scream.

9

SOFIE

This is not my husband.

He may wear his handsome face and use his deep, melodic voice. His palm may feel the same, smooth against mine.

But the more I pay attention, the more I catch the subtle differences.

The way his chocolate-brown eyes glimmer with cruel intentions.

The way the corners of his lips curl with a perpetual sneer.

The way he squeezes my hand too tightly, as if wanting to remind me of his unparalleled strength.

This is not *my* Elijah, and I refuse to think of him as such.

"It is a pity the rebels caused such damage. It will take weeks to get the stench of smoke out of these drapes and paintings," Malachi muses as we stroll up the aisle toward stairs leading to a dais. There are countless eyes on us in this packed throne room—of nobility and peasant alike, ushered in by the guards like cattle to pack every corner of the majestic space.

Tension cloys the air, and I cloak myself in a shield to ward off an attack. But Malachi is unfazed as he sidesteps a pool of blood. Countless puddles and smears still mar the hallways. The surviving staff are hard at work, scrubbing marble and dragging bodies to the waiting wagons—to cart away and burn.

There is blood *everywhere* I look, and yet after three hundred years of feeding off it, not so much as a twitch of hunger stirs inside me. A riddle I would like an answer to, but silent observation seems safest for the moment.

We climb the steps toward the two thrones. I keep my focus on the heavy skirts of this ivory dress I donned at his request, pulled from the queen's overflowing wardrobe. Malachi chose a black suit that hangs a little too large on his frame. The previous king had broader shoulders. He insists he'll have the royal tailor adjust everything, but we have yet to find the person who holds that title.

He doesn't need a tailor for the king's crown he found secure in the royal vault. That, he placed atop his own head, before setting a matching, slightly smaller crown on mine.

"You are quiet, my love." He gestures toward the queen's throne.

I choose my words cautiously, for this is Malachi, and even in flesh and blood, surely, he is formidable. "I am adjusting to this new world." And the deep sense of betrayal and discontent that clutches me.

I am no fool, so how did I not see this coming? Again and again, the Fate of Fire has used and abused me. And the clues were all there, laid bare. How much he enjoyed assuming a corporeal form during our visits, how often he talked about me as his queen.

Malachi regards the horde of people watching us, everything from fear and shock to calculating distrust on their faces, while the corners of his mouth tic. Never in my life have I sat in a room of so many immortals, let alone mixed with the lesser humans. They all look the same now—ragged after the city's turmoil, unwashed, their clothing soiled in varying degrees. It's as if they were pulled off the street and ushered in here at sword point to fill the room. Perhaps they were.

"Have no fear, my love. Your husband is not lost. I am merely borrowing him for a time."

A glimmer of hope strikes me. "What does that mean?" Is Elijah still in there, somewhere? Will I see him again?

But Malachi doesn't answer me, turning his attention toward the crowd. "My people!" He addresses them with open arms and a jovial voice. "Gone are the centuries of weak monarchy. I have arrived to bring you a new life. Under my reign, we will grow strong and wealthy."

A single cough buried in the silence answers.

"You do not believe me? It has already begun, has it not? Where is your thirst for mortal blood? Surely you have noticed it suddenly absent?"

Questioning glances dart around the room. Both immortals and humans seem equally mystified but for different reasons.

Malachi stands and paces around the two thrones. "You were

growing too dependent on the mortals, and with this wicked Ybarisan poison spawned by Aoife—a curse upon these lands!—you were vulnerable. That is why it no longer plagues you. Because *I* made it so."

"How?" a male voice challenges, the source hidden.

Malachi's gaze narrows. "Who asked this question?"

But no one raises their hand or steps forward.

His lips curve in a wicked smile as he leisurely descends the steps. He finds their fear amusing. "*I* have brought freedom to the people of Islor!"

One by one, the crowd erupts in polite applause, but there is no missing their wariness.

Their doubt.

The main doors swing open and the guards herd in five prisoners. Their clothing, though filthy, mark them as nobility.

"Ah, the eastern lords who have stirred so much trouble for my realm." Malachi holds his hands out in a welcoming gesture. "Remove their chains so they may come forward."

The prisoners exchange uneasy glances with one another and those in the crowd as they're unshackled. They take measured steps down the aisle.

Malachi regards them one by one for long beats. "Swear fealty to me, and you shall live."

A lord with black hair and pale skin clears his throat before he plasters on a wide, fake smile. "Your Highness, if I may be so bold as to ask what your claim to the—"

With a flick of Malachi's wrist, a rope of flame lashes out and slices through the lord's throat as precisely as a blade. His head topples from his shoulders a second before his body buckles to the floor, the lethal wound cauterized by the fire.

Screams fill the throne room as the head rolls along the aisle.

My stomach clenches. Fates know I am no delicate flower where delivering death is concerned, but Elijah has always played the diplomat, choosing words over violence. He would never serve a punishment so callously.

Malachi pats the air, calling for calm. "Now, now. Let us not pretend that we do not all know of Lord Adley's treachery. He has long since proven he cannot be trusted. It is unfortunate that neither of the previous kings had the gall to do what needed to be done, but I promise you, I shall not allow such a poison to seep into my realm." He turns his attention to the young, raven-haired female who stares at the decapitated body in horror. He must have been someone special to her. "Lady Saoirse of Kettling."

It's a moment before she seems to hear the address and then her head snaps up. "Yes, Your Highness?"

"Do I have your fealty?"

She drops to her knees without pause, bowing her head, and the other prisoners follow an instant after.

Malachi nods with satisfaction. "In answer to Lord Adley's bold question, my claim to the throne is that it is mine, as Islor has always been mine, for I am King Malachi, and I am here to rule that which I created." His deep, booming voice ricochets around the room. "Now, let us all feast tonight, so we may rebuild Islor tomorrow. Peace has come at last!" He throws his arms up and every torch within the great room swells with flame.

A muted cheer rises among the ranks.

He turns and raises a hand toward me. "May I present to you, Her Highness Queen Sofie, the first key caster ever to wear Islor's crown."

Gasps fill the room.

"Come, my love," he beckons over the noise.

I collect my skirts and take the stairs slowly. It's been some time since I donned such a weighty gown. Centuries.

A guard charges in just as I reach the bottom of the steps. "My apologies, Your Highness," he stutters. "But the flying beast is back. It circles the city." He frowns. "Only, I don't know if it's the same one."

"I imagine we will have guests. We must greet them." Malachi hums, unconcerned. He takes my hand and leads me down the aisle, pausing at a frail, middle-aged woman in tattered clothes, her bandaged hand cradled against her chest. She sits next to a guard. A caster, I realize, sensing the buzz of her affinity.

She trembles under his attention, keeping her focus on the floor.

"I believe I have you to thank. You played a vital part in allowing me the opportunity to return."

The caster swallows, and then bobs. "Yes, Your Highness."

"Come," he orders. "Old friends are here to pay a visit."

She stands on shaky legs, sparing me nothing more than a fleeting glance before her eyes regard her feet again.

Malachi steps around Lord Adley's loose head and then pauses. "On second thought ... where are my manners? I should bring a gift."

1 0

ZANDER

"What have you let happen, my dear idiot brother."
Faint smoke clouds above Cirilea, but the streets are busy as survivors haul bodies off the cobblestone and sweep away debris. The rows of loaded wagons tell a grim story of the lives lost. Too many to guess.

After what Romeria described, of mortals dangling from light posts and children imprisoned within the ballroom, it's no wonder the people rebelled. In fact, I commend them for it. All the same, my chest aches for my city and my realm.

"Have you ever seen it so empty?" Abarrane, who shares the dragon's clutch with me while the other cradles Kazimir's broken body, forgets her nausea for a moment to point to Cirilea's port. Not a single skiff remains.

"Never in all my years of life," I admit. I suppose that is a positive. It means a great many people escaped with Romeria's help. Northmost will receive them in the coming days and, hopefully, they will return once they hear Atticus is gone.

We pass over the castle's outer wall where people fought to punch through and gain access to their children, and then over the royal garden, where both Gesine and Boaz perished. The former, I will mourn. The latter, I cannot for his aid in Atticus's betrayal, though he did serve my family honorably for many centuries.

"Fates." Was it Caindra's fire or Romeria's that cut the impressive swath of destruction, devastating everything within its path? Either option is terrifying. I would not wish to face them in battle.

"I know I have expressed my share of doubts over Romeria, but we are fortunate that she is an ally and not an enemy," Abarrane notes, complementing my unspoken thoughts.

"Land in the courtyard!" I yell, hoping the orange beast can hear me. When we left the east, I asked it to bring us to Cirilea and here we are, so it seems to understand my words.

Castle staff collecting rubble spot us descending and run for cover, their hands waving in panic. I cannot blame them for their fear. We all reacted much the same way the first time we laid eyes on Caindra, and this beast is far bigger.

The cobblestone and buildings around us shudder under the dragon's weight as it lands and releases us, while continuing to cradle Kazimir in its other claw. I wonder if Atticus's right-hand man still lives.

But that is beyond my control.

I am home.

That is my focus as my feet touch the ground of my city again.

Around us, guards and servants alike stand frozen and wide-eyed, uttering not a word. We must be a sight—the exiled king, returned and covered in beast blood, the largest creature they've ever laid eyes upon at his back.

The horses corralled in the stables kick at their doors, agitated by the daunting predator that fills half the courtyard.

"Do not eat *anything* here," I warn. That would be a poor start.

The beast snorts in response, which tells me it likely understands far more than we give it credit for.

A glimmer within the crevices of cobblestone catches my attention. I stoop to collect the golden cuff with my house's signature flame marking it. A royal servant's adornment, meant to remain within their ear. It was likely ripped out as they ran. But without the blood curse, are these even needed anymore?

With one night, everything has changed in Islor, and yet with the wrong leadership, I know that nothing will change. The rich and powerful immortals will do anything in their power to remain so while keeping the weaker human race enslaved.

That ends now.

I toss the cuff away and stand.

"Your ... Highness," a guard stammers, his eyes flipping between me and the enormous beast at my back. "You have returned."

"I have, and I am here to reclaim that which is rightfully mine—"

The castle doors creak open and behind the cohort of guards, two figures emerge.

The sound of Abarrane's blade sliding out of its scabbard fills the air, timed perfectly with the dragon's deep, low growl.

My jaw clenches as I take in the tall, dark-haired male—a stranger —who dons my royal suit and *my golden crown*. But it's the woman wearing the queen's crown beside him that raises my hackles. A female with copper-red hair, who looks eerily similar to a pencil sketch Romeria once drew, of the key caster Sofie.

"Fates." It's too late.

Malachi is here.

Movement in the shadows behind him draws my attention briefly to Wendeline—or a shell of who she once was. She's still alive, at least. Romeria will be happy to learn that.

"Exiled King Zander. My dearest son." Malachi smiles smugly. "I am pleased you are attending me with due haste. In honor of your arrival, a gift for you."

I was so preoccupied by shock, I hadn't noticed the grip of black hair within his fist and the head dangling from it. Malachi tosses it toward my feet. It lands with a sickening thud.

Lord Adley's dead eyes stare up at me.

"How kind of you," I manage, deadpan.

"After all the grief that one caused this realm, ridding us of him is the least I could do. It is a shame you did not bring the little mortal thief with you."

"I assume you mean Queen Romeria?"

"If that's what she's calling herself." He grins. "I would have preferred to accept fealty from both of you at the same time, but I suppose accepting it from one of you now will suffice."

Abarrane grunts. "Never."

He swings his attention toward my commander, who feigns bravery even as her fingers tap rhythmically against her pommel—a tell for her anxiety. "*Never*?" A wicked, dark glimmer flickers in his eyes. "That is a bold claim for such defenseless creatures. What ... you believe you have a formidable protector in Valk?" He regards the dragon behind us with unnerving ease. "I thought surely he would have lost that wing during our last encounter."

I struggle not to wince as the dragon—Valk, it seems is its name— emits a roar that pains my eardrum and sends everyone in the vicinity stumbling back. Clearly, they not only know each other but have battled.

The amusement slips from Malachi's borrowed face, leaving stone-cold resolve. "So foolish of any who think they lay claim to this throne, for it has been mine since the day Ailill first summoned me. I understand it will be difficult for you to accept this, so I present you with a choice. You may kneel before me now and I will make your death swift. Resist, and your suffering will last an eternity." He folds his hands in front of him and waits patiently for my response.

This is how it shall be—I am to battle the Fate of Fire himself if I have any hope of reclaiming my throne. I suppose I shouldn't have expected less. It was all too easy otherwise.

Romeria was right. Coming to Cirilea was dangerous. Now, it might prove deadly if we can't get out of here swiftly.

Before we do, though, I need one answer. I shift my focus to Sofie. "Tell me, key caster, how does it feel to know that you played pawn for centuries in hopes of reuniting with your husband, only to discover that you will likely never see him again?"

Raw pain flashes across Sofie's face before it morphs with unfiltered rage, and her emerald eyes turn silver, much like Romeria's do when she is about to unleash.

I've certainly said the wrong—or right—thing, and I'm about to pay for it. "Valk." His name is barely a growl under my breath.

The dragon sweeps a claw out to collect us, his wing closing around just as bolts of fire unleash from Sofie's slight form. He launches us into the sky with a screech.

And I hold my breath that we will escape her wrath.

We've cleared the borders of Cirilea's outer wall when Abarrane snarls, "You intentionally provoked a key caster. Are you mad?"

"Maybe. But I needed to test the waters." The stench of burned flesh curls my nostrils, but I cannot get a proper glimpse of where Sofie struck Valk. It doesn't seem to have hindered his ability to fly, at least.

"And what did you find lurking beneath? Something that will kill us or simply maim?" she mutters, unimpressed.

"Another victim of Malachi who might be swayed." There was no mistaking the anguish before her fury took over. But it is too soon to say if she will abandon her loyalty to him because of it, and Malachi with a key caster at his side is far from ideal.

To Valk, I order, "Let us get our injured passenger to the healers at the rift, so we may return to Ulysede tonight."

11

SOFIE

The terrace doors to the queen's chamber open, and Elijah strolls in wearing only black linen pants that sit low on his hips, revealing a honed body.

For a fleeting second my pulse races with need. But it's quickly chased by a crippling distress that threatens to tear me to pieces.

This is not my Elijah.

"There you are." Cold brown eyes find me in my bed. "I have been looking for you."

"You could not have been looking hard. I've been in my chambers for the past hour." I feign focus on a book I found in the sitting area as I pluck strands of all four affinities, weaving them into a tightly braided coil of silver, at the ready.

"You left the festivities without my permission," Malachi declares.

"I did not realize I needed permission." I can't help the surliness in my tone.

Tell me, key caster, how does it feel to know that you played pawn for centuries in hopes of reuniting with your husband, only to discover that you will likely never see him again?

The unseated king's words—and his arrogance—still burn beneath my skin, hours later. How dare he say such things to me? How dare he cut so close to the quick?

"Besides, you were busy with your subjects, *Your Highness*." A steady line of lords and ladies snaked through the great hall during the feast, coming to our table one by one to introduce themselves and preen at their new ruler's feet.

"They are your subjects too. Have you forgotten the crown that adorns your head? The one I placed there?"

I tense as he rounds the bed, settling on the edge. He collects the book from my grasp without asking. "*Samara's Quest*." Tossing it aside, his heated gaze drags over the black silk nightgown I found in the closet. Despite the uprising that saw countless sections of the castle destroyed, the king's and queen's chambers remained untouched. Overhearing the guards, it sounds like the rebels focused their efforts on searching for missing children. "You are angry with me."

"I am tired." It isn't entirely a lie. I am *exhausted*. Three centuries of waiting will do that.

"You lashed out at our visitors with far more than fatigue today."

I caught the side of the beast with a bolt of my affinity. I imagine they'll need the casters to heal the burn.

Malachi caresses my cheek with his palm before cupping my chin, as a lover would.

I flinch and attempt to pull away, but his grip tightens until it borders on pain.

His dark eyes are searing as they attempt to dissect me. "You think that because I have taken this physical form, I cannot sense what is going through that vindictive mind of yours?" His eyebrow arches with amusement, even as his fingers squeeze.

Tears well in my eyes, but they aren't for pain. Not physical, anyway. "I have waited nearly three hundred years, I have done all that you asked, and still you have not returned my husband to me."

"Did I not?" He shutters his eyes, a soft smirk curling his lips.

My affinity bubbles under the surface, begging to be unleashed. I could end this torture now.

When his eyes reopen, he blinks repeatedly, as if regaining consciousness after a long sleep. He focuses on my face and his eyes grow wide with panic. "Dear God." He releases his tight grip of me, pulling away as if burned.

Dear *God*.

The Fate of Fire would never say such a thing.

"Elijah?" I ask tentatively.

He breathes a heavy sigh and ropes his arms around me, pulling my body to his. "Yes, my love. This is me." Hot lips press against my forehead. "I am still here. I have been here the whole time. Ever since you found me in the Nulling." His voice is hoarse. "It is a never-ending nightmare. I can see and hear everything, but my body and words are not my own to control."

"But you can see *me*?"

"I see you. Your anguish, your heartbreak."

Hope explodes in my chest. "It is not too late, then. I have not lost you yet."

"You have not." His lips move to my cheek, then to my lips.

I relish their taste against mine for a long moment until my tears meld with our kisses. "This is not what I intended." I shake my head, sobbing. "This is not what he promised me."

"What did I warn you of Malachi, my dearest Sofie? That he was not to be trusted. That he would take everything from you."

The season for castigating has long since come and gone. "What am I to do?"

"I do not have the answer for you." Elijah's cheeks are damp with tears too. "But know that I am here with you. You are not alone. Your pain is mine." His kiss turns frantic, full of desperation and urgency, as if the clock is about to run out on our moment.

I match the intensity, our hands working away at each other's clothes until we're left with nothing but skin and the cool air flowing in from the terrace.

I cry out with Elijah's first thrust, a dreamlike feeling overwhelming me as the memories I've clung to for centuries rush back. My legs wrap around his hips as he pins me down, our fingers entwined above my head. I have waited so long to feel his weight atop me, and the delicious burn of him filling me so completely. I would sacrifice everything to hold on to this moment forever.

"See, my love? I did not betray you."

The hairs at my nape prick at the sudden change in timbre.

As quickly as Malachi left, he has returned.

His hips pause and he pulls back to show me his cruel smile. "Your husband is with you at all times." I gasp as he thrusts hard, his hands flexing around mine until they threaten to crush my bones. "And any harm inflicted upon me—by *anyone*—will be dually felt by him."

A not-so-subtle warning in case I had plans to take my revenge.

I swallow. "No harm shall come to you while I am at your side."

"I did not think so. And if you are a good servant to me, perhaps I will allow you to see him, from time to time." He rolls us over until I'm straddling his hips, his length still seated deep inside me. "Are you a good servant?" Warm hands stroke over my thighs, squeezing as he prompts me to continue.

I look past the monster beneath me to the male I love hidden deep inside. "I am." I roll my hips, earning Malachi's guttural groan.

I will protect Elijah until I can find a way to free him from this nightmare.

12

ZANDER

It's dusk by the time we descend on the entrance to Ulysede, and I gape at what I see. I should not be surprised, though. I've witnessed the healing power the nymphs unleashed upon our realms. Desolate lands at the rift long since punished by the fates' wrath have been blessed with a carpet of grass and trickles of water as of this morning's sunrise.

But this transformation? I stood in this barren wasteland only days ago, where soaring trees now line a road fit for royalty—fresh, as if newly laid.

Abarrane stumbles a few steps as her feet touch stone. "There *must* be a better way to travel by these beasts," she growls, sparing Valk a glare.

He all but ignores her, his rapt attention on Caindra and her smaller green companion who rest in a clearing nearby.

"Why don't you ask one of them?" We take in the daunting winged creatures who line the tunnel into the city. They're easily twice my size and surely twice as strong, their bodies swollen with muscle, clad in armor that bears the kingdom's two-crescent-moon mark.

But they don't raise my hackles. It's the pale-skinned warriors that form a wall, their black eyes affixed to us, that unnerve me.

"These are our allies?" Abarrane's tone hints that she shares my doubt. Nothing about their rigid stance suggests they are here to offer us aid.

But if Caindra is out here, then Romeria is in there, and I will cut through every one of them to reach her. "Valk!"

The orange beast swings his massive head toward us, his jade-green eyes narrow slits as he regards me. The charred scales along his back from Sofie's attack look less damaged than they did when we landed at the rift to deposit Kazimir to the healers. "Remain here until my return."

Valk's head tips back and he releases a shrill screech that rattles my teeth, loud enough to ricochet off every peak in this mountain range.

Abarrane's eyebrows arch. "Is that a yes?"

"More likely a 'go fuck yourself.'" And after I provoked Sofie, I wouldn't blame him.

We stroll toward the gate and the barrier of nymphs, and I prepare myself for an obstacle. Now that we're closer, I can make out the bones that protrude from their skulls like tiny, dull horns. They truly are hideous creatures. "I am King Zander of Islor, and I am here to see Queen Romeria."

One of these unnerving warriors steps forward. "You wear no crown," it says in a raspy voice.

Such a simple statement and yet it lands as painfully as an ax cleaving into my chest. Now that Malachi has arrived, the crown I rarely wore will likely never sit atop my head again.

"He is the one true king of Islor," Abarrane spits out, drawing both her swords. "And you do not wear *any* crown that allows you to speak to him in such a manner."

Faster than my mind can register, the wall of warriors have drawn their bows. Sixteen arrows are aimed at my commander, the metal gleaming with merth.

The creature smiles, showing off pointed teeth that remind me of a hag.

We didn't come this far to die because of bruised egos. "Abarrane. Stand down."

After a beat, she lowers her swords.

"What is your name?" I ask.

"Oredai. I command the Cindrae."

I ignore the fact that his voice is like glass breaking. "Well, Oredai, I suggest you allow us to pass through, unharmed. The queen is expecting me, and if she learns you have kept me outside, one of us will face her wrath, and it will not be me."

Oredai barks an order and the drawn arrows vanish as if never there. "She is waiting for you."

"Interesting. Why didn't you lead with that?"

His returning smile is hideous. "We will escort you to her."

"I MUST ADMIT, of all the things I did not anticipate today, this may be the most unsettling." I watch their sleeping forms from the doorway to Jarek's chambers, afraid to come any closer that I might wake them. Romeria looks the same as she did when we parted ways at the rift—matted with beast blood from head to toe. Jarek has been stripped and covered by a blanket. Even from this distance, it's easy to spot the wound across his abdomen that glows silver.

"Her Highness would not leave his side while the wisps worked on him," Corrin whispers. "Her bath grew cold, her meal dried out, and yet she remained there, fighting sleep until she no longer could."

"And what is the prognosis?" I ask. Zorya mentioned an especially toxic poison from a beast called a vrog—the small creature we could not identify.

"He will live, according to *him*." Zorya jerks her head toward Oredai, who waits soundlessly at the end of the hall.

Corrin's face pinches with disdain. "He knew Jarek was being poisoned from within and neglected to mention it until Jarek collapsed, moments from death. You tell me whether you trust his word, Your Highness." She clearly does not, but she distrusts everyone. It's likely why we've always gotten along.

"No, I do not think I do." Oredai would not respond to any of my questions on our trek from the gate to the castle, not about his role or about the variety of curious creatures that now inhabit Ulysede. When Abarrane reminded him that he was in the presence of a king, his smirk reeked of amusement.

"You should have heard Her Highness when he finally told us." Zorya snorts. "I think if she'd had any spark left, she would have incinerated him on the spot."

"I do not like him," Abarrane sneers his way. "I do not like *any* of them."

"How did I surround myself with such a suspicious lot?" I allow a smile before it falls off. "We do not have to like them to work with them, and now more than ever, we need allies. Besides, recall how much we detested Kienen and Radomir." And now I consider them among our most loyal. "You say these wisps are healers. That is good. We need that."

"You say this because you have not seen how they work." Zorya grimaces, her eyes still on her sleeping commander. "I prefer the casters' touch. They are far gentler."

I can't help my chuckle. "I recall a time I had to order you all to accept healing." Deep in Eldred Wood, after I lost Cirilea to Atticus and we were forced to run. "Be that as it may, these wisps repaired him when Romeria could not." My conflicting feelings for the legionary—mainly his bond with her and the way he challenges me constantly over her safety—does not diminish the fact that there is no one I'd rather have at her side when I cannot be there. Preferably *not* at her side in bed, though.

"We will move her to her room so you are with her when she wakes," Zorya insists.

The selfish side of me desires to disturb her now. There is so much I need to share, and comfort I could gain from only her presence. But I'm afraid news of Malachi and Sofie will steal rest she desperately needs. She's still so new to this world and this role of key caster and queen, learning more each day, and yet last night, no one could argue that she belonged at the rift. She attacked relentlessly, throwing everything she could find, conjuring weapons out of thin air, and she continued long after I was sure she'd depleted herself. "Everything I need to say can wait until morning." I carefully shut the door.

"I shall draw your bath, then," Corrin announces.

"There is no need. I am going back to the rift." I will not gain any rest tonight. I may as well put my sword to good use. "Do not shed light on anything I have learned when she wakes."

"You have not revealed anything to shed light on," Zorya counters.

"Good. I wish to be the one to inform her."

Abarrane falls into step with me as we march down the hallway. "You know she will tear a strip from your hide when she discovers you've gone back to the rift without her."

I grin. "I will hand her the whip."

13

ATTICUS

The steady drip of water is almost more torturous than being strung up by my wrists.

Almost.

Aside from the burn against my skin from these metal cuffs, I can't feel my arms anymore. They were numb when I regained consciousness and found myself in this damp cellar, stripped of my armor and trapped in a cage. In Ostros, I assume. I've drifted in and out, shivering in nothing but a loin cloth, though the air isn't especially cool. It must be my body's fight against my injuries. How long since they delivered me to this hole, I cannot say, but the ache in my side and back is noticeably less than it was on the ship.

My head throbs more, thanks to that Kierish brute's ax handle. I'm going to enjoy killing him when I get out of here.

"Have you lost your tongue in battle?" a deep, thickly accented voice calls out.

I blink several times and focus. A silver-haired man in red finery stands in the cellar with me. If the garments don't mark him as King Cheral, the jeweled crown on his head certainly does.

"I'm sorry, did you say something?" His voice must have been what pulled me from my stupor.

He flourishes a smile that doesn't reach his pale blue eyes. "I asked how it feels to be conquered by mortals?"

"I wouldn't know."

He strolls closer to the cage, allowing me a better glimpse of the fine lines around his features. How old must the mortal king be now?

Past his sixth decade, surely. "Even now, hanging from chains and with no one but rodents for company, the great Usurper King Atticus refuses to accept defeat."

"Is that what you call it? Defeat?" I offer a lazy smile. "Every eastern lord who supported your treachery is locked in a cell, and I can promise when my brother returns to Cirilea to reclaim it—if he has not already—he will rid Islor of them once and for all. Without them, you have nothing."

"I have *you*."

My chuckle is dark. "Zander would sooner barter for a lame horse than negotiate for my life." I claim this, but I'm not sure I believe the words.

I don't even know how to play draughts.

That caster's voice whispers in my ear often. I would have died that night outside of the Goat's Knoll if not for her. I am sure she is inexplicably linked to Romeria, who has every reason to wish me dead. So, why would she ask this caster to save me? "Unless Zander's so desperate to kill me himself, that is," I think out loud. It's the only rational explanation. "Then, you may earn a lame horse out of the deal."

"We will see." King Cheral's hard gaze drags over my battered body. "My men were surprised that you survived the battle. By all accounts, you should be dead."

"Remove these chains and they can try again."

"I am no fool. Your prowess with the blade is legendary." He snaps his fingers. "Clean him up! He stinks of death. I cannot bear standing next to him."

Two young female servants scurry out from the shadows with pails of water and washcloths. The guards unlock the cage door. It swings open with a noisy creak, and they step inside, their eyes downcast.

Was I imagining things earlier, on the ship? I inhale deeply, absorbing the scent of their mortal blood. But like on the ship, it stirs nothing inside me. No urge, no craving. Fates, how did Romeria pull this off? No matter. It seems Zander got what he has always wanted—freedom from Malachi's curse.

But at what cost, I must wonder.

The servants' pulses race with fear. Is this their first time near an Islorian? I make a conscious effort to remain still as they dip the cloths into the buckets and begin at my legs, hoping that will assuage their nerves.

Warm water sluices off my skin with their gentle strokes. It reminds me of the night I took the arrow to my chest and Gracen cared for me, bathing the blood from my skin and giving me her vein.

And her love.

Does she still wait for me within the castle? What will she say when she learns that I knew of the end of the blood curse when I was still executing mortals? I can't imagine I'll be forgiven for my part in it all. I should have stopped the killings the moment that letter landed in my hands. I should have responded to Romeria with something other than a taunt. That is what a good king would have done.

Perhaps it is best that Grace finds no more appeal in me. Without the blood curse, she will remain mortal and survive only a handful of decades, anyway. We are both better off apart.

"What has the usurper king's thoughts so grim?" King Cheral asks.

I snap out of my daze. "All those wives and you prefer to watch your servants bathe your prisoner?" The girls have moved to my torso, working quickly to wash away the filth.

He ignores my slight. "It has been days since your capture. You must be thirsty." He beckons forward another mortal in a simple gauzy white gown, her feet bare. "Give him your vein."

The two servants shift to the corners, making room for the third to approach me. She's a young and diminutive thing with flaxen-colored hair, her face barely level with my chest. She keeps her gaze there as she holds her wrist against my mouth.

I inhale the delightful scent. "Jasmine and lemongrass. That's a lovely combination." My lips graze her delicate skin with my words, stirring gooseflesh.

She waits a few beats and then peers up at me through green eyes. Her slight body trembles, but no fear stirs in her pulse. All I sense is the heady anticipation that I've sensed many times before from mortals offering their vein.

Interesting.

"Just water, if you will. Please."

Shock flitters across her face, then disappointment.

Also interesting.

"You are refusing her?" King Cheral's eyebrows arch with surprise, but then his shoulders sink as if with understanding. "Ah, yes, of course. You fear the poison. I assure you though, it has not crossed into Kier."

They have no idea what Romeria has accomplished. But why

would they? Still, it's best to keep that secret as long as I can. If they believe me weak from lack of blood, they'll eventually become lax with their guard.

"You'll understand if I don't accept assurances from a man who holds me captive."

He snaps his fingers and the young mortal darts away. "He cannot be trusted. Keep his chains on, and if he tries anything while they finish bathing him, shove a spear through his gut. See if he can withstand that." King Cheral leaves and the woman in white trails behind him, stealing a glance at me.

The guards who remain keep their weapons aimed as the two servants scrub away blood and dirt. I hiss at the sting from the wound I cannot see on my shoulder and one drops her bucket, splashing water at our feet and earning the guards' snarls. She's sent off to fetch a new one while the other continues. This one is not feigning anything as she moves to face me, washing the dried blood from my neck. No doubt she grew up hearing bedtime stories of Malachi's demons and believes every word.

"I will not harm you," I whisper, infusing as much sincerity in my voice as I can muster.

"No speak to her!" a guard barks, fumbling with my language.

I bite my tongue against a retort that will likely earn me a fresh wound. There's no point in any of it. Even if she did understand me, my words do nothing to ease her fear.

14

TYREE

I cover my eyes with my palm, the rising sun's glare against the sea especially blinding this morning.

"You may fare better with proper rest," Captain Aron calls out. "There is a second pallet in the cabin the princess occupies."

"Lie next to the Islorian who aims to slit my throat? I fare just fine where I am." I haven't moved from this spot on the main deck since the first night we set sail, save for the need to relieve myself. The wooden crates grant me a place to sit and a decent vantage point. The mast at my back holds me up.

It seems as good a place as any to die.

He sighs. "Suit yourself."

"You are one to speak. Do you sleep on your feet?"

Captain Aron rarely leaves the helm, never for more than an hour or two at a time.

He throws a smirk over his shoulder. "I don't think you want me lazing in bed. These waters promise many trials, and my second did not make it to the ship in time. The rest of this lot? I wouldn't trust to get us all the way there."

"Whatever you need to do." I unfasten Annika's silk belt and check the dagger wound on my thigh, grimacing as I note the trickle of blood. It's been days and there's no sign of stemming it. This is far worse than any of the wounds inflicted upon me during my weeks in captivity.

But I'm sure the princess knew what she was doing when she plunged the blade into my thigh. I study the smooth, bronzed handle of the dagger. A fate's token. Of course an Islorian princess would carry nothing less. It's deceivingly dainty, much like its owner. It will likely be my downfall.

Much like its owner.

Speak of the demon …

Annika emerges from the deck below, nibbling on a biscuit, her cascade of plump blond ringlets only slightly matted. Even several days at sea, donning a dress stained with my blood and a blanket half devoured by moths, she still appears regal.

When we first arrived in Cirilea ahead of my sister's nuptials and I laid eyes on Princess Annika Ascelin, daughter of King Eachann and Queen Esme, it took me a few beats to remember who she was—*what* she was—and why I had come to Islor in the first place.

Certainly not to bed her.

Annika's beauty is without equal, I will grant her that. It's no wonder she has an endless supply of fools crooking their necks and donating their veins. That she's royalty is the sharpened edge on a masterfully crafted blade.

"Did you bring me a biscuit?" I call out, my stomach growling.

She follows my voice and wrinkles her nose as if disgusted by the sight of me. "You know where they are."

"The stairs are a challenge with my injured leg." The truth is, I can barely stand, but I don't want anyone on this ship knowing how vulnerable I've become.

"Perhaps you should have stayed in your perfectly comfortable room in Cirilea, then."

If I had stayed there, I would certainly be dead by now. I shake my head. "You enjoy kicking a wounded animal when it's down."

"When that wounded *animal* plotted to kill me and deserves to suffer?" she snaps. "Gladly."

The end of a nearby hemp rope suddenly whips across my thigh, landing directly on my laceration. I scream, my vision blurring from the agony. For a moment, I think I might pass out. "Is that the best you can do?" I manage through ragged breaths. If only I could shed these blasted cuffs Atticus slapped on me to quell my affinity.

With a satisfied smile, she moves to the side of the sailboat, casting her pretty blue gaze out over the sea.

It's a good reminder that, as lovely as Annika may be to look at, her viciousness is without mercy.

I tuck the dagger into the sewn-in sheath in my breeches pocket.

"The wind has picked up," she notes, and I know she's not talking to me. Her tone doesn't bleed with hatred anymore.

Captain Aron nods a greeting. "Aye, we're making good time now."

"How far are we from Westport?"

"Another few days without interruption."

"And how long before the sirens find us?"

"Won't be long now. See that over there?" He points to a small jutting island. "That is known as the Tooth. Once we cross that, we are in their territory."

She shudders, and I know it's not from cold because the breeze that came with dawn is balmy.

"You're frightening her with tall tales," I call out before I can stop myself. Why do I attempt to soothe her nerves? Let her tremble. I'm *dying* because of her.

"Tall tales?" Captain Aron looks to me curiously. "Why do you claim this?"

"Because I have sailed from Westport to Northmost and back again, and I came out unscathed."

Annika snorts. "The only tall tale is his own."

"Okay. Whatever you say." I settle back against the mast, closing my eyes, feigning sleep.

One ... two ... three ...

"When was this little adventure of yours?"

I crack a lid to find her facing me, her eyes narrowed. "Nearly a century past." Long before Romeria's birth.

"In a ship?" I have Captain Aron's interest now as well.

"A small skiff with an elemental caster adept at manipulating the wind and sea. We stuck to the coastline. Nearly lost ourselves to the rocks a few times," I admit. "But we made it there and back without ever crossing paths with one of these dreaded sirens everyone is so frightened of." My father insisted it couldn't be done, but if by some miracle I succeeded and found myself infected by the bloodlust, I dare not return or he'd drive a blade through my heart himself. He wasn't exaggerating.

I was happy to prove the fool wrong.

Annika bites her bottom lip, torn by curiosity. "Where did you go?"

"I stayed in Northmost and the countryside. Traveling through Islor proved far too dangerous, given how much your kind loves the scent of my blood." Does it taunt her now? For an Islorian who hasn't fed in days, she reveals nothing.

"How boring," she drawls, but I catch a flicker of something else there that I can't read.

"It *was* a little, though I found suitable entertainment for a time."

Understanding flickers across her face. "What was her name?"

"I can't recall," I lie without missing a beat, even as jade eyes pierce through suppressed memories.

Annika folds her arms across her chest. "How long did you stay in Islor?"

"Long enough to see that Malachi's demons are as corrupt and revolting as we feared." I grit my teeth against the grim memory. "And nothing has changed since. You'll still do *anything* for blood."

She matches my sour face. "Do not pretend you value mortal life any more than I do. It is at your hands that so many Islorians have died. You are the one who peddled that poison around my realm. Do you have any idea how many mortals were executed because of it?"

Silence hangs thick as we stare each other down.

"Well, I hate to break it to both of you, but we don't have such powerful casters on this ship, and we are certainly not hugging the shoreline. You will hear the sirens' song soon enough, and then you cannot deny they exist."

I shrug. "I am dead, anyway. I'd rather it be to the sea than to this Islorian."

Captain Aron's gaze flutters to my thigh, then to my boot. The bugger knows I have jewels hidden in there, but he's not foolish enough to try to confiscate them from me. Yet. "Have you ever heard the story of Captain Finnigus, the first to face the dreaded sirens and live to tell the tale?"

"Something tells me I'm about to," I say dryly.

"It goes something like this." He returns his focus to the horizon. "Three ships left Cirilea together, heading for Skatrana to rejoin their loved ones, divided by the rift. Two of the ships had elven on them, while the third carried only mortals and supplies. One hot, sunny day, just as they passed the Tooth, they heard the most beautiful singing. It grew louder and more intoxicating until the captains of the three ships couldn't help themselves. They changed course and sailed deep into the sea.

"The sirens' song was so compelling, people believed they were listenin' to the fates themselves, and one by one, they dove overboard, desperate to get closer. That was until the people on the ships watched those below get pulled under the water and devoured by the creatures."

Annika winces.

"But even seein' that, the songs kept going and people kept getting dazed and divin' in, like they couldn't help themselves, even though they knew what was down there. So, they tied blankets and shirts around their heads, anything they could get hold of to drown out the sirens' song so they wouldn't be tempted to go for a deadly swim. It worked for the most part."

"That is all you need to do, then? Muffle your ears?" Annika asks, absently toying with the blanket around her shoulders.

"Surely that would be all, if it were only the sirens we had to contend with. It wasn't them who attacked the ship, according to Captain Finnigus, but a great scaly beast that came up in the waters. It tore apart two ships before vanishing into the sea. His ship—the one with only mortals—was left untouched.

"The distraught captain made it to Westport with half his men gone but his ship intact. The only explanation he had was that the sirens and the beast were after the immortals. He refused to sail ever again and spent his remaining days in Westport, warning everyone of the perils. Some listened. The ones who dared sail with your kind anyway were never heard from again."

"Great scaly beasts that will rip apart your ship and yet you agreed to take us to Westport for a handful of jewels." I scratch my chin with mock doubt. "This all sounds completely plausible."

Captain Aron winks. "I do like my jewels. And I've learned a few tricks along the way." He slides the loosely wrapped scarf from his neck and binds the material around his head, covering his ears. "Everyone, guard yourselves. The Tooth is comin' up!"

All around us, sailors follow suit, fishing out readied articles of clothing as if they've done this countless times.

Annika studies their steps and then tears her blanket in half and copies their binding. Somehow, she makes it look fashionable.

Captain Aron notes me sitting there and warns, "You may wish to do the same."

"I seem to be fresh out of scarves. *If only* someone had cloth to spare."

The other half of Annika's blanket dangles from her fingertips.

I hold out my hand, palm raised. "I know you care about my well-being."

"Sorry, I couldn't hear you! What did you say?" With a flick of her wrist, the material flies into the sea.

I expected as much. "It's fine. I'm not a sucker for a beautiful voice like the rest of this lot."

Captain Aron shakes his head at the both of us before returning his attention to the sea.

For the next half hour, I sit back and watch everyone fuss with their crude muffles and shout at one another to be heard. Annika remains quiet, leaning against the side of the ship, gazing at the horizon, her thoughts seemingly beyond it.

When the first sweet melody tickles my eardrum, it's so faint I'm sure I've imagined it, but I find myself leaning forward, searching for a repeat—a confirmation that it was real. It comes moments later, a musical and feminine high note that erases the clatter around me. I've never heard anything so beautiful, so mesmerizing in all my life, and I find myself closing my eyes and smiling as I listen to it grow louder.

"You hear them, don't you!" Annika startles me.

I crack one eye to find her hovering over me. "You don't?"

She scrunches her nose. "Barely. It's muffled."

"Remove your blanket."

"Of course you'd suggest that. You want me to get eaten."

A sly smile curls my lips. "Yes, I would quite enjoy that, but not in the way you mean."

"You swine." She spins on her heels, but not before I catch the flush of her cheeks, and rushes back to search the waters.

More sirens sing now, the soothing chorus wafting through the air in wave after wave, relaxing my body despite the throb in my leg. It's not long before I begin to feel the pull of longing, the urge to get up, to venture to the edge of the boat, to lean over in hopes of catching a glimpse of them for myself.

Maybe torn apart is how I would like to die.

Maybe I should end my suffering now.

"Radic. Get back from there!" someone shouts. "Radic!"

I turn in time to watch a sailor behind me jump overboard. A heavy splash sounds seconds later.

"The idiot didn't secure his scarf tight enough!" Captain growls.

"There! I see him!" Annika points to the water.

"It's too late."

"What?" She gapes at him. "He's *right there*! Give him a net!"

With a curse and a glance my way, Captain waves his hand and chaos breaks out as men rush to the side of the ship and cast a fishing net. They shout his name, trying to get his attention. Through all the commotion, the sirens continue singing, beckoning.

"I see something! I see it! Is that …" Annika pauses and then her mouth hangs open.

"What do you see?" I call out.

Her face twists with alarm. "How can something like that sing—ah!" She screams, slapping her hands over her mouth while several sailors shout and others recoil as if veering from a gruesome sight.

"This, I need to see." I struggle to stand.

"Stay where you are!" Captain Aron hollers, but my curiosity is piqued by Annika's terror.

Her profile blanches as a new level of fear grips her. "Fates, what *is that*?" She points to something on the horizon.

My attention is glued to her when a searing pain hits me.

15

ANNIKA

"I see something! I see it! Is that ..." Scales shimmer in the water—an iridescent kaleidoscope of pink, white, and green. First one sleek body, then another, then a half-dozen more, cutting like arrows through the water toward our ship.

These are the sirens?

"What do you see?" Tyree calls out, but I pay little attention, my focus torn between these mythical creatures surrounding us and the poor attempt to rescue the overboard sailor, who has no interest in reaching for the net they cast.

Suddenly, a round face emerges from the water's surface, and the sun's rays catch mottled gray flesh, like that of a rotting corpse. Cold white eyes scan the ship as it opens its mouth and sings. I barely notice the song, too horrified by the rows of pin-like teeth. "How can something like that sing—ah!" I stifle my scream with my hands as four sirens leap out from the depths to claim a corner of Radic, sinking their teeth into his limbs. A cloud of crimson billows below the water's surface as they pull him under.

My stomach churns as I avert my gaze from the massacre to the horizon.

A dark shadow cuts through the water, at least ten fins breaking the surface as it propels itself toward us. "Fates, what *is that*?" Forget Radic. Does no one see the coming beast? It must be two times the length of our ship.

No one is answering me. "Captain!" I holler. "There is something in the water, heading straight for—"

My words cut off as I discover the scene behind me unfolding—of three sailors binding a raw merth cord around Tyree's neck while another yanks off his boots and fishes out the rest of the hidden loot.

Six more have swords aimed at me. I have no hope of fighting them off.

"But we paid you in jewels!"

A few sailors have the decency to study the deck floor.

Captain Aron jerks his chin. "Hurry and be done with him."

I watch with mute horror as they lift Tyree and toss him over the side of the ship. A loud plunk sounds a second later.

With him gone, they focus on me, a fresh cord of raw merth dangling from one sailor's fingertips.

The sword points get closer and I back up until I have nowhere to go but down. "This was your plan all along?"

"Ever since you forced me to sail to Westport," Captain Aron admits without missing a beat. "Told ya I have a few tricks up my sleeve, and one of them is makin' sure your kind isn't on my ship when the beast shows up."

"That wasn't me, that was Tyree! I will gladly sail to Northmost. Turn the ship around!" I attempt my most commanding voice.

"It's too late for that." But guilt touches his face.

"You have no honor."

"Honor won't help us at the bottom of the sea, Princess, which is where we'll all end up if we don't rid ourselves of you right now." He snaps his fingers and a man seizes my wrist while the one with the silver cord readies my binding.

A wave of déjà vu hits, and I can already feel the pain of a thousand razors slicing across my flesh before the cord touches my skin. But this isn't a river outside Cirilea, and Romeria is not here to save me.

16

ROMERIA

I wake with a start, bolting upright in bed.

Jarek's bed, I realize, sizing up the room and then the body lying next to me.

The very naked male legionary body with—thankfully—a sheet covering his lower half. It seems someone attempted to wash the smears of black blood from his face but gave up halfway through. Eden, if I had to guess.

My memories of the night slam into me like a sledgehammer. It wasn't just a nightmare; it was real.

Jarek, screaming as the wisps dug deep within him to claw out the poison.

Me, shrieking at Oredai with tears in my eyes, demanding to know what they were doing.

The Cindrae leader, with that smug fucking smile of his, insisting Jarek would die without their aid.

Zorya and Loth, held down by the guards so they couldn't slaughter the wisps.

Me, gripping Jarek's hand in mine and thinking he might crush my bones while I sobbed, overwrought with helplessness.

I'm positive this night will haunt me for years to come.

But my affinities are replenished, vibrating like electric currents beneath my skin, taunting me to reach for them, to wield them. They're no longer a discomfort. Now, they're a safety blanket.

Gesine once promised me they would return stronger each time I depleted them, and the well would deepen. How deep does it go now? Could it be enough to break through Mordain's wards?

To defeat the fates?

It is certainly enough to finish healing Jarek.

I pluck strands of Aoife's threads and settle my palm on the fresh silver wound across his taut abdomen. Closing my eyes, I send them forward to take away any remaining discomfort. My ears catch a sharp inhale, but I focus on my task, letting the threads search for infection, for injury.

A warm hand pressed on top of mine breaks my concentration and cracks my eyelids.

"There's no need," he croaks, his voice even raspier than usual. "I'm fine."

"You said that yesterday and look what happened," I scold softly. "Are you sure?"

"Yes." He licks his lips. "If I die of anything, it will be from thirst."

I pull away to fill a copper mug with water from a jug waiting on the side table. "Here. Slowly." I hold it against his lips and keep it there, watching his Adam's apple bob with a few swallows before I take it away.

"You held my hand through it all," he says after a moment, his jaw tensing. "Did I hurt you?"

"No," I lie as I flex it. It's stiff but otherwise fine.

"All I can say is do not ask those little demons to bring you relief."

He's not wrong. Their method is horrendous. And yet ... "They healed you when I couldn't. You would have died last night, Jarek. I don't know what I would have done if ..." I can't finish the thought, the lump in my throat too painful.

His chest heaves with a sigh, and his gray eyes roam my face. I used to think them so hard and cold, but now all I see is wisdom and concern.

The corners of his mouth kick upward.

"What?"

Long, dark lashes flutter. "You should see yourself."

I wrinkle my nose. "That bad, huh?" Neither of us have bathed. Corrin will insist on burning these sheets.

"I've fought hags more appealing than you."

"Shut up." I laugh as I smack his chest, earning his chuckle. "What time do you think it is, anyway?"

His gaze flickers to the dim light beyond the windows. "Early dawn."

"What? *No.*" I scamper across the vacuous room, to the balcony, and see the sun rising, not setting. "What the hell? They let me sleep *all night*? Why wouldn't Zander wake me?" *Unless* ...

The door to Jarek's chamber creaks open and Zorya steps in. "Your Highness. I heard your voice." To Jarek, she bows. "Commander. It's good to see you ... not screaming."

"Where is Zander?" I demand without preamble, stalking forward. "Did he make it back to Ulysede?" Or did something terrible happen to him while I slept?

"He was here. He left for the rift last night."

"He went back without me!" What about that "kings and queens do not sit idly waiting for mindless beasts" speech he gave me yesterday?

"He felt you should rest." She grins. "Though your choice of bedfellows was a little perplexing to him."

I ignore her attempt at humor. "What did he find out? Is Atticus still alive?"

"He did not share news with us and was very clear that he would deliver it to you, himself."

"That sounds ominous." My stomach is in knots. "What if something happened to him at the rift?"

"He is impossible to kill. Have you not learned that?" Jarek eases up into a sitting position. "And he was right in his decision to go. He will benefit from Islor's armies seeing him fight alongside them, and they will benefit in kind. You have important places to be too."

"Yes, apparently a land full of witches." Zorya grimaces. "I am not sure if that is better or worse than remaining with these nymphs."

"*You* will remain here with Agatha," Jarek says. "And we are not going to Mordain until we have a plan to get *into* Mordain."

"Actually, I might have one." It's so obvious, and yet it never came to me yesterday, too exhausted and overwhelmed. "The stone doors in the crypt ... Lucretia said there was one that leads to Nyos and it might work once the nymphs return." Gesine knew where it was within the guild towers. "If I could get to Mordain through it instead of announcing myself at the gate, maybe this Prime wouldn't be able to bind my affinities. And then I could bring the scribes back through this stone like I brought the children from Cirilea."

"There are many ifs in that idea." Jarek casts his sheet aside and stands.

"Jesus." I whip around, though not before getting an eyeful. "A little warning next time?"

"It's nothing you haven't seen before. More than once, if I recall." An arrogant smirk laces his tone.

My cheeks burn at the reminder. Twice—once in the river in Eldred Wood after escaping Cirilea when he very much still wanted me dead, and then in Fernwich, while he was fucking a mortal in a wagon beneath my window. "So glad you're back to your old self."

"I suggest you wash the beast blood off you before we leave." Bare feet pad over the stone toward his bathing chamber. "Unless your plan is to frighten your way through Mordain."

I shake my head as I stroll past Zorya, who watches him, her eye cast at waist level, unabashed. "I didn't think *that* appealed to you." I'd only ever seen her show interest in Gesine.

She offers no more than a lazy shrug.

"YOU ARE A QUEEN NOW. You *should* dress the part," Corrin chastises as she weaves the last braid in my hair. When she saw how I planned to go—with my hair flowing freely—she filled the doorway with her little body, hands on hips, effectively barring me from leaving. I'm desperate to get to the rift—to Zander—but I agreed to the braids if she could do it in under ten minutes.

"Ball gowns work even less with dragons than they do on horses." I throw her a knowing smile. "Besides, I think this look fits a queen preparing for war." I found a section of tunics and breeches in my closet, as well as a new, pristine brown leather-and-metal vest that hugs my body. If the nymphs put it in there, clearly *they* deem it acceptable attire for the Queen for All.

"I do not like all this talk of war." Her face pinches with worry.

"And yet those are conversations we can't avoid." The only question is, who will we be fighting against? Possibly Mordain now, on top of everyone else.

A knock sounds, and Dagny and Gracen are ushered in, Gracen's arms filled with a sleeping baby.

"Her Highness is a *very* busy person," Corrin declares, her nimble fingers fastening the last braid. "She does not have time for frivolous things."

"It's okay, I asked them to come." I ease out of the chair.

"My, doesn't Her Highness look so regal!" Dagny exclaims, clapping her hands.

The tiny bundle in Gracen's arms stirs with a sputter that quickly morphs into a wail, earning Gracen's pained look and Corrin's scowl.

"Fates, look what I've gone and done." Dagny scoops Suri from Gracen's arms without asking for permission and begins strolling and rocking and cooing. The baby quiets quickly.

Gracen's shoulders sink with relief. She wears deep circles under her blue eyes, as if she hasn't slept in days.

"How have things been here?" I ask, admiring the smattering of freckles across the bridge of her nose. Untamed blond curls frame her pretty face.

"Wonderful, in some ways. Between Eden and Pan and the nymphs, Mika and Lilou are entertained from morning until night, passing out from exhaustion before I can get them into their baths. It makes the long nights with Suri easier. I think she's starting to teethe."

"But you feel safe?"

"Oh, yes. The first night when they came, well, that was terrifying." She laughs nervously. "But they like to play and so do my children."

"Good. With all that's happening out there, I'm glad you guys are in here. No Nulling beast is getting past those gates."

"That's good." Yet she wears a worried expression. "Is there any news of what is happening in Cirilea? And elsewhere?"

"Zander left to learn what he could, but I haven't had a chance to speak to him yet." I know what she's really asking, though. "He went to the east to look for Atticus. There was a large army waiting, one Atticus wasn't prepared for and did not have enough men to fight." In the last moments before Bexley abandoned her elven form for good, she warned that the only way Atticus would survive such a battle would be if someone found more value in him alive than dead, and he would not go willingly. I say as gently as I can, "I don't know that you'll see him again."

"I understand." Gracen blinks back tears. "I will remain hopeful."

I'm sure she will. She'll likely hold out hope for the rest of her days, keeping her life on pause while she waits for the improbable. But will Atticus even return to her, *if* he returns? She and her children have suffered so much at the hands of these elven. Will she suffer more, waiting for a day that will never come?

Gracen only ever saw one side of Atticus—the kind, caring version who saved her and her children from Lord Danthrin's malice.

I'm sure it was a dream—a mortal baker who sparked the interest of a king.

But there is—or was—a spiteful and arrogant side too. That side betrayed Zander twice. Not only did he steal the throne from him, but he would have stolen his bride had Princess Romeria not been scheming. And Atticus would have executed me.

That side of him, I can't forgive.

Is it fair that I sully this false image of a martyr for Gracen, though? Who am I protecting more by remaining quiet?

I hesitate, but I can't help myself. "You should know that we wrote to Atticus and told him about Ulysede and the end of the blood curse. He probably didn't believe us, but either way, he *knew* it was a possibility and he allowed the killing of mortals to continue. All those people ... they didn't need to die."

A small gasp slips from her lips, and the tears she tried to keep at bay flow freely.

A twinge of guilt pricks me now that the words are out, but I push on, softening my voice. "I'm not telling you that to hurt you, Gracen. He was very kind to you and your children. But if you're going to mourn Atticus, I think it's fair that you know who you're mourning." And if that makes me a villain in this scenario, so be it.

Jarek pokes his head in, freshly bathed, his braids redone. "He is prowling."

I don't have to ask who Jarek means. The disdain on his face says it all.

My stomach flips with nerves. "All right, let's get this over with." The sooner it's done, the sooner I can test that door to Nyos.

"Wait!" Gracen bursts out, wiping her palms over her cheeks to dry her tears. "Before you go—Wendeline told me something about Suri that you should know, Your Highness." She steals a glance at Dagny and the baby and then lowers her voice. "She said Suri was born with an affinity to Aoife."

My mouth gapes as I study the tiny sleeping bundle. "But ... How?"

She shrugs. "I was hoping you could tell me."

Could the nymphs' power have brought caster children back to Islor? But the baby was born *before* Hudem. "Honestly, I don't know. But there is someone who might." Whether she helps is another question.

With quick goodbyes, I step out into the hallway and find Oredai waiting.

The queen must attend the elders.

I grimace at his unwelcome intrusion into my thoughts as I wave a hand. "Yes, yes. Lead the way."

THE OUTDOOR COURT that houses my throne is exactly as it was before —an ancient, unkempt garden of clawing vines and weeping trees, the air warm and fragrant—only now it's occupied by wisps and those odd little goblin-like nymphs who lounge idly around the black stone pillars, pretending to tend to the many blooms.

The Cindrae march in single file, encircling the entrance to Lucretia's crypt.

But my focus veers beyond it, to my prickly throne of white branches and polished metals, and the circle of bony silver spikes that sits on the forest-green velvet seat. "My crown! How did it get here?"

The elders wish an audience with the Queen for All.

Oredai hasn't spoken a word out loud today and his focus is singular.

I dismiss the question of the crown's mysterious reappearance for now. "Yes. I am aware." I wish Gesine were here to guide me. I don't know what to expect, and Lucretia didn't prepare me. Is this meeting a formality or is there a purpose here?

Will these elders bow for me? Will they thank me for opening the nymphaeum for their return? *She who wears the crown will reign over all.* That's what the inscription on top of the throne suggests—that I am a queen for *everyone.*

Jarek is at my side when we move for the first step. Spears suddenly angle upward, aiming at his chest.

The elders wish an audience with the Queen for All, Oredai repeats. *We must honor their wishes.*

The message is clear, even if the words spoken in my head are not.

"No fucking way," Jarek growls, stepping forward until the blades dig into his leather vest. The Cindrae don't back down.

"Does your commander hope for the wisps' healing again?" Oredai croons, smiling. "Our weapons are dipped in vrog poison."

Jarek blanches, which is, I imagine, the reaction the Cindrae leader hoped for when he chose to speak out loud.

"Anyone who harms my commander will answer to me," I say evenly. But we don't have time for healing more injuries and delivering punishments. "Is Lucretia down there?"

The sylx serves her masters.

I'll assume that's a yes. "It's fine, Jarek. I'm rested. Besides, if they wanted me dead, I'm sure they would have had our best friend Oredai kill me in my sleep."

"Wait." Jarek trots up the steps to the throne, sending wisps and goblins scattering from his formidable form. When he returns, my crown is held gingerly in his fingertips. "These creatures seem set on ceremony." He places it on my head before meeting my gaze with a severe, warning one. "Remember who you are and do not hesitate to remind anyone who forgets."

"Got it."

"And do not think of going through one of those stones without me."

"Who's the queen here?" I say glibly. With a nod of thanks to him and a flat glare for Oredai, I walk past the guards and descend the spiral staircase.

I've taken this path and visited Lucretia at least a dozen times, and yet the moment my feet touch the stone floor, I have no idea where I am.

Once a dark and dank circular underground tomb that housed ancient statues, obscure carvings, and a devious serpentine creature, it is neither dark nor dank nor circular anymore.

I'm outside. Where, I can't say, but it feels almost ethereal, with a hazy blue sky for a ceiling above and grand white stone pillars lining a stretch of plush grass the size of a football field, each blade the same length as if by design. If there's anything beyond the pillars on any side, it's hidden by a dense fog.

Where are the portal doors? The ones to connect me to other places in this realm? Where is the door to Cirilea?

It's a fleeting thought as my focus gravitates to the forms who occupy four matching stone thrones at the center of the space.

Lucretia stands beside them, her lengthy auburn hair collected in a delicate chignon, her typical choice of lewd attire replaced by a modest, high-collared ivory ensemble. "Come forward." Her voice carries as if caught on an eerie wind.

There is an elder for each version of nymph I've come across in Ulysede, from wisp to Cindrae to whatever the goblins and gargoyles are called, and they're all layered in silky robes of muted colors. Bony, skeletal hands that peek out hint at their age, but nothing about them seems fragile.

There are no gestures of deference, no hint of emotion of any kind as I approach, feeling the weight of their hard, measuring gazes with each step. It's unnerving. Even my old crime boss, Viggo Korsakov, would smile before he raised his gun.

But I am their queen, I remind myself again.

"Your Highness, it is so kind of you to *finally* grace us with your presence, after my masters have saved your people from a fate's curse. *Two* fates' curses, if one considers the toxin." There's no mistaking the disapproval in Lucretia's tone; it's in direct contradiction to her address.

If Jarek were here, he'd yell at her. If it were just the two of us, I'd toss a snappy response. But the four ancient nymph elders stare at me, saying nothing, unmoving, and all I can focus on is the sound of my pulse in my ears. Maybe that's their goal—to rattle me. Either way, this feels more like a day of judgment than a greeting between queen and subjects. This crown on my head is pointless, a trinket. Lucretia may as well call me an impostor, nothing more than a naughty child playing dress-up.

Remember who you are.

I take a deep breath and let Jarek's words sink in. Even if I don't feel like a queen, I can play one. I'm a chameleon, after all. "I needed rest, but I'm here now."

"And how is my favorite servant? He must be thankful for the aid he received."

She means Jarek, of course. The sylx has an odd infatuation with him in particular. I don't need to ask how Lucretia knows about last night. She was being creepy again, floating around the castle, unseen and listening to conversations she shouldn't be hearing. "He's waiting in my throne room. Why don't you go and ask him yourself?" He'll likely choke her. It wouldn't be the first time.

She grins, showing off her perfect teeth. It's all part of the form she's designed—so much more appealing than the snake we first met. "I will do so later."

I make a point of looking around. "Where are we?"

"In the place where my masters congregate when they must congregate." Lucretia waves a hand at the nymph elders. "You see the healing brought to your world with my masters' return, have you not?"

"Yes." The nymphs' power is impossible to ignore. All I need to do is look outside Ulysede's gates.

"There is more yet to come. Wonders you cannot yet see."

Gracen's question stirs in my mind. It's one of many unknowns I want answers for. "A baby was born in Ybaris with an affinity."

Lucretia dips her head. "The first of a new age."

"Before Hudem, though."

"Before Hudem, but after you unsealed Ulysede, when my masters began restoring balance to the realms."

I glance around us. "What about the stone doors? You said they might work again when your masters return. They're *gone*."

"They are not gone. They are just not here."

Whatever that means. "Will they work again?"

"Some may. Some may not."

I clench my teeth. Thirty seconds here and Lucretia is dancing around her answers.

Taking a calming breath, I meet the four sets of cold and calculating eyes that bore into me. I came here with my thoughts in order and questions to be asked, but as I stand beneath their harsh study, I wonder if there's some formality Lucretia neglected to mention. "Thank you for your help with ending the blood curse."

None respond. They don't so much as twitch. If the Cindrae elder didn't just blink, I'd question if they were even alive.

"Valk and Xiaric's return have been helpful to you," Lucretia says suddenly.

"I don't … who are they?" I stammer.

Her lips curve with her typical condescending smile. "Caindra's mate and their offspring. A male. They must have been eager to reunite."

My mouth gapes. The chartreuse dragon is their *child*? Bexley had a mate and a child *all this time*? "How long were they in the Nulling?"

"Since Vin'nyla sent them to it, just before my masters left."

"But that's *thousands* of years." Tens of thousands, maybe. "Why didn't they come back when Farren tore the veil?"

"Because my masters were not here yet," she says matter-of-factly.

"And they take this form when the nymphs are here." I try to work out the logic aloud. Bexley said that with the nymphs' return, she would become what she is again—a dragon. If that's true, then whatever magic these dragons hold is ancient and tied to the nymphs.

"It is all connected," Lucretia echoes what she has said before.

"Why did Vin'nyla send them to the Nulling?"

"You would need to ask Vin'nyla." Lucretia's grin is teasing, her answer unhelpful.

"Was it a punishment or for leverage?" Malachi sent Sofie's husband to the Nulling and used her to do his bidding. So, if Vin'nyla wanted leverage over Caindra, what might her schemes mean for this realm?

"I do not offer speculation. But what does it matter? The Queen of All has reunited them. Caindra is more than a formidable ally. She is indebted."

Speaking of formidable things flying out of the Nulling ... "I saw Queen Neilina's body carried out of the rift. A wyvern saved her."

"You rule the Ybarisan realm now. Why do you concern yourself with the past?"

"*Why* did the wyvern save her, Lucretia?" My voice reverberates off the stone as I enunciate each word, my anger bleeding through. I've learned how the sylx works. She shares information when she chooses, not necessarily when I ask for it. In this case, I'm demanding an answer.

Lucretia meets the wisp elder's sharp eyes, holding them a few beats. "It did not."

"I know what I saw."

Again, Lucretia checks with the wisp elder before speaking. It dawns on me that they must be able to communicate as Oredai does, his voice leaking into my mind like cold water in my shoes. According to Jarek and Zorya, Lucretia is also adept at slinking into peoples' minds to communicate.

"The previous Ybarisan queen has not owned her life since the day she begged a fate for a weapon. She has long since been marked as a vessel and willingly accepted a token to aid in the transition."

"Aoife's antlers." It is as Agatha feared, that garish piece that adorned her neck. I shouldn't be surprised. It was Malachi's horn that Sofie used to bind me to this body I inhabit now.

"A more powerful gift from the fate could not be granted than the bone from their head or wing from their back, though in reality, it was not a gift for the queen but for the fate herself."

Because Aoife planned to walk this plane again, just as Malachi has. "So Aoife is *here*."

"Not *here*. Not yet."

"But she's coming."

"Perhaps. Or perhaps she will find suitable interests elsewhere. I cannot speak to her desires."

"Her desire is to rule. Anyone with half a brain knows that. And you're speaking in riddles again." My patience is thinning, despite our audience.

"I speak only the truth, even if you may not understand it. There are realms beyond that which you see and designs beyond that which you know. Regardless, the host body must mend first. Its wounds were grave. You ensured that with a well-placed dagger."

"The one you gave me." A token from Malachi that I embedded in Neilina's throat.

"That was a gift from my master." She nods toward the Cindrae elder. "It was meant to delay the healing process, to give you time. But it will not stop it entirely."

"So, you're telling me you knew Aoife was planning to return and you never said anything?"

"Your Highness, you are far too focused on the threat that isn't before you that you have not even asked about the one that is." Lucretia's musical laughter rings out.

My stomach tightens with understanding as I process her words. "Malachi is here." It's as much a statement as a question. We knew he would come. That has always been his purpose. I just didn't expect it to be so soon. "Where is he?"

"Where one would expect a fate desperate to play king to be." Lucretia's odd citron-colored irises dance with delight. "In an abandoned kingdom."

I shut my eyes with dismay. Zander went to Cirilea, didn't he? Does he know? I really need to get this meeting over with so I can fly to the rift and see him. "How do we defeat Malachi?"

Lucretia looks this time to the Cindrae elder. Whatever passes between them, she doesn't share.

"Why do you speak for them?" I ask suddenly.

"I speak for my masters now as I always have. It is my duty."

"They can't speak for themselves?"

Her lips quirk. "You would prefer they do not."

I groan. "Fine. How do we defeat Malachi?" I repeat, urgency in my tone.

"You are the Queen for All."

"But what does that mean besides wearing this stupid crown?" I throw a hand toward my head.

Lucretia's gaze wafts around the circle of elders, but when it returns to me, she offers me only silence.

My irritation swells. I try a different angle. "How strong is Malachi?"

"Not as strong in this form. Far stronger than your precious king."

Another nonanswer. I'm wasting valuable time. "Aoife and

Malachi were here once. Who defeated them and did the nymphs help?" They must have had *something* to do with it.

"It is not a simple—"

"I'm not asking you," I snap at Lucretia who is going to keep me chasing my tail for her own amusement. I turn my attention to the wisp elder, meeting her eyes. "You demanded an audience, so here I am. Your Daughter of Many and Queen for All." I throw out my hands. A challenge, maybe.

Humor flashes in the wisp elder's eyes and finally—*finally!*—her lips part in a mischievous grin.

We do not trouble ourselves with their wars.

I cringe against the shrill voice that erupts inside my head. It's nothing like the childish giggles I've grown used to, but more like a blade dragged across glass.

Lucretia tsks. "I warned you."

But my anger only flares. "Then why bother coming back?"

She stares at me.

"*Why* bother—"

Because you summoned us.

The raspy voice squeezes my eardrums. I cry out against the crippling pain, pressing my palms against my ears, but it grants little relief. Only when the throb subsides can I search for its source.

The Cindrae elder reveals pointed teeth much like Oredai's.

"I didn't *summon* you," I counter without thinking and then brace myself against his response.

But it's Lucretia who answers. "You opened the door to Ulysede."

"I didn't know what that meant." I hear how weak that excuse is the moment it leaves my lips.

"Your ignorance changes nothing."

"Thank you, Lucretia, for your scintillating opinion that I *didn't* ask for," I snap. "I'm asking for the nymphs' help as the Queen for All. Why won't they give it to me?"

"If Her Highness is unsatisfied with the aid provided by my masters, perhaps she should summon Aminadav or Vin'nyla for counsel."

"So they can know what Malachi and Aoife are up to, and crack the earth again? Are you *insane*?" Though a conversation with them might be less painful than this.

Lucretia's head tips back with her laughter. "You think they do not know where Malachi and Aoife are? You think they have not begun retaliating?"

A chorus of wicked laughter explodes in my mind, buckling my knees until they meet the grass. The pressure is agonizing, and I struggle to not scream as drops of blood splatter near where my hands press against the ground. More blood trickles from my nose until I taste a metallic tinge on my lips.

I'm seconds from blacking out when Jarek's words stir in my mind.

Remember who you are and do not hesitate to remind anyone who forgets.

They haven't forgotten who I am. They're toying with me.

My rage ignites and with it a swell of affinities. I grasp onto all four, weaving them until the silver cord coils, ready to lash out like a viper. "Enough!" I shriek.

The crippling sound cuts off instantly.

I stagger to my feet, wiping the back of my hand against my mouth. My affinities still ripple beneath my skin. Could I kill these elders with it? What would happen if I did? Would others take their place?

As one, they dip their heads. A sign of apology or respect? I can't tell. Nor do I care. "As much fun as this has been, I have too many places to be and enemies to defend against. Thank you for your help with the blood curse. If you don't see your Queen for All again, it's because I've been trapped by Mordain's guild, or killed by a beast, or Malachi has—"

The goblin elder opens its mouth and the shrill, layered scream it emits makes my teeth clench. Thankfully, this time it is out loud rather than inside my head.

"There are four factions and so there must be four offerings made to the Queen for All." Lucretia strolls to the far end where the gargoyle sits. In its massive grip is a bronze horn. She bows and collects it before handing it to me. "A gift from the *golle.*"

I study the enormous smooth bronze token in the shape of a bull horn. "What does it do?"

"When you find yourself in the deepest of perils, in your darkest, most desperate hour, put it to your lips, and relief will arrive. But do not waste this gift, as it may be used once and once only."

"What kind of relief?"

"The kind your people will need," she answers vaguely, and I sense that's the only answer I'll get.

"Thank you," I mumble, meeting the gargoyle—the golle—elder's eyes.

"There is one more. Perhaps the most valuable to you." Lucretia collects a set of thin gold bracelets that suddenly appear in the wisp elder's grasp. She hands them to me. They're similar in design to the ones Zander put on me when I first came to Islor, though far more delicate. "She who wears these shall never be separated from her affinities."

"Never be ..." My voice fades as I grasp her meaning. "Even against powerful caster wards?"

Lucretia dips her head.

A smile stretches across my face as I gingerly slip them on and squeeze the open ends together until they seal shut, fitting snuggly around my wrists. The seams vanish. I dip my head toward the wisp elder. "*Thank you.*"

"My masters have granted the Queen of All what she desired most and what she needed most." Lucretia's eyes meet the elders, each in turn. She bows deeply, and it's a long moment before she rises again. "Their obligation is now fulfilled."

I frown. "What do you mean by oblig—ation." My voice falters as I take in the sudden change in surroundings. I'm back in the dark, dank circular crypt. At my feet are chunks of stone where the statues broke apart. The pedestals sit empty.

"Where did they go?" I say.

"Their duty is fulfilled," Lucretia answers.

I search but can't find her. It's not the first time she's hidden in the shadows. "But what if I need them again? I thought I was their *queen.*"

"And they have bestowed the greatest offerings to you as such. The gift of obscurity from the *kaeli*, of time from the Cindrae, of relief from the golle, and resistance from the wisps. A kingdom for asylum, filled with the knowledge you seek. You have everything you need from them. Now it is time to fight your war." Lucretia finally emerges. She's changed out of her white coat, replacing it with an outfit that is a replica of mine, right down to the soft brown leather boots. Even her auburn hair is braided in an intricate weave that matches Corrin's work.

"What is *this*?" I drag a finger through the air from head to toe.

She looks down at her outfit. "Is this not what we wear to war?"

"It's what *I'm* wearing. Why are *you* wearing it?"

"My masters have released me from service. I am free to choose my path, and I choose to serve Her Highness."

"So, you'll admit you weren't *actually* serving me before."

"Have I not been helpful?"

I sigh. As frustrated as I've been with Lucretia, as many games as she seems to play, she is still the best source of information we have. My focus lands on the engravings that make up the carved stone doors. At least they've returned. "Which one leads to Nyos?"

She gestures to a rectangle on my left.

"And it works now?"

"There is only one way to know."

I close the distance. Adrenaline pumps through my veins as I drag my fingertip over the scripture …

Familiar childlike laughter touches my ear, and I sink against the stone with relief.

"My masters have healed it," Lucretia says, before quickly correcting, "my old masters."

Excitement explodes in me. "I have to get Jarek. With these cuffs, I can go in, get the scribes, and bring them back—"

"You cannot," she interrupts me.

"What do you mean? Why not?"

"There are powerful wards against entering the casters' realm, uninvited, just as there are powerful wards against entering this realm, uninvited. It will not allow you to pass."

"It *has* to." Even though I know about these wards from Solange and Agatha.

"If you doubt me, try."

Jarek and Zander will argue over who gets to kill me first if Lucretia is wrong and I end up in Nyos without them. But I *have* to know. Drawing on my key caster threads, I direct the bound cord toward it, bracing myself for either disappointment or new scenery.

The moment the cord touches, it fizzles as if burned, and my momentary excitement deflates.

"You still mistrust me, Your Highness?"

"What about from the other side? Can I bring scribes here?"

"The Queen of All may always return to her realm."

Well, that's something, at least. "What about the one in Argon?"

She gestures to another door carved into the wall.

"Where does it lead?"

"To the jeweled palace, but beyond that, I cannot tell you for I do not—"

I don't test the engravings this time, channeling into it …

And find myself in utter darkness.

Fear grips me instantly. I wrap an air shield around myself, hoping I didn't just do something stupid, and ignite a light orb. As it swells, chests of jewels and gold and gilded busts appear around me. I recognize the room for what it is—Argon's royal vault. *My* royal vault. It's not quite as large as the one in Ulysede, but it is undoubtedly impressive.

A heavy door sits at the far end of this vast room. I imagine there are guards outside. Who knows what else is beyond. For now, I have the answer I needed.

In moments, I'm back in Ulysede.

"Another wormhole, Your Highness?" Lucretia mocks.

But I'm rushing up the stairs, desperate to find Zander. "I'll be back with all the scribes as soon as I can!"

Jarek is waiting at the top of the steps. The Cindrae have stepped back. "What happened down there?" he barks, panic flashing in his eyes as he takes in the blood smears under my nose.

"Long story, but it's fine. We have more tokens. Useful ones. The golle gave us this." I hold up the bronze horn.

"For what?"

"I don't know, but this"—I wave my wrist to show off the gold bracelet—"stops the Prime from binding my affinities."

"And what is *she* doing out of her snake pit?"

I turn to where his attention—and scowl—has swung and realize Lucretia has followed me up. "She's serving me. Lucretia, why do you look so amazed? You've seen all this before." I doubt anyone knows Ulysede better than the sylx, and yet she gapes as she takes in the throne room.

"Seen it, yes." She shuts her eyes and tips her head back. "But I have not *felt* the sun in many millennia, my obligation to my old masters binding my corporeal form to that place."

I absorb her words with a wave of pity. She's been in that crypt as long as Ulysede has been sealed. When she was lurking around the city, unseen, it's because she had no other choice.

Jarek doesn't share my compassion. "What does 'serving you' mean, exactly?" The question is for me, but Jarek towers over her. "Are you saying I will have to look at her on the daily?"

Lucretia's eyes widen and anger I've never seen before ignites within. "Does my appearance not please you, servant? Would you prefer another?" In an instant, her face morphs into a replica of my old one, of Romy Watts.

Jarek's dagger is drawn in an instant, the tip pressed against her throat. "How dare you wear the queen's face."

"*This* is not the queen's face." Her lips stretch wide with her hiss.

"I know what you're doing, and I will execute you for this," he growls.

A drop of blood trickles from where the blade digs into her skin, but she shows no fear, leaning into it.

"Enough!" I shake my head. I remember the first time she did this, taking on Eden's form. It's even more unnerving now. And dangerous. "Lucretia, you are not allowed to wear anyone's face but your own. Do you understand?"

In another blink, she's back to her usual humanlike form—a beautiful female with high cheekbones and full lips. "I will not wear anyone's face but this one, Your Highness." But there's challenge in her eyes as she stares down Jarek.

Snarls and shrieks sound then, pulling our attention toward where a gargoyle—a golle, Lucretia called its kind—stares down two squealing goblins, or kaeli. With a swing of its fist, the golle sends both the pot-bellied creatures flying.

The Cindrae move swiftly with spears drawn, leading them all away.

"It will not be long now before the factions forget their peace accords." Lucretia smiles as if reminiscing over fond memories.

"Are you saying they don't get along?" What about that scene we walked into through the gates? Of kaeli and wisps splashing in fountains and browsing carts?

"They are usually at war with one another. It is inevitable."

I groan. I have enough to deal with. I cannot handle bickering nymphs too. "Is it safe having them in Ulysede?"

"It depends what you consider safe."

"There are hundreds of children in this castle, Lucretia. What would *you* do if you were me?"

She falters on her answer. It's the first I've ever seen her stall. "I would remove all nymphs from the castle grounds, Your Highness. The Cindrae will manage those within Ulysede with zero tolerance."

"And what about those not in Ulysede?" The ones who passed the golden gates and disappeared into Islor.

She grins. "Her Highness has enough to worry about."

"That's comforting," I mutter.

Would you like me to remove the nymphs from the castle as the sylx advises, Your Highness?

Oredai's question slides into my mind. After what I endured with the nymphs, it feels like a healing balm. "Yes. Peacefully."

Of course.

His responding smile sends shivers down my spine and makes me think our definitions of that word are vastly different.

"Let's find Agatha and then get out of here." I'm desperate to see Zander.

17

ANNIKA

I blink against the burn of saltwater as I come to, lying on a pile of rocks, my dress sopping wet and cold against my skin. Vague recollections of retching stir in my memory, but I will gladly welcome that for eternity if it means never feeling the agony of raw merth again.

Those bastard sailors ... I put up a pathetic fight against them, using my affinity to Aminadav to whip several with hemp ropes to no avail. I remember little else after they bound my wrist in the silver cord and heaved me overboard to join Tyree. That is the one positive of that toxic weed—I was so consumed by pain that my lungs ballooning with water and my body plummeting toward the bottom of the sea were secondary.

At some point, hands tugged at my waist and the pallid, hideous face of a siren filled my vision. I said a silent prayer of thanks to the fates that my suffering would end quickly on unforgiving teeth.

Only, it did not end that way. I was dragged through the water at speeds too fast to acknowledge. It seemed an endless journey. Eventually, I lost consciousness. And now I am on this rocky shoreline, free of merth, staring at a fractured ship in my blurry vision. Is it the *Tempest*? No, this one has been here some time, the gaping hull home to barnacles and black moss.

Wherever "here" is.

Where in fates am I?

A wave of nausea assaults me as I peel my battered and weak body off the jagged stone and breathe through the urge to vomit. I expelled half the sea if my aching ribs are any hint, and it's a struggle just to sit up.

An odd suckling sound draws my attention behind me, and I discover a gray-skinned creature hunched over Tyree, its spine protruding down its back in sawtooth spikes.

My shriek sends it leaping back on sinewy legs with a hiss, to glower at me through beady white eyes. It's a siren like the ones I saw in the water surrounding the ship, only now I can see its full, spindly form and all the gills and webbed folds of skin that allow it to thrive underwater. However this creature was created, all designs of beauty were poured into their song, for it is the most atrocious-looking thing I've ever laid eyes on, next to a daaknar. And it appears ready to pounce on me.

My fingers scrape blindly as I fumble for a potential weapon, landing on wood. "Go away!" I screech, waving the stick frantically back and forth. It will snap before it does any real damage.

But it works because the siren skitters to the water's edge and dives in. It vanishes into the dark sea without leaving a single ripple in its wake.

What was it doing to Tyree, hunched over like that? An unsettling thought rises. Having a meal, likely. I saw what they did to that sailor in the water.

Cautiously, I edge closer to him. He's eerily still. Is he even alive? His limbs are all accounted for. That's a small relief. But did he survive the ordeal?

I crouch down to check his pulse—it's strong—and note the silver cord still looped around his neck. He may be conscious, but he's paralyzed and in agony.

His trousers are torn wide where I stabbed him, the gaping wound on his thigh now packed with a strange green paste. Was that the siren's doing?

My dagger.

Frantically, I dig through Tyree's pockets until my fist curls around the familiar handle. It was not lost in our ordeal. With a smile of victory, I slip it out, and then weigh my options.

I could leave the Ybarisan prince who plotted to murder my family, let him suffer while awaiting the siren's return.

Or I could slit his throat and have some semblance of vengeance for the ruin he helped bring to Islor.

I search our surroundings, trying to find my bearings. All I see are rocks and more broken ships resting against the shoreline where they washed up, their splintered masts telling their tale. It's a nautical graveyard. Were there any survivors? If not, I could be stranded here alone. Would that be better or worse than being stranded with my enemy?

He's far more handsome like this, I'll admit. When his lips aren't flapping with gibes and his crystal blue eyes—so similar to his sister's —don't shine with cruel amusement. If he had arrived at court as an Islorian noble, surely he would have caught my eye.

"Oh, fates ..." As much as I hate Tyree, as much as he would deserve it ... Unlike him, I am not a murderer, and I know the pain he endures. I would spend too much time thinking about it if I left him here.

With my dagger and the stick I used to fend off the siren, I sever the knot in the cord and flick the merth away.

Tyree gasps, his eyes wild with panic as they search first the sky above us, and then my face.

"Do not make me regret this," I warn.

"What happened?" he croaks.

"Besides Captain Aron and his sailors outsmarting you?"

He blinks away the fog and I watch quietly as he puts the hazy chunks of his memory together. "I'm going to kill him."

"If you can find him. But hopefully the sea already took care of them." Did they toss us overboard in time to avoid the monster heading their way?

He pulls himself up with a groan, quickly surveying the surrounding ships. "Where are we?"

"You mean this isn't Westport?" I say with mock sweetness.

He spares me a glare, his gaze sliding over me, to the dagger in my grip, then to the silver cord strewn over the rocks. "You didn't finish me off when you had the chance."

"There's still time." And I'm far too close to him. I climb to my feet and step back, putting distance between us in case he tries to confiscate my weapon—again.

He chuckles. "Do not worry, I have learned my lesson." He frowns at the green sludge packing.

"There was a siren here when I woke. I was hoping it would eat you, but I think it was tending to your wound."

"It seems better." Stretching his injured leg out in front of him, a slow smile stretches across his handsome face. "Much better."

"Your charming healer went that way"—I point to the water—"if you'd like to thank it. Don't hurry back."

"Oh, my dear Annika, you had the perfect chance to kill me and you did not take it. I'm beginning to think you're all talk." He eases to a standing position and notes his socked feet.

"*So wise*, hiding my jewels in your boots."

He steps along the hard path, his wet clothes molded to a fit and muscular body. "Never mind. I'm sure there must be a suitable replacement somewhere—" He stops abruptly and holds up his hands.

Panic swells inside me. The cuffs Atticus bound him with are missing from his wrists. There are only two ways those could come off—if my brother removed them.

Or if he were dead.

Surely, Tyree knows this, for he meets my gaze as I blink back unexpected tears for a twin brother who has caused me more strife than anything else. I'm on this blasted rock as much thanks to Atticus as Tyree. He abandoned me to Cirilea and an uprising!

"Perhaps the sirens had something to do with this as well," he suggests in a soft tone I didn't think him capable of. "They healed my leg, after all, and that was by a fate's token."

"Perhaps." I swallow my brewing anguish as I pick a path along the rocks, heading in the only direction we can go.

"It's a good thing that I have access to my affinity. Who knows what we'll find here," Tyree continues, trailing after me.

"Yes, maybe you'll finally be of *some* use to me now." What is his elven affinity to again? I cannot recall; I've never deigned to care. I pray not Malachi, given there isn't a hint of flame to be seen anywhere.

For once—fates bless me—Tyree grants me silence.

18

ROMERIA

"Why do you punish me with mundane tasks again?" Zorya leads us through the library, sparing a glare for Lucretia. "I would be far more useful killing things at the rift than I am fetching books and guarding an impotent caster who limps about."

"Her Highness has commanded it," comes Jarek's sharp retort. This foul mood has trailed him from the throne room, his body drenched with tension. I assume it has to do with the sylx who *also* trails him.

"Agatha is the most valuable caster in this entire world right now, and I trust *you* to keep her safe," I amend, my fingers toying with the smooth gold over my wrist. "Lucretia, I need you to bring any book that talks about the time when the fates were last in this realm to the Master Scribe." If she's going to serve me, she may as well do it here. Also, that should keep her busy.

"The magic wielders of the past age were particularly verbose, Your Highness. There are many."

"Great. Bring them *all* to the Master Scribe."

"As you wish." She evaporates into thin air.

"There. That keeps her useful and it should give you time to remove that giant stick up your ass." I brandish a sweet smile at Jarek before strolling away to Zorya's laughter.

We find the elderly caster hunched at the very same desk Gesine occupied for hours on end, stacks of books surrounding her much like I found her pupil many times. My heart clenches as a wave of déjà vu washes over me.

And, much like Gesine, she is too engrossed in her reading to notice our approach.

"Find anything of interest?"

Her head snaps up. "Your Highness!" Setting down her magnifying glass, she braces her hands against her chair handle in her struggle to stand.

"No, don't get up."

She abandons her effort quickly. "You look well rested."

"Much better. Did you rest yourself?"

She waves off my words. "I will rest when death greets me, which will not be long now." Her eyes drift over the four floors of endless books. "You were not exaggerating."

"You can see now why getting the scribes to Ulysede is so important to me." There must be valuable information locked up in here. Why else would the nymphs preserve and protect it so?

"When do you leave for Mordain?"

"Today. I have these now." I hold out my wrists.

Agatha's gray eyes brighten as I explain their purpose, but by the time I've finished, her furrowed brow is back. "It is one thing to battle beasts. It is entirely another to face a guild of experienced casters when you are still learning how to wield. The Prime is not your only obstacle. I do not think you appreciate the dangers here."

"Maybe not, but I can't sit by while a hundred scribes are executed because of a prophecy involving me." I pull up another chair, settling next to her. How do I word this ... "Tell me everything *I need to know* about Mordain."

Her cheeks puff out with a giant breath. "Where do I begin ..."

"How about quickly," Jarek quips, hovering.

I spare him a glare. "Who can I trust?"

"That is easy," she says. "No one."

"Seriously?"

"It is the stance that will keep you safest, Your Highness." She sinks into her chair. "The new Master Scribe, Zaleria, is a strong proponent for prophecy and shares my views. She has kept *many* of the same secrets as I, which likely means she has faced the brunt of Lorel's interrogation. I do not know if she will have the capacity to withstand it." She pauses, swallowing hard. This Zaleria means something to her. "But you can consider her a strong ally. To an extent, the Second, Allegra, can be counted on. She aided our cause when others would not, though be warned she aspires to be Prime, and she does not shy away from conspiring. I can say that with a degree of certainty. Her role in all this was known by almost no one, though, so I do not know if she has faced the same scrutiny at Lorel's hands." Agatha snorts. "Who knows, she may deny it all and turn against us, in which case you *cannot* trust her."

"What about the other Second, Solange?"

A smirk appears with that question. "She will serve you frank honesty whether you ask for it or not."

"I've noticed." I laugh. "It's a refreshing change." Especially in this world where everyone spins lies to suit their needs, including Zander.

"Indeed. She respects order and chain of command, which is why she never acted against the Prime. But she also longs for a Mordain free of Ybaris's boot on her neck, which she has told you herself."

"I don't need or want a castle full of elementals." Dolls on shelves, Annika called them once.

"That is one large piece of it, but it is not the entire puzzle."

"Can I trust her, though?"

"Can you trust her to serve the Queen of Ybaris over a Prime whose interests serve only herself? For the time being, I believe so. However, if she suspects you are following in worn footsteps, you will find her loyalty wavering quickly."

I catalogue the scribe's invaluable words. I am beginning to see why Gesine trusted her implicitly.

"The Shadows command both respect and fear from the various caster factions. Those attempting to act against you will think twice with them at your side." Agatha holds up a gnarled finger. "But there are still plenty of casters remaining in Mordain who were not sent to the rift. Do not underestimate them because together, they can stifle your plans. There are casters who support Lorel and more who believe in a liberated Mordain. Who knows what lies the Prime has fed them to aid her cause."

"Got it." Agatha is making me more nervous by the second. "And where is the nymph door?"

She looks genuinely perplexed.

"Carvings, likely in a wall, that you wouldn't be able to read. Gesine said there is something like that there."

Her eyes light up. "A door! Is that what that is? I always knew it was something. Yes, well, it's in the scribes' hall beneath the tower, where we keep our scrolls."

"That's helpful. Thank you, Agatha."

"So, what *exactly* is your plan?"

"I don't have one yet. I'm hoping it'll come to me as I go."

"Because that always works out so well," Jarek says wryly.

I ignore him. "Zorya will stay with you. Ignore her surliness. You'll be safe. And I've asked the sylx to bring you any books about the fates. It might be helpful."

"Oh, is she here?" Agatha searches around. "I look forward to meeting her."

"That might change quickly." My irritation with Lucretia hasn't lessened since the meeting with the nymph elders. "Do you think Aminadav and Vin'nyla will punish us for what Aoife and Malachi are doing?"

"I would not be surprised if they did. Why do you ask?"

"Just something Lucretia said." I retrieve the bronze token from my satchel and hold it up. "Just before she gave me this. Also a gift from the nymphs."

Her eyes widen. "Aminadav's horn."

"Yes. But I don't know what it does." I repeat Lucretia's words about using it during the darkest hour. "What kind of relief could it bring?"

Agatha purses her lips as if she's holding back words. "Raw tokens like this are scarce, and usually tied to a summons. Often, unlocking their power requires sacrifice in the form of a life."

"Whose life?" Jarek demands to know.

"That is the fate's decision. The nymphs may have gifted this to you, but they received it directly from Aminadav. He decides the cost."

"Sofie stabbed me with a large chunk of Malachi's horn as part of whatever ritual she performed to send me here," I say, recalling the curved black object in her fist.

"And I believe Aoife claimed Neilina's life form with her antlers," Agatha notes.

Lucretia all but confirmed it. I see the picture Agatha is painting. "You're saying that if I blow this horn, someone is going to die."

"Someone or more than someone. In our archives, there is a story of Aminadav gifting his horn to a king in the face of war once, many years ago."

"And? What happened?"

"The king and his entire army perished in an instant. The war ended." Her smile is wry. "I suppose one might say they found relief in death."

My stomach sinks with dread as I shove the horn into my satchel and vow never to use it. "Good to know." I stand to leave.

Agatha holds up a finger. "One other thing I did not mention before but ought to, given your question of the fates' meddling. The wyvern has long since been considered Vin'nyla's creation."

I frown. "You mean, like daaknars are Malachi's?"

"Precisely, which makes me wonder why one would carry Aoife's vessel body from the rift. I doubt it is in aid."

I reconsider what Lucretia said earlier under this lens. "You think Vin'nyla has somehow sabotaged Aoife's plan to return to this plane?"

Agatha shrugs. "Once can only hope."

I can't decide if this is good news. "Thank you for sharing your knowledge with me. I would be lost without you."

"Of course." She bows. "I am here to serve the Queen for All."

My back is to the caster when she calls out, "Your Highness!" She hesitates, fumbling with a locket around her neck. "There is a young scribe. A boy, really. Cahill is his name. Might I ask, if you find him in Nyos, can you bring him here? He is dear to me, and I would very much like to have him at my side."

My instincts tell me there is more to this story, but I simply nod. "I'll make sure he comes."

"Be careful, Your Highness!" She wrings her hands. "Our realms cannot afford to lose you."

———

THE SCENE at the rift is far different today from when I descended with Caindra the first time. The two armies that arrived yesterday have doubled our force, their tents stretching beyond the perimeter of the original camp, all the way to the forest's edge. And despite another night of battle, the camp is alive with activity—smoke from cook fires swirl in the air, fresh stacks of wood await tonight's burn. If soldiers aren't washing last night's battle off in the nearby river, they're working in teams to heave carcasses over the edge of the cliff.

It has definitely earned its Valley of Bones title by now.

Caindra glides in smoothly, Xiaric flanking her right. The two were entwined and asleep when I emerged from the gates today—Caindra protecting the smaller dragon's body within her own. Any doubt that he could be her child vanished at the sight.

With a deafening screech, the orange dragon—Valk—propels himself off the stone wall roost, wings spreading as he soars toward us in greeting. I cling to one of Caindra's claws as she swerves, barely avoiding a collision. They circle each other once ... twice ... almost as if in a dance.

Below us, horses buck and soldiers struggle to keep them in place, their wary eyes on the sky as we descend. Those in our path rush to get out of the way before the dragons touch down, the ground shaking beneath their weight.

As always, Caindra sets me down with ease, allowing me a moment to gain my bearings so I don't stumble like a drunken fool. And as always, save for yesterday when she showed gentleness toward a poisoned Jarek, she tosses him like trash. He's ready for it and lands with a graceful roll.

"You're getting better at that," I tease.

"Not a skill I strived for." He pulls himself up, dusting off his pants. "When can we return to traveling by horseback?"

"I second that." Abarrane steps out from a tent, weaving her lengthy wheat-colored hair in a thick braid. "Your Highness. You look well rested."

"And you look ... clean."

She grins. "You should have seen me an hour ago."

"Where is Zander?" I search around us. These two are never far apart.

She nods toward the tent she just vacated. "He has finally drifted off after days without rest. I would give him an hour before you wake him. Anything beyond that and the fool will fill my ear with complaints for days."

My shoulders sink. I'm desperate to feel his arms around me, but she's right. He needs rest.

I take in the camp again from ground level. It buzzes with adrenaline—or perhaps it's my own adrenaline that invigorates me. "How was last night?"

"Not as eventful as the first, though we fear the beasts have begun crawling up elsewhere." Abarrane secures her hair with twine. "Only two wyverns emerged, but the great winged beast scared them off. Where they go to, I wish I knew." She juts her chin at the orange dragon soaring in the sky. "He has a name, by the way."

"Valk."

She frowns. "How do you know this?"

"Lucretia. How do *you* know?"

Her lips purse with hesitation. "That is a story best shared by His

Highness. Come, I have something of interest to show you." She leads Jarek and I deep into camp.

I GRIMACE at the desiccated corpses, stripped of their armor and weapons. "You thought piles of skeletons would interest me."

"These are the bodies we could not explain before." Abarrane stands between the two heaps. "Some of them have turned to dust."

"Did you find the beast that does this?" The soldiers will need to avoid it as readily as they should avoid the vrog that poisoned Jarek.

"In a manner of speaking." Her face turns grim. "Lord Rengard's army was marching toward us at the height of Hudem's moon when the change happened, as it did for us. They were far from any Nulling beasts when a dozen of their soldiers suddenly collapsed, dead. Same thing with the eastern army. And even within our camp, soldiers noticed those near them falling before the first attack."

"So, it *wasn't* a beast that did this?" I struggle to follow her thinking.

"We believe these soldiers were turned Islorian immortals. Not born by the nymphaeum's blessing. When the nymphs reversed Malachi's blood curse, all those who lived immortal lives because of the blood curse returned to their mortality."

"Because they weren't born this way." And in mortal years, I'm sure many of them were several hundred years old.

"Exactly. We did not come to this conclusion until last night, after we received word from Lyndel that Lady Telor had succumbed to the same fate."

I gasp. "Lord Telor's wife is dead?"

"Yes. And His Highness knew intimate details of her ... path to immortality, shall we say." Abarrane gives me a knowing look. "After some pressing of those closest to the dead, we feel confident this is the answer."

Gesine did warn me there might be unforeseen consequences to the end of the blood curse. I guess this is one. "But Elisaf is alive and *we know* he was turned." By Zander himself—a secret kept to this day, though the law preventing it no longer matters now that the blood curse is gone.

"Aye, he *was* turned." Abarrane nods. "That fact stumped His Highness for a time, too, until he started to ask what makes Elisaf different from the others and the answer is you."

"*Me?*"

"He was healed by a key caster after a grif shredded him to pieces."

"So you think *I* saved him from this?" I hear the doubt in my own voice.

"Lord Telor should have been dead before they reached him, and yet he is now resting in Gaellar's tent. The elemental could sense traces of something powerful while she was healing him. She found the same thing in Elisaf. There is something special about your touch." She shrugs. "Ask her yourself, but that is the only explanation we can find for any of it."

I think back to all those I've healed. Elisaf, Lord Telor, Zander ... Atticus. Will he benefit from this too?

"On second thought, I think I will accept that healing you suggested this morning." Jarek holds his hands out to the sides, wearing a smug grin.

"As long as that is *all* that was suggested this morning while sharing a bed." Abarrane narrows her gaze at her previous Second. "Speaking of those who should be dead ..." She leads us to another tent, throwing the flap aside. "Look what we found wallowing in his own filth when we went to search for Atticus."

A male lies on a cot, his olive complexion ashen, his lengthy brown hair in disarray. The skin around his shoulder is marred by angry red streaks.

My mouth gapes. "I know him." *Know* is not the right word. "He was there the night Atticus took the arrow. He was the one who tried to stop us from leaving."

"That is Kazimir, Atticus's arse licker," Jarek confirms.

"Kazimir can hear you talking about him," the man croaks, cracking his eyelids and rolling his head toward us. Dried blood speckles his beard. "*You*, I know, unfortunately." His gaze veers from Jarek to me. "And you, I escorted from the rift to Cirilea, so I know your face well, and I did not see it outside the Goat's Knoll that night."

Of course he would recognize Princess Romeria. "Different face, but I promise you, it was me." How close is he to Atticus, anyway? Does he know what his dear friend did with his brother's betrothed on that escort south?

"That's a trick I'd like to learn." He pulls himself up with a wince. "I heard whisperings of the new Ybarisan queen with silver eyes while they thought me unconscious. They say she is a key caster and that she killed her own mother to claim the throne."

"I killed Queen Neilina to stop a war we don't need so we can fight a war we have no choice in fighting *because* of Queen Neilina," I counter evenly.

"And which war is that? The one you caused with your blood?" There's challenge in his tone.

I'm beginning to see why Atticus kept this soldier so close—they're both smug asses who always have an answer. "The poison is no longer an issue, in case you haven't noticed."

"I may have." He runs his tongue over his teeth as if a reminder. "And why is that?"

Because I opened the nymphaeum, unleashing all our new problems. The weight of that truth is not lost to me.

"His Highness insisted we bring him with us to see what he could share of Atticus." Abarrane sneers at the soldier. "I was happy to leave him there to suffer."

Kazimir smooths a hand over his jaw, but it doesn't hide the smirk. "Always a joy to be in your presence, Abarrane."

"Did you find Atticus?" A quick glance around shows me he isn't here.

"No." Abarrane shakes her head. "Kazimir witnessed him struck down in a deadly blow from an ax. We searched for his body but could not find it."

"Kier took it as a trophy," Jarek says.

My insides twist at the thought. There's no love lost between us—especially after what I observed in Cirilea under Atticus's reign, of mortals dangling from city lights—but it would wound Zander.

"A king's corpse does King Cheral little good," Abarrane counters. "But we do think he might have survived. Romeria healed him. That might have been enough to keep him alive until he reaches Kier."

"Do they have healers there?" I feel Kazimir studying me.

"I do not see how. It is a mortal realm, and the waters between Ybaris and Kier are impassable. But our connection with Kier was severed many centuries ago. We know little and have cared little of what goes on across that border."

"How do we find out if they have him?" I ask.

Abarrane shrugs. "We go to Kier."

"When?" Kazimir blurts, urgency filling his voice. Atticus is obviously important to him.

"*You* are not going anywhere but to the rift to help Islor defend itself," Abarrane snaps. "Something *your king* should have done instead of ignoring pleas for help and giving traitors room to tear our realm apart."

"That began long before Atticus sat on the throne and you know it," Kazimir throws back, defending his friend. "And he did not ignore anyone. He sent half our army here to aid you, weakening us for the battle in the east. *That* is why Kier was able to defeat us."

He's not wrong on all those accounts, but this is not the time or place for this fight. "Our focus has to be on the good of all people, not just one." I add more quietly, "Even if he is Zander's brother."

Kazimir's jaw clenches, but he doesn't lash out. "And what of the people in Cirilea? I hear the situation is grim and they"—his eyes cut to Abarrane—"will tell me nothing."

"You deserve nothing," Jarek retorts.

That he seems to care draws my sympathy. But it's another update I still need from Zander. "We helped a lot of them get out before the rebellion, but many more remain."

"There were children in the ballroom—"

"They are safe *now*." Playing tag with pot-bellied nymphs until recently.

"He gathered them there so they would be protected," Kazimir counters. "He feared they would be dosed with the poison if he did not."

"We wrote to him! We told him that the poison wouldn't matter after Hudem."

"And why would he believe you? You've never given him any reason to."

"Because he should have *wanted* to believe me!" My voice cracks with my eruption. "He should have looked for any excuse. But instead, he killed *all those people*. I saw them! I *saw* their bodies hanging in the streets!"

"Romeria …," Jarek whispers.

I take a deep breath, trying to rein in my emotions. What good does yelling at this guy do? He didn't make these decisions, and what's done is done.

"For what it's worth, Atticus struggled with the right path forward, and near the end, he did try his best to protect the mortals," Kazimir offers. "Really, his biggest mistake was relying on Boaz to oversee the problem."

"It's a good thing Her Highness killed Boaz then, isn't it," Abarrane says.

A twitch of Kazimir's eyebrow is the only sign of his surprise. "Good. I never liked him, anyway."

I sense we've gotten all the helpful information we will from this one. "If there's nothing else useful you can share about Atticus—"

"What of the baker?" he interrupts.

"Who? Gracen? She helped me get the children out. She and her family have left Cirilea and they're also safe."

He sighs. "That is good news. Atticus was ... fond of that mortal."

If I had to guess, Atticus isn't the only one fond of Gracen, but I'm not surprised. She wins hearts without trying.

"Well, unless you'd like to give me some of that special healing, I think I need more rest." He lies back on his cot and closes his eyes, effectively dismissing us.

Abarrane's face contorts with fury, her hand reaching for her blade.

I shake my head at her. I know these types of assholes; the reaction is what he wants. We duck out of the tent.

Elisaf and Lord Rengard march toward us.

I look to my old night guard and my first friend in this inhospitable world. The very idea that Elisaf could have been another body in that pile of bones has me throwing my arms around his lanky frame.

"Not the greeting I expected, but I will take it," he murmurs, squeezing me back.

"I'm so happy you're okay."

"Yes, it sounds like I have you and a grif to thank for that. Who could have imagined?"

I feel gazes upon us as I peel myself away. Maybe it's not considered appropriate for queens to hug guards, but I've never been one to follow rules, and I'm not about to fall in line now. "Lord Rengard." I dip my head in greeting. He looks as regal as usual—not a hair out of place, that stripe of gray cutting perfectly through his otherwise jet-black mane.

"Your Highness." He bows. It's not deep, but it feels genuine.

The Islorian soldiers around us follow suit as they pass.

Lord Rengard notes them. "It appears the tide is changing in your favor. The common whisper among camp is that Zander won your cold Ybarisan heart over and you two have been scheming together against Queen Neilina to save Islor all this time."

"I wouldn't say they're wrong." Except my cold heart was that of

Romy Watts of New York, the thief abandoned by all loved ones and fighting for survival.

He grins. "I've heard many tales of your bravery since we arrived here. At first, I thought they might be exaggerating. But now I should think they are more accurate than not."

My cheeks burn with what I'm certain is a compliment. "Just trying to fix a lot of wrongs." How much has Zander told him about my past and my purpose here? They're good friends and Lord Rengard has proven his loyalty time and time again, but would Zander divulge my deepest truths?

Lord Rengard studies the activity in camp. "I hear there is a fleet of ships from Cirilea arriving in Northmost tomorrow."

"If all goes well, yes."

"Common folk traveling through Venhorn to get to this hidden city of yours may not be wise. Especially with all these new creatures crawling out of the rift."

"I know. I was thinking about that too. The people might need to stay at the port."

"I am afraid Northmost is not equipped to accommodate that many, especially when the season turns cold. But Bellcross is a relatively short march south. I am sure we could welcome them there for the time being."

"Really? You would open your city to them?"

He dips his head once. "Consider it done."

I recall the day we were within Bellcross's walls—the square of jesters and merchants selling their wares. Elisaf said it was probably the most progressive place in all of Islor for its mortals, mainly due to its lord. "You are a good friend to Zander."

"Anything for the rightful king of Islor." He hesitates. "*And*, it seems, the queen of not one but two realms. I hope I receive an invitation to visit this secret Ulysede."

"Once all this is over? Absolutely."

He smiles. "Now, if you will excuse me, it seems I have some letters to write in haste."

"So do I." Plus I have jewels to deliver to the captains for their help with rescuing Cirilea's citizens. A promise I made to Seamus that I intend to keep.

"My city should be prepared within the week." With another bow, he marches off.

"How is everyone doing here?" I'll get a different answer from Elisaf than I will Abarrane. "I heard Lord Telor will live?"

"He will, though his recovery may take longer, according to the caster. Two near-death injuries within mere days of each other ..." He shakes his head. "Otherwise, the camp seems in decent spirits for the most part. Some confusion over the sudden absence of the blood curse, but that is to be expected, given it's all they've ever known. Most are anxious to close the rift and get back to their loved ones."

"If only it were that easy." There is no closing it, not while the nymphs are here.

"Yes, but some truths are better left unsaid," he says, raising his eyebrows with meaning. "Radomir has carved himself quite the audience while sharing tales of last night's escapades, which sounded far more exciting than they likely were. He is a natural storyteller." Elisaf grins. "But he knows more about these beasts than any of us ever did. There was certainly value in inviting the saplings to join our cause. I do not think we could have fought them off so effectively otherwise."

"That's why I did it, of course. Because I *knew* how valuable he would be."

"Yes, of course. No one doubted your acumen." Elisaf hums and slips his arm through mine. "Let me lead you through camp, Your Highness, so we may discuss the land and lordship you plan to bestow upon me."

My bark of laughter turns heads.

ANTICIPATION TRUMPS my guilt as I part the canvas flap and duck inside. The tent Zander sleeps in is small and plain—nothing like the marquee tents during the crown hunt, with rich furs and furniture adorning the king's quarters. But it's private, and that's all I care about.

The seams allow just enough daylight to spot his still form, lying face down on a cot, a charcoal wool blanket covering the bottom half of his bare body. My pulse races as I approach, so eager to see him that I nearly trip over the folded stack of leathers laid out on the ground next to his weapons. One of the camp servants must have cleaned his clothing for him.

I reach for his shoulder, but hesitate. Maybe I should let him sleep another—

"You would make a terrible cutthroat," he croaks, humor lacing his voice.

I climb onto the cot and cover his body with mine. "I agree, I'm a far better thief." I tease the back of his neck with a soft, open-mouthed kiss, earning his hum of contentment. Meanwhile, I slip my dagger from its sheath and replace my tongue with the blade, pressing just hard enough for him to feel the sharp prick. "But I'm a quick learner."

His deep chuckle vibrates in my core. "I stand corrected. You simply have a different method for getting close."

I abandon the weapon to the ground. "You came to the rift without me." I can't help the accusation in my tone even as I lay another kiss, this one on his shoulder. His skin smells of fragrant soap. He must have bathed in the river earlier. Hopefully not *with* Abarrane, but I don't ask. Modesty isn't something these Islorian immortals waste time on.

"You needed your rest." He pauses. "Besides, you had your bedfellow for the evening."

His voice is unreadable. Is he upset with me? "I fell asleep there while the wisps were healing him. And if you saw what they did to him—"

Zander turns abruptly, cutting off my words with a kiss. "Relax. I know who your heart belongs to," he whispers, rolling his body until he's on his back beneath me.

His breath hitches as our lips find each other in the dim light, his desperation palpable as he deepens the kiss with skilled strokes of his tongue.

"You're not wearing anything," I manage to get out.

"And you're wearing far too much. Though that can be easily rectified."

Our mouths are a messy tangle as his hands make quick work of laces and buckles, helping me out of my elaborate vest and the rest of my clothes until they're in a scattered pile next to his.

I climb back onto him, our bare bodies flush, the strain of his hard length pressed against my apex. No one has ever made me feel the way Zander does, like I could never get enough of him, like the simplest touch—even his fingertip along my shoulder—might set every one of my nerve endings on fire at any given moment. Now, my entire body tightens with the anticipation of feeling him inside me again.

Until I sense him wincing through our kiss.

I pull back. "What's wrong?"

"Nothing." He leans in to capture my lips again, but I move out of reach.

With barely a thought, I weave a light globe with my affinity. It swells, drenching the tent in light. I pull the blanket away, to reveal the bloodied cloth tied around Zander's thigh.

"It's nothing," he dismisses. "Just a hag caught me off guard, but it's healing."

I grab one of his daggers from beside the cot and slice off the bandaging with the honed blade. A deep, yawning gash across his leg stares back at me. "Zander!" My face must be filled with horror. It's no longer bleeding, but it's far from healing itself. "Why didn't you ask the casters to fix this?"

"Because there were others far worse who needed attention."

"Ugh! It looks serious! And painful! And ... and ... Why are you all so goddamn stubborn!"

He flops back on the cot with a grunt.

Drawing on threads of Aoife, I begin knitting his flesh back together, pushing aside his complaints and my frustration so I can concentrate on the task at hand. When I'm finished, only a thin silver line remains.

Zander lies so still, I wonder if maybe he's asleep, until his Adam's apple bobs with a hard swallow. "You shouldn't deplete yourself for me."

"I haven't depleted anything. And you're welcome," I add in a clipped tone.

His head rolls and hazel eyes shine bright in the globe's glow. "Thank you." His crooked smile stirs flutters in my stomach and melts my annoyance.

"*That* is why I don't want you coming to the rift without me." I trace the ridges of his taut abdomen. A more exquisite male body, I have never seen.

"I will keep that in mind. Now, where were we?" Reaching down, he wraps his palm around his length and strokes himself a few times, igniting a fresh wave of warmth and anticipation inside me.

Strong, rough hands seize the backs of my thighs. He yanks me upward, his forearms straining as he lifts me onto him. The feel of his tip against my center draws a gasp from my lips. It's followed closely by a cry as he pulls my hips down, sinking deep into me.

His eyes never leave mine as he fills me completely, my body stretching to welcome him in. "You are my entire world," he whispers hoarsely, his hips lifting and falling in tandem with mine.

"I don't want to be apart ever again." Even though I know the chances are high that we'll be pulled in different directions very soon.

Every muscle in his torso flexes as he sits up to meet me, his hand clamping over my nape as his lips move forcefully. I roll my hips to pull him deeper into me, and the guttural sound that escapes his throat is almost my undoing.

What follows after is not our usual graceful, rhythmic dance. This is lust-filled and desperate, our fingernails raking along each other's skin as our slick, naked bodies keep searching for purchase, as if we can't find it.

I know what drives this overwhelming urgency in me, this frantic need to erase all space between us—it's the foreboding feeling that every time together is the last. So I don't temper my cries or slow my lips or let my thoughts slip anywhere beyond this perfect being who has made me whole as I come apart with his touch.

My LIMBS ARE boneless as my body relaxes against his and I revel in his arms. Outside, there is a massive army and a heavy threat hanging in the air. The buzz of voices and clang of steel is near constant.

But in here, it's just the two of us.

"I don't like being apart either," he whispers, fingers stroking a pattern of swirls across my back.

I inhale the scent of him again. Let it burn into my senses, absorb into my skin. "Abarrane told me you think Atticus is in Kier?"

Zander groans. "Can we not remain in this blissful bubble for just a while longer?"

"Fine." I fold my forearms and rest my chin there to stare at him, waiting.

He sighs heavily. "If he is alive, he is in Ostros by now, and we have far bigger problems to deal with than rescuing him." He taps my wrist. "Who has been giving *my queen* jewelry?"

"I wondered how long before you noticed."

"I noticed the moment you landed in my bed, and then you distracted me." His palm smooths across the curve of my ass cheek before sliding back up my body to test the gold. "A token."

"From the nymph elders. I went to see them this morning." I quickly fill Zander in on the strange, airy field I found myself in and the painful exchange.

He curses. "How are we to withstand not one but two fates?"

I shake my head. I don't have the answer to that. "But Lucretia says Aoife isn't our concern. Malachi is. He's—"

"In Cirilea. Yes, I know. I was going to tell you."

"You saw him?"

"More than saw him. I spoke to him. Abarrane and I landed in the castle courtyard after assessing the city from above. I was ready to stroll in and reclaim my throne, but there he was, waiting for me, a tall, thin, dark-haired male I've never seen before, wearing my crown and my clothes." His hard swallow fills my ear. "Foolish of me to think it would be that easy."

That sounds like the man I saw lying in the stone box below Sofie's castle. "What about Sofie?"

"She was at his side. There is no mistaking her. She looks exactly like that sketch you drew."

The one Zander stole while I slept and passed around Cirilea's guard to be on the lookout, thinking she was a caster in Ybaris or Mordain. My stomach clenches with memories of that enigmatic woman in the green silk gown, and the version that followed not long after—a precise and fearless killer who will do anything to get what she wants—her husband. "What happened?"

"Our conversation was brief. He called me 'son' and demanded I pledge allegiance and die swiftly or rebel and die mercilessly slow. Oh, and he tossed Lord Adley's head at my feet as a gift." Zander smirks. "Which frankly *is* a gift."

I find little humor in this. "And what did *you* say?"

"I denied him, of course. And then I provoked Sofie."

"You did *not*." My fingers grip his shoulders, as if clinging to him will somehow squash my growing anxiety. "And what did she do?"

"Tried to kill me, naturally. Valk swept us out of there before she succeeded. That's the orange dragon's name. He seems to be healing from the wound he sustained."

"And Xiaric is his child with Caindra. Lucretia told me," I say dismissively, my thoughts hitched on what he just said and along with it, my anger. "So, she *nearly* succeeded, is what you're saying?"

"But she didn't—"

"And then what? You'd be dead and where would we all be? How would we go on?" How would *I* face this without him? Anguish flares inside me with the thought. "Why would you bait her? She's dangerous." And I haven't even seen what she can do as a key caster. I've only seen the aftermath of her slaughtering Korsakov and his men without earning a single scratch, despite their guns against her single sword.

"Because I needed to know how she felt about Malachi claiming her husband's body." Zander's tone bleeds defensiveness. He doesn't like his choices questioned. I suppose that comes with the territory of being born and bred a king.

"*And*?"

"I do not think she is pleased."

A small twinge of satisfaction stirs inside me. After what Sofie did, I'm glad it's not all going as planned for her. "She's still standing beside him, though."

"Yes, but it could work to our advantage, if we know which levers to pull. I *needed* to know, Romeria. I did not see any choice in the matter."

I sigh heavily and focus on the reality that Zander is still here. "Please promise you won't go back to Cirilea without me."

His chest lifts with his deep breath. "Fine. As long as you promise the same."

I think back to those nymph doors, and how easy it is for me to slip in and out of the city. "Fine."

The sudden swell of tension between us ebbs.

"How did Malachi get to Cirilea and seize the throne so quickly, though?" Not even a day has passed, and he's claimed a kingdom?

"He has spent how many millennia trying to get back here? Watching and waiting, scheming. I am not at all surprised." The muscle in Zander's jaw ticks. No wonder he came to the rift while I slept. He needed to blow off steam.

"He saw an abandoned kingdom." I hear Lucretia's voice in my head. All eyes elsewhere. It couldn't have been easier. "What is he like?"

"Honestly? Charming, even while he was threatening my life."

Silence hangs over the tent. "What are we going to do?" I ask the question, but I don't really expect an answer.

"For now, he holds Cirilea and all those who remain there. There are barely enough guards to maintain order in the city, but I imagine he'll use fear to keep the people in line. Carrying Lord Adley's head around will certainly help with that," he adds dryly. "We hold the might of Islor's and Ybaris's armies, as well as that of Mordain's casters, and the nymphs—"

"Don't count on that. They gave me a horn that we can use *once*. They said to save it until all hope is lost and it will bring relief."

"That sounds ominous."

"Right?" I relay what Agatha told me, earning Zander's curse and urge that we throw it into the rift.

"Even without the nymphs, we have the dragons. They are possibly our strongest allies. And we have *you*, the Queen for All." He draws an aimless pattern across my back. "We must keep Malachi's influence isolated to Cirilea while we win favor everywhere else, and once we know how to get rid of him, we move in."

"You've given this some thought."

"It was a very long night." He pauses. "I saw Wendeline. She does not appear well, but she lives still."

My heart leaps with that bit of good news. I may still not forgive her for what she did to Zander's family, but I know she didn't do it out of hatred for them. "Can we get her out of Cirilea?"

"Not if Malachi keeps her at his side. But we are likely better off leaving her there. The priestess might be our only ally within those walls."

"You think she's an ally now?" There was a long stretch of time when Zander swore he would never trust another caster again.

"To the greater good of Islor? I think I've been proven wrong on more than one occasion. Perhaps she will still be of use to us," he admits, his jaw tensing. "I have no idea where Annika is. I fear what will happen to her if Malachi finds her."

"She knows how to survive," I say for Zander's benefit, but I'm not entirely sure anyone can outsmart this fate.

Zander stares at the tent ceiling. "Am I to be all that remains of my bloodline?"

I don't know what to say, so I attempt to distract him with my lips over his collarbones, over the muscular pads of his chest, grazing his peaked nipples with the tip of my tongue, earning his sharp inhale.

"I know what you are trying to do," he murmurs.

"Is it working?"

"Keep going and I will let you know." His fingers toy with my mussed braids a moment before pushing my head down his body.

"Your Highness!" Abarrane hollers from outside the tent flap.

"Who is she talking to?" I whisper against his stomach.

"I do not know, but if neither of us answers, perhaps she will return later," Zander whispers back, earning my giggle.

"*She* is tired of waiting for you two to finish your *business*," comes Abarrane's stern voice as the flap flies open and she moves into the tent.

I scramble to pull the blanket up and give us a modicum of privacy.

"What earns such a rude invasion, Commander?" Zander drawls. "I do not hear any roaring beasts."

"The Shadow leader has sent word to meet with you. Dire news arrives from Mordain."

Zander rolls out from beneath me and sits up, reaching for his breeches. "About what?"

"Dire usually means one thing." Abarrane notices me glaring pointedly at her and averts her gaze as Zander stands to pull up his pants, though not without rolling her eyes first. "Someone has died or is about to."

Panic flares in me. Lives there were under threat to begin with. "I have to get those scribes out."

"*We* have to get those scribes out. You are not going to Nyos alone," Zander corrects, yanking his tunic over his head.

"But you can't get through the gates."

He freezes. "What *exactly* does that mean?"

"They've been warded against Islorian immortals ever since Rhionn took Farren."

He stares at me with incredulity. "Who told you this? When were you going to tell me?"

"Uh ... now?" I gave him only topline details yesterday and we haven't seen each other since.

"But that means Jarek and Abarrane can't either. So ... the dragons will protect you." He nods, as if satisfied with that solution.

I bite my bottom lip. "Actually, they can't fly there either."

Zander looks at me like I've gone mad. "You are not going into Nyos *alone*, Romeria. That is not an option. I forbid it."

"I'm sorry, you *forbid* it?"

A sliver of light flashes as Abarrane ducks out of the tent without a word. For once, she senses a fight brewing and wants no part of it.

I toss the blanket off and collect my clothes. "I won't be alone. Solange will be with me."

"Solange is a caster. And Mordain's second-in-command."

"Who has been nothing but helpful."

"Who could decide to trap you within a city I can't enter." He shakes his head fervently. "I do not trust her."

"You don't trust *anyone*." It's been the common theme since the night I met him.

"Fine, then let Solange and her Shadows free the scribes without you. There is no need for you to go there."

"But *I* can take them through the stone, directly to Ulysede."

"All hundred of them?"

"I've done it before." Except this time, I can't make multiple trips as I did from Cirilea. There's no in-and-out privilege.

He shakes his head. "We will figure out how to defeat Malachi with Agatha and Lucretia's help."

My mouth drops as I grasp what he means. "I am *not* leaving all those scribes there to die!" Many of them had no involvement in this prophecy scheme to begin with. They're as innocent as the priestesses Atticus slaughtered because of Wendeline.

"So that *you* can die? No, this is too risky." His voice rises. I'm sure anyone within a ten-foot radius of our tent is listening to this fight.

"You know what was also too risky? You going to Cirilea yesterday!" I throw back, yanking on my pant legs. "You, taunting Sofie! She nearly *killed* you."

"But she didn't."

"And they won't kill me either. Have some faith in me."

"It has nothing to do with faith in you." He pinches the bridge of his nose as if pained. "You don't even have a viable plan."

"I *might*." I rush to fasten all my buttons and ties and tug on my boots. It's a scrap of a plan, really. I spent the flight over considering it.

He pauses, watching me dress. "And? What is it?"

I pull my tunic over my head, not bothering to tuck it in. "I'm still working out a few details." Mainly, how not to get killed.

That earns me a flat look. "Am I going to like it?"

"Probably not. But it's a good thing I'm not asking for your permission." I fling the flap up and storm out of the tent, my fancy vest in my clenched fist.

Abarrane waits with Jarek and Elisaf next to a group of horses, their expressions revealing nothing.

"Which one's mine?" I snap.

OUR HORSES MAKE A STEADY, slow path across the bridge toward an approaching Solange and Kienen, a row of Shadows and Ybarisan soldiers behind them. The rift is a yawning canyon beneath us, promising an endless fall should one of our horses suddenly spook.

The only concern my gelding seems to have, though, is the tiny green bird that flutters by, stirring a twitch in its ear. "What kind of bird is that?" It's identical to the one that caught Caindra's attention outside the gates of Ulysede yesterday.

"We are crossing over the Valley of Bones where any manner of beast may emerge at any given moment, and her focus is on the tiny sparrow," Abarrane mocks.

"*That* is not a sparrow."

"I do not recognize its type," Zander says, ignoring Abarrane's acerbic gibe, his hard gaze ahead. It's the first words he's said to me since emerging from our tent.

Not that I've made an effort to speak to him either.

When we meet Solange and Kienen at the center of the bridge, I almost wish she were wearing her mask, so I wouldn't have to see the grim look on her face.

With a gesture, the Shadows form a solid, unmoving wall from end to end, those closest to the edge showing no hint of fear. Kienen and Solange guide their horses forward.

"Your Highness." Kienen bows. "I trust you have regained your strength."

I smile at my Ybarisan army commander. "I have."

"Good, you will need it." Solange holds up two folded letters. "From Nyos. The first is from the Prime. She is ordering the withdrawal of all casters and commanding them to return to Mordain's borders."

I steal a glance at Zander to see the muscle in his jaw tense. It's as Solange warned just yesterday. "Will they follow it?"

"Not until *I* order it, which I have no intention of doing. But once Lorel realizes I am acting against her, she will strip me of my rank and replace me with someone who will do her bidding." Everything is always very matter-of-fact with Solange.

"How long before that happens?"

"Before she learns of my treason? The Shadows will sequester the messengers for the short term and quell any official communication that isn't my own, but more than a day of silence will raise alarms with the guild masters, who receive regular updates from their factions. Regardless, when my Shadows do not arrive with Agatha tonight, she will grow suspicious. By tomorrow, she will assume much."

"So, basically, we have to get her to reverse her orders today."

Solange dips her head. "It is only a matter of time before messages make their way into camp and casters here begin to choose which side they are on."

"You're saying they'd *abandon* the rift?"

"I'm sure many would be happy for any excuse to return to their warm beds."

"Do they not teach loyalty in Nyos?" Jarek quips.

"They are not soldiers," Solange snaps.

"What's the second letter about?" Zander asks, his voice stony. He's remained quiet, listening, up until now.

She spares Jarek a glare. "It's from a trusted source within Nyos who says the Prime has started executing scribes. Four by pyre, in an attempt to force Zaleria to divulge all she knows."

I curse. "We need to go now. The dragons can get us there within hours."

"If we have any hope of minimizing the damage Lorel can cause, yes," Solange agrees. "But Lorel will bind your affinities the moment you touch shore—"

"She can't while I'm wearing these." I hold up my wrists, showing off the gold bands. "From the nymphs."

The Shadow's eyebrows arch. "Fine ...," she says, not pushing for more details. "So she cannot bind you, but she can launch an attack against us that even a key caster would not save us all from. There are at least a hundred casters aside from scribes and students within those walls, and they are all highly skilled."

"What if Romeria strikes first? With her full power, as she did in Cirilea?" Jarek asks.

I wince at the memory of the damage that caused. I don't know if I could even do that again. It was during a moment of raw agony, after watching Gesine die, my rage with Boaz blinding.

"I am sure Romeria could cause untold damage and kill many. Is it your intention to decimate Nyos, Your Highness?" Solange asks evenly. "There are children within those walls, and many innocent people. I doubt you will win the hearts of my people by doing this."

"No." I grimace. Forget the casters, I could never live with myself.

"What about moving in unseen?" Jarek tries again. "You could use your cloaking ability to—"

"It will not work," Solange interrupts, shaking her head. "There are wards against channeling affinities as you pass through the gate."

"These witches have thought of everything," Abarrane complains. "So, basically you are saying that if she sees us coming, it's over."

"It is not over, but it will end in war."

"We do not have time for these games," Zander speaks up. "We are fighting an endless battle against the Nulling beasts that will spill out over our lands, two fates now walk this plane in flesh, and one has claimed my throne."

At that, Solange and Kienen both gasp. I guess news hadn't reached the other side yet.

"And instead of uniting as one to face this great threat to all our people, there is a small group of casters sitting in a room on their warded little island, grasping for more power and wasting our precious time." Fury oozes from each word. "There is only one end to this. Kill the Prime and anyone who supports her."

I can't help my sharp inhale. This isn't the Zander I just spent an intimate morning with. This is a cold, calculating king who has lost too much.

Solange dips her head. "I agree, they must be stopped."

Zander's gaze narrows. He doesn't trust her, and he's looking for any hidden meaning within her words.

I study the line of quiet Shadows, hiding behind their menacing black veils, the black metal masks revealing nothing more than their eyes.

"I know that look." Jarek watches me. "What scheme are you hatching?"

I bite my bottom lip in thought. One that Romy Watts would be proud of.

19

ATTICUS

"Sleeping on your feet. That takes talent."

The heavily accented voice startles me awake. "I'm a talented individual," I drawl, digging deep for the strength to grin. In truth, I simply can't remain conscious anymore. I don't know how long I've been hanging, but my body has grown numb. I'll certainly collapse the moment I must rely on my legs.

A female in sweeping red robes stands before the cage, the likes of which I've never seen before, with golden skin and faded scripture written across her forehead—illegible to me. I can't guess her age—other than to say not young and not old, and yet in her black eyes is an eerie sense of wisdom.

She nods to the guards, and they open the door to my cage.

"I have never heard an accent such as yours," I say as she steps inside.

"Have you heard all the accents there are in the world?" Her hairless eyebrow arches.

"I'd like to think I've heard a lot of them."

The smile she returns is smug. "Tell me, usurper king—"

"Atticus," I correct her with a hint of annoyance in my voice. That title grows tiresome.

She nods once. "Atticus." My name sounds harsh on her tongue. "Have you ever been to Kier?"

"No," I admit. "I've never had the need."

"Then I imagine there are many things you have not heard yet." She rounds my dangling body until she's hovering at my back.

I tense. Why is she here? What does she want from me? "How's the gash from that fucking ingrate? I haven't had a chance to look at —" My words cut off with a yell as sharp pain splices through my shoulder. "What are you doing?" I growl between gritted teeth, struggling to twist out of her reach. Because she's definitely doing *something*.

"Stay still!" one of the guards barks.

"You heal well for someone who should be dead. And faster than I have ever seen anyone heal."

"Have you ever been to Islor?" I ask, throwing her question from only moments ago back at her.

"I have not."

"Then there are many things you haven't seen yet either."

She comes back around. A mysterious smile touches her shapely lips as her eyes crawl over my bare chest, studying me. "I have seen much of your realm and your people." She drags a lengthy golden claw that caps her fingernail across the silver scar left behind from the arrow. And inhales. "Who repaired you?"

"A caster." Technically two, but I don't think she's referring to Wendeline, who came in to finish whatever that silver-eyed one did to keep me alive. "Do you like my scar? A mercenary from Kier gave it to me."

Her eyes close as she presses her palm against the scar, her lips moving with soundless words.

A warmth blooms inside me, swelling from my chest, into my limbs, easing some of the aches I'm plagued with. Is that ... I watch with fascination as the script on her forehead glows ever so faintly.

She opens her eyes abruptly and pulls away, taking the pleasant feeling with her. "You must be thirsty." With a snap of her fingers, a guard brings a copper bowl forward and hands it to her. She holds the bowl up to my nose, and the metallic tang touches my nostrils.

I turn away. "I prefer my blood warm and my source identifiable." At least that's how I did before this last Hudem.

"Very well." She tosses the bowl aside, its contents splashing in the corner. "Thank you for seeing me, Atticus." She glides smoothly out of the cage.

"What is your name?" I dare ask.

She pauses, her back to me. "Tuella."

"Thank you for the visit, Tuella." For what reason she came, I can't figure out. Assessing me for the king, I'm sure.

She speaks to the guards in their language as they lock the door behind her.

The guard on the left pulls a lever and suddenly, the chains relax.

I fall to a heap on the ground.

WHISPERS WAKE me hours later as I lie sprawled on the cold stone floor. It's the most comfortable I've been in days.

I crack an eyelid to find the same servant who offered her vein before standing over me now. "I was having a lovely dream."

"Up your feet," the same guard who released my chain barks, his choice of words almost comical.

"Yeah, that'll be a minute." Or an hour.

He charges toward the lever, and I brace myself for the pain of having my arms ripped from their sockets. But the servant says something to him in their language and holds up a hand, as if asking for pause.

He falls back, dipping his head in a bow.

Interesting. I've yet to see a guard listen to a servant so. Aside from Gracen, when gossip spread about our relationship, that is.

She waits patiently as I struggle to pull myself to my feet, my legs wobbling as if made of that vile fruit-filled jelly my sister loves so much. The temporary relief Tuella granted my aches and pains didn't last long. "We must dress you for presentation to the king," she says, her words stilted as if she's searching for them.

"Already met him. Remember? You were there."

"But to stand before him within the palace, you must be acceptable." She nods to another guard, who hands her a tidy stack of white linens. "Remove his chains."

He responds in their language, and she rattles off a retort that sounds sharp.

"Do not try thing," the guard warns, glaring at me.

"He is still very weak, and he is not a fool. Right, Atticus?" She peers up at me, giving me a good look at her eyes. They're not just green, as I quickly dismissed before, but a kaleidoscope of emerald and jade and aqua, with flecks of gold sprinkled through. They are as beautiful as she is, her features feminine and delicate.

Not a hint of fear radiates from her.

"Many would disagree with you on that front." I smirk, but then add, "I know when I am beat." I also know how to bide my time for the right opportunity.

I sigh with relief as the biting metal cuffs slip off my wrists and fall to the ground.

"Leave us," she says to the guard.

He opens his mouth to argue, but with a single look from her, he spins on his heels and marches out, followed quickly by the other. They station themselves outside of the doorway, within earshot.

"What is in that metal?" I ask.

"Something strong." She drops to her knees, holding the linen pants in her hands.

"I can manage this."

"But I am already here." She tips her head back and, I swear, the grins she flashes me is laced with impure thoughts. It's a good thing I'm starved and in pain. Otherwise, this delicate mortal kneeling in front of me might stir baser needs.

"If you insist." I grab hold of the cage wall for balance as I lift first one foot, then the other. "A woman visited here earlier. Tuella, she said her name was."

"The conjurer from Udrel."

My eyebrows pop. "*Udrel*?"

"Yes. Have you not heard of it?"

"I have heard of it, but honestly I thought it was a fable created by the seers." Along with Espador. That would explain the accent, though, so different from anything I've ever heard.

"It is no fable, but it is very far away. His Highness's men traveled there on an expedition twenty years ago. They were away for more than twelve moon cycles—so long that everyone assumed them lost at sea. But they returned with the conjurer. Tuella has served as advisor to the king since."

"What can she do?"

"Interesting things." The servant climbs to her feet, drawing the linen pants up with her. "Some, I am sure you will see soon enough." Her fingers fumble with the ties on the loin cloth, loosening them until the material falls away. She takes a long, unabashed look at me before fastening the buttons.

I can't help but chuckle. It's been a while since I've faced a mortal so brazen. "What is your name?"

"Satoria." Her eyelashes flutter. She's flirting and making no effort to hide it. Collecting the tunic, she orders, "Bend forward."

I lean down toward her, inhaling that fragrant blend of jasmine and lemongrass again as she slips the gauzy shirt over my head.

"Will your people try to rescue you?" she asks.

"*My* people? I do not know who is left." Kazimir's was the last face I remember seeing as I fell.

Sparing a furtive glance toward the entrance, she steps in close and drops her voice to a whisper. "There are ways out of the palace."

"Is that so." Why is she telling me this?

"With the right guide, you could find your way out beyond the city wall." Her cool hands graze my flesh as she fumbles with the buttons at the collar, her eyes darting back and forth between her task and my face. She has freckles across the bridge of her nose that remind me of Gracen.

"And let me guess, you are the right guide?"

She doesn't answer, but the look on her face says as much. I imagine part of the bargain would be that I take her with me. This servant is not what I expected.

Movement in the doorway catches my attention. The guard, shifting position. Or trying to eavesdrop. "And what happens to you if you get caught helping me?" I whisper.

"It is worth the risk."

"Is it really that bad here?"

She bites her lip in thought. "I wish to see other lands. I could serve you."

Or she could run at the first chance. "I am not sure I would like your death on my conscience, if we got caught." She'd not likely end up in a cell. Disloyal servants aren't worth keeping alive.

A throat clears near the entrance.

"There." She smooths her hands over my tunic, over my chest, and then steps back. "You are now ready to see the king."

"Thank you for your help, Satoria." I offer her a heated smile, pushing aside my guilt for my shameless flirting. Finding allies here is critical and, even if I don't use her for an escape plan, she could prove a valuable source of information if I nurture this interest she clearly has in me.

Her cheeks flush as she rushes away and the guards return, spears out and ready.

"A TEN-GUARD ESCORT. My reputation precedes me," I drawl as King Cheral's soldiers lead me along palace corridors that are open to the outside. Where Cirilea has welcomed a seasonal chill, a pleasant, humid warmth clings to the brine-coated air in Ostros.

The blunt end of a sword against my wound buckles my knees, and they hit the ground with a jarring thud. My vision blurs as I breathe through the agony.

"Your reputation tells a different story than the disappointment we faced on that grassy knoll," the brute declares with a laugh.

That voice ... It is the same man from the ship. The one who defeated me with his ax.

I grit my teeth against the urge to groan as I stand. "I will have to remedy that." *Soon.*

But for now, I shut my mouth—because that fucking hurt—and learn what I can about my surroundings.

At one time, long ago, Islor and Kier were amicable, trade between Cirilea and Ostros flowing steadily. That was until my father made the mistake of visiting at the king's invitation. When the third wife of the king entered his chambers to present her vein and herself that night, he accepted. How was he to know she didn't have the king's blessing?

Islor has not concerned itself with Kier for centuries, which is the main reason I know little of it. It is a hostile mortal realm divided from us by mountains, the city of Ostros banked by staggering cliffs. The only viable way here is by sea, and they guard their waters with systems designed to burst ships who don't carry a trading invitation from King Cheral himself.

That weasel Adley garnered such an invitation for Kettling, while Islor's crown family remained enemies. My father permitted it. A tactical truce, he once called it. An olive branch that might root and grow to benefit all of us one day.

One of many mistakes he made that ended up costing him his life.

I see now that turning a blind eye to Kier might have been a mistake. The soldiers have proven themselves formidable, even as mortals. There is fortune to be had here, if the palace is any evidence of that. It is more splendid than Cirilea's castle, I hate to admit, the many spire-topped towers and buildings clustered together around pools of turquoise water and cascading fountains. And I presume they've built this without the aid of casters.

Giddy laughter echoes from behind grand doors, and when the guards open them, I'm overwhelmed by children. At least two dozen dressed in white run barefoot around the lengthy room.

The space is mostly empty of furniture, save for the center of the room, where a circle of oversized chairs are stationed. King Cheral occupies the largest as he watches me.

The doors slam behind us and the children freeze, a mix of wariness and interest in their eyes. They range in age—one still wobbly on his legs while the oldest girl is filling out with feminine curves. How often are prisoners paraded before them?

"You'll have to excuse their curiosity. All they know of Islorians, they have learned from bedtime tales." King Cheral says something in his language and the children dash toward a door on the far side, two little ones slowing long enough to place kisses on his cheek, which he accepts with a soft chuckle.

They must be *his* children. Little princes and princesses.

And the four women in white occupying the chairs around him must be his wives.

Tuella hovers in one corner, dressed in the same red garb as before, dissecting me with her black eyes.

"Come forward, usurper king of Islor." He waggles two fingers, gesturing to an open space in the horseshoe of chairs.

I have no time to react before the guard behind me jabs my back with his pommel.

I breathe through the pain as I stroll toward my assigned spot, unwilling to give them any satisfaction. "Inviting me to meet your whole family? I am honored."

"That? That was not all of them. I have thirty-two children and, what is it now? Sixteen grandchildren. One was just born last week. Obviously, they were not all here."

My eyebrows arch, earning his laugh.

"It must be so unusual to you, given your kind's struggles. This is one of their great weaknesses, you see," he says to his small audience, but loud enough for me to hear. "They take only one wife and then they must fuck on a stone under a special moon four times a year and hope the gods see it in their heart to gift them a child. Can you imagine?"

A chorus of titters carries.

"Actually, it does not surprise me in the least to see a mortal king with so many offspring. Mortals breed like hares and you've taken *four* wives. But I doubt you satisfy any"—I falter over my words as I meet gazes with Satoria, seated in one of the chairs, and wearing a white gown to match the others—"of them."

Clever king, sending one of his most trusted—a *wife*—to impersonate a slave and loosen my tongue. Risky, though. I had the opportunity to kill her several times over.

Satoria smirks—at my shock or at my slight, I cannot tell. She truly had me fooled.

King Cheral leans back, ignoring my insult. "Your reign in Islor, though short, has brought with it delightful tales. Is it true you chopped a lord's head off in your throne room, in front of everyone? And in the name of a mortal servant?"

The smile I wear is genuine, the satisfaction of that moment enduring. "He was a minor lord and, believe me, he had it coming." I have many regrets. That is not one of them.

"And then you tossed all of your eastern lords and ladies into prison cells."

"The tower. I see someone's been receiving messages." I locked the gates and stifled all communication earlier that same day, which means Cirilea's gates must be open again.

Zander must have reclaimed his throne. Or perhaps Annika has taken the crown for herself. Za'hala knows I deserve that level of betrayal from my twin sister.

King Cheral watches me mentally work my way through the possibilities. He's enjoying this. "Many. A few at first and now they are pouring in. Are you surprised to hear that Cirilea fell to rebellion only *hours* after you left for the east?"

His words are like a swift punch to my gut. I recall the tension brewing in the air the day we marched out, the deathly glowers from Cirilea's citizens. "No, that does not surprise me." But it pains me. If I had stayed, would it have made any difference?

"There was a concerted effort led by your people and aided by Ybarisan allies. Many mortals left by ship, the captains bribed with priceless jewels. Others stormed the castle gates, looking to find their stolen children and punish all those keeping them prisoner."

I can't help the sharp inhale. Gracen would have been in that ballroom with the children. Would they have painted her friend or foe? "And the result?"

"By all accounts, they did not find them. The children were gone. Disappeared."

I frown. "That is impossible." There were hundreds, far too many to simply "disappear."

"But perhaps the most surprising message I received is this one, though. It arrived this morning by a spirited messenger fowl." He slides a folded paper out from his vest and holds it up for me to see the wax seal and the flame stamped into it. Cirilea's royal seal, broken. "From the king of Islor."

The urge to dive for it—to learn what has happened to my city, my realm since I left—is overwhelming and yet I restrain myself. "I do not recall writing to you. Must have slipped my mind."

By King Cheral's amused expression, he knows his taunt is effective.

"What does my dear brother have to say for himself?"

"I have no idea. It is not your brother who tests the king's quill but another."

"What?" I don't bother hiding my shock. "Who would dare claim that title falsely?"

"Besides you? This one calls himself King Malachi."

I snort. "A usurper of a usurper and he presents himself as a fate." An act long since forbidden, even in the days before Islor's existence. To take a fate's name is to be condemned to Azo'dem.

"You do not know this new king?"

"This fool? No, I cannot say I have any inkling who would be so audacious."

King Cheral studies me a moment, as if searching for a lie in my words. "Audacious or not, he has released the eastern lords and ladies and claimed peace in Islor."

"*Peace*. With my brother free and commanding our army at the rift." For Zander surely has won the soldiers' hearts over with his idealism. "This is too far-fetched a tale for me to bite on. But I applaud your attempt." I clap my hands slowly.

"You do not believe me." He holds the letter out.

I move for it but then stop. Is this a tease? An excuse to approach him so his guards can beat me mercilessly in front of his wives? I note the overzealous one from the battleground hovering nearby.

"Go on … They will not harm you." He shakes his head curtly at them.

I step forward and collect the letter, my thumb skating over the flame imprint in the wax. As familiar as it is to me, the scrawl inside is foreign. King Cheral and his brides' gazes burn into me as I devour the single page's contents. "He claims *he* has rid us of the blood curse?" I read out loud. In her letter, Romeria painted herself the catalyst of this change. So, was she working with this King *Malachi* who has now stolen my throne? Have they done it together?

After all that, did she betray my brother?

"That is why you refused Satoria's blood, is it not? Because you no longer need it. That is quite the secret to keep."

At mention of her name, my eyes dart to the wife in question to find her watching me. "I would not have taken it, anyway. I do not feed off those forced to offer." Though something tells me she would gladly supply me. She's not nearly as diminutive as I once thought.

I return my attention to the letter, reading the last line out loud. "'All will bow before me.' Interesting letter for the king of another realm to receive."

"Clearly, he does not understand much of our borders and political systems." King Cheral holds out his hand, a wordless request for me to return the correspondence. But there's a flicker of something in his eye—is it worry?

With one last glance at the floral writing—it looks feminine—I comply.

"According to Tuella, you have been healed by the one power," he says, changing subjects.

"I have been healed many times."

"This was no ordinary wielder," Tuella edges forward from her corner. "This one is a creator of all four elements."

"You mean a *key caster*?"

"If that is what your people call them."

I shake my head. "We haven't had one in two thousand years. Mordain and Ybaris have made sure of it."

"And yet the wound in your chest was healed by one."

I falter. That caster with the silver eyes. I'd never seen her face before. Could she have been kept hidden from Ybaris? From Mordain?

"You really have no idea what is happening in your realm." I note a hint of sympathy in King Cheral's tone, even as he mocks me.

I could come up with a quippy answer, but for once I'd prefer the truth. "Care to enlighten me then, since you seem to be all knowing?"

He stands, smoothing a hand over the shoulder of the wife on his right—a stunning brunette and the oldest by appearance. His first wife, if I had to guess. "One of the problems I have with your kind is your arrogance." He rounds the cluster of chairs and moves across the room, toward a golden pedestal. "You believe yourselves above all, taking what you wish from anyone, be it a royal or a slave. Even as a king, you made no effort to educate yourself beyond your own borders. Tuella's homeland of Udrel is a … what did you call it? A *fairy tale*? No, it was a fable."

It's good to know our conversations are repeated, word for word. Did Satoria explain to her husband how long she stared at my cock?

"All must cower before the great and formidable Islorian ruling class." He embellishes his words with a theatrical bow, followed by a sneer. "You are but specks like the rest of us, bending and breaking to a higher power's will." He beckons me forward with a waggle of his fingers, as if I'm a slave.

My fists ball at my sides. Funny, one of the problems with this mortal king is also his arrogance—specifically, ignoring the reality that I could snap his neck long before his guards reach us. But saying that out loud will likely earn me a fight I don't know that I can win, injured as I am. Besides, I can sense the energy radiating from across the room. Whatever King Cheral wants to show me, it excites him.

I take my time joining him. "My mother had a birdbath much like this. She spent hours watching the warblers cool off in the hot summer months." This one has a pool of water, too, but it's twice the size and in its center sits an opaque white sphere.

"A gift from my temple." Tuella is suddenly beside me, startling me with her soundless approach.

"I have seen a similar stone before." It reminds me of the dull gem within the ring Zander gave to Romeria as a symbol of their betrothal, though much larger. I'll admit, my curiosity is piqued. "I assume it is more than decoration in this case. What is its purpose?"

She rests her palm against it. "We call this a seeing stone."

"Because you see things through it?"

Tuella smiles as if she was waiting for me to ask and then closes her eyes and mutters unintelligible words. When they reopen, her black irises and pupils have vanished, leaving an opaque white in their place. The tattooed script across her forehead glows.

"It is something, isn't it?" King Cheral whispers, drawing my attention from the conjurer's peculiar appearance to the pool of water that now reflects an image—of Islorian soldiers building bonfires and fixing tents. "This is Islor's rift army."

I gape at the view. "How is this possible?"

"Through the eyes of a kell. A tiny, unobtrusive bird that goes mostly unnoticed but sees all."

I'm glued to the image reflected in the water as the kell swoops in, speeding past a dead nethertaur, to a group on horseback. I know them all. Elisaf is there, along with several legionaries, and—

"Stop! Go back!"

But the bird is moving on.

"It will take her a moment. It is not so simple," King Cheral says, patting the air. "These kells can be wayward."

The image in the small pool wavers before expanding. The bird is climbing, giving us a panoramic view—of the thousands of soldiers and countless corpses, both beast and Islorian, and the odd golden-crested armor that I do not recognize as Islorian. Far in the distance, on the Ybarisan side, waits another army. Queen Neilina brought her armies to attack on Hudem, after all. Did they battle?

I gasp as three great beasts of scales and wings appear, perched atop the bridge's stone walls. "Fates, what are those?"

"Ancient creatures of another age, according to Tuella," King Cheral whispers, as if not wanting to disturb her concentration. "It seems they are allied with your realm. They've even been seen shuttling Islorians from one place to the next."

What else has Zander been hiding from me? From this vantage point, high up in the sky, I begin to grasp just how many Nulling creatures litter the ground. There were obviously far more hiding than we ever imagined. "What drew them out of Venhorn to attack?"

King Cheral peers up at me with a mixture of pity and amusement. "They did not come from the mountains. They came from that gaping crack in the ground."

"That is impossible. That would mean the Nulling has been opened, which would mean ..." My words drift. It would mean a key caster opened the nymphaeum door. Likely the same one who saved my life. "Have you seen this key caster? Do you know who she is?"

His smile is reserved. "We have. And we do."

The bird finally loops back around and dives toward the company as it moves past the stone gate, onto the bridge. "Where are they going?"

"To the Ybarisan side, I presume."

The kell follows, feigning interest in a horse while giving me a clear view of their faces—Zander and Romeria riding side by side. She is as beautiful as ever, dressed in the leathers of war, Jarek and Abarrane at their flank.

My chest tightens at the sight of my brother—and the many memories soured. "So they've allied with Queen Neilina. Zander has betrayed his realm and his people and—"

"Queen Neilina is dead."

My eyes widen with shock. That news, I was not expecting. The Ybarisan ruler has been a bane to Islor for nearly five hundred years and believed impossible to kill, thanks to her wall of Shadows and elementals, and her ability to choke the air out of one's lungs before they ever got too close. "How?"

"According to our sources, by her daughter's own hand. Queen Romeria now rules Ybaris, and it would seem she and the exiled king work together." His pause is lengthy. "She is your key caster."

"What? No, that is impossible! She is Ybarisan, elven born." I lean on the pedestal for support as I absorb his claim. Even as I deny it out loud, in the back of my mind, I think I'd already put together the pieces. Romeria herself had told me as much, hovering over my bleeding chest outside the Goat's Knoll.

I don't even know how to play draughts.

Ever since the night she was brought back to life by the High Priestess, there has been something inexplicable about her. Wendeline warned me that she was not the same Romeria who arrived here from Ybaris. That blasted, conniving priestess. How long did she know?

"Impossible, and yet it is true. Tuella watched the battle on the night of your blood moon and there was no mistaking her silver eyes or the way she fought alongside your people with the elements. All four of them."

I have no response.

Has Zander known what she was all this time? Is this why he protected her? Is this why he was willing to lose *everything*? Because she could bring an end to our blood curse, a dream he'd carried for too long. And look at that, he succeeded. But what will be the cost, now that the Nulling is open? Our people and our lands will be plagued by monsters for the next fifty years? A hundred? Who knows how long.

Was it worth it?

"Show me Cirilea," I demand, adding a soft, "if you wouldn't mind."

The image in the pool of water goes dark as Tuella shuts her eyes.

"She is searching for another kell. We have many in your lands," King Cheral says softly.

"What else can she connect with?"

"Wouldn't you like to know." He watches his conjurer with admiring eyes. "Isn't she a marvel? I was skeptical at first, when my men returned from Udrel with her. But she has proven herself beyond value many times over."

"You knew of Cirilea's plight, even while the gates were closed and messages halted, didn't you?" Because he has Tuella and these birds at his disposal.

He hums his answer. "Of Cirilea, and of the hidden golden city in the mountains."

"Ulysede?"

"If that is what it is called. Unfortunately, since your blood moon, our kells can no longer get too close. The creatures who live within do not allow it."

Tuella's eyes open again and a new vision appears in the pool, of Fortune's Channel and the great stone wall of Cirilea ahead.

The bird sails past the docks, showing empty ports. There isn't so much as a skiff to sail. The quiet streets beyond wear scars of a recent clash—char marks where fires erupted, peasants tossing buckets of water over the cobblestones to wash away blood, debris uncollected. Wagons brim with bodies, but I can't be sure if those are from battle or the mortals I had executed. The odd body still dangles from a light post, here and there.

The devastation grows worse the closer we get to the castle grounds—the obvious target of this rebellion.

"What did *that*?" A path of destruction mutilates the royal garden, splintering trees and shattering stone fountains. A large swath of it has turned to ash. Workers attempt to clean, but it is far beyond repair.

"This happened before your blood moon, when our eyes were on the eastern lands," King Cheral admits.

I'm unable to help myself. "You mean when your army of cowards massacred soldiers sleeping in their tents rather than meet them on the field."

The guards behind me shift. Surely, I'll pay for that gibe when they escort me back to my cell.

"*That* was the price of war, when every advantage is necessary. Whatever or whoever did *this*, I would not want to make them my enemy."

The kell swerves toward the quiet castle. A figure stands on the terrace of the king's chamber, overlooking the devastation, the sun's rays gleaming off the crown atop his head.

My body tenses. "May we get a look at this new impostor king? Perhaps I might recognize him."

Tuella—and the kell—obliges, soaring closer, until it settles on the terrace wall, mere feet from the male, allowing me a good view of his dark hair and hard features. He stands regal—in *my* clothes, nonetheless—as he overlooks the grounds.

As if he is meant to be there.

My fists clench as my chest burns with fury at this pretender who has stolen from my family, who has claimed what does not belong to him by any stretch. "I've never seen this male before in my life."

Cold, brown eyes reflect in the water as the male notices the bird. He crooks his head as if studying it and then holds out his hand and makes a clucking sound. The kell hops over, accepting the upturned palm.

A slow smile stretches across this King Malachi's lips as he lifts the bird to eye level. "A favorite of the Udrelians, I believe." His voice is deep and smooth. "Who has come to spy on me, little bird? A king from Kier, perhaps?"

"How does he know?" King Cheral whispers. "How can he tell—"

Suddenly, the image in the pool erupts in flames before vanishing altogether.

Tuella gasps as if coming up for air after being underwater for too long. Her black eyes have returned and in them, I see a mixture of relief and fear.

"What happened?" I wait impatiently for her to catch her breath.

"How did he know we were watching?" King Cheral pushes.

A bead of sweat trickles down her forehead. "There is great power in him."

"Elven?"

She shakes her head. "He is a creator of the flame."

"You mean a caster." Islor has been seized by a powerful male caster who calls himself King Malachi. My brother is also powerful in wielding the flame—but not creating it.

Tuella meets King Cheral's gaze but doesn't respond. I suspect there is more to it than that, but she won't share while I'm here.

His steps are slow and methodical as he strolls around the bird-bath. "It seems your realm has quite the obstacle to overcome."

I chuckle, though nothing I've learned warrants humor. "Please tell me you are not foolish enough to believe this problem ends at a border. If the rift is truly open, no one is safe."

"Plenty for them to occupy themselves with in your realm." But he frowns as if he doesn't buy his own words.

"And that?" I point to his pocket where he slid the letter. "That alone should be a warning of this king's intentions."

"With the rift open, this King Malachi does not have time to *attempt* to conquer Kier."

"Maybe you're right. Tell me, how many of your soldiers remain in Islor, waiting for instruction on how to proceed?" Bexley warned of a vast Kier army. There is no way they've abandoned their cause, especially not with a realm in turmoil.

Cheral's lips purse, answering my question whether he means to or not.

I hum. "Sounds like your men will be occupied too. Wait until they meet a hag."

"I had hoped your brother would reclaim the throne. There could have been a negotiation for your release. Now, I do not see the value in keeping you alive." He says this, but he watches me closely, and I sense a challenge behind his words. *Give me a reason to keep you alive.*

"This impostor may wear the crown today, but I can assure you, it won't be long before my brother comes to reclaim it."

"Tuella just confirmed, King Malachi is powerful."

"My brother is powerful." Far more than even I realized. "And he has a key caster by his side, by your own admission, one who now wields the power of Ybaris and Mordain and this secret Ulysede and those scaly winged beasts. And frankly, fates know who or what else." Who has Romeria won over with her charm? The clearer the picture I paint, the more I begin to believe it.

Zander and Romeria will take back Islor.

And the realm will be the better for it.

"You stole his crown from him. I can't imagine he wants anything from you but your death."

And I will deserve it. "You're right, he most likely wants me dead. But Romeria saved my life only days ago, despite that betrayal. The only reason I can think of is that my brother insists on delivering my punishment himself. If that is the case, he will come looking for me. If he discovers you stole his opportunity for vengeance ..." I let the words hang for a few beats. "Imagine what those winged beasts could do to this beautiful palace and your lovely family."

My attention drifts over the pillars and painted ceiling. "On second thought, with your vast army in Islor and his ability to fly here, he could claim Ostros as his own. There wouldn't be much of a defense." I meet King Cheral's gaze in challenge.

He studies me through shrewd eyes. "Surely, something to ponder," he says, waving his guards over. "Return the prisoner to his cell."

I can't help my smile as I'm escorted back to my cage, though it's empty. The realm is in shambles and, if there is anything King Cheral just taught me, it's that I know nothing at all.

20

SOFIE

"Your Highness." The greeting is a constant chorus as I stroll along the corridor of gilded pillars and candelabras, the lords and ladies bobbing and bowing like bleating imbeciles while the mortals scurry out of my path.

But it's the whispers trailing that charge my spirits.

"She's a key caster."

"The first we've had in two thousand years."

"She must have ended the blood curse."

How thrilling it is to be in a world where my power is revered, not hidden from weak mortals who cannot wrap their tiny brains around its existence. I will gladly accept at least some credit for their recent fortunes. It was *me*, after all, who sent Romeria to this realm. It was *me* who suffered for three centuries in the dark as part of Malachi's game.

It is I who suffers still, sitting idly by while my beloved husband is trapped in yet another hell.

But these fools had a key caster in their midst for months and hadn't the first clue. Then again, that silly girl lived twenty-one years with no clue what great power waited inside her either.

I march through the grand entrance doors of the castle. The dress I've chosen today—a wine-colored silk gown with ebony boning—squeezes my rib cage. This will take time to adjust to. I've grown too accustomed to modern fashion.

"Your Highness." Two guards slap their heels together in a stiff stance and bow.

"Which way to the sanctum?" I ask without preamble.

"Through those gates." The one on the left nods toward the twisted metal. A team of blacksmiths have been working to repair them since the morning. It will likely take them weeks. "We will escort you for your safety."

"My safety?" I snort. "I could kill you both with nary a thought." And no one would dare say a word to me about it.

Fear pumps through his lanky frame while the other guard pales. "But His Highness insisted."

My hands clench. "Very well. I would not wish you to be punished for not following his orders. But you will remain outside the doors." I will not tolerate spies and tattletales.

They bow again, and spinning on their heels lead me down a path.

Fools.

All of them.

WHAT I WOULD HAVE DONE to have such a place to worship in.

I pause to admire the splendor of Cirilea's sanctum. The exterior is a sight to behold—a Gothic vestige built to honor the Fate of Fire, its obsidian walls dominating the gleaming gold, silver, and bronze trim —nods to the other fates but, in their eyes, likely a dismissal. Bold on the part of these Islorians. It isn't a wonder Malachi pined for this throne. These people have already deigned to grovel at his feet.

But inside is equally splendid, the gold mosaic ceiling glittering in the sunlight that peeks through the many small windows, highlighting how much dust has collected over the mahogany pews. From what information I have gleaned so far, I imagine the sanctum was pristinely kept before the last ruler slaughtered the priestesses.

Save for one.

Bowed heads line the first six rows of pews. I'm sure if I closed the distance, the stench of unwashed bodies would assault my senses. It's difficult to decipher the common mortals from the exceptionally destitute in this world—the luxury of running water and soap seemingly nonexistent. Thankfully, the ones living in the castle have better grooming habits.

The person I am looking for—the reason I am here—sits in a chair within the sanctum's circle, the grand sculptures of the fates towering over her. Gone is her tattered dress, replaced with a white robe trimmed in gold. I suppose she has an abundant supply hanging in closets of empty rooms now, her sisters all gone. Her neck is bent forward in prayer, her injured hand cradled within her lap.

She must feel my eyes upon her because suddenly, her head snaps up and our eyes meet. With a faint nod, she rises from her seat and makes her way down the steps toward me.

I momentarily consider shielding myself. What if this feeble priestess is waiting for an opportunity to exact revenge for her suffering? But the closer she gets, the more I see the husk left behind after her ordeal. Perhaps once she could have been a formidable threat to the unsuspecting.

More than one head turns in the pews, and the glares aimed at the caster ooze with venom. Do they blame her guild for what has befallen them, or her in particular? She has certainly earned their hatred.

"Your Highness." She bows, her shoulders hunched—from trepidation or the weight of all she carries, I can only guess.

"Walk with me, Priestess." I lead her down the aisle, away from prying ears. "Is the sanctum normally filled with so many mortals?"

"It has been some time since we've seen so many patrons of their kind." She follows my gaze.

"And what has inspired this sudden influx?"

"Some are here to praise Malachi for ending the blood curse."

"But not all?"

"Not all. Many lost loved ones in the rebellion. Others have not seen their children since they were rounded up by King Atticus and pray to be reunited."

"They have little love for you, it seems."

"They blame me for doing the king's bidding when I helped root out those with tainted blood." She says more quietly, "I cannot fault them for that."

I jut my chin toward her bandaged hand. "Something tells me you were not given much choice in the matter."

"There is always a choice, Your Highness."

"Comply or die?"

"Still, it is a choice." In her eyes is a forlorn sadness that I have seen from time to time when I look in the mirror.

I gesture to the last pew. "Please, after you, *Wendeline*." It took no effort to gather information on the only caster left in Cirilea, at one point a trusted advisor to the royal family. From there the stories fray in different directions, but all end in the same conclusion: she betrayed many.

Wendeline slides in. "I wondered when you would come."

"And why is that?"

"You are the key caster who sent Romeria to us, are you not?"

"I am." This one is intelligent, though I'm not surprised. "What did Romeria tell you about me?"

"Nothing for a long time." A tiny smile tempts her lips. "She held her secrets close."

"She's a smart and deceptive little thief." As I knew she would be. "Where is she now?"

"Now? I have no idea."

"But she was here, only days ago, was she not?" The tales of the attack in the royal garden—of a powerful caster with glowing silver eyes and a flying beast much like the one the exiled king arrived with yesterday—point to Romeria, though witnesses swear it was not her face they saw.

There are also rumors floating that it was me. I haven't dissuaded them.

"If she was, she did not cross my path." Wendeline's throat bobs with her hard swallow. At one time, I am sure she was adept at lying. How else did she deceive so many?

"You tell the truth, and yet you hide what you know. Given your current situation, I would think you wise enough to appease a powerful ally. As difficult as your time has been, I assure you, it can be much worse."

She lifts her chin. "I have served my purpose, and I am prepared to die. But I will not be a part of any scheme meant to lure or betray Romeria or His Highness, the true king of Islor." There is no waver in her voice, no falter in her heartbeat. She speaks the truth now.

"You are prepared and yet you are still here. Honestly, I am stunned you haven't plunged a dagger into your own heart."

Mild amusement skims her expression. "Who says I won't?"

"Because you believe you could still be of use to your beloved king." When Malachi ordered the guards to release her, I expected her to run from these city walls before the sun set. But she skulked to the sanctum and here she has remained. It's the only answer that makes sense.

I *could* have the guards imprison her to avoid an unseemly end at her own hands, but I imagine she'll be of little use to me then. She is a valuable source of information and a connection to Romeria, even if I can't trust her.

I ease back into the pew. "I've always thought it silly that we have all this power to heal others and yet cannot help ourselves. Give me your hand."

She hesitates but finally relents.

I unwind the gauze, revealing the angry red stump where her smallest finger used to be. "I imagine you weren't privy to much in the way of poultices and clean water during your time in the dungeon."

"I made do."

"Still, it is difficult to reverse the damage done." The hint of rot lingers. "Your guild is a great distance from here, is it not?"

"I would not call them 'my guild.' They have long since labeled me foe. But yes, Mordain is leagues away, across another realm and a channel."

"You work against them, and yet you could not have master-minded this grand plan on your own. I have only just arrived and already I have heard the stories of murderous complicit casters and a tainted princess created by Aoife herself who won the heart of a king, only to betray a realm."

It's a moment before she relents. "Yes, I had much help, from those who value prophecy and a higher purpose than power and wealth."

"I did not know such beings existed." I draw forth a weave of healing, directing it into Wendeline's injury. It's mere moments before she sinks against the pew, some of the tension dissipating from her limbs as the flesh knits together smoothly, the redness fading to a faint silver. I release her hand. "There, you could have earned that injury years ago by the looks of it."

"That would have taken me an hour to mend on someone else," she admits, smoothing the pad of her thumb over the stump. "Thank you for the kindness," she offers after a delay. "You do not have marks."

"Hmm?" Her question catches me off guard.

She slides her sleeve up to reveal a small glowing emblem of gilded horns. "To indicate your affinities. You do not wear any from what I can see."

I turn my wrist to confirm my bare forearm. "No. In my old world, casters hide who they are. It is safer for them that way."

"You must greatly prefer this new one. Not only a key caster revered but also a queen."

"It has its benefits." And I have little time to waste. "What do you know of *my* purpose here?"

"Besides aiding the Fate of Fire in raining havoc?"

"Do not accuse me of things you are equally culpable in." My voice turns sharp and carries too far, earning looks from several sanctum patrons. A swift glare from me has them ducking their heads.

With one last glance at her deformed hand, Wendeline gathers the used bandaging as she collects her thoughts. "I know that Malachi sent your husband to the Nulling. I can speculate that it is because you summoned him to preserve your fleeting life in hopes of matching your husband's lengthy one. It seems he granted your request, but at a very steep cost."

"I suppose that wouldn't be too hard to piece together." Still, some praise should be granted to Wendeline—and perhaps Romeria, for managing it. "What else?"

"You waited a long time to reconnect with your husband. I am not sure you expected this result."

"That my beloved Elijah would be trapped, sharing a body with Malachi himself, you mean?" A hint of bitterness laces my tone.

Wendeline's gaze travels upward tentatively, as if afraid I might turn her to stone with a single glance. "This must be difficult for you."

My responding laugh is mirthless. "Do not play sympathetic to me. I know where your allegiances lie." With a heavy sigh, I ask, "What does your guild know of fates who walk this plane in flesh and blood?"

"I am not the right person to ask, truly. I never spent much time with the scribes and had little familiarity with prophecy before I was contacted by someone far more skilled and knowledgeable of it. If there is any insight, she will be the one who can provide it."

"Her name?"

"Gesine. She was with Romeria, the last I heard."

"Do you have any way to reach her?"

She shakes her head. "Not anymore, I'm afraid. Those who helped me carry messages have all abandoned Cirilea with the outgoing ships."

The sanctum's doors swing open.

My body stiffens as Malachi strolls in, pausing a moment to admire the statue of himself on the dais.

"Proper devotion. That is what I like to see." He closes the distance to me with quick strides. "There you are. I left you with a quill and paper for a moment and when I returned, you were gone."

I smile while my rage simmers. For a moment, my ass. After

releasing Elijah briefly last night—just long enough to prove he was still in there—Malachi had me record his words in a letter and then left me with orders to pen duplicates and spirit them to kings and queens and lords and ladies of Islor and nearby realms with the help of the castle fancier and my affinities.

I haven't seen him since.

"The letters went out at first light."

"You must have given those messenger birds' wings something extra. I've been visited by a nosy kell for a neighboring realm."

"You wished for a swift delivery."

"And what might my love be doing here?"

He plays at easygoing, but I have spent enough time with him to know it is all a ruse. He may turn as quickly and fiercely as a storm at sea. "I thought I would heal my fellow caster."

He hums, sizing up Wendeline, who bows deeply and murmurs, "Your Highness." But I sense her body turning rigid with fear.

"Come. I have need of you now." The demand is soft, but it is a demand, nonetheless.

And while he calls me his queen, I am not foolish enough to believe I am anything more than his servant.

"Thank you for the kind gift of healing, Your Highness." Wendeline dips her head. "If only I should be able to return the favor one day, though I fear I will be of little use to you."

"If ever a need, I know where to come." It's as much a threat as a promise.

Malachi snaps his fingers and barks, "Now, Sofie."

"Do you remember the wisteria that climbed the stone walls in our place in Belgium?" I ask as we walk the crumbled path in the garden. "It lives still, even after all these years."

"Hmm?" Malachi frowns, then dismisses my wistfulness, his focus ahead.

I expected as much. I'm not reminiscing for his benefit. Elijah would tend to it daily in the warmer months, pruning and training the clambering vines.

If Elijah must be held hostage in his own body, the least I can do is remind him that I know he is still in there.

The nymphaeum comes into view, a solemn rectangular stone surrounded by pillars and trees, skirted by an altar.

"Send us through again," Malachi commands, sliding his hand into mine.

"Back to the Nulling's entrance? Why?"

"You question me, loyal servant?" The edge in his tone is unmistakable, and when his fingers clamp over mine and squeeze, I know I walk a precarious line.

"Of course not, my love." Pushing aside my trepidation, I channel into the stone and take us through.

And gasp.

Once a vacant cave that we passed through on our journey to Cirilea, the space is now crammed with a horde of beasts.

Malachi grins with satisfaction. "Behold my army."

"You have brought demons to this world."

"No, I have brought Saur'goth soldiers. My own creation and utterly devoted to me. Marvelous warriors. They do not tire, they do not stop. They are beautiful creatures. I have been gathering them for centuries."

I fight the urge to cringe as I peer up at their bloodred irises and barbed horns. In no eyes could these things be admired for their beauty. They remind me of the demon Malachi unleashed on Romeria's father all those years ago, in a dark parking lot one cold winter's night. The male elemental caster tipped over the brink of madness after that, succumbing to the change. All a part of Malachi's calculated plan, I realized later.

As is *everything* he does.

Saur'goth soldiers part, making a path for him as he strolls into the flock, undaunted. "I learned much from my last experience here. Namely, that one cannot rely solely on those who kneel before them, for it is not me they bend a knee but for themselves. No ... I need an army that is devoted to me and me alone."

I trail behind him. "How many are there?" A sea of helmets reaches deep into the cavern, as far as my vision stretches. Far beyond, surely. I have never seen so many beasts.

"Enough to overwhelm this mountain range and crush any army that challenges me. No enemy will have the strength to defeat me." He stops before a soldier larger than all others, with streaks of black and red paint across his chest and a necklace of fangs dangling from his neck. Clearly, a leader of sorts. "Mal'Gar, my loyal servant. It is time."

I shudder at Malachi's words. He said something similar to me once.

"Sire." The Saur'goth leader's voice is sinister and deep, the two-syllable word delivered in layers that vibrate within my chest.

"Send the first wave now. It will take them time to get into position."

"As you wish, Sire." He shouts, drawing the attention of two other warrior-beasts wearing necklaces of fangs. His officers, I presume. They share a series of grunts and snarls in their language as he gives them their orders.

"What is the aim of this army?" I ask Malachi.

"What is the aim of *any* army?" he answers vaguely as Mal'Gar returns. "Have you brought what I requested?"

Mal'Gar waves a gauntlet and the horde parts.

Malachi smiles. "You have done well."

My stomach twists with disdain as the warriors present him with his prize, and the pathetic, terrorized souls drop to their knees, begging for mercy.

I helped with this.

I didn't even ask questions.

Will Elijah ever forgive me for the depths I've sunk in his name?

Malachi watches me closely.

"A truly formidable army against your enemies, my love." I force a guise of adoration in my features.

"And now let us bring it home." He gestures toward the stone.

2 1

ROMERIA

"What are the odds of this working?" Zander asks as our ship cuts through the water, Mordain's port growing in our line of sight.

"Better than the odds of anything *else* working?" It sounds like a question rather than a statement. "If the Prime has no reason to see us as a threat, then she won't be ready with an attack."

He searches my wrinkled face—Agatha's face, thanks to my silver mask. His eyes are the only part of him I can identify behind the daunting Shadow disguise. "You are right. This is a good plan. I'm sorry I doubted you."

When I first suggested this scheme, Zander couldn't imagine me fooling anyone into believing I was an elderly scribe, but as soon as I transformed, he demanded Solange secure Shadow armor for himself, Jarek, and Abarrane.

"It's only half a plan." We've figured out how to get into Mordain. The getting a hundred scribes out part is still a little murky.

"Lucretia said the door would work, did she not?"

"She said, 'The Queen of All may always return to her realm,'" I admit reluctantly, because I don't want to give Zander any more reason to worry.

"There is always room for deception in the serpent's words," Jarek says from behind his matching costume.

"Our immediate problem is not getting the scribes out but dealing with the Prime," Solange says. "She believes me still at the rift, preparing to march home with the casters. This plan only works until she discovers I am here."

We were careful not to reveal our scheme to anyone in Ybaris, ordering the Shadows who sacrificed their armor to remain in Islor. All messenger casters have been sequestered. Her second-in-command, a Shadow named Mannix, is the only other who knows of what is happening in Mordain, and Solange assured us he would fall on a spike before he betrayed her.

We traveled by dragon and landed well outside Argon to avoid raising alarms that could reach Mordain. After procuring horses, we rode the rest of the way, sending Caindra, Valk, and Xiaric back to patrol the rift—far from us.

"Then we must not let her find out until it is too late," Jarek says matter-of-factly.

"*You* cannot do anything. If you three try to pass through the gates, you will find yourself striking an invisible wall, and I doubt it will be painless. Romeria and I will be on our own against them."

Zander's jaw must be clenching beneath that mask. He hasn't dared "forbid" me again, but the anxiety swirling around him is potent enough to choke a corpse.

"What does this Ring of Minerva look like?" I ask, steering the conversation away from any chance he has of letting Solange know exactly how much he doesn't trust her.

"Nothing you might expect. A simple band made of gold and engraved with the old language that few can decipher, save for a handful of scribes."

"From the age of the mystics?" The elemental wielders here before the casters, according to Gesine's time in the library.

She shrugs. "I do not know who inspired it, but it is underwhelming to say the least. Regardless, it gives the Prime all the strength she needs and never leaves her finger."

"Then it is simple. Cut off her finger first." Abarrane has been quiet since the flight over. The moment her feet touched the ground, she declared she would ride a horse back before ever flying again. I imagine her complexion has returned to its healthier, less green shade by now.

"Spoken like a true Islorian fool." Solange scoffs. "*If* we manage to get close enough to cut off the Prime's finger before she discovers the ruse, it will not stop all the faction masters and remaining casters from pouncing in an instant to defend against an attack, and we will have yet another battle on our hands. We must do this quickly, but also wisely. The best way is to meet alone with the Prime."

My stomach roils. She's talking about killing people as if it's a checkmark on a list of to-dos for the day. Will it come to that? Or will I be able to reason with these casters for the greater good?

"Abarrane has a bad habit of hastily removing body parts," Jarek says wryly. "Ask Lord Isembert of Norcaster."

"He was not going to give us anything," Abarrane snaps, shooting daggers from the narrow slit in her mask.

"Now, now, *children.*" Zander grips the rail as our boat rocks against the waves.

The channel between Ybaris and Mordain is narrower than I expected, given the grim story Wendeline once shared. "Did Neilina actually ship three skiffs of dead babies across this stretch as a message?"

"They were alive when they left port. She used her wind casters to steer the boats, leaving them out there for days," Solange confirms. "We'd already been cut off from our kind for decades. It took nearly seventy years to fill Nyos's walls with grown casters again once we relented."

I grimace. "What a monster."

Solange's gaze sears into my profile. "And what lengths would you go to as queen if Mordain refused the aid of elementals to your cause? Say, for a battle at the rift that you could not win without them?"

It's a fair question, given our current predicament and the reality that we're sailing across the channel with plans to kill the Prime. "I would start with honor and diplomacy. I sure as hell wouldn't murder babies."

"Do not forget that we had two honorable kings from two realms, and look how well diplomacy worked for us," Zander says grimly.

"That was all Neilina, which is why she had to go." I have yet to be hit by the guilt of killing her.

"And why this Prime must as well," he counters. "She has denied truths in Neilina's name for her own benefit. She is not a good fit for a leader. I know your head and your heart, Romeria. You are looking for ways around what must be done. But do not make the same mistakes I did as king. Remove all threats as soon as they make themselves known. Kill her the first moment you safely can."

Even hours after he first declared this, I can't digest it. "Doesn't that make me a tyrant? Running around, killing people?"

"No, it makes you a queen who knows what is truly at stake. With Malachi here and Aoife who knows where, the realms need Mordain's aid. If this Prime won't grant it, make room for someone who will. Name someone you can trust."

"The only person from Mordain I've ever trusted is dead."

"Elementals cannot be made Prime," Solange cuts in. "It is too dangerous to bind Mordain's power to a mind that will fracture."

That leaves Agatha, but I need her in Ulysede. "Why not let Mordain choose their own Prime?" Wouldn't that be the way to step forward?

"Now is not the time for breeding diplomacy. There are beasts spilling into our lands and a fate sitting on a throne. Every day we waste is a day our people suffer and another day Malachi is given to grasp for more power." Zander's tone brokers no argument.

"He is not wrong," Solange says, giving me pause.

I turn to the Second. "What would *you* do if you were named Prime?"

"Do you wish honesty or vague promises?"

"I don't have time for anything but honesty." The shore is approaching fast.

"I would tell you that Mordain is willing to work with Ybaris as allies, but we serve it no longer. I would insist on keeping our elementals here, rather than collared and locked up in a tower to be used as the queen's playthings." She pauses. "But if you are asking me if I want the role, my answer must be no."

That, I didn't expect. "Why not?"

"My Shadows are my focus, not the politics of this place."

"Some would say that is precisely why you should be named leader," Zander counters.

"I hold a place as Second so I may press the Prime for her decisions. That is my purpose on the council. I am not adept at kissing anyone's arse, not even a queen's."

"In case you haven't noticed, I don't surround myself with anyone who kisses my *arse*."

"You could claim it." Zander's words cut into all other thought.

"Me? No—"

"Why not? You are the most powerful caster they have, and you will not suffer the same fate as a mortal one. And you know what is at stake better than anyone."

"*No.*" The single word is delivered with as much force as I can manage without yelling. "I'm not running around killing people and collecting crowns. That does make me a tyrant. I am not Genghis fucking Khan."

Zander's chest rises and I brace myself for an argument.

"As much as it pains me to say this, Allegra would be an effective Prime," Solange cuts in, much to my relief.

"The other Second?"

"Yes. The one who aided the scribes in their mission. She walks a fine line between what is right and what is beneficial to her, but her heart is with Mordain, and she values prophecy and the scribes' purpose." She adds quietly, "I think the last few days have proven how wrong our people have been to dismiss their value."

"And you like her?" I ask cautiously, recalling Agatha's words.

"*Like* Allegra?" Solange chuckles. "I cannot stand the caster. She is far too conniving. Still, I pray she is well within those walls. You need a suitable replacement for Lorel. Unless she has betrayed the scribes, she is your best hope."

"And if she has betrayed them?" Zander asks.

"Then you will need to replace not just a Prime but also a Second." Her tone leaves little to wonder. Solange will slaughter the Second herself if she must.

I peer back at the jeweled castle now in the distance. The turrets could easily be spotted sparkling in the late afternoon sun, long before Caindra landed. Now I've witnessed firsthand why Argon is talked about often and by many.

Unfortunately, there was no excuse for four Shadows and a Master Scribe to stop there on our way to Mordain. I'm curious to see what secrets it holds, of Neilina and her plans. "When the Prime is dealt with, Argon is our next stop," Zander says, as if reading my mind.

My nerves form a hard ball in the pit of my stomach as I consider the mammoth stone wall ahead. It reminds me of a great dam, except smooth—surely built by stone casters. Beyond it, spires reach into the evening sky like jagged fingernails. They're dark and Gothic and unwelcoming, nothing like the splendor of Cirilea or Argon. Maybe that's intentional, though. A deterrent.

"This is *all* Nyos?" I ask, regarding the sloping hill before the wall, peppered with colorful houses and thatched roofs and gardens.

"Yes. Beyond the wall is the guild and school, but most have homes outside of it."

"And everyone who lives here is a caster?"

"That is correct. The children sent from Ybaris are placed with new families here. When they are old enough, they attend schooling, but we've always felt it important that they feel at home in Mordain. Many of them are swiftly cast out by their mortal Ybarisan families, who want nothing to do with a child touched by the fates."

"Wendeline told me about that."

"This is the place most long to return to while they spend their lives serving Ybaris." There's bitterness in Solange's tone.

Three lethal figures dressed in black emerge from a stone hut.

My affinities hum inside, begging to be unleashed. Something inside me has changed since the night of Hudem's moon, as wave after wave of seemingly endless power unfurls. This thrumming energy is intoxicating.

Solange warns, "Do not forget, you are an old scribe with no power. The moment you reveal your silver eyes, this charade is over."

I resist the tendrils reaching for me like a small child's fingers, begging to be clasped.

"The Shadows are mine to lead, and they will listen to my command above all others. But one can never know who or what is listening, and word travels fast, so I will do the talking. Remain quiet, all of you," she hisses as the front of the boat slides into its slip.

Several young boys of maybe twelve scramble to grab the ropes.

A Shadow meets us at the end of the dock, dipping their head in a curt bow. "As one we stand," she recites, her voice feminine and youthful.

"As one we fall," Solange responds. Clearly a code of sorts.

"Master Shadow!" Her body stiffens. "We were not aware that you would be home today."

Solange leaps out of the boat in a smooth step. "Plans changed, and I had urgent need to return on the Prime's directive." She lies so smoothly.

"Yes, we have been told to escort your party to the gates." The Shadow's large russet-brown eyes touch me briefly before ducking.

Abarrane and Jarek hop onto the dock, keeping their backs to the young girl to avoid raising curiosities about which Shadows have returned with Solange.

I collect the skirts of the beige gown I conjured for myself—Agatha's garb when I met her—and step up onto the dock after them.

Solange dives in, grabbing my forearm. "Allow me to help you, Master Scribe"—she emphasizes her words with a squeeze—"given how *difficult* it is for a caster of your age to climb out of this boat."

"Yes, of course. *Thank you.*" I curse myself as I hunch my shoulders, mimicking what I remember of Agatha's stance. "I wouldn't want to fall overboard before the Prime has a chance to chop off my head."

Solange's eyes flare in warning.

Right. Wrong method. "How are the pyres coming along?" It's a weak attempt to distract from my many gaffes.

"Lead the way, Fatima." Solange gestures ahead and then waits one, two, three beats before following. "Are you *trying* to raise alarms?" she whispers.

"I should have warned you. Following instructions is not her strong suit," Jarek answers from behind us.

I make a point of pursing my lips—a silent promise that I'll stay quiet from now on.

With a heavy sigh, Solange guides us toward where the three Shadows wait. "One escort will be more than plenty. Fatima, you will accompany us. You two, remain here." She drops her voice. "And mention nothing of my return to anyone."

"Yes, Master Shadow," they chirp in unison.

We fall into step, Solange ahead with the young Shadow, Zander and Jarek flanking either side of me, Abarrane at the rear.

This Fatima steals frequent glances at Solange but says nothing as we climb the steep cobblestone street. The houses are small and quaint, like little cottages, each with thatched roofs and little fences surrounding them and gardens of herbs and tomatoes. The insides are brightly lit for evening, the windows showing families at dining tables or in chairs with books in hand, seemingly oblivious to the world's turmoil.

"What is it you wish to say, Fatima?" Solange asks suddenly. Clearly, she knows her well enough to drop the caster title.

"How do we fare in battle?" she stammers.

"It is far grimmer than expected."

"I see." A pause and then, "Thank you for answering, Master Shadow."

The great wall approaches ahead, solid and foreboding. "We must pace ourselves for the scribe's slowness," Solange says without looking back, halving her speed. "How is the mood in Nyos?"

"Dour."

"I heard there were executions."

"Yes. Scribes. There will be more in the morning. It was announced not long ago."

"What reason does the Prime give?" Solange is pumping this young Shadow for information, and the girl is happy to share it.

"They are saying the scribes have betrayed Mordain and have joined forces with Islor."

"*Who* is saying that?"

"The Prime herself. She declared it from the height of the tower, for all to hear. Is it true?" she asks Solange, but she turns her head to glance at me.

"No, it is not true," I blurt before Solange can answer.

"Queen Neilina is not dead?" There's hopefulness in Fatima's voice.

I sigh. "No, that part is true. But the scribes had nothing to do with it." Not directly, anyway.

"The Master Scribe is rather chatty for someone about to face severe judgment for her crimes," Solange warns.

I clamp my lips shut.

"The only caster to betray Mordain is the Prime herself, and it is for ignoring Queen Neilina's own treachery when she ordered Caster Ianca to summon Aoife on her behalf," Solange explains, laying the accusation bare on the table.

Fatima gasps. "Do the Masters know?"

"We shall soon see, won't we?"

"The Prime claims the Ybaris throne has been stolen."

"It cannot be stolen if the heir to Ybaris has claimed it."

"Do you mean Princess Romeria is still alive?" There's unrestrained hope in her tone, like a child, seconds from squealing with excitement. I'm having a hard time believing this young and effervescent girl is also a lethal warrior.

"*Queen* Romeria is alive, and she is still a pain in the arse." Solange *must* be smirking with that dig. "What else has the Prime claimed?"

"That the new queen will be the downfall of Mordain."

"Do the casters believe this?"

"They have no reason not to, Master Shadow. It is the Prime herself who speaks." She hesitates. "Is it not true?"

The pause lingers so long that I begin to doubt Solange's stance. "No, it is not true. If anything, Mordain's future looks brighter than it has in centuries. As bright as can be under the current circumstances, anyway."

I can't help the satisfied grin as we approach the line of Shadows at the wall.

"You are returning for your execution," Zander reminds me, wiping it from my lips in the next moment.

My insides churn.

"Shadows," is all Solange says, and as one they stiffen, realizing their leader is back. A unified echo of "Master Shadow" slips from their lips before stepping aside.

Much like the stone walls banking either side of the rift bridge, blocks in this wall begin moving and sliding. I marvel at the impressive process as a passage opens. I can see now why Solange said there was no way in without an invitation.

"Where is the Prime?" she asks.

"Meeting with the guild council, Master Shadow," a deep-voiced guard responds.

I stifle my curse. They're *all together*. I had hoped to be able to meet the Prime alone.

"Very well. I will bring Master Scribe Agatha to her. You three may return to the docks." Solange tosses the order over her shoulder and moves forward, assuming her Shadows will listen.

As one, Zander, Jarek, and Abarrane step forward toward the gate.

And just as quickly stop dead in their tracks, soft grunts slipping out.

I guess Solange wasn't lying about that ward either.

"Master Shadow, a word before you go," Zander calls out through gritted teeth as the three of them back away.

Solange pivots and, with a quick order to Fatima, she returns, ushering us farther back, away from prying ears. "You did not believe me. You had to see for yourselves, didn't you," she hisses. "How did that feel?"

"Fucking wonderful," Jarek quips, pain lacing his voice.

She shakes her head. "I can assure you, I will not let anything happen to her. I have several Shadows to rely upon. Fatima will be of great aid. She is one of my most promising."

"That newborn foal? You expect me to entrust Romeria's protection to her?" Zander counters, venom in his voice.

Solange steps forward until they are inches apart. "I expect you to trust that I have been frank in my goals and that I well know we need this queen should we have any hope of surviving Malachi."

"Stop fighting now or you'll blow *everything* before we even get through the gate," I whisper.

Zander steps back, his shoulders sinking. "Forget the Prime. Get the scribes through the stone."

I frown at his hurried words. "But you said—"

"I know what I said, but that was before you were facing the entire guild alone. *Mostly* alone," he amends. "The scribes are your priority. They do not deserve this punishment. We will find another way to deal with this Prime." His hazel eyes meet mine and in them I see a silent apology for his words earlier. But I also see his doubt. He knows this isn't the right plan, but he can't push beyond his fear of losing me.

"We must go while we still have the element of surprise." Solange dips her head. "I will meet you at the dock as soon as it is done."

"And I'll find you in Argon as soon as I can," I promise.

"Make it fast. And Solange? While you are in there, we are out here with the guilds' loved ones. If something should befall *my* loved one, I will not feel the same urge for diplomacy that she does."

A not-so-subtle threat.

"Understood."

I turn to give my back to the Shadows at the gate so I don't have to guard my—Agatha's—expression. "I'll be fine," I reassure him. "I know how to protect myself."

"If something happens in there, I cannot get you out." Desperation bleeds from his voice. "If it comes to it, use *everything* you have. Do not hesitate. There are too many people counting on you."

"I won't." I wish I could hold him, touch him. Even just see his face again. "A kiss before we go?" I pucker my—Agatha's—wrinkled lips.

A twinkle of humor stirs in his eyes. "I think that would raise a few alarms."

I stifle my snort. "Probably."

He moves forward a step, dropping his voice. "Promise you will return to me."

"Deception is what I'm good at, remember?" With a wink to mask my trepidation, I rejoin Solange.

Together, we walk through the passage and into the Casters' Guild.

2 2

TYREE

I grit my teeth as a jagged rock digs into my heel. Those blasted sailors could have had the decency to redress me after they robbed me. Not that they expected me to survive the plunge into the siren-infested waters, let alone need boots to traverse a stony peninsula on some island for hours. But if I ever see Captain Aron again, I'll enjoy returning the favor, beginning with my blade slicing through his bare toes.

"Thirty-two," Annika whispers.

"What are you counting? The times you've thought to stab me in my back with that dagger?" I joke.

"The ships," she snipes. "The urge to stab you is at least thrice that."

"And yet you didn't kill me when you had the most perfect opportunity."

"There will be more. I have faith."

I bite my tongue against the impulse to goad her. Annika's temper erupts faster than a young man with a whore's practiced hand on his cock. But I'm not a fool to think it's because she favors me. Until there are signs of other life, I am her only companion.

"I do not doubt that." I spare a glance over my shoulder to offer her my best smug grin. By the way her eyes flare with annoyance, I'd say it's effective.

Fates, how does a female who's been dragged through Azo'dem look so good? Annika's hair has dried into plump ringlets that cascade down her back. I've felt the itch to fondle them more than once—to test if they're as soft as they appear. Her dress is in soiled tatters and yet still flatters her feminine curves.

"What?" she snaps.

And the momentary fog of stupidity I caught myself in dissipates.

I turn back. "Nothing." Her mood is especially foul today. I can't decide if it's our dire predicament or the likelihood that her twin brother is dead, or that she's craving her blood fix. If the two of us are truly the only living creatures in this fates-forsaken land, it will only worsen as the days pass. Eventually, she might decide to feed off me just to end her suffering.

A few moments of silence pass before I hazard conversation again. "Unless I'm mistaken, that is a mountain range." I draw a line against the horizon with my finger. "Or it's the clouds."

"That could be days away."

"At least you have shoes to weather the distance."

"You would, too, if you hadn't stolen all my jewels and stuffed them in your boots like the idiot you are," she scolds, but I catch the hint of raggedness in her breath, the beads of sweat on her brow. We've been walking for hours over difficult terrain and, while I am accustomed to lengthy treks, Princess Annika certainly is not.

"Would you like to stop?"

"For what?"

She'll collapse before she admits to needing a rest, and then I'll have to carry her stubborn arse. Shoving my ego aside, I ask cordially, "Would you mind if we pause here for a moment so I can give my feet a rest?" Each must wear at least a dozen cuts.

"Since *you* need it ... fine." But a soft sigh of relief follows her bitter tone.

Shaking my head, I steer us toward a smooth outcrop of rocks shaded from the sun by a ship's hull. A half-rotted wooden crate sits nearby. I perch myself on it, groaning with the momentary respite.

A tiny green bird flutters past. A good sign that there is more than rock and water nearby.

"It is like a graveyard here." Annika ropes her arms around her middle as she studies the moss-covered ship. "Do you think these are all from Ybaris and Islor?"

"I don't know where else they would come from. Skatranan and Seacadorian sailors are too smart to sail with our kind." I add quietly, "So are captains like Aron, it would seem."

She hesitates. "I saw something large heading straight for the ship moments before they threw us overboard. It had at least ten fins sticking out of the water. Maybe the tale of the sea monster wasn't so far-fetched."

"If a sea monster had struck these, they would have sunk, not washed up here." I consider the alternatives. "I'll bet the sailors dove to their deaths with the sirens' song and then the ocean's current carried the empty ships here, where they broke apart on the rocks." If that's the case, this merchant ship might still have something useful inside. Who knows how long it has sat here, though, steeping in seawater.

Still, my curiosity gets the better of me. With a wince, I stand and pick a path through the cool shallow water. It's a blessing to my wounded feet.

"Where in fates are you going now?" Annika exclaims.

"Inside."

"You can't go in there!"

"Why? Are you worried for my safety?"

"No." She scoffs. "But it's pure idiocy. You may as well climb into a coffin."

I smile at her, perched on a rock, looking regal. "Do not fear, I will return and our wedding will go forward as planned." I ease past the ship's wooden frame before she can throw a barbed retort. Surely, she's grinding her teeth.

It's dark inside, the air ripe with a damp, earthy aroma. As I expected, the wooden crates are submerged and long since rotted. If these merchants were hauling anything of use, there is likely nothing of value now.

Splashes sound behind me. "Anything useful?" Annika's voice echoes in the cavernous space.

I stifle my surprise that she would venture inside here. "No, and there is not enough light to explore."

"For *you*, perhaps." She wades in until all I can make out of her is her golden hair in the last few tiny streams of sunlight.

And then she's too deep for me to see even that.

"Find anything?" I squint into the pitch-black as I edge forward.

"Not yet," she mutters as if annoyed. A moment later, she yelps. It's followed by a heavy splash.

"Annika?"

"I'm *fine*. I tripped over this stupid piece of wood. Now I'm soaked *again*, thanks to *you*—ah!" Her bloodcurdling scream has me running blind into the darkness.

23

ANNIKA

"Annika!" Tyree's roar echoes in the vacuous ship's hull and heavy splashes sound behind me.

"I'm okay," I call out as I stare at the corpse caught in the netting, my heart pounding. "I was just startled. I wasn't expecting a body."

He slows. "What kind of body?"

"A dead one," I snap back, watching as Tyree fumbles blindly toward me. "Take two steps to your right or you'll—"

He trips over the same hunk of wood I did and tumbles into the thigh-deep water.

"—fall."

Pulling himself up with a grimace, he edges around the hazard. He is sopping wet, his tunic and pants clinging to every hard curve of his muscular body.

If only he weren't such a lecher.

"Where are you?" His eyes search the dark.

"Over *here*. I knew my kind was far superior, but is your Ybarisan sight really *that* lacking?"

He grins as he veers toward the sound of my voice. "Just keep saying those sweet things and I'll find you in no time."

I roll my eyes, though he can't see it. "There are two small wooden crates hanging within the netting, out of the water. They seem intact."

"I was hoping for that." He closes in on me, his hand fumbling through the air until it grazes my hip. Still, he moves closer until he's standing inches from me.

So close I can pick the flecks of silver in his eyes as he searches the darkness, and the scent of neroli teases my senses.

Too close. I take a step back.

"And the body?" he asks, unbothered.

"A soldier, by the looks of it. But he's long since dead. Nothing more than a skeleton now. It's on your left."

He waves his hand until his fingers catch the net. "Can you reach him through this?"

"*Reach him*? I am not touching him."

He sighs with exasperation. "*Fine.* Guide me and I will." He holds out a hand in front of him, palm up.

I stare at it. Aside from when I've fought Tyree off, I've happily avoided any contact with him until now. "What do you want with him, anyway?"

"His boots, if he wears any."

"He does." They appear to be fine leather. I grimace. "You would wear a corpse's clothes?"

"And you would not, if given no other choice?"

I bite my retort. Atticus always did say I was too pretentious for my own good. Besides, I saw how Tyree was hobbling out there. The rocks must be punishing his socked feet.

With a heavy groan, I collect his wrist and guide it through a sizable hole. "I suppose this is better than carrying you."

His deep chuckle curls inside my ear. "I would enjoy seeing you try."

I ignore how close the move brings us together again, or the strong pulse I feel beneath my fingertips. "There." I peel away from him.

"That wasn't too awful, was it?" He slides his hand down the length of the skeleton's boot, finding its heel. "If he's old enough, this should come off ..." His words drift as he tugs.

One of the crates in the netting shifts with the sudden jerk and an ominous crack fills the air above us.

Before I can shout a warning, Tyree pulls free of the netting and plows into me, tucking my head to shelter me in his arms. Every muscle in his body tenses as he braces for impact.

A rotted beam drops down, landing in the water with a heavy splash.

Silence surrounds us again. "Are you okay?" he asks after a beat.

My face is pressed against his chest. "I'm fine. I thought you couldn't see me." I'm surprised by not only how quickly he moved but how quickly he did so to protect me.

"I can't. But it would seem that I'm acutely aware of you even in complete darkness." He loosens his grip but doesn't release me, his palm grasping the back of my head. The humor that normally laces his tone is absent.

This is far too close for me. I shove against him with my palms. The netting must have been anchored to that beam because the ends of it now lie open for easy picking.

"Your corpse is free for looting. Have fun." I trudge through the water toward the daylight, suddenly needing air.

"THAT WAS CERTAINLY WORTH THE TROUBLE," Tyree declares with renewed energy as he hops from one stone crop to the next. Is it the leather boots or the dull merth sword at his hip that excites him so? He heaved the netting with the cargo tangled inside and laid it out for pilfering. The crates proved disappointing—casks of stale spice and soured wine—but Tyree was thrilled as he slipped the sheathed weapon from the skeleton's hip. Dislodging stiff bones from the boots was trickier, but he managed and slid them on with a boyish grin.

"Speak for yourself. There was nothing of value for me, and I'm drenched in seawater again." Beads of sweat trickle down my neck as I struggle to follow, the terrain now a steady incline.

"You're nearly dry. And I think my ability to walk *and* save us from any dangers we come across benefits you greatly."

"I do not need you to save me."

"Could have fooled me back there." His voice is smug and taunting.

My annoyance flares. "How do those boots fit you? Because that soldier had *very* small feet."

Tyree's head tips with his boisterous laughter. "His toes had crumbled off! And come now, Annika, I thought you were cleverer than that." Tyree spares a smirk over his shoulder. "Don't tell me I've given you too much credit."

I pause long enough to collect a stone, closing my fist around it, the urge to whip it at his head overwhelming.

Tyree stops at the ridge crest, his hands on his hips. "There. What did I tell you? I knew there would be more than rock if we ventured far enough."

I'm out of breath when I match his stance, to look out over the expanse of greenery. Trees with dangling fronds tower over a lush forest of broad leaves. Far beyond is the darkened outline of a mountain range.

For the first time since coming to this cursed land, my heart beats with excitement as I feel my affinity thrumming to life. "Have you seen anything like this before?"

Tyree shakes his head. "Though it reminds me of illustrations I've seen in books based on Seacadore."

"You read?"

"Occasionally."

"While also plotting regicide. Impressive."

He ignores my quip. "Come, there must be something edible growing in there. Maybe we can find an innocent mortal for you to drain so your sour mood improves."

I feel his sideways glance, but I don't meet his eyes. "Yes, let's."

I SLAP my palm against my neck, squashing another of these wicked flying, biting bugs. The air has grown warm and sticky within this jungle, coating my skin in a sheen that they seem to like because they're congregating where I'm sweatiest.

"So willing to take but never to give." Tyree tsks. "I knew someone like that once. The relationship did not last long."

"Was it the Islorian immortal you fell in love with during your secret journey?"

It was a hunch, but the way Tyree stops dead for several seconds before continuing without a word tells me I've struck a chord.

I grin, victorious. "What was her name?"

Still, he doesn't respond.

"Gosh, if I'd known this is how to get you to shut up, I would have brought her up *hours* ago." After another lengthy moment of silence, an impish part of me can't resist. I reach out with my affinity to grasp hold of a vine and tangle it around his ankles.

Tyree trips and falls to the forest floor.

The cackle of laughter that erupts from me is louder than I anticipated.

He dusts himself off as he stands, turning to face me. "The Islorian princess wishes to play games, does she?"

The wicked gleam in his eyes is the only warning before the forest around me comes alive, vines and branches twisting around my limbs. With a squeal, I'm dragged backward until I'm pinned against a tree, my arms stretched out on either side of me. I reach for my affinity to free myself, but the bindings don't relent. I'm not strong enough.

"You are connected to Aminadav?" I whisper, shocked. And he's powerful. I should have suspected as much, given Romeria's affinity to Aoife is strong enough to explode stone water fountains. "But I thought you had an affinity to ..." My words fade. I don't have an answer.

"Anything you may have heard about my affinity was surely a lie." Tyree strolls toward me until he stands an inch away, his breath skating over my cheek. "Not so amusing now, it seems."

"Release me immediately," I demand.

"Oh, I don't know." He mock frowns. "I kind of like seeing my future bride trussed up."

I wrestle against my constraints, and they tighten in response, almost to the point of pain. "This is *not funny*, Tyree."

His expression turns serious. "Since you asked, her name was Jada. She was beautiful beyond compare, and desirable, and convincing, and she whispered all kinds of sweet promises. In the end, all she cared about was getting a taste of my Ybarisan blood." His voice is hard, but in his gaze, I catch the tiniest flicker of something else. Something that resembles hurt.

But that can't be because it would mean Tyree has a heart.

I harden mine. "And you bought her lies like a fool."

His jaw clenches. Another chord struck. "Any male would have found himself equally foolish."

"Whatever you need to tell your ego to soften the blow."

"And you're saying you would be different?" His focus drifts downward over the deep V of my dress, before climbing back up to my lips. "That, if my blood weren't laced with poison, you wouldn't be spewing all sorts of sweet lies for a taste of it?"

"I wouldn't." *Because I don't need it anymore.* Even if I can still smell it—like a delightful fragrance I can't help but chase with a second, long draw. But I bite back the urge to confess that. I like holding on to the inexplicable secret. "I don't feed off those who disgust me."

"Is that what I do, Annika? Truly? I disgust you?" He moves in closer, reaching up to toy with one of my curls. "It's even softer than I imagined," he whispers, winding it around his fingertips.

"You've imagined touching my hair?" I attempt a mocking tone, but instead it comes out shaky.

Long, dark eyelashes flutter as he peers down at me with a heated look that stirs my pulse. "I've imagined *a lot* of things where you are concerned."

I swallow against this unwelcome reaction stirring inside me. I *hate* Tyree. He is a Ybarisan, a murderer, a kidnapper. I hate him with every stitch of my—

A rustle sounds in the trees, and Tyree's attention whips away from me. A boy of maybe ten in soil-stained clothes stares wide-eyed at us from beneath a branch, like a doe caught in the crosshairs of an arrow and aware of it.

"Hello," Tyree says calmly, stepping toward him. "Can you tell us where we are—"

The boy turns and bolts in a flurry, earning Tyree's curse.

He starts running after him.

"Hey!" I yell.

"What?" He peers back and, as if remembering he has me bound to a tree, he curses again. The vines fall to the ground.

He takes off after the boy. "Hurry, or he'll get away!"

We tear through the dense forest, flat leaves slapping at our faces no matter how often we duck from them. Eventually, Tyree grabs hold of my arm and stops. "He's just a boy. How did he outrun us?"

"He's short?" I scan the trees, looking for movement, my breaths ragged.

"He can't have gone too—"

Branches snap to our left.

We take off in the direction of the sound, me at Tyree's heels, until we emerge in a clearing where the dense foliage has been cut back. The boy stands in the middle of it, his chest heaving.

"He's mortal," I whisper. I can hear the telltale heartbeat from here.

"No wonder he's running. He's terrified of you."

"As if he knows the difference between us," I snap. *Idiot.*

Tyree holds up his hands in a sign of surrender. "We will not harm you. We just want to talk."

The boy shouts something in a language I don't recognize before taking off with a leap.

Tyree groans, and we give chase again.

I can't say if it's him or me who trips the wire, but suddenly we're entangled in a net and dangling high in the air.

24

ROMERIA

It takes every ounce of my courage to not arm myself with my affinities as Solange leads me inside the walls of Nyos's Casters' Guild.

While the towers that loom ahead are imposing and unfriendly, at this level, the view is far more welcoming, with winding stone paths and manicured grounds of low hedges and glowing lanterns that give off a charming light.

Solange and Fatima are silent as they lead me down a main street, and I steal glances at the many buildings and alleys between them, making a mental map, should I need to rely upon it later.

The street opens into an expansive square. My eyes are drawn immediately to a bronze statue of a male that stands at least fifteen feet tall. "Who is that?" I ask.

Solange shoots me a warning look. "Is the Master Scribe's memory lapsing? How do you not remember Caster Yason?"

That name rings a bell. "Ah, yes … the proud bull." Wendeline once told me about the male elemental who studded hundreds of children in Nyos's attempt to spawn a key caster, back when Mordain prized the rare power instead of culling it.

Fatima regards me. If she knew who I really was, would she be so loyal to her leader?

I'm quickly distracted from those thoughts by the display at the far end, where four scorched heaps of wood sit, the charred remains of a person tied to beams on each. Fresh pyres wait nearby for the next round.

"Who were they?" Solange demands.

Fatima lists names I don't recognize. None are Zaleria or Allegra, at least. But it doesn't ease the tightness in my chest. These scribes did not deserve this. "Where are the others being held?"

"In the dungeons, Master Scribe Agatha," Fatima answers, and I sense a hint of familiarity in her voice. "Except for Caster Zaleria. She is being questioned in the Prime's study, I believe."

"And the Second?" Solange asks.

Fatima shrugs. "With the guild, I assume?"

"Assumptions will lead you astray more often than not."

"Yes, Master Shadow." She dips her head.

A soft huff sounds behind Solange's mask as she peers first at the pyres and then at the towers looming above. "I think the Master Scribe would benefit from some time in the dungeon before meeting with the guild. Perhaps seeing the fear of her fellow scribes will help loosen her tongue. We will escort her there now." She grips my elbow, leading me several steps toward a dark entrance. I know what Solange is doing—heeding Zander's revised orders to get the scribes out rather than deal with the problem of the Prime.

But this will likely be my only chance. I can't let Zander's fear dictate my actions.

I lock my feet. "Actually, I would much prefer to meet with the Prime now."

Solange stalls. "Along with the *entire guild*? Are you positive, Master Scribe?" She's trying to warn me off.

"Yes. Let's get this over with so we can move on to more important things."

THE BREEZE CHILLS my face as we cross the parapet high above the ground toward a corridor. Countless lanterns burn along the path, unaffected by the wind.

"You were a pupil of Master Scribe Agatha's before you joined the Shadows, were you not, Fatima?" Solange says.

"Yes, I was."

"Were you surprised by what the Prime has claimed she and her fellow scribes have been party to?"

Fatima sneaks a glance at me. "Astonished, to be honest. Master Scribe Agatha was always patient, and fair, and she taught me much. She was my favorite teacher."

"I'm not dead yet. *Soon,* likely." I imagine Agatha would say something like that.

Fatima's eyes crinkle. "No, Master Scribe. You are certainly not."

Solange does a cursory glance around but lowers her voice, anyway. "Given your own experience with the Master Scribe, do you believe what the Prime claims to be true?"

She falters. "Earlier, you said—"

"Forget what *I* said. What does your gut say?"

My ears catch Fatima's hard swallow. "I would accept *any* reason not to believe it."

"Good. I hope you will see that reason soon, firsthand." We round a bend, and her next words come quick and clipped. "You will accompany Master Scribe Agatha inside."

"Me?" Fatima squeaks while I exclaim, "What?" my feet stalling. Solange is abandoning me the first chance she gets?

She spares me a look. "Yes, Fatima. *You.* And if asked who escorted her here, the answer is Shadow Dain. *I* am still at the rift. This is very important. Do you understand?"

She blinks. "Yes, Master Shadow."

"And when you deliver Master Scribe, make to leave, but do not. Find a corner and stay within it. Their attention will be on her, not you. Whatever you do, *do not leave.*"

"But ... yes, Master Shadow."

"And Fatima? Whatever Caster Agatha reveals of herself in that room, know that she works for the good of Mordain." Solange turns her attention to me. "I will find my way inside."

"*How?*"

"Quickly, given your loose lips will foil this scheme within thirty seconds. Now *go.*" With that, she splits off down a narrow hall, and we continue around the next bend.

Ahead, two Shadows stand guard outside grand doors.

Fatima's breathing is shaky. She's nervous.

"Don't worry. You're not the one they want to burn at the stake." How in the hell Solange thinks this girl is going to protect me, I would *really* like to know.

With a deep inhale, she approaches the two guards. "I am here to deliver Master Scribe Agatha, as ordered by the Prime." It's barely audible.

This does not bode well for me.

But it's too late now. The guards open the double doors without a word, leading me in.

And suddenly I'm standing in a room of tall pillars and guild casters around a table, each wearing an expression that says they believe Agatha deserves to die. I'm sure all would be even more willing to kill the key caster hiding beneath this mask.

Every seat but two are filled. Solange's and Agatha's, if I had to guess. Which one is Allegra?

The caster at the head of the table stands, her eyes locked on me. I don't know anyone within this room, but I know this is Lorel before she opens her mouth.

"Shadow, send for the others at the helm of this treachery," the Prime barks.

There's a pause—the poor girl is struggling between conflicting orders from her Shadow Master and the Prime—and then a weak, "Yes, Prime."

I can't resist checking the dark corners as the heavy doors shut behind Fatima, but Solange is nowhere to be seen.

I am utterly alone.

With that order delivered, the Prime shifts her fierce gaze to me again. "*Caster* Agatha, your travel across Ybaris was swift."

My affinities call to me, begging me to latch on, but I fight the urge. Solange was right. If I strike the Prime down now, I'll likely have to keep going around this table of accusatory faces, slaughtering each one.

I offer a stiff dip of my head, as I recall Agatha doing. "As swift as you demanded, Prime. It seems your Shadows weren't too concerned about comfort for my old bones."

"And *you* weren't too concerned about those old bones when you left Mordain. Imagine my surprise when I beckoned the Master Scribe to my study, seeking an update on my important request, and Caster Zaleria arrived."

"I left her in charge. She is a more than suitable replacement."

"*I* appoint the Masters!" Her voice is borderline shrill. She gestures to the empty seat on the far end of the table. "As you can see, *I have not* appointed a new Master Scribe. It has been quite the task, rooting out all those with their hands soiled in your schemes to betray our realm in the name of Islor and Princess Romeria."

"Don't you mean *Queen* Romeria?"

"Come forward, Agatha," she seethes. "Face all those you betrayed in the light."

I ease around the table. I should have asked for descriptions of everyone so I'd know who was who. But I wasn't supposed to be confronting all of them together.

"How do you like the changes I've made so far?" The Prime waves a hand at the lanky, stern-faced man beside her. "My new Second."

"You've replaced Allegra."

"*As if* she would retain her position after betraying the guild!" The Prime scoffs. "She will be punished for her part in this vast web of conspiracy that we are *still* working to unravel."

I guess that answers the question about how much Lorel knows about the Second's involvement in all this.

"Caster Gaian has replaced Barra as Master Messenger." She waves a hand at a stalky male who squirms in his chair under the attention.

Two casters I can't trust because Lorel clearly does.

"So? After eight decades of life, your legacy will end with a tale of great deception, two realms now under attack from Nulling beasts because a key caster *you* nurtured and protected released the nymphs. What do you have to say for yourself, Agatha?"

"I should ask you the same. Twenty-five years ago, Queen Neilina ordered Ianca to summon Aoife, to create a weapon against Islor. Don't tell me you didn't have any idea—"

"I had no clue!"

"Then you're a fool and a terrible leader."

Anger bursts in her eyes.

In the next instant, shards of something razor-sharp pelt my body. I double over from pain as at least two dozen tiny ice daggers drop to the floor in front of me. Along with them are splatters of my blood. She attacked me without so much as a flick of her wrist.

I breathe through my nose as my affinities vibrate like a live wire, begging me to unleash them. If I look up now, I'll give myself away. I'm also liable to incinerate her.

"Tell me, how did you convince Caster Wendeline to abduct that elemental baby and travel to Islor?"

I keep my eyes on the floor. "I didn't need to convince her of anything. Caster Wendeline left with Margrethe of her own free will because she couldn't murder an innocent child. She raised her as her own."

"That *innocent* child summoned Malachi at Caster Gesine's behest to bring the Princess Romeria back to life as a key caster."

Finally, I dare look up. Satisfaction shines in the Prime's eyes, as if she's proud of herself for uncovering that piece. What she must have done to dig it out of Zaleria ...

"The princess is an impostor, a plant by Malachi himself, bringing war to us while serving Islor."

"That is a lie and you know it," I force through gritted teeth. "'When she rose again as a Daughter of Many and Queen for All, only then could there be hope for peace among the peoples.'" I recite the words Gesine first spoke, while huddled in a tent, fleeing Cirilea.

The Prime's eyes flare. "Yes, Caster Zaleria seemed adamant that performing the ramblings of mad seers would somehow prove her salvation."

"You mean, *prophecy* that has come true?"

The Prime is spinning her own story away from facts.

I look to the Masters. They can't all be lost causes. "This is the leader you support?" Zeroing in on the new Second, I push, "Someone who has conveniently ignored *everything* since the day Queen Neilina killed her own husband and blamed an invisible Islorian assassin?"

Barro's expression remains stony. The previous Master of Messengers surely knows ... he knows but chases a climb in rank over truth.

Of the six remaining Masters, two avert their gazes, but four watch me closely—one, a tiny, wispy-haired woman with intense curiosity. Can she somehow see through my guise? "Did the Prime tell you about the secret nymph city that Romeria opened? Because she knew about it days before she tortured the answer out of anyone."

"That is a lie!"

"Queen Neilina's taillok saw it. The Prime came to A—" I falter, nearly blowing my cover—"me, asking if the seers had foretold of it—"

"And you lied to me!" The Prime's shrill scream fills the room. "You told me you had no idea what this vision could be!"

I can't help the smug smile that stretches across my lips. "So, you admit to believing there's truth in what the seers see."

Her eyes narrow, realizing she's outed herself. "If you had informed me of what you knew then, I could have warned Her Highness. She would have known that her daughter was not hers any longer, and she would have protected herself on that bridge. It is because of *you* and your plotting that the Ybarisan queen is dead."

"Queen Neilina is dead because she started a war. And besides, you've never believed in prophecy. You didn't care about it even then. What would you have done with that truth?"

"I would have—"

"Denied it." My own voice rises, my temper loosening. "If I had told you that the heir to Ybaris is now also a key caster, allied with Islor's exiled king—who lost his kingdom to protect her—and she is guided by our own scribes in hopes of repairing the harm that the fates and Queen Neilina have brought to our lands, what would you, a Prime whose *only* concern is remaining Prime, have done?"

Her nostrils flare.

"Queen Neilina got what she deserved." I brace for another round of ice daggers as I add, "The only reason you care is because the new queen will not allow you to keep that ring for your part in this."

The Prime's hand balls into a fist. "The princess died months ago. The heir to Ybaris is Prince Tyree," she says through a hiss.

"And where is he right now?" Dead, likely, and she knows it.

"That does not matter. Mordain will recognize *no one* else."

"Really? Does your entire council feel the same way?" I study their faces, and I see a multitude of expressions.

"*I* speak for Mordain!" The Prime shouts, all semblance of control whittled away with my accusations.

The doors swing open then.

I gasp as two prisoners are half dragged, half carried in, their clothes soiled with sweat stains but, surprisingly, no blood. The one on the left, wearing a plain brown gown much like Agatha's, stares at me through empty eyes. That must be Zaleria.

What has the Prime done to them to leave them like this?

A third—a young man in his late teens with tawny skin—is ushered in last, walking on his own and coherent. Terror-filled, sage-green eyes rake over the council of hostile faces. When they land on me, there's instant recognition, and then confusion and guilt and a flinch of … betrayal, is it?

"It took some time and careful *questioning* before the casters divulged useful information, but they've been most cooperative since." The Prime's composure has returned. "The biggest surprise discovered was your dear budding *scribe, Cahill.*"

That name. This is the boy I'm supposed to bring back to Ulysede, the one very dear to Agatha.

The Prime tsks as she dangles a silver pendant in the air. "Hiding a male elemental caster right here in Nyos beneath our noses."

Cries sound around the room. Clearly, this was a well-kept secret.

I struggle to hide my shock. Why didn't Agatha warn me?

The Prime glares at the boy. "What do you have to say for yourself, Cahill?"

"I didn't know, Prime ...," he stammers. "I swear it!"

The slightest movement catches my eye, a black cloak behind a pillar in the far corner. Solange has found her way in. And good timing, because my gut says things are about to implode.

"See? Caster Agatha didn't even tell him! Will we ever get to the bottom of *all* your deceptions?" The Prime paces around the two hunched bodies, held up by the Shadows who brought them in. Neither show any clue that they know where they are or what's happening. "Do not worry, his powers are useless to him here, not that he has any clue how to use them. I was going to execute him with these two, but he can serve a purpose still. He will give us a weapon to fight against the impostor queen."

I realize instantly what she means. "You're going to *breed* him." She's going to use the poor guy as a stud horse like they did to Caster Yason.

"And you were not?" she retorts with a scoff. "You planned on hiding a second key caster in case yours didn't support your fantastical prophecies."

"I did not," I deny, though honestly, I have no idea what the wily old scribe intended with Cahill. Maybe that's *exactly* what she planned all along.

"You and *Gesine*." She practically spits her name. "I should have known that an elemental more interested in silly tales would prove dangerous. Wait until I get my hands on her, I will light the pyre myself—"

A thread of air leaps up and out of me, slamming into the Prime. She flies backward, colliding with a pillar before collapsing to the floor, unconscious.

The Masters stare at me—a silver-eyed scribe who can barely create a flame—with shock that will no doubt swing to suspicion, then reaction, in seconds.

I guess this charade is over. I arm myself with all four affinities, forming a shell of air that I pray these casters can't break through.

"Shadows, hold!" Solange appears from behind a pillar, her mask and cloak removed. Somehow, she looks even more fierce.

Gasps sound around the table, all startled to discover their Second lurking, unseen.

She uses that moment to our advantage. "Shadow Fatima, secure them so they may not do something *unwise.*"

The girl's eyes glow a brilliant green.

I frown as I try to figure out what she has done. It takes a few seconds to notice that the Masters haven't so much as twitched. It's as if they're frozen in place.

"How ...," I hear myself ask, enthralled.

"Time is limited. Use it wisely," Solange says curtly. "Perhaps allow them their tongues. I would love to hear what our new Second's excuse is for sitting idly by and allowing the Prime to declare herself above a queen."

However Fatima is doing it, she eases her hold. Grunts and wheezes and a few exclamations of outrage erupt.

Solange ignores them all, her focus solely on Barro. "What do you have to say for yourself, Master of Whispers? How many times have you ignored truths and curiosities that arrived at your door, biding your time in hopes of landing in this very seat one day? How long ago did you first hear of Queen Neilina's summoning?"

If he's at all guilty or fearful, he doesn't show it. "What do you hope to achieve for this treason, Shadow? A ring for yourself?"

Her head falls back with dramatic laughter, though there's no mirth in the sound. "If it was a ring I wanted, I would have secured it long ago. And I am a Second. You will address me as such."

"I will address you as nothing but the traitor you are—"

His words cut off with a gargle as Solange's dagger embeds itself in his throat.

"Would anyone else like to accuse me of betraying Mordain?"

The Masters around the table gape as the light extinguishes from Barro's eyes, his body still frozen in place.

The Prime is stirring, her eyes blinking repeatedly. "What is the meaning of this?" She struggles to pull herself to her feet with a wince.

"You have reached too high, Lorel, and you will pay the price for that." Solange's hand settles on her sword. I've seen how quickly she can strike another down.

"Agatha, your eyes ... since when ..." Even stupefied, the Prime fumbles for the band on her finger, her lips moving with inaudible words.

"Trying to bind me? You can't." I slip off my mask.

The Prime's eyes widen with horror. "Fates, it's *you.*"

I hold up the silver token. "Thanks to a gift from the nymphs who've returned, just as *prophecy* foretold."

She struggles to regain her composure. "What have you done with Caster Agatha?"

"She's safe in Ulysede, not that you care."

"Well then … what do you want? Why are you here?" Her gaze flitters from me to the table of powerless Masters, stalling on Barro. Her eyes flare.

"You know what I want. If you had given me the scribes I'd asked for, instead of burning them in the square, we would not be having this conversation."

"Fine. Take your scribes and go." She waves a hand dismissively. "I will not stop you."

I almost laugh. This is *almost* funny. "I *will* be taking the scribes with me, as well as Allegra, who I am naming Mordain's Prime."

"She is a traitor." Lorel sets her chin. "And Ybaris will no longer dictate Mordain's will."

"Something you and I agree on. But right now, we need Mordain's help, and since you've proven you are unwilling to give it, I am replacing you."

The Prime glares at her council. "An impostor queen is seizing control of Mordain and no one has *anything* to say about this?"

The silence in the room is deafening.

"I think that says a lot, don't you?" Though it might have more to do with the corpse at the table with them.

"I would not waste time with this one, Your Highness," Solange warns, and I know it's as much a reminder of Fatima's ability to hold the Masters in place—the glow in her eyes is waning.

If Zander were here, his sword would be aiming for the Prime's neck. But, despite everything, I can't bring myself to reach for a dagger. "You can either take off that ring, or we can remove it from your body. You decide." I hold out my hand, palm up.

The Prime glares at her Second. "History will name you as Mordain's downfall."

"That's funny, I thought *I* was going to be Mordain's downfall," I quip.

"Only if you hold the quill, Lorel. But you will not be here to witness it either way," Solange sneers, drawing her sword. Her arm is poised to swing down when suddenly she drops to her knees, the weapon clattering to the stone. Blood blossoms on her skin like tiny drops of sweat—first a few, then a few more, and then too many to count. Whatever she is doing, she is killing Solange.

I blast the Prime with a silver coil of my affinities. Not with the same rage I felt for Boaz, which incinerated him and everything in his surroundings. Just enough to see the look on her face as her heart stops and her body collapses in a sickening thud. I rush to where Solange lies.

"Took you long enough." She pants, her face coated in a layer of her own blood as if someone painted her in it.

"You need healing."

"Later." She pulls herself up off the floor, grimacing in pain. "Right now, we must get the scribes and Allegra out of here before your beloved burns down every cottage out there in his impatience to know you are safe." Solange nods to the two guards still holding the limp casters. "Take them to the port. Three Shadows will transport them to Argon, where they can be healed." But the mask of worry on her face as she regards her counterpart is troubling.

"Master Shadow," Fatima calls out. One glance at her shows her eyes back to their plain green.

I shield myself in an instant and turn to face the guild head-on, letting them see my silver eyes.

But the Masters remain where they are, none in a hurry to attack.

"Go, now!" Solange barks, and the guards leave.

"Your Highness," the wispy-haired caster who watched me curiously before, calls out. "They will need special healing for their injuries. *I* can provide that, if you will allow it."

"Thank you, Master Healer Brigitta." Solange's eyes flicker to me, giving an almost indistinguishable nod. The healer is telling the truth. "You will accompany me to Argon. And if the three Islorians with us sense that your goal is not genuine, they will tear your spine from your body."

The healer's face pales.

I stifle the urge to shake my head at Solange's words—only Abarrane would do that—as I bend down and gingerly slip off the gold band from the Prime's finger. The Ring of Minerva is as unremarkable as Agatha suggested. No stones, no gleam, nothing to suggest it's the most prized trophy on this island of caster power. I tuck it into my pocket for safekeeping.

Solange's attention swings to a cowering Cahill, pressed against the wall. Her jaw sets with determination.

"He's coming to Ulysede with us." I step in front of him, forming a barrier.

"Male elementals are dangerous," she warns.

"You've been saying the same about key casters for two thousand years."

"And look what has happened." But the corner of her mouth curves in a smile. With her bloodied face, it looks sinister.

Despite towering over me, Cahill somehow shrinks.

"We don't kill people for being born a certain way. Not anymore. That must change."

After a pause, she offers a dip of her head. "As you wish, Your Highness."

"Come on, Cahill. Agatha is waiting for you."

"Excuse me, Your Highness?" His voice is low but timid. "Do you think I might need the necklace Master Scribe gave me?"

The one she must have used to hide his elemental caster affinities, just as Sofie hid mine from me and everyone else with that ring.

"He's only bound within Nyos," another caster, one with down-cast lips and eyes too close to each other, confirms. "Once he leaves Mordain, he will have access to his affinities."

"Right." I fish through the Prime's skirt pocket like a corpse-robbing thief until my finger catches the chain. I hand it to him.

"Thank you, Your Highness." His fingers fumble with the clasp to replace it around his neck. He has such rich, innocent eyes.

They would have killed him the moment I left here.

"Let's go." I hesitate at the door. "I hope that the next time we cross paths, you'll see me as the ally that I am." Barro's body slumps against the table, his blood leaking into the grain. Solange was right. We could not have left him alive. I know his kind. He would have claimed the role of Prime, ring or not.

"My advisors insisted I kill the entire guild council and start fresh with casters I can rely on to help fight this war, but I refused because I think you all know the right path. Don't make me regret that choice." I let my words hang as we leave the guild tower.

THE DUNGEONS below the towers are not quite as bleak as the ones in Cirilea, but they're far smaller and they are packed. "There are so many of them." I scan the terrified faces. A stench of cold sweat lingers in the air.

"And Lorel would have burned every last one." Raising her voice, Solange announces, "Queen Romeria, the new ruler of Ybaris, has come to free you." She waves at the guard to unlock the doors.

Cautious scribes eye me as the doors swing open, no one rushing to move.

"You can stay here if you'd like, but I can't guarantee your safety. If you come with me to Ulysede, you'll have warm beds and food and an entire library to study. Your Master Scribe is there waiting."

A low murmur erupts.

A young girl of no more than fifteen stares at me through bright blue eyes.

"Do you know where the nymph scripture stone is?" I ask.

"You mean the lines on the wall? Yes, Your Highness." She caps her words off with a curtsy.

I smile. "Perfect. Take me to it."

"THIS IS IT?" Solange sneers.

"Yes, Second. Unless there is another stone wall of scripture that I am unaware of?" the young scribe stammers, her furtive eyes darting from Solange's blood-covered face.

"No, this is what I was looking for." It looks like the ones in Ulysede. "You've honestly never seen this?"

"I had better things to do than lurk under the guild towers, staring at walls." Solange grimaces at the low stone ceiling as if it might close in on us at any moment, trapping us here. "As I do now." A not-so-subtle hint to get a move on.

Taking a deep breath, I trace my fingertip over the curved lines as I've done so many times before. And sigh with relief as the familiar and welcome laughter rings in my ears.

"It is as you expected?" Solange asks.

"Yes." At least I hope so. There's only one way to know for sure and, once I pass through, I can't come back.

How often did Gesine stand in this very place, tracing these curves?

Wondering about the past.

Hoping for the future.

When this is all said and done, someone will write a book to immortalize her. I will make sure of it. "I need every scribe here to hold another's hand," I say. "They cannot let go or they'll be left behind."

"I will see that it is done, and you are through, and then I will meet you in Argon," Solange promises.

"Are you sure?" The guild seems stunned after the deaths of their Prime and Second and in no rush to revolt, but as Solange once warned, there are plenty of casters and motives still within these walls.

"I am the highest-ranking guild leader in Mordain at the moment. I cannot abandon Nyos in this state. Besides, someone must meet His Highness at the dock to tell him you are safe, and it cannot be Fatima."

She's right. He'll believe the worst—that the guild sent a young Shadow out there while they tie me to a pyre. Besides, she's not asking my permission. "Tell Zander I'll see him as soon as the scribes are in Ulysede, safe."

"I would hurry. Argon may have received word about Ybaris's new queen, but if the guards discover who is under those Shadow uniforms, they will not hesitate to attack."

"Right. Thank you, Solange, for all your help. And your faith in me."

She hesitates. "As you said to the council, Your Highness, I hope you never give me reason to regret it."

25.

ATTICUS

I t is well into the night when my ears catch soft whispers in the hallway outside my dungeon cell. I stiffen in my cot—a welcome but unexpected addition when I returned from my palace visit—and listen intently for steel sliding against scabbard.

Is this how King Cheral delivers my death?

While I sleep soundly in a bed for the last time?

A slight, feminine figure rounds the corner, the lantern in her grasp reflecting off her white nightgown as she fumbles with the key to my cell. Satoria. The king's *wife*.

Where are the guards and why would they allow this?

I watch with a mixture of curiosity and apprehension as she slips in and sets the lantern down in the corner.

"If you're here to kill me, I feel I should warn you that the element of surprise is gone," I drawl, my voice laden with sleep.

"I am not an assassin, Atticus." My name hangs off her whisper as she reaches up to her shoulders and unfastens the clasps there. Her gown tumbles to the floor.

"And yet you will surely get me killed for this." I admire her naked curves as she crosses the cell, tendrils of flaxen hair loose around her shoulders. How many of those thirty-two offspring has this delightful body carried for the king? I look for hints of childbirth —silver stretch marks, wider hips—but can't find any.

"What if I told you His Highness sent me?" She climbs onto the cot, straddling my hips with her muscular thighs.

"I would say that the wife of a Kierish king once told my father the exact same thing, and it turned out to be a terrible lie." *Well played, Cheral.* An effective reminder of past betrayals.

She rolls her hips in answer. The swell of her breasts and pert nipples are highlighted in the lantern light, begging to be touched.

I groan. Thank the fates they allowed me to keep these clothes. If I were still in those scraps, I would be in grave trouble. Still, if she keeps this up, the ache in my shoulder and thoughts of Gracen might not serve as effective wards.

I grimace from pain as I pull myself up to a sitting position, bringing us to eye level with each other. That delicious mixture of jasmine and lemongrass is faint now, and it does nothing to mask a muskier scent. Even if King Cheral sent his wife here to seduce me, she is a willing participant.

I collect her face in my palms and study her parted lips, wondering if I have gone mad. "You are beautiful, Satoria, and I am surely a fool for declining, but I must."

Something unreadable dances in her gaze. "Who is she?"

I smirk. "You assume that is the only reason I am turning you away?"

She looks down at her naked form and then back up at me. "That is the only logical reason I can deduce." Her eyebrow arches. "Unless you prefer my husband over me."

"I assure you, that is not the case," I say with a chuckle, my hands drifting from her cheeks, down over her bare shoulders and arms.

Her smile is soft. "Is it the female you beheaded that lord for? The mortal servant?"

I hesitate, but find myself admitting, "Yes."

"What is her name?"

"That is of no concern to Kier."

"You think I am here as a spy for His Highness."

"I think you played servant earlier to learn what you could about my current standing with my people. Now that I know who you really are, I think you are here to give your husband a reason to kill me and be done with it." I pause. "That, or you have mistaken which king's lap you belong in."

"You are a king no more. And I assure you, I can tell the difference." There is a nervous energy flowing through this one's veins. Adrenaline. "Do you plan to wed the mortal?"

Marry Gracen ... For a short time, I did toy with such a fantasy. I do not know if she will speak to me once she learns the truth. *If* she still lives. But the grand life I could have given her is over. "I am currently a prisoner. The only plan I have now is to remain alive, something you seem intent on challenging."

Satoria bites her bottom lip, waiting for my resolve to weaken, perhaps.

Gooseflesh has erupted over her bare skin. I stroke her shoulders and arms with my palms to warm her. "It is cool here at night. You should really redress."

Her face falls with seriousness. "And what if this is your last night?"

My hands stall. "What are you trying to tell me, Satoria?"

"His Highness needs no excuse to execute you. I heard him speaking earlier to his officers. He has made plans for tomorrow."

I suppose I shouldn't be surprised. "That would be reckless of him, but if his mind is made up, there is not much I can do, is there?" Except fight my way out or die trying.

She deftly pulls my palm inward to cup her breast. "There is *one* thing you can do." Leaning in, she skates her lips over mine. They are soft and plush, and the feel of her warm flesh and peaked nipple in my palm is enticing.

If Gracen's freckled face and green eyes didn't appear in my mind every time I closed my eyes, I would likely not be able to resist, regardless of who her husband is. "You are right. I can take my last breath knowing I honored those I love." I press a gentle kiss against Satoria's temple, not wishing to insult a king's wife. "Good night, Your Highness."

"Good night, my usurper king." She slips off my lap and, quickly redressing, she slips out of the cell and disappears into the night.

I study the cracks in the ceiling and plan my final stand.

26

ROMERIA

A small horde of scribes trail me through Ulysede's library in a daze, their shuffling feet the only sound.

I suppose it's to be expected. One minute, they were crammed in Nyos's dungeon cells, awaiting certain death for a crime most of them were oblivious to, and not fifteen minutes later, they're free and strolling through the halls of a castle in a long since hidden realm, led by a new queen.

"Fates! You've made it!" Agatha drops her magnifying glass and eases out of her chair. Zorya joins her as they approach, the warrior surveying the horde of casters through shrewd eyes, no doubt searching for a threat.

At the sight of their old Master Scribe, the scribes perk up, rushing toward her, drowning one another in a flurry of questions. Their voices swell through the silent, vast space, giving it life.

I smile as I watch them all. At least we've accomplished *something* today.

Dismissing them as a threat, Zorya rejoins me. "Where are the commanders and His Highness?"

"On their way to Argon, which is where I'm about to go. How have things been here?"

"Quiet within the castle walls, now that Oredai has removed all the nymphs."

"And where is our favorite Cindrae now?" I managed to avoid him and am relieved for that.

"Somewhere within the city. The various groups do not get along.

I've told Cirilea's mortals to stay within the castle for the time being. I do not think they are in any danger. The nymphs mostly ignore them, too busy squabbling amongst each other. But there are fewer and fewer in the city each day."

Which leaves anyone to wonder where they're going.

Zorya's gaze wanders over the crowd. "This is far more than the thirty scribes you promised."

"More hands to help you find books?" We have plenty of room for them all.

"You were concerned for the battle-hardened warrior, stuck babysitting the elderly in this tomb. How thoughtful," she deadpans.

"This is what Gesine wanted, you know. The scribes here to sift through all this. She asked me for help." And I denied it.

Mention of the elemental caster wipes the hard expression off Zorya's face. "Now you can take the sylx with you."

"Where *is* Lucretia, anyway?" I frown, searching for her slinking form. I would have thought she'd be the first to find me.

"Probably building another tower that will kill the old witch should it topple." She gestures to a stack at least four books deep and ten feet high.

"Those are *all* about the fates?"

"You'd have to ask *her*." Zorya juts her chin toward Agatha. "Though she's still working through the first. This will take ages."

"Not with thirty scribes who can read the text."

Agatha notices our attention and peels herself away from her faction to join us, bowing. "Your Highness, it is a relief to see you. What of Zaleria and Allegra?"

By the time I'm done giving a quick rundown of what happened, Agatha's face has lost all color.

"Corrin is sorting out rooms and meals for everyone. I thought I'd bring them here so they could see you and know that they're safe."

"Yes, they've been through quite the ordeal." She wrings her hands, still racked with guilt. "I knew Lorel would not take kindly if she found out what we had been up to."

"Speaking of being up to things ..." I point to Cahill, who's occupied by a prattling Pan. They're about the same age, though where Pan is scrawny, Cahill stands tall and broad-shouldered. "That's quite the necklace."

Agatha's eyes widen before she's able to school her reaction.

"Don't worry, he's wearing it again." How long before he takes it off to test these hidden affinities of his? I still recall the first time I removed my ring while standing on the terrace overlooking the royal garden and the strange, buzzing energy that claimed my senses.

"I should think so. He would be crawling out of his skin by now otherwise. Who else knows?"

"The guild and a few Shadows. And Cahill, now." He and I are more similar than he has any clue of. Both of us had no idea what we were capable of, our skills hidden by others.

"I'm surprised Lorel didn't kill him on the spot."

"She was going to breed him."

Agatha gasps, her face filled with disgust as she looks at the young man, no doubt still seeing the little boy she rescued. "I have only ever wanted to protect him, since the day he arrived in a caster's arms. But I suppose that truth cannot be put back into the box."

"How powerful is he?"

She falters on an answer, her jaw clenching as if afraid of admitting to the truth.

That tells me all I need to know. "He'll be safe here, but you need to train him before he decides to take that pendant off and learn by himself."

She waves my words away. "Cahill is a sweet and innocent boy. He will do as I say."

"Train him, Agatha. It's better for all of us." I hold up the Prime's ring. "I have to get to Argon and give Allegra this."

"*Allegra.*" Her eyebrows arch with her slow nod.

"Solange recommended her."

"Huh! Well, now I can die in peace for I have truly seen it all." She gazes over all the scribes, some venturing down aisles, their curiosity getting the better of them. "Do not worry. While you are there, we will hunt for answers in here." She dips her head. "I am grateful that we have been gifted a queen with a kind heart. Thank you for bringing them back safely to me."

"You can thank me by finding the answers we need."

ARGON'S royal vault is exactly how I left it. With a nervous flutter in my stomach, I weave around the various chests and crates, intent on the heavy iron door that leads to the castle and Zander.

"This is a fine piece."

I yelp in surprise and spin around, arming myself with my affinities.

Lucretia hovers by a gold bust adorned with a layered necklace of gold and diamond, her fingertip skating over the gems.

"How did you get in here?"

"I followed Her Highness through the wormhole."

"It's not a—never mind." I shake my head.

"Why do they create such fine pieces, only to hide them in a cellar?"

"The same reason you hide fates' tokens. Because they're valuable. Why are you *here*?"

She abandons her interest in the jewelry. "I serve my master."

"You were serving me by helping in that library. The scribes need you."

"I have delivered a vast selection of tomes they may find value in. There is more than enough to keep them occupied. Now I must serve my new master." She bows. "I am of use here."

"How?"

"In various ways."

I sigh heavily. I don't have time to peel through layers of Lucretia's ambiguity. I also can't waste time shuttling this conniving sylx back to Ulysede's library. Zander and the others will reach the port soon. Besides, knowing her, she'll vanish and follow me back to Argon, anyway. "Fine." I move for the door. "But keep *this* form."

"It is the one I favor."

"And no more vanishing." I raise a finger in warning. "And do not antagonize Jarek."

"I enjoy our friendly banter, though." She smiles wistfully.

That's what she calls friendly banter? He genuinely wants to kill her. "Stay out of his head. *And his dreams*." I know they have something to do with me.

Her pretty face furrows with confusion. "But those are a reward to your most valued advisor. I give him that which he desires most but cannot have."

"That's not … what he wants." I stumble over the denial. I *hope* that is not what Jarek wants, but deep down, I fear there may be truth to her words. Regardless, I wish only happiness for him. As much happiness as I have with Zander. "Do not mess with his head anymore or I will relegate you back to your crypt like your last masters did." I have no idea how to do that, but my threat seems to have the desired effect.

Lucretia sulks as I channel Aminadav into the lock, picking it from the inside. It opens with a jarring sound.

The lanky guard on the other side jumps back, a dazed look on his face. "Your Highness!" he exclaims. "But … how did—"

"Long story. A group is arriving from Mordain with wounded casters who need tending. Take me to the port."

"Yes, Your Highness." He quickly falls back into obedient stiff-guard mode, leading us out.

"HOW MANY THERE ARE?" I squint into the darkness. "I can't tell."

"It is difficult, Your Highness. Especially with Shadows on board," says the guard closest to me, seemingly in charge. I heard someone call him Yardley. "It moves quickly, though. By the grace of Vin'nyla, I would imagine."

I huddle in my jacket, the cool night wind creating whips out of my braids. When I insisted on meeting the boat at the docks, Yardley barked orders and suddenly, twenty-five guards were marching down the path with me, the sound of their metal armor daunting.

"I count twelve standing and two wrapped in blankets, lying on the floor, Your Highness," Lucretia purrs. Her unusual eyes have earned countless wary looks from guards and servants alike as we marched through Argon, but I'm sure the sylx enjoys the attention. "Seven Shadows and five others."

One must be the Master Healer. Who are the others?

Lanterns mark the slip for the boat as it slides into position, dock-hands rushing for ropes to tie it in place.

"Stay here!" I order, my impatience winning out. I take off running, my feet scattering loose pebbles.

A Shadow leaps out onto the dock and collides with me where wood meets rock. I know it's Zander even before he yanks off his mask and kisses me.

"That wait was agonizing. My mind conjured a dozen terrible scenarios," he whispers.

"I was ready to drown His Highness in the channel to put him out of his misery," Abarrane confirms.

He ignores her, roping his arms around me. "You did not listen to a word I said at the gate."

"I listened. I just didn't agree with you." I smile. "You were right. We needed *all* of Mordain allied with us, not just the scribes. This was our only shot, so I took it."

He leans down to press his forehead against mine. "We heard what happened. Are you okay?"

Am I okay with having more blood on my hands? "Lorel would have killed Solange. I had no other choice." But never in a thousand years could I have thought I would one day rationalize taking a life so easily. That person I left behind in New York is so far gone. I could never return to her—even if I wanted to.

Jarek leaps out of the boat with ease, having shed his mask. "*She* insisted we bring all these witches with us." He hauls a caster out by her cloak, earning her yelp of surprise. The others avoid his reach, clambering out on their own.

"Master Healer Brigitta is the best one to try to undo what Lorel has done, but she cannot do it on her own and our elementals are at the rift." Solange strolls forward, her bloodstained expression hard. The Shadows follow her with Allegra and Zaleria in their hands, bundled and deathly still. The casters trail, a somber, quiet line.

I fall into step next to the Master Healer, Zander at my side. "They *can* be healed, though, right?"

"If there is hope, it must be done now." But her eyes are laden with doubt.

2 7

SOFIE

M y fingertip traces the tines of my fork as I study the scene in the vacuous dining hall before me. It's almost comical, playing out like a skit written and rehearsed. A band strums an upbeat tune as servants shuttle platters of food for greedy lords and ladies, and others keep their mugs of ale and wine brimming. Everyone wears smiles.

And *everyone* pretends to ignore the terrifying Saur'goth soldiers who stand guard around the room, but fail terribly, their nervous eyes darting furtively to the beasts—their armor, their weapons, their fangs—as they devour morsels of roasted meat and other delectables.

I spent the afternoon shuttling Malachi's army into Cirilea. There must be at least a thousand here now, infiltrating city streets and terrorizing peasants and nobility alike. It's a small fraction of what moves through the rest of the realm, unbeknownst to anyone.

"Are you not enjoying the meal the servants have prepared for their queen?" Malachi asks, tossing a bone to his plate.

"I am not hungry."

"Eat," he barks.

It does me little good to earn his displeasure, so I stab at a carrot and pop it into my mouth, chewing slowly so I have an excuse to not speak. Elijah was never one for sitting at the head of a table like this, waiting for constituents to climb the steps and kiss his ass.

But as I look at the fate who has possessed his body, his eyes alight with giddy mischief, his smug grin dripping with pomp, it is clear this is what Malachi has longed for.

My beloved trapped inside must loathe every second.

A silver platter clatters to the floor. It doesn't take long to find the source—a young female servant who lost her balance or her nerve under the scrutiny of the Saur'goths. Now she scrambles on her hands and knees, collecting loose buns, her fingers narrowly avoiding the boots of the noble couple on their way here.

No wonder I have no appetite. My teeth grind as I prepare to digest their drivel.

"Your Highness," they echo, their bows deep. "We are Lord and Lady Spire of Fernhoth," the male introduces. "It has been forever since a Cirilean ruler has treated us to such a lavish affair."

I barely stifle my snort. "Perhaps one was thrown while you two were locked in the tower for treason against your king." I recognize his pinched face from the other day.

His eyes flash—with anger or fear, I'm not sure—but he quickly disguises it behind laughter. "A simple misunderstanding."

"Which part?" He reeks of deceit.

Malachi chuckles as he settles a heavy hand on my shoulder. "I apologize for my love. She is very protective of me. But there is no need. No one here would be reckless enough to scheme against us."

The male's eyes widen with exaggeration. "Of course not!"

The lady echoes his words with a fervent shake of her head, as if I can't see through her lies too.

"We will not disturb your meal further." With bobs and bows, the two scurry away.

"You have much to learn about ruling a kingdom," Malachi chastises.

I know better than to ask, and yet my curiosity overwhelms me. "Such as?"

He takes his time answering, ripping off a chunk of roasted duck with his teeth. Juice dribbles down his chin.

Elijah would have swiftly wiped that off with a napkin. Though, he would never eat like an animal.

Swallowing the mouthful, Malachi says, "You do not begin your rule with fear. You begin with compassion and benevolence. You lull them with charm."

"So, when you beheaded that lord in the throne room, was that benevolence or charm?" I couldn't care less about that sniveling fool —I'm sure he deserved it. "And what about the guard outside upon our arrival? And your threat to kill the exiled king?"

"Simple lessons. I delivered them with a smile, did I not? And I did not threaten to kill Zander, I promised to do so, and I gave him options." Finally, he dabs at the grease. "Only use fear when they think you are weak."

"And what of these Saur'goths, then?"

"They are proof of my strength."

He has an answer for everything, warped or not.

Malachi's intent gaze is on a youthful blond servant as she passes with a tray of roasted vegetables. "Things have changed much since I ruled here last. The slaves wore far less then."

"Why would it matter what she wears?" I snap before I can rein in my jealousy. I know *that* look—I have seen it countless times, in my crumbling sanctum, when I was forced to submit my flesh for Malachi's pleasure. But it has never been through my husband's eyes. Elijah would *never* admire another female in such a way, not since he met me.

"Because I wish to appreciate that which I have had a hand in creating." Anger etches into Malachi's features. "Does my loyal servant feel I should not be permitted to do so?"

Fear cords my muscles. The one time I dared question the Fate of Fire's intentions so bluntly, his punishment was swift and brutal, his blazing hand against sensitive flesh delivering an agony I did not think I would recover from.

I never dared question him after that.

I dip my head and remind myself yet again—this is not *my* Elijah. "You are permitted to everything you have had a hand in creating, Your Highness."

A noblewoman with a curtain of shiny black hair bows before our table then. "Your Highness, I am Lady Saoirse. I wish to thank you for bestowing upon me the gift of governing Kettling."

Ah, yes. The city whose lord Malachi beheaded. And here is his daughter, grinning for her father's executioner.

"Lady Saoirse." Malachi regards her. "I am certain that whatever the previous ruler conspired to accomplish, you had no involvement in."

"Certainly not." Her hair swings with her vehement headshake. "I was betrothed to King Atticus and intended to be queen. For what reason my"—she falters—"*the Lord Adley* chose to plot is beyond me."

I clear my throat. It took me all of half an hour to learn the deep-rooted hatred between Cirilea and Kettling, and that all the accusations against those thrown into the tower were likely true.

Her eyes flitter to me for a second before plowing on. "If I might be so bold as to ask about the eastern armies that King Atticus sent to the rift. The Kierish soldiers have invaded my lands, and they are still there."

"You wish me to send them back to the east."

"If it is feasible. I worry for the safety of my people. I received troubling news today of a large enemy encampment claiming the village of Baymeadow."

"From what I've heard, the encampment has as many Islorian soldiers as it does soldiers from this enemy realm." I recall addressing a letter to Kier's king. I don't imagine he appreciated Malachi's closing line.

"They are traitors to Islor and a threat to you, Your Highness."

Malachi twists his lips in thought. "Have no fear, Lady Saoirse. My Saur'goth warriors will decimate them soon enough."

"Of that, I am sure, Your Highness." Lady Saoirse dips her head again.

Between the beasts crawling out of the Nulling and his warriors, there will be no one left to rule over soon enough, but I bite my tongue.

"But I appreciate your concern for my kingdom." He leans forward on his elbows. "You are even more exquisite up close."

The fool beams. "You honor me greatly, Your Highness."

My insides churn with disgust, the single carrot in my stomach threatening to reappear. "I seek fresh air. I will be outside in the garden if you require me, though I'm sure your guards will remain dutiful." No one would attempt anything with these fucking demons ready to pounce.

"Leaving your king at dinner is rude, my love. It will cause talk."

The last thing Malachi cares about is gossip, but I hear the underlying disapproval in his voice. If I were smart, I would remain where I was, shovel my dinner into my mouth, and smile like a good little queen.

"As you have said, I have much to learn about ruling a kingdom." I rush away before he can stop me.

My HEELS CLICK on the stone pathway as I meander through the garden, igniting cold lanterns with flame as I pass. This must have been a lovely place once. I suppose it still is, save for the hideous scar that splits its center. The bodies have been removed and mortals tinker away at the stone fountains day and night, preparing to rebuild. But the swath of damage from dragon's fire cannot be fixed by any mortal with their cart of tools.

I glance over my shoulder at the castle behind, half expecting to see a cohort of Saur'goths marching to drag me back to face Malachi's wrath. But he is suitably occupied by all the preening idiots who stroke his ego, allowing me a chance to breathe out here.

I pause by a vine that reminds me of our beloved wisteria, though this one boasts flowers in fuchsia and violet hues of a tropical beach sunset. At least it did. Only a few blooms remain now, while the rest wear a coat of ash. It will die without help.

I weave strands of Aoife and Aminadav together and channel it into the roots of this poor, abused plant. Moments pass and then the ash flakes off, revealing new wood beneath. Fresh buds erupt on it, promising another burst of blooms.

I move on to the next vine.

This, I can do.

THE LAST THREADS of my affinities flutter, frayed and dim, as I climb the steps to the queen's chamber. My legs wobble from the exertion. I should not have drained myself so thoroughly for the sake of trees and vines, and yet once I began, I could not stop, the simple act of healing as satisfying as it was therapeutic.

Two guards hovering at my door step forward in unison. "You must attend His Highness in his chamber," the one on the right says.

Oh, fates. I barely stifle the groan. There is only one thing this could be for, and I am spent. "I am far too tired to—"

"He insists," the one on the left cuts me off, collecting my elbow, the metal of his gauntlet digging into my skin.

"You *dare* touch me?" I have never been skilled at containing my temper, and now is no exception. I lash out with my last threads of Vin'nyla, dragging the air from the guard's lungs. He releases my arm in a fit of coughs, his face turning red as he struggles to breathe.

It holds only moments before I lose my grip of him, my affinities dwindled to nothing. But it's enough.

Gasping to refill his lungs, he gestures ahead, now keeping his distance.

"Do not lay a hand on me ever again or I will be the last female you touch," I warn crisply. Perhaps making enemies of the guards is not smart on my part, but they should not forget what I am. Pulling my shoulders back, I walk the rest of the way to the king's chamber where two Saur'goths wait.

My guards want even less to do with them than me and linger at the corner.

Releasing a heavy sigh of annoyance, I stroll in. "Your Highness, you summoned me?"

"In here, my love," comes his deep, velvety voice from the direction of the bedroom.

My stomach drags on the marble floor as I move through the expansive sitting area of opulent gilding and moody, soot-black Baroque décor and into the bedroom.

I freeze at the horrid scene before me, grabbing the doorframe to keep from buckling.

This is not Elijah, I remind myself, rage and pain warring inside me as I watch Malachi use my husband's body to pleasure that simpering Kettling fool, sprawled out on his bed.

"There you are." Elijah's deep voice fills my ear. He holds her legs in place as he kneels over her. "I was wondering when my queen would gather enough 'fresh air,'" he says between thrusts that are growing in intensity by the second.

Lady Saoirse lets a cry slip, and then tips her head back and offers a coy smile. It disappears when she sees my face.

I hope she enjoys fucking my husband tonight because tomorrow I will hunt her down and—

"You can undress now." Malachi cuts into my murderous plot. "I will be done with this one shortly."

This is not Elijah, I remind myself as my heart constricts. But Elijah is an unwilling participant. He would never touch another woman, and yet he is forced to do it with me watching. He must be in agony, seeing my reaction to it.

This is Malachi's style. I knew he would make me suffer, but I should have expected this. "I have been healing the garden all evening and I am tired, Your Highness. I would very much prefer to—"

My words die as my skin ignites in flame, pain slicing through my flesh in an instant, searing every nerve ending. The burn is unbearable, and I have no defenses left, save for my shrill screams.

Just as quickly as the coat of fire arrived, it vanishes.

I stare at my smooth, uncharred flesh, my hands shaking. The stench of singed hair fills the air, but when I paw at my head, soft strands meet my touch.

Did I imagine that? Malachi was skilled at playing mind games—one moment Elijah lay in his tomb, the next he did not.

But Lady Saoirse has abandoned all pretenses of pleasure, gaping at me in horror. Whether she saw the flames as I did or not, surely, she heard my screams. My throat is raw.

"You were saying?" Challenge sparkles in Malachi's eyes.

"Yes, Your Highness." I reach behind me for the fastener at the top of my dress.

With a grin of satisfaction, Malachi flips Lady Saoirse over onto her hands and knees and reenters her as I disrobe.

28

ROMERIA

Z ander pauses, inked quill in hand. "How did I get roped into writing letters to Ybarisan nobility I have never met?"

"I haven't met them either." I pop a raspberry into my mouth. I can't remember the last time I ate. The castle came awake as soon as word spread that Queen Romeria had returned, with lady's maids rushing to prepare a bath and meal. "Plus, you're *so much better and faster* at it than I am." Writing that letter to Atticus took me forever.

"Flattery might get you somewhere with me." He smirks. "Anything else you'd like to add?"

"Depends." I pause in my pacing to admire the castle spires from the window of Neilina's chambers. "What have I said?"

"That Queen Neilina is dead, and you are the crowned ruler of Ybaris. You have allied with Islor to defeat the Nulling's beasts and Islor's impostor king, who will bring ruin and suffering to all."

"Do I need to add something about expecting their fealty and all that other *stuff*?" I wave a dismissive hand.

"As Ybaris's queen, it is implied."

I shrug. "Okay. Then I guess I have nothing to add."

His eyebrow arches. "Nothing *at all* to help bolster *your* people's confidence in you and in our union?"

"Fine. Tell them what a good lay the king of Islor is."

He leans back in his chair. "I'm glad you are taking this seriously."

"I am! I just don't see the point while there's an actual war going on out there. Everyone's at the rift, risking their lives, and we're sitting here, writing letters from this sparkly castle. I mean, the roof *literally* sparkles." I point out the window to where lantern light ignited by caster magic reflects off multifaceted rubies and sapphires and diamonds.

"One taste for battle and suddenly she can't get enough." He sets down the quill and stands, his expression stony. "Do not underestimate the value of what you have accomplished. What you *will* accomplish." He rounds the desk. "Islor was facing not only a civil war but also one with our neighboring realm. You ended both."

"And now we're fighting a war against fucking monsters, and you've lost your throne."

"I had already lost my throne, remember?"

"Yeah, I remember. To your brother, because of me."

He collects my chin between his thumbs and forefingers. "And if I had to endure it all over again, I would make the same choice." He leans in to brush his lips against mine. "Just this morning, Mordain's Prime was executing scribes and cutting off support from the casters. So, you devised a brilliant plan and went in there *on your own*—"

"With Solange's help."

"—saving them all—"

"Not *all*."

He groans through another kiss, this one hard. "Stop interrupting me while I sing your accolades."

I roll my eyes dramatically.

He releases my chin to tug my braid. "And you have secured an alliance with a realm who has been killing key casters for two thousand years."

"*If* Allegra survives." The casters whisked her and Zaleria off to a room in the elementals' tower and told us they would know more by morning.

"Give yourself credit where it is due, Romeria."

"What about your throne? What about Malachi?"

"There is not much we can do at present. Arriving unannounced in Cirilea has proven a bad idea, and killing him will not be so easy with Sofie as his shield." Zander smooths a hand over my hip. "He wears my clothes and my crown, but he seems more interested in playing king than destroying the realm."

"For how long, though?"

"Only time will tell. But that is why we must focus on winning the loyalty and hearts of our people—both yours and mine—and proving to them that we are joined in our aims for peace and prosperity, so that when the day comes, we are united." He leans down to peck my nose with his lips. "Hence the letters."

A grating sound suddenly fills the queen's chamber. Zander's sword is in his grip and my affinities bubble in mine as a panel in the wall slides open.

We both sigh in relief as Jarek's broad frame fills the gaping passage beyond. He and Abarrane have been scouring the castle since we arrived, searching for anything that might interest us. "Look what I found."

"What *you* found?" Lucretia's voice sings from the darkness. "You have a short memory, *Commander*." She's been calling him that since they arrived tonight.

His jaw tenses. To say Jarek wasn't pleased when he saw Lucretia at the port would be an understatement. "You will both want to see this."

I MARVEL at the windowless room, lit with lanterns—fueled by caster magic that ignited as soon as Jarek pulled the hidden lever. "How in the world did you find it?" I walked through Princess Romeria's quarters earlier and noticed nothing other than the mundane taupe silks and general lack of evil aura one might expect to linger in the personal space of such a duplicitous villain. The trigger to open it is carved into the molding on the opposite side of the room from the entrance behind the fireplace.

"I am a skilled legionary. I miss nothing."

"And *I* did not miss the way the serpent led you there, practically holding your hand as you pulled," Abarrane muses. "It's as if she knew where it was all along."

"I do not know what is built within these walls, warrior. I have never been to this place before." Lucretia's eyes sparkle with delight as they drag over the floor-to-ceiling shelves.

I sense a half-truth in her answer, but it's not worth chasing yet. "So, this secret room has doors into Neilina's and Romeria's chambers?"

"And Prince Tyree's as well—here." Abarrane points to a panel in the octagonal-shaped room, sitting open a crack. "But not the king's, from what I can see."

"His chamber is too far away. And I imagine they did not want him privy to their scheming." Zander fumbles through a stack of loose paper on the expansive table in the center. A map much like the one in Zander's circular war room fills at least half of it.

"Look. They even had portraits drawn of you." I hold up a sketch of Zander. "Not bad, though whoever drew this made your eyes too small. And I wouldn't have used charcoal. The lines are too heavy."

Zander collects the portrait of himself for closer examination before his gaze drifts to the array, pausing on his parents for a beat longer than the rest. "Annika is missing from here."

"They didn't consider her a threat worth studying." Jarek holds up a jar to the lantern light, showing off the dark liquid inside. My tainted blood, no doubt.

"Then they seriously underestimated my sister." Zander's frown is deep. I know he thinks about her often, worries about her. I wish I could have found her and brought her to Ulysede.

"Messages from her many spies." He flips through a stack of unfurled letters in various handwriting. "There must be hundreds of them here. Maybe more."

Abarrane holds up a page. "From Lord Muirn."

"A well-deserved death. What did that snake have to say?" Zander mutters.

She scans it quickly. "Nothing we did not know or suspect. Information on Hudem's festivities, access into Cirilea ..."

I wander over to the bookshelf to check the spines of various leather-bound books. Biographies of kings and queens, royal families, mostly.

"Is there anything of interest here, Your Highness?" Lucretia asks.

"A lot of boring stories."

"You should look more closely at the shelf below it."

I pick up the quill that rests there. "This?"

"Perhaps. There is something here."

"How do you know?"

"Because it glows in silver light, and that means someone has touched this with their affinity."

"You can actually see an affinity?"

"The marks it leaves, yes. Even you wear faint traces, Your Highness, from the wielder who bound you to this world."

Jarek pauses in his inspection of the map. "Wait, was there a light on the lever out there?" He jerks a thumb toward Princess Romeria's chamber.

"Yes. And a trail of it along the wall leading to the fireplace. I saw it right away."

"But we were in that room for almost an hour."

"Yes. I enjoyed watching you search." Lucretia's musical laughter fills the room.

Jarek tosses a flat "Look what I have to put up with" glare my way.

But I'm more interested in what might be hidden in here. Inspecting the quill for a moment and then dismissing it, I turn my attention to the shelf, poking and prodding, the base, the sides, the back panel … looking for anything.

Suddenly, it pops open.

Zander notices. "What have you found?"

"I'm not sure." A book and four stone figurines of the fates sit inside. I slide out the book and flip through it, noting the dates and the feminine scroll. Each page is signed off with the initial *N*. Recognition has my heart racing. "I think this is Neilina's journal." Or something like it. It's not a daily recounting. Months pass between entries, years, even. And the entries span … I do a double take at the first record, to ensure I'm reading this accurately. It reminds me how old she was. How old *I* will be one day, living in this elven body.

"Has she admitted her role in her husband's death? Or perhaps her exploits with Tiberius?" Zander smirks.

"I don't think it's that kind of journal." As I scan the first entry and then the second, a sinking realization takes hold. "Oh my God." I cover my mouth. *Of course.*

How could we not have assumed as much?

"What is it?" All humor has slipped from Zander's voice.

"Ianca wasn't the first elemental to summon the fates for Neilina."

Tyree grunts. "*Stop* elbowing me."

"I'm not elbowing you. I'm shifting my weight to get *away* from you." It's not working. Our bodies are tangled in this net, thighs and shoulders and ribs pressed against each other, as we hang high in the air above a growing audience of mortals. I can't even say for how long anymore. The sun left and came back, my stomach growls, and my bladder threatens to burst.

"Yes. By using *your elbows*," he hisses.

"Would you prefer my knees?" I say with mock sweetness, lifting my leg.

His thighs clamp down hard, stopping me just short of connecting with his groin.

I struggle to jerk my leg out of his grip, but he holds me there with his flexed muscles, and I'm capable of doing little else besides rubbing my body against him.

A lazy smile curls his lips. "Yes, I think I prefer this. A little higher and more to the left."

"Release me, pig," I demand through gritted teeth, giving up.

He chuckles, a glimmer of amusement in his eyes. "Or what?"

I slide my dagger from its sheath and hold it up in a silent threat.

Tyree spears me with a warning glare. "You wouldn't dare."

"Wouldn't I? We're in this mess because of you." I sigh dramatically. "But I won't because I don't want to listen to you whine again."

He rolls his eyes. "Here, let me see if I can cut through this netting.

I've never seen such a metal. I do not know what it is made from." He holds out his hand.

I glare at it. "I am *not* granting you my dagger. Use your sword."

"How am I supposed to draw that given our current predicament? Besides, it's dull." He waits, his gaze boring into mine. "I'm giving you a choice to be amiable, Annika. You don't think I could strip you of it if I wanted to?"

"Not if I know you are going to try—"

With a lightning-quick move, Tyree clamps his fist around my wrist.

"No!" I try to wrestle it away, the move bringing him farther on top of me.

"Would you *let go* so I can—"

I do as asked and the blade falls.

The mortals waiting below jump back with shouts, several uttering words in that foreign tongue as my dagger lands in the grass with a thud. A man rushes forward to collect it.

I assume it's as good as gone forever.

"Now look what you've done," I complain, acutely aware of Tyree's weight on me and where my thigh presses between his legs.

"What *I've* done. If you had just—" His jaw clenches. "You are the most obstinate person I have ever had the displeasure of knowing in all my—oof!" His words cut off with a groan of agony as I swiftly lift my knee.

"I'm sorry, what were you saying?" I smile up at him.

He breathes through the pain. "I was trying to see if I could free us. Traps like these are not set for welcomed visitors, and those caught in them aren't treated well."

When he says it like that … I study where the net is affixed to the tree above us. "Can you not break that branch with your affinity?" Based on what he displayed earlier, his connection to Aminadav is powerful. Far more so than mine.

He peers over his shoulder to where I'm focused. "Not a bad idea. In this position, you would bear the brunt of the fall."

"You say that and yet earlier, you dove to protect me from that beam. Do not think I didn't notice." I raise my eyebrow in challenge.

"I also conspired to kill your entire family. Did you not notice that?"

That reminder stays my tongue.

Tyree sighs. "On second thought, there is nothing to say breaking that branch will untangle us from this netting before those people attack."

I angle my head to get a better look below. "That's a lot of pitch-forks," I agree.

"Even simple farmers can do serious damage under threat. And do you smell that stench in the air?"

"Besides you?" I throw back without thinking, earning his scowl. In truth, Tyree doesn't smell unpleasant at all—like orange blossoms mixed with clean sweat and seawater. I may not crave his blood anymore, but still appeals to me. "Yes. What is it?" Besides some-thing foul.

"Burning flesh."

I shudder. "It has lingered all night." The crackling flames of the pyres have played as background music.

"It can't be anything good. And that language they speak—I have never heard it before. Have you?"

I shake my head.

"Perhaps it is a Seacadorian dialect—"

"*That* is not any dialect of Seacadore. We have enough of them living in our city that I would know."

"In any case, I prefer our odds up here rather than down there. I think our best plan is to hang until we come up with a better plan." His gaze drifts over my face, stalling on my mouth.

"Anytime you'd like to move ..."

He rolls onto his back, fitting beside me. "Better?"

"Not much."

He shuts his eyes.

"What are you doing? *Sleeping*?"

"May as well. Nothing else to do." He pauses. "Unless you'd like to go back to humping my leg. Our spectators seemed entertained."

"More like horrified on my behalf."

"Suit yourself, but I will be well rested."

My stomach chooses that moment to growl.

"What Princess Annika would do for one of those dreadful sea biscuits now, I imagine," Tyree muses. "Here, will this help?" He stretches the collar of his tunic to expose the hard lines of his collar-bones and the pad of muscle peeking beneath. "You're welcome to it." A playful grin touches his lips as he tips his head to the side, his eyes still closed.

Such a thick, columnar neck for a treacherous villain. It's one of my favorite parts of a male, and it has nothing to do with the pulsing vein that runs through it. Though, that always helped …

Zander chastised me for indulging in blood daily rather than building up a tolerance, and I laughed at him. I'm a royal princess. Why would I deprive myself of such a need, as well as a pleasure?

Since the poison took hold, I saw merit in his scolding. But now, it no longer matters.

It's not the first time Tyree has taunted me like this, but it's the boldest. If my thirst for blood hadn't mysteriously vanished, if I truly were suffering right now, this proximity—an attractive male neck, offered—would be torture after this many days, poison or not.

My spite flares, coaxing me to lean in and inhale deeply. "Maybe the siren healed you of more than your leg wound," I whisper. "What if that poison is no longer there?"

Tyree's body stiffens. "That is not something you should risk finding out, Annika."

"Why not? You wanted me dead, anyway." I flatten my tongue and slide it across his jugular, tasting the salt on his skin.

His breath hitches, and his heart rate leaps. It's not the speedy pulse of fear, and it's certainly not hatred. Though, he can still hate me while wanting to fuck me, I suppose. But he knows what it feels like to be fed upon—he admitted as much. This Jada who wounded his heart for his blood, I'm sure she taught him how intimate the act could be, and I'm sure he thoroughly enjoyed it.

"If I am to die soon, anyway …" I repeat the tongue drag, this time letting my teeth scrape along with it.

Tyree seizes my chin within his grasp, pulling my face far enough away to check for fangs. A shallow breath skates across my cheek. "You are teasing me."

The simple but dominating move stirs a need deep in my belly. I've always preferred a male with a little fight in him—a rare treasure to find when you're a princess in line for the throne, bedding mortals and foolish elven with lofty ambitions. "As you are me, except your version is far crueler."

Long lashes flutter as he meets my gaze, showing me odd sincerity. "You are right. I am sorry."

Any response I could dig out from my gaping mouth is cut off as heavy footfalls approach. I recognize the sound of armor. We twist in our net sack to see a horde of soldiers marching forward.

"Let me do the talking," Tyree whispers, studying them intently.

"Oh, you suddenly speak their language?"

"They're soldiers. Trust me, they'll manage to get their point across."

With violence, he means.

The one at the front barks something at us.

When we don't respond, he yells it again while patting his sword.

"We do not understand," Tyree calls out in a deep, authoritative voice, reminding me of that day he was hauled before Zander in Cirilea's throne room, a captured enemy, bloodied, but still somehow regal as he demanded a parley.

The soldier removes his scabbard, points at us, then drops his to the ground.

"He wants me to surrender my weapon."

"Don't do that!"

"And what am I going to do with it otherwise?" Tyree hesitates long enough for the soldier to yell at him again, his agitation growing.

Unfastening his sword is as tricky as Tyree anticipated, forcing him half on top of me again as he squirms. Finally free, he feeds it through a hole in the netting and lets it fall.

Another soldier swiftly collects it and moves out of the way.

The leader issues a command, and another draws his sword, moving for a rope affixed to another tree.

Tyree grabs onto my hips. "This is going to—"

The net gives away and we drop to the ground, landing in a heap.

"Hurt," Tyree groans, somehow having positioned himself beneath me to take the worst of it.

Before either of us can move, soldiers collect the corners of the sack and tow us through the clearing.

"Where are they taking us?" I wince as stones and twigs scrape and tear at my skin and dress.

For once, Tyree doesn't have an answer.

Past the row of trees are small huts with thatched roofs, surrounded by wagons and washbasins. Clotheslines hang between the houses, draped with linens. This must be the farmers' village. Small children in ragged tunics and breeches cling to their mothers' legs as they watch the parade of soldiers drag us past.

A wooden door sits in splinters, likely broken apart by force. A few houses down, another. Other houses are marked with raking claw marks on their sides, from some manner of unruly beast. It appears a battle was fought here recently.

And that stench grows stronger.

Angling my neck, I get my first look at the firepit ahead. It's sizable, the flames licking wood stacked high into the air, and it blazes, even in the day.

That's ... a foot in there. And another. And an arm.

There is no mistaking the charred limbs stacked within, feeding the fire.

Human limbs.

Or maybe elven.

And the soldiers are moving toward it.

Terror seizes my lungs. "Fates, they're going to burn us." I should have given Tyree the dagger; we should have risked pitchforks to break free. We should have done *everything* we could to escape. "I endured an uprising and a kidnapping, and sirens and the sea, and now I am to be burned alive?" I grapple at my affinity, aiming to tangle the soldiers' boots in the lengthy grass, to pelt them with the stones, but I can't grasp anything, my hysteria too strong. "Do something, Tyree! You have your affinity. Use it to stop them—"

"Annika!" Tyree's palm lands on my cheek, forcing my eyes to meet his. "Calm down. They are not taking us to the fire," he assures me, nodding ahead to a nearby wagon I hadn't noticed in my panic.

Sure enough, we're towed up the wooden ramp by four soldiers. I wince against the rough grain as soldiers climb in and surround us, their blades aimed at our faces.

The two soldiers closest to me ogle my chest as they utter something in their language.

"They won't lay a hand on you," Tyree whispers in my ear, startling me. I'm surprised he even noticed.

"How do you know that?" Because the way the soldier on the left stares at me, I would argue otherwise.

"Because I won't allow it. I am your betrothed, remember?" Tyree ropes an arm around my waist, pulling me closer to him. He meets their leers with a murderous glare.

For once, I don't fight him or his ridiculous claim, huddling closer as the wagon rolls forward along the bumpy ground, the wheels creaking.

The sun sets and yet the journey continues, plodding along. Eventually, I have nothing better to do but drift off.

I WAKE with a start to gruff voices in that strange, abrasive tongue. My head is nestled in the crook of Tyree's arm. The air has chilled considerably since yesterday.

"Good morning, Princess," he murmurs, his voice husky from sleep.

"Don't call me that." I blink away the bleariness and note the pale pink sky above. Somehow, we slept through the night.

"Isn't that what you are?"

"Yes, but you're not using it to respect my status. It's nothing more than a pet name, and I despise pet names." I pull away, but he tightens his grip, keeping me in place.

"As you wish, *Your Highness*. But you are free to refer to me as your prince in case you were wondering."

"I was not."

"Or Ty. That is what my friends call me."

"You do not have any friends."

My head lifts with his heavy inhale, and when I steal a glance at his face, I find him grinning. "What are you so happy about?"

"Just thrilled to share another sunrise with your delightful company."

Before I can throw back a suitable barb, the wagon halts and the soldiers pile out.

Tyree's mirth from a moment ago evaporates with a groan. "Get ready—"

Our sleepy, aching bodies jerk forward as they drag us out by the netting. Again, Tyree manages to pull me on top of him before we hit the ground with a thud. His head smacks against the stone.

The sound draws my wince. That would have been *my* head had he not moved to protect me. "Are you okay?"

He answers with a moan, slipping his fingers to the back of his skull. They return with drops of blood.

The leader barks, and the netting is unfastened and thrown off. With the sharp ends of a dozen swords pointed at us, he orders us to our feet with an "up" gesture.

I must not move fast enough, my body stiff from this neverending ordeal, because a nearby soldier jabs my thigh with his sword pommel. I cry out from the pain.

"Do not touch her!" Tyree shoves himself between us.

With a sneer, the leader draws his sword back for a swing, his intention clear. But he's stopped by a deep holler from somewhere unseen. They all, leader included, snap to attention.

The pause gives me a moment to gather my bearings. We've left the rainforest and entered a city of tall stone buildings and streets lined with onlookers who watch quietly—peasants, by their drab wool clothing and sunken faces.

A loud creak sounds as the grand golden gate swings open. It's as tall as Cirilea's castle. The road beyond it disappears into a dewy, thick fog.

A group of soldiers emerges, these dressed in gleaming armor and moving in formation. I've seen my share of royal guards to recognize this as one. Their faces are unyielding as they tug two grimy men along, led by chains bound to their wrists and ankles. Prisoners, by the looks of it, and by the various gashes marring their arms and legs, not treated well.

Is this to be us?

A soldier with a black plume sticking from his helm strolls up, directing the others to bring the prisoners forward with a wave. He must be the captain. He reminds me of Boaz, his expression equally hard.

The two mortals shake as they're shoved toward us. With a one-word command, the keepers of their chains draw hooked blades.

I slink closer to Tyree.

But the weapons aren't meant for us. With quick swipes, the throats of both prisoners are carved wide open. Crimson gushes out in a steady flow as they gurgle their last breaths and a metallic tang fills the air.

Cries of dismay erupt from the spectators around us as the two men collapse, their blood seeping into the seams of the stonework where they land. They were likely known to these people.

The guard with the plume gives an order and soldiers step forward, yelling at us in their native tongue.

"We don't understand you!" Tyree snaps, using his arm to herd me behind him. But a sword point in my hip has me yelping and jumping back in place. Three more at Tyree's neck freeze him from whatever next move he wishes to take.

A soldier grabs hold of my jaw, squeezing until my mouth is forced open with my cry of pain. He shoves his thumb under my upper lip, pulling it up.

I realize what they're doing—checking for fangs. If I still had them, there would be no way to keep them in after that bloody display, repulsed as I am.

Tyree gets the same treatment.

The captain, seemingly satisfied, barks another order and the soldiers step away, dropping their swords.

The next seconds are a blur.

Tyree spins on his heels, throwing elbows and fists that crack jaws and noses before he strips the closest soldier of his sword. In a blink, he cuts through three with deft swings of the blade and impales a fourth, finishing with his sword's edge pressed against the captain's throat. "Release us, or I will kill him and every one of you!" Tyree yells, fury flashing in his blue eyes.

I believe him. Witnessing what he just did, he *could* kill every last one of these guards and escape. I've never seen anyone fight with such skill, and I've watched my brothers spar. How our legionaries ever captured him in the first place is beyond me.

I hiss at the sharp prick against my neck, cutting into my flesh. A soldier stands behind me, growling something in their language that is likely similar to Tyree's ultimatum.

Tyree curses as he sees my predicament. His wild eyes dart around us, assessing, until they settle on a nearby horse. He could make it to that. It's close enough that he could run, mount it, and gallop away, leaving me to my fate.

He grits his teeth.

Fates, he's considering it. The bastard is going to leave me here to—

He tosses his sword to the ground and raises his hands in the air.

The captain answers with a hard punch to his cheek that snaps Tyree's head to the side. He winds back for a second.

A sharp cry from inside the gates stalls his swing.

Suddenly, the soldiers are retreating, the one holding me hostage moving swiftly away. They part into two lines on either side of the gate, forming a corridor to pass, and bow their heads. Their entire demeanor has changed, from combative to obedient.

The captain gestures wordlessly toward the opening, the order clear. If it's even an order. Where does this lead? Are we better off trying to run?

I meet Tyree's gaze, only to see my confusion reflected in his eyes.

He sidles up next to me, his head on a swivel.

"Did you honestly think you could kill all twenty of them?" I whisper. His cheek is split, the blood running in a rivulet down his face.

"It was worth a shot." He sizes up the line of soldiers behind us, waiting to usher us in. "Okay, on the count of three, you are going to run for that horse as fast as—"

"*Kal'ana.*" A man in luxurious red robes appears at the gate's entrance. He bows and then hobbles forward, his skeletal hand gripping a knotty-wood cane for support. "It is a great honor. Please, come forward. You will be safe within these gates."

Tyree and I exchange looks.

"Thank fates, *someone* we can understand," he speaks softly.

"But can we trust him?"

"We don't have to trust him to get information from him. Would you rather fight through their armies?" The brutes who dragged us here hover in the background, waiting.

I sigh. "I suppose we do not have much other choice."

Slowly, we move past the guard, side by side.

The man who waits is ancient. I cannot guess how old—his hollowed cheeks, sparse white hair, and age-spotted scalp suggest he lives far beyond his mortal kind. But it's his eyes that are the most unsettling, his irises reminding me of a murky swamp. At first, I wonder if he can even see, but the way his pupils bore into me, I'm sure he can.

He bows again. "We have prayed for the kal'ana to arrive, and here you are." His accent is thick and harsh, but Tyree is right. It is a relief to have someone who speaks our language.

That's the second time he's used that term. I open my mouth to ask what this kal'ana is.

"Where are we?" Tyree cuts in, skipping pleasantries.

The man smiles, showing off gray, decayed teeth. He seems unfazed by Tyree's brusque manner. "You are inside the gates of the Temple of Light, and you are safe here."

"Yes, but which realm?" Tyree pushes.

"You are in Udrel."

30

ATTICUS

The metal cuffs dig into my ankles and wrists as the guards usher me along the corridor, the chains scraping stone. They rushed into my cage this morning as I was drifting off after a night of mentally playing through escape scenarios. With seven swords pressed against my body, I had little choice but to lie still while they affixed them.

It's as if they knew what I had planned.

At least the journey to my execution is picturesque. Morning rays highlight drops from last night's rain on the petals and leaves of a nearby garden, where small children chase birds. This humble side of the palace is different from the ostentatious one I saw yesterday. More peaceful, even with fifteen guards at my side.

"Up!" The guard prods my back with his gauntlet, directing me toward yet another set of stairs to the top floor. Whatever Cheral has planned, it will happen up there. "Faster!"

"It's not easy, you know." I take my time—much to their annoy-ance—but, really, I'm straining against the chains with each step. I've had years of practice escaping similar binds in training. Whatever this metal is, it will not break, and it bites.

Heavy doors wait ahead, with more guards on either side.

My adrenaline rushes with my anxiety as they usher me inside.

It's the same sitting room as yesterday. There are no children or wives today, though. There is only King Cheral, sitting in his customary white chair. This is far too nice a room for an execution.

But I did behead a lord in my own throne room, so who am I to judge?

"*Our guest* seems on edge this morning." King Cheral takes a long sip from his mug. "Did you not sleep well?"

"My sleep was delightful. Thank you for asking," I lie.

"The guards said you seemed restless. Are the accommodations not to your satisfaction?"

I snort. Is *that* what the guards said ... I would be foolish to think the king doesn't know about my visitor. He likely has his conjurer spying on me through the rodents.

"Come," he beckons, waving me toward him. "Enjoy a morning tea."

"*Tea.*"

"Yes. That is what we call it. Is that not what Islorians call it?"

What is this new game he plays, trying to lull me into a false sense of safety?

"Oh! I almost forgot. Take those off." He waves a dismissive hand at his guards, who comply without hesitation, removing my manacles.

Suddenly, I'm free, and more confused than ever.

I roll my shoulder, testing it. Each day brings significant healing where I took the ax, though I don't know if I'm strong enough to fight fifteen guards. I suppose I'll find out soon enough.

A guard jabs my back with his hilt, forcing me forward in a stumble. I grit my teeth. Him, I will kill first. "Your men could use some lessons in manners around your *guests*," I drawl, crossing the room at an even pace.

Movement in a corner catches my eyes.

Tuella is here. Observing me or protecting the king, or both. I have no idea what the conjurer is capable of, but I must assume she's proficient in stopping me from killing her mortal king, especially since the guards remain at the door.

"Please. Sit." King Cheral gestures at a chair.

I can't help but frown as I slide in. This is not the start to the day I toiled over in bed last night after Satoria's visit.

He fills another mug before setting the pot down. "An old favorite family blend. A mixture of beetroot, cardamom, and apple. Some find it bitter." He motions to the bowl of cane sugar.

"Please do not take this the wrong way, but do you offer your favorite blend of tea to all you plan on executing? Or is the tea your method? A poison to burn me from the inside out."

King Cheral's eyes flash with surprise, but then he chuckles. "The tea is simply tea." He doesn't deny his plans for execution.

When I still don't reach for my mug, he makes a point of recollecting the pot and filling his own mug to brimming, then taking another long sip. "King Malachi has executed Lord Adley of Kettling."

"Did your kell tell you this?" My gaze flickers to where Tuella stands, silent.

"No, I received word early this morning. The king killed him in the throne room, with a flaming whip that appeared out of thin air."

"Sounds like a tall tale."

"After what you witnessed with the seeing stone yesterday, does it truly?" He peers at me over the rim of his mug.

I use the tea as an excuse, taking a long sip as I consider that. "I planned to execute Adley when I returned from the east, so this king has done Islor a favor."

"Islor, perhaps, but not Kier. My kingdom sacrificed much to amass such an army, and now it waits for orders to invade, and I hesitate about what to tell them."

"That is easy. Leave my realm and return to Kier. Or let them stay there to fight off the Nulling beasts when they travel deeper into Islor, which they will. I'm sure you won't lose more than *half* your men to those things."

King Cheral smiles, but there is sadness and disappointment in his eyes. "I was promised the spoils of rich lands if I aided Kettling's cause. Something tells me that is unlikely to come to fruition now."

"Are you looking for sympathy from me? You, sitting here in your pristine palace, drinking your tea? Because you will not see it, not even at the end of a sword's blade. I could have told you never to forge an alliance with the likes of Lord Adley."

"And yet you yourself did, when you proposed marriage to his daughter."

"A terrible attempt to keep my enemies close, which is why I made a terrible leader." I hoist my mug up to toast the air before letting the warmth slide down my throat. Fates, this *is* bitter.

"Politically, yes. But your achievements leading an army on the battlefield have been touted far and wide."

"And it is where I should have stayed."

He cocks his head. "Why didn't you? Why did you betray your own brother? Was it the glory of a kingdom?"

"I had more than enough glory to satiate my ego. No ... I thought

I was saving him from himself while also protecting my realm. But it is clear now that I may have caused more harm than good." It may have been Romeria who cursed Islor with her tainted blood, but it also seems to be Romeria who works to save it now. Which version of her, though, remains a mystery to me. "What do you know of the fates?"

"Your gods with their horns? Have you seen any grand statues around my palace?"

"During one of my many tours?" My voice drips with sarcasm.

He takes a sip. "If you were to ask a Kier or a Skatranan about Islor, I imagine they would at first claim they have never been. But then they would fill your ear with information about the people, the land, the curse."

"Your point?"

"Islor has only ever been interested in Islor, and you believe your way is the only way." He smirks. "I know what I need to of your fates, but I do not concern myself with them. Kier follows the way of Udrel."

"And which way is that?"

Tuella emerges from her corner. "The way of shadow and light. Our beliefs are rooted in that of balance, both that which we can see and that which we cannot."

A vague explanation, but my curiosity is piqued. "If I recall my childhood teachings about Kier—which you assume I have had none —that was not always the case."

"That is true," King Cheral admits. "Once, long ago, we were influenced by our neighbors to believe differently. Mordain's wielders used to arrive at our shores to educate us on the way of their creators. And most in Kier welcomed such notions. But these fates of theirs who grant children connected to the land's power have never bestowed Kier such consideration, have never given us an opportunity to converse with them, to ask them for gifts. So what reason would we have to honor them with sanctums and statues made of precious metals and stone?"

"Islor has not seen a caster born within its borders in two millennia either."

"And yet you still bow at their feet," Tuella asks. "Why?"

Her question gives me pause. "I suppose because they are all that we have ever known."

"And now that you know me?"

"Honestly, I do not know what or who you are."

"That is understandable. Not everyone in Kier has embraced the way of shadow and light yet."

"And if Udrel's conjurers aren't born by the grace of these fates' power, how do *you* exist?"

Her small smile borders on smug. "We are chosen."

"*Chosen.* By whom?"

"By the light."

I shake my head. "Listening to you speak, it is as if I am looking outside at that sky that is clearly blue, and you are insisting it is green."

"And yet both our convictions would be equally strong."

Something tells me I could talk in circles around this one and never get to the center unless she wishes me there. But I need answers. "What do you know of our fates and what is happening in my realm?"

She glances at King Cheral, who nods once, as if granting permission.

"The balance has shifted. I felt it even before your blood moon, but since that night, light and shadow both radiate, almost as if in competition with each other."

"What does that even mean?"

Worry pinches her features. "I do not yet know, except to say there is much shadow and also much light. Too much of either does not allow balance."

King Cheral sets his mug down. "I received word from my general. The day after your Hudem, as you call it, his scout spotted one of those scaly winged beasts landing in the plains, at the site of the battle."

A change in subject. Fine. I can't understand what this bloody conjurer is talking about, anyway. "What did it do here?"

"Besides swallow a horse nearly whole? Nothing. But a male and a female flew within its clutches. They searched the bodies thoroughly and then left with a soldier."

"Alive or dead?"

"My scout did not specify, other than to say they seemed very interested in that one in particular. I wonder why that is." He watches me evenly as I process this bit of information.

Could Zander and Romeria be looking for me? In that case, who would they have taken? I know who *I* would collect—the male who knows me better than myself in some ways. Kazimir. But there would only be one reason to take him—if he was alive to give answers.

"I suppose it is a good thing they didn't continue farther east. They would have happened upon your Kierish army. Imagine the destruction that beast could cause."

"Yes, it is a blessing. I think that shall be all. Guards, please take our guest back to his accommodations."

I set my mug on the table and stand. "No execution today, then?" Were the chains a ruse or did he change his mind when I got here?

"Not today. Perhaps tomorrow." He studies his fingernails. "My wife claims I am too indecisive to be pragmatic. Satoria, that is. You recall her, do you not? She is the one you refused." He pauses. "When she offered her vein."

Right. "The wife outfitted as a servant." Though she wasn't dressed as such last night. She wasn't dressed at all. I bite my tongue against that taunt, though something tells me it wouldn't come as a surprise to him. "I know you have three others to console you, but I find it odd that you would present her so freely to a prisoner such as myself. Her vein, that is."

The corners of his mouth curve upward, and then he flicks two fingers toward the door, dismissing me.

This is the game we shall play.

So be it.

31

ROMERIA

Dawn peeks past the sheer window dressings when I reach the last page of Neilina's diary, my eyes bleary from lack of sleep. "Eight times," I call out into the quiet room.

Zander looks up from the desk. A stack of sealed letters sits in a tidy pile, ready for Mordain's messenger casters to deliver on swift wings. They're not only to Ybaris's ruling class, though. There are letters signed by Zander and addressed to Islorian lords and ladies, announcing our alliance and his intention to reclaim his throne.

"Neilina had her elementals summon the fates *eight* times." Wendeline once told me that to summon a fate as an elemental, you were basically bound to them for life. But Neilina had access to hundreds of elementals over her years as queen. She could reach out to *any* of the fates with no limits. Except Malachi, of course, because those with an affinity to him were all killed at birth.

"They answered five of them." Three summons were ignored, much to Neilina's fury, based on her scathing entries. She blamed the elementals and had them poisoned in the night, with false claims they had succumbed to the change and died within hours of falling ill. "No wonder she insisted on keeping them here, on a leash."

"It is not a surprise that a ruler with access to power would use it, despite laws and oaths against doing so. We should have assumed as much." Zander stands and makes his way to the grand bed where I've settled, peeling layers of clothing and weapons off as he approaches. "Nor is it a surprise that the elementals would agree to save their own skin." The featherbed sinks with his weight beside me.

"Two refused. She executed them for treason."

"A subject who does not submit is of no use." His eyelids are growing heavy, despite the topic. His kind can run on little sleep, but he looks tired. "So, what did she ask of the fates?"

"Once for Aminadav to heal the farmland damaged by the rift he made."

"He certainly didn't do that."

"That's the thing. Apparently, he did. For a hundred years, the land produced again."

His eyes flash open. "An apology from a fate?"

"She doesn't say anything about an apology. She asked and he answered, and they had crops again. People built homes and entire villages around the outskirts, trade picked up. And then suddenly, everything toppled again. At first, the farmers thought it was a strange blight, but the next year, nothing grew. So, Neilina made another elemental summon Aminadav again and asked him for more." *Demanded* it is more like it, if the words in her journal are anything like what she said to him. "She insisted that the fates owed her after what they had done to her realm."

"And?" Zander listens, intrigued.

"And they woke up overnight to all these fields bursting with new crops."

His eyebrow arches. "Aminadav gave her what she wanted again?"

"She thought so. Neilina told the people it was her elemental casters who healed the land. The Ybarisans praised her and named a harvest festival in her honor. And then people started getting sick. Stomachaches and fevers, feeling like their insides were burning. Mordain's healers kept healing people and then they'd get sick again. They couldn't fix it. No one tied it to the crops until the dead middle of winter, when people stepped into their storerooms and found everything turned black with rot, overnight."

"Telling a fate they owe you is not the way to win favor."

"It says the only thing that survived Aminadav's blight were the oats."

"Which is what the people of Ybaris survived on for many years. But even the oat fields have given way to the rot in recent decades, according to King Barris." Zander shakes his head. "Mordain should have clued in to what Neilina had done."

"They did. The Prime at the time, named"—I flip through the pages to find the entry—"Circe, she questioned Neilina. She wanted to know which elementals healed the land, but Neilina knew Circe suspected the truth." There is a six-page entry about it in the journal. "So to cover her tracks, Neilina had the Prime and the elemental executed that same day, announcing that they had schemed to poison the Ybarisans."

"And Mordain bought that?"

"No. They stopped sending her elementals." There is one fury-laced page of Neilina's plans to cut off Mordain from Ybaris and its gifted children, to keep and train them for herself, using those she trusted. She would build her own Mordain within Ybaris.

"That's what instigated the war between Neilina and Mordain." Zander hums as pieces fall into place. "Was she foolish enough to summon Aminadav again?"

"*No.* She swore him off and moved on to Vin'nyla, assuming that because her affinity was to her that she would be favored. Three different elementals summoned Vin'nyla on three occasions before she gave up." And killed them for their failure—or simply to silence them. "So she summoned Aoife, who answered immediately."

"And gave us the gift of Princess Romeria?"

"Not yet. The first time they summoned her, she begged Aoife to heal Ybaris's lands. Aoife told her that she couldn't undo what Aminadav had done, and that the only way forward was to reclaim Islor. Aoife convinced her that it was rightfully theirs and they needed those lands if Ybaris was to survive. So, she persuaded Barris to wage war. It took time but finally, he agreed."

"Yes, I recall," Zander says dryly. "One century ago. They lost."

"And she blamed him for that." Her loathing for her husband and his wishes for an allegiance practically leapt off the pages. "She summoned Aoife again and this time asked her for help in defeating Islor."

"Princess Romeria."

I shake my head. "That was the last summoning, when she asked for a weapon that would kill them all." It happened just like Ianca told Gesine it had, with Neilina and her queen's army commander fucking on the altar in the sanctum before a fate they could not even see. The only visible proof that she'd been there was the golden antlers in Ianca's hand—a valuable token for protection and healing that Neilina must always wear. That and the baby that arrived nine months later, with blood that would one day start a war. "This second summoning, Aoife promised her an ally."

"The saplings?"

"Kier."

Zander frowns, considering that. "Islor and Kier have been at odds for centuries. Are you telling me Neilina was behind this army invading from the east? That she was working with Adley?" His voice is heavy with shock. "That's impossible. Even he would not partner with her."

"It doesn't say anything about Adley in here. All it says is what Aoife told Neilina through the caster, that"—I flip to the pages to where her curly penmanship marked down the words—"the way to defeat Islor would be to weaken them first so they could not fight off threats from two sides. Aoife would poison Kier, forcing them to look to Islor to solve their problems." If Neilina was keeping tabs on the goings-on of Kier, she didn't include them in this journal.

"Look to Islor, not Ybaris."

"That's what it says."

Zander studies the ceiling. "King Cheral has never approached us for aid of any sort. Neither did his father. Look to Islor *how*?"

"Doesn't say. Maybe Kier's king was working with Neilina and Adley didn't know it. But poison seems to be Aoife's thing."

"There would need to be a reason for Kier to ally with *anyone*, so what did Aoife do to them? We should have kept closer tabs on that realm."

I study his handsome face as he bites his bottom lip in thought.

He inhales sharply. Something important has clicked. "The best spot for Lord Adley to battle for territory and win would have been at the Sanguine River. Between his men and Kier's army, they could have claimed that side of Islor and held it for themselves without issue. But they crossed the Sanguine and headed into the Plains of Aminadav. They wanted that land. Or what it could produce."

"Isn't the harvest what your father and King Barris negotiated for in exchange for Princess Romeria?"

"Yes, it is valuable. But Kier has an abundance of rich and fertile lands. They've traded with Kettling for years. Why risk sending a vast army of mortals into a realm with a blood curse to fight someone else's cause unless you are gaining something valuable in return? Something you don't have." He taps his bottom lip with his index finger. "There have been raiding parties from Kier at harvest time, bands of thieves and misfits. Atticus has plenty of stories. The captured would all sing the same tune, complaining of a king who didn't share his bounty. But if the king himself is willing to send a vast army through, like the size Bexley described, perhaps he no longer has his bounty."

I'm beginning to see where his thoughts are heading. "Because Aoife poisoned the land."

"The fates have done it before. The proof is in that book." He nods to the journal in my hand.

If Aminadav used the earth against Neilina ... "Aoife's element is water," I think out loud. "So she contaminated the water that feeds the land. The rivers, maybe?"

"Maybe. The only way to find out would be to go to Kier to ask the king himself." This time when he blinks, his eyelids settle for a few seconds.

"We *could*, you know. Go and see this King Cheral."

"You just want to witness my brother in chains."

"Call that a bonus." I smirk. But I know Zander thinks of him often. I can sense it.

He sighs. "Let us sort things out here first. But something tells me Aoife has been scheming for as long as Malachi to return." His eyes shutter again.

And yet she isn't here. So where is she? I stroke a stray hair off his forehead but keep my thoughts to myself. He needs sleep.

Through the window, a dark shadow cuts across the pastel sky, its wings stretching out on either side of its beastly form as it patrols from above.

Sliding off the bed, I rush to the windowsill. And smile. She's returned in the morning, like I asked her to. "Caindra." It's not a yell. It's barely above a whisper.

Her massive body pivots in the air, angling toward Argon.

I throw up an arm and wave, hoping she might spot the motion in the window, so she knows where I am, knows that I'm safe.

She answers with a layered screech that sets the hairs on the back of my neck on end and stirs shouts of alarm from down below.

"I probably should have warned the guards about her, huh?" When I don't get a response, I glance over my shoulder.

Zander is fast asleep.

Less than thirty seconds later, Caindra lands on a spire, her claws raking for purchase. Precious jewels of Argon's famed castle roof rain down.

Master Healer Brigitta is waiting for us when we arrive in the infirmary an hour later, sparing a guarded look for Zander and the legionaries. The bags under her eyes are heavy, the whites of them bloodshot. All signs of a healer who depleted their affinity helping another.

"Where is Allegra?" Zaleria is asleep in one of the beds, but the Second is nowhere to be found.

"She is awake and with the other Second in a room down the hall," Brigitta confirms. "She will make a full recovery."

I sigh with relief. All our plans around Mordain have hinged on Allegra surviving this. "What about the scribe?"

She leads us over to the still form tucked under blankets. "I fear there is nothing more we can do for Caster Zaleria."

"What if I try?"

Her smile is gentle. "That is kind of you, but it is not so simple as healing tissue and bone, Your Highness."

I study the still caster. Her eyes are shut. "What did the Prime do to them?"

"She picked through their minds, thread by thread, searching for information. Allegra was strong enough to resist, but Zaleria's mind has been ... shredded, for lack of a better word. It is more fractured than that of a seer now, and those minds cannot be healed, even by a key caster."

"I had no idea casters could do that."

Brigitta pats Zaleria's forearm. "It is a special skill that one with an affinity to Aoife can master, if they so choose. Most of us spend our efforts learning how to heal with our gift, not destroy. The Prime saw value in the latter."

My shoulders sink. "This is going to crush Agatha."

Zander smooths a comforting hand over my back. "You have done all that you can. This is beyond your control. We must look ahead."

Brigitta watches us. "So, it is true, then. Ybaris has allied with Islor."

"I don't think you've officially met." I gesture between the two of them. "Master Healer Brigitta, this is King Zander."

"Your Highness." She dips her head in greeting. "I must say, an Islorian king dressed as a Shadow was almost as shocking as a Ybarisan queen masquerading as an old scribe."

"And you did not attempt to strike me dead in the skiff on the way over. I will consider that progress," he muses.

"I am not a fool." She hesitates. "I heard an interesting story from

Caster Serenis. She is an elemental and one of our most proficient healers."

"Red hair. I met her at the rift. She crossed to our side to heal the injured soldiers. She was working on someone very important to us," Zander says with a frown, likely wondering where this is going, as am I.

"Yes, well, she has plum rooms in the caster tower here, one with a large window that overlooks the royal wing. It grants a view into His Highness's chambers when the curtains are not drawn. Such was an occasion on the night of Hudem's moon, when king and peasant alike observe the silver light. Serenis was perched on her windowsill when she heard a scuffle. Queen Neilina and the commander were in the king's chamber. Serenis saw the queen plunge the dagger into King Barris's chest while Caedmon Tiberius held him down."

Zander's eyebrows pop. "She witnessed the murder. And by Neilina's own hand."

"There was no Islorian assassin in sight. Needless to say, Serenis was terrified of what she had seen."

"Did she tell anyone?" I ask.

"Yes. *Me*. And I instructed her to remain quiet until such time as it made sense to speak. There was no point, other than to get herself killed."

Given all that I just read in that journal—about the lengths Neilina would go to, to hide her crimes—it was good advice.

A slow smile touches Brigitta's lips. "Now, I think it might be time to speak. People should know the truth. They should know Islor is not to blame."

Zander dips his head. "Thank you for your help, Master Healer."

She answers with a bow. "As you've so wisely put it, we must all look ahead."

"And on that note, it is time Romeria named your new Prime." He turns to me, his expression determined.

SOLANGE MEETS JAREK, Zander, and I outside Allegra's room. All traces of blood from last night's ordeal with Lorel have vanished, and the Shadow leader moves as if it never happened. "She is awake but weak and traumatized. She does not remember much. Certainly not what happened in the guild council chamber."

"Is she aware the Prime is dead?" Zander asks. "And of her new role in Mordain?"

"She is aware of the former. As far as the latter is concerned, she seems to think I have coerced my way into the position." Solange smirks. "I did not correct her false assumption yet, as I felt that news would be best coming from Her Highness. You may speak to her and decide she is not the right one."

"My options are limited." And this ring sits heavy in my pocket.

"What about Mordain? Any word from there?" Zander asks.

"Gaian sent a message early this morning, to inform Her Highness that Ybarisan villages are coming under attack by Nulling beasts. Several in the past days. They have little defense, given the bulk of our army is fighting at the rift."

"We can assume the same is happening in Islor." Zander curses. "Do you trust this caster?"

"That his reports are accurate? Yes. But he is no fool. Gaian is attempting to separate himself from his predecessor but also to curry favor with Her Highness and the new Prime. But it is not a bad thing to have Gaian attempting to please you. He is well respected among the messengers and likely has cultivated as large a network of informants as Barro himself."

"And he would have heard the same rumors and did nothing," I add. But he wouldn't be the only one. There was an actual eyewitness to King Barris's murder who also said nothing for fear of her safety. It's becoming clear that everyone, including the Prime herself, seemed to know that speaking out against the queen would earn them a death sentence.

"We spent the night addressing letters to the lords and ladies of Ybaris and Islor," Zander says. "We must be certain they are delivered with both urgency and accuracy. Can we trust your messengers to do that under this Master Gaian's direction?"

"Yes, I believe you can," Solange says with grim certainty. "Especially if the request comes from the new Prime."

"Then I suppose we should get on with it." Zander reaches for the door handle.

Allegra is standing in front of the window, dressed in robes, her focus outward.

"You have guests," Solange announces, startling the Second enough that she jumps before turning around to face us.

I hadn't realized last night how young she looked compared to the Masters. She must be in her early forties, at most, with caramel-colored hair that sits loose and unkempt at her shoulders. Her complexion is still pale, but her evergreen eyes are lucid as she assesses each of us, stalling on me.

Allegra may have helped Agatha and Gesine, but what does she truly think of having a key caster not only breathing but as Ybaris's queen?

It's a moment before she seems to catch herself and bows. "Your Highness." She nods out the window toward Caindra, still on her perch, basking in the sunlight. "I heard there is a sylx lurking about the castle and that an ancient beast returned to serve as ally."

"I wouldn't let her hear you call her that, if I were you," Jarek warns, drawing Allegra's attention to him, fleetingly.

"I recall a tale or two but never imagined any truth in it. Childhood stories, you know." Her gaze drifts to Zander. "Just as I could never imagine witnessing an Islorian king standing beside Ybaris's queen in Argon's castle."

"Or an Islorian king standing across from two of Mordain's highest guild members. You are no more surprised than I," Zander responds evenly. "But I suspect you will witness a great many things you never imagined possible in the coming months."

"Something tells me you are right." She hesitates. "I was told that I have you all to thank for my rescue."

I nod toward the Shadow leader. "Solange played a big part. So did Agatha."

Mention of the Master Scribe brings a soft, genuine smile to Allegra's lips. "She found you after all. I knew she would."

"That wily one made it all the way to the rift before I discovered her," Solange mutters.

"And how many times has she mentioned her imminent death?" Allegra asks.

I laugh. "At least five times. A day," I add after a beat.

Allegra chuckles. "She was fascinated by news of your great nymph city behind the wall. She would be happy to end her days there if permitted."

"She's in the library, combing through books with the rest of the scribes." And one annoyed Legion warrior.

"Don't be surprised if she asks to be buried with them." She pauses. "And what of Gesine?"

A prick strikes my chest. "She was killed in Cirilea while we were freeing the mortals."

Allegra's brow furrows. "Fates rest her soul, then."

Fuck the fates, I want to say. They're the reason for this disaster. I step deeper into the room. "That library is full of books that we believe hold the answer to how to get rid of Malachi. The scribes are looking for any clue."

"Solange told me he has claimed Islor's throne. And that Aoife is also somewhere, but we do not know where, or what her plans may be." Worry mars her forehead. "What of Malachi's actions?"

I shrug. "Not much, though I doubt that will last."

"He has made no move to claim the armies at the rift yet," Zander adds. "But he has a key caster at his side."

Allegra's eyes flare. "There is a *second* key caster?"

"Because one wasn't bad enough, right?" I say wryly. Let's call a spade a spade. I spent too many months hiding what I was to protect myself.

Zander shoots me a warning glance. He really should learn to appreciate my humor. "Romeria has ended the blood curse and united our two realms. But yes, she is a key caster, and we know the lengths to which Mordain has gone to keep such power out of reach. What is *your* stance on all this?" He watches her closely. I know that look well. He's searching for all the things she doesn't say in her next words.

"I would much prefer one as an ally than an enemy." Allegra bites her bottom lip. "It was inevitable, was it not? The seers foresaw the nymphs return in the age of the caster. If it was not by Her Highness, it would be by another. Prophecy always finds a way."

A wave of déjà vu ripples through me. Gesine said those exact words, more than once.

"The fates are not bound by time as we are. For whatever reason Malachi has to wish to rule here, he would not have stopped in his attempts. That is why I helped Agatha and the scribes in their cause. What Neilina made Ianca do was reckless, but the wheels were in motion the moment a fate wished to walk this plane. Denying or ignoring the seers' visions would have helped no one, despite Mordain's position."

"Those wheels have been in motion a lot longer than we thought." I hold up Neilina's journal and explain what I spent the night reading.

The Seconds' curses are simultaneous.

"A summons is an open invitation to wreak havoc. Who knows how Aoife chose to grant such a request!" Solange spits, fury marring her face.

"We will find out soon enough. But first, things must be in order with Mordain. Do Ybaris and Islor have your full support?" Zander pushes.

Allegra opens her mouth, but hesitates. "What if I said no? What would you do?" She stares at him in challenge for several beats before relenting to the silence. "As the guild's Second, yes, I support any cause that resists the damage a fate may inflict upon our realms. But I do not speak for Mordain. Only the Prime dictates Mordain's position." She looks to Solange.

"Except Solange isn't Mordain's new Prime." I dig into my pocket and pull out the unassuming ring, holding it out to her. "I'm naming you Prime, Allegra. You have helped the scribes and prophecy. We need you to lead Mordain now."

She stares at it, unmoving.

"Your assumption that I care for politics was amusing," Solange says, her voice flat. "I declined the offer."

"Solange is the one who recommended you," I add.

That raises the Second's eyebrows higher. "That is … unexpected."

"Do not waste too much time being honored," Solange says. "And spend even less time deciding, for there is much to do."

Allegra takes a step toward me, but then stops.

"Well?" I hold the ring a touch higher.

A few seconds pass and then Allegra says, "I must decline, Your Highness."

My spirits deflate as my arm flops to my side. "Why?"

Shrewd green eyes meet mine. "Because it is your role to claim."

My head is shaking before I even get the *no* out. "I don't want it."

"'When she rose again as a Daughter of Many and a Queen for All, only then could there be hope for peace among the peoples.' You are this person, you are this hope." She moves forward, her voice growing stronger with each word.

My heart races in my chest, the urge to run from this overwhelming. I turn to glare at Zander. "Did you have something to do with this?"

"As if an Islorian king could sway two guild members." He chuckles. "But you know where I stand."

He wants me to rule Mordain.

"Solange has told me of your vision for our future, as an ally to Ybaris rather than a servant," Allegra says. "You can win the casters on that alone."

"Yes, but—"

236

"Take the Ring of Minerva, and you will wield our full power against Malachi. *You must.* You are the queen for all peoples of this plane—mortal, caster, and elven."

I falter. Beside me, Zander vibrates with energy. I can practically taste his urgency in the air. "But I don't know anything about Mordain."

"You know nothing about Ulysede or Ybaris either," Jarek retorts, earning my sideways glare.

"I will assume the role of Mordain's steward for you," Allegra offers. "I will ensure the guild acts in the best interests of the people. And Solange will lead the casters where you need them most." She looks to her counterpart, her eyebrows raised as if to say "Right?"

Solange steps forward, and together, they kneel. "Mordain is yours to rule, Prime."

My hand shakes, the slight gold band suddenly weighty. I already have two crowns. This modest ring is basically a third.

"We need their might, Romeria," Zander whispers. "You may not want it, but you must take it. At least for now."

I meet Jarek's gaze and he dips his head. He agrees.

I think my blood might gush from my ears at any moment, as hard as my heart is pumping. "Fine. You can call me your Prime if you want, but I won't wear this ring. I'll keep it safe for you, and when this is over, Mordain's guild will decide who should lead. This is the only way I'll agree to this."

The Seconds exchange looks.

"Then we have an accord."

Zander's slow sigh fills my ears.

They climb to their feet, Allegra much slower, with Solange's hand to help her.

I feel faint. "Did you know Allegra would decline?" I hear the accusation in my tone.

The corner of Solange's mouth twitches.

"I *hoped* she would, and I knew you would not claim this of your own volition. You made that very clear," Zander says.

I tuck the band in my pocket for safekeeping. "What now?"

"Now, we write another letter."

I groan.

He slips an arm around my waist and leads me toward the door. "By the way, who is this Genghis Khan?"

A LOW WHISTLE slips from Jarek's lips as he pulls something from a chest in the royal vault.

I let Abarrane, Zander, and Lucretia pass me and pause next to him to see what he's admiring—an Ottoman bracelet studded with sapphires. "I didn't think sparkly things impressed you."

"They don't." His thumb smooths over the stones. "I remember my mother wearing something very similar. Only on special occasions. I imagine she was buried with it."

I've never heard him speak of his family before. "They lived in Lyndel, right? Elisaf mentioned it."

"Of course. The nosy guard who gossips more than the kitchen staff." He frowns, displeased. "Yes, for their entire lives. My father was an army officer until his death."

"In the last war against Ybaris." Jarek was just a boy, according to Elisaf.

"Yes." He sets the bracelet down gingerly.

"You can keep it, if you want." Ybaris won't miss it.

"And what would I do with a bracelet, Romeria? All that I own is on my body."

"Give it to Eden." She would cherish it.

His eyes snap to me. "Why do you say that?"

"Uh ... I don't know?" But I've clearly said the wrong thing.

"He has ended his salacious affair with the servant girl," Lucretia purrs in my ear, suddenly there. "She is heartbroken."

"How do you know that?" Jarek snarls at her while I exclaim, "You did *what*?"

If looks alone could kill, the eye daggers he's stabbing Lucretia with would murder her ten times over.

"What happened?" I ask gently.

"Nothing happened. She is a mortal, and she will live a happy mortal life without me in it." Spinning on his heels, he charges toward the nymph door.

I struggle to keep up. "Jarek!"

"—and I will happily die with my blade in my hand, whether it is tomorrow or years from now. I have no interest in the life she wants. Now that the blood curse is over, she does not need me. And that is all I will say on the matter, Romeria."

I raise my hands in surrender. Dropping my name is as good as telling me to fuck off.

Zander spares a curious glance at my seething legionary. "Let us be done with Ulysede quickly."

I beckon my affinities and feel them twining together like a nest of snakes.

"Your Highness!" A metal fist bangs noisily on the outside of the vault door. "Are you still there?"

That's Yardley's voice. "Yes. Why?"

"The dragons! There are three of them outside now."

"But I just sent Caindra to meet us in Ulysede." I watched her fly away.

"She is back and with more. They seem agitated, Your Highness."

We all share a look.

Zander's face turns grim. "Something must have happened at the rift."

"This is not Udrel."

"And you know this because ..." Annika arches an eyebrow, waiting for an explanation.

"Udrel is to the east, and we sailed the western shores." I graze a fingertip against the gash across my cheek and wince. It might be worse than the split where my skull collided with stone. At least I'll heal quickly, now that my body is no longer plagued by merth-induced wounds.

I could have made it to that horse.

I could have escaped.

I hope she realizes that.

Annika's eyes flitter around as if checking for those listening, but no one has seemed interested in speaking to us since we began the arduous trek—first by carriage, then by a contraption operated by a pulley that carried us far up, until the haze blurred the ground below and my lungs reached for air. Still, she drops her voice. "We have no idea how far those sirens carried us, or in which direction. And have you ever met anyone from Udrel? Because I have not. I have never even seen a map of it. Where does the Endless Sea truly begin and end?"

"I suppose."

Annika lifts her chin in that triumphant way of hers, as if she's seen reason where no one else possibly could. When I don't want to throttle her, I find it rather adorable.

But I have questions. "What happened back there at the gate, when they killed those prisoners?" Or, more importantly, what *didn't* happen? From what I know of the Islorian immortals—and Annika, specifically, who is known for imbibing like a sailor at port and daily —that much blood pouring free should have drawn her fangs. If it had, would they have killed her?

"I have no idea what you are talking about." But her eyes flare, betraying her lie.

My smile is wide, letting her know I see through her. I'll get the truth soon enough.

"This temple has stood for tens of thousands of years. Maybe longer," our guide announces, waving a flourishing hand around. "When the haze has lifted and the sun shines, the temple's crown of pillars can be seen far and wide. It serves as a beacon of hope for Udrelians."

I've heard people say similar things about the jeweled spires of Argon. I've also heard them say many things untowardly about our city and its rulers when not aware who was listening. "What city are we in?"

"Orathas, the capital city of Udrel."

I pause, waiting for him to ask where we're from and how we washed ashore. He asks neither. "You speak our language. How?"

"You mean the ancient tongue. Yes, all who reside within the temple know it to some degree. There are places within the realm that still use it, though less with each generation that passes."

"And where we were found, which side of Udrel is it? The east or the west?"

Our guide smiles, as if he can sense where my questions are leading. "I believe it was the south, based on the village where you were discovered."

That doesn't help me orient myself much. And discovered? I snort. "You mean imprisoned."

"I do apologize for any harsh behavior. The people in the outer villages can be unsavory."

Unsavory is one word for them. "They were burning bodies. Piles of them. Why?"

"This latest *Azokur* brought with it much turmoil. The people must now recover."

I share a look with Annika, who doesn't hide her frown of confusion.

"Azokur," she repeats. "What is that?"

"When light and shadow battle, and the shadow wins." He laughs at our expressions. His sunken face is especially hollow from this angle. "I imagine you come from a land of different truths, but do not worry, all will be explained in due time."

"Do you not care to know where *we* are from and how we came here?" I blurt.

"You came from across the great waters and were delivered by the *sea wraiths*, were you not? From whereabouts exactly, it does not matter. You are here now, and soon you will have the highest honor of standing before King Hadkiel." His nostrils flare with disdain. "But not like this."

"Is ... GOOD?" the servant asks tentatively, her eyes everywhere but on me.

I smooth my hand over the leather vest I found folded neatly on my bed, along with a tunic and breeches made of fine material, when I finished bathing in the adjacent chamber. "Yes. Thank you." I wiggle my toes within the soft boots she also brought. It's as if they were custom made for me, and far better than the dead sailor's. "All I need are a few swords and daggers and I will feel like myself."

Her gaze flips to mine for a moment before dropping again. I can't be sure she understood me.

"You know, weapons." I mock parry the air with my hand.

Her eyes brighten with understanding, and then she shakes her head. "Soldiers, yes. You, no."

"I thought so." I wander over to the gaping window. They don't bother with glass panes here, though I can't say I mind. The chill is welcome compared to the stickiness of the jungle. The dense fog has not relented, masking any view beyond my arm's length. Still, given how long we traveled, I imagine we're high up. My affinity can sense nothing but moss clambering on the stone facade. "What is your name?"

"Ilyth?" She says it as if it's a question.

"Ilyth," I repeat. "That is a pretty name."

Her cheeks redden, telling me she understands that much. That or maybe it's my smile. It's the one reserved for Argon's female servants. It's gotten me into a lot of welcome trouble.

"Ilyth, do you know where they've taken Annika?" The guards shoved me into this modest chamber and locked the door before I knew what was happening. Now they wait on the other side—five of them, based on what I saw when Ilyth arrived.

She shakes her head, her stare blank.

"The female I arrived with." I drag my hands down from my head, twirling my fingers in an attempt to mimic Annika's long curls.

Ilyth's mouth makes an *Oh* shape and she gestures at the wall.

"She's there? One room over?"

She nods.

I lean out my window. The next one is some distance away, but I could probably make that jump, using the ledge for leverage. If I miss, though …

I would have heard Annika's screams if anyone had tried to have their way with her, so they must be treating her well enough. An unexpected sigh of relief slips from me. For some inexplicable reason, I feel responsible for the Islorian princess's well-being. Maybe because I'm the one who got her into this mess in the first place.

She pretends to be fearless, but I know she's far from it. I can still hear her terror when she convinced herself they would burn us alive. The sound of it replaying in my head helped keep me awake in the wagon, which was a blessing, given I didn't want to drift off with those leering soldiers hovering over her. A prisoner who looks like her would be difficult to resist for some of these "unsavory" people.

If I'm being honest, the feel of her warm body pressed against mine was far from my worst experience. In fact, it was pleasant. Not that I'll ever admit that to anyone.

"Please." Ilyth gestures at a chair. She holds a small jar in her hand.

Curious, I settle in.

Unscrewing the top, she collects a finger's worth of the clear salve and gingerly spreads it on my injured cheek. "Will help."

I inhale the scent of *yeri*. It's a favorite plant among those without access to healers, to help mend minor scrapes and cuts. Many of the soldiers used to carry a jar with them. "Thank you."

Her eyelashes flutter as she meets my gaze before averting.

"Can you tell me about Azokur? What is it? What does that mean?"

"Uh … In sky." She points out the window. "Night with two …" She searches for her next word.

But I've found it for her. "Moons." Of course. Hudem just passed in our realms; it only makes sense it would exist here as well. They have another name for it, though. "And what happens here on Azokur?"

She stalls, and I can't tell if she's struggling with her words or how much she should divulge. "The change."

"The change. Who changes? How?"

The door to my chamber flies open and two royal guards step in. "Come now," the one on the left barks.

"Or what?" I stand and hold out my hands in challenge. They were both at the gate earlier. They've seen what I'm capable of.

A gentle hand lands on my biceps. "Please." Ilyth nods toward the door. "No trouble."

But it's not her soft voice that goads me forward. It's the irritating one in the hallway.

33

ANNIKA

"I demand to know where you are taking me. And *stop* manhandling me. Do you have any idea who I am?" I jerk my arm out of the guard's grip, doing my best to squash any hint of fear. Of course, he doesn't know who I am. None of them do, nor do they seem to care.

"Glad to see a bath hasn't washed away your swollen ego."

I spin to find Tyree standing in the doorway. A sigh of relief escapes me before I can stifle it. I knew he was in the next room over, but I didn't know when I would see him again. Despite my better judgment, I feel safer when he is around.

"You clean up well." His gaze drags over the lavish red and gold gown the servants presented after I climbed from the bath, adored by rhinestones and billowing to the floor in a cascade of luxurious layers.

"And you are clean." *He's more than that*, I admit silently. They've dressed him in basic but decent clothes. His black hair sweeps back in a wave, showing off his crystal blue eyes. I suppose they don't trust him with a blade because his carved jaw is coated in scruff that I find more appealing than I should.

He smirks as if he can read my inner thoughts, and my palm itches with the urge to slap that look off his face.

A slight and pretty servant slips out from Tyree's room.

"I hope you will return later, Ilyth? I am sure I will have needs for you to tend to." He winks.

"I ... Yes." She curtsies, her cheeks flushing furiously as she darts past us.

"That way." The guards gesture in the opposite direction, giving Tyree's shoulder a little push.

"Really? After all we've been through, *that* is what you have on your mind?" I hiss.

"That is what is usually on my mind. And given I was held prisoner for weeks, by *both of your brothers*, I'd say I'm due."

I harrumph. My servants didn't speak a word to me. Meanwhile, he has her name and everything.

"What's wrong?" Tyree falls into step beside me. "Jealous?"

"Oh yes. Very much so." I roll my eyes.

"Honestly, though, you look ravishing." He slips a hand around my waist and leans in.

I stiffen as his plump lips graze my earlobe with a soft kiss.

"Let me do the talking," he whispers quickly before pulling away. The kiss was clearly a cover to pass along that message and yet his hand remains in place, its warmth bringing me comfort—an unsettling reality.

"Why? So you can give them a reason to execute us?" I throw back, not caring if the guards hear—and understand—me.

Tyree merely chuckles in response, squeezing my side. What game is he playing now?

I fight the urge to shove him away as the guards lead us down a web of gilded hallways and stairs, the air thick with the smoky lemon-pine scent of olibanum.

Finally, we reach a grand hall. Tyree and I tip our heads in unison to take in the extraordinary mural that forms the ceiling above—an artistic jumble of every manner of creature, both mortal and winged, some I have never laid eyes on before.

"Have you ever seen anything like it?" Tyree murmurs in awe.

I shake my head, unsure where to settle my concentration.

"They say it is our history and our future," a deep, melodious voice calls out, drawing our attention to the right, to a man dressed in black and red finery. "We do not know its origins other than that its construction was before our time. But it remains pristine with no effort from us. Truly a sight to marvel." The man shifts his admiring gaze from the ceiling to me, revealing the prettiest robin egg blue eyes I have ever seen. "As are you, *kal'ana*."

They keep saying that word.

Tyree never removed his hand from my waist. Now, his grip tightens. "Who are you and why do you call her that?" There's a dangerous edge in his tone, much like the one he used just before he attacked the soldiers outside the gate.

"I am King Hadkiel, and I call her that because that is who she is." The man smiles, showing off perfect white teeth. In fact, all of him is perfect, from his sculpted square jaw to his full lips, to the way his silver-gray hair frames his handsome face. He stands with confidence, his broad shoulders relaxed, despite there being no guards within the room and himself wearing not a single visible weapon. "'The new kal'ana will arrive with Azokur, and the people shall be bathed with mercy,'" he quotes.

Tyree's jaw tenses. "According to whom?"

"The lights of the night sky foretold it," a female voice laden with the same harsh accent answers a moment before a figure cloaked in red sweeps in. Eight others trail behind her, moving like a pattern of geese. Their skin shimmers with gold paint.

"This is Yidara, my most skilled conjurer," King Hadkiel introduces as they close in.

Yidara bows. "I am most honored, kal'ana." She lifts her head and I stare, first at the odd, glowing scripture scrawled across her forehead, and then into soulless black eyes that seem to draw me into their depths, until I feel as though I'm sinking.

Tyree steps forward, putting himself between us in a move I would call protective—if it were anyone other than Tyree. It breaks whatever momentary daze I was caught in, leaving me feeling cold and bare.

"I am not familiar with this term. What does a conjurer do?" he asks evenly, steering the conversation.

Yidara's lips curve slightly, as if she finds his blatant distrust amusing. "Many things, in light and shadow. We guide, we educate. We assess." She lifts a hand toward him, revealing fingertips capped with odd gold-metal claws.

He seizes her wrist before she can touch him, the vein in his forearm rippling with tension. "I did not ask for a demonstration," he growls before pushing her aside and stepping backward into me, goading me farther away.

"Your mate is protective," she croons.

"He is *not* my mate," I blurt, earning Tyree's warning glare.

"No?" Her hairless eyebrow raises and she steals a glance toward the king. "Your defender, then. That is good."

If only she knew our history.

"No harm is to come to our kal'ana, I assure you." King Hadkiel's eyes have never left me. "She is a gift from the sea and the stars and serves the highest purpose to the people of Udrel. She is to be honored and revered." He hesitates. "And, if willing, she will become their queen."

I inhale sharply as the king drops to one knee and bows his head as his words take hold.

The flock of red conjurers mimic him, and a clatter of metal at the doorway hints that the guards have as well. Soon, Tyree and I are the only two left standing in the grand hall.

I have never seen a king kneel before *anyone*. And was that a proposal?

He rises with a sheepish smile that is boyish, despite the etched lines around his eyes and forehead. "I apologize. I was so excited to meet you that I have forgotten my manners. You must be famished."

My stomach grumbles in answer.

"May I have the privilege?" He holds out his hand, palm raised. I feel myself gravitating toward it, his words a soothing balm after all I've endured these past days. Finally, someone treats me with the respect I deserve.

"It *has* been a while since we last ate." I shrug off Tyree's hold and slip my fingers into the king's.

A WARM BUZZ of conversation churns in the dining hall. Well, *hall* is not the appropriate term for this room and the lengthy, oval-shaped table that fills most of it. Twenty strangers sit around it with us—certainly nothing like the nightly affair in Cirilea—sharing jovial stories of children and grandchildren, and the latest household gossip that servants giggled about during daily tasks. It's all very quaint and familiar, and nothing like I am used to.

Beside me, King Hadkiel has remained mostly quiet, listening and smiling, stealing glances at me often.

I find myself wanting to strike up conversation. "So, these are your advisors?" I pick off a piece of succulent meat from the bone. The table is laden with platters of various roasts drenched in gravies, root vegetables, and breads, and endless carafes of wine. I'm so ravenous, I'm struggling to remember decorum.

"Mostly." King Hadkiel dabs a napkin at the crumbs on his lips. "Plus a few special guests who heard of your arrival and rushed to the city to see you for themselves."

"No family?" Tyree watches us evenly from across the table, having barely touched his meal, sparing a frequent glance at the conjurers who stand sentry around the room as one would expect of the royal guards. His distrust seeps into the air.

"I lost my children and wife long ago. I am alone, unfortunately." Blue eyes land on me. "Though I hope to change that soon."

He is a brave and assertive mortal, I will give him that. He is a king, after all. But would the Skatranan boy-king my mother promised me behave with the same confidence?

Tyree scoffs. "You don't even know her name."

I take a deep, calming breath to keep from snapping at the buffoon. It's as if he's *trying* to insult the king, who has fed and clothed us, and shown nothing but kindness. And this is after he killed four of his royal guards! "It's Annika."

"Annika," King Hadkiel repeats, my name lovely on his deep voice.

"You have no idea who we are or where we have come from, and yet you are *so sure* she is your savior. Why?" Tyree challenges.

"Because we have beseeched the sea and the stars for her, because she arrived on the heels of Azokur." There's an edge to the king's tone now. "And because my people have been without a queen for too long. They need hope."

Tyree is undeterred. "And mercy, apparently. Why do they need that?"

"Because they live in shadow." King Hadkiel's sinewy forearms tense as he meets Tyree's steely stare with one of his own.

I remember the farmers' children, clinging to their parents' legs with fear, and the peasants outside the gate, their forlorn expressions. Was that poverty or something more?

"A ship once arrived at our shores, carrying explorers from a distant land." Yidara steps forward, cutting into the growing tension. Everyone falls quiet to listen to the conjurer's words. "They had traveled a great distance to reach us, and their hull brimmed with fine gifts from their ruler. They wished to open means for trade. They stayed as guests, learning all they could of our realm, our people, and our customs, and the way of shadow and light. And we in turn learned much about them—about the various realms of their lands, and the peoples who inhabited it. This terrible blood curse, as they called it, a punishment by their gods."

Tyree's eyes bore holes in my face. Will he out me?

They must not know *everything* about the elven race, or they would be questioning why I—a supposed vegetarian—am able to devour half a boar without keeling over in agony.

"Eventually, they sailed home with promises to return one day." She glides around the table. "It was centuries before another ship arrived from this distant land, again filled with valuables but also a letter, pleading for a conjurer. The distant land had adopted our way of light and shadow. The ruler wished to have one at his side so that he could face the shadow taking over his land, to help bring them into the light. A sister left with the sailors nearly twenty years ago." She ends her stroll at Tyree's back. "So you see, we know where you have come from, Defender of Kal'ana. But you are here now, as a gift from the stars and the sea."

"Only two decades." Tyree folds his arms across his chest. "And what was this ruler's name?"

"King Cheral."

Surprise flashes across Tyree's face. By his smug expression when he asked the question, he wasn't expecting an answer. "You are saying Kier has one of your conjurers?"

"If their ship survived the journey. It is too far for a messenger to travel."

That seems to give him pause. "And there are no casters here, in Udrel."

"Not for thousands of years. A blessing. They tend to bring nothing but trouble to everything they touch."

"I cannot disagree with you there." Tyree taps the table's surface, his thoughts elsewhere.

"I'm sure I speak for all when I say this has been an exciting but tiring day. Tomorrow will be ten times this as we begin our grand celebration, presenting the kal'ana to the people of Udrel. They will travel far and wide to witness this miracle. The pillars of our temple will shine, even through the fog." King Hadkiel stands, and everyone rushes to their feet a beat after.

Everyone except Tyree, who leans back in his chair and picks at his blueberries.

A ghost of a smile passes the king's lips. "I trust that your accommodations will be far better than previous nights. My royal guards will escort you when you have finished your meals." Collecting my hand, he raises it to his lips. "Good night, kal'ana. Sleep well. Tomorrow, you will bring hope to many."

King Hadkiel strolls out of the dining hall, trailed closely by his conjurers. The guards move in.

"Kal'ana." The plume-feathered leader gestures toward another doorway. I guess it's time for me to return to my room. That's fine, I'm finished and I'm exhausted.

"Don't stay up too late, oh blessed one," Tyree mocks.

On my way past, I pluck a slice of juicy roast and dump it onto his plate over his potatoes, hoping the meat juices soak in and make him ill. "Enjoy." With my head held, I march away.

THE SERVANT HANGS a crisp white robe much like the style the conjurers wear on a hook by the dressing mirror and then ducks out of the room.

"Good night," I mumble.

The bolt on the other side clicks in answer.

With a frown, I return my attention to the mirror. I would prefer a royal chamber, but otherwise, King Hadkiel hasn't spared expense. The gown tonight was immaculate. The nightgown I wear now is made from the softest spun material my fingertips have ever grazed, the scooped neckline trimmed in a delicate fine lace.

Unscrewing the jar the servants left on the dressing table, I smooth the night cream over my cheeks, hoping it might erase evidence of my recent trials so I may be ready for my "presentation" tomorrow to these people I am to rule. The scent is pleasant—of rose petals and lavender.

It reminds me of the royal garden at night. Thoughts of that stir a twinge of longing. I doubt I'll ever see Cirilea again, certainly not how I have always known it.

Is there anything left there for me?

A soft thump sounds behind me. "You're right at home here."

I jump at the sound of Tyree's voice and fumble the glass jar. It slips from my grasp.

He dives to catch it a split second before it shatters on the ground. The move puts his face inches from my chest, his hand braced on my bare shoulder.

"How did you get in here?"

"Through the window, naturally. Lower your voice." He pauses, his breath skating over my flesh. "Primping for the king?"

"Maybe. Jealous?"

He snorts.

"I thought you would be occupied with your servant by now. What was her name again?"

"I can't recall. Get changed. We're leaving." He's heading back to the window, his newly acquired gray cloak billowing out around him.

"For where?"

"Away from this fucking place. Don't tell me those conjurers don't make your skin crawl." He leans out, assessing the plummeting fall below.

I will admit, they are unnerving with their soulless black eyes and prowling. "We have food and clothing and a bed. We're safe here. Why would we leave? So we can end up dangling from a net again? Or maybe this time they throw us into that firepit. We can't even speak the language outside these walls!"

"Trust me, there is something off about this place. I knew it as soon as they began spouting prophecy. And this shadow and light nonsense?" His handsome face screws up. "We will find our way back to the sea and sail to Kier. It is possible. Yidara herself told us."

"For mortals, yes. Who is to say the sirens don't bring us right back?"

"It is worth the risk. Speaking of what we are ..." He marches back to settle his hands on the arms of my chair, caging me in. Piercing blue eyes study me. "What happened back there, at the gate? With the prisoners."

I sigh. There is no point in keeping this from him anymore. "I don't know."

"Annika—"

"I don't know! Really!" My eyes dart to the door, expecting the guards to burst in. I temper my voice. "The night of Hudem, my craving stopped."

He falters. "That's impossible."

"And yet it is true."

"So, you do not need blood to survive anymore," he says slowly, as if processing this.

"It doesn't seem so. I can still smell your Ybarisan blood, but I do not want it."

"All Islorian immortals? Or just you?"

I shrug—the only answer I can give.

"What has happened to cause this?"

"I have no idea, Tyree." I hold his assessing gaze, letting him see the truth in my words.

Finally, he relents, releasing me. "I knew there was something happening. A plot of some sort." He paces back and forth in front of my chair, his footsteps soundless. "Two elementals fled from Argon. According to Romeria and Atticus, they came to Cirilea and helped your brother and my sister escape. Who knows what else they were up to."

"Mordain have been scheming," I agree. "Wendeline played her role in my parents' death, though she swears she had nothing to do with what Ybaris was planning."

"She did not. In fact, her actions foiled much that day. That one ... Gesine, she is known to be particular about those basement-dwelling scribes. They live and breathe prophecy."

I can hear the disdain in his voice. "For a royal family who relies so heavily on the power of casters, you seem not to like them much."

"*My mother* relied on them. *I* would have much preferred they remained on their island. She didn't trust them not to cause havoc which is why she kept the elementals in the tower."

"That's rich, considering she's the one who used them to summon a fate."

He shoots me a sideways glance. "Again, I had nothing to do with that."

"And yet you went along with it, shuttling your sister's poisonous blood all over my land, ending untold innocent lives."

"As opposed to the untold innocent lives lost in Ybaris through centuries of starvation, while your kind flourished from rich soils in Aminadav's name, the very fate who continues to punish us, season after season?" He adds, "And half sister. We do not share the same father."

I gasp. "I knew it. Who is her father?"

"It does not matter. We must leave, Annika. Tonight. Now." He rummages through my wardrobe. "Why is there nothing in here for you to wear? Not even another dress, let alone sensible clothes." He pushes the doors open to show me a bare cupboard.

"Perhaps the seamstress is preparing such things." That dress must have been his late wife's. I push aside the shudder with that thought. "And leave to go back to what? My parents are dead. Presumably my twin brother is dead too." Should I have felt the moment it happened? Mortal twins always talk about a bond, a connection, they feel to each other, but if I have ever felt it, I'm unaware. "If Zander is alive, he is exiled and off in the mountains with Romeria. Islor has fallen to rebellion. What am I rushing back for?"

"You may be the sole heir of your realm."

"Of what? A kingdom in flames? And besides, the last I heard, your mother was crossing into Islor with an army we could not beat, fractured as Islor is. I imagine I would return home to her sitting in my throne. Oh, but you could deliver me to her!" I exclaim with mock excitement before letting my face fall flat. "No, thank you."

"So what? You wish to stay *here*?"

I shrug. "You heard the king. He will make me queen."

"*That* is who you want? That fossil of a human."

"He is not *that* old. And, as if who *I* want has ever been a topic of conversation. My brother tried to marry me off to *you*."

He cocks his head. "Oh, come now, would that have been so bad?"

"Worse than terrible," I toss back, though I will admit, I don't feel the same abhorrence as before. Tyree has proven to have *some* good qualities. And this is the first civil conversation we have ever had.

He shamelessly studies the plunging neckline of my gown. "You cannot even bear his children, Annika."

I blush under his gaze. "I cannot bear yours either."

"Who knows, with this latest development. Maybe that has changed too. I wouldn't mind trying." He winks.

I ignore his overt flirting. This is the Tyree I know, and it means nothing. He'll kill me in the next breath if it serves his purpose. "Udrel's throne will be mine when King Hadkiel passes on in, what, twenty years." A blink of an eye.

All humor fades from his face. "You are actually serious."

"Yes. I can't think of a good reason to go."

He seems to ponder this. "I will not force you—"

"Really? Not like in Cirilea?" I quip.

His jaw tenses. "I did not have a choice. Plus, you stabbed me."

"So ... we're even?"

The corner of his mouth quirks. "I will not force you, but I will not stay."

A prick of unexpected disappointment catches me off guard. "That's probably for the best. You would make a lousy defender."

He smirks. "So, this is where our journey must end, Princess Annika of Islor, soon to be Queen Annika of Udrel. Or is it Queen Kal'ana?" He hesitates and then leans in and presses a kiss against my temple, the bristle on his jaw scratching my skin. "You will always be Annika, a royal pain in my arse."

"Goodbye, mongrel." I inhale the scent of him one last time, relishing the feel of his lips *far* too much.

"You don't need this, do you?" He holds up my horsehair brush.

"No, but *do you*?" Maybe that's the secret to his lush locks.

Shoving it into his cloak's pocket, he marches toward the window and throws his legs over the ledge. "Enjoy your new kingdom." He salutes me and then vanishes.

What in fates … I rush to the window. There is nothing out there but darkness and … I reach down past the windowsill and my fingers run over moss.

34

ZANDER

"Fates."

The great city of Lyndel smolders, countless plumes of black smoke marking the buildings that still blaze.

This is why the dragons arrived in Argon to collect us.

Plans changed quickly. Romeria shuttled Lucretia through the nymph stone door with the Ring of Minerva to secure in the crypt and Neilina's journal to give to Agatha, and then we ran to meet the three agitated beasts that filled the castle courtyard. No sooner had we stepped out the doors than they snatched us in their claws and took off across Ybaris, their wings stirring gusts of wind that toppled over guards, their screeches sending citizens scurrying for cover.

I assumed something terrible had happened at the rift.

This? This is far worse.

"Fly in closer!" I shout.

Valk dives, the other two dragons following at his flanks, to give us a better glimpse of the city's destruction, and the scores of bodies that lie in the streets—both guards and civilians. Swarms of two-legged creatures rush along the parapet like ants for the ballistae that Lyndel always has at the ready.

What manner of armor-clad beasts are these? I have never seen them before. They certainly aren't the typical brainless things that crawl out of the Nulling, if they managed to infiltrate a fortified city.

"There are people down there!" Romeria shouts, pointing to huddles of women and children, corralled in the main square, in alleys, and along the inside of the wall, kept in place with swords.

Hostages. Another tactical move that typical beasts don't do.

A streak of green catches the corner of my eye. Xiaric, flying in far too close to the wall.

With a loud crack, an arrow fires into the sky. Valk swerves and narrowly avoids it.

"Pull back!" I roar as three more ballistae sound, launching their arrows.

A pained screech rings in my eardrum.

Xiaric struggles to regain control below us, his one wing pumping uselessly as he spirals toward the ground, his other impaled with a bolt and hanging limp at his side.

Valk banks hard and plunges to position himself beneath the smaller dragon. His body jolts as he bears the brunt of impact, changing the momentum of Xiaric's fall. We careen toward safety outside the range of Lyndel's weapons. My stomach has moved to my throat—Valk is flying too fast for a safe landing, and Abarrane and I are completely at his mercy.

He releases us in midair. I brace myself as I plummet before tucking and tumbling to my feet.

The ground shudders as Valk hits it. Unable to control his momentum, Xiaric skids through the grass and dirt before coming to a rest near a group of soldiers who have scattered.

Abarrane and I share a look of flustered relief a split second before Xiaric releases another agonized cry.

This one is answered with a screech that rattles my insides and turns my blood cold.

We watch in horror as Caindra swings around and aims for the city wall, deftly maneuvering her body as bolts fly.

"Romeria!" I roar, my panic surging.

Caindra's maw opens and a stream of flames spew as she coasts past, blasting the length of the rampart.

"Fuck." I cover my mouth with my hands. The enemy will perish but so will the city and its remaining innocents.

I can just make out Romeria's screams of "No!" as Lyndel's great wall erupts in fire and bodies topple over it, falling to the ground.

Caindra swerves back around. The enemy soldiers who remain scramble to reload those ballistae not damaged by the ruthless dragon fire.

"She is a mother seeking revenge. There will be nothing left of the city or its people by the time she is done." Abarrane's voice is hollow as she echoes my fears.

Caindra's giant maw opens again and another punishing blast sails out.

But this time it ricochets off the city wall, forcing the beast to bank hard to avoid her own flames. From between her claws, a glint of silver flashes. Romeria is channeling, protecting the city with a shield.

I'm momentarily struck by awe. Gesine once warned me that Romeria's strength will be greater than anything I have ever witnessed. I'm seeing the truth of that unfold before my very eyes.

Her interference seems to quell Caindra's urge for revenge. The dragon steers away from Lyndel, the sun glinting off her indigo scales as she speeds toward us, joining the other two dragons.

We run to Romeria and Jarek, staggering as they attempt to gain their footing.

"Are you harmed?" I ask, panicked.

"Define 'harmed.'" Jarek studies the singed ends of his braids.

I dismiss him, chasing after Romeria as she sprints to Xiaric. I grab hold of her wrist, stalling her to check for burns. "That was reckless. Brave, but fucking reckless." Anger seethes through me despite my relief that she seems well.

"I couldn't let all those people burn!" She adds sheepishly, "But I didn't expect the fire to bounce back like that."

Xiaric bends his long neck to sniff at the barbed bolt anchored firmly through his wing.

"They hit that exact spot that immobilizes wyverns, according to Radomir." Was it by fluke or skill? Since when do beasts have the latter?

"Your Highness!" a soldier shouts.

Both Romeria and I turn.

He points to a body lying near Xiaric's open claw. It's one of the enemy beast soldiers. The dragon must have snatched it off the wall before he was hit.

"Is it alive?" I ask.

The soldier pokes its arm with his sword, scoring its skin. "It doesn't appear to be."

"Secure it, anyway." I note the crimson blood that seeps from the wound. That is odd. Nulling creatures bleed black, not red.

"Forget that thing." Romeria worries her lip in thought. "How do we get that bolt out of his wing so I can heal him?"

"Without him killing us? He's a wounded animal. They all respond the same." Jarek looks doubtful.

"Give me a spark." If there is one thing I've tested, it's how hot my fire burns.

In a split second, one dances on the tip of Romeria's finger.

Collecting it, I channel my affinity, allowing the flame to meld into the metal until it glows orange. Within seconds, the solid structure disintegrates and the top half of the bolt topples off, rolling to the ground.

"Now the hard part." With a half-dozen warnings and assurances, Jarek and I ease in under his wing.

"One … two …" Jarek counts, and together we yank out the bottom half of the bolt.

Xiaric responds with a pained screech, but Romeria is there, her eyes glowing silver. He stretches out on his belly, allowing her close access to his injury.

"I need to reorganize our position given this new development …" My words fade. She's not even listening to me anymore.

With a smile, I leave her to her task.

"THEY CAME IN THE NIGHT, closer to dawn than dusk." The squire stands before a line of us within the shelter of the newly erected tent, shaking, his face smeared by soot and blood. He was one of the few to escape Lyndel before it was completely overrun. He raced for the rift on foot. "I do not know how they got in. One minute they were not there, and the next they were … *everywhere*."

"How many?" Abarrane demands to know.

He shrugs. "Hundreds, thousands. More."

I curse. "They must have been in the mountains, waiting." There were too many of them to be anywhere else.

"There is a small hidden cave entrance southwest of the city. We used it often. It is close enough to move in after dark," Radomir confirms. "And they could have evaded notice, given the few remaining eyes left in Lyndel were facing the opposite direction."

"But this all suggests that beasts from the Nulling are capable of, what … organizing?" A pale-faced Lord Telor leans on a makeshift crutch. When he heard his city was under attack, he heaved himself out of his cot and demanded Elisaf bring his horse.

"*These* are not simple Nulling beasts." I point to the corpse lying in the middle of our tent. We peeled off the armor to uncover a creature with yellow fangs and mottled flesh the color of ash, its body honed with muscle, its claws sharp enough to tear out throats. Standing on its feet, it would tower over any of us. "They are an army, and I am certain Malachi brought them here." There is no other explanation.

The tent erupts as questions pile on top of each other.

I raise a hand for silence. "I do not know how or where they are coming in. Certainly not through the Valley of Bones."

"I fear creatures have found other paths. The rift is long, and we have received reports of an attack on villages farther east." Gaellar wears a new silver scar across her cheek.

"We've received reports of the same on the Ybarisan side," Kienen confirms.

"How did you fare at the rift last night?" I ask.

"Busy, but nowhere near so as the first." His brow furrows. "I've heard rumors amongst the casters of problems in Mordain."

"There *was* a small problem, but the issue has been resolved. We have more pressing concerns to focus on."

"But we have the Prime's support?" he pushes. "They will not abandon us?"

I see where his worries lie. "Romeria is now Prime so, no, Mordain's casters will remain. The Shadow leader will return soon."

Both Kienen's and Elisaf's mouths are agape, earning my chuckle, despite the dour situation.

"For now, we must decide how to proceed here. It would appear they plan to hold the city."

"With innocent people trapped inside." Lord Telor's teeth clench.

"Yes, it seems they are using them to keep us from destroying the city in a blaze with the dragons. For now," I add quietly. I have never met a beast who shows kindness or mercy.

"I don't suppose there's much room for negotiation with them." Theon stands with arms folded, a worried mask marring his typical calm.

"Who wishes to attempt to parley with that?" Abarrane points at the corpse.

"I will go." Lord Telor's jaw sets with determination. "It is my city, and these are my people. We must know what the enemy's goal is here."

I settle a hand on his shoulder. "And I will go with you, friend."

"Not without me." Romeria ducks in past the flap, her eyes red-tinged from her efforts healing the dragon. Jarek is on her heels. No one needs a reminder to bow as she passes.

When she spots Elisaf, her face splits with a wide smile.

"Have you ever imagined a queen so happy to see you," Elisaf murmurs, matching her joy.

"Me? Of course. Not many can resist this face." Radomir smooths a palm over his trim beard.

I chuckle, appreciating the moment of levity. "How is Xiaric?"

"Healed, though he'll have a scar. Just like his father."

"And Caindra?"

"Still looking like she's two seconds from flying back to torch the entire city." She nods toward Lord Telor. "It's good to see you up."

"I am beginning to think I am more resilient than a daaknar, thanks to you." He dips his chin in greeting. "How do you fair, Your Highness? The last I laid eyes on you, you were helping to dismember a nethertaur."

"She has been busy dismembering Mordain with her clever tricks since." I smooth my hand over the back of her neck.

"Yes, Prime now too?" Kienen mock frowns.

"Just call me Genghis," she mutters, earning confused looks from others and a laugh from me. She is hardly a tyrannical, murdering conqueror. "So, what's the plan?" she asks, sparing a disgusted sneer for the dead soldier on the ground.

"Simple. We divide our forces between the rift and Lyndel, so we can keep them in the city rather than having them close in on our backs at night. Then we need to figure out what they hope to achieve here." Is it merely a show of Malachi's power, or is it tactical?

"We will ready everyone." Gaellar and Kienen bow and depart swiftly.

"Speaking of threats." Lord Telor slips out a letter tucked inside his breastplate. I instantly recognize the seal with the flame imprint. "A squire delivered a letter from Cirilea yesterday."

Romeria shares a look with me. "King Malachi?"

"Yes."

"I imagine one sits in Bellcross, but I have not yet received word," Theon adds.

"May I see it?"

With a nod, Telor hands me the letter.

I have ended the blood curse. I am your new ruler. All will kneel before me.

My jaw tenses. "Very short and to the point. Almost not worth the effort." I hand it to Romeria.

"He's claiming that *he* ended to blood curse!" Indignation sparks across her face. "He caused *all of this!*"

"Islor is not the only realm who has received such a message."
Elisaf's expression is almost apologetic. "Kienen confirmed that a
similar one arrived at the front line only hours ago, by messenger
bird."

Romeria's eyes widen. "He sent them to Ybaris too?"

"He has his sights set on more than Islor. Do not be surprised if
Mordain and Kier hear from him as well. There could be one waiting
in Argon for you."

Romeria says something incoherent under her breath as she
studies the letter closer. "Nice penmanship."

"Great care in those rounded strokes," Elisaf agrees. "Dare I say,
feminine."

"He didn't write this," she says. "Sofie did."

"You're likely right," I agree. As if the Fate of Fire would sit at a
desk and write out letters to those he deems beneath him. "And there
isn't any mention of the war at the rift or his plans for Islor."

Romeria hands the letter back to me, determination blazing in her
eyes. "Let's go meet his army and find out for ourselves."

MY GELDING reels as I rein it in, stalling the line. "This is as close as we
get." A quick glance confirms Caindra hanging back. Far enough to
allow for a parley, close enough to pounce as needed.

From here, the destruction to Lyndel's outer wall is glaring. Large
strips are charred black, the stone crumbling and cracked. Areas still
smolder, the embers hidden inside enough to kindle my affinity. I
can't imagine what devastation lies beyond the wall.

"Lyndel has withstood invasion for millennia, and yet it fell in the
hours before daylight, with merely a whisper." Lord Telor shakes his
head. "Thank the fates Erwynn isn't alive to face this."

Romeria shakes her head. "I don't know how you thank the fates
for anything."

"You are not wrong, Your Highness." His jaw clenches tight
against emotions that must be rising. "At least she can rest peacefully
in the next life, not knowing the truth of what her son attempted."

I offer him a wordless pat on the shoulder. As a lord, he put his
king and realm first. But as a father, he no doubt sees his son's
betrayal as his own failing.

A row of soldiers appears on the rampart, bows in hand and
ready.

"Do they even know what a parley is?" Jarek asks.

"I guess we will soon see." I search for a leader but find no crests or plumes to identify one.

Romeria's eyes shine silver with a shield as we wait for the main gate to open.

"Between Mordain and Caindra, we could overcome these vermin," Abarrane notes.

"And every innocent person in there would die," Romeria retorts.

"They will likely die, anyway."

"Likely does not mean definitely."

I'm about to order them to cut their bickering when the spring of a catapult launch sounds. Several objects sail up, into the air. They land nearby, scattering. One rolls to a stop by our horses' hooves.

Lord Telor sighs as he peers down at the head. "That was my steward."

"I suppose this is their answer about a parley." I give him a moment to say a silent prayer for his subject's soul. "This is your city. What is your preference?"

His face is grim. "To kill every last one of them and reclaim Lyndel."

"Then that is what we will do."

35

TYREE

The inside of the ramshackle tavern smells of bone broth and unwashed bodies. Precisely what I was looking for. There isn't a better place in any realm to ferret information and cajole a guide than a shady watering hole lined with drunks.

I sidle up to the bar, my hood still drawn. The barkeep spouts off a string of words in his tongue that I don't understand, but when I point to the keg behind him, he sets to pouring me a pint.

He slaps it on the counter with a grunt of a word, the ale sloshing out over his hand.

"Do you understand me?" I ask.

The answering scowl and headshake says he doesn't. Or doesn't want to.

I expected as much. Fishing the hairbrush I confiscated from Annika's room out of my cloak, I set it on the counter in front of me. Anyone could take half a glance and see the value in the solid gold handle.

Sure enough, the barkeep's eyes widen. This is worth more than what this poor sod makes in five years. He reaches for it with a meaty paw.

But I'm too quick, snatching it a split second before it's in his grasp. I waggle my finger. "I'll be over there." I point to a table by the window—a good vantage point to watch the door as well as the street outside. "Find someone who can understand me." I collect my mug, and weaving around the tables, I settle into my corner to wait. It

264

could be awhile, given what our guide said, about the ancient language not spoken much outside the temple.

Leaving King Hadkiel's castle was easier than I expected. They were too busy watching for people trying to sneak in. Luckily, the side of the tower they stuck us in was covered in moss. Not my favorite, but I fashioned a sturdy ladder with my affinity and climbed down. From there, I slipped past the guards and tossed a strategically aimed stone at the back of one's head as a group of city dwellers ambled by. The guards ran out to accost them, and I slipped past the gate.

The mortals here are as simple-minded as the ones in our realm.

I sense what King Hadkiel said earlier, about them living in shadow—whatever that means. There is a somber cloud hanging over these people, their shoulders hunched, their voices flat. There isn't even music playing to help mask the dour mood, as several steal glances my way, either out of curiosity over a stranger or because they heard about the valuable prize in my pocket and are searching for my weapons.

For all our sakes, I hope they stay put. I need a way out of here, and they need not die tonight.

I watch as the burly bartender saunters over to a small, cloaked figure, hunched over the end of the bar. He leans in and whispers in their ear, then jerks his chin in my direction.

The person doesn't bother lifting their head. They slide off their barstool and make their way to my corner, stumbling a touch. "What do you want?" The female mortal punctuates her blunt question with a hiccup before peering at me through glossy eyes, half veiled by a heavy fringe of black hair.

She's small enough to be a child, and yet I would put her in her late twenties.

And she's drunk.

"Please, join me." I gesture to the adjacent chair.

She misses it on the first try but smacks her palms on the table, catching herself before she falls. With a mutter in her own language, she drops heavily into the seat. "You are not from here."

"I am not."

"That is yours?" She taps my mug.

"Yes."

"Why do you not drink it?"

"I was saving it for you." I slide it across the small table and into her greedy little hands. "I am looking for safe passage out of Udrel."

I wait as she takes a few generous gulps, stealing a glance at our matchmaker at the bar, giving him a "Really? This was the best you could do?" look.

He goes back to wiping the bar with a rag.

"That is simple. Travel seven days north to the ports. The ships leave for Espador once a month."

I pause. Another distant realm I have heard of but assumed may not be real. "Not Espador. Kier."

Her eyes widen. She slaps the copper mug down so hard, ale splashes out onto my tunic, and she leans in to whisper, "How do you know about Kier?"

I guess the tale Yidara shared tonight isn't common knowledge. "How do *you*?"

She hesitates, glances around, and then pushes her bangs up, just long enough to reveal the faded ink script across her forehead.

I falter. "You are a conjurer." This, I did not expect.

"*Was.*" She holds up a finger, and burps. "Not anymore."

"But your eyes, they aren't … like the others." They're a warm amber, and they don't make my skin grow cold when they touch me.

At this moment, they're crossing as she struggles with her focus. At least her speech isn't slurred. "Because I am an outcast." Her hood has fallen back, revealing an odd, bowl-shaped haircut. "Did another ship arrive from Kier?"

"Sure. Why did they cast you out?"

"I did not conform. And the red robes did not suit me." She takes another large gulp. "Ask too many questions, and the chosen becomes unchosen."

I should focus on my purpose here and press her for information on how to get to these ports while she's still conscious. But what are the chances of finding another exiled conjurer with vital information about what is going on in that temple? Because I am certain not all is as it seems. Even though Annika made her choice to stay, I wear the discomfort of leaving her there like a jacket full of pins. "What is your name?"

"Destry. What is yours?"

"Friends call me Ty."

She grins, displaying oversized front teeth that are oddly charming on her.

"What do you know of the kal'ana, Destry?"

She lets out an exaggerated moan that draws attention from a nearby table. "Not you too. That is all I have heard *all day long*. This new kal'ana that washed up on the shore."

"It seems important."

"Sure ... sure ..." She waves a hand.

"You do not believe she is important?"

"Oh, I know how important she is. I lived in the temple, remember?" Despite her inebriated state, her words are clear, the meaning behind them sobering.

I lean back, folding my arms across my chest to feign a casual pose. Meanwhile, my unease grows. "What do you mean by that?" Because I met a handful of conjurers who bowed to Annika and seemed to readily embrace this world of sea and stars, light and shadow.

"Why do you ask?" Her eyes narrow. "Have the *Azyr* sent you to search for detractors?"

"No. I am honestly curious. And who are the Azyr—"

The barkeep interrupts us, his voice gruff as he spews words.

Destry twirls her hand in the air. "He is asking what you want for that gold."

"Information that you are giving me, and safe passage to the port, leaving tonight. When I'm satisfied that I have both, I will give it to him."

She relays my words.

With another grumble, he ambles away.

I watch him go. "Do I need to worry about him double-crossing me?"

She waves a dismissive hand. "Ledric likes gold, and he is grumpy. But he is also smart, and he says you carry yourself like someone who is deadly even without a weapon. Why do you ask about the kal'ana?"

"Let's say I have a vested interest in understanding what she means to these people." That interest has long blond curls the color of corn-husk silk, blue eyes like the earliest spring flowers, and a tongue as sharp as a barber's razor.

Destry shrugs. "For too many years now, every new Azokur that passes, more are lost to the shadow. She gives them hope for a reprieve."

"What does that mean? Lost to the shadow?"

Her eyes squint as she sizes me up. "You truly know nothing about Udrel."

"I truly know nothing about Udrel."

I watch as she processes this. Until she gasps. "You are the defender! They spoke of him arriving with her and killing fifty royal guards before he and the kal'ana passed through the gates!"

"Fifty." That is quite the exaggeration.

"Are you one of her kind? One of those ..." She frowns as she searches for a word. "El-ven?"

"Yes, and no." Though what is Annika now, without the blood curse?

"But ..." She struggles to wrap her drunken brain around this. "How did you escape the temple?"

"It was easier than you would think."

She searches the bar. "And where is your companion?"

"She chose to remain. She aspires to be queen, and it seems King Hadkiel is amicable to the idea." *More* than amicable. He was practically salivating when he laid eyes on her. I wish I had an ale to wash away the sudden bitter taste in my mouth.

Destry's face falls. "Oh no. No, no, no ... *my friend.*" Her head shakes back and forth. Concern shines in her glazed eyes. "That is not a throne she wishes to claim."

36

ANNIKA

When I stir, it's still nighttime. I sense the dark shadow hovering a split second before a hand clamps over my mouth, muffling my scream.

"Shhh. Annika, it's me."

I still at that voice. *Tyree?*

He leans down to whisper in my ear, "I am going to take my hand away, but *be quiet*. You do not want to alert the guards." His breath skates over my skin, sending shivers through me. "Promise you will remain quiet."

Not until I nod does he move his hand, but he remains close, his face inches away.

"What are you doing back?" I inhale. "And why do you stink of ale?"

"A mortal I met in the tavern spilled it on me. She was a tad inebriated."

I snort. *Her*. Of course. The fool runs from here and straight to a brothel.

"Annika, listen to me. This King Hadkiel is not what you think he is, and this throne is not what you are expecting."

"How do you know this?"

"From a reliable source. Well ... reliable enough. It is a long story. For now, I need you to trust me."

"Are you kidding?" I scoff. "You know I will not. And I am not going anywhere with you."

"You must!" His breath hitches, and he lowers his voice. "You *must*." There is urgency in his tone.

"Why? So you can use me as a bartering chip to find passage on a ship again?" Knowing Tyree, that's what this is about, and he has to convince me to go willingly because there is no way he'll be able to carry me out. "I have not screamed yet, but that does not mean I won't."

"And I promise, you will regret doing so for every moment of every day for as long as you breathe."

The sudden ominous tone in his voice gives me pause. This isn't one of his thinly veiled threats. He's genuinely afraid of something. "I demand to know what is going on."

He sighs heavily. "How did I know you would be a stubborn mule about this? Fine, Annika. I will show you what it means to be the kal'ana. Come. And put on your slippers."

Curious, I slide my feet into the soft shoes by the bed and follow him as he tiptoes toward the window, narrowly avoiding a side table in the darkness.

"You think I am climbing down your moss ladder?" When I discovered how Tyree escaped, I will admit, I was impressed.

"Why not? It's sturdy enough."

"Until it's not." The chill raises gooseflesh on my bare arms.

"Here, take my cloak. They've left you nothing to change into and that nightgown will glow in the dark." He slips the heavy wool over my shoulders before affixing the clasp with gentle fingers that graze my collarbone.

"How far down is it?"

"Far. But first we go up." Without asking, he grabs my arm and leads me over the ledge, guiding my hands to sink into the soft plant.

My pulse races with apprehension. "How did you build this?"

"Easily. There is more moss on this stone wall than I have ever encountered in all my life." He fits himself behind me, his feet one rung down, his arms caging me in, his body pressed against mine.

I do my best to ignore it. "But how do you keep it together?" Anything I weave with vines falls apart the moment I'm distracted. Having him so close to me would definitely land in the category of distraction. Meanwhile, he left and came back and his ladder remains.

"Talent." Humor laces his voice, but it falls quickly. "We have to climb three stories."

I peer up into the dark void. The dense fog remains, hanging like a veil between us and the outside world. "To *where*?"

"It is best if you see for yourself. Climb, Annika."

Despite my better judgment, I do as ordered, my focus on one rung at a time and nothing else. Certainly not the plummeting fall I sense below us.

And not on Tyree moving with me, his chest at my back.

"So this mortal …"

"She is the reason we are here now. You will meet her soon enough."

"Can't wait."

He reaches up, his fingers crowding mine.

I swat his hand away.

And my foot slips off the rung.

Tyree is quick, his muscles tensing to keep us on. "Don't worry, I've got you," he whispers in my ear. "Keep going."

"Why did I agree to this?" I grumble, continuing on.

"Because deep down, you know you can trust me." His face is beside mine. "And because I came back for you."

"I'm sure there is a self-serving reason. If you cost me this throne that you insist I do not want, I will *never* forgive you."

"I thought you already would never forgive me," he mocks, his voice teasing. It's followed by a "shhh" as we pass a darkened window and continue up.

"For what it's worth, I argued with my mother that we would be better off holding you prisoner," he whispers after a moment, suddenly serious.

"After slaughtering the rest of my family and stealing my throne. Am I supposed to thank you for that?" I resist the urge to elbow him. He could fall, and then where would I be? "You have never once apologized for all that you've done to me. And I will bet you don't even know the half of it. Were you aware one of your saplings bound me with merth and tossed me into the river, tied to a boulder?"

"I was not," Tyree says after a pause. "What did he look like?"

"*A sapling*. They all look the same. Grotesque." I cringe at the memory of his face hovering over me. "Romeria, of all people, is the one who rescued me." I think back to that night. "And then she saved me again, from the daaknar."

"Twice in one night."

"I would certainly be dead otherwise."

He's quiet for a moment while we climb. "What do you know of Romeria—the version after that night?"

"She was not the same. Atticus believed she was not even the same person." A tightly held secret among my brothers that I was warned not to speak of. I doubt it matters anymore.

"And you? What did you believe?"

"I despised the version before the attack. The one after?" I smile as I remember our garden walks and her genuine naivete—that I was sure was an act at first. But there was something truly different about her. "I grew quite fond of her."

"You forgave her for what she was a part—"

Tyree loses his footing.

I gasp as he scrambles to regain purchase, feeling the tug on the moss ladder as he grabs hold and returns to his position. "Let's focus on getting to the top without dying for now." His breathing is a touch ragged.

We continue the rest of the way in silence until the ladder ends at the top.

I pull myself over the ledge, Tyree following closely after.

"The temple is built directly into the mountain. This is the top of it."

I huddle in Tyree's cloak but it does little good against the wind cutting through. And yet, naked candles burn bright from their crooks on the wall. "What happens here?"

"According to Destry, the mortal, it is where the conjurers seek guidance from the stars." He points upward, bringing my attention to the ring of white stone pillars looming. How high they reach, I can't tell. They vanish into the mist. "And that is the temple crown."

I reach out to touch the odd white stone that makes up the cap of this mountain, illuminated in the candlelight. "Is there no one here?"

"No one who will bother us at this late hour," Tyree answers cryptically, setting a hand on the small of my back to guide me forward, into the main area.

A small, round tarn sits in the center of the pillars, carved into the white stone, its glacial blue water shimmering as if lit from within.

But it's the form who floats under the surface in the middle that turns my blood cold. "Who is that?"

"*That* is the last kal'ana to arrive in Udrel." Tyree meets my horrified stare.

We edge in closer to get a better look at the naked skeletal body, the tissue and fat eaten away. Her skin is like soaked paper draped over bones, and wisps around her skull are all that remain of her hair. Chains bind her ankles and wrists to the stone, her arms and legs stretched out like a starfish.

"They call this their pool of life," Tyree says.

"They keep *death* chained in their pool of *life*?"

At my question, the corpse's eyelids peel open. Startling white eyes roll toward me.

"Fates," I gasp. "She is still alive!"

"Barely."

"How long has she been like this?"

"The sirens brought her to Udrel's shores two thousand years ago. She was named queen. Technically, she is still Udrel's queen."

My jaw drops.

"The conjurers keep her living in this state to feed their connection to this light. She is elven. That is the secret, apparently. They've tried this with mortals but none survive. This one, though, has birthed children during her time here. Many, long ago, when she was still strong."

A sinking realization hits. "This is supposed to be *me* next."

"*Kal'ana* means sacrifice." Tyree lets that hang heavy in the air.

"But ... *why*?"

"Why do any of us suffer, Annika? Because casters existed here once, and we all know what happens when casters and kings are together."

"They summon the fates," I say on an exhale.

"And the fates answered by cursing these people. Every Hudem, or Azokur as they call it, select mortals change into demons. There is no rhyme or reason to who is affected. Child or elderly alike, anyone can turn. The Udrelians call it the demon moon," he adds bitterly.

"As opposed to our blood moon and our blood curse." Nausea claims my stomach. "This all comes down to another case of the fates meddling?"

"It's how it started. But whatever these Azyr conjurers do *here*"— he waves a hand at the pool and our surroundings—"is to keep the curse at bay. And apparently, it has worked for thousands of years." Tyree shakes his head. "This kal'ana's life is all but depleted, and the curse is returning, getting worse each time. Now, on the night of Azokur, the citizens are required to chain themselves in their own homes until the morning and those who turn are executed, their bodies burned."

"The bonfires in the village."

He nods.

"There were so many of them." So many limbs stuffed into the flames.

"And there will be even more next time."

The weight of his words settles on me. "So, if I do not agree to *this*, then what?"

"There is no *if*, Annika." Tyree turns to me, anger flaring in his eyes. "You are not anyone's *sacrifice*. We are leaving *now* and getting as far from here as we can before they realize we are gone." As if trying to temper his harsh tone, he collects my face in his hands and says softly, "This will not be something else you have to endure because of my actions."

I nod, my voice momentarily lost. I regard the shackled female. "We can't leave her like that."

"We have no choice. Destry warned me that the Azyr will know the moment she dies, and there will be little chance for our escape."

"But—"

"No, Annika. She is almost gone, anyway, and we must be far away from here by sunrise." He collects my hand and leads me to our escape route.

37

ATTICUS

The approaching footsteps are a touch louder tonight, the effort to unlock the door less stealthy.

"Still not an assassin?" I watch Satoria set her lantern down and cross the floor of my cage.

"What do you think?" She keeps her nightgown on, but she may as well not, given how sheer it is. I won't complain—it is easy to confirm she has no weapons hidden anywhere.

"I think you are still trying to get me killed."

"And I think you can accomplish that just as well on your own." She slips into bed beside me.

Despite my better judgment, I lift an arm to allow her the crook, and she nestles her slight body flush against my side as if we were lovers.

"You smell nice," she purrs.

"They allowed me use of the bathing pool tonight." And brought me fresh clothes.

"Because I ordered them to." Her fingertip trails over my chest, tracing the curves. "How is your injury?"

Her question triggers my need to roll my shoulder. "Nearly healed." I pause. "I thought the king was supposed to execute me today. Instead, he gave me tea."

"His family's ancient blend? I'm surprised you didn't beg for a sword through your gullet after tasting that."

I chuckle at her glib answer and enjoy a moment of peaceful quiet before asking, "Why am I still here?"

"Perhaps he likes you."

"I am a highly likable sort."

"Or he sees value in keeping you alive."

"Just as he sees value in sending his wife here to seek information?"

To that, she has no answer, but her teasing hand shifts farther down, to settle above the waistband of my loose-fitting linen pants.

"Tell me, Satoria, how many children do you have with him?"

"None."

My eyebrows arch. "Four wives and thirty-two offspring, and *none* are yours?"

"I am incapable of having them. The conjurer says my womb will not produce."

"That's ... I am sorry."

"I am not. Minding children has never been my passion, and he has enough of them."

An answer I was not expecting, especially from the wife of a mortal who boasts about how many children he's sired. "When did you marry the king?"

"Nearly five years ago. I am his youngest wife, by far. The one before me did not survive her seventh child's birth, which is why he claimed me. Royal custom decrees that the king of Kier shall have four wives to bless his realm with an abundance of life. Now that I am confirmed barren, I am of little use to him, but to execute me without cause is strictly forbidden."

"Is that why he sends you to me? To give him cause?" Or was he hoping I would kill her for him?

"His Highness is not a cruel man."

"Then why does he keep sending you here? Is it to torment me?"

She climbs and stretches out on top of my body, her face hovering inches from mine. "Do I torment you?"

I wait for a real answer to my question. The weight and feel of her pressed against my cock isn't helping my resolve for celibacy.

"He has heard the many rumors and myths of the great Islorian battle commander, and sees the version of you who believes he is moments from death." Her fingertips toy with my curls. "Now he wishes to know who you *really* are, in the quiet, dark hours when no one is watching."

When the guards are gone and naked mortal flesh—my capture's valuable property—is presented to me on a platter, for me to use, to abuse, to exact revenge. "And why is that?"

"Because a good leader knows when he is defeated. An even better one knows when to seek aid."

I frown curiously at her answer. "And so who am I? I assume you will be the one to tell him."

Pressing her lips against mine, she whispers, "Good night, usurper king. I hope you survive tomorrow."

She slips away as quickly as she came, leaving me to make sense of her cryptic words.

"You can remove those from our guest." King Cheral pours tea into two cups on the table in front of him as the guards unfasten the manacles around my wrists and ankles.

Tuella waits in her same corner, watching.

He gestures wordlessly to the seat across from him. Today is a repeat of yesterday. Is it meant to lull my apprehension so I don't expect the blade until it is through my back?

I make note of the guards' positions before I cross the room and settle into the chair.

"You seem well today. Stronger." He peers at me over the rim of his cup.

"I had a pleasant sleep," I lie. It took forever for me to drift off, my mind toying with Satoria's words from every angle, trying to make sense of them, to deduce what the king might have planned for me.

"I'm glad to hear it." He smiles behind a sip, his eyes noting that my tea still sits on the table, untouched.

King Cheral obviously sees value in my life. The question remains, for what? Will his fourth wife continue to visit me each night until she whittles away whatever he searches for? Will he string me along with manacles and bitter tea until I break from the never-ending anticipation of my death?

I decided last night that candor would be my next defense. "I enjoy a good game of cat and mouse, but that is because I've always played the cat. I do not make a good mouse, so how about you tell me what *exactly* it is you hope to achieve here?"

King Cheral takes his time, adding a teaspoon of cane sugar to his tea, then another, his spoon clanking the sides of the porcelain. "Kier is a vast realm of fierce fighters and rich lands."

"Yes, I am well aware. Kettling has benefited from trade with you for many years that my father foolishly allowed. And I personally have stuck my blade through your raiders when they pillage, so I know they are not so easy to kill. As far as mortals go, anyway. Though, they do claim you a stingy king and their people starving."

"Yes, the less flattering rumors have reached my ears. I can see why they would believe that, even if it is not the case. Not truly, anyway. We ration our realm's harvest, but it is not without cause." His lips purse as if he is weighing his next words.

"Someone has invited the shadow to seep into this realm." Tuella steps forward. "Each season, its hold grows stronger."

"Again with this shadow and light. You will have to be more specific if you wish for me to follow."

"Our best soil sits at the base of the range north of here, where the streams run down to feed the land," King Cheral explains. "The farms there have provided for most of Kier for thousands of years. But our fortunes have changed. Blights ravished crops of tomatoes, grains refused to sprout. Year after year, the poor harvest returned, each time a larger swath of land affected. We could not make sense of it. Not until Tuella arrived from Udrel. She could sense the shadow that had infected the mountain's water."

"Water," I echo.

"Yes. It is slowly poisoning our lands and, thus our crops."

"There is only one way that the shadow touches us, and that is by your fates' design," Tuella adds.

"They are not *my* fates." I wasn't so much as tapped by any of their affinities. "You think a caster summoned Aoife to smite Kier."

"That is the only explanation for it."

I settle back in my chair. How did Islor have no idea about this? At least, Cirilea did not. *I* certainly did not. "Given Queen Neilina had every elemental collected and collared, it would likely be her who spearheaded this plan. What did you do to earn her wrath?"

"I have never so much as exchanged a letter with Queen Neilina during my entire reign. However, the queen did once write to Kier, asking for our alliance when they went to war with Islor a century ago. Her hope was that an invasion on two fronts would split Islor's forces, granting them victory. The king, my grandfather, declined. He wanted nothing to do with Islor and its blood curse."

"So you think Neilina summoned the fates against you out of spite." I nod. "I would believe that."

King Cheral sighs. "The past decades have grown increasingly difficult. This rot that eats away at our best lands has moved through the realm, and there is nowhere that is untouched by it. Those living in poverty are plentiful, and those who go hungry far outnumber those who don't. This is why, when Lord Adley offered a share of the harvest from Islor's fertile fields in exchange for the might of Kier's vast army, I agreed."

"Lord Adley had no right to offer a share of anything that did not belong to him," I snap.

"Maybe not Lord Adley, but *King* Adley ... he certainly could. Is it not always the case that land belongs to someone else before it belongs to you? Islor was once Ybaris before your family claimed it."

"That is different. We were exiled. They built a wall to keep us there."

"And now another has claimed it as his. And he will accuse the next king or queen of thievery."

"That next king will be my brother."

"You are so sure." Something unreadable flitters in his gaze.

"He commands all of Islor's armies, save for the offenders hiding in the plains with Kier. As queen of Ybaris, Romeria commands both Ybaris's army and Mordain's casters, not forgetting that she is a key caster, wielding great winged beasts." What she can do remains to be seen. "Yes, I am sure he will reclaim the throne and then swiftly deal with anything within Islor that threatens him, including those who squat on Islor's farmland."

King Cheral purses his lips. "I've toyed with the notion of recalling Kier's army, but that would signal failure to my people, and then Kier will face rebellion before too long. Already, there are skirmishes almost daily. My family and I cannot leave the palace, not even to walk the streets of Ostros. My biggest challengers grow bolder each day. My reign in Kier depends on my people's hope."

"And how will your reign fare when you no longer have an army at all? I assure you, Zander will not hold off on slaughtering them all for my sake."

"There you go again, giving me a reason not to keep you alive. Come, I have something that may be of interest to you." King Cheral gestures for me to follow him to the golden birdbath, Tuella on our heels. "She has been keeping an eye on things in the west for me so I can plan accordingly."

An image appears in the pool of water.

I quickly recognize the city I'm seeing. "That is Lyndel. But ..." The fortified wall has taken severe damage, the ramparts charred and crumbled in places. The kell dives in closer, giving me a better look at the red-eyed beasts standing guard along the top. My stomach sinks.

Lyndel has never fallen to an enemy before. "Where did they come from?"

"They are not of this realm. Tuella says they are born in the shadow."

The kell swerves away from the city wall and back around, giving me a look at the horde of soldiers gathered below.

I quickly spot colors and crests from Bellcross, Kettling, and Lyndel, as well as that unknown golden armor. A cluster of Shadows in their black garb stand alongside them. Ybarisan soldiers too. "They have truly united." Even the scaled beasts are there. I can't pick out Zander or Romeria, but there is a sizable tent erected. I assume they are inside, strategizing.

"They are splitting their forces between this city and the rift. It is quite a remarkable thing, from all that we've heard of the long-standing hatred between your kinds."

"They will reclaim Lyndel quickly." How could they not, with the power of Mordain and those beasts beside them?

"I'm sure you are right. Tuella," King Cheral calls softly, and the reflection blurs. A moment later, another appears.

I inhale sharply as a sea of these red-eyed soldiers fills the water's surface, charging through a forested area. The higher the kell climbs, the farther the image extends, all the way to the mouth of a cave. More pour out of it. "Where is this?"

"Leaving your western mountains and traveling south."

"Toward Bellcross?"

"I do not know your realm well enough to say."

The kell swerves back around, giving me a complete view, and my stomach sinks with dread. I've never seen an army that size before. Running alongside them is the odd grif and nethertaur, bound in chains and hauling ballistae on their backs.

The bird speeds toward the billows of smoke ahead as if it needs to show us what's there. Northern villages pepper these remote forests, filled with mortals who wish to live cuff-free and not fed upon. I know what we're about to see before the kell looks down to share the view of burning huts and bloodied bodies.

I doubt these beasts broke their stride as they tore through, slashing and killing. They move as if on horseback, racing toward a finish line. At this speed, they could reach Norcaster by nightfall.

"Does my brother know about this force?" I ask as the image blurs and Tuella's black irises return.

King Cheral shrugs. "He and the new Ybarisan queen are preoccupied."

"On the other side of the mountain range, so likely not." I curse as I pace around the pedestal. "An army that size will decimate Bellcross and all in their path." They could split forces, one half ravaging Islor while the other half wraps around and hems in Zander. I don't know that all the realms' might will be enough to stop what's coming. "We need to warn my people."

"*We* do?"

"Do not show me the imminent destruction of my realm and then play games with me!" I roar.

The guards rush forward, fists gripping their sword hilts.

King Cheral lifts a hand to stay them.

I temper my anger. It will get me nowhere and fast. "There is only one reason for an army that size."

"To conquer a realm," he agrees.

"*Realms*," I correct, my voice booming through the vacuous space. "What do you think is going to happen after they sweep through Islor? You honestly believe this king will stop there? With an army like *this*? 'All will bow before me.'" I recite the closing line of that letter.

"The usurper king speaks the truth." Tuella's cold gaze is on Cheral. "This King Malachi does not walk in the shadow. He exists in it."

King Cheral folds his arms across his chest. "What do you suggest, Atticus?"

I can't tell if he's being genuine or an arse. "We need to send word to them now, as fast as we can, so Zander can plan accordingly. Perhaps use those beasts of his to attack. Carve their numbers, stall their pace. He needs time."

"You think he can win against a great army of this size with time?" King Cheral's voice is laced with doubt.

"I cannot say it will be enough," I admit. "My brother is the most intelligent person I know, but his talents lie in diplomacy, and there is to be none with a king who brings an army like this." Where the fuck did he come from? I'm sure Zander and Romeria would know.

"What about *you*?"

My responding chuckle is grim. "I do not aspire to reclaim the throne, if that is what you are suggesting."

"Not the throne. I agree that wearing a crown is not your forte.

But wearing a sword and leading an army … that, I doubt anyone is better at."

"Careful, or you might accidentally flatter me." I smirk. "Zander will never hand me the reins of Islor's army again, not after what I did to him."

"What if you held the reins to twenty thousand soldiers?" King Cheral watches me closely.

I falter. "What are you proposing?"

He ambles over to the balcony, to look out upon his palace's pools and waterfalls. "That I release you so that you may lead a sizable army of Kierish and Islorian soldiers to serve your brother in defeating this shadow that threatens us all, in exchange for a percentage of fertile land within your plains."

"You wish me to negotiate my release." I bark with laughter. "I am a captured usurper king. I can make all kinds of promises that I will never be able to grant you. You realize that, yes?"

"I do." King Cheral smiles. "And a less honorable prisoner would not have admitted that so quickly."

"Or perhaps a less foolish one." Still, the prospect of my release, of bringing an army of twenty thousand soldiers to turn the tide of the storm that is about to hit … "Look, if I survive this battle and if my brother reclaims the throne and if he does not swiftly execute me, I can promise you that Kier's aid will not be forgotten, and its current plight will not be dismissed." Kier will never be granted land, but favorable trade terms? That may be feasible.

"Those are a lot of ifs."

"That is all I have to offer."

He returns to my side. "Then that shall have to be good enough." He extends his hand.

I hesitate a moment before accepting it in a firm clasp. Is this really happening? Is Kier's king releasing a valuable hostage and handing him control of his own army?

To his guards, he orders, "Bring Arturo in."

The guards disappear and return a moment later with a tall, gangly male of maybe thirty. When he sees me, he lifts his chin and puffs out his chest.

I stifle my laugh.

Behind him, Satoria floats in, dressed in the white robes of a wife.

I wait until this Arturo looks away before I wink at her.

The corners of her mouth curve ever so slightly.

"Atticus, this is my eldest surviving son. Arturo, this is the commander of Islor's army, and for a time, the king of Islor itself."

Arturo dips his head, but just barely.

I show him the same respect. Just barely.

"Atticus has agreed to lead our army and provide aid to his brother and Ybaris's new queen."

Arturo's jaw clenches. Clearly, he does not agree with this decision, but at least he knows better than to open his mouth.

"As first in line to the throne, I am naming you regent to Kier, to govern in my absence," King Cheral announces.

His meaning hits me as my eyes flash to him.

He chuckles. "You do not think me *that* reckless, do you?"

"Actually, it is a smart move. Why else would your soldiers listen to my orders, if not for their king standing beside me?"

He dips his head. "My thoughts exactly."

I doubt that, but I don't call him on the lie. The man has given me an army to steer, even if he has a hand on the yoke. "When do we leave?"

"Our ship will be ready within the hour."

For the first time since I set foot on this blasted land, my smile feels genuine.

38

ROMERIA

Z ander hunches over a makeshift table of wooden crates in the tent, studying a map that shows a rough sketch of Lyndel's city streets and passageways. Lord Telor sat for hours, scribing for a young cartographer who worked fast with her pencils, explaining the complex maze of underground tunnels hidden deep below, meant for the nobility and the guards to move about. Now he leans on his staff next to Zander, answering questions as they plan for this battle that has my stomach in knots.

"These beasts must have entered through here, here"—Lord Telor notes, dragging his index finger—"and here. Though I do not know how they were aware of those entry points. Very few are."

"If Malachi has a hand in this, then you must assume there is nothing he doesn't know. But we must find a way to get the people into these tunnels so they cannot be used as shields. Otherwise, we may as well let the dragons burn the entire city down, for it is lost." Zander looks up from the page to note me standing there. "Is there an issue?"

"No, I was hoping to talk to you for a minute?"

Lord Telor hears what I don't say. *Alone.* "I must speak to my men." With a bow, he hobbles out of the tent.

"I thought he would be completely healed by now."

"Serenis said the internal damage from the beast might be too severe to heal completely."

"Maybe I can try?"

"Good luck. He will tell you that you've wasted enough of your energy on him." Zander stretches his lean, muscular arms over his head before pulling me into his chest for a brief embrace.

I sink against him, enjoying the feel of his body, even if for a fleeting moment. I imagine that's all we'll get for the next few days, at least.

His lips press against my temple. "How do you feel? Did you rest?"

"Surprisingly, yes." I found a cot, sure I wouldn't be able to sleep, but the next thing I knew, Jarek was shaking my shoulder to stir me awake. "I'm better." Shielding Lyndel from Caindra's fire nearly drained my affinities. Whatever I had left, I sapped healing Xiaric and creating that shield for the parley.

But the elemental threads ripple beneath my skin once again hours later. "Maybe next time I'll block the giant flying bolts instead of an angry mother dragon."

He chuckles. "We need to avoid a next time if there is to be a city left."

"How is the planning going?"

"Honestly?" His hazel eyes rake over the drawing. "I wish my brother were here. He is far better than me at strategizing battles. He could see a pitfall and would pivot before anyone else knew what was happening."

I remember that day at the royal hunt, in the tents, where they hovered over a map of Eldred Wood. Zander deferred to Atticus's recommendation to use Gully's Pass for their nethertaur hunt.

But he hasn't always taken his brother's advice. I also remember them trading blades in the castle sparring court. It was basically a pissing contest of egos. "I'm sure you and Lord Telor will come up with the right plan."

Zander bites his bottom lip. "What did you wish to speak to me about?"

"I just ... Something doesn't feel right about all this."

"About what? Reclaiming Lyndel?"

"No, about why Malachi would bring an army through the Nulling just to have them seize a city so close to the rift."

"He knows we will fight to reclaim it and lose soldiers in the process."

"Then why not attack us from behind while we're focused on the rift? Or in the morning, right after we've been fighting all night?" I remember the dawn after Hudem when the eastern army arrived, everyone bloodied and battered. If they had come to fight, we would have lost thousands of soldiers, even with Caindra's help.

"It doesn't seem like the wisest move if he aims to deplete our strength," he agrees. "Perhaps he wishes to defeat our spirit as well. Lyndel is iconic. It has never fallen. Losing it to the enemy so swiftly is a blow to Islor's morale. Did you see those soldiers when we arrived earlier?"

"Yeah." A mixture of shock and anger painted their faces. "But his army is now surrounded in a fortified city ... for what?" My gut burns with warning. "What if this is to distract us?"

"You think he has something bigger planned that he wishes us not to see?"

"It's Malachi. He's a god. For him to plan all that he has, just to come here and sit in a castle, sending out letters, while his beast army sits behind that wall?"

Zander scratches his chin in thought. "There is no way to find out what he is up to, short of going to Cirilea to see what we can learn."

"I was hoping you'd say that."

He shakes his head. "It's a bad idea. I narrowly escaped last time."

"You weren't discreet when you showed up." I give him a knowing look. "But if we were to use the nymph door ..." I let my words drift.

"Malachi will have the nymphaeum heavily guarded."

"Probably, which is why Jarek and Abarrane would come with us. And if it's too dangerous, I pull us right out of there in an instant." I shrug as if it's not a big deal. Meanwhile, my pulse pounds in my ear, and I know he can sense it. "Those doors are meant to get answers, and that's what we need. Answers about what Malachi is planning, what his angle is."

Zander's jaw tenses, but I can see the flittering thoughts behind his eyes, the calculation. "The guards could prove useful for information."

"Malachi will assume we're occupied with retaking Lyndel. We could be in and out before he had any idea we were there. Plus, we could ask about Annika."

I've said the magic name. Not knowing where his sister landed in all this—if she's even alive—is a heaviness he can't shake.

He purses his lips. "If we are going, we must go now. Ailis will not wish to hold off securing Lyndel much longer."

I stretch onto my tiptoes to plant a kiss on his lips. "I'll meet you by the dragons." My soft chuckle follows. "Something I never imagined myself saying."

THE WRINKLED shadow wielder wishes to speak to you should you return.

Oredai's intrusion slips into my mind, unwelcome, the moment we cross the threshold into Ulysede's castle. "I assume you mean Agatha?"

The Cindrae escort falls into step with us as we move toward the library.

We do not bother ourselves with learning their names.

"Right, I can see how that would be inconvenient for you," I say dryly. "Why did you call her a shadow wielder?"

Because that is what she is.

"His voice box doesn't work today?" Zander sighs, annoyed.

"I guess not." Even if it did, I doubt his answers would be any clearer.

"Where are all the nymphs?" Abarrane looks down another empty hall.

Oredai drags his black eyes over her from top to bottom, as if deciding whether she is worthy of an answer. "They were removed from the castle upon Her Highness's orders. Those within the golden city who could not abide the orders of civility have been exiled."

"But there are practically none left in the streets. Are you telling us they couldn't stop fighting?" Jarek asks. He's right. We passed maybe a dozen in total. Ulysede has become a ghost town again.

The Cindrae grins, flashing his jagged teeth. "That is their nature, much as it is your kind's nature."

"Where did they go?" I ask.

Wherever they feel they belong.

Another nonanswer. We reach the library doors.

"Thanks for the escort, Oredai." That we didn't ask for. "You can remain out here." I don't bother smiling before we march into the library. I still haven't forgiven him for not warning me about the poison in Jarek before it was almost too late.

Three young scribes scuttle past, their arms filled with books. They attempt bows, their wary gazes on Jarek and Zander. I imagine it'll take them time to trust the Islorian immortals after all they've been taught.

I smile at their backs. "Looks like they've been busy."

"Yes, and hopefully they have found answers, but we need to make this quick. Lyndel is our priority." Zander vibrates with impatience.

Zorya sees us approaching and rushes to meet us. "Please tell me you are here to rescue me."

"It can't be *that* bad." Jarek smirks. "I'm sure you've found someone to occupy your nights with."

The one-eyed glare she answers him with would make most people cower. "Your favorite serpent is here. Let me go and find her for you," she hisses, and stalks away.

I shake my head at my commander. "*Way* too soon."

He winces. "I wasn't thinking."

We find Agatha in a different area—a section with rows of tables and lanterns burning. It's filled with scribes, each with a stack of books of their own.

She beams when she sees us. "Your Highness! That vile creature gave you my message. Good. I did not think he would."

"He did. And Lucretia gave you the journal?"

Agatha's eyes widen. "Yes! The scribes have long suspected Neilina of using the elementals for her own whims. Now we have the proof in her own handwriting. We will have to dig up records of these casters and adjust their histories to reflect—"

"We do not have much time here," Zander cuts in.

If Agatha's bothered by his rudeness, she doesn't let on. "Oh, are you heading back to Argon? How is the new Prime?"

I falter. Lucretia hasn't filled her in. Why am I surprised by this?

"She's fine. And no, we are heading to Cirilea to see what Malachi is up to. Do you have something for us?" Zander answers for me.

"A lot of *somethings*. Bits and pieces of this and that." She waves a hand toward the huddled heads. "They have been working tirelessly, scouring, and translating, oh, I couldn't even tell you how many texts. Each time we finish one, there are four more waiting!" But she doesn't seem daunted by this. A new energy radiates from the travel-worn caster I met at the rift. "There is an entire section about these mystics who once occupied Ybaris. They had affinities to the elements much like us, except they were not born to the mortals."

"Yes, Gesine told me about them. Does it say anywhere what happened to them?"

"We are still investigating. But!" She raises a gnarled finger. "We have just discovered an entire section in the back that I think bears closer investigation, about a people who could wield the power of the nymphs. They existed in our realm at the same time as the mystics, and it does not seem like they got along particularly well."

"What does that look like?" From everything Gesine told me, whatever power the nymphs have, it's also rooted in the elements, which is tied to the fates.

"It is not entirely clear yet. These conjurers, as they called themselves, did not idolize the nymphs directly, but they were devout believers in this concept of light and shadow—the light being the nymphs, and the shadow being—"

"The fates." It clicks. Oredai called Agatha a shadow wielder because she has an affinity tied to a fate, however weak it may be.

"Yes. They talk about seeking light to balance the shadow."

"The nymphs to balance the fates." Or their effects on the realms, more likely. "But that would mean the nymph elders are, what, gods too?"

"I suppose ... yes?" Agatha's face wears the same uncertainty that I feel.

"Why do you sound so doubtful?" Lucretia appears suddenly. Today she has mimicked Zorya's outfit and hair, right down to the legionary's eye patch. "You have stood in the elders' presence. You have witnessed their power. Why would you see them as anything but the deities they are?"

"I guess. I just never thought of them like that." Two sets of gods who seem to work against each other, but who also balance each other out. "Do these conjurers still exist anywhere?"

Agatha shakes her head. "I have not seen anything in the seers' visions, past or present, that spoke specifically of them. But we also never saw anything of this great city other than the two-crescent emblem, so perhaps there are hints that we have not correctly interpreted."

"Lucretia?" I ask.

"There are distant lands where my old masters' power is still revered," she confirms.

"Can these conjurers defeat a fate?" Zander asks.

Lucretia laughs wholeheartedly, as if his question is hilarious. Sometimes I think she cycles through a selection of memorized reactions without knowing what they convey.

Zander rolls his eyes. "Then they are of little use to us and our pressing matters. Romeria, we must go."

He's right. "Okay, thank you for the update, Agatha. Keep looking."

"Certainly, Your Highness. Be safe, everyone!"

"Zorya!" Jarek snaps his fingers at the warrior, who is casting daggers at Lucretia. "Feel the need to kill something tonight?" A peace offering for his thoughtless gibe earlier.

Her eye lights up.

"WE WILL HAVE NO MORE than a few seconds of surprise before we lose the edge. Be ready to return us here at my command." Zander settles a palm on my shoulder, the other gripping his sword. Everyone follows suit in a line, their weapons of choice drawn.

"Lucretia?" I call out. And wait. "I know you're here."

She materializes at my side, her hand on my other shoulder, though I felt nothing. She's lost the eye patch, at least. "I can be of great use in gathering information, Your Highness."

"I know. That's why I'm asking you to come with us and find out what you can. But stay hidden."

Her grin stretches. "I will stay hidden and learn important things."

My pulse races in my ears. I haven't been back to Cirilea since the night we rescued all those children, since Gesine died. So much has changed.

Weaving the strands of my affinities together, I reach out to the stone.

39

SOFIE

I swallow my revulsion and infuse concern into my voice. "Is your meal not to your satisfaction, my love?"

Malachi waves a dismissive hand as he chews his meat, his face twisted with displeasure. "The meal is fine."

I wouldn't know; I haven't had a bite of mine. Not that he notices. I hesitate. "Then what troubles you?" He has been in a mood all day, pacing the terrace, barking at the servants. This afternoon, he insisted we stroll the city to remind people who they bow to, and when the guard didn't present his preferred horse to him, he had him beheaded in the castle court.

"Why have I not yet received word from the Saur'goths?" His brown eyes burn with fury as they meet mine. "They should have claimed Lyndel by now, and the main force must be moving swiftly south, and yet they do not deem to keep their king informed?"

"They may be fierce in battle, but I cannot speak for their intellect." I eye the Saur'goth nearby. I'm pretty sure I saw him ambling down the hall earlier with a rat tail dangling from his teeth. "Would you like me to send a messenger to Mal'Gar, demanding an answer?"

"Yes. Though that should have been done hours ago."

"I am sorry to disappoint you." I keep my eyes on my plate so he can't see the lie in my words.

After a moment, he admits sullenly, "I cannot see what is happening elsewhere in the realm."

"A downside to this mortal form you've taken, Your Highness."

His inability to watch and scheme from the outside looking in, as he has done for an eternity.

"If I had one of those winged beasts, I could fly to them," he growls, tossing his fork to his plate with a clatter, his bitterness evident. "I should have killed Caindra when I had the chance."

Because that would make her mate and child fly straight to you upon leaving the Nulling, you arrogant fool? I bite my tongue.

Lady Saoirse sashays to our table.

"Your Highness." She bows deeply in front of Malachi. "It is a pleasure to see you again." When he doesn't acknowledge her, she turns to me. "Your Highness. You are looking ... well."

My mottled and swollen cheek is dreadful, but it is far better than last night, when Malachi's fist split my skin because I did not display enough eagerness upon climbing into his bed.

It takes everything in me not to snarl at her. It is one thing when Malachi claims what he wants. It's another when these devious nobilities invite it, and she is under the unwise notion that because he fucked her once, she is suddenly in his good graces. "What do you want?" Besides my husband, who is not really my husband.

She clears her throat. "The lords and ladies have been discussing a growing issue of their servants abandoning their roles. They have even gone so far as to remove their cuffs from their ears and leave them on their keepers' doorsteps. It is an insult! One household lost half their staff last night alone, after years of providing for the ungrateful lot."

"Servants who are treated well do not flee in the night."

"Yes, well ... with this recent change in the servants' purpose, and with a new king and queen on the throne, these mortals seem to think their service is no longer required."

"Are you suggesting that I am to blame for these issues?" Malachi asks coolly.

"No, Your Highness. Absolutely not." Her curtain of perfect black hair swings with her headshake. "I ... *We*—" She waves a hand behind her toward the rows of tables, where the nobility pretend not to hang on every word of this conversation. Did they send this simpering idiot here because she rules the second largest city in Islor or because she spread her legs for the king and queen like a monkey performing? She clears her throat, her cheeks burning with embarrassment. I almost pity her. "We were hoping you could decree that all servants remain with their keepers or face harsh punishment for abandoning those who have spent years protecting them."

Malachi leans back in his chair.

Saoirse squirms under that heavy gaze.

"You are right." He snaps his fingers and the rat-eating Saur'goth closes in. "Take twenty of your warriors and round up any mortals who do not wear a cuff. Bring them to the dungeon. Do not concern yourself with being gentle."

"As you order, Sire!" he barks in that throaty, deep voice and then marches off.

"Thank you, Your Highness." Saoirse's bow is even deeper this time. "I will be leaving for Kettling in the morning—"

"So soon?" He cocks his head. "I would not wish you to miss the festivities tomorrow."

"Oh? I had not heard of any such celebration."

"That is because I just decided that we shall have one." He raises his voice. "Everyone!" The room silences instantly. "We will gather in the arena at sundown tomorrow. It is time for a royal competition." His broad smile and sudden exuberance sparks their round of applause.

Meanwhile, my stomach twists. They have no idea what they cheer for.

"Thank you for bringing this to my attention. That will be all, Lady Saoirse." He returns to his meal, and after a brief falter, she rushes off.

"What will this competition entail?" I ask lightly.

"Reminding people who is king," he says through a mouthful.

A pair of servants arrive then with carafes of wine and a fresh platter of poultry.

The one aims to fill my goblet with wine until she notes it's still full. "Would you prefer ale, Your Highness?" she asks in a timid voice. She is young and pretty, with innocent eyes and full lips.

"No. Be off now," I reply curtly, hoping she will scurry away before Malachi, who is temporarily distracted by choosing a duck breast over a leg, notices her.

No such luck.

"I would love more wine," he purrs, holding up his goblet, his hungry gaze tracing her curves.

The stupid girl trips over herself to fill it for him, not seeing the danger she has just invited, the cruelty she will face tonight. But I suppose, why should she? The servant he ordered to his chambers last night did not live to talk about what he did to her.

What he made me watch.

What Elijah was forced to witness his own hands accomplish.

"If I may be excused, I must send that message to your army." With one last pitiful look at the servant, I rush out of the dining hall, glad to be away.

THE AIR IS frigid in the garden tonight. I pull my cloak tighter around my shoulders as I take the long way, along winding paths and through the cedar labyrinth, stalling at the roses to check last night's work. I won't know if it was enough until the new season when the sleeping bushes awaken. The servants ramble about their splendor in the warm months.

On and on I continue, wishing for one night I could lose myself in here until dawn and avoid whatever cruel lesson Malachi will no doubt wish to teach me. But I must endure it for Elijah's sake, for what he has endured is far worse.

A shout sounds somewhere beyond my vision, and then blades clash. More than one. There is an attack happening within the castle grounds.

I rush to follow the sound of the ruckus, weaving through the labyrinth until it opens to the nymphaeum ahead. Five forms stand over the six dead Saur'goth soldiers stationed at the stone door we use to travel back and forth to Soldor—two males, including the exiled king who arrived on his dragon, and three females.

One is a young woman with silver eyes.

My shield is up in my next breath, and my affinities crackle under my skin. I know who this is. "The little pilgrim has returned." And she knows how to use this door. Though I suspected as much when I heard rumors of hundreds of children disappearing the day of the rebellion.

They adjust their stance, blades raised and their intentions clear.

Romeria's face pales slightly as she watches me approach, the hem of my black silk dress—her dress once, likely—dragging through the damp grass.

"It is good to see you again."

Her eyes narrow. "The feeling's not mutual."

So this is how it will be then, little thief ... "I will say, I prefer your previous form. She was prettier."

"That's the best you've got? Petty insults?" she throws back. "I thought you had more class."

I answer with a toothy smile. "I am dealing with a clueless child, after all."

"Not anymore. And you? You're a monster. You stabbed a *clueless child* in the chest and sent her into the body of a princess who killed the king and queen. Do you have any idea how many times I've nearly died since that night?"

"I had faith you would not." And besides, Malachi gave me so few details, I didn't know exactly how dangerous it would be.

"How could you do that?" she seethes.

Enough of this. "You know why I did it. Do not tell me you would not do the same if *he* were held in an eternal abyss for *three centuries*." I jut my chin toward Zander, acknowledging him finally. "I am surprised you returned."

"To my kingdom?" he says coolly. He is exceptionally handsome. I can see why Romeria would be smitten with him. In another life, I might have been too.

"Well, what with your many current preoccupations." What has happened in the fortified city? Did the Saur'goths secure it as Malachi expected them to? "How did your dragon fare?"

"Valk is fine." He smiles as if he knows how much his taunting question from the other day still sits under my skin. "Tell me, how are you enjoying your husband these days?" His eyes flitter to my damaged cheek.

I clench my teeth to keep from showing my rage and granting him a victory, and quickly assess the situation. Three warriors flank their sides. One wears an eye patch, but I doubt that makes her any less deadly. The other two look like seasoned fighters. I am not overconfident enough to believe I could challenge any of them with a sword and win.

My strikes will have to be with words. "I see that you are no longer the oblivious street rat." I tsk. "I still cannot believe you had no idea what you were."

"And I can't believe you had no idea what Malachi was going to do." Romeria whistles, grim humor dancing across her face. "Three centuries, and I figured it out in, like, three weeks, give or take."

"You can be exceptionally bright at times," the male warrior with braids standing next to her deadpans, his steely gaze never leaving me.

"Why, thank you. I appreciate your kind words—"

"Enough!" I cut off their nonsense. "If you are here to kill Malachi, you will need to get through me, and I did not come this far to lose Elijah now."

Romeria studies me. "I wonder what your husband would think of the things you've done in his name."

"Who are you to judge me?" I snap.

"Nobody special. Just another one of your many victims." Her sneer is full of challenge. "As for getting through you, I have Mordain, Ybaris, at least half of Islor, Ulysede, and three dragons as allies. Who do you have?"

Something skates across my ear, like a soft breath, startling me enough that my shield slips for a moment before I secure it again. I spare a glance to my left, but there is no one there. The tension must be getting to me. "Foolish girl. You think you will have nothing more to face than a handful of these Saur'goths? You think Malachi didn't come here prepared for fierce defiance?" I let my mocking laughter go, hoping it will seep into their bones and keep them up at night. "You have *no idea* what is coming."

Romeria and Zander share a look.

"So, why don't you tell us?" Zander asks, his gaze again touching my bruised cheek.

"And spoil the surprise?" I pause. She mentioned having the favor of the guild, which means she could still be of use to me, if I play this right. "I met your priestess, Wendeline. She has been through much. She is quite skittish."

Panic flashes in Romeria's eyes. "What did you do to her?"

"Nothing. Yet."

"If anything happens to her, so help me God …"

The priestess is clearly important to the little thief, so perhaps she is even more useful to me than I thought. "What if I said I would bring Wendeline here and you could take her back to wherever you came from so she can live out the rest of her sad, lonely existence in peace?"

Romeria studies me. "I would say I don't believe you."

"Come now. Have I ever lied to you?"

She snorts.

"I was not permitted to tell you more than I did." And Malachi only told me what he felt I needed to know. "I will bring your priestess here on one condition." Am I showing too much of my hand? Not that it matters. I have no other choice. "You must find out how to extricate Malachi from Elijah's body without killing my husband."

Romeria's brow furrows. "How am I supposed to do that?"

"As you've said, you have the guild in your pocket. Surely, someone there has answers." They followed their prophecy this far. "Gesine might know."

Romeria flinches. "But what if it's impossible—"

"It isn't!" I inhale sharply to calm myself. It can't be. "Elijah is trapped, this time in his own body. I need him freed."

"And if we find out how, you will help rid us of Malachi and walk away from my throne?" Zander asks.

"This is not an alliance you can add to your long list. Just get me the answer I need. I am here each night, fixing all that you and your winged beast destroyed. Do not return without the information I seek—"

"I want to see her," Romeria blurts. "Wendeline. Bring her here tomorrow night."

I grit my teeth at her pomp. My, but she has grown. "Perhaps that can be arranged. Now, I suggest you leave so I can clean up this mess, or the next time you come through that stone, there will be fifty Saur'-goths and Malachi himself waiting for you, and there will be nothing I can do."

"What about my sister?" Zander asks.

"I have not met any sister to the king."

"Her name is Princess Annika. She has long, blond curls."

"There is no one here by that name or description. She must have perished in the rebellion."

"If they had found the princess's body, it would be well known," the one-eyed warrior says.

"True." The king is desperate to find this missing sister. I am not above gathering owed favors. "I can ask around."

Zander hesitates. "Thank you."

"The five of us are leaving now," Romeria announces. "We'll be back tomorrow, to see Wendeline and maybe with an answer for you."

"Good. Run along, then." I have no idea when more Saur'goths might wander in.

With another long, lingering look, they vanish through the stone.

I drop the shield and allow myself a deep breath.

Now to deal with this mess ... I set to work, disintegrating the beastly bodies with fire until nothing but cinders and metal remains. The ash, I scatter with a gust of wind. Their armor, I bury under a surge of earth, hiding all evidence with fresh grass.

With nothing but an unguarded sanctum remaining, I return to the castle.

A small spark of hope ignites deep inside me.

40

ROMERIA

"How did he get those Saur'goth beasts to Cirilea?" Zander demands the moment we cross back to the cold, dank crypt in Ulysede. "They were nowhere to be seen when I was there days ago."

"Likely the same way he got there so quickly." Abarrane studies the gore on her blade with intense interest.

"How many are there?"

"Lucretia?" I call out and wait. Nothing. "Okay, good. She understood." That, or she was being a defiant pain in my ass. But when I clearly specified that the five of us would leave, I hoped she would catch my unspoken order. "We'll have answers tomorrow night."

"Finally, she is useful," Jarek mutters.

"There is nothing better than an invisible spy," Zander agrees.

"As long as Malachi can't sense her." I know nothing about the sylx's abilities except what she is willing to show us.

"Something tells me she knows well how to survive. But the important thing here is that Sofie is on our side."

"On our side? She was two seconds from incinerating us," Jarek argues. "And will likely incinerate us two seconds after she has no use for us."

"Yes, but for now, we are of value to her. And whether she wishes to call our agreement an alliance or not, she will do for us what we may not be able to do for ourselves," Zander counters.

"Yeah, if we can figure out how to perform an exorcism of a fate." Is it even possible?

"That is what we went to such great lengths to bring these scribe minds here for, isn't it? So, let us give them their task and plan to return to Cirilea tomorrow night to deal with Sofie. Until then, we have a city to reclaim."

41

TYREE

I pull the canvas back to steal a glimpse beyond at the foggy, desolate road. Dawn approaches, the sky turning a murky gray. "Are we clear of Orathas?"

The burly farmer steering the supply wagon and its workhorses peers over his shoulder at me, giving me a good look at the nasty scar that runs from the center of his forehead down, deforming his left nostril and top lip. An unfortunate strike, one I'm surprised he survived. He points behind us. "Orathas."

"Thank you." I spare the young woman riding beside him a nod before ducking back inside. "I think he understood me."

"If only we had someone who could communicate with them." Annika looks pointedly at the balled-up form at our feet, who hasn't moved since we left.

I grin. "We'll give her another hour or two to sober up."

"I do not know how she sleeps through any of this." As if to punctuate Annika's point, the wagon jolts over a pothole, rattling my teeth and shaking the contents of the stacked wooden crates around us. It's a good thing Destry is so small because our travel quarters are tight. We had to shimmy through the front and wedge ourselves in the cramped space among the supplies. But I won't complain. To the unaware, this looks like any other trade run, which is precisely the kind of cover we want.

"I think there is more ale than blood flowing through her veins." Destry had a fresh mug in her fist when Annika and I arrived at the meet spot, after climbing down my moss ladder and retracing my escape route. I didn't have the luxury at that hour of using passersby to distract the guards at the gate and was forced to kill them. We ran, our arms laden with their swords and daggers.

Ledric was waiting alongside this supply wagon and its drivers—his brother and niece, Destry explained. His meaty fist sat open for his payment, which I gave him after Destry translated a clear threat about what would happen should he utter a word to anyone. It was all for show—I'm not that concerned. If he had intentions of betraying me, he wouldn't send his family with us, and deducing that brought me comfort.

"Why don't you try to get some rest." I shutter my own eyes.

"Sitting up on a wooden box? That is *impossible*."

It's not unless you are a spoiled princess who travels with servants by golden carriage. But I don't say that because we're semi-civilized with each other for once, and it's a nice change. "You can rest your head here." I pat my thigh.

If her eyes could shoot actual daggers, my groin would be eviscerated. "As if I would fall for that."

"My intentions are pure." Though, now that she puts that thought in my head, my eyes drift to her full lips and a mental image stirs my blood. "I'm serious. I will stay awake."

"No, thank you. As if I could sleep. Every time I wake up lately, I feel as though I've landed in Azo'dem." She tugs her cloak closer to her body. Peeking out from beneath it is that silken white nightgown that had me gaping like one of her fawning suitors earlier.

"We will stop to find you more suitable clothes as soon as it's safe."

"Will *anywhere* be safe? Any one of these people would be willing to hand me to the king if they knew what I was, and I wouldn't blame them."

"They would have to get through me first."

She has no answer to that, regarding me shrewdly before her attention flitters away. "Do you think they've discovered us gone yet?"

"Yes. I didn't hide the dead guards well, and they would find them gone at shift change."

She rests her head against a crate. "What do you think King Hadkiel will do?"

"Send his guard out to comb through the city, looking for clues about which way we went. It won't be long before they figure out that we headed for the port. They'll send messages ahead to the various lords and ladies, demanding they scour every corner with orders to kill me and detain you." That's what I would do, anyway.

"How many days is it to this port?"

"Seven."

She worries her lips, and I know what she's thinking because I'm dwelling on it too—seven days is a long time. Much can go wrong. "And then we get on a ship, only for the sirens to bring us right back."

"Fleeing to Espador is our best option for now."

"And what do you know of it?"

"Nothing," I admit. "But it can't be worse than what will happen to you if we stay here. We have no choice. We have to leave Udrel. If we can escape without notice." Annika may as well have rays of sun shining down upon her, so easy she'll be to pick out of a crowd. "Come, sit on this." I tap my foot against a short crate between my legs.

She glares. "I told you that is *not* happening."

I groan, my frustration surging. "Would you trust me, please? I think I've earned an ounce of that, have I not?"

Her lips purse.

"Come take a seat, with your back to me."

With slow reluctance, she moves and settles in between my parted thighs, her posture stiff. "Why am I doing this?"

I smooth her cloak's hood out of the way. "Because we can't be seen in public with the way you look."

"And how *exactly* do I look?" She attempts haughtiness, but I catch a hint of curiosity.

I smile. "Fishing for compliments today?"

"Would it pain you so much?"

At one time, yes, very much. Now? I don't know how to describe my feelings for this Islorian, but it is certainly not the disdain I used to carry.

She peers up at me, her blue-purple eyes shining as she waits for my response.

"You look like someone begged the fates for the most beautiful creature ever born, and they granted that request." I don't intend for my answer to sound so somber.

That gaze flitters over my face, stalling on my mouth for the briefest second before she turns around with a shaky sigh.

I gather her long locks in my fingers, reveling in their silky texture. "You cannot walk around with this hair. You will be easily identified."

Her head whips around, panic filling her expression. "If you think you are cutting a single strand—"

"Relax. I am not." I smile. "But we must tame it. I will plait it for you."

Her eyebrow arches. "You know how to braid hair?"

"It's not that difficult."

"*I know.*" She hesitates. "Though I have no idea how." Presenting her back to me again, she asks, "But how did *you* learn this?"

I divide her hair into several sections, letting my fingertips graze her nape. "It makes for excellent foreplay."

Her body stiffens. "Tyree—"

"I am teasing." But I don't miss the gooseflesh that crawls along her slender neck, which goads me to tease more. "Here, this is in the way. I need to …" Slipping a hand around, I unfasten her cloak's clasp and coax the wool down, my thumb brushing her bare, pale shoulder. I'm rewarded with more gooseflesh. "One of my mother's collared pets taught me, actually."

She clears her throat. "An elemental?"

"Yes. Her name was Inez." I begin weaving strands of Annika's hair, tugging the curls straight so I can plait them properly. "It is a funny story. I was a young boy and completely smitten with her. She had hair the color of spun gold. Much like yours but straight as a feather's quill. I followed her around like a puppy for years, fascinated by her affinities.

"She was equally smitten, often saying how, if she could bear children, she wished to have one like me. Considering how little I saw of my mother, Inez filled that void." I smile fondly. "She used to tell stories about fantastical beasts and distant lands, stories that she had been told as a child. Bedtime was my favorite part of the day. And then one night, I woke to her hovering over my bed with a dagger at my throat, uttering nonsense about how I must be stopped before I unknowingly feed my heart to the gilded doe."

Annika gasps. "She went through the change."

"Yes, and the first thing she wanted to do was kill me. But I was deft with my blade by then and fought her off. I put her own dagger through her chest and held her until she died." My father caught me shedding tears for her and called me weak.

Silence hangs in the wagon for a few beats.

"I thought you said it was a funny story," Annika says.

"On second thought, I guess it wasn't much of one. Hold this." I hand her the end of the first braid, her fingertips grazing across mine. Using a dagger to slice off a piece of hemp string from one of the crates, I secure her hair and move on to another section.

"She could not help what happened after the madness took over."

"I know." And yet it shattered my young heart all the same.

Annika turns, giving me her profile. "Is that why you hate elementals?"

"*Hate* is a strong word. But I certainly keep my distance from them. From all casters, really. And after Gesine and Ianca conspired against Ybaris, can you blame me?" To what end, I would love to know.

"I suppose not."

My fingers work deftly through Annika's hair as the wagon bumps along. Little by little, she relaxes, until she leans, her shoulder blades resting against my inner thighs. Because I love testing her boundaries, I take every opportunity to skate a fingertip across her bare skin.

She doesn't complain.

Destry stirs as I'm finishing off the last plait—a thick braid that combines all the smaller ones. She pulls herself up off the wagon floor to peer at us through squinted eyes. The wood's grain has indented her cheeks.

"Good morning." I smile. "How much do you remember from last night?"

"Other than the kal'ana escaping from the temple? A bit here and there."

"At least you remember the important things."

Destry's face pinches. She looks likes she may vomit as she pushes past us in the tiny space, clambering through the curtain. She exchanges words with the driver in their tongue while Annika and I swap amused expressions.

Finally, she slips back, taking a seat on the crate Annika occupied —the only one available. She closes her eyes.

"What did he have to say?" I ask.

"We should reach Garm's Pass at nightfall. There is a small village there with a place to sleep."

"Can't we just keep going?" Annika asks.

"If you enjoy laming horses." Destry cracks an eyelid. "That won't work. She is too pretty. You would be better off shearing her. Even that might not help."

"*Shearing* me?" Annika's tone is rank with indignation. "What am I, a sheep?"

Destry rubs her forehead, revealing the faded ink. She shutters her eyes once again.

Annika's body is tense as she glares up at me in a "Why did you saddle me with this idiot?" way. "What are we supposed to do?"

"Don't worry. I will smear dung on your face and teach you to walk with a hunch."

She rolls her eyes, but I catch the corner of her smile as she turns back to Destry. "So, you are one of these Azyr?"

"Not anymore," comes the croaky reply in that harsh accent.

"What can you do?"

"Sleep, drink, and pretend I was never one of them."

"She was friendlier last night," I mock whisper. "What do you know of our driver, Destry?"

"He is Ezra, Ledric's brother. She is Uda, his niece."

"Yes, that was established. What else?"

"They travel across Udrel, selling honey. They were not supposed to leave for a few weeks, but with what they'll get from that golden brush, they agreed to leave early."

Annika's mouth drops. "*That*'s what you wanted it for? To barter?"

"Well, yes. What else would it be for?"

"I don't know! To keep that mane of yours looking so …" She purses her lips as if she doesn't want to finish that sentence.

"*So* what? Luxurious? Sensual? *Thick*?"

"Shut up," she snaps, her cheeks pink.

"You two are far too concerned about your hair," Destry notes.

"And you are clearly not at all," Annika retorts, eyeing the ex-conjurer's dark mop.

I give Annika's shoulder a squeeze of warning. This is our only ally. "Do you know what happened to him?" I drag a finger down my face, mimicking the scar. "In battle?"

"No. His wife."

My eyes pop. "What did he do to earn that rage?"

"It's what he did *not* do. One Azokur, four years ago, she turned, and he could not bring himself to slay her. She broke free of her chains and killed their son before he struck her down with his sword."

"Fates." I grimace. "These people have lost so much."

"He no longer hesitates to do what must be done."

My heart pounds in my ears. More than anyone, Ezra would want a new kal'ana in place.

"They will not turn you in," Destry says, as if reading my mind. "They despise King Hadkiel."

"Why?"

"For many reasons. The king is known to cull entire villages when too many beasts are born there on any particular Azokur. He sends his royal guard around to herd and slaughter them without remorse. Then there are the rumors about what the Azyr do in his name. Some are fables, but some are true. I know because I have seen them for myself. But mostly, Ezra despises the king because his oldest daughter was taken by the temple and put to the test, and she did not survive."

"Speak to us as though we have no idea what you are talking about." Because we don't.

Destry smirks. "Conjurers are chosen by the light."

"So, they are not born this way? With the ..." I tap my forehead.

"No, they are not. I wish they were. It is a painful process."

"And what does the test entail?"

She sighs heavily. "Nothing I will describe, let alone live through again."

"'Ask too many questions and the chosen becomes unchosen.'" I quote her words from last night.

"Not by the light. By the Azyr."

"So ... politics." Annika slips her cloak back up around her shoulders, cutting off my pleasant view.

"Yes. Politics and power." Destry's grin is sour. "If only we could rid the realm of kings and queens."

"Wouldn't that be nice." Annika shoots me an amused look. This exiled conjurer has no idea she's sitting across from the spare heirs to two great kingdoms. I doubt she'd care one way or another, though. Destry doesn't seem the type to bob and bow for anyone.

I toy with Annika's braid as I say, "It would be impossible. Someone would always rise to take their place."

"Then we keep killing them." Destry wiggles as if to get comfortable, but there is no chance of that among the wooden boxes. "Did you see the sea wraiths who brought you to Udrel?"

"We saw them." Though I remember very little of the ordeal, too blinded by pain from the merth bonds. "We call them sirens, though, for their song."

"They are more hideous than I could ever imagine. Gray skin and white eyes, and spikes for a spine." Annika shudders for effect. "But they do have the most beautiful voice."

"To lure you in." Destry hums. "They are guided by the Azyr to hunt for the next kal'ana. Did you know that?"

"We didn't know *your kind* existed until yesterday. As far as the sirens go, they have hunted us in those waters for two thousand years, ever since they escaped the Nulling."

Destry's brow furrows. "What is this Nulling you speak of?"

How to describe it? "A place between worlds where beasts wait before they spill into our lands after the fates have meddled."

"I do not know of this place, but I know that the wraiths have hunted you far longer than two millennia."

"That is not true." Annika frowns up at me. "Is that true?"

I shrug. "I was always told that they came from the Nulling, but I hadn't heard of Captain Finnigus and his enthralling tale until just recently, so what do I know?" If Finnigus was the first to live to tell the tale, maybe all those broken ships against the rocks are evidence of the many who didn't when the sirens came searching for their latest sacrifice.

"Believe me, it is true. The demon curse first plagued us thousands of years ago, and the wraiths have delivered a kal'ana to our shores ever since, one every few hundred years, until they stopped coming. They have searched your waters ever since."

I ponder this new information. If the sirens sank a ship every three or four hundred years in search of their sacrifice and then left our waters, it's not a wonder we didn't know about them until they couldn't find what they wanted and tormented us. "The elven stopped openly sailing the realms once the fear of the sirens took hold. That, and when our blood curse arrived and split our lands in two. Ybaris wanted nothing to do with the lands south of us for fear of infection."

"Yes. The wraiths brought several of your kind to our shore, only to discover they were not truly your kind. When we realized the creature the infected turned into, we quickly cleansed the population of everyone they touched."

"The prisoners at the gate. The ones they bled." I nod, understanding now.

"They needed to be sure."

"If the sirens wanted *me*, why did they save Tyree?" Annika asks, which is a good question. "He was not long for death when the sailors tossed him overboard. The siren did something to his wound that healed him."

"The *sirens* cannot decipher between male and female. They bring all your kind to our shores. As for what they did, they are an interesting creature of the light, said to have fallen from grace and plagued by a curse of their own. If you were wounded by the shadow, their power can counter that."

"You keep saying shadow and light. What does that mean?" Another very good question from Annika.

"The shadow is what lives inside you. And him." Destry nods toward me. "It is what you were born with."

A shout sounds outside, interrupting our conversation. A moment later, a dull thump hits one of the crates.

I recognize that noise. "Was that an arrow?"

Ezra barks something in his language and the horses speed up.

I pull back the curtain to see Ezra and Uda both holding shields up to protect their sides as we rush along the misty road.

Destry presses a hand against a loose crate by her head. "This road is known as Thievers Highway for a reason."

"Then why did we take it?" Annika exclaims, panicked.

"Because *my friend Ty* said he wanted the fastest route." She gestures at me. "This is the fastest route."

"Not if we are dead!"

In the fog ahead, a row of forms materializes, their spears aimed upward.

Ezra yanks on the reins, and the horses skid to a halt with loud whinnies. A crate topples over somewhere in the wagon, and the distinctive sounds of glass shattering fills the air.

I slip back so these bandits can't see me. "What will they do when they realize we only have honey?"

Destry is hunting for something within her tunic. "Take the horses and the wagon. Kill the men and keep the women for their enjoyment."

Annika's face twists with horror. "I would rather die."

"But then who would I tease mercilessly?" I squeeze her shoulder as I steal another peek. Seven mortals. I can manage them easily enough. Slipping one of the daggers I confiscated from the guards out of my boot, I place the handle in Annika's palm and whisper, "Try not to use this one on me, yeah?"

Her blue eyes flash with something I can't read.

"You have a weapon, Destry?"

She doesn't answer. Her head is bowed, her fist clasped around a pendant as if in prayer. That will do little, but if that is her only defense …

I leave a second dagger on the crate beside her. Quietly, I slip two swords from their scabbards.

A gruff voice sounds from our right, and I grit my teeth to avoid my curse. I can see what's in front, but how many surround us? I cannot use my affinity blindly.

A crow caws, followed by another, and several more, until a deafening cacophony of squawks make me wince. Shouts sound. Through the curtain, I watch the large black birds swarm the bandits, pecking at their heads, their necks, their arms.

Annika's fingertips dig into my calf, pulling my attention back. She nods toward Destry, and I see what has her so rattled. The tiny mortal's hazel eyes have vanished, replaced by solid whites. In the slivers of skin peeking out between her thick bangs, the script glows.

She must be steering these crows. However she manages, the distraction is welcome. Now is my chance.

I grip my pommels. "Wish me luck."

"Don't die," Annika rushes to say.

When I arch a questioning eyebrow at her, she shrugs. "You are still useful to me."

"And you are still too stubborn to admit you do not hate me anymore."

The corner of her mouth quirks in that cute way she has, when she's trying not to smile.

An overwhelming bout of insanity claims me—that is the only explanation for leaning down and pressing a quick, hard kiss against Annika's lips. I rush through the curtain before she has a chance to stab me with that dagger.

42

ANNIKA

I stare in shock where he was sitting a moment ago.

Tyree *kissed* me.

I will have to yell at him later for that indecency, *after* he has saved us.

I scramble to the crate Tyree abandoned and peer through the curtain to watch him sprint along the wagon tongue, leap over the horses, his swords swinging as he flies through the air.

He cuts down the closest bandit, who's too focused on the three crows trying to peck his eyes out to notice the lethal warrior coming for him. The second is another easy kill, but by the time he reaches the third, the others have fended off the crows and surrounded him.

I hold my breath as they take turns lunging, weapons aimed.

Ezra shoves the reins into his daughter's hands, draws a short sword, and with a roar, clambers down, the wagon lifting with the loss of his girth.

All around us, loud, angry clashes of steel ring, one after another, as the men fight and crows attack. Uda grips the reins in one hand and her shield in the other as if it is the only thing that will keep her alive.

"It will be fine. Tyree will protect us. He will kill them all," I say, though she can't understand me. Maybe I'm comforting myself with those words.

A wiry mortal clambers up into Ezra's seat then, his vile stench making me gag. He shouts something and reaches for the reins.

Uda jerks them away, her face defiant even as she trembles.

With a sneer, he draws a blade.

My pulse races in my ears as I slip out through the opening and drive my dagger downward into the back of his neck with so much force, the end juts out the other side.

He lets out a gurgling sound and then slumps over.

Uda stares at him in shock for one ... two ... three seconds, and then she kicks his body off the bench with a hard shove of her feet.

Ahead of us, Tyree slides his blade through one last bandit and then suddenly all is quiet again, eerily so. Even the crows are gone.

I crawl farther through the opening, far enough to take stock of the scene.

My jaw drops. Twelve bodies lie scattered on the ground, seven by Tyree's hand, three by Ezra, one by the crows, based on his pecked-out eyes ...

And one by me.

I've never killed anyone.

Tyree slows long enough to yank the dagger from my victim's neck, wiping the blade clean on his clothes. "Was that more satisfying than that time you stabbed me?"

"Hard to say. He whined less about it," I quip, but my hands shake.

Tyree brushes his palm across his forehead to trap a bead of sweat. I can't see so much as a scratch on him. I shouldn't be surprised, though. He is a marvelous fighter, in league with my brothers.

He catches me assessing his body and smirks.

I remember then that the mongrel kissed me.

Uninvited.

I open my mouth to scold him when Destry calls out, "We must move quickly," before saying something in her language.

"We can't leave these bodies like this." Tyree grabs hold of one's arms and drags him into the bushes.

Ezra was not as lucky in his battle. He allows Uda to finish binding a gash across his forearm with a rag and then follows suit, hauling the dead men into hiding.

I slide back inside the wagon and settle onto the crate. "What did you do with the—crows?" I falter, startled by Destry's black eyes. They're just like the Azyr. It's the only thing about this odd little mortal that gives her away. Even her thick fringe of bangs hides the scrawl beneath.

"It happens when I reach for the light." She tucks her pendant back into her tunic. "Do not worry, they will return to normal soon."

Five minutes later, Tyree pokes his head past the curtain. "Slide down, Annika."

"But this seat is more comfortable. I can lean back!" I pout.

"You can lean back down there too. I don't bite, remember?"

"Neither do I, *remember*?" I respond crisply.

"Fine. I will take the lower seat and happily fit myself between your thighs." His grin is salacious.

With a huff, I shift down, ignoring the way his words stir a flutter in my stomach. That blasted kiss. How dare he!

Tyree slips inside with ease, dropping his cleaned swords to the floor with a clatter.

The wagon jostles as Ezra settles onto the bench and then we're moving again, the wheels rolling with a noisy creak.

"Look what I found you." Tyree holds up a brown tunic and black wool breeches. "Should be about your size."

I frown. "Where did you find those?"

"From one of the bandits."

"You are giving me a dead thief's clothes?" I stare up at him, appalled.

"Why not?" He shrugs. "He doesn't need them anymore."

"If my mother could only see this now ..." Though, I imagine she'd take issue with more than ratty old garments.

"What are you two to each other?" Destry asks, her eyes still that eerie black.

"She's my betrothed," Tyree says while I blurt, "He abducted me."

She studies us for a beat. "So, it is complicated."

"You could call it that." Tyree chuckles. "What did you do back there, with the crows?"

"I used the light to guide them. It is a handy trick of the conjurers, both for defense and for information."

"You're all able to do this?"

"Yes, to varying degrees. If you see a small green bird following, it means the Azyr have found us."

A shudder runs down my spine. "I do not think I like Udrel much."

"We will be gone from here soon." Tyree reaches down to squeeze my shoulder as he has done before, but this time his hand lingers, his thumb stroking over the back of my neck.

Reminding me yet again that he kissed me.

That Ybarisan mongrel *kissed* me.

And I didn't hate it.

TYREE OPENS THE CURTAIN, revealing the wooden gate ahead and the thatched roof cottage beyond, firelight glowing from within its windows. "Whose home is this?"

Destry calls out in their language and after a lengthy rambled answer from Ezra, she says, "A merchant and one of Ezra's best customers in Garm's Pass. He is always good for many jars."

"I hope not too many," Tyree grumbles. "We need as much cover as possible."

"Speak for yourself. I cannot wait to get out of this thing. I am desperate for a hot meal, a warm bath, and a soft bed." The day has been long, the journey cramped, but at least we've reached our destination with no more attacks.

"You will get none of those tonight. Ezra does not wish to risk his friend's life by knowing too much. You two will stay in the barn with the horses and the wagon."

My mouth gapes. "The barn?"

Tyree bursts with laughter at my reaction.

"Shut up." I swat his thigh.

"What? It's better than a metal net dangling twenty feet in the air."

"Also better than the pool of life," Destry adds, killing his mirth.

A gruff male voice sounds outside, and she puts her finger to her mouth, silencing us.

The mortals fall into jovial conversation, Ezra laughing several times, as if he didn't kill three bandits today and doesn't have two highly sought-after fugitives hiding in here.

I hold my breath as the canvas flaps at the back and the men shuffle crates, the glass clanking as they unload.

Tyree's hand clamps around his dagger, but Destry scowls and waves him off as the men go about their work. Thankfully, there are still two rows of boxes when they finish and our hiding place remains secure.

With another laugh, Ezra climbs into his seat and directs the horses forward, into the barn. My nose twitches with the potent smell of hay and farm animals.

"The stable hand has left for the night. Wait until the doors are shut before you come out." Destry pushes past me first, then Tyree, before clambering through the opening as if she can't get away fast enough.

"And where are you going?" he asks.

"They have good mead here. I will try to bring food for you."

Try? "Wait!" I collect the clothing Tyree stripped off the dead man and hold it out. "Wash this." I couldn't bring myself to put them on.

She looks from the rags to me and back to the rags and then continues without another word.

Tyree's shoulders shake from his silent laughter.

"I am so glad I entertain you." I toss them at his face, which only seems to amuse him more.

A gentle hand suddenly appears through the curtain, turned upward. Uda smiles and nods at me as she collects the clothing from Tyree, saying something in her language that I hope means "wash."

"Thank you." I flash her a broad smile. "See? Some of these mortals are civilized."

"She isn't offering because she serves you. She is offering because you saved her life today. Not all mortals are beneath you."

I sniff. "But I am of royal descent." Technically, *everyone* is beneath me.

"That means nothing here." Tyree sighs. "Come on, *Your Highness.* Let's see this loft we will be spending the night in."

"*I* will be spending the night in," I correct.

"And where will I go?"

"I'm sure there is a pen for the swine somewhere in here."

His laughter trails me.

DESTRY'S odd little face appears at the top of the loft ladder. She regards the makeshift pallet of hay and a wool blanket Tyree rooted out of a chest in the tack room below. "You have your soft bed after all."

"I suppose." Though it is far from comfortable.

"Where is Ty?"

His nickname sounds odd on her tongue. "I do not know. He went out the back."

"He is not supposed to go anywhere." With a deep sigh, she sets a parchment-wrapped package on the floor.

"I was sure you had forgotten about us." My stomach growls to punctuate my irritation.

"Are all of your kind so ungrateful?"

"No, that's just the spoiled princess in her," Tyree calls from below, having returned.

I roll my eyes. "What did you bring?"

"Bread and cheese. It's all I could take without someone noticing. I also have a jug of mead below. It is not bad. Not as good as Ledric's ale. Do not burn down the barn." She nods toward the chamber stick flickering nearby—another find by Tyree, along with a fascinating tiny metal box that ignites a flame when you push a lever—and then she disappears down the ladder. "Where did you get those?"

"From the neighbor's yard."

I scramble to the edge of the loft, curious. Tyree has used his tunic as a crude basket, but I can't see what's inside. "What are they?"

"Grapes."

I gasp. "I *adore* grapes."

"I guess you'll have to be nice to me for a change." He grins up at me, his eyes twinkling with mischief. He washed up somewhere. The smears of travel dust he wore earlier are gone, his dark hair swept off his face as if pushed back with wet hands. And his jaw is clear of stubble. Even in the dim light, I can make out the dimple on his cheek.

"You risked our lives for fruit?" Destry scolds. "Word spreads of the kal'ana's escape. Letters to local governance have arrived. People will be watching. Soon, soldiers will begin searching door to door. You *must* remain inside."

"I did not go far, but you are right. I apologize." Tyree sounds oddly genuine.

She shakes her head. "We leave before sunrise. This is from Ezra, as a thank-you for saving Uda's life today. I pray you do not cost it tomorrow." She thrusts a jar of honey into his grip and stalks off.

Tyree watches her go, consternation on his face. "Here. Catch." He tosses the jar up.

I fumble but manage to grab it before it hits the floor.

Collecting the pitcher of mead, he carries it and his tunic-basket of grapes up using one free hand on the rail.

"You have a lot of experience climbing up and down ladders?"

"Lately? Yes." He reaches the top and my focus drops to the exposed skin above his breeches, to the taut ridges of his abdomen and the hard cut of muscle disappearing below his belt.

"Thirsty, Annika?"

My eyes dart upward to find him watching me. A beat later, he holds out the jug. "For mead, I mean."

316

I yank it from his grasp and take a long, leisurely sip, ignoring how my cheeks burn from getting caught ogling him.

Tyree settles down beside me and busies himself with unwrapping the parcel of food, before smoothing out the paper for a place to set the looted grapes.

I pluck one off the stem and pop it into my mouth. Sweet juice explodes against my tongue, and I fight the urge to moan.

"Well?" Tyree's eyebrow arches, waiting.

"They will do."

A tiny smile forms on his lips, as if he knows I'm lying.

"Where did you wash up?" I ask, collecting a fistful of grapes and stretching back into my pallet, to lie on my side.

"In a trough out back."

"Cold water?"

"Freezing." He joins me, wordlessly handing me a piece of bread with cheese.

We savor our meager meal in comfortable silence until Tyree opens the jar of honey and jabs his middle finger into it.

My mouth gapes. "Have you no manners?"

"I have plenty of manners. What I do not have is a spoon." He sticks his tongue out to catch a drip of the sticky substance before stuffing his entire finger into his mouth to relish it with a deep hum of satisfaction. The act is far too suggestive to be unintentional.

I roll onto my back to force myself to look away before I get caught staring at his lips. "The last time I spoke to Zander or Romeria, I was eating grapes." The day of the tournament, when Atticus turned the army on Zander and stole his throne from him. "Though, those were from Seacadore. They are these delicious little things, bluish-black, and so sweet, they make your mouth pucker. Have you ever had those?"

"I can't say that I have."

I examine the last fruit in my palm. "I suppose you wouldn't. They barely survive the trip to Cirilea. They would never reach Ybaris before they spoiled."

I feel Tyree's gaze on my profile as I study the barn's trusses.

"Do you miss him?"

"Who, Zander?" I smile. "Yes, very much so. He always had time for me growing up, even when he was busy playing king-to-be." He never complained when he would return from a day of training to find his annoying little sister sitting in his room, her draughts board on her lap, waiting. I wonder what he's doing now. What they're all doing. Has anyone even noticed that I'm gone? "What about Romeria? You never talk about her."

"There is not much to talk about," he says. "We did not get along."

I roll onto my side again, propping my head up on my bent arm. "Is that why you smashed her face against the bars?"

"No. That was because she betrayed me. I may have lost my temper," he adds sheepishly.

"*May* have? I heard the priestess worked on her for hours." Speaking of people who have betrayed us ...

"Yes, well, do not worry. Your brother made me pay. I still wear the burn marks on my legs. And then there are these." He slides his sleeve up to reveal the silver scars that riddle his sinewy forearm.

"Abarrane does enjoy doling out punishment." On impulse, I run my fingertip along one of the ridges. A tiny thrill stirs inside me when the dark hair on his arm prickles and gooseflesh erupts. "At least she didn't mar your face."

A knowing look dances in his blue eyes. "And why is that?"

"Because then you would be even uglier than you are now."

He bursts with laughter, and I find myself smiling at the sound.

"Zander said Romeria was to inherit Ybaris's throne as is custom, even though you were the elder."

His mirth fades. He turns the jar of honey in his hand, this way and that, as if exploring the consistency against the candlelight. "I'm honestly no longer sure what my mother's strategy was. The way she spoke, it sounded like she planned to outlive us and rule *everything*."

"Maybe she did. Who knows what else she summoned the fates for." I say this casually, but I watch him for any reaction that says he knows more than he's letting on. "What is she like?"

"My mother?" His eyebrows arch as if my question startled him. "I've heard many describe her as cold and distant. I suppose that is a fair assessment. Though, she *is* a queen."

"My mother was neither and she was a queen, too."

"Here. Try some." He thrusts the honey jar toward me. His way of changing the subject, perhaps.

"No. You've tainted it with your dirty hands."

"My hands are probably cleaner than yours, Annika. Try it. It is quite something. Ezra knows what he is doing with the bees." He waves it under my nose.

The potent floral scent beckons me. "Fine." Poking the tip of my index finger into the jar, I mimic Tyree's earlier move, letting the thick syrup drip down onto my tongue before I slide my finger into my mouth with a moan.

Ever aware of Tyree's intense focus.

"You are right. That might be the best honey I have ever had in my life."

"You missed a spot." His voice is gruff as he slides the pad of his thumb over the corner of my mouth where a tiny stream dribbled, smearing it outward.

"And you made it worse."

"*Did I?*" He rubs his honey-coated thumb across my jawline. "Now *that's* definitely worse."

"Stop it!"

"Stop what ..." Another swipe of his thumb over my cheek has me smacking his arm away.

"You're making me sticky!"

"I've never had anyone complain about that." He shifts onto his back, reloading his finger and devouring another mouthful of the sweet honey, his grin boyish and playful.

I admire his profile, wondering what Queen Neilina and King Barris looked like and which attributes of each he inherited. Whatever else they were, they made a beautiful son together. Queen Neilina then took that son and molded him into someone hateful and vengeful. At least, I had assumed that's all he was capable of.

"Why are you staring at me?" he asks.

"You are not what I thought you were."

"I will take that as a compliment."

"Why did you come back for me?" He could have been long gone. King Hadkiel would not chase him. The Azyr don't want *him*. They want me, and he puts himself in danger by remaining with me.

He frowns. "Why would I not?"

"*Really?* Must we have this conversation *yet again*?"

"Oh, right. The whole 'my family plotted against yours' situation." He tucks his arm behind his head. "Let me ask you something. Would your father have honored the arrangement made with King Barris?"

"Yes," I answer without hesitation.

Tyree purses his lips. "I spent my entire life hearing about Islor's vicious and cruel immortals who enslaved and abused humans and punished Ybaris with their summonings. And then my mother went and did the same. By her actions, thousands of mortals have died and many more still will. And I helped her. Who am I to judge anyone else?"

"So what? Am I to believe you are suddenly a friend now?"

"I am *your* friend. If you will allow it." He holds the jar out to me, his expression somber.

An overwhelming urge hits me. I coat my finger in honey up to my knuckle and then smear it across his face, painting his cheek, his nose, his lips. "There. We're even."

"You call *this* even?" His tongue slips out to catch his bottom lip, and then a look of grim determination takes over as his blue eyes meet mine.

"*Don't,*" I warn, shimmying backward, out of his reach.

"When I am through with you—" He cuts off mid-threat, his head swiveling right.

Gruff voices sound nearby, just outside the barn door.

Diving on top of me, he reaches over and extinguishes the candle with his fingertips, throwing the loft into darkness. Our breath melds between us as we wait, Tyree's body stiff with tension, his pulse a heady thrum.

I stare up at him brazenly, appreciating the design of his handsome face—the hard, masculine angles coupled with appealing features—knowing that his Ybarisan eyes don't grant him the same ability.

Finally, the voices fade before disappearing altogether, the threat averted.

Tyree fumbles for the metal box, relighting the candle. "Just in case ..." Bales of hay slide to form a wall along the edge of the loft, closing us in.

The way he uses his affinity with ease still enthralls me, but right now I'm focused on the fact that he hasn't moved yet. "Is there a reason you are still lying on top of me?" I whisper. Not that I'm complaining. I don't mind his weight at all, though he's braced some of it with his elbows, landed on either side of me.

"A reason? No. A wish, perhaps." His shaky breath skates across my face. "How many times must I save your life before you will begin to trust me?"

"I don't know." But that's a lie, because somewhere along the way, Tyree became someone other than my Ybarisan captor and the person I most hate. "Why did you kiss me today?"

His eyes drop to my lips as if reminded of it. "Because I thought we might die."

"And now that we are still alive?"

He leans forward a touch, until his nose grazes mine, leaving a splotch of honey on my skin. "I want to kiss you even more."

My heart pounds in my chest at his frank honesty. "What if I still craved your blood?"

"Then I would regret ever having ingested that poison." He pulls back to meet my eyes. "I know what it feels like, Annika. How good you can make it feel."

Because it's rarely ever *just* feeding when we take a tributary. My last one, Percy, would eagerly strip off his clothes and present his vein the second he stepped inside my room. But it was more than fucking. An intimate bond formed between us—between all of my tributaries and me. They were entirely devoted, which is not at all uncommon.

"You mean, with Jada." The Islorian temptress broke his heart and turned him against the rest of us, and she wasn't even feeding off him for need. It was all for lust. A spike of jealousy stirs inside me, knowing she had him in a way that I never will.

I *never* will.

I gasp suddenly.

"What's wrong?" Tyree watches me warily.

"Nothing. It's just … I have not *been* with anyone when I did not feed from them. What if it isn't the same?"

His deep chuckle stirs my stomach. "That is what you are worried about? That the fucking won't be as good?"

"Well …" I bite my bottom lip to try to hide my smile. "*Yes*."

His eyes light up with mischief. "There is only one way to know, isn't there?"

A suggestion thrown out.

A proposition made.

The air between us electrifies as I search for the right answer. I could reject him, I could treat it as another of his flippant jokes. But the warmth blooming through my body holds my tongue.

I'm not the only one affected. I can feel his heartbeat pound through his chest, and the suddenly hard press against my thigh is not his dagger.

"Since we will probably die tomorrow, anyway …" I let the insinuation linger.

"Not if I can help it."

"You're not aiding your cause, Ty," I purr, trying out the moniker for the first time.

He leans in, dragging his tongue along my jawline where he smeared honey earlier.

I close my eyes and revel in the feel of his mouth. "You're getting more on me."

"Like I started to say, by the time I'm done, there won't be an inch of you not coated in *something*." He shifts, his face dipping down to my neck, leaving a trail of honey as he tugs on the clasp of my cloak. The ends fall back. His fingers work over the buttons at the top of my nightgown. I smile. Tyree wears no hesitation and excessive amounts of confidence, but I'm beginning to admire that about him.

"I'm glad you kept this on," he says, splaying the material apart. Cool air caresses my bare chest, peaking my nipples.

"Why is that?"

His eyes light up as they rake over my breasts. "Because I had to undress a corpse for those other clothes. It might have ruined the mood for me."

"If you continue to talk, you will ruin the mood for me." I grasp the back of his head and pull his face down to mine. Our mouths collide in a tangle as he fits his body squarely between my thighs and I weave my fingers through his silky hair.

"How about this? Does this help your mood?" He rolls his hips against the apex of my thighs, the hard press of his length straining within its confines.

I gasp and he deepens the kiss, his tongue stroking against mine, letting me taste the mead and honey he ingested.

His fingertips toy with my braid, slide along my jawline, over my neck, cupping it gently as he kisses me with abandon, as if he could get lost in my lips alone.

But imagining his hands and mouth elsewhere on my body stirs a throbbing pulse between my legs that I can't ignore. Using strength I always hide around mortal males so as not to bruise their frail egos, I flip Tyree over onto his back, climbing on to straddle him.

A sly grin curls his lips as he sits up and tugs his tunic over his head, revealing the honed body I caught a glimpse of earlier, his shoulders cut and shapely, his arms carved with muscle. "I am not one of your mortal conquests you can command."

I lift an eyebrow in challenge. "Are you saying you will not give me what I want?"

"I will give you *everything* you want, Annika. You simply must *let me*." Heat flares in his eyes as he tugs the hem of my nightgown up until it pools at my waist. Strong hands slide around my back, pulling my hips against his, earning both our moans as the thin barrier left between us proves nearly nonexistent.

On impulse, I grip his jaw to angle his face away, giving me access to his columnar neck. My thumb sinks into the smear of honey I gifted him earlier.

"Do you miss it?" He pants, his throat bobbing with his hard swallow.

"I don't know." I lean in, dragging my tongue back and forth over the spot where I would have sunk my teeth in, inhaling the delicious spicy orange blossom scent of his blood. I could never have kissed him here without drawing my fangs before.

"You can pretend." Tyree's hand skims my inner thigh. "I trust you."

I let my teeth scrape across his jugular as I revel in his hot skin and the way his pulse begins to race with anticipation against the flat of my tongue. And I admit to myself that, yes, I would beg the fates to allow me such an intimate act, so I could share it with Tyree.

His fingers slip beneath the fabric of my undergarment and into my slick core.

I moan at the sudden intrusion.

"Annika." Tyree's voice has turned gruff. Fisting my braid, he gently but forcefully guides my body backward until my back bows.

My eyes meet the ceiling as his teeth clamp over my nipple, the sticky sweet honey coating on his cheek and chin smearing over my skin with abandon as he sucks, all the while his other hand continues rubbing my sensitive flesh with a skilled touch.

I fumble with his breeches between us, unfastening the buckle, granting me access.

"Still looking for that ring?" He chuckles against my flesh.

"I am. Do you have it in here?" A sigh sails from my lips as I slip my hand inside to grip his hard length, his skin hot and velvety smooth, his size pleasing.

His mirth cuts off with a curse. "Fuck, Annika." He releases his grasp on my hair, allowing me to make a show of sucking the honey from my thumb as he watches intently.

Suddenly, I'm on my back again, with Tyree on his knees, working my nightgown and undergarments off me. He tosses them off to the side. His gaze rakes over my naked body splayed before him. "You are a hundred times more beautiful than all the stories across the realms ever suggested."

An answer to a summoning, he had called me earlier, in a moment that stalled my heart and made me question how he could be the same Tyree I've hated for so long.

Kneeling before me now, the candlelight glinting off his honed form, his chest heaving with his ragged breaths, surely the same could be said of him.

Ignoring the gooseflesh that has erupted over my skin, I stretch my arms over my head and part my legs wide for him, inviting him in. "Do not be afraid to worship me."

His easy smile fades, the only warning I have before he seizes the backs of my knees and drags my body down, bending my legs in a vulnerable position that I can't free myself from. "How is this for worshipping you?" Holding my eyes, he leans forward.

My back arches at the first swipe of his tongue across my center, vaguely aware of the stickiness from the honey on his cheek and jaw coating my skin, but not caring as he laps again and again with skilled strokes, his fingers digging into my flesh, just short of painfully.

"Fates," slips out on a breath as I close my eyes. He is even better at this than he is swinging his sword. Reaching down, I collect a fistful of his hair, pulling his mouth flush with my skin as I strain against his hold on my legs.

His groan vibrates deep inside me, stirring a need that quickly morphs into a rush of intensity as pleasure surges up my spine. Tyree's tongue has brought me to the edge in seconds—seconds!

He pulls away. "Too soon." His breath skates across my sensitive flesh, teasing me as I wait with anticipation for the next lick.

Releasing one of my legs, he guides it over his shoulder, freeing a hand. After a torturous pause, he drags his finger through my slit.

I feel something wet and sticky trailing with it. I peer down to watch him stick a honey-coated finger into his mouth to suck it clean.

"You did *not* just do that!" I admonish, feeling a dollop of honey oozing down my center.

He answers with a wide grin, and then his face is buried again, his fingers joining his tongue to working relentlessly over my sensitive flesh, the strokes hard and purposeful.

My hands grasp at the blanket as I stare up at the barn's rafters, the intensity of his attention overwhelming. It's not long before I'm grinding and bucking against his mouth, overcome with wave after wave of euphoria.

My body is limp as he climbs onto me, having shucked his breeches in the hazy aftermath of my orgasm. "Still worried about whether you'll enjoy fucking as much?" he whispers against my lips, his glistening and tasting of my pleasure and Ezra's honey.

Every time he says that word ...

I devour his mouth, no longer caring if he knows how attracted I am to him. He matches my passion, the tip of his cock teasing my entrance before he pushes inside me with a gentle thrust.

My lips fall apart with a cry as my body stretches to accept him.

"Shh," he warns through a kiss, his hand slipping beneath me to cup my nape as he sinks deeper into me. "I doubt anyone will believe these sounds are coming from the horses."

I bite his bottom lip in answer, earning his growl. "Shh," I mock warn. Meanwhile, my body is aching for him in any way I can have him.

He presses his forehead against mine, and our bodies move against each other quietly, like a dark secret shared between just the two of us. My fingernails rake over the web of muscle across his back, over his backside, touching every inch of him I can reach on the outside as he touches every inch of me inside. And, all the while, we never release each other's gazes, as if we'll miss something important if we break for even a second.

Ybarisan or not, conspirator or not, Tyree is a beautiful creature. Just looking at him sparks desire in me. But this is dangerous, what we're doing. I know this, and yet I cannot stop, my body aching to climax beneath him.

At some point, we forget caution, our bodies thrusting against each other at a frantic pace, our skin glowing with sweat and sticky from honey, the sounds impossible to disguise should anyone be standing outside the barn doors.

I know the moment Tyree's pushed over the edge of no return, when his thrusts grow erratic, and his grip on my nape tightens, and his muscles clamp down.

"Annika," he groans, driving into me one last time before I feel him pulsing deep inside in a trembling surge, his cries raw and guttural. The sound of him unraveling sparks an overwhelming wave of spasms that consumes me.

And his pretty blue eyes never leave mine through it all.

43

ROMERIA

The faces inside the tent wear shock, disgust, and confusion as they stare up at my towering form.

Zander grimaces. "I think I preferred the shriveled caster to *this*."

Next to him, Jarek's nostrils flare. "She even smells like one."

Lord Rengard mumbles, "Pardon my manners, but ..." He reaches up to poke my shoulder with his finger and declares, "Remarkable." When we suggested this plan, Lord Telor declared it couldn't work, and Lord Rengard looked at me as though I were mad, but they haven't seen what Vin'nyla's token can do.

"It'll work, though, right?" I spent a good twenty minutes studying the Saur'goth corpse that Xiaric brought back before attempting this.

Elisaf frowns. "What did she say?"

I slip off the silver mask and return to my own form, earning several sharp inhales.

Lord Telor shakes his head as if not sure of what he's just witnessed. "It will get you past the wall and perhaps buy us a few crucial moments. Beyond that, the fates only know if you can make it to the tower, and that is where you *must* be stationed if this has any hope of working." He still sounds doubtful.

I hope the fates don't know *anything* about what we have planned.

"You have your reservations about this scheme, Ailis. I understand. But a frontal assault will tie us up for days, and we'll likely have little success." Zander's brow furrows, and I know what he's worried about. In the back of his mind, Sofie's vague warning plays in a loop. What else is Malachi up to? "It will deplete our soldiers, and it will still likely cost every innocent their lives. But a stealthy approach while they do not expect it is to our advantage. We are in the late hours of the night, and they think our focus is on the rift." The dragons made a point of flying north shortly after we arrived from Ulysede to help sell that idea. Meanwhile, they swung around to wait within range for the signal to attack. "But we must move soon."

"Going in with just a handful of casters and legionaries?"

"Not merely casters, Lord Telor. Shadows," Solange responds crisply. I was so relieved to discover her here when we returned, delivered by Valk who we sent to Argon to fetch her while we were in Cirilea.

"But how will you reach the entrance without being seen?" he pushes. "They wait on the ramparts, watching."

"We will get there. Of that, I have faith." Zander smiles at me. "Romeria has a few more tricks up her sleeve."

That I've never tested to this extent, but I keep my nervous thoughts to myself.

"Have I ever told you about the night she escaped a ring of legionaries to visit the Greasy Yak in Norcaster?" Jarek deadpans, sparing me a headshake.

MY BODY TREMBLES from adrenaline as our line of fifteen presses our backs against Lyndel's south outer wall.

Zander squeezes my shoulder. A silent command, or wordless praise. Maybe both, because seven Shadows, five legionaries, Zander, Elisaf, and I just crossed the expanse of open ground without a single shout of alarm or arrow launched our way, thanks to my ability to cloak us—a discovery Gesine made that I am especially thankful for on this night.

I spot the trigger to open the passage immediately. It's a smaller, square block, much like the stone casters used to mark the secret way into Bellcross, but someone—or something—has smeared it with blood.

"You remember the plan?" Zander whispers.

"Of course I do. It's my plan." This part, anyway.

He leans in for one last, quick kiss and then I slide on my silver mask, and everyone readies their weapons, stepping back.

Zander presses the square block and a passage opens up through the wall.

I take a deep breath and amble through, my form's broad shoulders so wide, the metal armor scrapes across the stone. This beast body *feels* so real.

I stifle my gasp as a Saur'goth warrior steps out, his sword drawn. He's the only guard at this entrance from what I can see, though, which is a bonus.

"You're late!" he barks.

"I got lost." It's a vague enough response.

By his grunt, it seems like an acceptable one. "Report to command for your position."

"Where?"

"The tower above the square."

I stifle a curse. Exactly where I need to go, and where I saw the bulk of those hostages.

"What are you waiting for!" He's already turning away.

"For him." I step aside and Zander's blade swings out, cleaving through the beast's throat with a precise swing. The Saur'goth falls to the ground with a clatter.

A curt whistle sounds and our line moves stealthily inside, splitting in two rows and spreading out, looking for the next threat.

"Their general leads from the tower above the square. He will raise the alarm if he sees us," Zander whispers.

"Oseph will take care of him." Solange nods to one of her Shadows, who, she explained earlier is like Fatima, with an affinity to fire and a talent for manipulating the oxygen needed in that split second before the burn to freeze an individual.

"We move for the tunnels now. You know the plan." Zander nods. "Good luck."

She dips her head. "May the fates be merciful." They vanish down the path.

Zander gestures in the opposite direction, settling his hand on my shoulder. The others follow suit until we've formed a train. "Lead the way, beautiful."

The closest underground tunnel entrance Lord Telor mapped out is inside a bakery, only fifty feet away, but the alley to get there feels like five hundred as we step around debris and slain Islorians and over the sprawled legs of enemy warriors, asleep propped against walls. We may be concealed, but we're not invincible—a fact I'm reminded of when I accidentally kick a Saur'goth's boot, stirring them awake with a confused snarl.

The second we've stepped into the empty bakery, I release the cloak and sigh heavily.

Zander presses a finger to his mouth, then points to the shattered windowpane.

I fill the space with my gargantuan Saur'goth form while Jarek slides his palm along the brick wall, searching for the trigger.

"We could really use Lucretia right about now," Zander whispers.

I agree, but hopefully the sylx is proving useful with gathering information in Cirilea.

A click sounds and a panel in the wall next to the oven swings open. Abarrane snaps her fingers to beckon us and then disappears down the narrow stairs.

"You will not fit like that," Zander whispers.

I slide off my mask. "Neither will the Saur'goth soldiers, which means these tunnels are clear."

He smiles, ushering me ahead of him. "Exactly."

The five of us rush down, Elisaf shutting the secret door behind him.

"*Not* exactly." I freeze at the bottom of the steps, Jarek herding me to stand behind him with a wordless swat of his hand against my thigh.

Abarrane is pinned against a wall with three swords aimed at her throat, her chest, and no more than an inch from her eye. Torchlight flickers in the tunnel, revealing a huddle of guards surrounding us. More guards stretch out beyond them, lining the wall. The air is rank with urine and sweat.

Zander eases in front of me, he and Jarek forming a protective wall that I can barely peek around.

"Your Highness, please inform these imbeciles that I am your Legion commander and if they do not back down immediately, it will not end well for them," Abarrane growls.

"These imbeciles bested you," Jarek teases.

"It was that or I kill them all."

The soldier in front, an Islorian with lengthy brown hair tied at his nape, lowers his blade and the others follow suit a beat after. "Your Highness?" His attention flips between Zander and Jarek, not knowing who he is addressing.

Zander steps forward. "And you are?"

"Adar, Your Highness. I lead Lyndel's guard now. What's left of it, anyway."

"How many of you are down here?"

"Nearly two hundred."

"That's not *nothing*," Elisaf murmurs from behind me.

"Down here, it feels like it. We have been trapped since the attack. The enemy destroyed most of the tunnel exits. Only two are accessible beyond this one, but it's impossible to move without being spotted. A few scouts have gone out and not returned. We have not been able to exit for a coordinated assault."

"You would all be dead if you had tried. The city is overrun with the enemy."

Adar frowns. "Pardon me for asking, Your Highness, how did *you* get in?"

"With the help of casters," Zander answers vaguely. "What about the tunnel closest to the gate?"

"Destroyed. The closest one is two alleys away, in the smithery."

Zander's jaw clenches. "That will have to do. What about the one leading into the tower?"

"Intact, and I do not think they know it exists. But it is heavily fortified."

I curse. "I have to get up there, or this plan all goes to shit."

"We will get you there, but we are quickly running out of time. The Shadows will not be able to hide forever."

"If you have a plan, then you have our swords, Your Highness." Adar dips his head. "What do you need us to do?"

Zander shifts into king mode. "Split your men into two groups, one for each exit. Elisaf, you will lead one group to the gate and open it upon Romeria's signal. Jarek and Abarrane, lead the others to free as many of the hostages as you can and get them back into these tunnels or at the very least deep within a building. You do not want to be above ground when the dragons arrive."

Adar's eyes widen.

"Through that door and then straight ahead and up the stairs," Adar whispers. "But there are at least two dozen of those creatures waiting and more outside. Hundreds of them."

"We will take care of them. Your soldiers must focus on getting as many civilians into the tunnel as possible," Zander orders.

"Yes, Your Highness."

Gruff shouts sound somewhere in the city, signaling that either Elisaf and the others have attacked or the Shadows have been spotted.

"Stay and fight with them. I'll be fine."

"Romeria—"

"They need you down here. And I have my mask. Besides, I trust the Shadows to do what needs to be done."

Tension ripples through Zander's frame as he peers down at me. "If anything still lives in that tower, kill it without hesitation. I will meet you there. Ready?"

I reach for all four affinities, letting my glowing silver eyes answer, even as my panic ignites.

Jarek drops a hand on my shoulder—a silent gesture to protect myself—and then he, Abarrane, and Zander charge out with blades swinging. I follow closely behind them, an air shield around me for protection.

Chaos erupts.

I run through the clash of blades, narrowly avoiding a flying Saur'goth body as Jarek cuts him down. The clatter of pounding boots rises behind me as a hundred of Lyndel's soldiers rush from the tunnel, heading for the square.

Once inside the tower, I slip the mask on and then hurry up the uneven, steep stairs that remind me of Cirilea's gray prison tower, except this one is even higher. But fear and adrenaline drown out the burn in my thighs.

When I reach the top, I find six Saur'goths dead on the floor, and the one I assume is the leader is toppled over a table.

All have arrows through their eyes.

The top of the tower is as Lord Telor described it—a circular room with two bridges connecting each side to the ramparts. The one on the right is no longer intact, crumbled after Caindra's attack. I can see the entire city from here, including frightened faces that peek from the windows. There are still people hiding within.

From the corner of my eyes, a flitter of black moves. A Shadow, perched on a nearby roof, their arrow aimed at me.

I hold up my hands in surrender before slipping off my mask, my pulse racing.

They quickly find another target and fire below, hitting their mark with deadly accuracy. Is it their affinity or their immaculate skill? I would love to learn how to do that. But for now, I will simply appreciate it.

There are more Shadows stationed around the city, like dark blurs on the clay tile roofs, picking off Saur'goths below. The ramparts are littered with dead bodies, hunched where they fell, the ballistae unmanned. They've cleared the way for us just as Solange promised they would—without raising a single alarm—and no one below has any clue.

I blast a white light up into the sky, as high as it will go. Now for Elisaf to get that gate open.

Islorians and Saur'goths clash below, the Islorians outnumbered three to one. But Abarrane and Jarek join the fray, two blades each, spinning and lunging with impossible speed that the Saur'goths can't match as they cut a vicious path toward the huddle of women and children in the center. There must be at least a hundred of them, some lying face down and still, many with torn clothing.

My rage foams, looking for revenge.

A rush of Saur'goths charge in from an alley on the left, heading toward the square. That is where I center my anger now, scattering them with bolts of fire.

The two Shadows hovering directly above finish the attack for me. The entire group erupts in a ball of flame, their screams distracting the others, making it easier for our people to cut them down.

I pick off the enemy one by one with icicle daggers aimed at their throats, clearing space closest to the tower's entrance while some of Adar's men usher the mortals to relative safety.

Footfalls pounding up the steps distract me. I spin around, ready to shield myself from an attack. But it's Zander, smears of blood on his cheek and splatters over his clothes. None that is his, from what I can see. "They are moving the people into the tunnels, and Jarek holds the tower. How is it up here?"

"It's working, but there are still so many of them." I can hear them around the buildings, in alleyways, shouting, their blades clashing.

"They will be outnumbered shortly. I saw your signal." He leaps over the beast bodies to join me, his eyes raking over the empty rampart first, then to the gate ahead, crawling open, and beyond.

"Can you see Telor and the others?" All I see is darkness.

A smile curls his lips. He must be so happy to see this plan fall into place "Yes, they are in position. I think it's time you call in our winged friends."

I step out onto the intact bridgeway. "Caindra!" I call out, knowing that, by some design I can't understand, she will hear me.

Twenty seconds later, a chorus of earsplitting screeches reverberates through the night sky and three dark forms soar toward us from behind the mountain ridge.

I remember the first time I saw that wingspan above, how terrified I was. Now, I am in awe.

My ears catch the sound of horse hooves pounding on hard ground a moment before Telor's cavalry rushes through the open gate. The Shadows ride in front, forming shields that bulldoze the waiting Saur'goths. They fan out as planned, driving the enemy back toward the square.

"Look!" I point to a dozen who have made their way back up to the rampart from a set of stairs and are charging toward the ballistae.

Zander draws a second sword and moves for the bridge, but stalls as a Shadow materializes from seemingly nowhere. Their eyes glow as they swing their arms out and bring them back together with a clap. Half the Saur'goths lose their balance and tumble over the edge to their deaths.

"They used the air," I marvel.

Zander shakes his head. "I am so happy we have them as allies."

The Shadow stretches their arms out a second time, but then freezes and looks up, just in time for Xiaric to swoop in for his pass, snatching three up in his maw while knocking the rest off.

Beyond the wall, a ball of fire ignites as Valk hunts down fleeing Saur'goths.

"Should we go down there?"

"No, they have a handle on it." Zander settles his arm around my shoulders, pulling me against him. "Lyndel is ours once more."

We watch quietly as the sun rises and the enemy falls.

And neither of us say it, but I know we're both wondering what Malachi has in store for us next.

44

SOFIE

The morning peeks through the stained glass windows of the sanctum, bathing the patrons in dappled light.

"Your Highness." The priestess Wendeline's bow is slow and deep. When she rises, her eyes dart to my battered cheek. "Did you come for healing?"

"That is kind of you, but it will be gone by tomorrow." And I would never allow a caster, even as weak as this one, to touch me with her affinity.

Malachi let me rest last night, dismissing me when I arrived in his chamber to discover him mid-copulation with that young wine maid. *That is not my husband*, I told myself repeatedly, tears streaming as I drifted off.

I slept both fitfully and soundly, my dreams inundated with intimate memories of Elijah that I had long since forgotten. They were so vivid, I could feel his touch on my skin when I woke with a start, my body aroused and my blood racing.

As for the wine maid, I asked around discreetly this morning for her whereabouts. No one seemed to know where she went, but the maids who cleaned Malachi's room were as pale as the bundled bedsheets in their arms. I'm sure there will be a new servant pouring wine tonight. Ideally, someone less appealing to their king.

I slide into the same pew we occupied the other day.

Wendeline slips in beside me, her hands folded in her lap. She still cradles the once injured one, though it is as healed as it ever will be. "What brings you here today?"

"I thought I would see more of this city I now rule," I lie smoothly. The last thing I care about is playing queen alongside a mad king.

"That is a fine idea. I believe the market is open today. If you travel past the apothecary, you will find it. It is not what it once was, but it is still something. I saw a few carts rolling in before daybreak." She is trying her best to appear cordial, but she cannot hide her fear and disdain for me. I see it in the way she avoids my gaze, in the way she sits stiffly, ready to flee at the first opportunity. Is it for what I am or for what I did to her precious little thief?

"I will keep that in mind. Thank you." It's still early in the day, but people huddle in the front, their heads bent in prayer. "I hear the mortals are abandoning their keepers in droves."

"There have been rumors of that, yes." Her eyes flicker to the front, to a family who cowers in the corner. They're too far away to glimpse their ears—to see if they wear cuffs—but the way the parents steal petrified glances this way, I would suspect they have either taken them off or plan to. "Now that the blood curse is over, many do not see why the old system should prevail. The keeper no longer needs them to live."

"They are still seen as property, and no one likes to lose property." Certainly not that which provides both manual labor and status.

Wendeline nods but says nothing.

The faintest breeze grazes my ear, and I instinctively turn into the emptiness beside me, the hairs on the back of my neck standing on end. It is the second time this morning I have felt that. I felt it last night, too, when facing Romeria and her clan. It's almost as though someone sits close beside me.

On impulse, I let a tendril of Vin'nyla's thread reach out, searching.

There is nothing there, nothing that my affinity touches.

I must be going crazy.

"What do you know about the exiled king's sister's whereabouts? Annika is her name."

Wendeline's eyebrows pop at the sudden change in subject. "I have not seen or heard about Princess Annika since before the attack. But I have not spent much time in the castle."

"I do not think she is there, and there was no mention of her body found after the rebellion."

"Surely, you would have heard about that," she agrees.

"I wonder then, does she hide within the city?" I watch Wendeline's face closely for tells. "Perhaps here?"

"She is certainly not in the sanctum. If she were, I doubt I would be left alive."

"Fair point, given how you betrayed her family." Either this caster is telling the truth or she has reclaimed her masterful skills in deception.

Wendeline hesitates. "May I ask, what use does the king have of her?"

I waffle over how much I wish to trust this one. But she has proven loyal to this exiled Islorian. I imagine she would do anything to help them, still. "King Malachi would have many uses for the sister of the exiled king who leads the army and seeks to reclaim the throne, and none of them would be good." The things he would do to her ... I stifle my shudder. "Which is why I have not reminded him of her, nor have I sought information around the castle." Word would reach him, and then I would have to explain why I was asking.

And if he didn't like or trust my answer ...

I close my eyes against the excruciating memory of that invisible fire. Sometimes I can still smell my skin.

"Would you like me to ask around, see what I can find?" Wendeline proposes.

"That would be helpful, yes."

"I do not know how effective it will be. Many of my connections have left Cirilea. Even the Goat's Knoll sits abandoned, its owner gone. Such a vibrant city ... such a marvelous sanctum ..." Her sad eyes drift upward over the mural that adorns the ceiling—of a kingdom bathed in riches and honored by their gods. "It is an empty shell now."

I laugh. "If you were to see the sanctum *I* spent the last three centuries contemplating in, you would not sneer at yours."

"It is not the walls and splendor that makes it whole. It is the people and the faith you share it with." She hesitates. "I can imagine yours has been quite lonely too." She meets my eyes with a gaze that penetrates and haunts.

It leaves me cold.

"Find out what you can and do it discreetly. Come to the castle at last light and meet me by the main doors of the garden. Wait there until I arrive, and if anyone asks, you are answering my summons to help heal the roots."

Her brow furrows. "But I do not have the necessary skills to—"

"Those fools do not know that," I snap, standing.

She follows quickly, slipping out of the pew to make room for me, her bow deep. "I am honored by your visit, Your Highness."

I pause, studying the little family again. "The guards have been out, looking for mortals without cuffs. I fear the results if they should be found, and I would not assume the sanctum will protect them."

Her eyes flare with understanding—both of my words and my benevolence. "Yes, Your Highness."

There. Perhaps that will earn me some trust with the conspiring caster.

"I will see you tonight." I stroll down the aisle toward the double doors to the city beyond.

SOLDOR'S vacuous cave is much quieter when Malachi and I pass through the stone doors with six Saur'goths. They carry a large empty cage strapped to metal poles that he has not yet explained.

Dozens more warriors laze by the stream, the bones of half-devoured carcasses strewn around them. Of what creatures, I cannot tell. They scramble to their feet when they see us, barking greetings of "Sire!" and then dropping to a metal-plated knee.

"They are still arriving?" The opening into the rift allows a glimpse of afternoon light from above into the murky cavern.

"And they will continue to for many years before they are depleted. I have forged an army that can replenish itself twice over. No army of this realm shall defeat it." Malachi passes them without so much as a glance, heading toward the other side. "Remain here. We will return soon."

The warriors who arrived with us set the cage down.

"Where are we going?" I ask.

Malachi collects my hand, squeezing it in a viselike grip as he leads us into a corner where even my eyes can't cut through the darkness.

The air shifts and suddenly a dense fog materializes around us.

The hairs on my body rise as I realize what it is—the entrance to the Nulling that we arrived through, that he is now leading us back into. I reach for my affinities, but they are gone, my access cut off.

"What are we doing here?" I ask, my dread growing.

"Sometimes my subjects need guidance to emerge. We will wait until one senses me. It should not be too long." Malachi is at ease in this place between realms, this hell without time or dimension.

I search the murkiness. I don't know what's more disorienting—that I am basically blind to the dangers around us or that I cannot defend myself once they come. This feels like falling from the sky and not knowing when or if I'll ever reach the bottom.

Much like falling into the rift, I suppose.

It's the breathing I hear first—a raspy, guttural, inhuman sound.

The stench of rotting flesh hits me next.

And then suddenly, the beast looms before us, its red eyes glowing within the mist.

My mouth goes bone-dry. This is not the first time I've faced a daaknar at Malachi's request, but I've never been this close, and certainly not without a way to defend myself.

"Come, my loyal servant," Malachi croons in a soothing voice, leading me backward with slow, easy steps. "I have a job for you."

With a deep, rumbling snarl, the daaknar follows on sinewy hind legs, its tattered wings hanging limp from its back. This one's skin looks especially charred, the pale-yellow pus oozing from the cracks like dribbles of custard.

"I thought they lived in Azo'dem," I whisper, afraid that speaking too loudly will goad it to lunge. We are utterly defenseless here. Has Malachi lost his mind?

"They do, but I cannot summon them within my current form."

"So you sent them to the Nulling to wait for you." Clever fate.

"Yes. I have found them *very* useful in this realm. The Saur'goths are effective and listen to my commands, but they are not invincible. These special creatures, on the other hand, do not fall to a blade and strike fear like none other."

He is right about that. My heart is racing.

"They do not like it in the Nulling, but they know I am their way out, so they will not attack us while we're in here. Shield now," he commands as the fog dissipates.

I reach for my affinities and they leap to me, forming a barrier just as the daaknar charges, its fangs slamming into the invisible block. That only angers it more, and as we move backward and away, I extend the shield to protect us on all sides.

It quickly loses interest in us, swinging its attention to the waiting Saur'goths. They've barely drawn their swords when it reaches the first, tearing off its arm with its barbed claws. Two others sink blades into its flesh. It releases a pained roar that reverberates through the cavern before raking its claw across their stomachs, cutting through armor to spill their innards onto the stone.

Idiots. They could stab it a thousand times and it will not die. Now, it is even angrier.

"Drop the shield," Malachi commands, and I do so reluctantly, ready to rearm.

"Enough!" A flaming whip materializes, striking the daaknar's wings, earning a deafening screech as it veers its hateful gaze back to us.

A silver cord of power waits at my fingertips, ready to unleash and send it back to Azo'dem. It takes everything in my power to keep from lashing out.

"Obey me!" Malachi booms, cracking his flaming whip again.

I recoil on instinct. If I close my eyes, I can see the Fate of Fire standing before my crumbling sanctum, a menacing form of blazing horns and dominance.

The daaknar answers with a snarl, its lips curling back to flaunt its yellowed fangs. But then it lumbers over to the open cage, climbing in.

My heart thumps in my ears as the Saur'goths latch the door shut and, collecting the metal poles, lift the beast to carry it toward the passage back to Cirilea.

"Our entertainment for tonight is secured." Malachi smooths his palm over my back.

I beam up at him while inside, a voice screams.

"See? Not an empty seat. This is what the people wanted." Malachi throws a casual hand toward the crowded arena before leaning back in his chair, holding up his wine goblet in the air, his wordless demand for the servants to refill it.

"Yes, my love." I resist the urge to remind him that his Saur'goth soldiers stormed the streets, banging on doors and demanding that people attend the competition tonight or face the penalty of death.

The slightest breath grazes my cheek, drawing my attention to the vacant seat beside me, then up to the black and gold banners above, the heavy brocade flapping with a cool wind.

"Who are you?" I whisper, searching the emptiness with a probing thread of Vin'nyla. Still, it touches nothing, but I know someone is there.

"Who are you speaking to?" Malachi asks.

"Hmm?" I force a giggle as I turn to him. "Oh, just myself."

He reaches over and collects my hand in his, kissing the back of it.

It's in these fleeting moments that I can almost forget who I'm really speaking to, when I can imagine that I'm with my Elijah again and all is well. "I miss you so much." It slips out.

He frowns curiously. "But I am right here."

Not you.

I smile. "Of course you are."

"I suppose it is time to begin." Releasing my hand, he stands and moves to the edge of the royal partition, high above the crowd, and waits. A guard blows a horn and a deathly silence falls over the arena.

"Citizens of Islor! Behold, your king who has brought you peace and prosperity!" He holds his arms out wide, presenting himself to them like a puffed peacock. With a wave of his hand, the Saur'goths usher dozens of mortals through a gate at sword point and into the center of the arena. Men, women, children. The young and the old. Entire families. "These mortals wish to be free of their keepers' rule! So we will free them."

Another set of doors opens beneath us. I lean forward and my stomach drops as they carry the cage with the hunched daaknar within it.

Gasps erupt.

Including mine, as I realize his plan. "You cannot."

"I can, and I will." There's a dangerous edge to his voice. He regards the faces in the stadium. "The spark of rebellion must be extinguished before it has a chance to catch. These are all dangerous sparks."

I take in the huddle of mortals, the terror in their eyes, how the children cling to their mothers' gowns. My heart has never particularly bled for these creatures who hunted my kind and made me hide in the shadows, but I look upon them now as one might look upon defenseless puppies. My chest tightens with dread at what we are about to witness.

The Saur'goths have all backed away, lining the perimeter of the arena.

Malachi turns to regard me. "Open the cage."

I hesitate.

"Open it!" he roars, his fury crackling in the air, the two words echoing through the arena.

Forgive me. I shoot a stream of Vin'nyla, striking the latch. The door swings open with an eerie creak and the daaknar eases out, pulling itself up to its full height with a growl.

The women and children begin to cry. The men usher them to their backs, as if that will help.

But it won't. Nothing will.

I close my eyes.

"Watch."

"I cannot—" My words are cut off by Malachi's powerful hand clamped over my jaw. He drags me to my feet to stand beside him. "You are their queen. Let them see your crown."

A boy of maybe twelve cries out, attracting the daaknar's attention.

"Have mercy on them," I beg as it lunges.

WENDELINE WAITS by the main doors to the royal garden, exactly where I told her to. "Your Highness." She bows. "You are pale. Are you feeling ill?"

"Just tired." And unable to dislodge those screams from my mind's ear. I fear I will hear them in my sleep for years to come. I begin walking down the stone path.

She falls into step beside me. A group of Saur'goths grunt at us and she flinches.

"Ignore them. I do." There seem to be more of them and fewer of the Islorian guards each day.

Wendeline hesitates. "I heard there was an event in the arena tonight."

"Yes. An event." More like a massacre. "Did you not attend?"

She shakes her head, her eyes downcast. "The last time I stood in that arena was ... not a good night."

"Yes, you began marking the mortals with the double crescent moon. Where have you seen such a thing, anyway?"

"In Mordain. The seers were known to draw it but without explanation. It was the first thing that came to mind. I had no idea what it meant. I certainly did not expect its ties to this secret kingdom in Stonekeep, which I am sure you are aware of by now."

"I am. But let us tend to the plants, and I will tell you about the people who wear that same symbol in my old world."

Her eyes light up.

"So, these People's Sentinel ... they hunt casters?" Wendeline pauses to smooth a finger over a vine. All hints of her fear for me have faded as we stroll deeper into the garden and I tell her about the old world, how different it is from this one.

"And burn them. They also hunt those who feed off mortal veins, though there are few of us left. They consider themselves disciples for the human race, rooting out evil."

"And they are permitted to do so? No one questions this? The guild does nothing?"

"The mortal population, which greatly outnumbers our kind, does not know. It is all very clandestine. The Sentinel does not discuss it with nonbelievers, which is most of society. If they did, they would be labeled delusional and medicated to scare their demons away. We are mythical creatures. Fictional villains. The guild is happy to maintain this illusion, for our safety." I pause. "Romeria's mother is a disciple of their order."

Wendeline gasps.

"Yes. Ironic, isn't it, given what her daughter is? Not that she had any idea. But she tried to recruit Romeria. Brought the girl to a burning. That's the night Romeria ran and never returned. She lived on the streets of a busy city for years." I watched from afar, struggling not to intervene, my anger flowing. I knew Malachi had an interest in this family, but I didn't know for what purpose until much later.

"And her father is, or was, a seer."

"*Is*. Eddie is still alive. Though, I hazard, not for much longer. Not only did Romeria's mother have no idea what she bore, she had no idea what she married. Him, I feel sorry for. As difficult as a life for a seer is in this world, you are far better off dead in that one. But Romeria's mother? She reaps what she sows." I could have killed that mortal a hundred times over and not lost sleep. Malachi forbade it. "But it is interesting, is it not? That the same symbol can mean two entirely different things in two realms? Though, I suppose in both cases, it hinges on protecting the mortals. Or seemingly so, given how many I heard were executed here because that very symbol uncovered their secret."

Wendeline flinches at the reminder of her part in Cirilea's demise. "I had hoped Atticus would approach things differently. But he is not his brother."

"You are loyal to this *Zander*." I hear the distaste of his name on my tongue. That smug Islorian, taunting my misfortune with such relish. If he had not had that beast there to whisk him away, he would be dead. But then I would have no leverage with Romeria, so perhaps I am the fortunate one for failing to kill him.

"I have always been loyal to him and his family, but mostly to his cause." She smiles softly. "I've heard him speak often about a realm where all people live equally. Mortals and immortal alike."

I guffaw. "That will *never* happen, in this realm or any other. There will always be those with power who wish to keep it, those with wealth who refuse to relinquish it. Tonight's disaster in the arena was sparked by a noblewoman's table-side complaint that her servants were abandoning them. Now, with the king's demonstrated support, those with influence will take matters into their own hands, believing they have license to. They will use the fear of the arena as a tactic, and it will work."

"Perhaps it was too idealistic," she agrees. "Still … a noble cause for a noble king."

Our path through the garden is quiet for a long moment.

"Where did these People's Sentinel first see such a symbol and decide to claim it for their own?" Wendeline wonders out loud.

"Likely from one of the seers they burned."

A soft chuckle escapes her, even as her face pinches with consternation. "Yes, you are right. It is all quite ironic."

It feels oddly therapeutic to have someone to speak to so freely about our kind. I have not had anyone in my life to do that with for far too long.

But I have a purpose here, and it is not friendship. "Do you have any information for me about my earlier query?"

"I do, Your Highness, for what it's worth. More than one person saw the princess boarding a ship that left before all the others on the day of the rebellion."

"And what are the chances they mistook her for someone else?"

"It is not likely. Princess Annika is beautiful beyond compare, and her blond locks are distinctive. Also, the ship she was on was nearly empty. One source claims she was held at knifepoint by a male with dark hair. A regal-looking elven."

I frown. "A lord, perhaps?"

"They did not know who he was."

That is certainly curious. "Did they know where she was sailing to?"

"They did not say. But options would be limited. Either they sailed to Seacadore or to Northmost. Anywhere beyond that and they would face the sea sirens. No captain would risk it."

"Sea sirens." I shake my head. There is still so much for me to learn about this world. "So she might still be alive, then."

"Yes. And safe from Cirilea."

"Safe is a relative term." There is an army of Saur'goth warriors rushing south from the mountains and they will obliterate anyone and anything in their path. How long before Romeria and her precious exiled king discover that? Not long now, I imagine.

I lead us through the cedar labyrinth, past the circular rose garden, and toward the nymphaeum, checking the position of the moon as my heart hammers in my chest. All day I've waited for Malachi to mention something about the missing guards at the nymphaeum last night, but either he's been distracted or the Saur'goths never noticed their comrades missing. Or perhaps Malachi wishes to catch my treasonous hand in action, so to speak.

"Where are we going? The bulk of the damage is the other way." Wariness touches Wendeline's voice.

"It is, but I need you to come with me this way first. There is something you need to see." *Or, more accurately, someone who needs to see you.*

45

ROMERIA

"Where is she? We cannot stand here all night," Zander grumbles.

"We've been here for two minutes." But he's not wrong. The pile of beast-guard corpses will be hard to explain should someone stroll by.

"I'm surprised there weren't more after last night." Jarek hovers near one side of the nymphaeum while Abarrane takes the other, their eyes grazing the shadows. "Unless she and Malachi are scheming and this is a trap."

"I'd hope Lucretia would be here to warn us if that were the case." If she didn't somehow give herself away. "Regardless, I've shielded us." The entire nymphaeum is protected by an invisible dome. Of all the tricks Gesine taught me, that might be my favorite.

The slightest rustle in the cedar hedge sounds, setting everyone into a fighting stance.

Two forms step out.

I nearly lose my grip of my affinity at the sight of Wendeline. She was always slight, but now she looks frail, like a strong gust of wind could knock her off balance, her white priestess robes hanging off her skeletal frame. In just a few months, the threads of gray in her hair have multiplied, taking over the corn silk blond. She looks tired and worn, as if she has been dragged through a figurative hell and back.

Still, when her eyes land on me, they sparkle with surprise. "Your Highness!" She takes a step forward.

Sofie's hand locks onto her wrist, keeping her in place.

I gasp at Wendeline's missing pinky finger.

"You've left me with another mess to clean up." Sofie's eyes glow as they drift over the corpses. She's wearing a red satin dress that I remember seeing in the closet here—one of Princess Romeria's gowns —and her hair is collected in a simple but elegant chignon. She looks every bit the queen and as stylish as that first night I met her, at the charity ball when I was sizing up a set of cuff links and she was sizing up me. The bruising and gash across her cheek from last night are almost healed.

"Tell them to stop guarding the nymphaeum and we won't have to keep killing them," Zander answers coolly, his gaze on Wendeline. What is going through his head?

"That is not an option. But luckily, they seem too disorganized to notice guards missing from their posts. Have you found my answer for me?"

"Not yet. It's only been a day. The scribes are scouring the library in Ulysede. If there's anything there, we'll find it." Though part of me doesn't want to give Sofie her husband back after all she's done.

"If you'd like anyone left alive in this city, I suggest they look faster," she snaps. There's a different air about her. Where once she oozed confidence and calm, now urgency and impatience lace her tone.

Zander's body stiffens. "What does that mean?"

She takes a deep breath, as if trying to collect herself. "The mortals have begun abandoning their keepers. Malachi sees that as a sign of rebellion and has made examples of dozens tonight, in the arena."

"How?" His voice is steely.

"How do you suppose? With his favorite pet."

My blood turns cold. "There's a daaknar here?"

"That is right. You fought one bravely and survived. How are those scars?" Sofie studies my shoulder as if she can somehow see the marks through leather and cloth. "I've heard they are hideous."

I ignore her petty taunt. "We've swapped one king executing mortals for another. How is this better?"

"Believe me when I tell you, the last king's hangings were far more humane." She shifts her focus back to Zander. "Since you asked, the rumor is that your sister escaped Cirilea in a ship."

Zander pauses a beat. "To Northmost?"

"We do not know, but the ship was mostly empty, and she was held at knifepoint by a male with black hair."

"She was taken hostage, then. She is likely in Northmost."

"That is for you to discover, but the information is my gift. I have kept up my end of the bargain." She gestures to Wendeline. "See? Alive and well enough. Now it is your turn to hold up your end."

"Let her come with us!" I blurt before I can quell my urgency. "Please." I know Zander wants her here as a potential ally, but seeing her now ... Wendeline isn't the only one who played a role in everything that's happened, but she seems to have suffered the most for it.

"I cannot. If the priestess is missing and the king should ask, it will raise alarms. I have enough to cover up with these nightly visits of yours." She sets her jaw with determination. "Do not return until you have an answer."

"What if it is not the answer you hope for? What will you do then?" Zander challenges.

Her eyes narrow. "I will protect my Elijah until the right answer arrives, whether that is today, tomorrow, or three centuries from now."

"At what cost?"

"Any!" she snaps, her composure fraying again, like a worn rope that can no longer bear the tension it holds.

"And will he accept that?" Zander steps forward, testing the boundary of my shield. "When Elijah learns all that you have done in his name, do you think he will fall to your feet in praise or in agony? I know how I would feel if Romeria sat idly by and allowed the murder of innocent people. I could not live in my own skin after that."

Sofie's eyes glow brighter, as if she's about to strike. "Do not be reckless enough to think that if you were to kill Malachi today, that you would be protected from him tomorrow, when he finds the next suitable host waiting within the Nulling. As long as the rift is open and he wishes to walk this plane, you will *never* be free of him, in one form or another." Her posture stiffens. She looks ready to pounce. "But if you harm my husband, you will also *never* be free of me." Suddenly, her head whips left. "Someone approaches. You must leave now," she hisses.

"Metal. Soldiers' footfalls," Abarrane confirms.

"Lucretia?"

The sylx materializes at my side, her hand on my shoulder.

Sofie's mouth hangs.

"We will find an answer," I promise, offering Wendeline one last smile that, I hope, says, "Hang in there" before I whisk us back through to Ulysede.

46
SOFIE

I will dwell on that creature that appeared out of thin air later.

For now ... There's not enough time to incinerate the bodies.

Drawing on every thread of Aminadav I can find, I force the grassy ground to swallow the half-dozen Saur'goths whole, burying them deep in the dirt. The last ripple in the grass moves just as two more round the corner.

Wendeline shrinks under their looming forms.

"Your Highness," the one on the left barks. "Where are Mal'Rot, Mal'Sur, and the others?"

"How should I know? I am not their keepers. But a group of six passed us on our walk, talking about joining the hunt for mortal deserters. Perhaps that was them?" Meanwhile, I silently curse. These brutes *all* have names? This was easier when they were mindless beasts.

"Mal'Rot should know better than to leave his post," the one on the right grumbles.

"Then you should go and seek this *Mal'Rot* in the city and let him know. That's an order, as your queen."

With grunts, they turn, giving me their backs.

They never see the ice blades coming.

Wendeline yelps as the two massive bodies topple, their heads hitting the ground a split second after. I don't waste time, burying the bodies deep in the ground where they fell. In moments, there isn't the slightest hint of my crimes. "Huh."

"What is it, Your Highness?" Wendeline asks timidly, falling into step beside me as we head back through the labyrinth.

"It just dawned on me that the Saur'goth leader's name was Mal'Gar. Their names are *all* prefixed with Mal. An ode to their sire, *Mal*achi, likely." He is truly that arrogant that he had them name themselves after him.

"That is … interesting."

"Not really." But I smile. It feels good to slaughter his new pets.

DREAD GRIPS my every limb as I step into the king's bedchamber, bracing myself for what I might see on this night, for which specific way Malachi uses my husband's body to punish me or wound Elijah.

I inhale sharply at the sight of a young male sitting naked on the edge of the bed, servicing Malachi with his mouth. The pile of finery on the floor—a tailored jacket with a crest, a sword and dagger holstered in leather—marks him a ranking nobleman. I shouldn't be surprised that a lord would be as eager to suck a king's cock as those simpering ladies seem to be.

"Pleasant time in the garden, my love?" There's that edge in Malachi's voice that tells me I will not escape to my chambers unscathed.

"Yes. Peaceful."

"Good." His head tips back, his fist curling through tonight's lover's hair. "Undress."

I know better than to hesitate. Strolling over to the nearby chaise, I unfasten my dress and remove my underthings and lay them there while listening to the sound of Malachi's pleasure build.

He climaxes in the nobleman's mouth as I'm settling on the bed.

"Spill your seed in her," he commands.

The male turns to regard me with a lust-filled gaze.

My stomach drops. "No—"

Malachi's eyes snap to me. "No?"

"I mean … I am devoted to you." *Elijah.* I have never been with another, except within the sanctum, but that was to save my husband and it was with a fate, not this bootlicker.

"If you are devoted to me, then you will obey me." He nods toward my closed legs.

"Yes, Your Highness."

Too eagerly, the male lord kneels on the bed and, grabbing my calves, drags me over. Without any preamble, he pushes into me and begins thrusting.

I wince, my body resisting the intrusion.

"Are you not enjoying this, my love?" Malachi's smile is wicked as he stands over us and makes Elijah watch this male—this stranger —defile me.

"I am. Very much." But I can't even summon a fake moan.

Malachi shuts his eyes, and I brace myself for whatever torture he is about to inflict. He is always creative.

But when they open again, they are suddenly the soft, warm brown eyes I recognize from so long ago. In this moment, I see my Elijah staring back at me, just long enough for him to focus, for me to see the revulsion , the flinch of pain as he watches me beneath another male, and then he's gone, and Malachi is back in time to hear the lord empty himself into me with a series of grunts.

What if Zander was right?

The doubt that bastard Islorian king planted in my mind begins to sprout, its roots winding deep to take hold. Will Elijah thank me or doom me for all the ways I have made him suffer, first within the Nulling and now, as the unwitting hand and voice delivering Malachi's cruelty?

A tear streams from the corner of my eye, the only reaction I allow Malachi to see as he kneels on the bed, prepares himself, and then thrusts into the waiting lord.

47

ROMERIA

My shoulders sag with relief the moment the crypt walls appear. "I was worried you wouldn't make it back."

"You were worried about me, Your Highness?" Tonight, Lucretia wears a brown leather outfit to match Abarrane, her hair in three identical braids. "I am touched."

"Tell me you learned something."

"I learned *many* things."

"About Sofie and Malachi and what is happening in Cirilea," I press. I know Lucretia's game well by now.

She slinks around Jarek, pausing to tip her head to admire his face. "Hello, Commander. I missed you."

The muscles in Jarek's jaw ticks. "Answer her question or you are no longer of use to us."

She grins as if she was baiting him to get that hostile reaction. "The new queen of Islor misses her husband dearly."

"She's not Islor's queen!" Zander snaps.

Lucretia frowns with genuine confusion. "But she wears the crown."

I squeeze Zander's arm. It's not worth arguing semantics with the sylx. "Tell us what you saw."

"The king fornicated with a mortal and then ended her life."

I share a look with Zander. "In front of Sofie?"

"No. Well, the fornicating part, yes. But the not-queen of Islor left to her chamber and I stayed for the end." She slides her fingertip over Jarek's vest and he slaps it away. "It was quite something to watch."

351

"That must have been difficult for her to see," Zander admits.

If Malachi took over Zander's body and made me watch that? "It would be soul-crushing." No wonder Zander's words about Elijah needled her.

"He does it nightly, according to the servants who whisper when they think no one is listening." Lucretia waggles her eyebrows as she slinks around the vacant stone pillars. "Sometimes they are servants. Sometimes they are lords and ladies. Those, he does not kill."

We don't need explicit details on Malachi's sordid sex life. "What else did you learn?"

"She cried herself to sleep last night longing for the male trapped within the male. I gave her dreams to help console her, much like the ones I give to you." Lucretia smiles up at Jarek. "She enjoyed them as much—"

"What else? What is important for us to know?" I cut her off before Jarek pulls his daggers out and chases her off.

"Are they executing the mortals with the daaknar? Is it true?" Zander jumps in.

"Yes, and it was a slaughter. Both young and old. They died and everyone watched. They keep the beast in a cage. That is the only way to control it. There will be another event tomorrow night, and every night after until the mortals learn their place."

Zander curses. "And what about Annika? Was that also true?"

"The source of that information was the wielder, who communicated it to the not-queen tonight while they were on their way to you."

"There was a ship that left before everyone else. Seamus told me about it," I confirm.

"So we will go to Northmost tomorrow. See if we can find her." He scratches his chin. "I cannot imagine who the lord would be who held her hostage."

"An easterner who escaped and used her to gain passage out?" Abarrane suggests.

"Yes. Maybe." Zander paces around the stone circle. "What Sofie said about Malachi finding another host and returning ... How are we to rid ourselves of him if this is the case? If he can simply return in another form and then what? Are we to live this nightmare over and over again for all of eternity?"

"Is it true?" I ask Lucretia.

"I cannot tell you what the Fate of Fire will choose to do."

"But *can* he turn around and come back through the Nulling if he wants to?"

"Yes. The passage is open."

"And we can't close it."

"You cannot do anything. Only my previous masters can choose to close the Nulling."

"And how do we make them choose to do that?" Abarrane demands.

"You wish them to return to exile after they have done so much for your kind?" The smirk on Lucretia's face is infuriating.

"Why not? I mean, where are they, anyway?" I throw my hands out. "I don't see them anywhere!"

"There is as much that you do not see as that which you do." She smiles. "Perhaps Her Highness should summon Aminadav or Vin'nyla for counsel."

"*No.*" Why is she pushing for that?

"It is your choice to not heed my advice." She shrugs. "The not-queen uses the wormhole."

I falter at the sudden change in topic, and then process what she's telling me.

Zander frowns. "What does she—"

"The nymphaeum door." God, I wish I had never called it anything but that. "What do you mean, Sofie uses it? She can do that?"

"Of course she can. The not-queen of Islor is a powerful wielder like you. These passages were built for them and the rulers they served."

"Can Sofie come *here*?" I point to the door that leads to Cirilea, momentary panic setting in.

Lucretia's musical laugh carries. "These will not open for anyone but the Queen for All."

With a heavy sigh of relief, I ask, "Then where does Cirilea's door lead for Sofie?"

"To a place deep within a cave where the Fate of Fire can collect more soldiers. There is a stream there and a gateway to the Nulling."

"Fates. I know where it is." Zander closes his eyes for a moment. "Radomir showed me a nymphaeum door in Soldor. There's a gaping hole in the side of the mountain. I was going to tell you, but with everything else going on, it slipped my mind. That must be where these Saur'goths are coming in."

"And how Malachi and Sofie got to Cirilea so fast." It makes sense now. "Where else can she go?"

"The not-queen's path is limited by the designs of those who used these doors when they were created."

"The nymphs."

"And their people. But the Queen for All is not limited." She gestures around the room.

"Which one leads to Soldor?"

"That one, there." She points to a carving across from Cirilea.

The itch to reach out with my affinities is strong. "If I were to go through there now, what would I find?"

"I cannot say. Possibly nothing, possibly a grave threat."

"How many of these Saur'goths has he brought through?" Zander asks.

"I do not have a number."

"Do you have a thought?" he snaps.

Lucretia grins and then in the next instant, she morphs into Sofie.

Zander and the legionaries draw their swords in a split second.

"They are still arriving?" she says, her French lilt perfect.

In the next second, Lucretia's form morphs again, this time into the man I recognize from the stone tomb beneath Sofie's castle.

"And they will continue to for many years before they are depleted. I have forged an army that can replenish itself twice over. No army of this realm shall defeat it," the male standing before us says in a deep, accented voice before he vanishes, and Lucretia reappears.

Silence hangs in the crypt as the weight of what we just heard—a projection of what the sylx witnessed firsthand, I have to assume—settles on our shoulders.

"That mine weaves through half of Venhorn," Abarrane says. "This army could be moving through it and we would not know."

"No, especially when we've been so distracted with the rift and Lyndel and Mordain." Zander curses as he paces, his hands on his hips. This is what we have been waiting for. This is what Malachi has been planning.

First things first. "How do we destroy Soldor's nymphaeum door?"

"Destroy it?" Lucretia's pretty face puckers. "You cannot."

"Can the nymph elders?"

"You would have to summon them to ask, and there would be a cost."

I cringe at the idea, the painful memory of interacting with them still too fresh. "How do I summon them—"

"No." Zander shakes his head. "The nymphs were said to barter in lives. That is what Gesine once told me. I doubt this will be a cost we are willing to pay. We must find another way."

I wait for Lucretia's mocking retort, something about how little Gesine knew about anything. For once, though, she remains quiet, which only heightens my fear that what Gesine said was right.

"So what's the play here?" I ask.

"We cannot allow Malachi such easy access for his soldiers to move through Islor." Zander grits his teeth with determination. "We will take down the mountain around it."

DAWN BRUSHES the sky in shades of lavender and spun sugar as we march through the halls of the castle, adrenaline pumping through my veins. "For the record, I think this plan is nuts and you are crazy."

Zander's lips twitch. "Then it seems I am paying you back for all the insane schemes you have dragged me into."

I cast a sideways glare. We brainstormed late into the night before resting for a few hours, knowing today might require my full well of power. "We need Mordain's best stone casters for this to work."

"I am sure Solange will comply with her Prime's order."

"Don't call me that." I raise a finger in warning. "And I know. I just hope they aren't too tired from fighting at the rift last night." Because the sooner this is done, the better.

"You know they will just find another path out of the Nulling." Jarek flanks my other side, checking and rechecking the multitude of weapons strapped to his lethal frame while ignoring Lucretia who trails him.

"Maybe, but they won't have a door to Cirilea beside it."

"Your Highness! Please, a moment!" Agatha calls out, rushing down the hall from the wing dedicated to the scribes' sleeping quarters, a book tucked under her arm.

My hope blossoms at the urgency in her voice. "Did you find an answer about the host body?" I had emphasized the importance of that when we returned from our first visit to Cirilea with Sofie's demand.

"No." She pauses, resting her hands on her knees as she catches her breath. "But we discovered more about what happened to the mystics."

"Okay?" I wait patiently.

"Much like us, the mystics could create with their affinities, and those with more than one affinity could summon the fates. The conjurers were a different sort entirely. They also had connections to the elements, but they wielded them differently, more subtly. I do not have a good grasp of it yet, but that is not what is important. What *is* important is that the mystics would summon the fates, who would grant requests that the conjurers would then actively work to counter, causing much friction between the two sides."

"Are you saying conjurers could reverse what the fates delivered?"

"Not reverse, but quell, for a time at least. They were called curse breakers by the people and revered. The fates did not like that, so they convinced the mystics to wage war on them. In the end, the mystics slaughtered all the conjurers."

"And more weren't born?" Zander asks.

"Conjurers are not born, they are *made*. It is an arduous and painful process to become one and not all survived. With no one left to perform the ceremony, soon there were none left in the realm. Understandably, the nymphs were not pleased.

"Then Malachi decided he would enter this plane and rule. Soon after him, Aoife followed suit, and the two wreaked havoc on the lands. The mystics summoned Vin'nyla and Aminadav for help, and each time, the fates punished them in some way. They realized the mistake they had made, ridding the realm of the conjurers who could have helped offset the many plagues being brought upon them.

"And then an elemental wielder with affinities to all four elements was born. Her name was Nyxalia, and she became the ruler of the mystics. She summoned the nymph elders and pleaded for their help to reverse all these plagues once and for all, and rid them of the fates that ruled in these lands. The nymphs said there was only one way to do this."

"They had to leave and close the Nulling."

She nods. "And without the nymph elders here, the fates could not remain."

"So, you're saying it was the nymphs who got rid of Aoife and Malachi." Not a brave warrior or a key caster, or a king. Not even a dragon.

"Yes. But the cost was steep. The nymph elders demanded the mystics' lives. *All of them.*" Agatha whispers as if it's a secret. "As well as their history and their learnings. The age of the mystics would be over. Some other version would come along one day, the nymph elders promised, born from the lands and the elements within them, and they would call the nymphs to return. But, if the entirety of the nymphs had to surrender their freedom, to lock up their power within this realm of Ulysede that they created, then the mystics had to pay the price for all their crimes."

My stomach sinks. "And the mystics agreed to this?"

"Nyxalia did." She holds up the book. "We found it tucked away behind a special case. It is all in here, in her own words. She says she deliberated for years and during that time, the masses only suffered and starved more. There was no other way to stop it, so she finally agreed, without ever telling anyone. She was sentencing her entire kind to death, after all, and knew they would try to stop her.

"But her one requirement was that the mystics' library be preserved here so that one day when the nymphs came back as they said they would, the next age would learn the truth of what happened and be warned against following in the same footsteps."

"The next age being … us." The casters.

Me.

"The nymphs agreed. The last entry in this book is on the eve of Hudem, when Nyxalia walks through this grand library, taking stock of her people's history. There is nothing after it." She flips open the book to show us the blank page. "But we must assume the world was rid of Aoife and Malachi, along with the mystics, and the nymphs, and beasts stopped crawling out of the rift."

"I'm sure the people rejoiced." But Zander's brow is furrowed. "If only our own people took such care in documenting knowledge as these mystics did."

"They likely documented it, but it was destroyed in the aftermath. Kings and queens are known to influence what the realm may remember of them and the gods they serve, and sometimes society chooses to erase history as if it never happened rather than confront the dark side of it. Mordain has been guilty of the same. Most have never heard of the knowledge discovered in those tomes from Shadowhelm, and it is because the Primes of the past did not wish it to be known. But—" Agatha holds up the book. "We can be thankful for Nyxalia's consideration."

"Yes. Thankful. But this is … a lot to take in." Standing in a hall as the sun rises, learning the deepest secrets hidden within Ulysede for tens of thousands of years.

"I thought it was important you hear it."

"It was. Thank you, Agatha."

"Who have you told about the contents in this tome?" Zander asks, his voice lowered.

"Only those standing right here."

"It *must* remain this way." He levels her with a hard look. "No one from Mordain is to know."

I open my mouth to argue that Solange and Allegra should be informed.

"Yes, of course, Your Highness. *I understand* the danger this information presents for Her Highness where my people are concerned. I will keep this with me at all times." She clutches the book against her chest. "Best be on your way to whatever it is you are doing today. We will keep searching for answers to that other question." With a bright smile, as if the information she divulged wasn't loaded with doom, she marches in the direction of the library.

"What are the chances that the nymph elders would demand the end of the casters for their help?" Zander asks Lucretia.

"I cannot speak for them."

"Guess," Jarek hisses, his teeth bared as he glares down at her.

"To ask them to leave after they have given you so much would require a substantial sacrifice." Anger zags across her face.

And what other way do the nymphs barter but in lives …

My chest tightens. What if all else fails and I'm forced to make that bargain? Aminadav's horn still sits in my satchel, waiting for our darkest hour. But what consequences will that bring and will they be worse than what the nymphs offer?

Zander heaves a sigh. "Let us go now. We have a cave to collapse."

———

I'VE ONLY EVER SEEN the rift from high above, looking down as Caindra flew over. Now I cling to her claw as she dives into the chasm, my stomach in my throat at the bottomless pit below and the anticipation of falling into it. Valk and Xiaric follow closely behind, carrying Jarek, a stone caster, and two Shadows Solange chose for this mission.

"There!" Zander shouts and points to the left.

Earlier, when he described this harebrained plan of his and I told him he was insane, he insisted this was the best way—the only way— but that the dragons would not fit within the opening in the cliff wall. I see now that he was right.

"Dear God," I moan, arming myself with my affinities and bracing as Caindra swoops.

With a deafening screech of warning, she tosses us in. Zander rolls and has two swords drawn in seconds. I'm not nearly as graceful, smashing my knee against a rock. By the time I've hobbled to my feet with a wince, Jarek and the stone caster—a small man with a receding hairline and a face full of terror that matches what I feel—are behind us. Not five seconds later, the Shadows land with smooth precision, nothing but their glowing eyes visible.

The cave is empty.

Jarek steps in deeper to investigate, nudging a half-eaten carcass with his toe. "I was expecting a battle."

"Be thankful we do not have one, and hopeful that one does not find us. This way." The Shadows hang back while Zander leads us around the corner, to the nymph door.

"This is it?" The stone caster frowns as he cocks his head this way and that, studying the nymphaeum scrawl.

"Yes, and it must not be accessed. If they come through, I want nothing but an impenetrable wall waiting for them, something even a key caster cannot unravel," Zander orders.

I offer a wide smile, trying to balance Zander's clipped tone. "Solange said you were the best Mordain has."

"I am," the caster says without missing a beat. "How much time do I have?"

"Until a beast crawls up here and tries to kill us." Jarek's head is on a swivel. "If you could finish before then, that would be ideal."

The stone caster's eyes widen with panic.

I shoot Jarek a warning glare. "The dragons are watching the rift for any threats, but if you could work quickly, that would be much appreciated."

"I will start now, but I need room."

We step back and watch as he bows his head, as if in prayer. And then his hands begin moving, the sleeves of his beige cloak billowing with the motion. It reminds me of a person working through a Rubik's cube, his wrists twisting this way and that, back and forth.

Perfectly cut cubes begin sliding out from the cave floor, stacking and clicking into place around the nymph door, surrounding it snuggly with first one layer and then another, and then the next. Quickly, the door within begins to disappear.

"This is amazing." Gesine said stone casters were a rare and fascinating breed.

Zander folds his arms. "Yes. I can't say I have ever had the opportunity to watch one of them work. It is fascinating."

The sudden clash of steel breaks our admiration.

"Protect him!" Zander shouts, rushing around the bend with Jarek, their swords drawn. A flurry of sounds erupt, and the shouts and grunts multiply to concerning numbers.

Keeping one eye on our caster, I edge backward to get a look at the other side of the wall.

Two dozen Saur'goth soldiers battle against our four.

My panic swells as I lash out with fists of air and flaming arrows to pick off the four closest to me, dropping them in an instant. The others, I can't get to as easily with Zander, Jarek, and the Shadows in the throng, moving too fast for me to anticipate their next position so I can help them.

A blade slashes across Zander's arm, earning his hiss.

The Saur'goth moves for another swing, but before I can react, Jarek drags his sword across the beast's neck, dropping it.

And opening himself up to an attack on the other side that the enemy sees and aims to take.

I send it flying backward, crashing into the cliff wall. Bits of stone fly with the impact.

Unfortunately, that attracts the attention of several Saur'goths, who charge toward me.

I unleash a wall of fire that stops them in their tracks.

From behind, the Shadows make quick work of them with their swords.

Within minutes, the cave is quiet again, save for the sound of stone dragging into place.

I rush to Zander's side to investigate the wound on his arm.

"It's fine." He waves off my concern. "Where did they come from?"

"We are not sure, Your Highness. They appeared suddenly," one of the Shadows—a female—answers.

"That's what Bexley said used to happen before the rift was created. They'd just appear out of the Nulling, one here, one there." Not like cockroaches crawling out of the rift, which I've seen firsthand.

"This was not one here, one there. It was two dozen all at once, Your Highness." The other Shadow edges into the corner, his sword at the ready as if preparing for another sudden attack.

Zander points toward the tunnel that leads deep into the mountains. "Keep an eye that way too."

Jarek wipes his hand across his forehead, smearing the splatter of blood there. "Tell me he is nearly done?"

I return to our caster in time to see him set the last layer of stones.

He steps back and admires his work.

"She can't open that?"

"No one can open that from the inside." He grins, showing off a gap-toothed smile. "The lever to unlock it is here." He taps two blocks, one after another, and the stone begins shifting and turning, a cacophony of clicks and scrapes until the nymph door appears inside. He hits the stones again and the wall reforms. "If what you describe of how these doors work is true, then she cannot use the one power to dismantle this until she is through, and she cannot pass through."

"Right. Okay. Perfect." I smile. "Thank you …"

"Margeer, Your Highness."

Zander drops his hand on the little man's shoulder, and he jumps. "Well done. You will head back with Jarek—"

"He can go with one of the Shadows," Jarek counters.

"The Shadows are needed here. You are not."

Jarek's jaw tenses. "I am not leaving Her Highness's side."

"You can, because *I* am by her side, and surely there is nothing you can do for her that I cannot," Zander answers coolly.

Jarek adjusts his stance as if he's preparing for a fight.

I step in between them. "Okay, enough of this. Jarek, I need you to get the stone caster to safety so the Shadows can do what they do and then we're *all* getting out of here."

His gray eyes lock on me, anger flaring in them. And something else I can't pick out. "What did I say about asking me to leave your side when you are in a dangerous situation?"

That he would never do it.

"We're a minute behind you, I promise. Please, get Margeer back to camp," I beg. "You're the only one who can do it."

"Is that an order?" he says evenly.

I sigh. "Yes." If that's what it has to be.

Jarek snaps his finger and heads toward the cliff's ledge. Margeer scurries behind, likely happy to be leaving.

"Watch where you step or it will crumble under your foot." Zander adds, "We would not want you plummeting to your death."

I spare him my scowl.

Jarek picks his path to a stable part and whistles.

Valk answers with a screech.

"Ready?" He grabs hold of the caster's robes.

"Yes, but how will—"

Jarek drags him off the edge just as Valk flies past, snatching them in midair.

I feel the blood drain from my face. "Please tell me we don't have to do that?"

"You want me to lie?" Zander flashes a grin before it falls off quickly. "Let's finish this now." He nods to the female Shadow, who studies the area around the nymph door.

A rumble beneath our feet is the only warning before the ceiling caves in, burying the entire alcove.

"We also need to collapse the passage that leads east. We can't have whatever army Malachi has brought in using Venhorn as its home and pouring out toward the rift."

"Is it safe to be standing in here while they're doing this?" I ask.

"They are experts in bringing down both stone and people. But no, probably not." Zander collects my hand and leads me backward toward the opening.

"You take that side, I'll do this one," the female Shadow proposes to her male counterpart. "Your Highness, you may wish to shield yourself."

I do as suggested. We watch with fascination as stalactites crash down a few at a time, exploding as they hit the ground. The columns topple over each other, splitting into chunks that build up.

"That is all we can do while we stand in here, Your Highness," the male Shadow says. "Once we are flying with the beasts again, we can—"

His words are cut off with a gurgled sound, snapping our heads in his direction.

A daaknar stands behind, its barbed talons impaling his neck.

A cold dread washes over me as I'm transported back to that terrifying first night in this world.

"Soriel!" the female Shadow screams, launching a boulder at the daaknar's shoulder that barely nudges it.

It tosses the Shadow's lifeless body away and then lunges.

I release a bolt of fire, sending it flying toward the wall. Only the beast doesn't collide with the stone. It disappears into the darkness.

I frown. "Where did it go?"

"I think we just found the entrance into the Nulling that Malachi has been using for his army." Zander steps forward. "This is how the Saur'goths came through too."

"But it looks like ... nothing."

"It's certainly not nothing." Zander squints. "If we can bury this in rubble—"

The daaknar reappears then, charging at Zander with a snarl, its tattered wings spread wide, its talons angled for his chest.

Terror seizes my every nerve as I sweep Zander away with a gust of wind, and then I hit the daaknar again, this time with all my affinities combined. The answering shrill scream is like nothing I've ever heard. It bursts into flames—just as Annika described happening— and then vanishes.

Zander struggles to pull himself to his feet.

"Are you okay?" I cry out.

He waves me off, bracing his hands on his knees.

The female Shadow runs to her comrade, kneeling to check his pulse.

"Anything?" Zander asks.

She shakes her head.

Pain splays across Zander's face. I know he'll blame himself for this. It was his plan after all.

Easing upright, he waits another few beats before saying softly, "I do not wish to hurry you with your grief, but we should leave here before another one crawls out of that space."

"Yes, Your Highness." Sorrow fills her voice. Hauling Soriel's body over her shoulder with a grunt, the Shadow moves for the rift and whistles. Seconds later, Xiaric flies by, scoops them up, and continues.

"Ready?" Zander leads me to the edge, his arm tight around my waist.

"Caindra."

She answers with a cry, swooping down.

"No matter what, she will catch us," Zander promises, squeezing me tight against him.

But I'm too focused on what might materialize out of thin air behind us to worry about anything else.

We leap ... and land within her clawed grasp.

She sweeps upward before pivoting, beating her wings just enough to allow us to hover.

"You'll need to finish this," Zander says. "Destroy it all. Leave no space for these creatures to fit through."

I draw deeply on threads of Aminadav and Vin'nyla and launch it into the cavern. The sounds of the mountain inside collapsing is deafening and the sudden billow of cloud that explodes out of the opening has Caindra propelling us up and away.

"We can check back when the dust settles. For now, let's return to camp, and then we can go find Annika."

If I had not been here …

If I had reacted a split second later …

With a nod, I sink my head against Zander's shoulder and say a small, selfish prayer of thanks that it was the Shadow and not him.

"WHAT NEWS OF LYNDEL?" Zander asks after a chorus of greetings inside the command tent.

"The casters are working to help secure and repair the damage. They have closed off the secret passages so no enemies can use those," Gaellar confirms. "They believe they can have a new bridge to the rampart finished by tomorrow. There is also the matter of …"

While she gives an update on the goings-on at Lyndel and the rift, Elisaf edges in to nudge my arm. "Has Her Highness been playing in the dirt today?"

I wipe a thumb across my cheek and find dust on it. "Sort of." I give him the quick rundown of what happened in the mine.

He scratches his chin in wonder. "To be a fly on the wall when Malachi and this key caster realize what you've done."

He will be furious. "I'm not sure how many have gotten through already, but at least no more will flood through there, right?"

Abarrane throws back the tent flap and charges in. Jarek is behind her, barely treating me with so much as a glance. His mood was sour when we landed, and it turned icy the moment he heard about the daaknar. "Your Highness. This just arrived." She holds up a letter.

"From whom?"

"I do not recognize the seal." She hands it to Zander.

"Kier." His eyes dart to me before he snaps it open. And exhales. "This is Atticus's handwriting."

Abarrane barks with laughter. "See? That silver-tongued fool goes from captured to writing letters."

Chuckles fill the tent as everyone waits to hear what the treasonous brother-king has to say.

"Fates." All blood drains from Zander's face. "Theon, when did you last receive word from Bellcross?"

48

ATTICUS

I inhale Islor's crisp country air, free of the brine that clings to the coast.

"How does it feel to ride a horse across your own land again?" King Cheral canters beside me, a modest cloak draped over his finery to hide his station as our group of twenty moves inland along the Sanguine River like common raiders. Given the new king in place and the potential of blades aimed upon our arrival, we avoided the trading port east of Kettling and chose the narrower, quieter gulf on the west side, coming ashore in the night.

"I would prefer my own horse, though I imagine it did not survive the battle. Unless your conjurer can resurrect him?" I lean forward to find Tuella, who rides stiffly on King Cheral's other side. It reminds me of Romeria's early days on horseback. Clearly, she doesn't spend much time in the saddle.

"The light cannot reach beyond the realm of the living, usurper king," she says.

"And what *can* it do?"

"Fight the shadow."

"Still with that." I roll my shoulder to test it. Nearly healed. I can't imagine the gnarly scar that merth ax left behind. "And what am *I* to fight with? My winning personality?"

King Cheral's laughter is jovial. "It has done you well so far."

"You will have to allow me a weapon soon enough."

"Have I not already? I gave you a quill and ink after all, did I not?"

"And hovered over my shoulder, dictating my every word."

He shrugs. "I had to make sure you did not layer a secret message within."

"And what would that be? 'Please, do not kill me, Dear Brother, though I probably deserve it'?" Would the letter have reached Zander by now? Likely. And, if he hasn't seen the colossal danger heading his way, he will very soon.

"Trust is earned, not granted, especially not to an enemy."

You trusted me well enough alone with your wife. I bite my tongue, stealing a glance behind us. Satoria rides easily, a secretive smile on her lips as she takes in the rolling hills leading to Aminadav's plains ahead. There's no woodenness in her form.

"The cabin on the ship was a nice touch." I waited for Satoria to slink in, even just for the few minutes of company, but she never did.

"I thought it better than being chained in the hull," King Cheral says.

"Oh, I don't know. I do miss the delightful company I had on the way to Ostros."

The soldier who buried his blade in my back smirks and says something in his language. The other soldiers laugh and sneer until I grin back and their amusement withers.

Maybe they can read that look for what it means—that I'm going to enjoy killing them all.

"How much longer?" King Cheral tugs at his cloak collar as if uncomfortable.

"It depends. The plains are vast." And he has been tight-lipped about where the army has camped. "If I knew where we were headed, I would be able to give you an idea."

He peeks at Satoria. Whatever wordless exchange they share must be enough to convince him to loosen his tongue. "They have found adequate ground outside of a village named Baymeadow. Have you heard of it?"

I smile. "I have." It's where Gracen grew up. I check the position of the sun. "At this pace, we should arrive by nightfall." The wagon that carries Tuella's golden bird bath has set the leisurely pace.

King Cheral nudges his horse with his heels, goading it faster.

49

TYREE

"You have a little ..." I drag my finger over my collarbone, in the spot where hay clings to Annika's skin. Our wagon bumps along the road at a clip, the countless honey jars rattling. Destry is curled up on the floor by our feet, stinking of mead. I'm not sure she even made it to her bed last night, given she stumbled into the barn before the sun rose to announce that we were were leaving in five minutes.

Annika frowns as she peers down, angling her head. "Where?"

"Right ..." I reach over and pick it off her, allowing my fingertips a moment to slide across her skin, reveling in the softness of it. "Here."

She groans. "I have been finding it everywhere."

"I can't imagine why," I say with a sly smile.

Her eyes flash with heat, but she covers the reaction with a mask of annoyance. "Because we slept in a barn like wild animals."

My smile stretches. "Like wild animals. Yes. Definitely."

She hooves my shin with her new boot—a gift from Uda, along with a fresh tunic, breeches, and cloak that were not pilfered from a corpse. The mortal must have traded the others for clean clothes.

I chuckle, even as I wince. I guess we're going to pretend that didn't happen last night? So be it.

She wraps her arms around herself as if she's cold. "How long do you think we will travel for today?"

"We will stop in Basinholde," comes a grumbled reply from the wagon floor. "It is a small city deep in the valley."

I gently nudge Destry's thigh with my toe. "You are awake, my friend."

"It is impossible to sleep with all your gabbing." She adjusts, curling up into a ball. "And mead makes my head pound."

"Really? I quite liked it. And the honey. You will have to express my deep thanks to Ezra for the jar. I can promise, it was much enjoyed." I study Annika's reaction as I add, "Perhaps we can have another tonight."

The corners of her mouth twitch, ever so slightly, but she refuses to relent to me.

I grin, letting her know that I see through her little charade. There is no point in pretending it was anything other than an unexpected but pleasurable night for her as well, not when I had her naked body undulating beneath my touch.

"Ezra is stingy. You will need to fight off another attack for that."

Panic fills Annika's face. "Will we be attacked again?"

"Not by bandits. We have moved away from Thievers Highway. If we are attacked, it will be by soldiers. May the light help us in that case. Ezra has fresh bread and cheese if you are hungry." She groans, as if the mention of food stirs her nausea.

Annika's nose wrinkles with disgust. "Do you always drink yourself to sleep?"

"Only when I am fortunate." Destry tugs her cloak over her head, dismissing any more questions.

Annika frowns at me.

Who are we to judge, though? Clearly Destry is running from demons of a sort, but as long as she helps Annika and me escape this place, she can stay inebriated. "Hungry?" We didn't get the chance to eat before we stuffed ourselves into this coffin.

"Famished."

I draw the curtain back. The sun is shining—a welcome respite from the dense fog and misery of the last few days, but also an opportunity to see more of this realm we were brought to. The horses plod along a snaking road that cuts through forest, moving downhill. In the distance is a range of jagged mountains that reach beyond the cloud cover.

A dark shadow weaves around one of the pinnacles, earning my shock. "Is that a wyvern?"

Ezra spares me a shrug.

I point ahead and flap my hands, mimicking wings. "A wyvern."

He follows my focus and then nods as if understanding. "Wroxlik."

I repeat the word, committing it to memory. He doesn't seem shocked by it or concerned. "What is it doing there?"

He shakes his head, then juts his chin to Uda, who digs out a loaf of bread and hunk of cheese from her satchel.

"Many thanks." I wink as I accept it from her, and her cheeks flush with her smile.

Ezra rolls his eyes at his daughter.

"Do not give her too hard a time. She can't help herself. I am far too appealing to ignore." They have no idea what I'm saying. "Isn't that right, Annika? I believe you said that very same thing last night before you climbed onto my—" I grunt from another hard kick to my shin.

"WHAT DID you say this place was called again?" Annika peeks out of the curtain, having swapped crate seats with me earlier so she could get air.

Destry pulls herself up off the floor with a stretch. It took the entire trip for her hangover to subside, but she seems more energized now. "Basinholde. Ezra usually spends two or three days here, selling his wares at the market and resting his horses before the steady climb up the other side of the valley. Given our purpose, he will sell what he can this afternoon and evening, and we will leave in the morning."

We're certainly somewhere far busier than where we've been. The sounds of life—men shouting, babies crying, horses plodding—carry outside.

"Here, let me have a look."

Annika pouts. "But I like this seat."

"That's fine. You don't have to move." I tuck in behind her on the crate, my chest pressed against her back as I watch the view. She stiffens but doesn't pull away. We've continued this charade all day, where she pretends nothing happened between us last night. I shamelessly flirt and she studiously ignores, and every time my gaze is somewhere else, I feel hers dissecting me.

The streets of Basinholde are narrow and crowded, lined with shops below and half-timbered homes in the stories above, the windows draped in greenery and blooms. Stables of horses are plentiful.

"It reminds me of Port Street in Cirilea, except without the port. A busker!" Delight fills her voice as she spots the man on the corner, juggling five daggers.

"There is a canal, though." I point to the narrow passage between buildings.

"That is the Hag'nin. It feeds from the mountains and flows through the city," Destry explains. "You can hire a skiff. People say it is romantic."

I stifle my chuckle at her apathetic manner.

Above the busker is a balcony where half-dressed men and women showcase their bodies, waiting for clients. "*And* there are brothels."

"Lucky for you," Annika murmurs.

I lean in to whisper in her ear, "How much longer must we play this game?"

To that, she says nothing.

"There are numerous inns and *other* establishments," Destry says, sounding every bit a guide for visitors. "Basinholde is one of the busiest hubs in Udrel. Many roads to different corners of the realm pass through here."

I catch the clanging of metal boots and pull Annika back from the curtain, letting it fall. A moment later, soldiers bark orders nearby. "Is this a good idea, being in a place so busy and crawling with guards?"

"Don't do anything to attract their attention, and you will blend in." But Destry pulls her pendant out, closes her eyes, and begins to chant indecipherable words. When her eyes flip open, they've turned completely white.

Annika flinches. "That is disturbing."

"And yet useful."

We wait quietly for Destry to do … whatever it is she is doing. When her eyes shutter and reopen a moment later, they've turned black again. "There are many guards, but they do not seem to be searching for you here yet. They must think you are still within the capital."

"What did you do there?" I ask.

"I used the eyes of the birds to see what we cannot." She says it as if it's the most natural thing to do.

My eyebrows arch. "I am impressed."

"This only allows for a small range." She holds up the pendant to show me the white stone. "It is made from the temple in Orathas. Every Azyr receives one."

Annika studies it. "It's the stone at the top, where the kal'ana is."

"Yes. It channels the light. The larger the stone, the farther the reach. The Azyr within the temple can reach all of Udrel and beyond. To the seas, and the wraiths within them."

"So they knew we had washed up."

"Yes." She tucks her pendant away. Already, her eyes are returning to normal. "We should be safe enough in the city. For tonight, at least."

The wagon halts and Ezra shouts something. A creak sounds and then we're turning and plodding along again.

"We will stay in the inn tonight," Destry says. "The owner is a friend of Ezra's."

Annika sighs heavily. "Thank the fates. I am desperate for a bath." She grimaces as she touches her neck, where I smeared honey on her.

I chuckle as I slip my fingers beneath her braids and pull out another strand of hay. "He has a lot of friends."

"Ezra is the honey man. He is well known."

A dainty hand slips through the little window, two bands made of a dull silver resting in its palm.

"You must wear those," Destry announces.

"Excuse me?" Annika gapes.

"They are commitment bands—"

"Yes, I know what they are," she snaps. "Why must we wear these?"

"Because we will tell the owner of this inn that you are a married couple from the islands in the far west. The dialect there is so different, it is basically another language. Besides, the wife is a traditional sort and if you are to share a room together, you must be pledged."

Annika scowls. "There is an easy solution to that. We are *not* sharing a room together."

"Yes, we are." Enough is enough. "I am not leaving your side until we are safely out of this realm. Unless spending the next thousand years as their kal'ana sounds more appealing than listening to me snore." Not that I will likely get much sleep.

Annika purses her lips but doesn't argue as I collect the bands. "Thank you, Uda."

The instant I slip on the larger one, I feel the burn. "What is this made of?"

"A special silver from the mountains north of here," Destry says. "Where the wroxlik live."

"The wyvern. I saw one earlier today."

"Yes, they live up there, usually high within the clouds."

"Why does no one seem concerned by these things? In our realm, if one is spotted, everyone runs for cover and we order the Shadows to hunt for it until it is found and killed."

"If we do not bother them, they do not bother us." Destry shrugs. "That has always been the way."

I shake my head—this realm is odd—as I study the band again. "The net they captured us with was made of this same material, wasn't it?"

"Likely, yes. We use it to make nets and cages to capture loose beasts after Azokur. They cannot break free of them. It is too strong a material."

"It sounds like merth," Annika notes.

"Except it does not paralyze us. See?" I collect her hand and slip on the ring.

"Not even a proposal first?" she deadpans but then winces from the burn.

"I know, but it's not too bad."

"What is this merth you speak of?" Destry asks.

"It's a material that grows in our lands. Very dangerous to our kind."

"Where did Uda get these?" Annika looks at her ring with disdain.

"From Ezra, who would have collected them from the corpses of the turned on Azokur."

Annika blinks. "We are wearing dead people's commitment bands."

"Yes. I hope they fit."

Annika gives me a flat look. "Well, if that is not an omen for our grand future together, I do not know what is."

I hold up my index finger. "But you will admit that we *do* have a future together."

"I SUPPOSE THIS WILL DO." Annika scowls at the mouse running along the rafters of our attic chamber in the third story of the inn.

Uda was right to insist we brand ourselves a western couple. Ezra's merchant friend and his wife assaulted us with a barrage of questions that we were able to skirt entirely with smiles and nods.

The stocky woman will no doubt talk about the husband and wife who visited their inn to anyone who will listen.

"Of course, it will do. It has four walls, a roof, and a good-sized bed. *And* that bath you are so desperate for." I gesture toward the two servant girls who lug in pails of water and dump them into the copper tub that sits next to the bed. It looks like hard work. I will admit, I miss the faucets at Argon that bring water with the twist of a wrist. "Which I will leave you to."

"Why? Where are you going?" Annika asks, her voice a touch urgent.

"For a short walk around, to see what there is to see. Unless you would prefer I remain here." I look pointedly at the bed.

Her throat bobs with her hard swallow. "So you can watch me like a lecher while I bathe? I think not."

"Very well, my darling wife." I lean in to press a kiss against her temple. I could pretend it's for the servant girls' benefit, but really, I'm looking for any excuse to have my lips on Annika's skin again. "Keep your dagger near you at all times. Lock the door behind them when they leave and do not open it for anyone."

Her eyelashes flutter as she peers up at me. "Not even for you?"

"Open *only* for me," I correct, squeezing her waist. "But I know how much you like to."

I feel her blue eyes boring into my back as I draw my hood and leave to find Destry.

"THE BROTHELS ARE THAT WAY." Destry jams her thumb in the air behind us.

As is the barstool and ale she salivates for, no doubt. "Thank you, but I am not looking for one."

"Then what *are* you looking for?" Her short legs rush to keep up with my stride.

"A few odds and ends that Annika will appreciate." We pass a stand with baskets of fruits and breads. "Do you know if they have small, sweet grapes here? They are bluish-black in color."

"That does not sound like anything I have seen." She frowns. "I am struggling to understand your relationship with the kal'ana."

My head pivots this way and that, checking to see if we've caught anyone's attention, before I scold the tiny mortal. "Do not use that name. Ever. She is simply Annika, and nothing else." Though there is nothing simple about the Islorian princess who now seems to rule my every thought and decision. How did I end up here, serving as her rescuer and protector, on the hunt for treats to draw her smile while I pine for another chance to feel her bare skin against mine?

My mother would be distraught to learn what I've become. Then again, she has already expressed her deep disappointment in me and all but abandoned her children to their fates. I no longer seek her approval.

"Our relationship is ... complicated," I admit after a long moment.

"Because she hates you during the day and fornicates with you at night?"

"Who says we *fornicate* at night?"

"Is that not what you call what you did in the barn?"

"How do you know what happened?" I pause, my gaze narrowing on the conjurer. "Were you spying on us?"

"*No.* Though I may have used a rodent to check on you a few times." She grins. "Do not fret. Mice are difficult to control. I saw little."

I waggle my finger. "*Do not* do that again. And *never* tell Annika you did it in the first place."

A peddler ahead has a basket of flowers.

"Have a coin I can borrow?" I hold out my hand.

Begrudgingly, Destry slips one into my palm and I swap it for a bouquet of tall stems with blossoms that remind me of Annika's eye color. I hold them to my nose, but they carry no scent.

"So, she stabbed you in the thigh, but you care for her." Destry tests a knit blanket between her fingers before we keep going.

"I deserved to be stabbed, so I will not hold that against her." I give a vague and short explanation about our family's histories and crimes against each other. Though the crimes are beginning to seem more and more one-sided. In fact, maybe *all* one-sided. King Ailill may have caused the rift, but how many generations must pass before you are forgiven for your ancestors' wrongs?

I never asked myself these questions before getting to know Annika. Now, I struggle to condemn her for any of it.

"You are telling me that you are both heirs to your realms' thrones." Destry stares with disbelief.

"Spare heirs. We have siblings who are in line before us. In Annika's case, one is likely dead. I'm not sure about the other." I pause at a clothing stand with fine leathers, admiring a tan-color vest that would complement Annika's blond locks and fair skin.

"Do not ask me for coin for that," Destry warns.

"Have no fear, my friend. I would not want to deprive you of your ale." But I wish I had pilfered more than that one gold brush now. I could use my affinity to knock that stand and distract the merchant's attention, but she's an elderly woman and I imagine those weathered hands spent countless hours on this stitchwork.

We keep going.

"What happens if by some miracle, you return to your realm? Will you be at war?"

"That, my friend, is a very good question." There are clearly things at play that we know nothing about.

We round a corner and come upon a group of six guards at a stand selling cured meats. I can't understand their words, but it's clear they're arguing with the young boy merchant.

"What is going on there?" I ask.

"They do not feel they should pay full price. Keep moving," Destry whispers. "Do not do anything to stir questions."

"Give me some credit." I wander over to a nearby fruit stand to study the elderberries. Annika might like these. I hold out my palm. "I will pay you back, I promise."

Destry scowls as she digs through her pockets.

Meanwhile, I'm keeping one eye on the exchange across the street. The noisiest of the guards reaches into the coin purse tied to his belt and flicks the payment at the boy, letting it sail over his head. As the boy spins and scrambles to fetch the money from the dirt, the guards each collect handfuls of linked sausages before walking away.

The boy's shoulders sink as he discovers he's been duped.

My anger simmers.

The fruit merchant passes me a small pouch of the berries with a nod of thanks.

"Hold this for a moment, please." I hand it to Destry. Unsheathing a short dagger from my belt, I stroll past the guards who laugh and gnaw on their pilfered goods, using my affinity to splinter a wooden post that holds up an awning. It comes crashing down, distracting them for the split second I need to slice the leather strap securing the guard's coin purse.

Really, the fool made it too easy.

While the guards attempt to make sense of what happened, I mosey up to the kid, pointing at the smoked sausage and holding up three fingers.

His jaw drops as I slip more than enough to cover it and what the guards stole. With a wink, I move on.

Destry scrambles to catch up with me. "You enjoy tempting fate."

"No, I enjoy delivering fortune, both good and bad, depending on the person. Here." I fill her pocket with coins before securing the purse inside my cloak. "May you drink all the ale your tiny body can handle and not tumble off your stool."

She mutters something in her own language but then flashes me a toothy smile.

50

ANNIKA

The last rays of a setting sun flood in through the window, illuminating my naked flesh beneath the water's surface. I was not impressed with this attic room when the innkeeper's nosy wife first led us in, with all its dust and cheap fabrics and tiny bed. But it grows on me the longer I soak in the tub. One might even call the little nook charming.

I hold the bar of soap up to my nose, trying to pinpoint the scent. Rose, definitely. Verbena maybe? And … I inhale again. Is that pepper?

Whatever the combination, the rich lather smooths onto my skin like butter to wash away the stickiness from last night's honey. I think I've gotten it all off.

Fates, I cannot believe I allowed that to happen with Tyree. Of all people!

And then he spent the day not letting me forget it, not that I ever could.

I smile as I think of our time in the barn loft, how forthright he was with his compliments, how revering he was with his hands and his mouth.

If I didn't know better, I would think the Ybarisan prince might care for me. What a wild turn of events that would be. Oh, how my brothers would disapprove. But I would quickly remind them that one of them gave up his kingdom for Tyree's co-conspirator, and the other was courting a servant.

Not that I will get to feel my twin's disappointment. Atticus is very likely dead, a thought that stirs my melancholy. Perhaps I should have made more of an effort with him.

The only warning I get is a clicking sound before the door suddenly swings open.

I sit up with a start, ready to lunge for my dagger in case of an attack.

In strolls Tyree, his cloak's hood pushed back.

My shoulders sink with relief. Quickly following it is annoyance. "How did you get in? I locked that from the inside."

He pushes the door shut and latches it. "Have you forgotten what I'm capable of?"

Right. The metal would be easy enough for him to manipulate with his affinity. "No, I am well aware."

He flaunts that sexy, crooked smile that makes my heart skip a beat now.

"What are you hiding behind your back?" His left arm hasn't appeared since he stepped in.

"Wouldn't you like to know." His eyes touch my bare shoulders, and I see the lust spark in them.

"Fine, don't tell me." I make a point of turning around and settling back as if having Tyree in our chamber while I'm bathing has no effect on me. "I am tired of games."

"*You* are tired of games." His deep chuckle vibrates in my chest, but I ignore it and pretend that the way the floor creaks as he approaches doesn't affect me at all. Meanwhile, my pulse races as he moves in behind me where he surely has a prime view of my body in the tub under the waning sunlight. "You've unraveled your braids."

"Yes, I needed to wash my hair. There was honey in it. Find anything interesting at the market?"

"A few things."

I keep my eyes shut and my head resting against the tub's back as I listen to him shuck his cloak and weapons, and kick off his boots.

A delicious, smoky scent wafts to my nose, and I inhale. "What is that?"

"Provisions for the road." He waves the wrapped meat in the air before setting it on a nearby table.

"But you do not eat meat."

"No, but I know how carnivorous you are. I found these." He holds out a pouch for me to try.

I gingerly stick my hand in and pull out an elderberry.

"I also have bread and cheese, and a carafe of wine." He sets them on the table as he lists them. There's some more rustling behind me and then a bouquet suddenly appears in front of my face.

"You brought me flowers?"

He drops them into a nearby water pitcher. "The color reminded me of your eyes."

His words steal my breath. I swallow, unsure how to respond. Plenty of hopeful suitors have tried impressing me with blooms—too many to count. But for my would-be murderer and kidnapper to do so ... "What did you buy for yourself?"

"A leather satchel to carry everything. Are you finished with your bath?"

"Almost. Why?"

He sticks his hand in to test the temperature and I realize that he's removed his tunic. "Because I need one."

I reach out to draw a fingertip across the multitude of white scars along his forearm, and wince at all the days I meandered around the castle while he sat in a cell, alone and injured. Not that he didn't deserve it, or that my brothers had any other choice. But now that I've seen an entirely different side of Tyree, guilt gnaws at me for any part I may have played in it—even as an accessory by royal association. "You wish to bathe in my tepid, dirty water?"

"I bathed in a horse trough last night, Annika. I would call this a vast improvement." He smiles down at me, his gaze dropping to gather a leisurely look at my nakedness before he pulls away.

"There are servants to refill it."

"Yes, young girls, lugging up pails of hot water. I will not make them suffer through that twice in one day."

"How chivalrous of you." I climb out and reach for my towel to dry myself off, hyperaware of his eyes on me.

"Don't worry, I make up for it in other ways." With a grin, he drops his breeches.

My body thrums with anticipation as I study his honed, perfect form and the impressive length hanging between muscular thighs that gave me so much pleasure last night.

He seems unbothered by my gawking as he sinks into the bath, easing back with a groan, his legs bent to fit. The burns he mentioned before are visible—tiny pink marks peppered over his skin, buried within the dark hair. Zander *really* should have had Wendeline heal those. Maybe a caster still could.

He shutters his eyes, appearing relaxed, though surely he's always on high alert.

I pause for a moment to admire his broad chest, remembering what it felt like to touch those curves last night, and then wrap myself in my towel to ward off the chill in the air.

Venturing over to the side table, I sample more elderberries and then lean down to check the blooms for a floral scent. I've never seen such flowers before.

"It's faint. You need to get very close to catch it," Tyree says, his voice gravelly.

I lean in more, inhaling deeply. "I still do not smell anything."

"You'll need to get closer."

"What?" Tipping my head, I discover his heated eyes locked on my backside, my towel doing little to cover the view at this angle. "You mongrel!"

His laughter fills the room.

I collect the bar of soap from the stool and whip it at his chest.

"Thank you. I was going to ask you to pass that to me."

"You are insufferable." Meanwhile, I'm struggling to hide my smile.

"I rather like you too." He chuckles as he lathers soap and smooths his hands over his throat, his chest, his arms. All places I gladly caressed last night.

That, if I'm being honest with myself, I'm craving to touch again. *Twice, Annika?* Once, fine, but allowing it to happen a second time can no longer be blamed on the dire moment.

I distract myself with a new leather vest laying on the bed. "This is far too small for you."

"I should hope so. I bought it for you."

"Me?" I test the soft leather with my fingertips.

"I thought it would look good on you, with your hair color."

The craftsmanship is impeccable. Even Dagny would be hard-pressed to produce something so exquisite. "Did you steal it?"

"You offend me." He splays his bent legs in the tub, allowing me a fine view of his sculpted torso and the gift waiting for me, begging to be stroked. "I stole a purse of coin from a guard who was abusing the young meat merchant and bought it with that."

I snort. "You have no shame."

"You benefit from my lack of it."

On impulse, I slip off my towel and try on the vest. "Well?" I turn around, modeling it for him. "Were you right?"

His Adam's apple juts from his neck as his eyes rake over my body. "Yes. Very much so."

380

With a smile of satisfaction, I peel it off and gingerly set it on the table. Collecting the elderberries, I stroll naked to the far side of the bed and slip under the blankets.

"Are you not going to eat more than that?" he asks.

"Maybe later. I need sleep. You allowed me so little last night." I roll onto my side to study the darkening sky, the sun now set. In truth, I am tired, but I couldn't possibly drift off, not with the heady charge in the air between us, like those moments before a bolt of lightning strikes.

The sound of splashing water fills our quiet room as Tyree bathes himself. I could be wrong, but it seems he's traded his ease of earlier for speed because he is out of the tub within minutes.

I admire his firm backside through the reflection in the window as he towels off his body in a hurry. The bed sinks with his weight as he climbs in on the other side.

And then suddenly, I feel him *everywhere*—his bare, damp body molded against my back from my ankles to my shoulders, his cool nose and hot breath burrowed in my neck, his strong hand kneading a breast.

His hard cock pressed against my tailbone.

I inhale. Yes, that soap mixes delightfully with his skin, even if he bathed in my soiled water, and more so with the orange blossom scent of his blood. I run my tongue along my teeth, searching for the sharp points that are no longer there. Would I be able to control myself if they were? I no longer think so.

Tyree's thumb strokes across my pebbled nipple. "You are going to make me beg tonight, aren't you?"

I smile into my pillow. "Is begging beneath the Ybarisan prince?"

"*Nothing* is beneath me when it comes to you, Annika," he whispers, his voice unusually gruff, his words as blunt as a hammer's strike. He pushes aside my curls so his lips can find my nape.

I shiver as his tongue drags across it.

"I seem to be completely at your mercy," he whispers.

That's funny, because I feel like I'm completely at yours.

His hot lips trail down my spine, all the way to the crevice of my backside, the hand that was roaming my breasts following his movements, splayed as it traces my curves downward, over my abdomen and my hips, until it lands at the delicate place at the apex of my thighs.

His fingers slip over my slick center before sinking deep inside my core.

"See? You can play games all day, but you can't hide the truth from me here." With a quick movement, my leg is suddenly thrown over his shoulder and his face is inches from where I want it buried.

My heartbeat quickens as I wait for that first stroke of his skilled tongue.

"Should we pause for the night? I wouldn't want to be accused of stealing your much-needed sleep."

"Tyree, if you do not put that busy tongue of yours to good use—" A moan sails from my lips, cutting off my words as he grants my request with a long, deliberate stroke, followed by another, and another.

I steal a glance down, to see his blue eyes dark and shiny, watching my reaction. So I spread my thighs wider, granting him better access.

He pauses, pulls back, his lips glistening. "You know, as intoxicating as my blood may have been for you once, I imagine tasting you is just as addictive for me now."

"I wish I could still taste you," I admit. Not because I want to feed off him, but because it was another way to be intimate, and right now I feel the compelling urge to be as close to Tyree as possible. I would climb into his skin if I could.

"You still can, just not in that way." A wry smile touches his lips and then he leans forward, shuttering his eyes.

I tip my head back and cry out as his tongue sinks deep inside me.

With each stroke afterward, he plays my body like a skilled musician, drawing tension out like chords of a slowly building melody, until I'm writhing across the bed, my breasts heaving with each ragged breath, begging for him to end my agony.

He finally relents, his fingers joining his mouth to push me over the edge, his hair trapped within my fists as I buck against him, chasing the pleasure as it rolls through me.

I've barely come down when he flips me onto my stomach.

"I cannot be expected to return the favor in this position," I murmur, my words garbled, my body sluggish.

"Soon, but not yet." He settles on top of me, guiding my arms upward, holding some of his weight off me with his elbow. "I would last all of two seconds with those beautiful lips around my cock and then I would have to listen to you ridicule me all day tomorrow."

"Your ego is big enough to handle a little teasing."

"True. But I prefer my odds this way." He nudges my leg upward with his own, bending it until I am open for him.

"You are so demanding sometimes ..." I smile as I allow him to do as he wishes with my body.

Pushing my lengthy hair off to one side, he leans down and drags his teeth along my earlobe. "Do not worry, I will gladly help you to your knees for me later." Slipping his free hand between us, he guides himself into me.

I sigh as my body welcomes him with ease, well prepared for the intrusion.

His fingers tangle through mine near the headboard. "Relax. Let me do all the work."

"I don't have much choice." The way Tyree has me pinned down, I can barely move, and so I revel in the feel of his hips rolling as he thrusts at a slow and steady pace, his face buried in my neck.

"I've thought about this all day," he whispers, teasing my skin with his tongue.

So have I, I answer in my head, unable to admit the truth out loud.

His body stills.

"Do not stop!" I demand in a breathy voice, angling my hips to push him deeper inside.

"Then do not grow quiet with me."

"And what would you like me to say?"

"Whatever your heart urges you to." Calloused fingertips pull back more of my hair. He grazes my ear with his teeth. "Do you still hate me?"

"No," I admit reluctantly.

"Do you like me?"

A weak chuckle escapes my lips. "At this very moment? I like one part of you *very* much."

He thrusts hard in answer, his length filling me, drawing out a cry.

"The truth is, I am beginning to like *you* very much. More than like you, even. Every part of you, especially your vicious tongue."

My chest tightens. What is this? Is Tyree about to profess his love? But ... "You helped kill my parents and destroy my kingdom," I remind him.

His hips stall again. This time, I don't chase after him to continue.

Suddenly, Tyree's weight is gone. He flips me onto my back, sprawled out before his kneeling, naked form. He scoops me up into his arms, my thighs straddling his hips. His cock is still hard and waiting, but he doesn't angle to push inside me.

Dismay twists his handsome features. "Annika, if I could summon the fates and beg them to undo all that my family has done, believe me, I would." His voice is hoarse, pleading. "But I can't change the past. All I can do is tell you how sorry I am, beg your forgiveness, and promise to spend the rest of my life trying to be worthy of you." My ears catch his hard swallow. "Because I am yours, even if you are not mine." He stares at me earnestly, waiting for my response.

I search for a shred of the hatred I used to feel for this Ybarisan so I can shun his words and protect my heart. I can't find it. But I also can't find it in me to forgive him. That feels like a betrayal to my family. Maybe one day I will be able to, as Zander has absolved Romeria of her crimes. But that day is not today, no matter how sincere his proclamations.

Still, I do not hate this Ybarisan prince anymore.

Far from it.

But I don't know how to voice these thoughts, so I say nothing, tilting my hips until the tip of his cock slides through my slit.

Tyree groans, his hands grabbing hold of my thighs. He yanks my body down onto him until he's seated inside me again, his eyes burning with something unreadable. "Okay, Annika," he whispers, his hand clamping over my nape as he presses his mouth against mine in a passionate kiss.

My hands roam his muscles and curves as our bodies chase our pleasure. The slow pace from before is replaced by a desperate one, my muscles tightening in anticipation, my fingertips digging into Tyree's shoulders as I search for purchase.

I may be struggling with my feelings but *this*, we do very well together.

My cries are the first to fill our tiny attic chamber as my body clenches around Tyree. He follows a split second later, emptying inside me, his length pulsing with the waves of my climax, his arms holding my body close.

We collapse onto the bed in a sweaty heap, our breaths ragged.

And then, perhaps because I am not ready to give Tyree answers I can't yet find, I untangle myself from his limbs and shimmy down.

Tyree's body stiffens with a strangled cry as I seal my lips over his sensitive flesh.

I STARE up at the ceiling, my body sated like it has never been before. My worries about unsatisfying sex are groundless. Or perhaps it's Tyree who makes them so. "What are we to do in this Espador?"

"What do you mean?" Tyree tosses an elderberry up at a mouse that sits in the rafters.

It scurries after the food. I guess it worked up an appetite, after watching us fuck for hours.

"I mean, based on what Destry has said about the sea wraiths, there is little chance of us ever returning home. We are members of royal families. What are we to do in a foreign land where we have *nothing at all*?" We may as well be paupers.

There is a long pause, and Tyree shifts onto his side to face me. "We have each other."

I roll my eyes, even as my heart flutters.

If my reaction bothers him, he hides it behind a grin. I think he has caught on to my act, though. "Where is your ring?"

"Which ring? My one-of-a-kind ruby that you bartered away to that traitorous captain, or the one that *burns* me?"

He reaches over and collects my hand, his thumb stroking my bare index finger. "I will get you a new ring that does not burn you, and you will promise to never take it off."

Another flutter stirs, this time in my stomach. "What are you suggesting?"

Pulling my hand to his lips, he kisses my knuckles. "Exactly what it sounds like I am suggesting. We can be anything we wish to be here, *choose* anyone we wish. Islor's and Ybaris's issues are no longer our concern."

No, just this league of Azyr and their goal to chain me to a pool for eternity. I shove those dark thoughts out, not wanting to ruin this moment. Tyree is making plans to stay by my side, and I will let him. "Will you steal the money to pay for the ring?"

"Perhaps." He chuckles, leaning in to brush his lips over mine once ... twice ... before granting me a tender kiss that transfixes me. "Nothing is too good for my Islorian princess."

A tiny pebble hits the windowpane. Moments later, another one.

"I think someone is trying to get our attention." Tyree slides on his breeches and heads over, unlatching the fixture and pushing it open. "What are you—" He cuts off abruptly.

A moment later, he's rushing back into the room, collecting my clothes and tossing them at me. "Get dressed quickly," he hisses, tugging his tunic over his head and reaching for his vest.

"Why? What's going on?"

"The Azyr have found us."

My stomach drops. "How?"

"It does not matter. *Hurry*, Annika. And do it quietly."

I rush to dress and collect our meager belongings, stuffing them into the satchel Tyree purchased at the market. The vest he bought me hangs loose. I don't have time to decipher the laces. My hair is another issue altogether. I was going to ask Tyree to braid it again, but there is no time now. I settle for drawing my hood up.

With a dagger in his hand, Tyree pauses behind the door to listen intently.

I move toward him, but he points toward the window.

"We are three stories up!" I mouth. If I gave voice to it, it would be a scream.

With an arm around my waist, he ushers me forward. "At least they're not castle stories. And it is our only choice. They are in the hall, waiting. Five soldiers."

"Waiting for what?"

"The Azyr and the royal guard, I imagine." He pushes the windowpane open all the way and eyes a wagon full of hay sitting in the alleyway below. "Hold my hand. We will jump together."

"But—"

"Have I not protected you this far?" I see determination in Tyree's eyes. "Trust me again. *Please*."

All I can manage is a nod and then we're climbing up onto the window ledge. I clench my teeth to stifle the scream as we leap out.

We land in the center and sink into the bales, Tyree, cradling my head in his arms, and then we're rolling, scurrying to the ground. Loose straw clings to my clothes once again. If we weren't in such grave danger, this would be amusing.

Destry hides in a corner, her pendant clutched in her hand.

"What is she doing now?" I whisper.

"Something useful, I am sure." Tyree's head swivels this way and that as he backs us into the shadows beside her, drawing his sword.

Moments later, a swell of crows swoops down, angling at the cluster of horses by the inn's gate. The lone soldier left there to watch them loses their reins as they buck and rear and scatter down the street.

"That should keep them busy." Destry struggles to get to her feet, stumbling a few steps toward the opposite direction where a gate waits. "There's a path this way."

"What about Ezra and Uda?" I ask. "We need them to get to the port."

"We cannot go to the port. There will be soldiers and Azyr lining the path from here to there. Besides, Ezra is likely the one who turned us in."

I frown. "But I thought you said—"

"Forget what I said. I have too much faith in people sometimes."

I share a worried look with Tyree. "So then, how are we going to get out of Udrel?"

Destry holds up a wavering finger. "I have an idea, but we must go now."

Fates, we are to be led to safety by a drunk. "To where?"

Her expression turns somber. "The Great Kaeli."

51

ROMERIA

Cold wind whips across my cheeks, drawing tears from the corners of my eyes as Caindra speeds high above the mountains, Valk and Xiaric at her flank. The dragons use the cloud cover to travel west and then south over Venhorn's range without any orders to do so. It's as if they know the grim reality of what Atticus's letter warned.

Zander and Abarrane fly with Valk, Zander's stony focus below us, searching for proof that his brother lies. That was the first thing he declared when he finished reading the letter from Kier—that it had to be part of some elaborate new ruse to distract him while Atticus, making a rash deal with his captor, attempted to regain Islor's throne.

But as everyone in the tent quarreled over the letter's validity and how Atticus could have any clue of this impossible army he claims is sweeping toward Bellcross when he is in Ostros, Zander met my eyes, and I saw the fear shining in his.

How Atticus learned of Malachi's plan doesn't matter. What does is that our efforts to stop this impossible Saur'goth army from reaching Islor have failed.

It's already here. I know it in my gut.

Without their usual screech to announce themselves, the three dragons dive in unison, breaking through the cloud screen that conceals us.

I gasp.

That's Norcaster.

Was Norcaster. Now it's a pile of rubble, the wooden wall that before encircled the town lying on the ground like scattered matchsticks. Bodies mark the grass.

"What should we do?" I yell. "Do we stop? Look for survivors?"

"Keep going!" Zander shouts, pointing south.

I nod. Right. There is potentially so much worse ahead.

Solange and another of her fire Shadows rest within Xiaric's claws, witnessing the devastation. Trampled ground, flattened houses, bodies cast aside by stables where the army pilfered meals. There's little evidence of overnight camps. Do these beasts stop to sleep?

Here and there, I spot a cluster of females, scrubbing blood from clothes or hauling bodies into a pile—likely to burn. But it seems all the men have been slaughtered.

"There!" Jarek points to the trees. From this vantage point, the movement is subtle, like ants scampering through grass, but the closer we get, the clearer the bleak picture becomes.

Thousands of Saur'goths charge ahead. And this is the tail end of it. As we fly on, the horde grows thicker, until the rolling hills that skirt Bellcross are moving, the blanket of warriors thick. "No ..." My stomach sinks at the plumes of smoke that rise from the pale gray stone towers. The gates have been destroyed, the enemy flowing through freely. Once a welcoming city, it's now overrun. Soon, it will be in ruin.

Caindra screeches and banks right, avoiding a bolt as it sails past us.

I was so distracted by the entire devastating scene, I didn't notice the ballistae set up within the trees below. They knew we would come, and they're waiting for us.

"Romeria! Shield!" Jarek yells as another bolt flies.

I manage to throw one up at the last moment, sending the arrow ricocheting dangerously close to Valk.

"Spread out!" Zander roars.

"I can't shield everyone when we're apart!" My words are lost as the dragons separate.

Below, the enemy is scrambling to reload and aim. Several more of these projectiles sail toward the dragons, one nearly catching Valk's neck. We're quickly losing our advantage.

My heartbeat is in my throat as I unleash all four affinities at the defense line below. A white light explodes as it hits, charring everything in its path—the enemies, their weapons, the trees—and leaving a deep gouge in the earth.

Caindra picks up where my path of destruction ends, dragon's fire bursting from her giant maw like a flamethrower.

Valk and Xiaric attack with fire from other angles, aided by Zander and the Shadows.

Saur'goths scream as they die.

But when we climb back out of reach to regroup, it's clear that as destructive as our efforts are, haphazard attacks won't be nearly enough to stop this. More defense lines wait, more bolts are aimed. Eventually, one of them will meet their target.

There are just too many. It's an endless army, built by a god.

I meet Zander's gaze. His dour expression tells me he has come to the same grim conclusion: that we are here to gain information, not to die. He points east, and I nod.

Staying out of range of the weapons below, we travel toward Cirilea, searching for the end of the horde.

I could be wrong—I don't know Islor all that well, but ... they don't seem to be moving toward the capital city at all.

The line curves north.

I think toward Lyndel and the rift.

I search for Zander in the sky to see if I'm misreading this.

The hard look on his face tells me I haven't.

With a shout and a gesture, Valk dives and the other dragons follow.

We aim for the bridge.

52

ZANDER

The mood in the command tent is morose as everyone listens to Romeria and I recount what approaches us.

"We've destroyed the Bellcross Bridge." The only clear passage across the river. It was as old as the city itself, existing for thousands of years, long before the rift split our lands in two and Islor became a realm. A grand testament to the history and alliance between Cirilea and Bellcross.

I made the decision in half a second, and Romeria shattered it in three. What remained, the dragons destroyed with their fire and their claws after dropping us off safely on the other side.

"That will slow them down, but it will not stop them." Though the river is wide, the waters are shallow and calm.

"How many?" Theon's voice is gruff. Telling him Bellcross was all but lost may have been the hardest news I've ever had to deliver.

"I could not even hazard a guess, but I have never seen anything like it. Not Queen Neilina's force that waited to invade us, not the battle we fought a hundred years ago. It was ..." My voice fades.

"Too many for three dragons and a key caster," Jarek finishes, his words solemn.

"Maybe if I brought Shadows who could shield each of the dragons," Romeria suggests, her red-tinged eyes betraying her weariness from exerting so much of her power. "Maybe then we could do some real damage."

"There were at least a hundred ballistae waiting for us," Solange counters. "Something would get through sooner rather than later."

"And you would burn out of your affinities long before they stopped launching." I shake my head. "You are powerful, yes." The swath of damage she inflicted with that one blast was as awe-inspiring as it was devastating. "But you cannot win this war for us."

Theon leans against the table as if he needs support. "Then who can?"

I bite my tongue against the urge to give an honest answer. *No one.*

"This Saur'goth army was not designed to conquer. Malachi brought it here to destroy, and from what we saw of the lands that stretch south from the mouth of Venhorn, it is effective in its task."

"How long do we have?" Lord Telor asks, his voice equally grim.

"If I had to guess, their front line will reach us in three days, even without the bridge."

Anxious glances pass around the room.

"What are your orders, Your Highness? While my city burns and my people die, what shall we do here?" There's a hint of animosity in Theon's tone.

Abarrane opens her mouth to scold him, but I wave her off. Let him have his anger and if I need to be its target, so be it. When I first read the letter from Kier, he called for his horse, ready to lead his men back to Bellcross. I ordered him to stand down until I returned with confirmation, and he wasn't pleased with me for it. He even argued—a rare occurrence.

But if I had let him leave, he and his entire army would be heading to certain death and Bellcross would *still* be lost. He and I both know it.

"I do not pretend to have all the answers, and I fear there are no good ones for this. If anyone has a suggestion, now is the time to speak up."

There is a painfully long pause.

Oh, how I wish Atticus were here now. He never hesitates to offer an opinion when battle is involved.

"We could take our stance on the other side of the rift. Take down the bridge if needed," Kienen calls out from the corner, silent until now.

"And abandon all of Islor? Cut ourselves off from ever returning?" I say.

"While cutting off this army from expanding beyond this border," he counters. "Alive in Ybaris seems better than dead in Islor." He adds, "In my humble opinion, Your Highness."

Which is how all of Islor's citizens will be left if we desert them.

"That sounds like a worst-case scenario option, but I will keep that in mind."

He dips his head. "We may find ourselves there soon enough."

"How do we hold the rift?" Gaellar asks. "If we remain in our current position, with a battle coming from both sides, we are doomed."

"I know. That is why we can no longer hold the rift. Not actively, anyway."

"You are suggesting we let the beasts crawl out, unchallenged?" Radomir's brow furrows.

"When you see firsthand what is coming, you will understand. We need all the blades we can get. And Gaellar is right. An enemy force of that size will drive us right into the rift."

"What about bringing Ybaris's soldiers and casters into Islor?" Romeria studies Kienen and Solange to gauge their reaction.

Solange frowns. "And where would we make our stand?" Something tells me the Shadow would rather remain on the other side of the rift, and I can't blame her.

"Lyndel." Jarek steps forward, studying the map of Islor. "They obviously took it as a battle advantage. We've reclaimed it from them. Now we use it to *our* advantage. Refortify it with the help of Mordain."

"Lord Telor, your thoughts?" I ask.

"Lyndel is not built to hold an army that size." Though he's not arguing with this idea.

"That is why we split our army and hide the rest in here." Jarek taps Eldred Wood on the map. "Come up from behind and fight them on two fronts, with casters on both sides. Force them to spread out."

I bite my lip as I consider this plan. The very northwest tip of the woods is a few hours' ride from Lyndel. With an army that size moving in, the battle may reach such a distance. "That could work. Elisaf? Thoughts?"

My ardent friend shakes his head. "We need more blades."

"I know where we can get them." Romeria gives me a knowing look.

I sigh. Twenty thousand, if my brother's word is to be trusted. "I suppose it is time we repay the east a visit."

53

ATTICUS

Cook fires glow on the plateau ahead, giving away the Kierish and eastern forces in the growing dusk. "I have had my men set camp there many times, when we were here at harvest, fending off your raiders." Though I never traveled with this many. "It is a good choice." There is a deep bowl surrounding the area. Few forces would stand a chance against the one who holds the higher ground.

"I am so glad you approve." King Cheral smirks. "I suppose we Kiers know *something* of strategy too."

Baymeadow's bell toll in the distance announces the evening hour. Lights mark the wooden wall that surrounds the village. Most who live there are farmers. Normally, they would be asleep by now, so they could begin an early day of tending to the fields. I doubt they rest well lately, though, with an enemy army stationed within an hour's ride.

More than anything, I would like to stroll through those streets like I have done many a time. Maybe if I'm on my best behavior, the king will let me venture in tomorrow.

A shout sounds in the Kierish tongue, and a scout steps out from behind a boulder, an arrow notched in his bow. I assume, a demand that we announce ourselves or die. By my count, a dozen soldiers hide strategically up the hill, ready to fire with the order. All Kiers. I do not know what they put in their water—besides the poison that wreaks havoc on their crops—but their soldiers are all substantial brutes.

King Cheral unfastens his cloak to reveal his finery without a word.

The scout's eyes widen. He drops to his knee, uttering apologies, I presume.

"All right, usurper king. Let us see how your people receive you."

"YOUR LAND IS BEAUTIFUL," Satoria muses, sidled beside me as we wait for King Cheral to return from receiving his general's brief. "I can see why you would want to lead the army that protects its borders."

"My brother would say I enjoy the swollen ego that goes along with leading the army far more than the noble cause." I nod toward Tuella, who kneels on the ground, her head tipped back. "What is she doing?"

"Reading the stars."

I frown as I look up. "It's not dark enough yet." There's a speck here and a blink there, but nothing like what she will see in a few hours, as the night climbs in the sky.

"I do not understand it myself." Satoria shudders and pulls her cloak tighter around her slight body.

The urge to offer her warmth somehow—rub her shoulders or pull her against my side—hits me, but I refrain. Another mortal owns my heart, whether she wants it anymore or not. Besides, this is King Cheral's wife, a truth I seem to keep forgetting. "Why have you come?"

"Do you wish me not to be here?" A tinge of hurt laces her voice.

"I am not saying that. But there is nothing but war ahead. Are you a master warrior and neglected to mention it?"

She smiles. "I am adept with my blade. But I have other skills."

"Like loosening the tongue of your husband's enemies and convincing them to fight for him?"

A laugh sails from her lips. "I do not recall having to convince you of anything."

"I suppose not. I cannot lie, it feels good to be home."

"I hope you hold that sentiment after you speak to your Islorians." King Cheral rejoins us. "Now that my soldiers' blood holds no draw for them, they camp together. You will find them over there, on the left."

"Yes, I can pick out my own kind." Many of them know who I am.

Some fought at my side before the eastern lords' schemes turned them against Cirilea. Are they worried? They should be. I have not forgotten their disloyalty. Their only saving grace is that they were following their lords' orders.

But I lost good friends to their betrayal.

"Who leads the eastern wing?"

"A male named Segland. Do you know him?"

"Well enough." I smile. This should be interesting.

"My general says they have not received word from Kettling's lord, or any other, since before last Hudem."

"That is not a surprise. Adley would have had difficulties sending word, given his incarceration and then his death. Do they not know about that yet?"

"They've heard rumors. You will have the good fortune of confirming it for them. It is interesting, though, that no one else has stepped up to fill his shoes."

"They are all spineless cowards, afraid of this new king." That doesn't mean they won't eventually pick up their scheming again.

"Perhaps we could learn a lesson or two in that regard. But between the silence and this unexplained end to the blood curse, they grow restless and ill at ease, according to my general."

"Delightful. Do they know Islor has a new king?" There were towns and villages in Islor still living under the assumption that my parents were on the throne, even while I had taken it from Zander.

"Again, they have heard the rumors. King Malachi's quill has been busy." He gestures toward the tents. "I will let you lead the way."

"And with nothing but my charming personality to defend myself, I assume?"

"Surely, that is all you will need. You have enchanted me, after all."

I chuckle as we stroll toward Islor's soldiers, a row of Kierish guards trailing behind us. "Just remember, if they cut me down, you have far less leverage to use with my brother and Romeria when they arrive."

"That is why I am here. They would not dare attack a king."

"I believe that's exactly what they did when I was last in the plains. Segland!" I spot the familiar bushy red beard at the firepit.

The brawny easterner looks up from his mug of ale, his eyes narrowing—with confusion or hatred, I can't tell. Probably both.

"Yes, I am still alive, despite Lord Adley's best efforts. Tell me, how is that pretty wife of yours? When can I see her again?"

Rage morphs his ugly face. Leaping to his feet, he draws his sword and charges for me.

I disarm and throw him to the ground in three easy steps. "Look what I found!" I hold up Segland's weapon for King Cheral to see.

His guards step forward, their intentions clear.

"You ask me to lead this army, and yet you do not trust me with a single sword. What message will that send?" I warn, twirling it in the air.

His jaw tenses—because he knows I'm right—and he orders them to stand down with quiet words in their language. "If you were hoping to earn their attention, I believe you have." He waves outward.

Sure enough, the Islorian side of the camp has fallen silent as soldiers crawl from their tents and stand from their seats to see what the commotion is about.

"I suppose now is as good a time as any." If Zander shows up here and I can't prove I have command of these men, I am of no use to him. I climb up onto a supply wagon, balancing on a stack of crates. It's a vulnerable position to put myself in—I could easily be picked off with a well-placed arrow—but I don't have the luxury of time and intimate fireside conversations to win them over.

"Some of you have known me as your commander and fought at my side!" I use the same powerful voice I've used countless times when rallying troops before a battle. "Others knew me as Islor's king for a short time. A few insist on labeling me usurper—" I flash a smile at Satoria, who hovers behind her husband. "And dear Segland here still blames me for what happened with his wife, but *I swear*, she did not tell me she was married." She desperately wanted to bed a prince.

A few chuckles pass through the crowd.

I let the banter slide as my expression hardens. "Whatever you call me, it matters not anymore. I stand before you now without my gleaming armor, promising you that if you do not follow me now, everything you have and everything you are will soon be lost."

Somber stares meet me.

"There is much I cannot explain, for there is much I, myself, still do not understand. But what I do know is the following—the Nulling is open and the flood of beasts is great." Gasps sound, but I continue. "Queen Neilina is dead, executed by her own daughter. Islor now has an enemy more threatening than the late Ybarisan queen and her army of casters, and more deceptive than the eastern lords who led you into a treasonous battle for their personal gain. In the days to come, you will see alliances forged that you never imagined possible. Including this one." I gesture toward Cheral. "A Kierish king whose men cut me down and who held me captive has seen the danger ahead and knows it for what it is—the end of us if we do not set aside our differences and stand together." I pause to let that sink in. "The one true king of Islor, King Zander Ascelin, will soon call upon us to fight those forces threatening to destroy our realms, and we will answer with our blades and our loyalty to the future for all!" I hop down from the wagon, my newly acquired blade dragging through the grass.

"That is it?" King Cheral studies the mulling crowd. "You will not demand their allegiance here and now?"

"A king demands allegiance. A commander leads them to it. Tomorrow will be the true test."

"You believe your brother will come."

"Oh, he will come. Of that I am certain." He will have no choice once he sees what awaits. "Now, will I be granted a tent, or is there a cage I should retreat to?"

54

SOFIE

"You have been busy." Malachi bends to collect a fallen leaf from the great oak that shows signs of new life after splitting in half as if hit by a bolt of lightning.

I'm surprised his heartless glance doesn't disintegrate it. "Yes, it has brought me much joy to repair what I can. Especially this tree."

"And why is that?"

"Because we had one just like it, outside the window of our chamber in Montegarde." It was under that tree that I was to be buried once I went through the imminent change to seer. Surely, Elijah remembers, which is why I mention it now. He planned to be buried beside me there. We talked about it often.

"I hope the tree survives."

"If not, you can plant a hundred more to replace it."

I do not want a hundred more. I want one. I want mine.

Malachi leads us down the meandering path toward the nymphaeum. "Soon, these kingdoms' predecessors will be all but forgotten, and we will reign. A new population will rise, one that knows nothing but my name as ruler."

Kingdoms. Plural. But I am not surprised by his ambitions.

A fresh horde of Saur'goths guard the nymphaeum, clueless to the ones buried in the ground they stand on. Two more empty cages await.

"We are bringing more daaknar from the Nulling?" I fight my shudder. When he woke me this morning and demanded we visit Soldor, I did not ask for what purpose.

"And more guards. They are fearsome warriors, but they do not seem to follow orders as stoically. There are rumors that they have been abandoning their posts to hunt." With a snap of Malachi's fingers, the Saur'goths hoist their cages.

"I will have to do this one at a time." Reaching for my affinities, I thread a silver weave into the door.

And choke on a mouthful of dust.

"What is happening?" Malachi demands to know.

"I do not know. It isn't working."

"Try again!"

I send another thread and yet we remain here. Tension claws at my spine. "I am sorry, Your Highness, but there is something blocking my access to the other side."

Understanding fills his face, and rage quickly follows. "They must have discovered what we were doing and sabotaged us. That is the only explanation. But *how*?"

A wave of guilt washes over me. *I* know how. That creature, Lucretia. She must have followed us through the portal. She saw *everything*.

I hold my breath as Malachi paces, bracing for him to lash out at me in anger. In this case, it would be deserved, even if he has no idea of the truth. "Is there another door we can use—"

"No!"

I purse my lips to keep from offering more suggestions that will earn me nothing but punishment.

"Any word from Lyndel yet?" he snaps.

"No, Your Highness. Perhaps my letter did not arrive." That these beasts are capable of reading is shocking to me.

"Or it means there was no one alive there to receive it. They failed at capturing the city or they lost it quickly after. That is the only explanation." Malachi nods to himself, his jaw taut. "Just as well. The main army moves swiftly for them, and it is time I joined. I have gotten too comfortable here, feasting and entertaining. My presence is needed on the battlefield."

Panic stirs. "But your army is unmatched. Allow them to sacrifice themselves in your honor. That is what Mal'Gar is for."

He shakes his head. "Sometimes, a king must lead the rabble."

"But why put yourself in danger?" That is Elijah's body he risks.

He smiles. "I will not be in danger, because you will be at my side to protect me at all times, at all costs, yes?"

I swallow as my worry swells. "Of course, my love. I will not allow anything to happen to you."

"It is time our opponents learned there is no hope for them." He snaps his fingers at the Saur'goths. "Gather the army. Inform the lords and ladies we leave within the hour, and they will be accompanying us."

55

ROMERIA

We descend toward the plains at first light, having left long before the hint of morning touched the sky. I feel nauseous. The last time I spoke to Atticus was that night in the Goat's Knoll in Cirilea, when he had no idea it was me behind the mask.

I can't imagine how Zander must feel. He hasn't faced his brother since the tournament, when Atticus betrayed him in front of the kingdom.

How will this exchange go?

Will it be cathartic?

Disastrous?

Did I save Atticus before only to be forced to kill him today? Warning letter or not, I do not trust him, that much I will make clear. But the letter does feel like an olive branch. If only he had valued the one Zander and I sent first.

The plateau ahead where Zander thought they might be is covered in tents. Beyond it, in all directions, is farmland, peppered with the countless villages whose residents tend to the crops. In the far distance is the rift.

Shouts erupt from below as the camp stirs, much like they would react at the rift when we flew in, soldiers scrambling for weapons that won't save them, gathering shields that won't protect them, should we be here to attack.

"Over there!" Zander points to low ground beyond the plateau, out of range of their arrows. It's a good plan. Atticus will have to come to us.

Caindra banks left with a deafening screech, and the three enormous beasts cast their shadows. The soldiers below duck, even as they watch with a mixture of awe and terror as we pass. We land in the clearing and take our positions in front of the dragons, Jarek and Abarrane closing in on our flanks, and Elisaf and Solange behind them.

Zander purses his lips, the tension visible in his shoulders. "Now we wait."

"THIRTY, BY MY COUNT," Elisaf notes as the group rides down the ridge.

Atticus leads them, looking as pompous as I remember, his blond curls framing his handsome face. "Is that King Cheral beside him?" He's much older and distinguished-looking, his silver hair and beard groomed.

"I would assume so, based on his armor and his age. Atticus's letter did say they traveled here together."

"When have you ever known the king of Kier to come to Islor?" Jarek asks.

"Never. Not since the blood curse took hold and certainly not after having the audacity to invade our lands."

"Then he needs something from you as desperately as you need strength from him."

Zander nods. "That is what I'm hoping for."

"Who is *that*?" I watch the form cloaked in heavy red robes, the hood drawn.

"A conjurer," Lucretia materializes out of thin air, startling us.

"I fucking knew you were with me. I could *feel* you," Jarek snarls.

"That is because I *wanted* you to, Commander," she purrs, earning Abarrane's snort.

"*That* is a conjurer?" Zander pushes, drawing our attention back to the approaching group. "Kier has a conjurer?"

"I cannot say where her allegiances lie, but that is what she is."

"And what can she do?"

"It depends how strong she is and what her intentions are."

He pinches the bridge of his nose. I'm not the only one irritated by Lucretia's vague answers. "Can you shield us until we can answer both of those questions?"

I draw on Vin'nyla, building a solid wall of air between us. "Done."

The group halts nearly fifty feet away, their guarded gazes on the beasts behind us as their lips move in quiet conversation. Whatever King Cheral is saying, Atticus doesn't seem to agree with it. He charges forward, earning a glare from the king before he follows, wagging a "come with us" finger.

The conjurer and another woman—a slight mortal in her twenties, by my guess—trail.

From the hill above, the soldiers watch as the group of four comes to a stop maybe ten feet away from us.

Atticus's blue eyes dart between Zander and me, then to the dragons. "I promised my dear friend King Cheral here that if your beasts want to kill us, we will be dead, whether we stand this close to you or with the soldiers back there."

"That is a fair assessment, *Brother*," Zander says coolly, emphasis on the label. Is it to remind him of what they still are or of how far they've fallen?

The two of them share a long, hard stare, like two titans taking measure, to see where the other stands.

The corner of Atticus's mouth flickers with amusement that disappears the moment his attention shifts back to me. "I've heard I have you to thank for my ability to breathe after that arrow, as well as for the countless beasts that now roam our lands?"

"You're welcome," I offer dryly.

King Cheral clears his throat.

"Where are my manners? This is the glorious ruler of Kier who made a risky and ill-gotten arrangement with the late lord of Kettling and now realizes his folly."

The older man cuts a scowl Atticus's way.

"This is my brother, Zander, once the king of Islor until his well-meaning but idiotic brother betrayed him. And *this* is someone who calls herself Romeria, but she has not been the princess of Ybaris for a very long time. I do not know if that is a blessing or a curse for us yet." Atticus meets my stare, an unreadable look in his. "She is also a key caster, the queen of Ybaris, and"—he frowns—"Ulysede?"

"You are rather well-informed." Zander smirks. "But you forgot Mordain's Prime."

That earns Atticus's raised eyebrows. "It seems congratulations are in order. Soon you will be as prolific at conquering realms as

Empress Roshmira. I believe Seacadore once had four kingdoms, each with its own ruler."

"No, thank you." I spear Zander a "See?" glare.

Zander analyzes his brother for a lengthy moment. "It is good to see your recent adventures have not deflated your obnoxious spirit. Well met, King Cheral."

Kier's king dips his head in greeting, but I catch his fleeting grin. "It is a pleasure to meet you both. We have watched your trials and achievements from afar with the help of Tuella." He gestures to the conjurer, who regards us through bold black eyes that leave me feeling cold. "This is one of Udrel's Azyr."

"Now it's your turn to be shocked, *I know*," Atticus says as several eyebrows arch. "Wait until she tells you how they don't bow to gods."

"Not even to the nymphs?" I ask, though Agatha alluded to as much.

"We bow to the light that brings balance to the shadow," the conjurer Tuella says in a thick, harsh accent.

"And yet you wear the nymphs' writing on your forehead," Zander muses. "That is what it is, isn't it?"

"Yes," I answer before she has a chance. I've spent enough time staring at those stones in the crypt to recognize the same swirls in the faded scrawl.

"They claim the gifts, but they do not honor the gifter," Lucretia says behind me, her serpentine eyes locked on this Azyr like an owl watches a mouse.

"What does devotion to these fates grant your people but pain and suffering?" Tuella responds calmly, unfazed.

"She's not wrong," Elisaf whispers.

"Who you bow to is of little consequence to us," Zander says. "Let us focus on the issue at hand, before our dragons grow restless and hungry. You are aware of this new king who has claimed Islor's throne for himself."

"King Malachi, yes. He has written to me," King Cheral says.

"'All will bow before me,'" Zander echoes the signing line. "From the sounds of it, he has written to all corners of the realms. I imagine he will wish to claim them all soon enough."

"It would certainly appear that way."

"Where did he come from?" Atticus asks, the usual humor missing from his voice.

"That is a long story, but it is *the* Malachi himself, and he came through the Nulling to conquer our lands."

"The creator of flame," Tuella says, and she doesn't seem surprised by that.

"So then you know how grave this situation is." Zander folds his arms, narrowing his gaze. "You say you have seen what approaches us. How?"

King Cheral pauses, as if deciding whether he wishes to admit the truth. "Through the Azyr's seeing stone."

Seeing stone? I bite my tongue against the urge to ask questions. We have more important issues to address besides curiosities.

"And what do you hope to gain for sacrificing Kier's army in our battle?" Zander asks.

"Is it not enough to recognize that if we do not join forces today, we have little hope for tomorrow and beyond?" King Cheral responds calmly.

"If you were not already in my lands, aiding Lord Adley in a scheme to split Islor in two, I might believe that. Why did you form an alliance with him? And before you think up a lie, I know your aim was to help claim the Plains of Aminadav for Adley's new kingdom."

King Cheral's lips twist as he pauses again. "He promised us bounty from the yearly harvest."

"Bounty for a realm with such rich lands of its own?" Zander watches him closely. He's testing this king. We have the answer. It was all but spelled out in Neilina's secret journal.

King Cheral sighs with reluctance and seems to age ten years, his shoulders sinking with a burden. "Once, yes. But our lands are being poisoned by the mountain streams. More of my people starve each year. When Lord Adley proposed the alliance, I saw it for what it was —my only option for my people to survive."

"You felt you had no choice but to look to Islor to solve your problems." Zander basically echoes what we learned from Neilina's journals. "I am sorry to say that your realm is a casualty in Aoife's scheming."

"How do you know this?" Atticus's eyes snap to me, as if I held the secret all this time.

"We found the answers in Argon," Zander answers. "The poison in Romeria's blood was not the first request Neilina made of the fates. She summoned them many times, inviting havoc of all sorts. One such consequence was apparently Kier's waters. They used your realm to force you to invade Islor and weaken it, to make it easier for Neilina to cross the rift and claim victory."

"You played right into her plot," Atticus muses. "How much satisfaction these fates must gain, pulling our strings like puppet masters."

"It would not have mattered. The balance between light and shadow changed on Azokur. Islor was doomed already," Tuella says, as if consoling her Kierish king.

I can't help myself. "What is Azokur?"

"The night of the second moon. You call it Hudem."

She means the night that the nymphs returned to this world, and both Malachi and Aoife stepped into it. The light and shadow. I think I'm beginning to understand this other way of thinking.

"So now you know why Kier is here," King Cheral says.

"And why are you here?" Zander asks Tuella. "That is a long way to travel."

"I came because my king ordered it." She smiles as if that explains everything.

"As you said yourself, Udrel and Tuella are of no consequence to our situation, and why Kier came to your lands does not change the fact that you need us now," King Cheral says. "Even though we might not be enough."

Zander regards him evenly. The king seems frank and honest, two things Zander respects. "No, it might not. But I will welcome all the blades you can bring to the east. If, by some miracle, we survive this and I reclaim my throne, I will not overlook your aid or your people's plight. That is the best I can offer at this time."

King Cheral peers at the young woman, and she shares an almost imperceptible nod. "We accept." He steps forward and holds out a hand.

Zander falters, eyeing Tuella.

"You need not fear me. I do not channel the light in the same way your queen channels the shadow, and I have no wish to die today."

After another long moment, Zander nods.

I drop my shield but ready my affinities and step forward with him. Relief envelops me as the kings clasp hands. One less enemy to face.

"You will need to leave immediately and move quickly," Zander says. "We will slow their approach as best we can, but we cannot hold them off forever. They will reach Lyndel the day after tomorrow."

"What is the plan?" Atticus sounds more like the commander of the king's army that I met that day in Cirilea's round war room, when I was still Princess Romeria, captive and murderess.

"Hem them in and attack from two sides."

"Lyndel and Eldred Wood, I presume? That allows for the most protection."

"Yes. Exactly."

Atticus nods and turns to King Cheral. "Send word to break camp. We are moving within the hour."

I half expect the king to remind Atticus who rules, but he snaps a finger and yells something in Kierish, and a soldier gallops up the hill on his horse.

"You will return at nightfall for updates, yes?" Atticus asks Zander.

"We have much to do, but ... you will hear from us before battle." Zander's jaw clenches. He must have so much to say, but now is not the time. "Tell the men not to piss themselves when they see us flying in."

"I cannot make any promises." Atticus's attention lands on the dragons, a curious look in his eyes. "What of Annika? She was in Cirilea when I left for the east."

"We were told she escaped the rebellion."

He sighs heavily. "That is good news."

"I am not so sure about that. She was seen fleeing by ship, held at knifepoint by a dark-haired lord, according to witnesses."

Atticus's face screws up. "Dark-haired *lord*? Who would that be? Who would ..." His words drift with a curse.

"What is it?" Unease laces Zander's voice.

"Tyree was being held in one of the rooms. The same one Romeria stayed in." Atticus pinches the bridge of his nose. "What are the chances he escaped and took her as a hostage to get out of Islor?"

"With our luck? I would presume quite good." Zander inhales sharply. "That is who it is, I know it. They likely sailed to Northmost. We were heading there to check on her when we got your letter. But we will go today. Now. We will find them."

I nod, though no one's asking me. Of course, that's where we'll go. I know how much Annika means to him.

"The last thing we need is that fucking Ybarisan prince running loose in Islor again." A crooked smile curls Atticus's lips. "Though, if he has our sister with him, I'm sure he is not having an easy time of it."

Zander chuckles. "Likely not." He hesitates. "We retrieved Kazimir. He is healing, but I am sure he will find his way to your side for the battle."

"Thank the fates." Atticus regards the dragons again. "These are quite the beasts you wield."

Caindra snarls, drawing his attention to her.

His eyes pop. "She understands me?"

"Yes." An impish impulse drives me. "Would you like to meet her?" I back up, sparing a glance toward Tuella, who watches with interest.

"It depends. Is this where I die?"

"I guess we'll see. What's wrong, are you afraid?"

"When you taunt me like that ..." Atticus eyes Jarek who shadows my side, his hand on the pommel of his blade, before moving closer.

"She *usually* doesn't eat people unless they're running from her."

Zander shakes his head, but there's a twinkle in his eye.

Atticus tips his head back to regard her. "What did you do to convince her to take orders from you?"

"I earned her trust. Caindra is my ally." I smile up into violet irises. "And a friend."

Caindra bows, her massive snout inches from him. She sniffs.

"Does she do this with all her victims?" He laughs, but there is no missing the way his body stiffens with apprehension. All she'd have to do is open her jaw and snap, and he would be gone.

"Depends what mood she's in." I wink at Caindra, enjoying our little secret.

"May I?" He holds up a tentative hand before placing it on her snout.

There is an odd, peaceful look in her eyes. I think Atticus meant something to the Goat's Knoll barkeep, whether she admitted it or not, and she's happy to see him alive. "The orange dragon is her mate. The green one is their child."

"Truly magnificent." Taking a step back, a pensive look takes over. "Do you know what happened to Gracen? The mortal baker who—"

"I know who she is. And yes, she and her children are safe, as well as all the other children we rescued from Cirilea."

Atticus's shoulders sink as he closes his eyes. "Thank the fates."

"The fates had nothing to do with it. Thank Romeria," Jarek snaps. "She put herself in grave danger to save them. She lost someone important to her."

Atticus dips his head. "I am sorry to hear that." He sounds sincere. Stealing a glance at the young woman—who is she?—he says, "If you see Gracen, please tell her I have thought of her often and that I am sorry for any pain I have caused her."

As much as I want to deny him that, there is genuine ache in his eyes. Regardless of his crimes, he does care for her, and he did protect her.

That's why I nod.

Atticus rejoins King Cheral, his mood more somber than when we arrived.

"We have a war to plan for and a sister to find, so unless there is something pressing, we will leave you to lead the men west," Zander says.

"We will see each other soon." King Cheral's mood, on the other hand, seems lighter, as if buoyed by relief.

They wait as we return to our respective dragons. Valk takes off with a terrifying screech, Xiaric following closely after. But Caindra lingers. It's as if she knew I wouldn't be able to keep my mouth shut.

"Oh, hey, Atticus, by the way, Caindra also goes by Bexley!"

The dumbfounded look on his face has me laughing as we soar through the sky.

THE APTLY NAMED Northmost port along the western coast of Islor is even smaller than Lord Rengard cautioned. I can see why he worried about the town bursting at the seams with so many of Cirilea's people seeking refuge.

The tension in my limbs slackens as we descend from the clouds. By all accounts, it looks as though Malachi's army didn't veer from their path south. The port is cluttered with ships, more moored in the waters around. The town is intact, if not bustling.

We direct the dragons to land on the outskirts, far enough away that panic doesn't erupt should the people filling the alleys and streets look up.

"This might not have been the best choice in locations." Elisaf watches Xiaric, whose attention is locked on the nearby field of cattle. "When did they eat last?"

I shrug. "They come and go. Who knows what they grab and where. But we'll be back soon. Please do not eat the villagers' livestock!" I call out to Caindra, who answers with a hot puff of air across my face.

The seven of us band together and head for the main gates.

"You said this mortal who helped you knows the captain of that ship?" Zander walks with purpose.

"Seamus, yes. He knew who it was." *I just can't recall. There was too much happening that day.*

"Then let us hope he is still here."

I hold up the bag of jewels I collected from Ulysede's vault. "Trust me, he's still here."

It took Abarrane two intimidating stares and one question to find out where all the sailors converge. The guards at the gate posed no resistance, far more concerned by the three dragons lingering in the field outside than who they were allowing in.

"This is where they are." She points at the tavern sign that reads The Screaming Siren. Inside, a fiddler plays a rowdy tune, earning plenty of cheers and jeers that carry through the windows.

"They have a sense of humor, I'll give them that much." Jarek pushes open the door, ducking as he passes the threshold.

Inside smells of sweat and ale and freshly caught fish, and I have to hold my breath to adjust as we weave through the dense crowd. We earn plenty of looks, some curious, some hostile. No one would recognize me as the one who brought them here, given I was wearing my old face. None seem to recognize me as Princess Romeria either, which is a nice change. Zander, on the other hand, earns more than a few double takes and whispers. Many of these people lived in his city, after all.

"Can I ask that we not have a repeat of Norcaster?" Elisaf covers my back while Jarek and Solange protect my sides. Lucretia has vanished and hopefully stays that way until we're back in Ulysede.

"If it involves a battle, know that you have an extra sword at your side," a deep, gruff voice announces behind us.

"And a big bastard at that." Jarek clasps hands with Horik, genuine grins plastering both their faces.

Even I can't help forget our purpose here for a moment, diving into the massive legionary's stomach for a hug. It's only been days since we left him at Cirilea's port to make sure the *Silver Mage*'s captain honored his commitment. "Kaders didn't give you issues?"

"'Course he did. Nothing I couldn't handle."

"And all the ships arrived?"

"Aye, they did, Your Highness, and we got your message. The people are growing restless, though, sleepin' in barns and streets. They push to go south to Bellcross."

"They will no longer be doing that." Jarek gives Horik a look before Zander steps in to greet the legionary. "Have you seen my sister here?"

"Princess Annika?" Horik shakes his head.

Zander purses his lips with disappointment. "What about the fellow named Seamus?"

"Aye, that one is right over there." He points to the little red-haired mortal sitting by himself in the corner, his stein nearly as large as his head.

Zander wastes no time, barreling through the crowd, earning more than one sneer that falls off the moment Abarrane appears in front of them, her hand on the hilt of her sword.

"Where is my sister?" he demands, fists leaning on the table.

Seamus pauses mid-sip, his eyes widening. "Your Highness?"

I squeeze in beside Zander before he causes a scene. "The south wind blows tonight."

Seamus falters. "And the north wind answers. But ... aren't you ..."

I retrieve the mask from my satchel. Slipping it on, I morph into Romy Watts.

He gasps. "You were the Ybarisan princess *all that time?*"

"You wouldn't have helped me if you knew." I dump the mask and fish out the sack of jewels. "We made a deal. I can trust you to give these to the other captains?"

His eyes light up as he tests the weight in his palms. "They'll skin me alive if I don't. I couldn't leave Northmost even if I wanted to."

I sense Zander's patience waning. "Listen, this is important. I remember you saying something about that ship that left ahead of everyone else."

"The *Tempest*?"

"Yes! That was it. I remember now. Did it sail here?"

"Aye. It did. After the rest of the lot, but they made it."

"And was Princess Annika on the ship?" Zander pushes.

"That, I don't know. But Captain Aron and some of the crew's right over there."

We follow his nod toward a table of four, just as a tall man with pocked skin stands and rushes for the door.

"Let me guess—that's Captain Aron," Zander hisses, charging after him. "Secure the rest of them!"

56

ZANDER

His heartbeat gives him away.

"You honestly thought you could hide from me behind a door?" Grabbing the sizable man by the neck, I haul him out from the stable. "Captain Aron of the *Tempest*, is it not?"

He holds his hands in the air in a sign of surrender. "I don't know what you want with me, but—"

"Oh, I think you do." I shove him hard, and he sprawls onto the dirt. Passersby in the street scatter with gasps and shouts, forming a spectators' ring around us. I could not care less who witnesses what I do to this mortal if he does not give me the answers I seek. "My sister, Princess Annika, left Cirilea on your ship, not by her will. She was taken by the Ybarisan prince. Are you denying this?" I slide my dagger from its sheath, twirling it in my grasp.

Aron winces as he stands, brushing the dust from his breeches. "Aye, they sailed with me. The prince was wounded, I believe by her dagger."

The one our father gave her for her birthday, no doubt. I demanded she always keep it on her. I think it's the only time she's ever listened to me. "Tell me more," I demand.

"They paid me in jewels to sail them out of Cirilea quickly."

"Which jewels?"

With resignation, he fishes into his pocket and produces the gold and white pearl pinky ring I gave Annika for her birthday. I recall it well. The craftsman, I found in a tiny village off the eastern coast.

I also know this wasn't the most valuable ornament in her possession.

With my blade against the captain's throat, I fish through his pockets, pulling out a sizable ruby ring and a pendant. Also hers. "It seems you were well paid to deliver them here. So, where are they?"

"They hired another ship to take 'em to Westport," he stammers, his erratic heartbeat fluttering.

"Why didn't *you* take her?" I hold up the ruby ring. "This alone is worth a trip."

"With the sea sirens? That is a death sentence!" He swallows. "I told 'em I'd bring them here and they'd have to find their way elsewhere. They agreed. Said they'd find someone else crazy enough to sail those waters with them on board."

"I do not believe you." I can taste his lie in the air. "You do realize the many excruciatingly painful ways I can get answers from you."

He shrugs. "I don't know what else to say. Go look in Westport. They might be almost there by now."

He's so convincing, for a split second, I'm tempted to dismiss my suspicions as that of a distraught brother. But then Romeria and the others close in, Abarrane hauling a bearded man by the scruff, blood trailing from his lip and a split across his cheek.

The pale look on Romeria's face sinks my stomach.

Even Abarrane's expression is especially morose. "This is Sye, the *Tempest*'s cook."

Captain Aron's eyes squeeze shut and a curse slips from his lips.

"Tell him what you told us," she insists.

The cook's lips flap but no sound comes out.

Abarrane kicks the back of his knee with her heel. He buckles to the ground with a howl, bracing his falling body with his hand. The two-crescent moon emblem glows.

I step forward, into the captain's face. "What is your cook trying to tell us?"

"Whatever it is, it's a lie." Beads of sweat trickle down his forehead.

"Speak!" Abarrane shouts, drawing her blade.

"The sirens came and they threw 'em overboard. Both of 'em!" Sye admits through his blubbering.

A burst of cold washes over me. "You fed my baby sister to the sirens."

"It was them or all of us!" Captain Aron explodes. "I wanted to sail here an' they wouldn't let me! I warned them, and they just kept pushing."

I step back, struggling to keep the tremble of fury and grief from overtaking my body.

Annika is gone. She survived Neilina's scheming, the near drowning, the poisoned blood—*everything*—only to succumb to the sea, at Tyree's doing.

And here, I found this captain enjoying his pint in the tavern, a king's ransom worth of jewels in his pocket, likely never losing a moment of sleep. "You figured that in the chaos, no one would miss a royal princess?" My voice has grown deathly calm.

"After all that you and your *royal family* have done to Islor, she deserved it, and far more." Captain Aron lifts his chin and throws out his arms. He knows he's about to die, so he figures he might as well say whatever he wishes. "Go ahead. You bring death to us all, anyway."

A sword through his gut would be too kind. "Abarrane, please escort the captain out of the gates." I flash a wicked smile. "Since he likes feeding beasts, I know of one that is hungry."

5 7

ANNIKA

"This way." Destry steers her horse left.

But Tyree halts, not following. "Do you actually have a plan?" Irritation seeps into his tone.

"I told you, we will seek refuge in the mountain."

"The mountain is *that* way." He points behind us, but there's no evidence of it. The misty ceiling is too dense.

I pull my hood down farther and, roping my arms tighter around Tyree's waist, I rest my cheek against his shoulder blade. "Wake me when you two agree on something." After darting along alleyways and through stables, we stole two horses from the outskirts of Basinholde and have been riding nonstop for hours, first through darkness and now through morning fog. We follow trail after trail through a densely wooded area with no pattern and no end in sight.

Tyree smooths a hand over mine, squeezing it with affection. "Perhaps we should rest."

"Not yet. We must keep moving while we have cover." Destry disappears down the path.

With a heavy sigh, Tyree guides our horse to follow.

I SETTLE AGAINST THE TREE, its gnarly roots forming an armrest to lean on while I savor a slice of cured sausage. For meat from a street merchant, it is quite good. I'm not sure I want to know what it's made of. "I did not see you grab the provisions from the table."

"Understandable. You were panicked." Tyree sits beside me, the satchel between his splayed thighs. "I have wandered the woods without food before, and it is not an enjoyable experience."

"I am not pleasant when I'm hungry," I admit.

"Yes, I've noticed."

"Bite your tongue."

"Bite it for me." He slices off another piece of meat and hands it to me with a smirk before his gaze veers to where Destry rests nearby, her cloak wrapped around her childlike body. She's been in that position since we stopped to water the horses at a nearby stream. "If she had not come when she had, I'm not sure what would have happened."

I can only imagine. I was so focused on Tyree, I wouldn't have noticed anyone until they were standing in our chamber. I shudder and lean over to forage around in the bag. "What else do you have in —" I gasp as I pull out a fresh jar of honey. "You stole this from Ezra!"

"And I don't feel an ounce of guilt about it if he traded us in."

"Maybe that's why he did. The man takes his honey seriously." I twist the lid and hold it to my nose, inhaling. The sugary floral aroma brings me back to the loft and Tyree's skilled tongue. A need stirs in my core.

Tyree's lips part as he watches me closely, as if waiting for me to dip into it.

I screw the top back on. "Maybe later."

A crooked smile touches his lips. "The vest fits."

I test the laces I strung while we rode. "Yes, it does. You chose well."

"I preferred how you wore it last night, though." He pops a soft elderberry into his mouth before tilting forward to kiss me.

I sink into his lips, slipping my hand around his nape to pull him closer, my mouth working over his with desperate abandon.

"Annika," he groans against me. "If you keep this up, I will not be able to ride a horse."

"I can help you with that problem *while* we ride if needed." I drag a finger over the ties of his breeches and the hard ridge tucked inside. Fates, two reckless nights and who have I become, flirting so blatantly with the Ybarisan scourge?

A flock of birds rushes past with noisy caws, and Tyree pulls away abruptly, trailing their path, his eyes narrowing slightly before his mouth returns to mine. But it's a ruse, because in a split second, he's on his feet, a tiny blade flying from his fingertips. A thump sounds as a bird falls to the ground.

"What is it?" I scramble to my feet and join him where he stands.

A small green bird lays dead, like the one Destry warned about.

"Destry, get up," he barks, moving for the horses. "We must go now."

THE FOREST HAS GIVEN way to a meadow of long grass and tiny pink and yellow wildflowers, allowing the horses to ride side by side for a change.

"What time do you think it is?" We've been riding for hours.

Tyree scans the sky. The sun is a hazy glow, obscured by a veil of mist, leaving the air warm but damp. "Midday. We are going the right way, at least." He points ahead at a faint dark outline of the mountain.

Beside us, Destry releases the stone pendant, her black irises returning. She's been doing this periodically for hours, checking our surroundings for danger. A few times, I was sure she would fall from her saddle. "The forest is dark and dense. Difficult to search. But there is a village about an hour away. It is best we veer before we reach it. No visitor goes unnoticed in these parts."

"And what happens when we reach this mountain?" I ask.

"There are caves to seek shelter within. The Azyr have seen them through the bird's eye. No one dwells up there, though. It is too harsh."

I frown. "Then how are *we* to survive there? Will these Azyr look upon our bones through the bird's eye long after we've perished?"

"We do not have to survive there. We must only reach as far as the wroxlik lives and learn if it will carry us out of Udrel."

My mouth gapes. "*That* is your plan?" That is what we've been riding toward? "We are to negotiate with a wyvern to *carry* us out? Is she still drunk, or has she gone mad?" I hiss into Tyree's ear. "Have you ever seen a wyvern before?"

"Not up close. Have you?" she challenges.

"Well … *no*, but my brothers have. They are terrifying and large and can kill twenty soldiers with a single swoop. There is no negotiating with a beast like that." I scoff. "You may as well invite a daaknar to tea."

"I do not know of this daaknar."

"It is a demon! One of Malachi's pets." I nudge Tyree's thigh, goading him to echo my concerns about Destry's *brilliant* scheme.

"Can you control a wyvern—or wroxlik—as you do the crows?" he asks instead.

"I have never tried it before. Birds are easy, but other creatures are not. Some are too wise and you cannot guide them at all, and others you must be close."

"How close?"

"Usually, to be *that* close to a wroxlik means you are already dead. No conjurer has done it to my knowledge, but I will try. I have nothing left to lose." She says this as if she's trying out a new hobby.

"Fates, we are going to die," I mutter, earning Tyree's chuckle.

"Inez once told me a tale of wyverns carrying passengers within their claws. The seers painted the illustrations. No one believed them, but I always wished it to be true."

"Maybe you will be the first," Destry says.

"Maybe *we* will be the first," he corrects.

"Can it even carry three people at a time?" I ask.

"I have seen one *shred* three people at a time."

I let out a strangled sound.

"Inez also said that the wyverns are thought to be Vin'nyla's pets, carrying out her misdeeds."

"Such as?" I ask.

"She never said. I'm sure there are fascinating stories."

The clearing ends, and we are forced back to single file as the trail is absorbed by a swath of trees and ground cover that allows for little light. Tyree takes the lead, guiding our horse through the thick bramble of thorny vines.

I pick off a burr that clings to my cloak, wincing at the pinch. "This path does not get much use, does it."

"More than I would like," he whispers, pointing to impressions in the forest floor, one where a boot sank into the moss, another where something *else* sank. Something large, with claws that gouge.

"How fresh are those tracks?"

"Too fresh." He draws a dagger from its sheath.

Unease slips down my spine as I twist in the saddle. "Did you check this area—" A scream tears from my lungs as I lock eyes with the beast slinking up behind Destry, she and her horse oblivious to their impending doom.

The next few seconds happen almost too fast for me to process. Tyree is out of the saddle, launching his dagger. It strikes the creature in its chest. The beast's resulting screech reminds me of the daaknar that night in the sanctum, after it bit Romeria, so shrill it scatters the birds roosting on branches.

Somehow in all of this, the reins landed in my hands. Tyree slaps my horse's rump, sending it rushing forward, away from immediate danger.

I crane my neck to watch behind me, frightened for him.

Destry follows, trusting her horse, her eyes closed and her pendant in her fist.

Tyree draws two swords.

But the creature has vanished.

"Where is it?" He spins on his feet, searching the bushes desperately.

My pulse pounds in my ears, though I'm not sure I'm breathing anymore. "Destry, where is it?"

Movement in my peripheral snaps my head to the right. My scream sits in my throat, unable to escape as it steps out from behind a tree, a low growl creasing its snout.

Tyree dives forward to place himself between us, his blades up.

It stands several heads taller than him, tufts of gray hair sprouting over its gangly body. The claws at the end of its arms are shaped like hooked daggers, surely capable of carving open torsos with a single swipe. Broken chains hang from its wrists.

But it's not attacking. It's easing forward on its hind legs as if in a daze, Tyree's dagger protruding from its chest.

Destry is controlling it, I realize.

"Kill it!" I hiss. "Before she loses her hold, and those claws leave you looking like Ezra." Or worse.

My words tear Tyree out of his own daze. He swings his sword, opening its throat.

It topples with a gurgling sound and a thud.

My heart still pounds in my chest despite the terrifying moment being over. "What was *that*?" And will we run into more while in these woods?

"It is a beast from Azokur," an unfamiliar female voice answers as a sharp point pricks my throat.

58

TYREE

Three conjurers waited for us, hiding within the trees, their red robes swapped for ones that match the color of the forest floor. Twenty soldiers are with them, dressed in leathers that blend into the bark and branches.

I grit my teeth in anger at myself. I should have seen it for what it was—a trap. They used whatever that thing was to distract us, so they could get close.

A soldier stands on the other side of Annika's horse, holding a blade to Annika's throat. An empty threat. She's the most valuable being in all of Udrel, but only if she's alive.

They must have hauled Destry from her horse in the seconds we were distracted, because now they hold her at knifepoint, her arms secured behind her back.

"That was an Udrelian, punished by the curse." The willowy Azyr with russet skin gestures toward the beast.

I startle at the sight. The creature I just killed has vanished. In its place, a young woman with tawny flesh lies in the bramble. A silver band adorns her ring finger. She was someone's mate. Now she's dead on a forest floor, her body to be picked apart by the vultures.

"These are the people who suffer for your selfishness, kal'ana." The conjurer's black eyes settle on Annika.

"I did not agree to be anyone's sacrifice," Annika spits out, her voice trembling.

"Not all have the luxury of making that choice. But your sacrifice will change the lives of an entire realm. It will give your life meaning." She shifts her focus to Destry. "We have been looking for you, Destrelia the deserter, who continues to betray her kind." Her bony hand yanks the pendant from around Destry's neck and stuffs it into her pocket. "We have wasted enough time. King Hadkiel awaits. Take the kal'ana. The other two are of no use to us."

Even a fool can read the meaning behind those words.

A thorny branch whips across the Azyr's eyes, drawing her cry as she shields her injury with her palm.

Annika lifts her chin with defiance.

"Good girl," I murmur. *I hope you can handle heights without me.* Coaxing the dripping branches of the willow trees around us down with my affinity, I rope them around both Annika's and Destry's waists, and haul them up into the thick branches. "Hold on tight!"

With them out of the way, I swing my blades.

59

ANNIKA

I hug the tree trunk as if my life depends on it—because it does—and watch with equal parts admiration and terror as Tyree cuts through these woodland soldiers, spinning and diving, his movements like a choreographed dance.

But there are too many for him to keep track of them all.

"Behind you!" I shriek.

He bends and swings, blocking the coming blade while he attacks with his other. The soldier collapses to the ground with a lethal wound across his torso.

"I feel so helpless up here," I moan in despair.

"Use the branches!" Destry pushes, followed by a shout of, "On your right!"

Tyree leaps out of the way from fighting one soldier, and the two cut each other down with their momentum.

I wish my affinity were stronger, but it's enough to injure that evil Azyr at least. She still holds a palm over her eye, but the other two are doing *something*, their hands folded over their pendants.

Something that will no doubt harm Tyree.

Straining, I focus on a tree branch above one of them, splintering its fibers at the joint. It snaps and tumbles down, clobbering her over the head. She crumples into a heap, her hand empty of her pendant, and a whirl of satisfaction grips me.

I squash it quickly because there is still one more.

Concentrating on the bramble around her legs, I use the thin, thorny branches as switches, whipping her thighs and calves over and over.

She releases her pendant with her yelps, running from her spot.

A well-placed dagger from Tyree into the back of her neck ends her flight.

He follows it with a blade swing for the Azyr I whipped in the eye, cutting her down. He kills the last three soldiers before his ragged breaths carry to our perch. "See any hiding?"

Destry and I scour the area, watching for anything, so much as a twinge of movement.

"I think you got them all." There are bodies *everywhere*.

"Good." Beads of sweat coat his forehead. "Now, I need you two to get yourselves down."

"That is amusing." The ground is at least thirty feet below us.

He tugs at his tunic, revealing a gash across his collarbone, and my stomach drops.

"You are not kidding."

"It's not merth, at least, but unless you wish to sit up there for the next few hours until it heals and my affinity works again, I suggest you either test your skills or your strength."

"Mine is not strong enough to carry us down."

"Fine." He juts his chin toward the trunk.

Destry shimmies and swings her lithe body from our branch, dropping to the next, and the next, landing on the forest floor with a soft thud.

"See? Easy."

"For a peasant child who played in the dirt, perhaps," I snap, my anxiety flaring.

Tyree gives me a mock shocked look. "Did the princess *never* climb a single tree in that royal garden?"

"Of course not. I did *many things* in those trees, but climbing them was not one."

"Yes, I've heard the stories." He grins. "Come on now, you can do it."

With a huff, I crawl across the branch like an inchworm, hugging it so tight, the bark picks at the fabric of my clothes.

Below, Tyree purses his lips to keep from laughing.

"Shut up!"

"I haven't said a word!" He sheaths his swords. "I was just thinking about ways you can use these moves on me later."

A burst of laughter slips from me, my nerves frazzled. "You are an idiot, Tyree."

"An idiot you adore."

"We *must* keep moving." Destry fishes through the Azyr's pockets to find her pendant. Three more dangle from her fist, two with bigger stones than her own. I suppose they have real value to her kind.

"Come on, try, Annika. I will catch you either way. I promise."

I know better than to question him. With a deep inhale, I copy Destry's earlier moves, far wobblier on my landings. I make it all the way to the last branch before my feet scrape past and I plummet …

And land in Tyree's arms.

"There you go," he whispers, setting me down.

My hands roam his body, checking for any other wounds besides the one he showed me. There are several, but none look that deep.

He presses a kiss to my temple, then my nose, then a lingering one on my lips. "As much as I enjoy you groping me, Destry's right, we need to go." He leads me to our horse, helping me up. After collecting a few extra daggers from the fallen soldiers, he joins me, taking the reins.

I hug him tight as Destry leads us forward through the grim battlefield.

"So, Destrelia the deserter …," Tyree calls out. "What's the story to that?"

"I left before they could kill me. That is the story." She picks up the pace, signaling the end of those questions.

60

ROMERIA

I t's early evening by the time we reach Ulysede. The silhouettes of the Cindrae's bony heads fill the inner gate as we ride through the tunnel. Jarek and the others hang back, giving us—Zander, really—space. He has said almost nothing since he dragged Captain Aron past Northmost's gates, shoving the terrified mortal to the ground in front of Xiaric and announcing, "A snack, but take your time."

The young dragon didn't need to be told twice.

The sailors of the *Tempest* were quick to set sail while their captain died, believing they could escape punishment. They made it past the last set of markers into the sea before the dragons descended, Valk igniting the ship with one pass before Caindra tore off the mast and punched a hole in the side with her claws. Those on deck died quickly. Any below are now sitting at the bottom of the sea.

We took the long way around the mountains, flying over Malachi's army to check for signs of their leader and gauge how long we have before they reach Lyndel. It was discouraging to see them wading across the waist-deep river with ease, barely slowed by the lack of a bridge.

We made two passes, attacking with streams of damaging fire before the bolts began soaring and we chose to retreat.

Now we are here, for a moment's respite, while we wait for the foreseeable doom. That's what it is beginning to feel like, anyway. The days and nights bleed together, and one gain leads into a devastating setback around the next corner.

"I do not have it in me to tolerate Oredai," Zander warns, his

426

voice empty, the pain of losing his sister radiating from his every limb.

"I know." All I have to offer is a sympathetic smile and a comforting stroke over his arm, my heart aching for him.

"Have the scribes left any new messages?" I ask the Cindrae leader when we reach him.

They have not, Your Highness.

That likely means no answer about a possible exorcism for Sofie yet. Which means there is no purpose for coming back here, except to give Zander—and all of us—a moment of quiet before chaos arrives.

Our group passes along the vacant streets to the castle without saying a word. This city once felt like hope, like a new beginning. But in reality, it has become just another distraction from the inevitable. What is the point of holding on to Ulysede if everything around it burns?

We step into the empty and quiet grand hall and I slip my hand through Zander's. "What do you need?" More than anything, I want to curl into our bed and hold him in my arms.

"Answers. I need to know how we will win this war so that all this wasn't for naught." The look in his eyes is pleading.

"We'll find a way," I promise him, infusing as much hope into my words as I can.

"You will not find what you seek in this library," Lucretia warns in her melodic voice.

"Which library do I have to go to, then?" I ask.

"None. The solutions are not in any library or any tome."

I sigh with exasperation. "Then where are they, Lucretia?"

She gestures down the hall, toward my throne room. "They must be granted."

Again, with this. "I am *not* summoning the fates."

She shrugs. "Then you will not get your answers."

Zander rubs his forehead. "I will be in our chamber while you make your rounds." He rushes up the stairs without waiting for my response.

My chest aches as I watch him go, wishing I could follow him.

Elisaf pats my shoulder. "He always held a special place in his heart for Annika. They were close."

"I know." I smile, thinking back to the night I broke out of the tower, only to find her at the bottom of the stairs, there to ensure I escaped. She was willing to betray her brother's order to protect him. "She hated me."

"Actually, she was growing fond of you by the end of our time in Cirilea. She told me herself."

"She did not."

"She meant to." He gives my arm an affectionate squeeze.

A lump swells in my throat, thinking about Annika now, about her tragic end. "Let's get some updates."

ZANDER IS on the balcony when I arrive in our chamber, dressed in only breeches, his broad shoulders hunched as he leans over the rail. "Anything from the scribes?"

"More of the same. I told Agatha about Kier's conjurer. She insists we bring her here."

"She'll likely dissect her to see what's inside. I have never met anyone thirstier for knowledge." He studies a small gold and pearl ring in his hand. "All this effort to get the scribes here, and so far, nothing they have uncovered has helped us in our fight against the fates."

"I wouldn't say that." I press my lips against his bare shoulder, inhaling the scent of lavender soap from our bath. His hair is damp, drying in the sun. "We know what the nymphs will demand if we ask them to close the Nulling, so that option is off the table." I hesitate. "I was thinking I should fly to Mordain and tell Allegra what we know."

"Do *not* tell her of this, Romeria." Urgency flares in his voice.

"But they should understand what's at stake, shouldn't they? And I'm not making any deals with the nymphs!"

"You did not think you would open the door either."

My jaw drops with shock. "That was unintentional, and you know it."

"You are talking about killing all casters. It is *not* an option, because *you* are also a caster, and the only way I will lose you is in battle, when I fall by your side. Not by sacrificing yourself." His jaw clenches. "But should I fall—"

"You won't."

"Should I fall," he repeats, "and Malachi achieves whatever he is hoping to achieve, you may find you no longer have a choice. One day, many years from now, your hand may be forced. How do you think Mordain would respond, knowing you have the power to end them all at any time?"

"But if it's the only choice left—"

"Then it is the only choice, and you will make the same decision as that mystic Nyxalia did, bearing the weight of it on your shoulders alone, because I promise you, Mordain will not make that decision, not for mortals or elven. And should we somehow succeed at defeating Malachi? One day, long after Allegra has passed, there will come a caster leader who does not appreciate your great power, regardless of where your heart lies. Agatha knows this. It's why she did not argue with me when I ordered her to hide the book."

That's also probably why she took the book to her room and had it with her when she found us. She knows some information is best kept hidden.

"I know you think I am too suspicious, but in this, please trust me."

"I won't say anything," I promise. As much as I hate keeping secrets from Solange and Allegra, my gut tells me Zander is right.

His body sinks with relief as he studies the pearl from the ring in the daylight.

"Was that Annika's?" I ask gently.

He nods. "He had all her jewelry in his pocket, like loose coins. The ironic thing is that he could have earned a hundred times this by protecting her from Tyree and bringing her to safety."

But the captain likely watched Cirilea burn as he fled and figured this family's time on the throne was over. He hedged his bets on a guaranteed prize now versus a chance at a lottery win later. I can't say I blame him for that. He didn't think that the exiled king might arrive, hunting for his sister with the help of dragons.

I guide his arm around my shoulders so I can slip mine around his waist and pull him close. "I'm so sorry, Zander."

With a hard swallow, he nods. "I must tell Atticus."

"We can go there tonight."

"We should be in Lyndel, to help strategize and prepare."

"Then we go to Lyndel first. I don't think the dragons mind flying back and forth across Islor." They definitely didn't mind setting swaths of Saur'goths ablaze. I only wish our efforts had done more. "Do you think Malachi knows what we did in Soldor yet?"

"It matters not. Look what he had time to bring through." He bites his lip. "I've been thinking about what Lucretia said, and she might be right."

"You'll have to be more specific. She says a lot."

"About summoning the fates."

I pull back to meet his eyes. "Speaking of doing things I promised I'd never do … Are you serious?"

"They are the only potential ally in all of this that we have not yet tapped."

"For what? So Aminadav can split Islor in half to stop the army from spreading?"

"What if the fates can block the Nulling somehow? What if they could stop beasts from coming through?"

"And Malachi from returning." I see where he's going with this.

"Otherwise, if we somehow manage to kill him, we will have no reprieve. He could have ten souls like Sofie's husband waiting in the Nulling for him to assume their body."

"And then there's Aoife to worry about too." We've been so focused on Malachi that it is easy to forget she's somewhere, wherever the wyvern has taken her.

"If we could stop things from coming through the Nulling, that would be half the battle, won."

"But there's nothing to say the fates will answer me."

"Something tells me they will not ignore the Queen for All if she summons."

My stomach flutters with nerves with the idea of facing Aminadav or Vin'nyla. "And how exactly will they solve our problems for us?" If Neilina's journal taught us anything, it is how the fates use every opportunity to further their own agenda.

Zander searches my features. "I fear we have little left to lose."

How many times have others been in this position, believing the fates might be their only hope? "Can I think about it first?"

"Yes." He leans down to kiss my temple. "But do not think too long."

ATTICUS

"I hear this is mine?"

The two Islorian soldiers erecting the command tent rush to their feet. "As ordered by Segland, Commander. Er ... Your Highness?" The one on the left falters, not sure what to call me.

Last night, I slept in a small tent surrounded by King Cheral's guards, but after the entire wing of our army witnessed me stroke that dragon's snout this morning, they seem to regard me with, dare I say, respect. That, or they believe me insane. Segland even apologized for his reaction and willingly surrendered his title and his tent.

"I will leave you to it, then." I wander through the camp, surveying the soldiers and our odds for survival. No one from Kier's side trails me tonight, another satisfying outcome from this morning's parley. I suppose King Cheral has finally decided to trust me too.

Tuella kneels at the outskirts of our camp much like last night, her head tipped back, her hand cradling a pendant.

I crouch beside her. "At least you have stars to look at now." A blanket of them paints the black sky above. We rode hard and left the plains behind, trading them for the highlands north of Eldred Wood, peppered with craggy rolling hills. It's far from ideal for a campsite, especially with the rift so close.

She opens her eyes. "There is that which you can see, and that which you cannot, usurper king."

I grin. "I so missed our conversations today." There was no time for idle chitchat once Romeria and Zander left. "Tell me, are you able to control one of those dragons the way you control the kells?" I watch her closely.

"Why are you so quick to betray your brother again?"

"I thought I was saving him," I snap, not expecting her to move so swiftly for my jugular. "And it is not me I am worried about."

She smiles knowingly, as if she knew that was where my thoughts were but chose to test me instead. "A kell's mind is empty, easy to manipulate. Others can be guided in the same way. But those winged beasts? They are ancient, and wise, and cannot be manipulated by anyone. If the queen has their dedication, it is because she has earned it."

She could be lying to me, but my gut says she's not. "Why did you agree to come to Kier?" A question that has been burning a hole in my mind all day, after meeting with Zander. "It is a long and dangerous route, and yet you arrived here alone."

"You assume I had a choice?"

"Your king ordered it. I understand that. But why? Kings usually do not sacrifice valuable assets simply for curiosities."

"I am not that valuable. Many more can replace me." Her attention returns to the sky. "Did you know that my kind once lived in these lands?"

"I did not. But there seems to be much I do not know," I admit.

"It is true. Many millennia ago, until the shadow swallowed the light." She narrows her focus.

"What do you see up there?"

"Promises and dreams. Omens and futures."

"Can you see my future?"

"Yes, and it is very short now. Your brethren arrive." She stands and, collecting her pillow, vanishes into the night, leaving me cold from her words.

I have little time to digest them, though, as shouts sound around the camp.

Two dark forms approach from the west, blotting out the stars beyond. I search for the third, but don't see it anywhere.

Someone calls for the archers to ready. "Don't fire at them, you idiots!" I yell, scrambling toward the clearing as the ground trembles with their landing. "That will do nothing but earn yourselves a quick death."

From the darkness, four solemn figures emerge, Zander and Romeria a step ahead while Jarek and Abarrane flank their sides. All four wear hard expressions.

I can just make out the shape of the beasts waiting behind them. Could that truly be Bexley, or was that some twisted joke? I think back to the owner of the Goat's Knoll, to her svelte curves and her fearless demeanor. I had explored every inch of that body. There is no possible way *this* was hiding within.

Is there?

"You have made good time," Zander says by way of greeting. So many sharp words must be cutting his tongue, waiting for release, yet he focuses on the pressing issue. A part of me wishes he would just lay it all out before me—every accusation and threat that bubbles inside him. I could accuse him of all the vital secrets he kept from me, truths that might have led us down a different path. But who am I kidding? If I had known that Romeria was a key caster, I would have acted sooner.

"We did. Have you found Annika?"

The pain that lances Zander's face at mention of our sister is unmistakable.

"I SHOULD HAVE KILLED him when I had the chance." I pace around my tent, my anguish blistering as I try not to visualize Annika's last horrifying moments, relayed by the sailors who helped kill her.

"Then she would likely be in Malachi's grips now, and I fear what he would have done with her," Zander says quietly.

I swallow against the lump in my throat. "Where is this captain now?"

"In Xiaric's belly," comes the cold answer. "The crew has also been punished. The *Tempest* will never set sail again."

Though it won't bring our sister back. I wish I had been kinder and made more time for her.

The tent flaps open and King Cheral enters without preamble, followed by Tuella. I'm surprised Jarek and Abarrane allowed them in so easily, but I'm glad they did. "Good evening, I heard you had arrived." Irritation laces his voice.

Zander holds up his hands in a sign of surrender. "No disrespect meant in meeting with Atticus first. I was informing him of our sister's fate, and I thought it best to do it in private."

King Cheral's expression softens. "I suppose that means the news was not pleasant."

"It was not." Zander replays what he told me.

"By sea sirens, you say?" Tuella asks, her black eyes revealing nothing. "That is certain?"

"Several sailors saw her pulled under." Zander's voice hitches, a rare display of emotion. It wears on him. *All* of this wears on him. That he has continued down this path, rallying for Islor when it all but chewed and spat him out, is honorable.

This is why he was always meant to be Islor's king. What a fool I was to think he needed saving.

"I am sorry for your loss." King Cheral bows, deeper than I imagined any king capable of.

Zander pauses, regarding him curiously. "Kier has long since been known for their brutish warriors and their lingering, spiteful memories. You are not what I expected."

"I did not believe the rulers of Islor gave much thought to Kier at all." He smiles sadly. "I am merely a king trying to save his people."

"In that, our goals are similar." Zander unrolls the map tucked under his arm, spreading it out on the table before me, affixing the corners with the waiting rocks. It's a roughly drawn configuration of our coming battlegrounds. "Half of Ybaris and Mordain are in Eldred Wood, shoring up defenses. They moved in this morning and will be ready to receive you by tomorrow, nightfall."

"We will be there, fates forbidding any setbacks," I confirm.

"Okay, then." Hazel eyes meet mine, and a wave of nostalgia washes over me, for the many years passed and battles planned as my brother and I faced each other across a table. "Tell me what we need to win this war."

I FALL into step next to Romeria as we escort their party through the camp, back to where the dragons wait. Zander is deep in conversation with King Cheral about the troubles Kier has faced. "Did you have a chance to speak to Gracen yet?"

"Her Highness has more important matters than relaying messages to your lovers for you," Jarek snaps.

"You know, in another life, I would have drawn my sword right here, right now," I warn, letting a sharp edge glisten in my voice.

He flashes his teeth. "And you would have suffered greatly for it."

"Care to test that theory?"

"*No.*" Romeria shakes her head at her right-hand shadow. "Give us a minute? Please?"

With a stiff posture, Jarek's pace slows, falling behind several steps. Still close enough to cut me down should the legionary feel the urge.

"He is rather protective of you," I note.

"He's doing his job."

That's more than duty that drives him, I would guess, but I'm not about to say that out loud.

"As for Gracen, I haven't had the chance yet. With the news of Annika and everything ... I will let her know, though."

"When you're next in ..."

Romeria cuts a look but doesn't respond. She still refuses to tell me where they are, but if I had to guess, I would suspect in that golden city of hers, beyond reach from everyone.

"I appreciate it." I smile. "How is that little imp Mika doing?"

She smirks. "Still an imp."

"And the others? The baby?" I can picture walking in on Gracen feeding the child in my bed the morning I left. What I would give to return to that day again and make different choices. But, had I stayed, we would not have King Cheral as an ally, and I would more than likely be dead. Maybe I am following the path my fate has laid out. Regardless, it's becoming clearer to me that the mortal baker and the usurper king's time together was meant to be fleeting.

"Suri? She is growing."

"Suri, yes," I echo, imagining her tiny fingers and the way she kicked and wailed that night the servants' quarters were searched for the poison.

Romeria hesitates. "You know, her actual name is not Suri."

I falter. "No, I did not. What is it?"

"Romeria." Her smile is smug.

"In honor of the queen who saved her." Gracen never revealed this secret, which means she never fully trusted me. I guess I can't blame her, given all that I did during my time as king.

"She hid the truth because she was afraid of being punished for her loyalties."

"That is ... reasonable." I push aside the hurt stirred by this information and drawl, "How was your ego after learning that?"

"It's *very* healthy." Romeria's beautiful blue eyes shimmer with her grin, but her amusement quickly falls off, as if she remembers who she's with.

We both must be thinking the same thing. "The escort south from the rift to Cirilea, that truly was not you?" I ask gently.

"You mean, the nights you *played draughts* with the princess?" Her eyebrow arches in meaning. "No. I mean, it was *this* body." She gestures at herself, drawing my attention downward over her curves, adorned with finery fit for a queen. I remember what it felt like beneath me. "But it wasn't me. I'm not from around here. Maybe I'll explain it to you one day."

"I look forward to the enlightening tale."

"Who says you deserve it? And for the record, you're an asshole for what you did to your brother."

"I do not disagree." My gaze drifts to Zander's back. "On many fronts."

She follows my focus. "You've seen what's coming. Do you think we stand a chance?"

"With all of Mordain and these dragons and a key caster behind us?" My chest tightens. "I do not know."

She bites her lip, as if holding back her next words while she decides whether to say them. With a flittering search around us to see who is close, she admits, "We're thinking of summoning the fates for help."

My eyebrows pop. "*Who* is?"

"Zander and I." Fear shines in her eyes. "We need to close the Nulling and we're out of options."

My attention falls to my brother again, strolling through the camp like the leader he naturally is. Zander despises the fates. He would likely be happy to follow the way of Udrel instead. So if he is considering this … it means he does not think we have any hope of winning otherwise, which is a scary reality. No wonder he's been so quick to welcome me back, though with tepid arms. He's desperate.

Romeria waits quietly, and I get the distinct feeling she's looking for my opinion. "In war, I would use every weapon at my disposal. The fates are weapons."

"But what about the consequences?"

"There are consequences to every choice. The blood curse was a consequence of a selfish request, and yet we have survived for two thousand years with it. We can live with consequences. Can we live with the alternative?"

"The alternative is death," she says with grim certainty.

"Exactly."

She nods, seemingly digesting my words.

We've reached the outskirts of the camp when shouts of alarm rise at the north end, the word "Grif!" escaping a moment before a stream of fire erupts. A two-headed creature appears in the glow of burning grass and trees.

It was only a matter of time before the beasts found us, but I suppose Romeria's caster abilities could have drawn it in.

With a screech, the dragons launch into the air, reaching it in seconds.

A devastating stream of fire sails from Caindra's maw, before the orange dragon swoops in to snatch the grif from the ground. Its body dangles from his mouth for a few seconds before he bites down, severing its two heads from its body. The pieces fall and scatter.

All is quiet again.

"You said that was Bexley's mate, right?"

"Yes, which means you slept with his wife," Romeria teases, stirring Jarek's bark of laughter.

Many, many times. I rub my forehead. "A common theme for me these days, it seems."

SATORIA SLIPS into my tent not long after I've settled, a lithe shadow moving through the dark as she struggles to see, her usual lantern absent.

I smile. "Good evening, terrible assassin. It's been a while."

She fumbles the air for my cot and when she finds it, she sheds her breeches.

I help her by lifting the blankets to allow her to slide in.

"I prefer your dungeon in Ostros. It was warmer, and you wore less." She rests her head in the crook of my arm, her hands roaming my chest.

I chuckle. "Once, when I was very young, during a routine campaign through the realm, I shed all my armor and had an enjoyable night with one of my tributaries, only to wake up in the middle of the night under attack. I fought them off with my cock hanging out and nowhere to sheath my blades. I will never make that mistake again."

Her slight body quakes with her giggle. "I would have enjoyed watching that."

"What are you doing here tonight, Satoria? I would think you should be warming your husband's bed instead, so what does he hope to gain from this? He has my sword and an allyship." I'm past the point of pretending Cheral didn't send her.

"I am here for you, not for him. I have long since stopped sharing his bed. I am barren and therefore undesirable." There is sadness in her voice.

"You are far from undesirable, believe me. If I did not have another in my thoughts, I would have been buried deep inside you by now."

She shudders with my words, her palm raking over my stomach, her fingertips slipping under the waistband of my breeches. "Where is she now?"

"I am not certain because Romeria will not tell me, but likely in her secret city, where she will remain and live a long, happy, mortal life. Without me, if the queen has any say." The more I replay Tuella's foretelling, the more I am convinced that I am not meant to survive the coming battle. And perhaps that is just as well. It is the price I must pay for my many mistakes and betrayals.

"We will be breaking camp in a few hours." I press my lips against Satoria's temple. "Good night."

She burrows into me, unwilling to leave.

That night I sleep soundly.

62

SOFIE

"Now I remember why I've avoided riding horses for so long." I wince as I adjust in my saddle.

Malachi chuckles from his perch atop a black stallion, the gold crown gleaming despite the drizzle that falls from an overcast sky. "Your body will adjust to this way of life again soon, my love." Raising his voice, he announces, "We will make camp here so the queen may rest."

I will get no rest tonight, I'm sure, but I force a smile.

The Saur'goths bark orders at the servants, directing the supply wagons to a flat area on our right.

I spare a glance at the lords and ladies who were ordered to accompany us. The first one to openly question what purpose they served in this battle earned a blade through their stomach. No one else spoke after that, quickly gathering their servants and supplies. Now they wear fake smiles to mask their discontent. We have much in common.

"Come, my love." Malachi reaches for me. "I have something to show you."

The last of the daylight fades with our ride to the top of the hill-crest, and by the time we reach it, cook fires burn at our camp below.

"Behold." Malachi gestures grandly, waving a hand toward the valley in the northwest. "My army."

I gasp. In the distance, firelight burns as far as the eye can see.

THE SAUR'GOTHS ROAR with laughter when we return to camp, drinking ale and gnawing on roasted meat—of what kind, I'm afraid to ask. They seem less like demons and more like our kind, despite their hideousness, each day.

Beyond them sit the supplies and several cages. Traveling with the daaknar has proven challenging, its reach through the bars farther than they'd anticipated. They lost three Saur'goths to barbed talons before Malachi lashed out with a whip to warn the daaknar to behave. I've caught its hateful red eyes glowering at him often since. It will kill him the second we release it from its confines, but I am ready to—happily—send it back to Azo'dem when it tries.

The mortal prisoners in the other cages cower, just outside the reach of the demon. They're past the point of fear and shock and are now waiting to die. "I do not think you will be able to control Romeria with them."

"You are wrong. She is many things, but she is still human, and that weakness will be her downfall," he says with confidence.

In that case, I should have insisted we bring Wendeline along.

A female shrieks, snapping my attention to the right, past a row of tents, to where four Saur'goths hover over a servant. All I can see of her is flesh and torn garments, but when I decipher the dropped breeches and thrusting motion, my rage ignites.

I send all four warriors flying with a blast of wind, scattering them like bowling pins.

The servant clambers to her feet and runs through the camp, her clothes hanging off her body.

With a grimace of disgust, I gather threads to burn the Saur'goths where they lie.

Malachi's hand landing on my shoulder stalls me. "Do not punish them, my love. Sometimes they get overzealous, but that is what they are made for."

I stare up at him as I struggle to interpret his words. "They are demon warriors. They were made to *fight* for you."

"Who will also spawn a new age." He smiles as the four brutes pick themselves up off the ground, the guilty one's pants still hanging down to his knees to reveal his engorged length.

"They can *breed* with mortals?"

"And elven. And caster. Any creature that has a womb."

"But casters cannot bear children."

"They will bear these. The Saur'goths will create entire new races. It has already begun. This world is changing before our eyes."

My stomach twists into knots. "What kind of realm will this be, then?"

"One that bows to me and me alone." He rests his hand on my nape. "Let us get to bed. We have a busy day tomorrow."

But the way his fingers squeeze my neck tells me it is going to be a very long night.

63

ROMERIA

We regard the black stone and vine-covered pillars in front of us.

"Are you sure you want to do this?" Zander studies me with concern in his eyes.

"Take advantage of every weapon we have, right? Why *is* there a sanctum to summon the fates here, in this nymph kingdom, anyway?" I've wondered that more than once.

"Because they knew the Queen for All would have need for it," Lucretia says, appearing beside us in head-to-toe black warrior's garb to match Jarek. "They have met all of Her Highness's needs so far."

"Except the one where they leave and close the rift," Zander mutters.

I take a deep breath. "Okay, Agatha. How do I do this?"

The caster has been hanging back. Now, she moves forward. "It is quite simple. Step into the sanctum and channel your affinity to the pillar of whichever fate you choose. In this case, either Vin'nyla or Aminadav. Direct all that you can muster and, hopefully, they will answer. If they do not ... try the other."

"That's it?"

"Yes. As I said, it is simple. You do not even need a full sanctum. Long ago, elementals used to carry small stone carvings in their pockets, so they could call upon the fates from anywhere."

"Neilina had a set of those with that journal we found."

Agatha snorts. "Why am I not surprised?"

My stomach flutters with nerves. "How long will it take before one of them answers?"

She shrugs. "Casters have waited from minutes to days, and longer. Given our dire need, I hope not that long."

"Okay." I take a deep breath. "Let's do this—"

"And *don't* ask questions." She holds up a wrinkly finger. "They do not like questions."

I nod. "Okay. I will try to—"

"And *don't* try to be clever. They like their subjects obedient and meek."

I groan. "I'm going to piss them off."

"You will not." Zander cups my face. "You will do well. Just … choose your words carefully."

"You mean, don't tell a god that they owe me?" How arrogant Neilina must have been.

He leans in to kiss my lips. "Return to me quickly."

"Always." I chase his kiss with my own and then break free, aware of our audience.

Jarek looms on my other side. "I am going to assume they do not share your sense of humor."

"Don't be a smart-ass. Got it."

His jaw tenses. "Be careful."

My heart swells as I squeeze his shoulder. "Hey, Lucretia, keep him company?"

Jarek rolls his eyes as the sylx slinks over. "Thank you so much for that."

With a wink, I step up onto the pavilion, studying first the stone altar in the center and then the two pillars I need to choose between. Vin'nyla ignored Neilina three times. Aminadav punished the entire realm of Ybaris because of her. I chew my bottom lip in thought.

Eeny meeny miny moe?

With one last smile at Zander, I pull a thread and reach forward.

64

ZANDER

"Where the fuck did she go?" Jarek barks, voicing the words a beat before I can.

One second, Romeria was standing there, smiling at me.

The next, she was gone.

Vanished.

"She is still there, but she is in a different plane of existence." Agatha smiles, but I see the worry in it. "That means the fate she summoned has answered her call."

"But she is in *there*." I jab a finger toward the sanctum and then move forward.

"Stop!" Agatha yells, freezing my feet. "That would be unwise, Your Highness. While you cannot see them, once you step into the pavilion, they can see you, and within those four pillars, the fates take a physical form. If you anger them, it will not bode well for her. It has happened before."

"*What* has happened before?"

"Various things. They sometimes *take* things. If they choose to demand it, Your Highness." She averts her gaze. "It is expected that the caster complies."

Her meaning dawns on me. "I should never have sent her in there." I charge for the sanctum.

Jarek's solid body blocks me. "It's too late. Now you must trust her."

"It is not her I do not trust," I hiss, struggling to get around him.

Abarrane steps in. "In this regard, I agree with Jarek. You are no help to Romeria in there."

Jarek shoves me back, setting his hand on his pommel. A warning that he will use it against me to shield her.

"You are a loyal protector, and I appreciate that. But if you do not get out of my way, I will kill you," I push through gritted teeth.

His eyes are cold and hard. "I think Romeria will have something to say about that when she returns."

She would never forgive me.

"Romeria will survive this. She always does. Listen to the old witch now." Abarrane steps between us, and I see the silent plea for me to stand down.

I aim my anger at Agatha. "You should have told us before!"

But Jarek will have none of that either. "She would have gone, anyway. There is no stopping Romeria when she gets an idea in her thick skull."

Agatha wrings her wrinkled hands. "The fates have been known to simply give. It has happened, sometimes."

"And other times?"

Her brow furrows with worry as she regards the black stone. "They take *everything*."

65

ROMERIA

I release Vin'nyla's thread, letting it slip away.

"Now what?" I say more to myself. Do I sit here until she shows up? "How long should I wait before I try ..." My words drift when I look back to find Zander and Jarek gone. So are Agatha and Abarrane. "Hey, guys?"

"You cannot see them, but they are there, child," a breathy female voice says.

I spin around.

And try not to gape at the beautiful, shapely naked female standing at the end of the altar, her silver wings fanned out behind her. She regards me through large eyes with irises that remind me of my mother's old tea set when it needed polishing. Her silver-white hair is pulled back in a tidy bun. She is ageless, neither young nor old.

"Hi," I stammer. This shouldn't be more nerve-racking than meeting all four nymph elders, and yet I struggle to regain my calm. Probably because I have no idea what kind of damage the nymphs can inflict on our world, but I've seen what the fates will do firsthand. "Thank you for coming."

The corner of her mouth twitches. "You summoned me."

"I know, but you didn't have to answer."

"Would you rather I did not?"

"No! That's not what I'm saying."

"Then what *are* you saying?" a deep male voice asks.

I spin around to find a tall, broad-chested male standing behind me, bull's horns protruding from his forehead. They look identical to the one the golle gave me, in size and shape and color.

"You're … Aminadav." I lock my gaze on his face. It's as handsome as the grand statue in Cirilea portrays, with a masculine jaw and a strong Roman nose. The rest of him is like the statue as well, and I'm doing everything I can to not gawk.

Eyes the color of copper pennies bore into me. "Is there anyone else I could be?"

"No. But I didn't … I thought I had to summon you?"

"You chose *her* instead." His eyes drag over Vin'nyla's form.

"No, I didn't." Oh God, I remember Wendeline telling me they were touchy about one being picked over the others.

"You didn't?" There's an edge in Vin'nyla's voice.

I spin back again. "No, I mean, I did summon you. But if you didn't answer me, I would have summoned him."

"So, I was your second choice," Aminadav purrs directly in my ear, his breath caressing my skin a moment before his hand settles on my shoulder.

I stiffen. Is this real? Are they standing in front of me, in flesh and blood? "I don't know what you want me to say," I admit.

"Stop toying with her," Vin'nyla scolds, though her smirk tells me she's enjoying this. "We knew you would come to us, and we made an agreement that we would both attend you. Now, why have you summoned me?" Her voice rings with irritation.

"We need your help."

"With?"

I don't know where to settle my eyes. They are both *very* naked. "With closing the Nulling."

"The Nulling must be closed by the nymphs and the nymphs alone."

"I know, but I thought you might be able to block it somehow so nothing can get through to this realm."

"You mean so a fate cannot pass through and exist in your plane."

I hesitate, unable to read her tone. Is she insulted by that idea? "Malachi, especially. And Aoife. But also grifs and hags and nethertaurs, and definitely the vrogs and wyverns—"

"What issue do you take with the wyverns?" Vin'nyla snaps.

I stumble over my response.

"You've made your point." Aminadav strolls past me, and I avert my gaze from his firm backside. Are they always naked or is this to make me uncomfortable? Agatha should have warned me. "What would make you think we can do this?"

"I thought ... so you can't?"

"I did not say that. Where there is a will, there is *always* a way." He passes by Vin'nyla, and they eye each other like two predators deciding if the other is worth fighting before they pounce on their prey.

Have I made a *horrible* mistake coming here?

"Why would we grant such a request?" Aminadav asks.

"Because we won't survive if you don't." It's that simple.

"And what makes you think you will survive, anyway?" His smile is beautiful and perfect and yet it still sends a shiver down my spine.

"I'm not sure we will," I admit. "But we will try."

"How?" Vin'nyla prods, calm again.

Agatha warned me not to ask questions. She didn't warn me that I'd be interrogated. Don't they know all this, anyway? "With help from everyone willing to help us. Elven, humans, casters, dragons. You, if you are—"

"We do not fight the wars of lesser beings. Wars are fought in our names." Aminadav's voice is deep and loud, and it reverberates in my bones.

I purse my lips. This isn't going well. I can't seem to say the right thing.

"The Fate of Fire's flame burns forever." Vin'nyla's eyes sparkle. "Be wary of *how* you choose to fight."

"Okay." I nod, though I'm not sure what that means.

"We have seen the great army Malachi has produced. The abomination he has created in these Saur'goths." Aminadav sneers as he paces. "They will taint everything in this world."

He probably said the same thing about the Islorian immortals when King Ailill was plagued by the blood curse, and then he went and cracked the earth in two to show his displeasure.

Aminadav rounds the altar, his palm smoothing over the stone. "You are an interesting creature. A human at heart, a wielder by skill, an elven in body." His fingers toy with the collar of my leather vest, his thumb grazing my skin.

When he meets my gaze, my stomach drops. I've seen that hungry look before. If he thinks I'm going to—

"Consider your request granted."

"Really?" I squeak. Just like that?

"I am feeling compassionate. And Malachi is testing my patience in ways I do not appreciate."

I swallow. "You'll block everything from coming through the Nulling?"

"For a time. Not for *all* time. My mercy is not limitless."

I nod. "I understand. Thank you. Both of you."

Vin'nyla hovers behind, dissecting me with her tarnished silver eyes. Wherever that wyvern took Neilina—Aoife—I'll bet all the jewels in Argon's castle that it was by this fate's order. "You are bound to us now, to call upon when you next have a request."

"Oh, I'm not summon—" I cut myself off before I admit that if we survive the coming days, I will never stand in front of these two again.

Their laughter rings out, Vin'nyla's a musical song, Aminadav's a lover's deep chuckle.

"She denies us while she wields gifts we tore from our very forms." Suddenly, his massive hand is in my satchel, pulling out the silver mask and the horn.

"The nymphs gave me those," I stammer.

Anger ignites in his eyes. "They were gifts from *us*! This is bone, ripped from my very skull!"

"They've been very helpful. Thank you." I should just keep saying this over and over again. Or better yet, shut my mouth entirely.

Aminadav drops the silver mask back in but holds the horn. "You do not even know what it does."

"The elders told me it was for when all hope is lost."

"Is that what they said?" He sneers. "You could use it today. Now."

I throw caution to the wind and ask, "What would happen?"

"There is only one way to find out."

"Would someone die?"

"Someone *always* dies in war." He cocks his head, surveying my face like an archaeologist might admire a perplexing find dug out of the ground. "You do not value my gift."

"I do! I just ... I'm afraid of it," I stammer.

"You are afraid of extraordinary power?" He holds the end of the horn close to my lips. "You could end your people's suffering right now. All it would take is a sacrifice."

I pull back a touch, afraid I'll accidentally blow into it. "What do I have to sacrifice?"

Again, Aminadav studies me as if searching for answers hidden deep within. "That is for you to tell me. *Who* is the Queen for All willing to exchange for peace in her realms? *Who* would she sacrifice to save the lives of her people?"

I resist the urge to shrink away as I process his words. Agatha was right in her warning. A gift of this magnitude would come at a significant cost. I suppose the fates aren't all that different from the nymphs. And there is only one answer to that question. "Myself."

His eyes narrow. "You would sacrifice your life for these people from this foreign land, many of whom would have killed you ten times over? Would kill you still."

I'm not doing this for them. "If you are saying the people of these realms will live…" Forget the ones who hate me, if we are in our darkest hour with no hope in sight and giving my life will save everyone I love … "Yes. My life for those of the realms. *All* the realms, including Islor."

Aminadav's gaze traces my features as he sets the horn in my hand. "That is a commendable sacrifice. An acceptable one."

My dread bubbles. What have I just agreed to?

"If there is nothing else …" Vin'nyla's voice trails.

I sense my time with these fates is running out. I hesitate, my fingers gripping the bronze token tightly. "Can I ask a question?"

"A question about a question." Aminadav's heavy eyebrow arches. "We are waiting."

"Malachi took over someone else's body, and that person is still alive inside. Is there a way to save them while getting rid of Malachi?"

He stares at me for so long that I squirm, afraid I've somehow offended him. "There is no scenario where he will survive."

I nod. "Thank you." Not the answer I wanted, or the one Sofie will accept, which means she's back to being our enemy.

Aminadav steps in, herding me backward. "Unless you are summoning us for another request, so soon after you promised you would not again." Strong hands seize my waist as he hoists me onto the altar and fits his hips between my thighs. "This one will cost you now, Queen for All."

I swallow my rising panic as the Fate of Earth's daunting frame looms over me, his meaning clear. He would break me in two. "I'm good, thanks."

"Then we are finished here."

I blink and they're both gone, but his grip still burns.

Footfalls sound and a moment later, Zander, Jarek, and Abarrane are at my side.

"What happened?" Zander seizes my trembling hands, the horn still within my grasp. "Which one did you see?"

"Both."

"Both of them!" Agatha sputters, easing up to the pavilion.

"I summoned Vin'nyla and Aminadav came too. They made some sort of deal." Did all that just happen or did I imagine it?

"I've never heard of such a thing!"

"That is because you have never met the Queen for All." Lucretia closes in. "My master is valuable."

"Did they hurt you or make you *do anything*?" Zander asks through clenched teeth.

I shake my head. But I can *never* summon them again, that much is clear.

His head bows with his heavy sigh of relief. "What did they say?"

"Aminadav said to consider my request granted. Not forever, but for now. He will block the Nulling for us."

"And you believe him?" Zander clearly doesn't, given the doubt in his tone.

I shrug. "We'll see what happens at the rift tonight before we celebrate."

"Did they say anything else?" Agatha asks.

"Yes." I struggle to pick through my frazzled thoughts. "Malachi's fire burns forever, and there is no way to separate him from Sofie's husband unless I wish to make it an official request of the fates, and that will cost me."

"No." Zander shakes his head firmly. "You will not be punished for Sofie's mistakes. What about this horn? Did he tell you what it will do?"

I peer down at the token in my hand. If Zander learns what I've just done, that I've sacrificed myself for the realm, he's liable to throw the horn into the rift so I can never use it. I can't tell him the truth. I have to bear the weight of this on my shoulders alone, in his own words. "Just that the cost will be great."

Jarek turns to Lucretia. "What does that mean?"

"My old masters do not explain themselves any more than the fates do."

"It means we do not use this unless we are moments from death." Zander takes the horn and tucks it into my satchel, and then collects my hands in his. His eyes shine with pride and something I haven't seen much of lately—hope. "For now, we will claim this victory, and it is not a small one, if the Nulling is truly closed. You, Romeria, have just given us a fighting chance."

I smile and nod.

But I don't miss the way Agatha watches me, her eyebrows drawn together with worry.

66

ANNIKA

"Tell me again why we are doing this?" I pant as we stumble and climb over the rock. Scrapes mar my knuckles and knees where I've slipped, the stone beneath our feet slick from a recent rainfall. We abandoned the horses long ago for this treacherous path, sending them galloping off to freedom with slaps on their behinds.

"Because it is the only way you will escape your fate, kal'ana." Destry leads the way, struggling more than me, her legs too short for some of the boulders.

"We should stop for the night," Tyree announces from behind, checking the sky. "The light is waning."

"Over this ridge ahead, I saw a cave that will work. We just need to keep going ... a little ... bit ... longer." She wipes at her brow with the back of her hand, leaving a smear of dirt.

"You lead the way, Destrelia," Tyree teases.

"Do not call me that," she snaps, sparing him a glare before continuing, the four pendants dangling from her neck like trophies.

"Behave," I warn. Clearly, there is much about her we don't know.

"I will." A comforting hand smooths over my lower back. "How are you doing?"

I groan in response.

His deep chuckle warms my insides. "Just a little bit longer."

"And *then* what?" What are we rushing toward? Another attack by these Azyr and their guards? Or by one of those hideous beasts from the Nulling? So far nothing has gone as planned.

"And then I'll give you some of that meat you love so much." Diving in to press a kiss against my neck, he slaps my arse.

Weak laughter sails from my lips. It's all I can muster. "You are a *pig*."

"I thought I was a mongrel." He grins. "Come on, you can do it, Annika."

Together we climb.

"THIS WILL WORK," Tyree declares, standing at the edge of the deep, empty cave, his hands on his hips, peering out over the ledge. Beyond it is a drop that would break every one of our bones. It was both daunting and relieving to discover. I didn't think we had climbed that far.

The valley below quickly fades into darkness. I fear what the night might bring.

"I saw debris out there." Tyree points back the way we came. "Hopefully, it is dry enough to start a fire."

"Is a fire wise when we are in hiding?" I ask.

"A very small one. The cave is deep. It will obscure it some. But we do not have a choice. This night will grow cold, especially for a mortal. But have no fear, Destry is keeping an eye out."

That didn't help us much in the forest, I want to say, but I bite my tongue.

"You two, get comfortable."

"Be careful," I call out.

"See how much she adores me now?" He vanishes before I can cast a retort.

I seek out a corner to rest in. There is nothing but rock. "I doubt another living creature has ever set foot in here." When Destry doesn't answer, I glance over. She's seated cross-legged at the cave's opening, her fist clamped around her pendants.

"I'll leave you to it, then." I dig out provisions from Tyree's satchel and settle in with my back against the cave wall.

IT'S pitch-black by the time Tyree returns, his arms loaded with rotted logs and bramble. "I have not seen a single berry bush or hare since we started this climb. We will have to ration our food."

"We will not stay long in these mountains." Destry hasn't moved from her spot. Wherever she was in her head, though, she has returned, her eyes black again. "If I cannot connect, we must devise another plan."

"Did you hear that, Annika? Shearing and dung, it will be." He dumps his scavenged goods into a corner and then drops to his haunches to build a small pile of twigs and grass. "Have you found a wyvern yet?"

"There are several above us."

Tyree's hands pause. "*Several.* Is that normal?"

"It is more than I expected. They hunt at night. The fire will attract them."

"In that case ..." He drags over a log. "Don't worry." He grins when he sees the fear splayed across my face. "They are too big to fit in this cave."

I watch as he sets to work building our fire, using the tiny metal box he confiscated from that first barn to light it. Before long, orange flames dance, casting light and warmth within our alcove.

Tyree eases down beside me, reaching for a hunk of bread.

"Let me see that wound." I unclasp his cloak and, unlacing his tunic, I push the collar away to inspect the gash. "It looks better." We stopped by a river to water the horses, and I made him clean it out. It was angry and gaping then, and I was worried.

"As far as you know." I feel him studying my face as I inspect a few other cuts, my fingers tugging at his clothes and prodding his hard, bare flesh without shame. "What?" I demand, meeting his curious gaze.

"If someone had told me Princess Annika would tend to me one day, I would have never believed them." There is an odd sincerity in his eyes as it roams my face. It feels too intimate.

"You are valuable, that is all." I move to pull away.

He grabs my wrist, tugging me into him. "I thought we agreed no more games?" he whispers against my lips.

My pulse races. "Where is the fun in that?"

His eyes sparkle. "Speaking of aches for you to tend to, I have a rather uncomfortable one I desperately need your help with." He guides my palm over his breeches to the hard length waiting for me.

"Really? *Now?*" I steal a glance over my shoulder. Destry is occupied with her stones.

His lips trail along my jawline. "With you? *Always.*"

I would be lying if I said I hadn't been thinking about this—about him—all day. "Can we move over there?" I jut my chin toward a more private corner.

"I hear them!" Destry exclaims, interrupting our moment.

Tyree groans but then grabs my hand and, pulling me to my feet, we rush to the cave's opening. "Where?" he demands, searching the darkness.

I watch as four dark shadows glide ahead. "There!" I step out onto the ledge as I trace their movement. "It looks like they're hunting in the valley." I hope those horses have found cover.

"How close must one be before you test this plan of yours?" There's giddiness in Tyree's voice.

"Much closer than that. I will wait until—"

The rest of Destry's words are lost to me as sharp claws dig into my arms and I'm lifted into the air, my screams echoing across the night sky.

67

TYREE

"Annika!" I roar, watching in horror as she disappears up into the darkness. Her screams fade.

And my heart plummets. "Where did it take her?"

"I do not know." Destry fumbles with her pendants. "Likely to its nest."

"*Where* is its nest?"

"Up there, somewhere?"

That's when I hear it.

My name.

It's so faint, but it's Annika, and it's coming from above us.

"Get your things. We are climbing." I rush into the cave to collect my weapons and my satchel.

"We will not survive the night, my friend."

"Neither will she, and I have no interest in surviving without her." The moment I admit that, I know it is the truth. I grab a lengthy branch and shove its leafy ends into the flames, holding it there until it ignites. "Stay here if you wish, but I am going."

With a sigh, Destry rises to her feet. "That will not burn long." Collecting the stones in her grasp, her lips move with unintelligible words. The inky scrawl across her forehead glows and with it, so do the stones. "There. That should bring the other wroxlik right to us," she says with a hint of bitterness.

"Perfect. Maybe they will carry us too." I lead the way, my pulse racing with fear.

68

ANNIKA

Terror grips my every muscle as the wyvern climbs, its wings pumping furiously. It's flying to somewhere within this mountain.

Probably to a place where it can eat me in peace.

"Tyree!" I shriek, hoping he will hear and place my voice. That he won't assume I am dead and move on. Yet.

Suddenly, it swoops and releases me from its grip midair.

I hit the ground and remember nothing else.

A cool breeze flutters my hair as we look out over Lyndel, observing the buzz of activity. Below, casters work to repair tunnel entrances, and soldiers sharpen swords and haul weapons to various stations. Lyndel's citizens collect food and other supplies that we might need to dig in and not give ground.

Just days after evicting the Saur'goths who stole the city, the air feels different. Vibrant, even as we all prepare for the worst.

Zander's attention is in the distance, across the expanse of land beyond the wall. It's too far to decipher what Ybaris and Mordain are doing on that side, but there is activity. "Atticus will arrive in just hours."

"My people are establishing defenses deep into the battlefield as Atticus suggested. Things the enemy will not see until it is too late." Solange sits on a ledge, peeling and slicing an apple with a curved dagger. "We have left a small group of casters at the rift tonight, to manage the worst of the beasts. They will have enough time to ride to the line before the enemy arrives."

Zander and I share a glance, the unspoken decision in that fleeting look. This isn't a secret we can keep from her without earning her distrust.

"We might not have to worry about things crawling out from the Nulling anymore." With a deep breath, I tell her what I did. By the time I've finished, her complexion has paled.

"You summoned the fates." Her voice is cold and full of accusation.

"I did." I can still feel Aminadav's breath on my neck, his piercing gaze dissecting me.

"We had no other choice." Zander jumps in. "At least now, if we manage to kill Malachi, he cannot come back."

"And what about Aoife?"

"We cannot worry about Aoife right now. We will deal with her when she reveals herself."

Solange shakes her head. "You have no idea what you play with."

"My entire existence here is because people decided to summon the fates. Believe me, I have an idea." My voice is harder than I intended, but I stared into Aminadav's eyes and forfeited my life for these realms—not that anyone knows that. I'm not in the mood to be scolded. "Aminadav also gave Ybaris a hundred years of healthy crops without any strings, so *he* is capable of mercy. And these Saur'-goths that Malachi created? Aminadav doesn't like them. He said as much to me. That works to our advantage."

Solange scowls at her apple and tosses it at Jarek, who snatches it out of the air and takes a bite. "Allegra wrote to me. She would like an update to share with the counsel. What would you like me to tell her?"

"The truth."

"And if any of them have an issue with it, we will gladly collect them from safety and let them witness what our realms are about to face," Zander adds cooly.

Footfalls sound, and a moment later, Lord Telor appears, shuffling forward with the support of his cane. "We will be ready by sunrise."

Elisaf trails behind, his stoic protector.

"Where will all the people go if the Saur'goths breach the wall?" I ask.

"Into the keep. Your stone casters have built us an impressive new locking mechanism that, I hope, will hold."

It's better than nothing, I guess. "I wish I could get them all to Ulysede. They would be safe there."

"It is a kind thought, Your Highness, even if it is impossible." He pats my shoulder in a fatherly way. "Do we know how far the enemy is?"

"We were just about to fly out and check," Zander confirms. "I am anxious to know if Malachi and Sofie have joined them. *If* we can get close enough to find them without being struck by ballistae."

"About that, I had an idea earlier." Elisaf taps his mouth with his index finger. "Your Highness, you cloaked fifteen of us the other night."

"Yeah ..." Where's he going with this?

"Could you cloak a dragon?"

70

SOFIE

"Should I have brought my love a carriage to lie in?" Malachi mocks, watching me squirm in my saddle.

"No, Your Highness. I am well." The sharp burn in my backside from last night's trials has faded to a dull ache after a day of riding. Gratefully, no one else was involved to witness my humiliation or face his wrath. "How long before we reach the battleground?"

"The front of the line should arrive by midday tomorrow."

An endless sea of Saur'goths leads us forward, speckled here and there with reluctant beasts hauling weapons on their backs. The villages in their path have been all but destroyed, buildings burned and bodies strewn, some missing limbs that have no doubt made it into the meal cart. But it is the females of childbearing age that twist my stomach in knots. I spot the odd one peeking through windows of the few remaining houses as we pass, their clothing torn and faces bloodied. Others are dragged into the nearby woods, out of the way of the main army so these demon warriors can spill their vile seed without interruption.

I can sense their racing heartbeats.

Their terror.

Given what Malachi said of his warriors' dual purpose, I imagine these mortals will wish for death before long, once they see what they have birthed.

And I helped accomplish *all* of this.

Forgive me, Elijah.

Those words are a constant silent prayer these days.

462

My listless gaze is ahead, dwelling on these dark thoughts, when the indigo dragon appears out of thin air. I have just enough time to shield us before its fire rains down, carving a path of destruction. The flames are so intense, I buckle under its pressure.

And then the dragon climbs into the sky.

With a cry of rage, I lash out, releasing a bolt of fire that disintegrates against its shield.

In its clutches are two figures—the exiled king and a raven-haired female. Romeria.

"She was aiming for us," Malachi sneers, taking in the hundreds of scorched bodies, the Saur'goths on the edges writhing in pain, burned to various degrees. He's right—there is no way that was coincidental. She knew exactly where we were.

She tried to kill Elijah.

Our arrangement clearly means nothing to her.

The dragon veers and dives again, this time on the far side of the army, delivering another devastating arc of fire.

Silver bolts fly into the air, some missing them entirely, a few hitting her shields.

Twice more, they dive.

Malachi seethes as he watches his army burn.

"She cannot maintain that for much longer." It is too taxing, especially for a beast of that size.

It flies within range.

With a roar, Malachi launches a ball of fire through the air at them.

It hits their side and the dragon jolts from the impact.

"You are right. Already, she weakens." He sends another one quickly after.

The dragon banks hard, narrowly avoiding it, and they disappear into the clouds.

He nods with satisfaction. "That should keep them away."

Groans and wails surround us.

"Move forward or fall on your swords!" Malachi urges his horse ahead, its hooves stomping on the charred remains of his fallen pets.

71

ZANDER

W e touch down outside Lyndel's gates and Romeria buckles, dropping to the ground in a heap.

I rush to her side, just as Abarrane, Jarek, and Elisaf close in, Solange close behind.

"I'm fine!" She holds up a hand to stall us. Her breathing is ragged. "That last hit got me good."

"Malachi." I thought Caindra would drop me, her massive body shuddering from the blow.

She nods. "It felt like, I don't know how to describe it … Like holding on to a metal bar that's been hit with another metal bar *really* hard. Like, it was vibrating through me and I had to let go. I can still feel it."

Elisaf's brow furrows with worry. "But did it work?"

"Yes, and no. They didn't see us coming, but Sofie had her shield up too fast." I shake my head. "We could have been rid of them both. Now, it will be impossible to catch them unaware."

"It was stupid. We should have come in from behind. I didn't think she could react so fast," Romeria says, disappointment radiating from her.

"Hindsight is always far clearer." I offer my hand and Romeria takes it, allowing me to haul her to her feet. "But they did well. There had to be at least a thousand dead."

"Yeah, only ninety-nine thousand more to go," Romeria mutters, and I sense her defeat.

Smoothing a palm over her back, I suggest, "Why don't we go inside and rest. There is a room set aside for us in the manor."

But she shakes her head. "How am I supposed to fight a fate when one hit from him did that?"

"You were defending, not attacking," Solange says. "There is a difference."

"There is? Will you teach me everything you know?" Romeria pleads, desperation in her voice.

"*Everything*?" Solange's eyebrows arch. "By tomorrow?"

"Until we run out of time."

"This reminds me of that day the princess fought a nethertaur after a two-hour lesson on how to not stab herself," Abarrane muses.

"I killed it, didn't I?" Romeria scoffs.

"No, *I* killed it. *You* stopped it."

"Right." Romeria dismisses the surly legionary. "So?"

Solange smirks. "I do not know how to fight a fate. No one has ever fought one and lived to tell the story. *But* I can teach you how to fight a powerful caster."

"Perfect, because I'm pretty sure Sofie is going to be really pissed off after that." Romeria squeezes my hand. "Give me a few hours and then we can fly to Eldred Wood to get an update from Atticus." They disappear behind Lyndel's gate, her ever-present legionary a shadow, and the sylx his.

"How did it look out there?' Elisaf asks.

My shoulders sink with dread. "If you have been sitting on regrets and wishes, I would settle them tonight." Anyone counting on us to lead them to victory will soon learn how fatal that hope is.

"That bad, then."

"Yes, that bad." We are thoroughly fucked.

72

ATTICUS

"The famed Eldred Wood." King Cheral canters to my side as he sizes up the forest ahead. "It looks peaceful."

"It is vast, stretching far south, almost to Cirilea. A great place for Nulling beasts to hide." I imagine there are plenty in there now with the rift's opening.

"Ybarisans and Mordain's casters now too."

"And soon, the Kiers. These are strange times, indeed."

He peers at the men. "We could not have reached this soon enough. The army has ridden hard and needs a rest."

We will all get plenty after tomorrow when we are dead, I refrain from saying. That's not the right attitude for heading into battle, no matter how hopeless. "Let us get to it then." Hazarding a glance up at the sky to note the late afternoon position of the sun, I nudge my horse with my heels and pick up the pace.

"AND HERE I WAS, jealous of my brother for having a fortress to hide behind," I jest, and yet the lengthy stone portico that travels along the tree line is jaw-dropping. The casters had only days to work with, and they built a wall and tower worthy of a kingdom, soaring high into the air and facing west toward Lyndel.

"No wonder Queen Neilina hoarded these casters for so long," King Cheral muses, his eyes lit with amazement.

"To be fair, Mordain wanted nothing to do with Malachi's demons either." Save for a few, like Wendeline. I wonder if the caster still lives.

Ybarisan soldiers line the rampart, watching our army approach. "Announce yourselves!" one of them yells.

"Really?" As if they aren't expecting us. "King Cheral of Kier, and Prince Atticus, commander of the king's army and once ruler of Islor! Where do we enter?" There is nothing but a solid wall in front of us, as far as the eye can see.

Stones grind and a large opening appears, earning gasps of astonishment from behind us.

A familiar figure stands in the center of it, a grin plastered across his bearded face. "What do you mean, *where*?"

I charge forward on my horse, leaping off at the last minute to collide in an embrace with Kazimir. "I heard you survived, you lucky bastard."

"Thanks to your brother and Serenis's remarkable healing abilities. She is talented." He gestures to a pretty female standing nearby, sparing her a wink.

Her face flushes with her demure smile.

I shake my head. "Leave it to you, Kaz, to bed the first caster who touches you."

"What?" He shrugs. "She wanted to make sure everything was working as it should."

"Right." I chuckle, my heart brimming with relief and joy that at least I have my best friend.

Our line of soldiers moves in slowly, King Cheral observing the sea of tents and campfires dotting the woods with interest from atop his horse.

"This is an unexpected twist." Kazimir regards them coolly, his attention stalling on Tuella for a beat.

I throw an arm around his shoulders. "Come, we both have much to tell."

———

THE SUNSET behind us bathes the expanse of land to the west, its last rays showering Lyndel in hazy golden light. From the top of the rampart, I can make out the great walled city that has served as Islor's first defense against Ybaris for centuries, feeding the rift army and guarding the bridge between our two realms.

And now our enemies of the past are here, allied with us for the future.

It's all because of Romeria.

"One of those carried me here." Kazimir nods to the great winged beasts that circle above Lyndel as if restless. "The orange one, I was told, though I don't remember any of it. I was all but dead."

"I should have died from that ax on the battlefield."

He leans over the edge, spying on the Kierish soldiers who set up camp and prepare their blades. "And the ax's wielder?"

"He's a delight."

"That his head is still attached to his shoulders is a shock. Are you sure you are the Atticus who fell in the Plains of Aminadav?"

I chuckle. "King Cheral has been oddly forgiving of many things, but slaughtering his soldier in front of the others would not be wise. As for who I am, that is a fair question as of late, given princesses are dying and returning as key casters. But I promise, I am the same version who has bested you at every sparring session since you grew fangs."

"And then lost them." He runs his tongue along his teeth. "Sometimes they feel like a missing appendage."

"And yet their absence has saved both us *and* the mortals. It was the only way."

"Romeria to the rescue yet again." His tone is unreadable.

King Cheral moves along the rampart toward us, escorted by a line of Kierish guards.

"It's the one behind him," I murmur, leaning against the wall.

"The brute with the stupid haircut. I remember him now." Kazimir's jaw tenses. "And I will not forget him tomorrow on the battlefield, in your honor."

"I have to say, I am impressed with what these shadow wielders have accomplished from dirt and rock," King Cheral says by way of greeting.

Kazimir's eyebrow arches. "Shadow wielders?"

"Long story, don't ask." I dismiss his question before responding to King Cheral. "And that is what you can see. There is much that you can't. Kienen, down there"—I point to Romeria's Ybarisan commander—"has walked me through everything, which I can relay to you. There are plenty of surprises for our enemy."

"I cannot wait to learn of them." He snaps his fingers and his guards step forward, carrying golden armor that gleams from polish, the flame crest on the breast plate familiar. "I believe this is yours."

I falter. "This is … unexpected." They cleaned and repaired it, and hauled it back to Islor.

"The commander of Islor's army should be recognized on the battlefield, no?"

Something tells me this alliance has been his plan since the moment I arrived in Ostros. A new level of respect blooms for this mortal and his scheming.

"They will bring it to your tent." He nods to my nemesis, who steps forward. In his grip is a sword.

My sword.

"Jimon has been keeping it safe for you."

The brute dips his head with the first sign of respect he's ever shown me.

I accept it, wrapping my hand around the hilt again. It would be poetic if I were to draw it now and kill the man before me.

Maybe that's why he looks at me the way he does—with a mixture of resignation and unease.

He knows he would deserve it.

Poetic, but supremely witless.

King Cheral smiles as if he can read my thoughts. "Wrangle these leaders of Ybaris and Mordain, and meet me within the hour in my tents." It's an order and yet, coupled with the handover of my belongings, it doesn't feel like it.

My smirk says as much. "Of course, Your Highness."

With one last roaming view of the land before us, King Cheral strolls away, his guard trailing him.

I lean into Kazimir. "Maybe do not kill Jimon too soon. He was just following orders, after all."

Kazimir's deep bellow carries.

A GUARD DUCKS into Cheral's tent as we're toiling over various strategies. "King Zander and Queen Romeria have arrived, Your Highness."

I don't wait, moving smoothly past him, the weight of my sword at my hip comforting.

Outside, the camp bustles. It's impossible to gauge the true size given the forest, but the delineation between troops—Kier and Islorian from Ybarisan and Mordain—is stark, like two halves with a solid line of space in between.

Zander chats with a tall, regal-looking male in armor with the infamous two-crescent moon symbol. I have never laid eyes on him before tonight, but he seems to command respect. I've heard several people call him by the name Radomir.

"There she is." Kazimir, who has not left my side since we reunited, points through the bustle to where Romeria and Satoria hover beneath a tree, exchanging words. Romeria's stance screams inquisition and Satoria stands defiant, her shoulders pulled back. I can't imagine what the two of them have to talk about.

Suddenly, as if feeling our gazes on them, Romeria turns. Her eyes narrow.

"Well, that can't be good," I murmur.

"Why? Does that Kier have something unflattering to share about you?"

"That is not any Kier. That is Cheral's fourth wife. As far as what she has to share ..." I lower my voice. "Let us just say I have had regular nightly visits that I did not ask for and did not relent to." But I don't know what picture Satoria might paint and how Romeria might interpret it.

I sense another set of eyes boring into me and turn to find Tuella nearby, her black eyes alight with a secret. "Good evening, conjurer. Are you keeping busy, surrounded by so much of the shadow?"

"It is enlightening. Enjoy the night, usurper king." She glides away.

Disquiet slips down my spine, her words from the other night like a bad omen.

Kazimir slaps my injured shoulder, earning my wince. "Lovely friends you've made, all around."

"He's clearly won over a few." Romeria closes in, her pretty blue eyes regarding me. "How's your shoulder?"

"I will live."

"Show me to your tent and I'll see what I can do." She spares Kazimir a look. "*Alone*. Let Zander know where we are when he comes searching."

He shoots an "Are you sure that's a good idea?" frown at me—he knows my history with the princess all too well.

I ignore him and lead the way, lifting the tent flap for her. "After you, Your Highness."

She ducks in, surveying the sparse space—the cot, the table, my gleaming armor. "I expected something way bigger to fit your giant head in."

I chuckle, not wasting any time, hoisting my tunic over my head and tossing it to the nearby table. I settle on my cot. "How bad is it?"

She sidles up behind me. "It looks mostly healed." Cool fingers trace the raw flesh. "It's going to leave a bad scar, though."

"If Tuella is right, I won't be here to live with it."

"Why do you say that?"

"Apparently, she has seen my death in the stars."

A long silence ensues. "Maybe she read them wrong."

I chuckle. "Maybe. But something tells me your one power, as she calls it, can only get me so far." I meet Romeria's gaze. "Where is Gracen?"

"Safe."

"I know. But *where*?"

Her lips purse.

"What am I going to do? We go into battle tomorrow, Romeria."

After another long pause, she sighs. "She's in Ulysede. Malachi can't touch her there." Kneeling behind me on my cot, she asks, "The conjurer. What do you know about her?"

"Not much. She can manipulate birds. And other creatures too. Not your dragons, though," I add quickly. "Unless she was lying to me when I asked."

"Let's hope not. Hold still."

Warmth blooms in my shoulder, spreading along my muscles and tendons, deep into my bones as her power knits whatever is still broken inside.

"I guess I wasn't as mended as I thought." I roll my shoulder when she finishes, testing it. It feels as good as new. "Thank you. Truly." I let her see my eyes, hoping she can read my genuine gratitude. "For *everything*." Saving not just my life but Gracen's and all those children I foolishly corralled in the castle before riding off to my near-death.

"Do not give me yet another reason to kill you, Brother." Zander strolls in. "You've already given me so many."

"He's fixed. Well, his arm is, anyway." Romeria flicks my ear before climbing off my bed. "I'm sure there's still plenty wrong with him."

I chuckle and redress. "Anything important I should know?"

"Malachi and his key caster are with the army. We tried killing them today, but Sofie is too quick." Zander inspects my armor. "They'll be moving in at dawn."

"And how long before they attack?"

"We shall see."

"How many will we bring for a parley—"

"No parley," Romeria snaps, her glare brokering no disagreement.

My eyebrows pop. I'm not used to seeing that side of her. "No parley. Got it."

"He and his creatures cannot be trusted to follow the rules of engagement. The rules of *anything*, really," Zander adds, more cordially.

"I took your advice," Romeria says after a moment.

"You will have to be more specific." I tuck my tunic into my breeches. "I give such great advice and a lot of it."

She rolls her eyes. "We summoned the fates."

My mouth drops, my hands stalled. "And?"

"Aminadav has granted our request to block the passage from the Nulling. I don't know how, and if there will be consequences. I guess we'll find out tonight." Her shaky sigh exposes her worry.

"This is a big deal."

"It is one problem solved," Zander counters, forever the pragmatist. "The other one is marching to our doorstep as we speak. Come on." He jerks his head toward the tent's exit. "Let us see how much ground they have made."

His meaning dawns on me instantly. "With the dragons?" I didn't mean to show so much enthusiasm.

Romeria snorts. "You sound like a kid on Christmas."

I frown. "Christmas? What is—"

"Never mind. *Yes*, with the dragons."

"I should probably tell King Cheral."

Zander cocks his head at me like I've lost my mind. "You are a royal prince and the commander of the king's army. Must you ask permission?"

"No, but … no." And yet I worry that Kier's king will consider it disrespectful.

Zander waits a beat. "Besides, I told him where we were going."

I shove him playfully, earning his laugh.

Behind us, Romeria wears a pensive smile.

"IT IS EVEN LARGER than I thought!" I yell as we soar high above the approaching army, their torches like a sea of stars on the ground. The horrifying reality below mutes the exhilaration of this experience. "Can we get closer?"

"No, it is too dangerous. They will be ready for us this time and Malachi's reach is considerable!" Zander yells back.

I cling to the dragon's claws. They look sharp enough to slice me in half and yet they haven't. The green beast that carries me is surprisingly gentle.

Bexley's child.

Who could have ever imagined?

Romeria shouts something at her dragon and it banks hard, the two others following a split second later.

WE COAST in formation along the rift, low enough to spot any movement within the crevice.

There is none.

Nothing emerges from the deep, dark well.

MY LEGS WOBBLE as they touch ground after soaring through the air for so long. "So *this* is your secret kingdom in the mountains." I stare up at the golden gate as it climbs open, anticipation feeding my body, the detour unexpected.

Gracen is in there.

I have no idea how she feels about me now. She may hate me for the mistakes I made with the mortals. I will have to live with that, for however long I survive. What I can't bear is not seeing her one last time.

Inside, the tunnel is lined with bulky winged beasts in armor the likes of which I've never seen.

"They're nymphs," Zander answers my unspoken question.

"Of course they are." This is all too surreal. "When I received your letter, Boaz was convinced it was all a sham to lure me away," I muse. "Where is he, anyway? Still in Cirilea?" I haven't thought of him since I left.

"His ashes are." By the cold look in Romeria's eye, I can guess who delivered that punishment.

Through the tunnel we march, and at the end is another gate and a different set of creatures, these sleek, the bony bulges from their skulls disturbing. They also have wings.

"More nymphs, I gather?"

"Oredai, this is Prince Atticus, Zander's brother," Romeria introduces us. By her tone, she isn't thrilled to see this one.

"Usurper king," the creature hisses.

"I will never live that name down." I dismiss him as I take in the splendor of this secret nymph city. But even that doesn't hold my attention for too long, as I climb into the saddle of a gelding.

The horses' hooves echo as we ride through the streets at a fast clip.

"Where is everyone?" It's deathly quiet in here.

"Most of the nymphs have left to go ... somewhere. We don't know where. The various factions don't get along with one another," Romeria says.

"What does that look like? Nymph factions not getting along."

"I'm not sure yet," she admits, worry marring her pretty face.

I have *so many questions*. For now, though, all I can think about is seeing Gracen again. "One problem at a time."

Zander cuts me a knowing look. Our father always used to say that to us.

We pass over a bridge and beneath two massive, winged statues. Ahead waits Ulysede's castle, which is as impressive as the rest of the city.

"Argon's jeweled palace was not enough. You had to claim this, too?" I tease.

"Do not forget Nyos's guild," Zander quips. "It is also remarkable."

Romeria scowls. "*None* were by choice."

"I will gladly take one off your hands," I joke.

"Are you asking or informing of your next coup?" Zander throws back.

"I deserve that."

"And I've only just begun," he warns, but the corners of his mouth twitch.

I pause in the grand hall to regard the little pot-bellied creature that dusts a pedestal—one of a dozen that sit empty within the vacuous space.

"I guess Oredai let one kaeli stay, after all." Romeria smiles at the mute thing as it goes about its business. "I'll bet this is the one that likes to play hide-and-seek with Mika."

I grin. "Mika's favorite pastime. He had every member of the guard searching the castle for him at one point or another." I remember the day I stumbled upon Gracen in the library. She was searching for the little rascal. That's the day he found the vial of poison and uncovered Saoirse's scheme.

"Come on. This way." Romeria leads me to the main set of stairs.

As the three of us move up the floors and down the halls, throwing casual barbs and quips at each other, I find myself longing for more time—to repair relationships, to explore this strange new world of no blood curse, of nymphs, of Ybaris and Islor united.

Romeria stops at a door. "These are her quarters. We're at the end of the hall. We'll need to leave before sunrise." She slips a hand into Zander's, and they turn to leave.

"Wait!" I call out, stopping them. "Does she know I'm coming?"

"No, because *I* didn't know I was bringing you until I spoke to the Kierish queen. She introduced herself and insisted I give you this night. You can thank *her*."

That is what Satoria and Romeria spoke about? "I will. Is Gracen angry with me?" I must know.

Romeria sighs heavily. "It's Gracen. She'll forgive you, even if you don't deserve it." They stroll away.

With a rush of nerves, I knock on the door, and then immediately regret it. The children must be sleeping. I probably woke the baby—

A shuffle sounds on the other side and then the door opens and there she is, wrapped in a robe, her mane of curly blond hair free and wild, the adorable smattering of freckles decorating her sun-kissed cheeks.

I've pictured Gracen's face too many times to count, and now that it's in front of me, I'm struck speechless.

Beautiful blue eyes widen. "Atticus?"

Just my name on her voice lulls my nerves. "I know I have a thousand apologies to give for my part and poor excuses, but—"

She launches herself at me, her lips cutting off my rambling words.

ROMERIA

"What I am most thankful for in all of this castle tonight is this bathtub." I close my eyes and settle back against Zander, hoping to soak away the never-ending tension that has encased me lately, or at least temper it for a night. It's as if the nymphs knew we would need this moment together. And maybe they did. They seem to have insight on everything else.

Zander's firm body cocoons me, his sinewy arms wrapped around my chest in a lazy embrace. "What made you want to bring Atticus here?" Pushing strands of wet hair off my forehead, he leans in to kiss my temple. Delicious stubble scrapes my skin. I ache for it to scrape me somewhere else.

"King Cheral's *wife*. She insisted that he was madly in love with Gracen and that I bring him to her." I'm glad I listened. Guilt would've clawed at me otherwise.

"I can't see Atticus professing that to the wife of his enemy. I wonder what the story is there."

"She couldn't keep her eyes off him, so it's probably a story I don't want to hear."

Zander sighs heavily. "Whatever. Let them be happy. Let them *all* be happy for one last night. Abarrane will surely land in Kienen's tent again."

I smile. "Solange was eyeing Jarek. I will bet you one giant gemstone from my vault that they hook up tonight."

"'Hook up'? Is that Romy Watts lingo?" he teases. "And from which vault? You have two."

"Aww." I mock sulk as I roll onto my stomach, my chin resting against his chest. "Are you still bitter about that?"

He chuckles, splashing a few drops of water in my face. "I hope Solange knows that Lucretia will be in the corner, watching."

I burst out laughing, but it morphs into a groan. "My god, the poor guy can't catch a break."

"I think Jarek is doing just fine." Zander studies my face. "What are we going to do when this is all over?"

"What, the war?" I pause. "I've never given it any thought."

"*Never?*"

"I mean … no. Everything we talk about, everything we do, it's all led up to tomorrow."

"What about after tomorrow?" he whispers.

"What if there is no 'after tomorrow'?" Fear bleeds into my voice. I have never been so powerful in my life as I am now, and also I've never been so scared. It's the first time I feel like I have so much to lose.

That bronze horn sits in my satchel, waiting for me to end this war with a single blow. Am I a coward for not using it already? Maybe, but I have no clue *how* it will end the war, and I can't take Aminadav's words at face value. That much, I am sure of.

I'm not willing to give up just yet.

I'm not ready to die.

"What about *after* tomorrow?" Zander repeats, trailing fingers down my spine.

I falter. "You tell me."

His throat bobs with a hard swallow. "I will reclaim Islor's throne." Back and forth, his fingers slide, reaching all the way down to the small of my back and beyond, teasing the crack of my ass. "We will root out every lord and lady who is determined to maintain the old ways of Islor and give their lands to the mortals, allow them the chance to rule. The keeper system will be abolished, and mortals will be free to live and work where they wish. Mortal villages will exist, and not ones that must hide in Venhorn to escape the king's rule."

As he speaks, my heart swells. It's everything he has ever wished for, everything we've talked about. I push aside my dread and let myself imagine. "The bridge between Ybaris and Islor will be open for travel, and I will figure out how to convince the nymphs to heal the lands without claiming lives. Not just Ybaris but also Kier."

"Until you do, the Plains of Aminadav will help provide for the people in all the realms," he says, bending his neck forward to kiss my nose.

"And I will empty Ulysede's coffers to trade with Seacadore. And Udrel, if we must," I promise. How long would it take to sail there? Could Caindra fly that far?

"Fine, but leave my gold pillars alone." A smirk curls his lips. It drifts with a pensive look. "We will have that wedding we keep planning."

I inhale sharply at the thought of marrying Zander. For real, this time.

Easing my body up to straddle his hips, I lay kisses along his throat, his jawline, his lips. Between my legs, his cock is hard and waiting. "And we'll take the stone on Hudem." Can a Ybarisan and an Islorian have children together? And is there any point to the ritual, now that the nymphs are here and the blood curse is gone?

He chuckles, his hands seizing my hips, positioning himself at my entrance. "With an audience."

My laughter dies as he slides into me.

"We'll divide our time amongst kingdoms." His hand slides between us, his thumb rubbing over my clit as he thrusts slowly, our mouths working together in a tantalizing dance of tongues.

"In Cirilea when the roses are in bloom." I sit up, his lip leaving mine to trail down to my breasts, collecting a nipple between his teeth. "And the dragons will fly us everywhere." I seize the sides of the tub for purchase, my breathing growing ragged as his teeth scrape across my flesh with a delicious bite just short of pain.

Words fade, giving way to moans and cries and the casual splash of water as our bodies rock against each other in an intimate dance, chasing a euphoria I once believed only existed in fiction. But all I had to do was fall in love with a king.

My king.

We climax together in a rush and topple into a heap.

And then continue planning out a life that we may never have a chance to live.

7 4

ANNIKA

I regain consciousness lying on the stone floor of a cave. My shoulder throbs. So does my head.

But the wyvern didn't eat me.

A wide opening in the ceiling allows in dappled light. It must be morning.

With a grimace, I heave myself to my feet, staggering before I gain my full balance and venture, checking the dark corners above for any beasts waiting to swoop down. From what I can see, I'm alone. But there are enough bones lying around to mark this for what it is—a lair.

I test for my affinity, but I can't grasp onto it. It must be because of the giant goose egg on the side of my head that stings to the touch.

How long before the wyvern returns for its meal? I need to get out of here.

I need to find Tyree.

There's a tunnel ahead. I bend and follow it through, into another cavern, this one long and narrow and lit by small gaps in the ceiling and a larger one on the far side. Too small for a wyvern. I aim for it but get distracted halfway by a stone fixture in a corner.

I've seen this before, in Cirilea, in the nymphaeum.

Could it be real? Or am I feverish?

Wandering to it, I trace my fingertip over the swirling lines. It is certainly real, and it even has the same engraving.

What is it doing *here*, in Udrel's mountains?

A fluttering sound stirs behind me. I glance over my shoulder.

479

And scream, jumping backward. My body slams against the stone.

Dozens of bald, pot-bellied little creatures with webbed feet surround me, watching through wide, curious eyes, their wings quivering. They haven't lunged at me yet.

I've seen these things before, I realize then. Or something like them, painted within the mural in the temple in Orothos. "What are you?" Does Destry know they live up here?

They say nothing, but one after another, they raise their gangly arms to point toward the other end of the cavern.

With a wary eye on these creatures, I follow their direction. Clearly, they wish to show me *something*.

At the far end, resting within a stone cradle layered in straw and twigs, is a female with hair like raven's feathers, wearing a shimmering gold and silver dress. Golden antlers claw at her chest, the points sinking into her flesh. A black dagger juts from her throat, embedded deeply.

She looks eerily like Romeria.

"Annika!" Tyree rushes through the opening, out of breath.

My pulse races as I charge toward him, into his waiting arms. "I am so happy to see you."

He holds me against his chest, his fingers tangling through my hair. "Thank the fates you are alive. I heard you call my name and we started climbing."

We? "Where is Destry?"

She steps in then, red-faced from exertion.

"We climbed all night. I heard you scream again now."

"I did, but ..." I frown, looking around. "Where did they all go?"

"Where did who go?"

"The little creatures. They were just here."

"I don't see any little creatures." Tyree winces as he inspects my head. "That is a nasty lump, but it will heal."

"I am not imagining things. I saw them! And there is a female here." I think? Taking him by the hand, I lead him to the end.

Tyree's grip goes slack. "Mother?"

TYREE

I blink several times.

Am I hallucinating?

"*That* is Queen Neilina?" Annika stares at the still form embraced among straw and twigs, and I realize that, for all the hate she and her kingdom have long since stoked for my mother, she has never laid eyes upon her. "Are you sure?"

"That she is my mother? Yes, I am sure. That is her. That is her token necklace. That is … her body. She is dead." A wave of numbness washes over me with my words. Dead … and in Udrel.

"What is she doing here?" Annika asks, voicing my inner thoughts.

"I cannot begin to guess." But given all that has happened, namely Annika's sudden and inexplicable lack of blood thirst, I can only imagine it has *something* to do with the fates.

Destry slinks in beside me to regard the scene, her hand clasped around her stones. "She is not dead."

"Excuse me?"

She leans in, studying the body from this angle and then another. "She is not dead."

"She has what appears to be a token blade through her neck and her own token embedded in her chest. Surely, you do not believe this." Has the altitude confused Destry's mind?

"The shadow lives in her. It does not live in dead things."

My heartbeat slows. What if Destry's right? Why wouldn't she be? "Who would have put her in here?"

"Those little goblin creatures?" But Annika shrugs, then winces, her fingers glancing over the goose egg. Dried blood mats her hair.

"What are we supposed to do?" As soon as I say this out loud, a thought hits me, and the urge to follow through is overwhelming.

Reaching down into the makeshift casket, I grab hold of the blade through my mother's throat, and I pull.

A deep, rattling gasp sails from her lips as her eyes flash open.

ROMERIA

The night sky hints at daylight as we emerge on the castle steps, our expressions somber. A crowd of mortals lines the stairs, much to our surprise for this hour, including Dagny, Corrin, Pan, Eden, as well as many of the scribes alongside Agatha.

While Atticus says his goodbyes to a tearful Gracen, I pull the old scribe aside.

"You look splendid this morning, Your Highness," she says.

"Thank you. I found this hanging on my closet door." A silver, black, and white suit of armor and leather. No wings attached this time. It makes me think there are still wisps and kaeli fluttering about, unseen. "If something should happen to me, this needs to get to Allegra." I set the Ring of Minerva in her palm.

Her eyes widen.

"I trust you will get it to her."

"I will find a way, Your Highness." With a nod, she tucks it into the safety of her breast pocket. "And I am sorry we failed at finding the answers that would help you avoid this terrible battle you must now face."

"You did find the answer. It just wasn't the one we wanted." I squeeze her shoulder. "Take care of everyone for me."

Her attention settles on my satchel. "May the fates be merciful to you today, Your Highness."

I sense a deeper meaning in those words, as if the old caster somehow recognizes the deal I made with Aminadav. "That would be a nice change." I turn my back on her.

"Gesine would be so proud of you," she rushes to add, bringing a lump to my throat.

Zorya and Loth stand in the middle of the steps, dressed in warrior's clothing, each strapped with a dozen blades. There's no question what they're angling for—a chance to die today rather than remain within the safety of Ulysede, babysitting scribes and humans.

I nod.

"Your Highness." They dip their heads and then climb into the saddles of the waiting horses.

The Cindrae wait in a line at the bottom of the steps, my crown resting in the palms of Oredai's upturned hands. The one I intentionally left on my throne not ten minutes ago, when I went into the crypt to fetch Mordain's ring.

Do not forget your crown.

Oredai's voice in my head is especially unnerving this morning.

"Right, of course." Collecting it, I study it for a moment. "What is this made of?"

The bones of elders.

"Huh. Bones. Really."

It is a necessity as much as an honor.

"Necessity for what?"

That which is coming.

That sounds like a warning. After Jarek nearly died, I now weigh everything Oredai says. But it also triggers something Aminadav said to me, about the horn being bone ripped from his head. A gift with a specific purpose. "And what does it do?"

He flashes his jagged teeth.

She who trusts the elders will walk in the light.

Another nonanswer, but I expected as much from him. I don't trust the elders, but I affix it to my head, anyway. It claws at my scalp. "Listen, if something should happen to me—"

There is only one ruler of Ulysede, and it is the Queen for All.

"That's not what I was going to say but ... Take care of them for me?"

His black eyes roam the mortals on the steps.

They are the people of this kingdom, Your Highness, and I protect the kingdom. No threat shall enter.

With that, the Cindrae pivot on their heels and march away.

"What did he say?" Zander asks.

"The usual. Things that don't make sense." But I do feel a little better, knowing Oredai will watch over them all.

Rubbing my neck with an affectionate hand, he calls out, "We must leave now."

Atticus kisses Gracen one more time and then takes the steps down, looking ready to choke on his emotions.

With a last wave at the sea of worried faces, people who have become like family to me, we ride for the gate and the war that waits beyond.

SHOUTS of alarm sound midmorning as I'm devouring a bowl of vegetable stew and a slice of bread in Lyndel's tower, oddly famished given the constant state of turmoil. My appetite disintegrates as I run after Zander along the bridge to the rampart and get my first clear look past Lyndel's outer wall.

A light drizzle falls as we watch Malachi's army move like a dark, slow wave over the grassy hill. A wave of ants that never ends, never breaks. For hours, it keeps rolling forward and spreading, until the land as far as we can see is alive with the enemy.

We've seen this army before, more than once, and yet now that they're here, with Malachi at their helm, it feels more ominous. This isn't a fly-by on a dragon, a hit-and-run attack. They are at our doorstep, and they aren't leaving until someone is defeated.

And their mass is terrifying. I roam the pale faces of the soldiers sharing the wall with us, trying their best to appear brave and confident. They had only heard of the coming force, but they hadn't seen it until now.

I know what they're feeling because I'm also feeling it—a surge of hopelessness that grows stronger the longer we stand here and witness this unfold.

Eldred Woods is a blur from here, but Atticus said they would be watching through their conjurer's seeing stone. Just in case ... "Caindra."

From the mountain ridge behind Lyndel, the three dragons launch into the sky with piercing roars to perform a wide loop. A signal to the other side that they can't miss but also a reminder to everyone that we are not weak.

My affinities crackle under my fingertips, begging to be unleashed with bolts of fire and devastating gusts of wind, but it's far too soon. Malachi hasn't appeared. So we stand with forced calm, seeing the enemy fall into place.

"Have you ever seen anything like it?" Lord Rengard scratches at his chin.

Lord Telor leans against his cane. "This is beyond my comprehension."

"The Fate of Fire has had many millennia to prepare," Lucretia purrs from behind Jarek. "He has prepared for *almost* everything."

"What *hasn't* he prepared for?" Jarek asks.

"The Queen for All."

I shake my head. "You give me far too much credit. His fire hit my shield once yesterday, and I could barely hold it."

Her lips pull back with a brilliant smile. "You were not wearing your crown."

Without thought, I reach up to test the spikey prongs. The nymph elders' bones. Have I been foolishly dismissing this as a simple ornament all this time?

"Look how they use the Nulling beasts." A mixture of admiration and dismay laces Elisaf's tone as he watches a Saur'goth ride a nethertaur, steering it with a chain to keep its tusks from gutting those nearby. Strapped to its scaly back are nets filled with silver bolts. There are dozens more just like this one. "Thank the fates they do not have wyverns at their disposal."

"Thank Caindra for scaring them all off. But where did they get all these weapons?" I ask no one in particular.

"I imagine they brought them. Malachi thought of everything. Now, where is he ..." Zander's gaze scours the tide, searching. This feels like a game of *Where's Waldo*, but I stifle my urge to say that out loud. It would make no sense to anyone here. "There." Zander points to a cluster of riders moving through the crowd, the Saur'goths parting to make way. A horde follows closely, carrying cages draped in cloth.

Even from up here, I recognize the man from the stone sarcophagus beneath the castle. Tall and regal and handsome.

Sofie walks next to him, dressed in an emerald ball gown.

"Not the wisest choice for a battle," Jarek muses. "You can spot her from anywhere."

Sofie is a lot of things, but stupid isn't one of them. "It's her way of saying this will be over before it starts." Or is it to announce how untouchable she is?

Was it even her choice, or did Malachi dictate it?

My heart flutters with a rush of fear, and for a moment, I'm back in the bowels of her Belgian home, listening to her spew nonsense about gardens and retrieving stones. Malachi didn't even trust her with the complete truth, it's clear now.

"Look, there." Zander points to a crop of riders on horses, farther back. "I believe those are the lords and ladies of Islor."

"Do you think they are here of their own volition?" Elisaf asks.

"I doubt it, but it matters not. They fight alongside the enemy, and they will die with them." Zander forces as much conviction as he can into his voice. "Let us not make ourselves an easy target. It is best we spread out."

"We will see each other on the other side, my friend. Here or in Za'hala." Lord Rengard bows to me and then marches to the right.

"May the Queen for All save us today." Lord Telor hobbles to the left.

His words steal the air from my lungs as dread washes over me.

A hand squeezes my shoulder. Jarek's. "Have faith that you are stronger than you think."

He always knows when I am doubting myself. I peer up at the looming legionary, allowing him to see my terror. "And if I'm not?" All these people are counting on me.

"Then we will likely be dead before we know otherwise. Either way, I am by your side until the end, Your Highness." His eyes roam my face, stalling on my mouth for half a beat before he stiffens and pulls away.

With a deep, shaking breath, I turn to face the line as Malachi and Sofie arrive at the front.

"They are just beyond reach of our archers," Abarrane notes.

"As intended." Zander leans against the rampart wall, his hands bracing him on either side, his steely gaze on the god who has claimed his throne.

Finally, Malachi strolls forward, throwing out his arms, palms up.

"He is asking for a parley?" Surprise laces Elisaf's voice.

"*No*," I snarl.

"Absolutely not," Zander agrees. "Let us give him the answer his new pets understand." Zander signals the soldiers manning the main catapult. A thump sounds, and a dozen Saur'goth heads sail through the air, raining down to hit the ground rolling.

Malachi answers with a wave to his side.

The Saur'goths march forward, setting the cages in front of him. They tug the cloth, removing the coverings.

The daaknar immediately attracts my attention, hunched over, its tattered wings waiting to fan out. Pitiful, almost, but I know better than to feel anything but hatred. It is likely the one Malachi used in the arena to slaughter those mortals who removed their cuffs.

"Who are they?" Zander asks, pointing at the two forms cowering in the other cages.

"Oh my god." I grab hold of the rampart wall to catch myself as my head swirls with sudden dizziness.

No, it can't be.

Here? In Islor?

"Those are my parents."

77

ATTICUS

"Who are those people?" King Cheral asks as we watch the reflection of Lyndel in the pool. Tuella hovers nearby, her white eyes and glowing forehead drawing the unsettled gazes of the casters.

"I have never seen them before." They clearly mean something to Romeria, who stands on the ramparts, her lethal crown perched on her head. She looks every bit the queen, but at this very moment, she appears seconds from collapsing.

"What are your orders, Commander?" Kazimir hovers, all semblance of my dear friend gone.

"Have the first wave of cavalry ride out to the line." Something tells me this king has a plan of attack and it is coming soon.

And we won't need a signal from the dragons to see it.

ROMERIA

They cower within the metal bars, filthy and gaunt.

My mother's head swivels this way and that, taking in the monsters that surround her. She warned me of them years ago. She dedicated her life—and lost her mind, or so I thought—to fighting against this world, and while I have felt no love for her for many years, now I can't help the raw pity and the grim understanding.

She may have been so wrong in the choices she made, but she *knew*.

She knew this world existed.

Eddie sits cross-legged, hunched over, as I've seen him so many times before—on curbs near the park, on corners of busy city streets. Oblivious, I always assumed. But it was me who was blind to what was coming.

I haven't thought about them in so long, having dismissed my old life and all that came with it. But now here they are—in Islor—and all kinds of thoughts and emotions flood me.

I wonder, for the first time, who Eddie's affinities were to.

And how would my mother have reacted had she known what I was?

She had no idea what her own husband was.

"Why would he bring them here?" I hear myself ask out loud. Through the Nulling, obviously. "He doesn't need them."

"He hides behind them like a coward," Jarek answers.

He's right. I've imagined myself launching my full power at Malachi before, but now that he is here, waiting, the bound cord of silver wavers, because I know I'll kill my own parents while Sofie protects him from harm. They are human shields to him, nothing more.

But to me, they were once the people who washed my scraped knees and cradled me while I cried and tickled me until I screamed. They were loving and kind, before the underworld of caster magic and beasts claimed them. Now that I've seen it all come to life first-hand, the anger that simmered in my heart for years as I struggled on the streets gives way to immense sadness, like a dam breaking and the water surging through.

Here they are, serving like a pinnacle in Malachi's grand scheme. How much more did we all suffer because of him plotting, with Sofie's guiding hand?

I feel Zander's gaze boring into my face. "What do we do?" I ask.

His jaw grows taut. He sees Malachi's plan as clearly as I do. "Either you give him what he's hoping for, or we wait for him to make his next move."

"We wait." There's no hesitation.

I half expect him to argue, to point out that this is two people versus an entire realm.

With a nod, Zander slips his hand within mine. "Do not do anything that could risk the people in the cages!" he orders, his commanding voice carrying along the wall.

Long minutes stretch.

And then a bloodcurdling scream rises up into the air.

My mother holds her hands out in front of her as she shrieks, the pain in that sound twisting my stomach, threatening to unload the stew that sits within.

"What is he doing to her?" I cry out.

Zander shakes his head. "I do not know—"

"Lucretia! Tell me *something* for once!"

"He uses the shadow. Her entire body glows." She cocks her head with curiosity. "She burns without burning."

I stare in mute horror as Eddie scrambles to his feet, grabbing hold of the bars to his cage, rattling them like the gorillas at the zoo. The faint, "Stop him, Romeria!" reaches my ears.

He knows.

He understands.

Rage ignites inside me and with it, my affinities surge.

"Romeria," Zander warns.

Tears prick my eyes. "I can't anymore! I feel like I'm about to explode!"

"Then hit him where he does not expect it," Jarek urges.

I lash out to the right, the blinding light carving a line through the army.

But Sofie was waiting.

Silver light hurls toward us.

79

SOFIE

Romeria blocks my attack at the last minute, saving her and her king from obliteration.

Malachi releases her mother from her torture, and the woman crumples to the cage floor, her hand resting mere inches from the hem of this absurd gown Malachi insisted I wear today.

Despite my revulsion for this particular mortal, I feel pity for her. I know what she just endured.

"She's quicker than you thought, my love," Malachi purrs, unfazed.

"And stronger." Though, I've never faced another key caster before, so I have nothing to compare against.

The Saur'goth army roars, the spectacle invigorating them. They look like bulls waiting behind a gate, ready to be unleashed.

The daaknar rattles within its cage, demanding to be set free.

Shrill roars from the winged beasts perched atop the mountain peaks answer.

The air thrums with anticipation.

"She is strong. But not strong enough." The glint in Malachi's eyes is the only warning I have before he launches a veil of fire that gusts toward the city wall.

ROMERIA

"Shadows, ready!" Solange bellows in the quiet moments after Sofie's assault as adrenaline strums through my veins. The sleek figures hop up onto the rampart walls, their cloaks fluttering in the breeze.

A roar rises from below, racing my blood. The Saur'goths ache for war.

The dragons respond with screeches that reverberate through the sky.

The air itself seems seconds away from igniting.

And that's when a giant wall of fire rushes toward us.

"Fates," Zander gasps.

With a battle cry, I throw out everything simmering in my well at it.

ATTICUS

From the tower, I watch as a brilliant white light shoots down from Lyndel's wall, into the army. Romeria, no doubt.

Another returns, exploding in a flash over a hard surface. Malachi's key caster, returning fire.

"That is the one power in its purest form," Tuella notes, her black eyes shining with fascination. "A show of strength."

My jaw drops as a burst of flame erupts. If there was any doubt that the Fate of Fire stood before us on this plane, we now have proof. A moment later, a deafening boom cracks as a radiant light collides with the fire, and the two sides surge against each other.

The dragons launch into the sky.

The battle has officially begun.

"Advance!" I command, pointing my sword tip at Kazimir.

He lifts the war horn to his lips, and a deep croon carries.

The ground rumbles.

SOFIE

M alachi finally relents, his fire extinguishing in an instant.

My mouth gapes at the pristine wall and the line of soldiers still standing. "She stopped it." I don't know that I could, even with all my affinities combined. The power that radiates off him feels impossible to contain.

"Those blasted nymphs," he hisses through gritted teeth. "They meddle where they should not, aiding her cause beyond what is deemed appropriate."

The casters cloaked in all black stand on the wall like grim reapers, their eyes glowing. But they haven't attacked us yet. It must be because of Romeria's parents. Malachi was right—that weak mortal fool cannot bring herself to do what must be done.

Chaos rises behind us as the dragons char lines of fire through the ranks, deftly avoiding the bolts flying toward them. But I note the faint sound of clashing blades. "I think there is a second assault—"

"Forget about them! Our battle is here," Malachi snaps, his fury seeping through his pores. He assumed he would be victorious already. He did not expect for the little thief to put up a viable fight.

"Tell me what you wish me to do, Your Highness."

"Nothing. I must do this." He heaves a sigh. "This will take longer than I anticipated, but she cannot match my power indefinitely. Be ready."

He launches another wave of fire toward the city wall.

ATTICUS

I watch from the tower with a mixture of awe and grim satisfaction as my battle recommendations come to life. Deep fissures crack the battleground, separating ribbons of the enemy army, making it difficult for them to advance in either direction. Beasts scream as they tumble into the crevices with no hope of crawling out.

Rows of stone towers rise from the ground on this side, scattering the enemies where they stand. Before they know what's happening, the casters emerge from the top to hurl fireballs and arrows made of ice.

The enemy hacks and claws at the stone structures with reckless abandon, oblivious to the first wave of cavalry that charges in.

All is unfolding as planned. There is nothing more I can do from up here.

Kazimir and I dash down the stairs, aiming for our horses.

King Cheral is waiting, Satoria at his side. "Goodbye, wife." He kisses her forehead in a peculiar—almost fatherly—show of affection, but given all she's told me, I'm not surprised. Climbing into his saddle, he leans down to offer me his gauntlet-sheathed hand. "I still haven't decided if I should execute you."

I accept his gesture with a grin. "We can discuss it more later."

His eyes sparkle. "Until then." With a kick of his heels, he rushes past the wall.

Satoria runs to me as I reach my horse. "Did the queen take you to her last night?"

I don't have to ask who she means. "Yes. Thank you for whatever it was you said to Romeria. And for everything else." On impulse, I lean forward and kiss her goodbye. "Work on your assassin skills for me."

Tears brim in her eyes as she nods.

And then I'm in my saddle and racing ahead.

84

ANNIKA

Tyree sits on the stone ledge next to Neilina as her flesh knits itself back together, the token blade from Malachi and that gaudy rack of golden antlers in his grip, his face full of shock.

After that initial gasp of air, she demanded with a raspy, barely coherent voice that he "take them out" and then collapsed, unconscious.

There was only one thing she could mean.

With gritted teeth, Tyree wrenched Aoife's token from her chest, the points leaving deep gouges.

"I would like to know who put that blade there," I whisper from the opposite corner of the cave where I sit on a boulder. *And thank them,* I add in my head. According to Tyree, she wore the antlers like a necklace daily. Regardless, my feelings for her son do not change the reality that I have often wished for her death, and do not believe for one moment that my heart will soften for her as it did for him.

"I am much more interested in how the queen of a distant land ended up here." Destry studies the replica nymphaeum stone beside her with intensity. She's been quiet since they arrived, and on edge.

We all are.

"Maybe the wyvern carried her here." But all the way from Ybaris?

"Who told it to do that?"

The fable Tyree shared earlier stirs in my mind. "Vin'nyla?" Who else could command one of these things but a fate? There's certainly no Azyr nearby to guide the beasts.

"And why would one of your gods do that?"

"Because Neilina has a collection of elementals to summon them for her." And we all know she isn't above breaking her own rules. "Maybe the wyvern dropped her body in its lair and those little goblins made that nest for her."

"But *why*?" she pushes, not challenging my claim about the creatures that vanished.

I shrug.

Desty is silent as she traces the swirling lines on the stone with her fingertip.

"That looks like the writing on your forehead."

"It is the script of the light."

"We have one of these stones in Cirilea. It has something to do with the nymphs but I have no idea what."

She hesitates. "The balance here is off."

"I have *no* idea what you mean by that."

"I sense both light and shadow in this cave. I cannot find the source of the light, and the shadow grows stronger by the minute." Her black gaze veers to the corner where Queen Neilina and Tyree are as she says this.

"Your eyes haven't gone back to normal. You know that, right?"

"I have reached for the light too much lately. They will remain like this for some time."

"Is that a bad thing?" I know nothing about this conjurer except that she has helped us immensely, at her own peril.

She worries her lips over her answer. "I did not ask to be made this way. I did not ask for any of it."

A dainty hand appears then, pawing at the ledge, and Queen Neilina sits up. Even from where I sit, I can see that the wounds in her chest and neck are closed. That is unheard of—to heal so quickly and from such devastating injuries without the aid of a caster.

"Mother." Tyree bows his head in deference to his queen.

"Fates, Romeria looks exactly like her," I whisper. Neilina's blue eyes are glacial, though, as they rake over her surroundings, barely acknowledging me. Whatever happened to her, it must have been awful.

"Where am I?"

"In a mountain in Udrel," Tyree says, drawing her gaze to him.

Her lashes flutter as she blinks, as if noticing her son there for the first time. "Prince Tyree of Ybaris." It's not a question, but it is an odd way to address your son. Then again, he did say people call her cold and distant.

A frown flickers across his forehead. "Yes."

"Help me rise."

He sets the tokens down and collects her hands, easing her to her feet.

She wobbles with her first steps, the skirt of her elegant gold and silver dress tattered and streaked with dirt. "How did I get here?"

"We do not know. We found you lying there with a blade through your neck." He gestures at the makeshift bed. "We are high in the mountains with nothing but wyverns."

"Wyverns," she hisses, and an odd look of comprehension washes over her. "This is Vin'nyla's meddling."

Destry and I share a knowing look. My guess may not have been wrong. But it doesn't explain why the fate would send the Ybarisan queen to a mountain in Udrel.

"Why are *you* here?" Neilina demands to know.

"That is a very long story, involving an escape from Cirilea, sea sirens, and conjurers chasing Annika." He nods toward me.

I stand and take a step forward, offering Ybaris's queen a polite nod. She may be dreadful, but she is Tyree's mother, and despite my better judgment, I have feelings for him.

Her gaze narrows. "You are one of Malachi's demons."

"This is Princess Annika of Islor." Tyree hesitates. "She is with me, Mother."

"She is one of his creations and is not to be trusted."

"*I* trust her." He takes a step toward me, then another, watching his mother closely.

"Very well. Bow, child," she commands.

I set my jaw. *Never.* "I am an Islorian princess. I do not bow to Ybaris."

Her lips peel back with a snarl. "Then I have no use for you."

I crumble to the ground in crippling pain, every vein in my body straining against my skin as if about to explode.

TYREE

"What are you doing?" I roar. Mother's signature move is stealing breath from people's lungs. She does it often. But this looks different, like Annika's veins are trying to crawl out of her skin. "Stop!"

"If she does not bow to me, then she bows to *him*," she sneers.

Blood drips from Annika's eyes while Destry gapes, frozen.

"I am in love with her! Stop!" I charge forward, reaching for her wrist. In the next moment, I'm flying, slamming into the stone wall. With a grimace, I pull myself up.

She is not going to relent.

She is going to kill Annika.

She may as well kill me next.

I cannot allow this. The token blade that was embedded in her throat is within reach. Grabbing hold of it, I launch it through the air. It embeds deep into her back.

With a cry, my mother buckles to the floor.

Ignoring the shock of what I've done, I rush for Annika, pulling her limp body off the ground, her eyes rolling. I cradle her head in my arms, wiping the tears of blood away with my thumbs. "Say something, *please*, Annika," I urge, my heart threatening to stop beating.

Her lips move, barely. "Your mother … is delightful."

I pull her close to me, resting my forehead against hers. "You are too stubborn to die. Stay with me."

"I will, only so I can hold this over your head for eternity," she whispers, her voice hoarse.

I chuckle despite everything. "You can punish me twice a day, morning and night. I will strip and hand you the flog."

She licks her lips. "You would enjoy that far too much."

"Perhaps. We will have to find out." Because if there is anything I am certain of, it is that this Islorian has stolen my heart and I will kill anyone who tries to separate me from her.

"She lives, still." Destry nods to where my mother struggles to ease herself up. "And I do not think she is who you think she is, my friend. Not anymore. The shadow consumes her." Her short sword is in her hand, her knuckles white around the hilt.

Whatever version of Queen Neilina this is, I will not allow her to harm Annika again. Easing Annika to the ground, I stand and stroll over, flipping this person onto her back.

She gasps as the dagger digs deeper into her.

"Who are you?" I demand, my rage overtaking any loyalty or love I might feel for the female who stares up at me.

She sputters a cough, blood dripping from the corner of her mouth. "Your only hope against Malachi. Without me, you are all dead." With another rattling, wet cough, she goes still, death meeting me in her gaze.

"The shadow no longer lives in her," Destry declares, confirming what I already know.

I hurry back to Annika, who has managed to pull herself upright.

"What did she do to me?" She holds up her arms. "It felt like she was leeching every drop of blood from my body."

I kneel before her. "My mother could not do that. But she's gone, whoever she was. You are safe."

Annika peers up at me with her beautiful blue eyes. "You thought she was Queen Neilina when you stabbed her. For me."

"Yes." Did she hear what I said just before that, when I was begging for her life?

Her fingertips trace my lips. "Thank you." She adds after a beat, "Again."

"I will gladly save your life a thousand times. Ten thousand times."

A screech sounds.

Destry scurries toward the tunnel. "The wyvern is back! This is our chance."

"*Please* let this work so we can get out of this fates-forsaken world," Annika moans.

Helping her to her feet, we rush to follow.

86

ROMERIA

Beads of sweat drip down my forehead as I battle against this never-ending wall of fire. But Malachi will not relent.

I understand what Vin'nyla meant now when she said his fire burned forever. She meant he would never yield and his well is bottomless.

I will break long before he does, and then he will destroy us all.

87

ZANDER

Romeria's face strains with her struggle to shield Lyndel from Malachi's devastation, even as Ulysede's crown atop her head glows with a white light.

"How much longer can she hold this?" Fear and despair twists Jarek's face. I have never seen the legionary reveal either.

Solange shares his worry. "Not forever."

"We are useless here!" Abarrane scowls at me, and I know what she is suggesting without the need for her to say it out loud.

She is right. If we are to make a difference, we must be on the ground.

Romeria meets my gaze. She *must* see the reality of our situation. Her nod is barely perceptible, but it's there. "Go," she mouths.

My chest constricts. "Elisaf."

"I will guard her with my life, Your Highness," he swears.

Sparing her one last look, I bellow, "To the gate!"

88

ATTICUS

My horse charges through the throng, my sword slashing the Saur'goths with abandon. Everywhere around me, blades swing and bodies fall—both enemy and ally.

Wherever these beasts came from, they were built for war, and I know that if I relent for even a moment, I will be quickly overcome. But we are making ground, the casters in the towers delivering crushing blows to the hordes below them while the dragons devastate beyond.

That wall of fire still burns at Lyndel. I don't see how Romeria can fight against that forever, but I know little of her abilities. I pray she is strong enough.

My horse takes a spear to its hind leg, toppling it. I leap off before I'm caught beneath its body weight and land on my feet, only to be swarmed.

Kazimir barrels through seconds later, driving several of the enemy back as I draw a second sword, fighting my way toward a tower. A bolt pierces the center of it, cracking it in half.

Two nethertaurs ram another tower nearby. The Saur'goths are beginning to use their brains.

Ahead, I spot King Cheral slashed in the stomach by a sword. Jimon is at his side, swinging his ax, but they're precariously close to a fissure and losing ground.

I fight my way to them, just as a sword impales Jimon in the neck. A killing blow. He's dead before he collapses.

I cleave his attacker's head clean off its shoulders.

"Kaz!"

"I'm here!" he hollers.

I grab hold of a groaning King Cheral, hoisting him up onto the back of the horse. "Get him to safety, now!" There are healing casters behind that wall who can still save him.

Kaz purses his lips, not wanting to leave.

"Now!"

He charges off, racing hard so he can return to me quickly.

A shadow passes over me and I look up, spotting the purple dragon soaring past. "Bexley!" I roar, waving my hands.

The beast's head swings my way. She dives, plucking me with ease in one claw while she snatches a handful of the enemy in the other. I watch as she squeezes and slices them apart, tossing their lifeless bodies to the ground below, all while she cradles me.

I will never not be in awe of these creatures.

"Take me to my brother!" I shout.

She banks hard to avoid a bolt and then carries me across the battlefield.

89

ZANDER

The Saur'goths charge Lyndel's gate the moment it draws open, giving our army little time to advance. The Shadows fall into formation, launching an assault of everything from flaming bolts to flying boulders. The rest of us fan out with our blades.

But I have one purpose here.

One goal.

And he stands ahead of me, his concentration still locked on the rampart above.

Jarek and Abarrane guard my flanks as we cut through, their blades carving a path of bodies until I'm within range.

I don't have to search for a flame source. It's *everywhere*.

With grim determination, I aim to ignite Malachi.

A body slams into me, sending me sprawling as a burst of fire explodes.

My head is spinning. I struggle to regain focus, faintly aware of Jarek lying beside me, before I can make out Lucretia's face. She grins at me through a bloodstained smile before dismissing me altogether, stalking toward Sofie.

90

SOFIE

I nearly had him.

The exiled king of Islor would be dead if not for that creature —Lucretia—who appeared out of thin air to save him and the warrior, taking the brunt of my assault. She should be dead!

"What are you?" I hiss as she prowls toward me, not waiting for an answer before blasting her in the stomach with another bolt of fire.

She crumples to the ground, only to unfold a moment later.

I gasp.

She's morphed into the spitting image of Elijah, save for her vertical irises. "Sofie, my love," he purrs in that deep voice, slinking closer. "Did you enjoy my visit the other night?"

Her meaning dawns on me. "How dare you play such tricks!" I knew there was something different. "How dare you pretend to be him!"

"You should thank me. I gave you a gift. A parting gift, for you will never be with him like that again." Her gaze cuts to my left, the only warning before I hear the spine-chilling grunt. Malachi's fire cuts off.

"Noooo!" I shriek as the daaknar sinks its fangs into Malachi— Elijah's!—neck, its barbed claws anchored deep in his chest.

I lash out with a whip of fire.

It releases him with a roar, swinging its furious red eyes on me.

Before it can lunge, I send it back to Azo'dem with a surge of fire, and then dive for my husband's mangled body, dismissing the battle around us. "I did not see it freed from its cage." But who released it? "This is why I hate these demons!"

Crimson pours from a ripped artery in Elijah's throat where the beast tore out a chunk of flesh with its fangs. But the gaping hole in his chest is far more concerning, revealing lung tissue and rib bones that will take hours to mend.

My hands shake as I attempt to stem the blood flow. "Hold still and I will fix this." Is there *any* way to fix this?

I reach for my affinities.

"No, my love." His hand clamps over mine, and soft, brown eyes peer up at me.

My breath hitches. "Elijah? Is that you?"

"Yes. He has abandoned this ruined body. As will I momentarily."

Tears stream down my cheeks. "No, you will not. I will heal you."

"No." He wheezes. "No more. I cannot bear what these hands have done."

"It was not *you*. It was Malachi."

A tear slips from the corner of his eye. "And I cannot bear what you have become in my name."

I choke on a sob. "But—"

Sharp pain explodes under my ribs. I gasp as I look down to see Elijah's hand slip from the hilt of the cutlass he just drove into my body.

"Three hundred years. No more, my love. Let us end this together. Let us have peace."

"But—"

"Promise me. *Promise me*," he growls through gritted teeth.

"Okay." An unexpected calm washes over me, knowing that after centuries, this is the end. I have my Elijah back, if only for a few moments.

"In Za'hala then," he rasps.

I lean forward to kiss him. "A fool's dream."

His lips pull back with a smile. "A fool in love." With one final rattling gasp, his heart stops.

I sink into his still body, pushing the blade in deeper, and let the agony turn to numbness, then to nothing, and the sounds of war around us fade away.

91

ROMERIA

E lisaf acts as my crutch, holding me up as we peer at the chaos below.

Sofie lies over her husband's body, protecting him, her green ball gown a silken heap of vibrant color among steel and death.

"Is Malachi gone?" The words sound hollow, unbelievable.

"I think it is safe to assume both he and the key caster are. They have not moved in some time."

"Who killed them?"

"I did not see the killing strike."

Because he was picking me up off the ground where I collapsed, a split second after the wall of fire broke.

Malachi is gone and yet the Saur'goth army fights on, the ruin Malachi has brought to this world is still very real.

The cage with the daaknar sits empty. The other two remain untouched, my parents curled into balls in the center as if to get as far away from any one side and a blade that might push through.

I want to protect them. I want to go to them. But I can't do anything. I have nothing left inside me. I can barely stand.

"Where is Zander?" I've lost him in the shuffle.

"There." Elisaf points out where he fights alongside Jarek and Abarrane. A dozen legionaries and Shadows surround them.

Drakon falls with an ax in his back.

Abarrane's left arm hangs at her side, useless.

Caindra circles them, fighting with fire. A glint of gold shines in her claws. She's carrying Atticus, and he's directing her to attack where it's most concentrated. He's trying to help.

But it's not enough.

"There are too many of them." Our catapults fly and our dragons burn but no matter how many Saur'goths fall, more flood in to fill the void. The casters' affinities will be depleted long before we run out of enemies to kill. "We can't win." The moment the words slip from my lips, my gut tells me it is the truth.

A pain-filled screech echoes, snapping my attention to where Caindra spirals down, two bolts in her wing. She skids across the battlefield, crushing dozens of fighters, but more swarm in. Her injured wing stays close to her side as she breathes fire.

I can't pick out Atticus's armor anywhere.

Valk and Xiaric dive to her aid, but they'll be of little use. She can't get back in the air and she's a sitting duck on the ground.

The fight isn't just outside anymore. Shouts to retreat to the keep sound below, inside Lyndel. They opened the gates and the enemy are pouring into the city. I see their helmets. They're rushing the stairs.

"Lean here." Elisaf props me up against the wall to free his hands. He draws a second sword. "Shadows!" His voice booms, but it doesn't veil his panic. He senses the impending end as surely as I do.

The dozen remaining casters on the rampart rush to our sides, forming a buffer.

"It's not enough."

This is it.

Our darkest, most desperate hour.

"Call the dragons! One of them can fly you to Ulysede," Elisaf urges.

And leave everyone else here to die? I don't think so.

A strange calm washes over me as I reach into my satchel, my fingers wrapping around Aminadav's horn. The smooth bronze bone that promises Islor's salvation.

I know what I must do. What no one else can do.

I steal one last lingering look at Zander, surrounded by blades and beasts, fighting for his people. "Elisaf?"

"Yes, Your Highness?" His eyes are on the rush of Saur'goths charging toward us.

"Tell Zander I will find him in my next life." I smile. Who knows? Stranger things have happened.

Elisaf breaks from his focus just in time to watch me bring the horn to my lips and blow.

92

ATTICUS

When Tuella warned me of my coming death, I assumed it would be with my sword in my hand, not crashing into the ground, clutched in the claws of a dragon.

A massive leathery wing covers my broken body as I struggle for breath, and Bexley burns everything within the path of her fire. She's trying to shield me as the enemy charges in. That's kind of her, given I can't even lift my arms, let alone a weapon.

Somewhere above, her mate and her son screech, speeding to her rescue. The thought makes me smile as I admire her shimmering scales. "Did I ever tell you how much your friendship meant to me?" I doubt she can hear me over the shouts, but I ramble on anyway, eager to get my thoughts off my chest before I no longer can. "I keep playing our last conversations over in my mind. It all makes sense now. Well … a lot still doesn't make any fucking sense to me." My attempt at a chuckle dies on a groan. "I wish I had listened to you." Would it have changed anything? Who knows, but I wish I had recognized who my true allies were.

Suddenly, all goes quiet. The clash of blades, the enemies' shouts, the dragons' roars.

All of it is gone.

And the sound Bexley releases bleeds with despair.

93

ROMERIA

My jaw drops as countless clouds of dust erupt and cascade to the ground.

The Saur'goths are gone, vanished.

So are the Nulling beasts that carried their weapons.

But I am still here, standing on the rampart, watching the tide of battle shift.

"He lied," I say out loud to no one in particular. Or misled me. Aminadav made me believe I was sacrificing myself for the good of all, for the sake of the realms. And I *did* make that choice.

Yet I am still here.

"*Who* lied?" Elisaf asks, his face filled with wonder, his swords lowered.

Caindra's forlorn screech brims with agony, drawing my attention to her.

"No," I gasp, searching the fields for their forms. But Valk and Xiaric are gone.

"Romeria." Elisaf's face pinches with consternation, his attention on the cages where Zander now stands, where my parents were. Nothing but piles of dust remain.

A heap of green silk is all that hints of Sofie.

They're *all* gone.

It dawns on me then. "It killed everything that came from the Nulling." Both good and bad.

Aminadav's horn crumbles within my grasp, coating my hands in bronze dust.

"What did you think it would do when you blew it?" Elisaf asks, suspicion lacing his tone.

"I thought it would save the realms." An accurate—and vague—response.

But Elisaf isn't fooled. "'Tell Zander I will find him in my next life'." His chest heaves with a sigh as he puts the pieces together. "All it would cost is you, right?"

"I did what needed to be done." What the Queen for All was meant to do. "But maybe don't tell Zander about this?"

Elisaf shakes his head and throws his arm over my shoulder, pulling me against his side.

A few cheers erupt, and then more, until a deep wave rolls over the land. The sound of victory.

Zander is below, his swords thrown to the ground at his sides.

We've done it.

We've saved Islor.

I smile as I slump against my dear friend.

ANNIKA

D estry and Tyree crouch at the mouth of the tunnel, Destry cradling her stones, her eyes solid white.

I lean against the wall, still regaining my strength, my body aching. "Can you see it?"

Tyree leans out, searching the cave ceiling. "It's there." He ducks back in a second before its massive leathery body swoops down. "How's it going, Des?"

She doesn't answer and he doesn't push her, settling a hand on my thigh instead.

"Here. Try this." I collect a stone and toss it into the cave. Wings flap somewhere above and then the wyvern lands, bending to sniff it.

"It's pretty," I admit, admiring the shade of its red scales.

"That's the one that brought you here. Same coloring."

"I'm surprised it didn't eat me right away."

"So am I." He winks. "*I* would have."

I sink into his side, desperate to be close to him.

"Wait, I think …" Tyree frowns at Destry, then at the wyvern, who sits idly, its head bowed. His eyes light up. "I think she's got it."

"How will we know?"

As if in answer, it turns its claw upward, resting on the stone. It watches us through narrowed slits.

"Let me test it out." Tyree unsheathes his sword.

"Careful!" I urge.

He approaches the beast, giving it a wide berth as he strolls around it before moving in closer.

It sits quietly, unmoving.

"She's done it." Tyree grins. "We are going to fly out of this forsaken realm. Take Destry's arm and guide her—"

Destry gasps as if coming up for air after too long under water.

The wyvern rears back with a screech, the claws waiting to collect us raking across Tyree's torso.

And then it turns to dust before our eyes.

"Tyree!" I scramble out of the tunnel and run to where he has fallen. "Fates. Okay ..." The slash is long and deep. My trembling hands cover it, attempting to stop the blood from flowing. Rivulets stream over my fingers. "Okay, so it is bad, but it'll heal."

"Liar." He grimaces. "It's a Nulling beast wound, Annika, and I do not see any casters."

"But it will be fine. It *must* be fine."

Destry is hunched beside me, her eyes returned to black.

"What happened? What did you do!" I cry.

"Nothing! I had it and then ... I did not."

I search the gaping entrance above for any hint of wings. There were four hunting last night. "We need to move him back to the other cave before another one shows up. Help me."

Tyree grits his teeth as we each grab under one arm and drag him through the tunnel.

"Okay, if we can get him up there, onto that straw and—"

"Stop, Annika. Stop." Tyree collapses to the ground.

I drop to my knees beside him. "But we have to get you up there!"

He collects my blood-drenched hand. "No bed of straw will fix this." His face is pale, his eyelids shuttering.

"No! You will not die on me. I forbid it!" I yell, my tears streaming down my cheeks as I clamp down on the wound with my other hand.

"Annika," Destry calls out, but I ignore her. "Annika!"

"What?" My voice cracks as I snap at her.

She nods to something behind me, her eyes wide.

Fates, please tell me Queen Neilina hasn't risen again ... I turn.

The little goblins are back, and padding toward us on their webbed feet.

"What are you ... no, no, no." I shoo their hands away from Tyree as they paw at him, fumbling with his clothes. But they do not relent, one hissing at me in warning.

"Let them." Destry grabs my shoulders and pulls me away with surprising strength. "They can help him."

"How do *you* know?"

"I sense it."

I'm momentarily distracted by the glowing script that peeks from behind her heavy bang.

We watch as they strip off Tyree's vest and his tunic, their hands moving for the gaping gash. "What are they?"

She smiles, showing off her oversized front teeth. "They are the light."

"Welcome back." Zander lifts my hand to his lips. His armor is gone, as is the enemy's blood from his skin.

"What time is it?" I croak.

"Evening. You've slept for more than a day."

The sheer rock wall through the window is drenched in the orange glow of a sunset. "We're in Lyndel?"

"In Lord Telor's own chamber. Only the best for the Queen for All." He strokes strands of hair off my forehead.

Someone has undressed me. My crown rests on a nearby night table. "It's truly over?"

"It is truly over. Everything that ever touched the Nulling has turned to dust. I assume that includes Aoife, wherever she was hiding."

It also includes my parents and Caindra's family.

"But Malachi and Sofie were already dead. Who killed them?" I ask, melancholy slipping into my mood as yesterday's events unfold in my memory. I wish I could have at least spoken to Eddie, had a chance to say goodbye.

"The daaknar killed Malachi. Lucretia released it and then distracted Sofie long enough for the beast to attack." He shakes his head. "Sofie sent it back to Azo'dem before attempting to heal her husband. I was behind her, my sword ready to swing, but he beat me to it, stabbing her with his cutlass."

I gasp. "Was it Elijah or Malachi?"

"Elijah. I heard his last words." His lips purse. "He begged for peace."

My heart clenches. "In the end, he might have suffered more than anyone else."

Zander sighs. "All that effort and planning on Malachi's part, only to be bested by his demon pet."

It is a poetic—if not anticlimactic—end for the Fate of Fire. And a sad one for Sofie. "You're telling me that *Lucretia* is our savior." Who would have thought?

"She also saved me and Jarek from Sofie's fire. We would certainly be dead otherwise."

"Then I owe her *everything*." I entwine my fingers in his as I consider Malachi. "How angry do you think Malachi was when he found out he can't come back through the Nulling?" He couldn't have known what Aminadav did for us until he returned to his ethereal form.

"Probably as angry as I was when I found out that you lied to me about that horn." A somber expression passes across Zander's face. "What did Aminadav tell you?"

I sigh. Elisaf is a traitor. "He gave me a choice. He let me decide who I would sacrifice for the realms, and so I said I would sacrifice myself. He said that was acceptable. But I'm still here."

"Perhaps the Queen for All's willingness to die for her people was enough for him. Regardless, we will discuss you keeping secrets from me later." The smile that stretches across Zander's face then is lighter than any I have ever seen before. "If you are up to it, there are many people who are asking to see the queen who saved the realms."

"Shall it be by guillotine? Pyre? Or will you give me more of that terrible tea?" I drawl.

King Cheral chuckles, smoothing a hand over his stomach where the enemy blade cut him. It has long since been healed. "You will wake one morning and wish you had a cup, I promise."

Behind him, Tuella and Satoria linger, watching with interest as Serenis knits the bones in my leg back together. The moment the casters built the first bridge over a fissure, Kazimir was riding across with her, searching for me. They spotted my armor beneath Bexley's wing and quickly rounded up men to carry me to Lyndel.

My body was all but crushed in the fall. Serenis has worked tirelessly ever since, and when she needed rest, she ensured there was another skilled healer to take her place. I do not know if her doting is because I am Islor's prince, or Zander's brother, or simply because Kazimir's cock was that pleasing to her. I'm appreciative, whatever her motivation.

"What do you think about the shadow now, huh?" I direct that to the conjurer.

Tuella smiles. "It has its benefits. I have never argued that."

"The stars lied to you."

"They did not lie. They just did not tell the whole story. I saw you fall from the sky with the great beast."

"And you couldn't have warned me?"

"Would it have mattered?"

"Likely not," I admit. With Bexley's help, I kept the throng of

Saur'goths from swallowing up my brother. I bought him time until Romeria could do … whatever she did. I'm still unclear about that.

A soft knock sounds on the door.

Zander and Romeria stroll in, hand in hand.

"I thought you would be sitting on your throne in Cirilea by now, Brother," I mock, though there isn't any hint of animosity in my tone. "Where you belong."

Serenis pulls away, her eyes tinged with red. "That should suffice, Your Highness."

I bend my leg, careful not to expose my naked body to an entire room of people. It's stiff, but I've broken enough bones to know I will be limber again within a day or two. "As good as new. Thank you, High Priestess. Get some rest."

With bows for Romeria and Zander, she and Kazimir depart.

"Have you been to see Bexley yet?" I've thought of her often since I was carried away, her forlorn moans playing on in my mind.

Romeria's smile is sad as she shakes her head. "She's gone. She flew off as soon as the casters healed her."

"She'll come back."

"I don't know that she will. Our alliance may be permanently damaged." Romeria's eyes water. "I killed her mate and her child."

"*You* did not," Zander corrects her in a stern tone. "And you were fed lies about that horn. You did not know the true consequences."

"When all hope is lost," she murmurs, more to herself.

I meet Zander's gaze, searching for any residual animosity there. I don't see any, but I imagine it will take more than one realm-ending battle for him to trust me again—if he ever can. "How many did we lose?"

"Many," Zander admits. "But not nearly as many as we could have. Lord Telor has named Radomir captain of Lyndel's army. He is gathering information on those lost for us."

"Yes, who is this fellow? I keep hearing his name."

"He was a sapling until the blood curse lifted." Zander chuckles when my jaw drops. "A story for another day. Suffice to say, he can be trusted."

"If a sapling can win you over, there is still hope for me. What of Cirilea?"

"We leave for the city in the morning to reclaim my throne. A few lords have survived the battle." He snorts. "And Saoirse, of course. How she continues to evade death is beyond me. It has become an art form."

"For a cockroach," Romeria mutters.

"If I were to give you one piece of advice, it would be to execute her now. Today." I give him a stern look. "Believe me, she has earned the honor of both our blades."

He pauses. "Consider it done, as my thanks to you for all your aid."

"This Saoirse … she is elven?" Tuella interrupts.

"Yes. Why?" I ask warily.

"Because she may serve a better purpose, for my people."

Zander crosses his arms, taking the stance of suspicious inquisitor. I've always hated when he does that to me. "And how is that?"

"It is a long story. Too long to explain now, but I believe your sister still lives."

"What?" I bolt upright, forgetting my lingering pain. "Where?"

"In Udrel. If she fell to the sea, the wraiths will have brought her there, where the Azyr would certainly have retrieved her."

In Udrel? "Why are you only telling me this now!" My voice booms.

"Because your focus was on the war, where it needed to remain," she counters smoothly.

I glare at King Cheral. "Did *you* know about this?"

"I did not." He shoots a reproachful look her way. "The conjurer does not reveal all her secrets to me either."

"If your sister lives," Tuella continues, showing no remorse for keeping this from us, "then perhaps this cockroach's life in Udrel may be better served than her death in Islor. My king has been known to barter."

"How do we get to Udrel?" I demand to know.

"We might have flown, if we had the dragons," Zander says, urgency in his tone. He wants to find our sister as quickly as I do.

"It is a lengthy sail," King Cheral admits. "Months at sea."

"Fine. Then I sail. I will go right now and I will bring her back to Islor." I throw off my blankets and then remember I'm naked beneath.

"There is a wormhole," a voice purrs, as the snake-eyed creature suddenly appears in the room.

97

ROMERIA

Zander's and Atticus's eyes are on my back, waiting impatiently as we stand on Lyndel's rampart. A fierce wind blows, scattering the dust from the battlefield. I can't help but wonder if it's somehow Vin'nyla, reminding me of her part in this.

With a deep breath, I call out Caindra's name. If she won't fly us to Ulysede, we'll be stuck riding by horse, and that's a week wasted, traveling. "I need your help one last time. *Please*. I'm begging."

We wait several long minutes.

Until finally a dragon's screech answers.

ANNIKA

"Here." I scoop another dollop of honey out of the jar with my finger and hold it up to Tyree's mouth, his head cradled in my lap. "Eat."

"I prefer the other way you served it to me in the loft. Can we do that instead?" he croaks, licking his dry lips.

I laugh to hide my fear. Whatever those little goblins did, they succeeded in bringing him back from the doors of Za'hala. But he has lingered here in this state of frailty since, and he doesn't seem to be growing stronger. We have no hope of leaving this mountain while he is this weak.

Footfalls sound, and a moment later, Destry climbs through the tunnel.

"Anything?" I ask. The sun has set and risen again, and there has been no sign of any wyverns.

"They are all gone," she confirms, but her face bunches with worry.

"What is it?"

"The Azyr have found us. They will reach us within the hour. King Hadkiel is with them, and many soldiers."

My arms tighten around Tyree.

"Get back to that corner." Tyree ushers me behind him. He's made it to his feet, but leans on his sword like a crutch, his complexion pallid.

"You cannot fight them," I hiss, while listening for the sounds of armor.

"Get back," he urges, pleading with his eyes.

Reluctantly, I follow the order, gripping the dagger I found where Queen Neilina's corpse used to be. Only a pile of dust remains. Whatever claimed the wyvern must have also taken her.

Destry hovers at the left side of the tunnel, her short sword ready.

They are both going to die for me today.

King Hadkiel's soldiers will kill them, haul me back to the temple, and tie me up in their pool of life, where I will suffer for fates know how long. "Do not let them take me alive." My voice cracks.

Tyree's throat bobs with his swallow. "With my last breath, I will not. I promise."

The first scuffle in the tunnel comes a minute later.

Tyree releases a battle cry as he swings his sword, cutting down the soldier who appears. That one is quickly replaced by two more, then another four, their blades blocking Tyree's furious swings and Destry's attempts.

As I cower in my corner, I wish I had accepted Zander's countless offers of lessons in the sparring court, though I don't know that it would help against this many. I do the only thing I can think of, drawing on my feeble affinity to pelt the onslaught of soldiers with loose stones from the cave, aiming for their faces.

It works for a time, distracting them enough that Tyree and Destry can slice and stab and cut them down. But suddenly, there are too many of them.

Tyree trips over a body, tumbling backward to the cave floor.

A soldier moves in, lifting his sword in the air.

"Stop, or the kal'ana dies!" I shriek.

They all freeze. They may not understand my words, but they understand the dagger I hold at my throat.

King Hadkiel appears, trailed by four Azyr, who look no worse for wear after clambering up a mountain. His gaze sweeps over the cave, stalling momentarily on the golden antlers cast aside nearby, and then gives an order in his deep, melodious voice.

The soldiers lower their swords.

"My dear kal'ana. Why did you run? I was going to make you a queen."

My anger surges. "You dare use a disappointed tone with me? I saw your last queen," I hiss. I can't believe I ever thought this mortal handsome, or that I considered marrying him.

"Yes, and she serves as the brightest light for all Udrel. She has saved countless lives. Do you not wish to be honored in the same way?" He takes a small step forward, and the Azyr edge in around him.

"Do not come any closer!" I snarl. "This is a token blade from Malachi, and it is deadly. I promise, you will get nothing from my body if I embed it in my neck."

He holds up his hands, staying his Azyr. "What would you ask of me?"

"*Leave.* Let us go."

His smile is soft. "I cannot do that. My people have suffered for too long." He takes another step forward.

I back up, pressing the tip of the blade into my flesh. The sting is fierce. "I would rather die than serve as Udrel's queen." My eyes flicker to Tyree. I pray he can read the request in them.

His jaw grows taut with grim determination as his eyes water. "I will meet you at the gates of Za'hala," he promises, gripping a dagger in his hand. He's proven his skill and speed, many times over. If I don't succeed, he will.

I nod as his fist tightens, readies.

"Stop!" Atticus's voice booms.

A rivulet of blood trails down Annika's throat as she gapes at me, stunned.

"Back away from her now," I command, strolling in with swords in each hand, ignoring the shocking fact that one moment ago, we were standing in a dank underground vault in Ulysede, and now we are in a cave filled with soldiers, a king, and a handful of conjurers.

And Tyree, sprawled out on the ground.

"I presume you are King Hadkiel?" We expected to find Udrel's ruler in a city named Orothos, not standing on the other side of Romeria's nymph door.

"I am." His cautious eyes flitter from me to Annika. "And who might you be?" His accent matches Tuella's.

"Prince Atticus. And this is King Zander of Islor, and Queen Romeria of Ybaris and Ulysede." I ignore Saoirse for the moment. Her introduction will come soon enough. "And this"—I nod toward a shaking Annika—"is our dear sister, who we are here to take home with us, so I suggest you step away, unless you'd prefer to lose your kingdom today." I flash a wicked grin. "Queen Romeria is collecting."

Behind me, Zander snorts.

One of the Azyr speaks in a low voice, in their language, but her black eyes are riveted to Romeria, her tone one of warning.

King Hadkiel takes a step back.

And then another.

And another.

The guards lower their swords.

"Atticus?" Annika sounds dazed.

I charge forward, gathering her into a hug.

"I thought you were dead." She squeezes back.

"And *I* thought *you* were dead."

"But Tyree's cuffs came off."

"That, I can't explain." I stroke her bedraggled curls. "So much has happened."

"The blood curse—"

"Is gone, yes, we know."

"And Queen Neilina—"

"Is dead. Romeria killed her."

"Then who was the person using her body because we found her over *there*." She peels away from my arms and points to the far end, where a makeshift bed of twigs sits.

"That was Aoife." Romeria steps forward, offering Annika a smile. "But she's gone now."

"Because Tyree killed her to save me," Annika says absently, staring at her. "Why are your eyes silver?"

"We'll explain everything later, Sister." I smooth a hand over her back. "Ready to go home?"

"Fates, *yes*." She rushes to Tyree's side, spearing King Hadkiel with a glare. "Come on." Pulling him up off the ground, she serves as a crutch, tucking herself under his arm to help him hobble toward us. Her hand rests affectionately on his chest.

"What?" she snaps, seeing my bemused smile.

"Nothing. I seem to recall you demanding his death the last time we spoke. Or was it wishing for him to suck on a vat of Romeria's blood?"

"Both, I believe." Tyree winces with each step. He is far from well. "I told you her tune would change."

Despite my hatred for this Ybarisan, I chuckle. "I cannot wait to hear this story."

Annika rolls her eyes. "Shut up, both of you. Destry! Are you coming?"

A tiny person with the black eyes of a conjurer rushes to Tyree's other side.

"Don't worry, they have good ale where we come from," Tyree whispers, ruffling her mop of dark hair.

King Hadkiel looks on with a sour expression.

"We know about your curse," Romeria says. "Tuella explained it to us."

"Yes, the people of Udrel have suffered greatly because of your kind, and we will suffer more, now that you rob us of our only hope, our kal'ana."

"She is not yours to claim. Your sirens stole her and brought her here." Romeria's voice rises with irritation.

"To dull the curse of shadow wielders like you. And now we arrive here and find the gilded doe has been in our lands, and I must wonder what new curse we will contend with."

Romeria falters. "What did you just say?"

"The gilded doe. Your Aoife." King Hadkiel gestures to the golden antlers on the ground. "You said she was here."

"Yes, but …" Romeria strolls over to collect the token, studying it intently. Dried blood stains the tines. "Find the gilded doe," she whispers, and a pensive smile touches her lips.

It's gone in the next moment as she returns her focus to Udrel's ruler. "We have no interest in making your people suffer, which is why we've brought you a new kal'ana."

Zander, who has remained quiet up until now, steps forward, his viselike grip on Saoirse's arm resisting her struggles.

King Hadkiel sizes her up with interest. "You offer up one so lovely as this freely?"

Zander and I exchange an amused glance.

"Lovely, yes," he says. "But her time in our realm has come to an end. She will gladly spend the rest of her lengthy life being of value to Udrel. Isn't that right, kal'ana?"

Saoirse sneers at my brother.

"I would bind her wrists if I were you," I warn. "Otherwise, you're likely to find a dagger in your back before long."

The foolish king smiles at her. "I would hope Udrel's future queen would not wish to harm her betrothed."

You have no idea.

"She is yours on one condition." Romeria steadies her hard gaze. "Your sirens stay away from our ships."

"As long as this kal'ana feeds the pool of life, the curse will remain at bay, and our sea wraiths will not need to search for another to replace her."

"Then I hope she lives a very long life."

Zander passes Saoirse to the guards, freeing his arms to slip around Romeria.

"We're done here." With a heavy sigh, she smiles up at my brother. "Let's go and reclaim your throne."

ROMERIA

I pause to listen and remove my shoes. A branch snaps to my right.

Taking off in the opposite direction, I run as fast as I can, stifling my giggles as I navigate the endless corridors of the labyrinth. The air is thick with the scent of cedar, thanks to a heavy rainfall this afternoon, and the ends of my gown grow heavy and wet.

Above, Hudem's moon shines bright, bathing the royal garden in enough light for me to navigate my way.

That doesn't mean I have any idea where I'm going. I falter at a split in the path. I could spend every night studying this maze and never end up retracing my steps.

Another branch snaps to my left, so I go right. Zander knows exactly where to go. He's toying with me, herding me along, but I'll play.

My bare feet revel in the wet grass as I run. My dress will be ruined and Corrin will scold me. I can hear her now: *What kind of queen runs through the mud?*

One who is madly in love with both her king and her realms, I'll tell her.

Everything has changed. Ybaris and Islor are at peace, and I have uncovered brotherly friendships with both Atticus and Tyree, despite our sordid and rocky pasts. Tyree now plays the role of regent to Argon with Annika at his side, and while Oredai has been explicit about no one but the Queen for All going anywhere near Ulysede's throne, he tolerates Atticus and Gracen running things in the golden kingdom as husband and wife, bringing mortals from all over Islor and Ybaris to populate it. The city thrives and has become a tourist destination.

Mordain is no longer an enemy to Islor, with casters choosing to remain south of the rift and begin new lives here. Others have settled in towns and villages throughout Ybaris, by choice and not duty. And many, including the elementals previously serving Queen Neilina, now spend their days in Nyos, helping Allegra rebuild Mordain with a new focus on knowledge and history.

Wendeline has returned to Mordain, to lead a quiet life in a cottage, surrounded by children in need of a home.

The wards are lifted, allowing me free passage in and out, which I only do on occasion, usually to shuttle scribes to and from Ulysede. Many of them have remained, devouring ancient tomes and putting quill to paper to ensure our own stories are not lost, while also trying to learn what they can of the nymphs. We still haven't scratched the surface of understanding how they work.

I visit Ulysede almost every day, if not to ruffle Mika's hair and see Eden and Pan, who have grown close, then to check on Cahill's elemental training and fill in the smallest details about Gesine for Agatha. She keeps warning me that she might die before she finishes writing it all down, but Solange insists the old caster will outlive all of us.

Not everything is perfect, though. There are those who long for the old days of keepers and blood currency, and others who do not understand why Islor should share our harvest with other realms, even after we explain that Kier's waters are still poisoned and Ybaris's crops are still prone to rot. We have yet to discover how we temper those problems without summoning the fates or the nymphs and paying a steep price. A solution may lie with the conjurers from Udrel, but there is still too much we don't know about them.

Bellcross struggles to recover from the Saur'goth army, as does much of western Islor. Lord Rengard faces looting and revolt as he rebuilds. I will remain hopeful that the city's magic, which I discovered that day in the square with Elisaf, is not lost forever.

Most people blame Sofie for the beasts from the Nulling, ignorant to where she came from and how I was involved. Others blame Mordain. Zander and I have not corrected the rumors. We have more important issues to focus on than problems of the past. Some people feel the exiled king and Ybarisan queen do not deserve to be anywhere near Islor's throne. They are the ones we watch closely, to make sure their criticisms don't turn into conspiracies, and then rebellion.

The aristocrats are not the only cause for worry. Countless stories of the Saur'goths raping villagers who now find themselves pregnant are rising, with concern over what grows in their wombs. Others are alarmed about the idea of uncollared elementals roaming free to summon the fates at whim. Thankfully, I think the ones who live today have no more interest in meeting their gods than I do. But what about the elementals of tomorrow?

And then there is the question of the Nulling, and of how long Aminadav's mercy might last. Fifty years? A hundred? A thousand?

Ten?

Only Zander and I, and a select few enlightened, know to worry about such a thing.

For now, Radomir and Gaellar monitor the rift while we stroke Aminadav's ego by praising him for his mercy out loud, and pray for centuries of relative peace.

The nymphaeum appears ahead. With an impish grin, I rush for it, my arms behind my back to undo the fasteners of my dress. I leave pieces of it here and there, a tantalizing trail.

By the time I reach the stone pavilion, I'm wearing nothing but the gold ring Zander slipped on my finger the night we married in a quiet ceremony, just days after the war.

I splay my naked body out on the altar, my arms tucked beneath my head like a pillow.

And I wait for Islor's king.

He appears from the shadows, his sleek form moving stealthily toward me, his hazel eyes blazing. "You wish to take the stone on Hudem?" He shrugs off his embroidered jacket, letting it fall to the ground.

"It's not like it makes a difference, does it?" Many Islorian immortals have discovered themselves pregnant over the past few months now that the blood curse is gone and the nymphs' power floods the land. We are not one such couple. Not that we're trying.

I arch my back, stretching with exaggeration. "I'm just enjoying a quiet night." We purposely suspended all Hudem's celebrations, namely Presenting Day, as we work to reinvent Islor in Zander's vision. Already, a dozen noble seats are filled by well-respected mortals. We tried to give Elisaf a lordship. He requested the deed to the Goat's Knoll instead.

Zander's deep chuckle behind me stirs my blood as I listen to him unfasten and kick off his boots. "And you are not worried that we will earn an audience?"

"Don't act like you didn't tell the guards to keep everyone out of the garden tonight." Otherwise, I would be concerned. Life in Cirilea will never be the same as it was before, but the one thing that hasn't stopped is the nobility and legionaries fucking in the trees after dinner. There just aren't any tributaries involved anymore.

"You heard that, did you?" He circles the altar, metal clanging as he casts away his sword and daggers. Unfastening his breeches, he lets them cascade to the ground, kicking them loose. He ends his stroll at the foot of the altar, his honed body and hard length on display for me. "And where is Lucretia?"

Warmth floods my core, being exposed out here in the open like this. "Harassing Jarek." Though ever since she saved him and Zander from Sofie's fire, he tolerates her more. I've even caught him smiling once or twice at her antics.

Thoughts of my legion commander bring a soreness to my heart. He came to me yesterday, asking for permission to explore Udrel and Espador on his own, to see what he can learn of the realms and search for Caindra, who we haven't seen since the day she carried us to Ulysede for the last time. For my benefit, he assured me, to learn more Udrel, and seek out any dangers before they can become problems for us. But he avoided my gaze. I can't help but feel he's been avoiding me in general. I'm not sure what's happening with him, but if he needs time away, I'll release him from his obligations as my commander.

I've agreed to transport him through the nymphaeum door to the place where we found Annika but only if he takes Lucretia to guard his side. He's agreed ... reluctantly.

I'll miss him, but my heart tells me that I need to let him go. Maybe he'll find his way back to me one day.

"Then we are truly alone." Zander climbs up onto the altar, his strong hands parting my legs, his palms sliding up my sensitive flesh as he moves into position.

I sigh with the weight of his body settling on mine, and my lips find his in a tantalizing kiss. "Except for the dozens of nymphs who are watching," I tease. After Annika's account of Udrel's mountain and the kaeli who appeared long enough to keep Tyree alive, I pressed Lucretia until she admitted that they live among us, and you never know where they might be or what they might be up to—both good and bad.

"Then I guess we ought not disappoint." Entwining my hands in his and pinning them down above my head, Zander's teeth scrape across my neck, biting down gently.

On the slightest breeze, a wisp's laughter carries.

Romeria—row-mair-ee-a
Romy—row-me
Sofie—so-fee
Elijah—uh-lie-jah
Zander—zan-der
Wendeline—wen-de-line
Annika—an-i-ka
Corrin—kor-in
Elisaf—el-i-saf
Boaz—bow-az
Dagny—dag-knee
Bexley—bex-lee
Saoirse—sur-sha
Kaders—kay-ders
Malachi—ma-la-kai
Aoife—ee-fuh
Aminadav—ami-na-dav
Vin'nyla—vin-ny-la
Ratheus—ra-tay-us
Islor—I-lor
Ybaris—yi-bar-is
Ybarisan—yi-bar-is-an
Brynn—brin
Theon Rengard—thee-on ren-gard
Sheyda—shay-da
Ocher—ow-kr
Ianca— I-an-kuh
Ulysede—you-li-seed
Tyree—ty-ree
Fearghal—fer-gull
Golbikc—goal-bik
Isembert—eye-sem-bert
Bregen—bre-gun
Eros—eh-rows
Barra—bar-ah
Taillok—tie-lock
Sylx—silks
Bragvam—brag-vam

Gaellar—gay-lar
Baedriya—bae-dree-ya
Cirilea—sir-il-ee-a
Seacadore—see-ka-dor
Skatrana—ska-tran-a
Kier—key-er
Mordain—mor-day-n
Azo'dem—az-oh-dem
Za'hala—za-ha-la
daaknar—day-knar
caco claws—kay-ko claws
Zorya—zor-eye-a
Jarek—yar-ek
Bodil—bow-dil
Horik—hor-ik
Danthrin—dan-thrin
Ambrose Villier—am-brose vil-lee-er
Eden—ee-dun
Drakon—dray-kon
Brawley—bra-lee
Mika—mee-kuh
Minerva—min-er-va
Norae—nor-ay
Cindrae—sin-dray
Oredai—or-eh-die
Golle—goal
Kaeli—kay-lee
Nyos—knee-oh-s
Orathas—or-a-thas
Azokur—a-zow-koor
Hadkiel—ha-d-keel
Yidara—yid-ara
Azyr—az-ear
Nyxalia—nix-ah-lee-a
Saur'goth—sar-goth

ACKNOWLEDGMENTS

Fate and Flame is a four-year passion project I am so proud of and already miss, even though pulling all those threads together sometimes felt impossible. As I wrap up Romeria and Zander's story, I must thank a few people who have joined me on this wild journey.

Jenn Sommersby, my incredibly talented editor, for talking me off a ledge once (or thrice.)

Hang Le, you are a true artist, and I am always excited to see what that clever brain of yours comes up with.

To the publishing teams around the world, including Del Rey (UK), TBR Editorial (Spain), HarperCollins (France), Filia (Poland), Alfa (Turkey), AST (Russia), Albatross (Czechia), Könyvmolyképző Kiadó (Hungary), and Tantor (audiobook format), for your efforts bringing Romy and Zander into readers' hands.

Nina Grinstead and the VPR team, for all facets of marketing and PR.

Stacey Donaghy of Donaghy Literary Group, thank you for your tireless efforts in bringing this series, which holds a special place in my heart, to readers worldwide.

My family, for being my anchor in this world, even when I'm living in another one.

ABOUT THE AUTHOR

K.A. Tucker writes captivating stories with an edge.

She is the internationally bestselling author of the Ten Tiny Breaths, Burying Water and The Simple Wild series, He Will Be My Ruin, Until It Fades, Keep Her Safe, Be the Girl, and Say You Still Love Me. Her books have been featured in national publications including USA Today, Globe & Mail, Suspense Magazine, Publisher's Weekly, Oprah Mag, and First for Women.

K.A. Tucker currently resides outside of Toronto.

Learn more about K.A. Tucker and her books at katucker-books.com

9 781990 105425